D1246614

COLD NEW DAWN

Also by Ian St. James:

The Killing Anniversary
The Balfour Conspiracy
The Money Stones

IAN ST JAMES

COLD
NEW DAWN

St. Martin's Press
New York

Library of Congress Cataloging-in-Publication Data

St. James, Ian.
  Cold new dawn / Ian St. James.
    p.   cm.
  ISBN 0-312-01748-0
  I. Title.
PR6069.A423C6   1988
823'.914—dc19
                                                      87-36888
                                                         CIP

First published in Great Britain by William Collins Sons & Co., Ltd.

First U.S. Edition

10 9 8 7 6 5 4 3 2 1

For Patsy, who else?

BOOK ONE

Keir

One

Keir Milford saw her first.

Half-way through that morning's English lesson he was sent to fetch a reference book from the school library. On the way back, taking a short cut through the Girl's School, he had almost reached the end of the corridor when Miss Bannister came round the corner. With her was a girl Keir had not seen before. What struck him first was that she looked foreign: French or Spanish, or at least the way he imagined French and Spanish girls would look. Her hair was a halo of thick, glossy, black curls; jet-black like a gypsy's. She had olive-coloured skin and brilliant, very dark eyes. Her slim legs were brown. Although she was dressed in regulation sweater and skirt, she wore the clothes with a style that made them look different. Keir felt his skin prickle all over.

'Morning, Milford,' said Miss Bannister briskly.

He answered without even glancing at her. His eyes were still admiring the girl. There was a brilliance about her, a lightness in the way she walked, and a gleam in her eyes that hinted at laughter. She smiled at Keir. 'Good morning,' she said.

Dazed, he almost bumped into her, stepping around her at the last moment but not without tripping over his feet. Then he was past her and turning the corner at the end of the corridor.

He heard Miss Bannister say, 'That was quite unnecessary. You had no need to speak to that boy.'

'I was being polite,' said the girl. 'You said Good Morning. He said Good Morning. I would have been rude to say nothing.'

Keir grinned. He was reminded of Dusty. Dusty would have answered like that; inviting a discussion, a discussion the other party might come to regret. The girl's voice stayed in his ears. It was so musical. And Keir had been warmed by her smile. An unexpected mood of happiness filled him, as if it were his birthday and Christmas rolled into one.

'What are you grinning at, Milford?' asked Clemence when Keir returned to the class.

'Me, sir? Nothing, sir. I think this is the right book.'

As he walked back to his seat, Keir caught Dusty's look of enquiry. Keir merely shrugged. For the first time in five years something had happened that he felt was best kept to himself. He was reluctant to discuss that girl even with Dusty. He wanted to keep her a secret.

Keir and Dusty had been friends from their first day when, along with a hundred other new boys, they had assembled in the school hall, everyone resplendent in freshly purchased blazers and flannels – everyone, that is, except the boy next to Keir. Even Keir noticed the lack of school-outfitter freshness which clung to everyone else. Not that he paid much attention. The truth was he was a bit overawed, especially when the masters filed in, all wearing academic gowns and mortar boards. Keir thought the gowns were quite something, as black as the robes of a judge but brightened by the coloured sashes of different universities. Most impressive of all was the Headmaster, from whose mortar board bounced a gold and red tassel as he walked up to his lectern on the stage.

Five minutes later, when the Headmaster was giving his speech, Keir felt a nudge in his ribs. 'My name's Dusty,' whispered the boy next to him. 'What's yours?'

Keir was taken by surprise. 'Milford,' he said.

'I know it's Milford. I heard them call the register. Don't you have a first name to go with it?'

Keir blushed. He blushed a good deal when he was twelve. 'Keir,' he mumbled. 'It's Keir Milford.'

'That's a funny name.'

People had been telling Keir that for most of his short life without him ever finding a quick answer.

'How do you spell it?'

Keir told him.

'Pleased to meet you, Keir,' said Dusty. Keir grinned back and was shaking hands with proper formality when the Headmaster bellowed down from the stage – 'Do I hear talking? You boys in the third row. Stand up! That's right, you and the boy next to you. Stand up at once.'

Keir stifled a groan. His first day and he was already in trouble. Miserably he rose to his feet, wishing the ground would open and swallow him.

'What's your name?' shouted the Headmaster.

Keir swallowed. 'Milford, sir.'

'Milford is it? I'll remember that. And you, the next boy, what's your name?'

'Miller, sir. Harry Miller, but everyone calls me Dusty. And I do apologize. It was completely my fault, sir. Nothing to do with Milford, not really, sir.'

It was the most grown-up speech Keir had ever heard from a boy of his own age, and in public too, with all the masters and a hundred kids looking on. But if Keir was impressed, the scowl on the Headmaster's face merely deepened. 'You were having a conversation. It takes two to hold a conversation.'

Miller shook his head. 'Not really, sir. I mean it wasn't a proper conversation. I was introducing myself. I told Milford my name and asked him his. That's all, sir,' he said confidently. His voice betrayed neither insolence nor fear.

The Headmaster narrowed his eyes and stared so hard at Miller's worn-looking clothes that he might have reached out and rubbed the material between his fingers. 'That's not a new blazer. Have you a brother at this school?'

'No, sir. I mean, I don't have any brothers, but this is a new blazer.'

Surprised whispers arose on all sides. Keir shared the same thought; a blazer so comfortably worn couldn't be new. It had been either handed down from an older brother or bought second-hand. The cost of school uniforms was horrific. Keir had heard his own parents complain. There had been one awful week when he feared he would start school in second-hand clothes. Thankfully, the money had been scraped together and he looked as band-box fresh as any boy there. In fact they all looked the same, except for Miller. Keir quaked, expecting the Headmaster to call Miller a liar.

But Miller spoke first. 'I know it doesn't *look* new. You see, sir, I wanted to settle in quickly. To look as if I belonged. So we bought the uniform six weeks ago and I've worn it indoors ever since, to sort of break it in. Like a pair of new boots, sir.'

It was a brilliant explanation. The Headmaster had been urging them to settle into school quickly. By almost echoing his words, Miller had extricated himself from trouble with a flick of his tongue.

Uncertainty was written all over the Headmaster's face. 'You'll settle in faster if you remain silent in assembly. Do you understand that, Miller?' he said sternly.

'I do now, sir, and thank you very much,' Miller answered politely, resuming his seat.

He had not been told to sit down. Keir remained standing until Miller tugged his sleeve. The Headmaster glared, obviously wondering whether his authority were being flouted. Expecting to be told to stand up again, Keir sat rigid. Finally, he risked a sideways glance at Miller. Then he relaxed, sensing the battle was won. Miller was returning the Headmaster's stare with a politely attentive look of his own. There was nothing defiant about it, but neither was it submissive. In time, every master in the school came to know that look of Miller's. It encouraged the speaker to continue, yet somehow it said 'I hope what you say is correct because if not I shall want to discuss it.' And discussions with Miller could be such bruising encounters that masters grew adept at avoiding his eye – just as the Headmaster did at that moment. He glanced down at the lectern and picked up his notes to signal the end of the incident. And with that one exchange, Dusty Miller had set his mark on the school, within an hour of crossing the threshold.

By the end of that first day, Keir Milford and Dusty Miller were already on the way to becoming firm friends. They would have travelled home together had they not lived in opposite directions.

'Hillingdon?' Dusty exclaimed in amazement. 'That's miles away.'

Which it was. Keir lived further from the school than anyone else. His journey took ninety minutes door to door, beginning with a long walk to the station, then fifty minutes on the train, followed by another twenty-minute walk at the other end. 'Imagine facing that for five years,' Dusty said dismally. 'Three hours a day, five days a week, say forty weeks a year. That's . . .' He paused. 'Six hundred hours a year, which is . . . twenty-five entire days. Over five years you'll be travelling for . . . a hundred and twenty-five days. Holy Christ!' Dusty always was a wizard at mental arithmetic, even when he was twelve.

As for travelling, Keir didn't mind. Pleased to have qualified for the Grammar School, he was full of excited tales when he reached home.

His parents owned a corner shop. Milfords wasn't exactly Fortnum and Mason, but then Hillingdon wasn't London's West End, and in the immediate post-war years, what with shortages and rationing, few grocers were making a fortune. Keir's father was forever saying, 'There's no money in this business unless you deal with those buggers on the black market, and I'll not do that. Bloody parasites, that's what they are. Undermining the system. Should be locked up, the whole lot of them. I didn't buy black market in the war and I'm damned if I'll start now. Joe Milford runs an honest shop.' There were times when Keir wondered if his father wasn't too honest. Not that he said so. He had once, and he could still remember his father's reaction. 'Too honest? How can you be too honest? You're either honest or dishonest. There's no in-between and don't you forget it.'

Joe Milford was a cripple from the waist down. He had been a train driver once, then there had been a horrific crash, leaving Joe without the use of his legs and facing a public enquiry into the deaths of six passengers. The Union tried to blame the owners but Joe's evidence so clearly placed the responsibility on an erring signalman that the Union lost the case. When the Union negotiators remonstrated afterwards, Joe had been un-repentant – 'I'll not tell lies for any man, and a legal action based on a falsehood is a disgrace to the whole Trade Union move-ment.' Consequently the negotiators had soft-pedalled Joe's own claim for compensation and the damages awarded had been less than they might have been. 'Better honest money than pieces of silver,' had been Joe's uncompromising reaction. He had used the money to buy the shop, expressing the view that 'a man's got to earn an honest crust somehow'.

The story of his accident summed up his whole life. A man of strong convictions, he believed in the British Labour Party, the Welfare State, free speech and the bettering of mankind. He had named his son Keir Hardie Milford after Keir Hardie, the pioneer socialist. 'A great name is something to live up to,' he told Keir. 'It's a big responsibility but I know you'll handle it.'

Born seven months after the rail crash, Keir had only known his father in a wheelchair. Just as he had only known him to be busy. Milfords stayed open all hours and Joe never stopped working. 'It's a living,' he said, without bitterness. 'There's many a poor devil worse off.'

Keir doubted the poor devils worked as hard as his parents. And Keir worked too, though he never counted it as work. He just helped out after school. There was always stock to be shifted, boxes to be lifted, jobs which defeated his incapacitated father and his overworked mother. 'Leave it for our Keir,' they said, and they did. Keir didn't mind. He had grown up as much in the shop as in the rooms above and behind it. He knew every inch of the place, the geography of which had been adapted to suit his invalid father. The original stockroom had become the main bedroom and that, with the living room, kitchen and bathroom, completed the ground floor. Upstairs was Keir's room and two further bedrooms which had been turned into stockrooms. Milfords – the shop on the corner, a shop with a good name. 'Never lose your good name,' Joe Milford was constantly telling his son. 'It's your most precious asset. You can lose money and make it again. You can lose time and catch up. But a man who loses his good name is finished.'

There was a lot of his father in Keir. They had the same colouring for a start: brown hair, blue eyes and a ruddy complexion. Both had open, honest faces. They even had freckles. And they shared a similar physique, for although Joe was wasted away below his hips, his shoulders were broad and his chest was deep. More importantly, they shared the same qualities of character. Joe's integrity and industry had been passed on to his son. 'A chip off the old block,' people would say, and Joe would answer with a shy smile, 'Aye, well, let's just hope the lad stays out of trouble. That's the most a father can ask.'

Keir's mother was less sure. She had nothing against honest work. The thought of her son engaged in anything else would have horrified her, but hard work by itself merely guaranteed a hard life in her experience. She rose at six every morning and rarely saw her bed before midnight, what with the book-keeping to do after supper, and the returns for the Ministry of Food, and making out orders for the wholesalers. 'Keir's got a chance to do better,' she thought happily when he passed the examination for the Grammar School.

Whether he would have done better without Dusty was hard to say. Some people said Dusty was a bad influence. Others said Keir had a mind of his own and wasn't easily led, by Dusty or anyone else. The important thing was that they suited each other. Keir's strengths were Dusty's weaknesses and vice versa. Where Keir was slow at mathematics, Dusty was as quick as a flea. Where Dusty was hopeless at languages, Keir became fluent in German and French. They soon developed a system for 'checking' each other's homework, especially after an incident in their first year. It was during an English lesson with a master named Williams – a sour, grey man with a waspish tongue whose delight was to make a boy look a fool in front of the class.

'Miller,' said Williams on this particular day, 'there are more spelling errors in your work than holes in a Gruyère cheese.' He paused, pleased by the comparison. 'In fact, there's a word to conjure with – Gruyère. How would you spell that?'

Most boys would have guessed and made a mess of it, but even at twelve Dusty was too cunning. 'I don't think I've come across the word, sir,' he said with that attentive look on his face.

'I didn't ask if you've come across it. I asked you to spell it.'

'Yes, sir, but that's like me asking you to describe my uncle's vegetable patch.'

'His what?'

'Vegetable patch, sir. You know – part of a garden –'

'Of course I know!'

'So can you describe it, sir? How big is it? What does he grow –?'

'I've never seen it,' Williams snapped, angry red blotches forming on his face. 'How can I describe something I've never seen?'

'It is difficult, sir, isn't it? Like me and this piece of cheese. What was it called again?'

Losing the argument made Williams lose his temper. 'Forget the cheese!' he shouted. 'Damn the cheese! The point is, your spelling is appalling. What are you going to do when you leave school?'

'About spelling, sir?'

15

'About earning a living!' Williams shouted, red-faced.

'Oh, I see. I shall go into business, sir.'

'What sort of business?'

'I don't know yet, sir, but I'll be a millionaire by the time I'm twenty-five.'

'A millionaire? You? And how will you cope with business correspondence if you can't spell?'

'By employing a secretary, sir,' Dusty answered as quick as a flash.

Williams gave up after that, but not Dusty. He plagued Williams throughout that entire lesson. 'Excuse me, sir. This piece of cheese. Is it from a place? As in Cheddar or Leicestershire cheese?' He was like a boxer driving his opponent round the ring – jab, jab, jab, and always with that piece of cheese – 'Excuse me, sir. This Gruyère. Is it French? You see that would explain things. We've only just started French. Perhaps that's why I've not come across it . . .'

Williams never picked on Dusty again. It was the same with the rest of the staff. One discussion was enough. They treated Dusty with caution after that, and because he and Keir were inseparable, Keir achieved the same status. The two became closer than brothers without ever being taken for such. Dusty had a great head of straight, dark hair, usually in need of a brush, and a large sensual mouth that was very expressive. And whereas the look in Keir's eyes was invariably trusting, Dusty's brown eyes were knowing and watchful. He had a characteristic way of pursing his lips into a sarcastic pucker and looking at people with a glimmer of irony in those dark eyes. Without being so good-looking as Keir, his clever face conveyed charm, and he was an inch taller, a difference that was to remain constant. Not that they were competing. On the contrary, they made a pact not to compete. It was a rule they established, never to compete against each other at anything. It became a point of honour, one of the reasons they became labelled the 'Team'. It was a funny nickname, especially for Dusty, to whom team games were anathema. Keir played football and cricket but Dusty avoided team games when he could and, although he became a useful middle-distance runner, he lacked real dedication. 'You could be a champion if you trained,' said Coleman, the sports master.

'It's good of you to say so, sir, but I don't think I want to be a champion runner,' replied Dusty politely.

That was what exasperated the masters – Dusty's unwillingness to put himself out. Unless something really interested him, he coasted along. And Keir adopted the same attitude. Too much his father's son to be lazy, he concentrated on only a few subjects and with everything else did just enough to get by.

'You could both do a lot better,' the Headmaster told them. 'Instead of which you drift along like two old colonels out for a stroll.'

Satisfied to be as they were, they complemented each other like two sides of a penny. If one of them wanted to do well in something, the other gave way. For instance, when they moved up to the Second Year, Dusty joined the chess club and Keir began to write for the school magazine. They competed against others but never each other. That was the basic rule of the Team. Most people said Dusty was the moving force and Keir was an amiable oaf who followed behind. If Keir knew what was said, he showed no resentment. He and Dusty had their pact and that was enough.

Leadership was a dirty word so far as they were concerned, especially with Dusty. 'Who gets blamed when something goes wrong?' he once asked Keir. 'The leader, that's who. So why set yourself up to be knocked down? Let them think it's their idea.' He was good at letting people think things were their idea. Dusty just influenced. Like that business of the blazer on the first day. Other kids copied it. They too wanted to look as if they belonged, so they stained and marked their clothes in all manner of ways. They overdid it and became a scruffy-looking lot in the process, but it showed how other kids emulated Dusty.

Distance split the Team at weekends. They each had 'home friends' and 'school friends' and geography alone kept them apart. Keir never visited Dusty's home so he could only guess what it was like, but he gleaned enough to know that Dusty would leave as soon as he could. His father had been killed in the war, at Arnhem. A sergeant in the Parachute Regiment, he had rescued three men under enemy fire and been killed as he dragged the third man to safety. Dusty's father was a genuine war hero, posthumously awarded the Military Medal. Where most boys would have boasted, Dusty kept it to himself. Even Keir found out by accident. One day, Dusty mentioned that he had a step-father, and Keir had probed away until the whole story came out. It was the one time that Keir saw Dusty close to tears. He went a sickly white and a note of bitterness crept into his voice. 'My Dad was a leader,' he said. 'He was marvellous, Keir, you'd have liked him, everyone did. People looked up to him and respected him. Then they killed him.'

Keir was shocked. 'The Germans killed him?'

Dusty shook his head. 'A German fired the bullet, but it was his friends who wanted him to be a hero. They made him set an example. And look where it got him.'

Keir was lost for a response. Despite the contemptuous tone, Dusty had clearly loved his father. Searching for the right words, Keir said, 'Men like your Dad won the war. They'll never be forgotten.'

'Huh! Six months after he was killed my Mum met this other man, and six months after that she married him. A year, that was all it took. Don't tell me my Dad won't be forgotten.'

Too young to imagine a widow's lonely despair, Keir could only understand Dusty's pain and resentment. It was as if Dusty had learned a lesson from his father's death. His father had been used. Dusty would never be used. He was determined that nothing like that would ever happen to him.

'So what's your step-father like?' Keir wanted to know. 'He doesn't beat you or anything, does he?'

'Fat chance. He's a weed. He wasn't even in the war. He had some sort of reserved occupation that kept him at home.'

Dusty's step-father was mean, not violent, especially about spending money on Dusty. That first school blazer had been second-hand. Keir was sworn to secrecy. 'I don't want his money anyway,' said Dusty, his scowl giving way to a grin. 'Besides, I handled that business of the blazer okay, didn't I?'

'I'll say. You were brilliant. No one knew, not even me.'

Perhaps having a penny-pinching step-father was Dusty's spur to make money. Certainly something spurred him on, because after two years in the school Dusty was better off than any boy there. In those days there was plenty of work. There were more jobs than people to do them. Nobody at school had trouble earning pocket money. Keir delivered papers before school every morning, and Dusty worked every Saturday at the American base.

Working for the Americans was frowned on by some people. Americans were frowned on. After all, Britain had stood alone against Hitler, Britain had won the war, the Americans had merely helped out, or at least that's what some people said. The sick thing was the Yanks had all the money. Every day newspapers compared the meagre rations in Britain to America's overflowing larders. 'Unfair,' said some people, but not Dusty. He liked Americans. He enjoyed working in the PX on the base every Saturday and in a way Americans even helped him start his first business. He became a dealer in American comics.

Every boy in the land collected American comics, which were thicker than English ones and printed in colour. Working at the American base gave Dusty a source of supply and at school he cornered the market. Dusty's wheeling and dealing would have gladdened the heart of any self-made millionaire. The result was that he always had money – which he lent at appropriate rates of interest to those who ran short.

And so the boys grew up, not unhappily, despite the rationing and the fact that the war had been over for only a few years. Most kids in the school could remember the London Blitz, some had been bombed out, many had lost relatives in battle – but they were the inheritors of victory, a new generation growing up with big expectations. None had bigger expectations than Dusty. He was going to make money in double-quick time. Ambition was the single difference between the two boys. Dusty was so sure, whereas Keir was uncertain. He thought writing for the school magazine might lead to a job as a journalist and was tempted to try that. On the other hand his father was forever telling him to seek a career in politics.

Politics were the love of Joe's life. 'It's all he ever talks about,' his wife grumbled. 'He's always going on about the government. As if I can do anything about it. Makes no difference who runs the country if you ask me.' Joe never did ask her. He *told* her from time to time, but never asked, and he was forever reading out snippets from the paper. 'Listen to this,' he would say, and anyone within earshot had no choice in the matter.

Keir grew up listening to his father discuss the state of the world. People were always dropping into the shop – like Bob

Cooper, Joe's oldest friend. They had worked together on the railways as young men. During the war, Cooper had been commissioned in the army and had risen to the rank of major. Afterwards he had turned down a good job in the city to become a Trade Union official. Another friend was Emlyn Hughes, the local librarian and secretary of the local branch of the Labour Party. Sometimes even the Vicar dropped in. Debates at the Milfords often lasted into the night, filling the downstairs rooms with the steady drone of voices discussing weighty events. Keir grew up listening to talk about the struggle for power in the world.

Meanwhile, at school, he and Dusty grew in stature and confidence. Their school reports were good for, although the Headmaster felt they could do better, neither boy was a trouble-maker. And they were rarely in a fight because the whole school knew that to fight one meant fighting the other. So they drifted along 'like two old colonels out for a stroll'.

Keir's mother was proud of him. 'He's growing up ever so nicely,' she said to her husband.

'Maybe he is, maybe he isn't,' was Joe's cautious reply, 'but don't you go filling his head with fancy ideas.'

There was little chance of that. What with his paper-round, the journey to and from school, helping in the shop and home-work to do as well, Keir was as busy as his parents. Life was too full for fancy ideas. He and Dusty were inseparable from Mondays to Fridays, and their reputations grew all the time. By the Third Year, Keir had emerged as the best cricketer in the school and his pieces in the magazine earned increasing praise and attention. Dusty, too, notched up successes. He won the chess championship for the first time and surprised everyone by exerting himself enough to set a new record for the half-mile. Both boys made light of their own triumphs while heaping praise on the other. 'I reckon you'll end up playing cricket for England,' said Dusty with a proud grin.

'And you'll run in the Olympics,' Keir would reply. Such was the charm of the Team.

Their friendship even survived a surprise in the Fourth Year, when Keir learned that among Dusty's 'home friends' was someone called Marcia with whom he went *all the way* on a Saturday night. Girls were still to be discovered by the majority of the boys, for although the school was co-educational, the two sexes were kept apart for most of the time. They came together for the annual play and a few other functions, but classes were segregated and the school was divided. At school dances they groped and fumbled, but to get a girl to go all the way was unheard of. Not that Dusty boasted, he had too much style to do that. Instead, casually, he let it be known that he was seeing a girl on a regular basis. What made it quite something was that she was seventeen, fifteen months older than he was. Seventeen made her grown-up. A grown-up woman who visited Dusty's house every Saturday when his step-father took his mother to the pictures.

Keir would ask, 'How's Marcia?'

Dusty would grin and say, 'Better than ever.' But he never elaborated. When one of the boys boasted about what he did with a girl in the cinema, Dusty would say with a superior smile, 'Those who do it don't talk about it. Those who don't do it, talk about it all the time.'

Keir took his cue from that. He never mentioned his weekends in the hope that his silence would be misinterpreted. It was, and the Team's prestige multiplied still further.

When they were seventeen, Keir and Dusty moved up to the Sixth Form. By now they were among the most senior boys in the school. Certainly they were the most popular. In effect, the Sixth ran the school and the Team ran the Sixth. Keir now edited the school magazine. Dusty won the chess championship for the fourth year in a row. Keir captained the cricket team. Dusty broke the record for the school mile. Whatever one did, the other gave his wholehearted support. One rule remained solid: nothing would induce the one to compete against the other.

Masters speculated on possible careers for the boys. Neither Keir nor Dusty planned to go to university, so they would both leave school the following summer. 'It's a pity,' said Matthews, the Headmaster, 'I wish they would go to university.' Coleman, the Sports master agreed. 'Especially Milford. If he could get into Cambridge he'd captain the cricket team. After that, who knows? He could play for the county, maybe even for England.'

'I suppose there's no chance of changing his mind?' asked Matthews.

'No chance. I don't think his family could support him. It's a matter of cash.'

'So what will he do? Have we any ideas?'

Clemence, the senior English master, smiled with self-satisfaction. Milford was his favourite pupil and it was pleasing to be the purveyor of good news. 'I sent some of his pieces to the local paper. The editor was very impressed. I'm sure I can get him in there.'

Matthews beamed with genuine pleasure. 'That's excellent. What about when he goes off for National Service? The paper will keep his job for him, I take it?'

Clemence nodded and the conversation turned to a discussion on the careers disrupted by young men having to serve two years in the Armed Services. 'The wretched system should be abolished,' Matthews complained. 'It's a confounded waste of time, messing up young lives just when they're anxious to get going.'

'Talking about being anxious,' said Clemence, 'reminds me I've not been able to do much for young Miller.'

Coleman laughed. 'What can anyone do with Miller? Except tap him for a loan. He makes a fortune on those comics, you know.'

They speculated on Miller's prospects for a while. Clemence suggested banking. 'After all, Miller's only interested in money.' But Matthews shook his head. 'No, I don't see Miller as a banker.'

The conversation trundled on until the bell signalled the start of lessons. It was Coleman who summed up what they were thinking as they trooped out of the Staff Common Room. 'I'll miss them, you know. Milford especially. The cricket team will collapse without him. And I know Miller can be a lazy bugger, but you can't help liking him. He's got a style all of his own has young Miller.'

'They'll miss each other,' Matthews said thoughtfully. 'In all of my years I've never seen two boys take to each other like those two. If this school has given them something, it's a friendship that will last for the rest of their lives.' Which was what everyone said. Keir and Dusty were closer than brothers. Just to see them walk down the street, generally with the taller figure of Dusty doing the talking while Keir nodded agreement, was to be struck by their friendship. In more than four years they had never once argued. Their friendship was set to last the rest of their lives.

And then came Dawn Wharton.

Two

'I wonder what she looks like?' Dusty mused. It was lunchtime and the whole school buzzed with talk about the new girl.

'Who knows?' Keir shrugged. 'Who cares?'

It was a lie. He knew perfectly well what she looked like. He could describe the way her eyes were set into her face at a slant, like the eyes of a cat. He could have said that, without being conventionally pretty, Dawn Wharton was strikingly different. He could have admitted that he had seen her in the corridor earlier. Instead, for the first time in his life, he told Dusty a lie. Not that it affected the outcome. Other boys felt compelled to tell Dusty. Ever since Dusty had first talked about Marcia he had been regarded as the expert on girls, so he and Keir were dragged off to the covered walkway that separated the boys' quadrangle from the girls'.

Keir shivered when he saw her. His first impressions were confirmed a dozen times over. He watched her walk down some steps with two other girls, neither of whom he could describe a minute later.

'Her name's Dawn Wharton,' one of the boys was saying to Dusty. 'She used to live in Bristol or somewhere like that. She's smashing isn't she, Dusty?' Keir felt himself wanting Dusty to say no. Another of the boys was asking, 'Are you interested in her then, Dusty?' while someone else asked, 'But what about Marcia?'

Marcia, so far as they knew, was still part of Dusty's weekends. She was eighteen now and worked in a hairdresser's. It was quite a coup for a boy still at school to have an eighteen-year-old steady. Marcia had become part of Dusty's image. All of which passed through Keir's mind as he waited for Dusty's

23

reaction. Surely Dusty wouldn't be interested? But one look at Dusty's face told Keir he was wrong. Dusty was staring with an unblinking gaze, much as Keir himself had stared in the corridor earlier. 'What about Marcia?' Keir repeated, trying to hide his concern.

Suddenly, unexpectedly, Dusty laughed and turned away. 'Come on, I've got customers waiting. I can't stand here gawping all day.' With which he set off for the corner outside the metal-working class, which was his pitch for doing business with his American comics. Keir's heart pounded as if recovering from an anxiety attack. Such was his relief that he giggled with nervous excitement. He wondered what had made him so anxious. It couldn't possibly be the girl. After all, he didn't even know her, he had only seen her twice . . .

Being a Tuesday, the Team stayed late after school, Dusty to play chess and Keir to collate articles for the magazine. Keir enjoyed Tuesdays. He liked to sit alone in the library, sifting contributions, writing his own piece and juggling with layouts. Hugh Clemence always checked the results but Keir had become so expert that his work was usually printed without amendment. Invariably, he finished at about seven and since the chess club finished at the same time, he and Dusty had established the habit of having a snack at the coffee bar down the road before going home.

But, for once, Keir's attention wandered as he sat in the library. The writing wouldn't come. Words refused to flow from his pen with their usual profusion. He kept picturing Dawn Wharton in the corridor, remembering her smile and the encouraging look in her eye. Trying to dismiss her from his mind, he started work, and re-started, and re-started again. He did try, but it was useless, and after an hour he gave up. For the first time in a year the magazine would be published without an article by Keir Milford. The defeat niggled him. Sighing with frustration he shuffled the other contributions into an acceptable order and put them in a file to give Clemence in the morning. Excuses began to form in his mind. 'Sometimes it won't come,' he grumbled. 'Writing's not like building a shed or painting a fence. If it won't come it won't, and that's all there is to it.'

With that he went off to the chess club, where he found Dusty, also in an irritable mood. 'I lost to a young kid in the Third

24

Form,' said Dusty in disgust. 'He caught me with the most stupid trap imaginable. I can't think what came over me.'

They adjourned to the Golden Paradise Coffee Bar where usually they chattered nonstop, but for once they were silent, almost morose. As a rule they so enjoyed each other's company they delayed going home, yet Keir felt strangely impatient to leave and he sensed similar feelings in Dusty.

Home early for a Tuesday, Keir set about his work in the shop, dragging cartons down from the stockroom to re-stack the shelves. The familiar tasks required unusual concentration and transferring the contents of even one carton exhausted him.

It was the same over supper. Generally, Keir was washed and at the table within an hour. Instead, he sat down late and only pecked at his food. 'Is anything the matter?' asked his mother. 'Did something go wrong at school?'

'No.'

Normally, he was such a chatter-box that he followed her in and out of the kitchen, relating his news, but for once he couldn't be bothered and, saying he felt tired, he went early to bed.

'That's right, love. You've probably been overdoing it. You'll feel better after a good night's sleep,' his mother said, comfortingly.

He was too restless to sleep. He was kept awake by thoughts of that girl. He remembered the warmth of her smile and the sway of her hips . . .

Keir's life was empty of girls. His weekends were absorbed by cricket or football, and what with delivering papers, school and homework, weekdays were a blur from Mondays to Fridays. He'd never desired a girl's company enough to sacrifice even an hour of his time, but he felt an urge to know Dawn Wharton. The problem was how. The whole school was talking about her. Someone would soon ask her out. No doubt they were already queuing up, vying with each other with their invitations. She would choose someone. She was that kind of girl. And she'd choose someone who mattered: she was that kind of girl, too. Keir's heart sank. She was bound to choose Dusty. After all, Dusty was a man of the world . . . Suddenly the idea of being 'the amiable oaf who followed behind' filled Keir with outrage. It had never been important before. After all, he and Dusty were the Team. They never competed against each other at anything . . .

After delivering his papers the following morning, Keir changed into his school clothes and set out for the station. Following his restless night, he felt listless and tired as he paced the platform, waiting for the train to arrive. He knew the journey by heart. The fact that he travelled further to school than others had long ceased to bother him. It was only when he was tired, as now, that he cursed the tedious journey.

Suddenly it turned into a blessing. A hand fell on his arm. 'Hello. I didn't know you lived here.' And there was Dawn Wharton, lighting up his whole day.

He stuttered that he had lived in Hillingdon all of his life.

She laughed. 'I didn't know anyone lived here. I'd never heard of the place until a few weeks ago. Now we've got a new house and I've got a new school. I don't know if I'm on my head or my heels.'

Neither did Keir, but for quite different reasons. Close up she was even more disturbing than from a distance. So dark were her eyes that the iris was indistinguishable from the pupil, giving them an unnerving intensity. But it was more than her eyes. When the train arrived and they found a seat, her regulation blue coat fell open to reveal the prettiest legs he'd ever seen. And he couldn't stop admiring her figure . . .

Never had the journey passed so quickly. He learned where she lived for a start. He actually passed her house on his way to the station. It was only a few roads from the Milfords' shop, only a few roads but definitely up-market, the sort of house that has a gardener and a cleaning woman to go with it. Not that it mattered. All that mattered was that this marvellous girl was almost a neighbour. This marvellous girl who was so full of questions about the school, the staff and the pupils. And of course he was an expert, being in the Sixth and being half of the Team. He was as informative and as amusing as he could be, basking in her laughter and growing so confident as they walked up the hill to the school that he said, 'You haven't heard the half of it yet. I'll tell you some more on the way home if you like.'

Her dark eyes laughed up at him. 'Why not? I'll meet you here, shall I, at the gates?'

Keir arrived in his class shaking with excitement, thrilled at the prospect of travelling back and forth, five days a week, three hours a day with Dawn Wharton. Meeting her like that changed his whole life. It was amazing to see the classroom still looking the same – the same desks and cupboards, the same boys, the same Dusty. Dusty! He knew he should go straight in and say, 'Dusty, the most marvellous thing has happened. Dawn Wharton lives round the corner from me. I'm going to ask her out. She's going to be my girl. Isn't it terrific?'

But the words stuck in his throat. His mouth went dry. Suppose Dusty said, 'I don't care where she lives, I'm asking her out. She's going to be *my* girl, not yours.'

Keir lost his nerve. The risk was too great.

'Hi,' said Dusty with a grin. He glanced up from sharpening a pencil. 'You okay? You look a bit . . . peculiar.'

'What? Me? No, tired that's all. I didn't want to get up this morning.' *What's wrong with me*, Keir thought furiously, *I can't even look him straight in the eye!* He sat down at his desk and opened his books. *Tell him later, there's no hurry.*

The morning dragged. *Tell him at lunchtime*, Keir promised himself. But at lunchtime he talked of everything he could think of instead of Dawn Wharton.

Don't make a big thing of it, he told himself, *mention it casually later*. But he failed to mention it later, even though the afternoon seemed everlasting.

Finally the school day came to an end. As usual, Keir and Dusty left together. Keir's heart leapt as he saw Dawn already waiting at the school gates. Then his pleasure turned sour. Three boys from the Fourth Form were with her, laughing and joking, almost standing on their heads to amuse her. Keir scowled furiously as the boys hurried away amid a flurry of waving hands and shouts of 'See you tomorrow'. Suddenly, the overdue explanation burst from his lips. Turning to Dusty, he said, 'I forgot. I met the new girl on the train this morning. She lives near me.' A look of incredulity came into Dusty's eyes but before he could say anything Keir had taken them to where Dawn was waiting. 'Hello,' he said, trying to recapture the confidence he had felt that morning. 'This is Dusty Miller.'

She smiled. 'What an honour. Am I to be taken home by the full Team?'

Dusty stared at her, absorbing every detail before shaking his head. 'No, I live in the opposite direction. I catch a bus at the bottom of the hill.'

Keir went weak with fear at the thought of losing her to Dusty. Dusty had the advantage of experience. He'd been going with Marcia for two years, going all the way with her every Saturday night. By Keir's reckoning he had fucked her a hundred times. Keir hadn't fucked a girl even once. He was still a virgin. Girls must sense these things. They must know . . .

Dawn's gaze was still resting on Dusty. She made a small moue, whether of disappointment or acceptance was hard to say. Keir took heart from one thing. She was unsmiling. So was Dusty. They were exchanging deep looks which Keir finally brought to an end by saying, 'Right then, shall we go?' So the three of them walked down the hill together for the first time – Dawn in the middle, Keir on one side and Dusty on the other.

Which was when Keir behaved very badly. He always waited for the bus with Dusty. It was never more than a few minutes. Usually they were still talking as Dusty clambered aboard. But this time, Keir deliberately walked past the bus stop with his hand on Dawn's arm. 'See you tomorrow,' he said, looking directly ahead. Dawn might have stopped had he slackened his pace. Instead she had no choice but to keep up with him, doing what he did. ''Bye Dusty,' she said breathlessly. Keir dared not look back. He could imagine the hurt in Dusty's eyes. He didn't want to see it. He didn't even want to think about it. All he wanted was to put distance between them, so he hurried Dawn into the station without even a glance over his shoulder.

His conscience was in an uproar when they boarded the train. He tried to put Dusty out of his mind, something that would have been impossible without Dawn at his side. As it was, she made it easy, especially when he learned how much she knew about him. She knew of the Team, and about him being captain of cricket and editor of the school magazine.

'Of course –' she laughed – 'you're famous, didn't you know?'

She was going to be really famous. She was training to be an actress. It was no idle dream either. She had been taught dance and the piano and singing from the earliest age. 'I'm joining RADA next September,' she told him, 'so I'm only at this school until summer.'

Keir had never heard of the Royal Academy of Dramatic Art. Neither had he met anyone who planned to go on the stage. Yet it seemed entirely appropriate that Dawn Wharton should contemplate embarking upon such a glamorous life.

'It's not as glamorous as people imagine,' she said. 'I've done some theatre work already, amateur stuff in Bristol, and it's pretty exhausting I can tell you.' Her talk about the theatre held Keir enthralled. He was in a daze when he left her at her gate. 'I'll call for you in the morning if you like,' he suggested with feigned casualness.

'Fine.' She caught his hand. 'And I'm glad you live here. I couldn't face that journey alone every day.'

He made himself walk to the corner before breaking into a wild run, leaping and skipping. He hardly dared believe his luck. Dawn Wharton lived in Hillingdon. They would journey back and forth together . . .

'My word,' said his mother taking one look at his face, 'it's easy to see you've had a good day.' His father swivelled round in his wheelchair. 'What's up, lad? Has the school gone on holiday?'

A holiday was the last thing Keir wanted. It would stop him from seeing Dawn Wharton. Tempted to tell them about her, somehow he couldn't. He felt shy. He had never talked to them about girls. He was afraid they might laugh at his excitement. 'So what's happened?' Joe Milford persisted.

'What? Oh, nothing special, Dad.' And then, because his father looked disappointed and because he was bursting with happiness, Keir wanted his father to be happy too, so he said, 'I was top in history today, that's all.'

It was a lie, another lie. For someone so truthful, Keir was beginning to lie with fluent abandon.

Three

Keir lived the following days in a state of continual tension. Being with Dawn became the most vital part of his life. Everything else – sport, the magazine, his school work and chores in the shop – fell by the wayside. Besotted, he sped to Dawn's gate in the morning and lingered with her on the way home.

At school, no other boy had a chance. Keir was at Dawn's side when she arrived and with her again when she left. His biggest worry remained Dusty. He would have trusted Dusty with his life. Loving him as a brother, he would do anything for him, yet deep down he feared him as a rival. On the horns of a dilemma, Keir knew that to keep Dusty and Dawn apart would make for an impossible life, yet unless they were kept apart Dusty might take over . . .

Dusty looked simply bruised and betrayed. The pain in his eyes was exactly as it had been when he talked of his mother re-marrying. Yet he said not a word. He watched Keir and Dawn arrive in the mornings. He accompanied them down the hill after school, to stand alone at the bus stop, staring after them as they hurried into the station.

In private, Keir was disgusted by his own behaviour, yet he seemed powerless to stop it. Torn apart by conflicting emotions, he was miserable about being disloyal to Dusty, but elated about being with Dawn. His quandary seemed set to last forever until, one evening on the way home, Dawn asked, 'What's Dusty really like? I mean he can't be as bad as he seems, not with you as his friend.'

Keir was taken aback. 'What do you mean, "as bad as he seems"?'

She shrugged. 'Oh, you know what they say about him and this what's-her-name – Marcia. And the way he looks at girls as if he's God's gift to women.'

'Dusty's not like that. He's great. He's my best friend. Don't you like him?'

Dawn tossed her black curls. 'I hardly know him,' she said with indifference, 'but he seems so arrogant. Nothing like you. I can't think why you're his friend.'

A great weight lifted from Keir's shoulders. How stupid he had been to worry about Dusty. Dawn didn't even like him. She thought he was arrogant. Keir's spirits soared. Dusty was not a rival at all. Suddenly, Keir was so happy that he rushed to his friend's defence with a torrent of words. 'He's great, really. He can be very funny at times . . . and he's ambitious . . . he's going to be a millionaire by the time he's twenty-five. He will be too. If Dusty says something, you can bet it will happen . . .'

When he went to bed that night Keir felt easier in his mind than he had for weeks. His conscience still plagued him about Dusty, but he vowed to end the coolness which had sprung up between them.

His chance came the next afternoon. Changing after sport, he and Dusty were the last to gather up their kit and the locker room was virtually empty when Keir suggested, 'Fancy a coffee on the way home?'

Dusty's grudging look was suspicious. 'What about your new friend?'

'We could ask her to join us.'

After a moment's consideration, Dusty shrugged. 'I don't know. Some of the girls say she's a snob. Stuck-up. Full of airs and graces.'

'No, she's not,' said Keir with hot indignation. 'She's not stuck-up at all.'

Unlacing the canvas bag which he used for his kit, Dusty jammed his running shoes inside. Finally, he smiled and the familiar ironic gleam returned to his eyes. 'I suppose I'm just spoiled. I mean what with Marcia being eighteen. After all, there's a hell of a difference between a schoolgirl and a grown-up woman.'

Keir flushed. People only had to look at Dawn to see she was more than a schoolgirl. 'She's got her whole life mapped out,' he said, 'just like you and your plans to become a millionaire. I bet that's why they say she's stuck-up. Mentally she's so much older than they are. I reckon most people would take her for eighteen . . .'

He got his way. That afternoon all three of them walked down

31

the hill and into the Golden Paradise Coffee Bar together for the first time – and if Dawn was reserved and Dusty was cautious, Keir was relieved that at least they were polite to each other. He felt very much better, and from that day on Dusty was never left alone to wait for his bus. Instead, Keir and Dawn waited with him, and only when he had clambered aboard did they walk arm in arm off to the station.

Keir treasured every journey, delighted when the train ran late because it gave him more time with Dawn. She had a way of looking at him that was irresistible. Her eyes rounded and grew even darker, and the suggestion of laughter gave way to a look that made him tingle all over. Everything about her intrigued him. He wanted to ask dozens of questions, but he was held back by his father's strictures on manners. 'Never pry,' Joe Milford had taught his son. 'If someone tells you his business, that's up to him, but don't ask personal questions. You've got to learn a bit of discretion.'

Keir bit back so many questions that days passed before he learned Dawn's story. He pieced it together slowly, gleaning something from one conversation and adding it to another until a picture emerged. It was a disturbing picture in some ways. Her whole life was dedicated to becoming an actress. Training consumed every weekend. She attended dancing classes on Saturday mornings and lessons in acting on Saturday afternoons. She had a singing class on Sunday mornings and elocution and voice training from two until four. He was appalled by the savage régime. 'Don't you ever get sick of it?'

'It was easier when Gran was alive. She made it fun,' Dawn replied.

Her eyes misted over when she talked of her Gran and hardened when she talked of her mother. Her voice too, usually so full of life, also went dead in a way that was as noticeable as the frown which came to her eyes. 'She blames me for wrecking her career. She might have been a famous actress if she hadn't had me.'

Keir's parents had never blamed him for anything. Having grown up feeling wanted he was horrified to learn that Dawn hadn't grown up the same way. 'Doesn't she want you to be an actress?' he asked.

'I don't know what she wants. Just to be rid of me I think. She's moving to Spain as soon as I start at RADA, so that will be an end to it. With luck I'll never see her again.'

Keir's ties with his own parents were so strong that he found her attitude hard to understand. 'But she does so much for you with these lessons –'

'She makes sure I do them, that's all.'

'And pays for them. They must cost –'

'They don't cost her a penny. It's Gran's money, left to me in a Trust. She feels Gran should have left it all to her, without any strings, even though Gran left her enough for a house and goodness knows what.'

Dawn's Trust Fund was limited. 'Just enough for my lessons and so on. Gran used to take charge of me. My lessons were a sort of hobby for her. I didn't mind because she got such a kick out of them. They were fun. We were always laughing and joking about me becoming an actress. There wasn't any pressure. I could skip a lesson if I had a cold or something. Not like now. I'd have to be dead first. My mother's in a fix with my lessons. She resents them because of where they might lead. On the other hand she's got to organize them because of Gran's Trust, so she forces the pace as a punishment. It's all a bit weird, I suppose.'

Keir thought weird was an understatement. 'Don't you argue about it?'

Dawn reflected before answering, 'In a way we never stop. In other ways we never argue at all.' Her voice fell almost to a whisper. 'We had a very bad row once,' she said, avoiding his eye.

Her smile was back a moment later. 'Let's not talk about it. After all, I *do* want to be an actress. It's for my own good. Nothing's for nothing in this life, you must know that by now. If this is the price for becoming an actress, I'll pay it. The sooner I'm an actress the sooner I'll leave home.'

Keir was reminded of Dusty who was also bursting to leave home. *Strange how alike they are in some ways.*

Dawn was still on his mind when he reached home. The shop was empty apart from the Vicar who was discussing politics with his father. Joe Milford paused long enough to greet his son, then continued – 'It's madness. I don't hold with this new West

33

German government at all. We'd all be a lot safer if Germany remained under our control. This new independent State is a mistake. Next thing you know the Jerries will want their own army. Then an airforce. We'll end up fighting them all over again. And all Churchill does is yak on about the Russians –'

Keir went through to the back and said hello to his mother before going upstairs to his bedroom. After throwing his blazer onto his bed, he went into the stockroom, picked up a carton and began to fill it with packets of tea.

His father and the Vicar were still talking when he returned to the shop. 'All this stuff about a Cold War is rubbish,' Joe was saying. 'The Russians don't want a war. They lost six million in the last one. Six million people killed by the Germans! So when the Russians say keep Germany weak and divided, I say thank God. The Yanks should have more sense than to support a strong Germany –'

Keir went back and forth, mechanically re-stacking the shelves, mindless of what he was doing, thinking only of Dawn.

'You ought to talk to Bob Cooper,' Joe Milford told the Vicar. 'All this trouble started at the Potsdam Conference at the end of the war. Bob was there. You listen to what he says –'

Oblivious to the political conversation, Keir finished his chores, and went upstairs to wash before supper, thinking only of Dawn.

Four

The following week Keir plucked up enough courage to ask Dawn to go to the cinema. Her face fell. 'Oh, Keir, I'm sorry – I'm not allowed to go to the pictures.'

Rejection was painful. She had turned his life upside down. He had been so well organized before – what with the magazine and cricket at school, and playing for a local side at the weekends, going to the pictures with the boys on a Saturday night. Now, none of it mattered. He'd swap it all for more time with Dawn.

'Not *allowed* to go?' he said blankly. He listened as Dawn explained her mother's views on the cinema. 'She hates it. She says none of them can act properly, not like on the stage. I don't count her opinion for much, but Gran used to say the same thing . . .' Keir hated Dawn's mother without even meeting her.

'It's not that I won't go out with you,' said Dawn, clutching his arm. 'It's just that going to the pictures would cause such a row.'

Feeling better, Keir was beginning to salvage his wrecked hopes when Dawn squeezed his arm with sudden excitement. 'There's a school dance in three weeks. I could probably go to that . . . I mean, if you wanted to take me.'

His spirits soared. *If I wanted to take her! I'll take her wherever she wants if she'll let me.*

Next morning, when Dawn met him with the news that she could go to the dance, Keir was elated. He couldn't believe his luck. She was going to the dance with him. For the first time since he'd met her, he began to feel he was regaining control of events. And then, quite out of the blue, came trouble with Dusty.

Since their first visit to the Golden Paradise Coffee Bar, the three of them had called back several times. It seemed to Keir that Dawn and Dusty blew hot and cold; friendly at times, yet cautious and watchful at others. One minute they were laughing and joking, then their eyes would meet and a wariness would descend to cause a change of mood that left Keir bewildered. Fortunately they seemed friendly enough that evening. They sat sipping coffee in the Golden Paradise when Dawn asked, 'Will you be bringing Marcia to the dance, Dusty? It's time we all met her.' The seemingly innocent question had a startling effect. Dusty flushed red in the face and shot Dawn a quick look of anger. To make matters worse, Dawn actually laughed. 'What's wrong? You're not ashamed of her are you?' she asked.

Dusty scowled, suddenly dark-faced and furious. 'Of course not, but she wouldn't be seen dead with a bunch of schoolkids.'

Keir looked on in amazement. Dawn laughed again, this time with a taunting gleam in her eye. 'Why not let her decide? I promise you, I won't look like a schoolkid. I'll wear a long skirt and all the trimmings. Marcia and I will be company for each other.'

'No.' Dusty shook his head angrily.

'Oh, come on,' Dawn teased, 'why not –'

'Because I say so, that's why. And I'll thank you to mind your own business!' With which Dusty pushed back his chair and stormed out of the café.

Keir was staggered. The exchange had developed so swiftly. Like a squall blown up out of nothing. Yet even as he looked askance at Dawn, he had the strangest feeling that something beyond his understanding had passed between her and Dusty. The incident made for an awkwardness when Keir met Dusty next day, but neither of them mentioned it. Obviously it was wisest to leave it alone, and it was seemingly forgotten by lunchtime when something else occurred which had a much more lasting effect.

Dusty was selling his American comics outside the metal-working class, when Dawn arrived. For any girl to have appeared in the boys' quad would have caused surprise, when the girl was Dawn Wharton the surprise was considerable. She couldn't walk twenty yards without attracting attention.

'Hello, Keir. I got bored. I wondered what you were doing.'

Keir savoured the envious faces around him. Swelling with pride, he led her to the stone bench by the bicycle sheds, where she gave him a mischievous grin. 'The truth is I couldn't wait to tell you my news.' The school's Drama Society had held an audition for their Christmas production of *South Pacific* . . . and Dawn had been offered the lead.

'Terrific,' Keir exclaimed, his blue eyes shining with pleasure. 'You must be very excited.'

She laughed, making light of it, although the blush on her cheeks betrayed her true feelings. 'Hardly. After all, it's not the West End and I've trained for the stage ever since I can remember. Mind you, some of the other girls don't think that should count.'

Apparently complaints had been made about a newcomer being given the lead. Keir patted her arm, 'They're jealous, that's all. I should ignore them.'

When Dusty finished with his comics, he came over to join them and, despite the exchange of the previous evening, he too offered his congratulations. In fact he and Dawn seemed anxious to make up; he took trouble to discuss the play and she asked polite questions about his business in American comics. Consequently, the three of them passed such a pleasant half-hour sitting in the September sunshine that the bell for afternoon lessons rang only too quickly. 'If those girls are as bitchy tomorrow, I'll be back,' Dawn said with a laugh.

And she was. Surprisingly, there was no outcry from authority. Dawn encountered some odd looks as she walked across the boys' quad, but no member of staff actually said anything. The reason became known a day or so later. Apparently nothing in the school rules stipulated that the quadrangles should be segregated. It was merely a convention that had grown up and, in the absence of unseemly behaviour, the staff were bound by the rules. So the pattern became established. From then on, Dawn spent every lunch hour with Keir and Dusty. They sat on the stone bench, talking about all manner of things; mostly what they'd do when they left school: Dawn would join RADA and then go onto the stage, Dusty would become a business tycoon, and Keir would join the local paper. Dawn and Dusty always had the most ambitious plans. When Keir thought of the future he did so in black and white, whereas their schemes were always in glorious technicolour. Dawn would say, 'You've got to have dreams –'

'Or you'll have nightmares,' Dusty would interrupt with a grin.

They were forever doing that, finishing each other's sentences. And a look would pass between them that Keir could never quite fathom. Sometimes he had the strangest feeling that they were older and conversing in a language he had yet to learn. It made him uncomfortable. Then Dawn would laugh or Dusty would grin and the moment would pass.

For the most part, however, Keir was pleased with the way things had worked out. It seemed to him that Dawn and Dusty had become friendly without becoming friends . . . and that suited him fine.

Another thing to work out well were Dawn's rehearsals for *South Pacific*. They were on Tuesday evenings; so on Tuesdays Keir laboured over the magazine, Dusty played chess, and afterwards they all adjourned to the coffee bar.

It all strengthened the theory that the bond between Keir and Dusty was set to last the rest of their lives. To the watching world, it seemed that not even Dawn Wharton could divide the

Team. On the contrary, she had joined it. Indeed, for a brief period, people wondered which two of the three of them would make up a couple.

Such speculation ended on the night of the dance.

Ranking with the summer cricket match against the Old Boys, and the school play staged every Christmas, the October dance was one of the high spots of the calendar. Everyone was there. Headmaster Matthews and his wife; Rene Bannister; Coleman acting as Master of Ceremonies; Hugh Clemence in charge of refreshments – all in their best bib and tucker.

Girls came in long dresses and precious sheer nylons, with burnished hair and painted lips. Many could turn a few heads. Penny Bridges had the lithe grace of the professional ice dancer she was soon to become, and Jenny Page had a sultry allure. Yet they were *girls*; girls dressed up for a party, girls who giggled, girls who blushed, girls who became self-conscious when a boy looked at them boldly. That was the difference between them and Dawn Wharton who carried herself with the assurance of a grown woman – and a grown woman who was there to be looked at. Her brilliant eyes flashed and laughed above lips that never stopped smiling . . .

Even Hugh Clemence, the English master, was prompted to observe, 'Keir Milford's a lucky young bugger.' Which was what everyone said. People changed their minds about Keir after that night. He was no longer 'the amiable oaf who followed behind'. With Dawn on his arm, he eclipsed even Dusty. The team was seen in a new light. Dusty lost status by his non-attendance. It was said he stayed away because he was jealous.

Although deaf to the talk about Dusty, Keir was not blind to the envious looks. They filled him with pride, and Dawn filled him with excitement. He couldn't stop looking at her. He trembled when he touched her bare shoulders and exulted when she clung to his arm. She was his girl and everyone knew it.

He hired a taxi to take them home. The mad extravagance cost a week's earnings from delivering papers but he thought the money well spent. Dawn responded to his kisses and only stopped him fondling her breasts when she saw the driver watching them in the mirror. 'Not now,' she whispered. 'Later.'

Later? Hardly daring to believe there could be more to this

marvellous evening, Keir paid off the cab and stood wide-eyed and waiting. 'Go into the garage,' Dawn whispered. 'I'll pretend to go to bed and join you as soon as I can.'

It was pitch black in the garage. Keir had to feel his way into the car, where he sat on the back seat, wrapped in a travelling rug, shivering from cold and anticipation. She came to him half an hour later.

The sixty minutes that followed were the most exciting of Keir's young life; an hour full of embraces and kisses, of whispers of joy and pleasurable sighs, of teasing fingers, mounting passion and blood-tingling excitement which culminated when she took him into her mouth . . .

Afterwards, warm in the blanket, they lay in each other's arms and talked in soft voices. Having experienced ecstasy, Keir wanted more. The problem was, how? Dawn's life was beset by so many restrictions. 'I know,' she whispered with a sudden idea. '*South Pacific!* I wish I could see the real show in the West End. I'm sure it would help my performance in the school's production.'

Keir had never set foot in a theatre. He hadn't even been to the West End, but when she said 'I wish', words fell from his lips. 'I'll take you,' he said. 'We could go together. If you'd come with me, I mean.'

'Of course I'll come with you, Keir.'

Even in the darkness, he could sense the smile in her eyes.

They went the following Saturday. Keir realized in advance that such an expedition would cost a good deal. He had saved hard until then. Two of his 'home friends' were keen cyclists and he had planned to have enough to buy a bike the following summer. 'We can go on holiday,' his friends had said. 'It won't cost much if we camp out and bike everywhere.' Keir had been enthralled by the prospect of spending long summer days exploring the south coast. His own needs were few. He neither smoked nor drank. His only expenses were cinema with the boys on a Saturday night – the cheapest seats – and a few snacks at the Golden Paradise Coffee Bar. His favourite recreations – cricket and football – cost nothing. Consequently, most of the money earned from delivering papers had been saved. It was all there, in his Post Office Savings Book, waiting to be spent.

He broke the news to his parents on the Friday evening.

'The West End?' His mother stared in amazement. 'Well, I never. Whatever time will you be home?'

His father grunted disapproval. 'That will cost you a pretty penny. You'll not get that bike if you waste your money on girls.'

Keir thought his father was stupid to compare cycling with the delights of being with Dawn.

Saturday night was marvellous. The West End was a new world, full of glitter and movement. Keir and Dawn walked down Piccadilly, agog at the flashing neon and the bustling traffic. They paused here and there to gape at lighted shop windows or at street vendors selling everything from fresh violets to hot chestnuts. In fact, so often did they stop that they grew anxious about reaching the theatre in time, so they quickened their pace and hurried until, turning a corner, they found it in front of them, with the actors' names up in lights and lots of photographs around the front doors.

The seats which had seemed so expensive to Keir were at the back of the dress circle, but the poor position was dwarfed by the thrill of being in a West End theatre. Dawn shivered with excitement as the curtain rose, rewarding Keir with a squeeze of his hand and a flash of her eyes before leaning forward in her seat, hardly daring to breathe.

At the interval they went to the bar, packed with people as excited as they were. Dawn ordered a dry sherry and Keir had the same, his first alcoholic drink to celebrate their first visit to the West End.

'Isn't it marvellous?' Dawn laughed, raising her glass. And since the second half of the show excelled even the first, the final curtain brought them to their feet to applaud until their hands hurt and all the strength drained out of their arms.

Still breathless, they emerged onto the street. Despite the late hour, they were amazed to find it still busy. The roar of the traffic was as loud, the lights as bright, the pavements still crowded with people. Keir and Dawn were delighted. Neither of them felt the slightest bit tired. There was so much to see. So they strolled arm in arm through the West End, discovering Shaftesbury Avenue and the outskirts of Soho. Which was when mouthwatering smells drifting from a restaurant prompted Dawn to exclaim 'Oh, Keir, I'm hungry. Wouldn't it be fun to have supper?'

All at once it seemed the right thing to do. Doubts disappeared when Dawn squeezed his arm and nestled against him. Hastily, he calculated how much remained in his pocket. To avoid any embarrassment he had drawn a quarter of his savings out of the Post Office, promising himself to return the surplus on Monday . . .

Dining by candlelight in an Italian restaurant was an adventure from the first moment. The Head Waiter broke into voluble Italian when he saw Dawn. He insisted she was from his country. Her laughing denials simply provoked another outpouring of words. The chef emerged from the kitchen and he agreed with the Head Waiter. Even Keir had to admit that Dawn's jet-black hair and brilliant dark eyes did give her the *look* of an Italian. *'La bella Signorina,'* sighed the Head Waiter before turning to Keir. 'The lady is beautiful, no? You are the luckiest man in London.' They gave her a white carnation which she put in her hair, and presented Keir with a bottle of chianti to drink with their meal. 'Compliments of the house,' said the Head Waiter with a flourish.

The dishes were unpronounceable, the prices appalling, but the ambience of the place set such a radiant smile on Dawn's lips that Keir was swept away by the adventure. Gypsy violinists drifted in and out of the tables. Waiters danced back and forth from the kitchen, carrying dishes on their arms, bursting into song, laughing and joking. Keir had never known anything like it.

They lingered so long over their meal that it was late when they left. The Head Waiter and three of his assistants lined up at the door. They all kissed Dawn's hand and one pinched her bottom. Where other girls would have been embarrassed, Dawn made everyone laugh by fluttering her eyelashes and rolling her hips. Keir was overwhelmed by her self-assurance. She bubbled with such gaiety that people at other tables craned their necks. 'She must be an actress,' someone said in a loud whisper.

'Oh, wasn't that fun?' Dawn laughed in the street. She hugged Keir's arm as they went in search of the station. 'Have you ever eaten such food? Or drunk such wine?' Apart from the sherry beforehand, chianti was the only wine Keir had ever tasted. What with the strong drink and the heady excitement he was intoxicated by the whole night. Even the bill, which had

41

amounted to a staggering total, failed to render him sober. How could he be sober when total strangers said he was the luckiest man in London to have such a beautiful girl on his arm?

But he sobered up at the station. The gates were locked. The station was closed. The last train had gone. 'Oh, Keir,' Dawn gasped in dismay. 'How will we get home?'

He had lost all track of time. Cursing himself for a fool, he ran back into the street to search for a bus, hoping to find one that would go at least part of the way. But the last bus had left an hour before.

Counting what remained of his money, Keir approached a taxi rank. The first driver refused to take them because Keir lacked the full fare. The second said the same. Keir was sweating as he approached the third cab in the rank. The driver listened and glanced over Keir's shoulder to where Dawn waited ten yards away. Indecision showed in his eyes. He checked his watch, then yawned. 'Okay, hop in. I live out that way. I was thinking about packing up for the night.' Keir gulped a great sigh of relief.

A moment later they were on their way home, leaving the bright lights of the West End behind them. Recovering her spirits, Dawn enthused about *South Pacific*, and went into raptures over the meal. 'Wasn't it wonderful? Hasn't the entire evening been fantastic?'

But Keir's attention had wandered. He was thinking about money, wondering how he had spent so much in so short a time.

'Tired?' Dawn asked, snuggling into him and kissing his cheek. 'Not *too* tired, I hope,' she whispered into his ear. 'The car's in the garage tonight.' Her hand stroked his thigh to send a surge of excitement through his whole body. She laughed softly, a husky sound no more than a whisper. 'What a night. It was wonderful. We must do it again. Keir, say you'll take me again. Please.'

'Sure.' He was incapable of saying anything else.

'Soon,' she pleaded.

'Soon,' he agreed.

'Next weekend?' She cocked her head in an appeal. 'Can we go again next Saturday, Keir?'

Keir smiled. With his eyes closed he was conscious only of her hand on his thigh and the pleasure it aroused. *You are the luckiest man in London.*

'Sure,' Keir murmured, 'we'll go again next Saturday.'

Five

'*Next* Saturday,' Keir's mother exclaimed in alarm. 'Up to the West End? Where's all the money coming from? That's what I'd like to know.'

'It's my money,' said Keir stubbornly, 'I earned it. I can do what I like with it.'

Joe Milford looked up from his paper. 'You'll never have enough for a bike at this rate.'

Keir's mother collected the plates from the table. 'You're being downright daft if you ask me,' she sniffed. 'Most girls would be pleased with a trip to the pictures.'

Keir remained silent, not wanting to argue. How could he tell them that Dawn was quite different from most girls?

'What about Jimmy Rogers?' asked his mother. 'He was round asking if you're going to the cinema with the boys on Saturday. You and Jimmy have been friends for years. Suddenly you've got no time for him.'

'I'll see him in the park on Sunday –'

'You didn't last Sunday. You were too tired for football. Whatever time did you get home?'

Before Keir could answer, his father said, 'Don't cut yourself off from your friends. You never know when you'll need them.'

'That's right.' His mother nodded. 'What happens when you fall out with this girl?'

Fall out with Dawn? The suggestion was absurd, even if Keir had to admit he seemed to be falling out with everyone else – his parents, 'home friends', and even Dusty . . .

Keeping the peace between Dusty and Dawn had turned into a headache. The constant undercurrent baffled Keir. They appeared to like each other one minute, only to act as enemies the next. Two clashes in two days had left Keir bewildered. The

43

first had occurred on Monday, when the three of them were in the Golden Paradise. Dawn was talking about Saturday night. She had told everyone that Keir had taken her up to the West End. 'I know I go on about it,' Dawn admitted to Dusty, 'but we had such a wonderful time. The food in this restaurant was out of this world. You never tasted anything like it. And the chianti! The chianti was nectar, wasn't it, Keir?'

Keir grinned happy agreement.

'Did you ever taste chianti, Dusty?' Dawn asked.

Dusty seemed bored. 'Maybe.' He shrugged. 'I can't remember.'

'You'd have remembered this. I'll never forget it. It was so –'

Suddenly, Dusty's indifference gave way to an outburst of temper. 'Trust you to keep talking about it! I'm sick of hearing about the chianti and the Italian rest –'

'Steady,' Keir interrupted in surprise. He glanced at Dawn, expecting her to be upset.

But she wasn't upset. Instead she was smiling, a triumphant look in her eye. 'It's all right, Keir, I suppose I was going on. Tell us about your weekend, Dusty. Did you have a good time?'

'It was okay,' said Dusty in a truculent voice.

'That's good,' she purred. 'And how was Marcia?'

Dusty gave her a look almost of hatred.

Smiling, Dawn finished her coffee and pushed her chair back from the table. 'Shall we go, Keir? I need some early nights if we're painting the town again on Saturday night.'

Dusty choked out, 'You're going *again*?'

'What's it to you?' she asked, tossing her head. 'I'm Keir's girl. I do whatever he wants.'

Keir's joy at her words was short-lived as Dusty whirled round to face him. 'You damn fool! I thought you had more sense.' Then he leapt to his feet and almost ran from the café into the street.

Astonished, Keir turned, and as he did so he caught the look on Dawn's face. He had expected her to look shocked. Instead there was a curious gleam in her eye. The suspicion entered his mind that Dusty's inexplicable loss of temper represented som kind of victory on her part, as if she had been baiting him . . .

'Don't be silly,' she said, 'I expect I did go on too long

about *South Pacific*. It's important to me because I'm in it at Christmas. I'll say sorry tomorrow. Don't worry, everything will be fine.'

Curiously enough, everything was fine the next day. Keir was baffled. He had never known Dusty to be so short-tempered, yet each explosive incident was swept under the carpet within twenty-four hours. Dawn and Dusty made a special effort to be nice to each other and behaved as if nothing had happened, which left Keir uncertain about what to expect and made him nervous and tense.

Not that he felt tense in the Golden Paradise the next day. Most of the talk was about chess, so it was hard to imagine anything less likely to lead to an argument.

'White to play and mate in three moves,' said Dusty. 'It's really quite easy.' They were discussing the chess problem for the school magazine. Dusty set one every week and Keir thought they were too difficult. He studied the sketch of a chess board with the pieces in play. 'You don't expect me to do it, do you? You should make them easier. More people would take an interest if they had a chance of solving them.'

'Okay,' said Dusty, 'I've another one here. Have this instead.' He withdrew his wallet from an inside pocket. Dusty was the only boy in school to carry a wallet and it always commanded attention. He opened the leather flaps and searched through the pockets, taking papers out and putting them back. One was a photograph and because of its shiny surface, it slipped and fell face-down on the table. On the back were written the words 'To Dusty with love, Marcia. The best you've taken yet.'

Dawn's eyes brightened. 'Oh, a picture of Marcia,' she said, reaching for the photograph. 'Did you take it yourself?'

'Yes,' said Dusty sharply. 'It's private.'

The mood changed in an instant. Smiling faces vanished, replaced by an angry scowl from Dusty and a look of triumph from Dawn as her hand closed over the photograph. Their eyes met in unmistakable challenge. Dusty remained quite still for a moment, then he shrugged, as if losing interest. Dismissing Dawn with a look of contempt, he resumed his search for the chess problem among the papers in his wallet. Even Keir was curious. He had heard about Marcia for two years without ever meeting her. Dawn said she doubted that Marcia even existed,

45

and sometimes Keir's suspicions had run along similar lines. So his eyes went to the photograph as Dawn turned it over.

It had been taken in a garden. Stone urns full of flowers flanked some steps on which reclined a girl with long blonde hair. Seen next to the Grecian urns the long hair gave her a slightly old-fashioned look. She had large eyes, a pert little nose, good shoulders, a slender waist and long shapely legs. By any standards she was good-looking, and if her smile was a trifle shy there was a very good reason. She was completely naked.

'Bloody hell,' said Keir in a low whisper. Dawn gave a little gasp. She tried to turn the photograph over but Keir caught her hand. His eyes travelled from the girl's perfectly formed breasts to the bush of pubic hair. Besotted with Dawn though he was, admiration shone in his eyes. 'Bloody hell,' he repeated.

'That's not a nice picture to carry around,' said Dawn, her cheeks pink and a hard look in her eyes.

'I like it,' was Dusty's laconic reply. He wasn't embarrassed. Setting the other chess diagram down on the table, he took the photograph from Dawn's hand and returned it to his wallet without as much as a glance. Instead he looked at Dawn, and this time Dusty's eyes gleamed with triumph.

Going home on the train, Dawn was in a thoroughly bad mood. *Penthouse* and *Playboy* had still to be born in the fifties. Girlie magazines did not peddle naked flesh on every street corner. Public nudity was a thing of the future.

'That shows what sort of girl she is,' said Dawn contemptuously, 'having a picture like that taken.'

'Dusty did say it was private,' Keir pointed out. Secretly he wished they had respected Dusty's privacy, just as secretly he felt a little bit of guilt and a whole lot of envy.

'I bet he's shown it to every boy in the school. I bet they've all drooled over it.'

'No,' said Keir. 'He hadn't even shown it to me.'

Dawn fell silent, but Keir guessed she was thinking about the secret game she played with Dusty, the rules of which were known only to them. It was all very puzzling, and Keir might have given it more thought had he not already been busy thinking about money. Another trip to the West End would decimate his savings. Going out with Dawn Wharton was proving to be very expensive . . .

The subject of money arose again on Saturday, when Keir met Dawn's mother for the first time. On previous outings Dawn had answered the door, and on school mornings she was out of the house before he was half-way up the drive. He had never been invited into the house, only the garage. So he was surprised when the door was opened by a woman with orange hair. 'Ah,' she said. 'It's you. Dawn's still getting ready.'

Keir blinked. He had never seen orange hair before. 'Oh,' he said. 'Thank you.'

Lost for words, he stood in the porch shuffling from foot to foot. The woman had orange hair and a large white bosom which threatened to overflow from a low-cut black dress. Wondering whether to say 'Good evening, Mrs Wharton', he decided against it. After all, she might not be Mrs Wharton.

'You'd better come in,' she said, turning on her heel and walking back down the hall.

Stepping inside, he took care to wipe his feet before hurrying after her. The hall was big and square, with a wide staircase rising to a half landing. Gilt chairs stood on a blue carpet. A large chandelier hung from the ceiling. Paintings in heavy frames decorated the walls.

'In here,' said the woman passing through an open door.

The drawing-room was well furnished. Two velvet-covered sofas flanked a marble fireplace. A grand piano took up most of a bay window. Vaguely aware of armchairs, bric-à-brac, and a sideboard loaded with bottles, Keir was mostly conscious of the woman who stood watching him.

'This is becoming a habit, isn't it? Three times in three weeks.' Her voice was as cold as her manner. Keir knew she was Dawn's mother by then. The portrait over the fireplace was clearly of her when she was younger. 'It's not a habit of which I approve,' she continued, taking a cigarette from a box on the mantelpiece.

Lost for an answer, Keir remained silent, rooted to a spot just inside the door. Lighting the cigarette, Dawn's mother walked over to the sideboard. Half filling a glass with gin, she added something from another bottle and swirled the contents around. 'See that?' she asked, pointing to a photograph in a silver frame. 'That was me when I was nineteen. And that one there was when I was twenty.'

Glancing at the photographs on the side table, Keir was

confused by some more which stood next to them. Beyond, on another table, was yet a different picture of Mrs Wharton, and on the grand piano were three more. Pictures of Mrs Wharton – full-face, profile, smiling and unsmiling – were repeated through the room like a wallpaper pattern.

'I had the world at my feet in those days,' Mrs Wharton said bitterly, 'then I threw it away.' Watching her gulp from the glass, Keir wondered if she wasn't the tiniest bit drunk. The thought shocked him. His own mother only took a sherry at Christmas and weddings. 'What's the matter?' Mrs Wharton asked suddenly. 'Cat got your tongue?'

He jumped. 'Er, no, I was . . . er, looking at the photographs.'

'Look and weep, that's what I do whenever I think of the life I could have had.'

Keir searched his mind for the right thing to say. He watched her return to the fireplace. Her hair changed to the colour of strawberries under the lights of the room. She was about Dawn's height but her figure, which might once have equalled her daughter's, had ripened into a comfortable fullness. The black dress was creased at the seat and tight enough at the waist to strain every seam. 'A lot of money has been invested in that girl, and I'll not see it wasted.'

Keir swallowed hard.

'She's had the best teachers money can buy. Nothing's been spared. So don't you get any funny ideas.' Mrs Wharton watched him with interest. 'You know what I mean by funny ideas?'

Although Keir could guess, it seemed prudent to remain silent. He swallowed again, feeling uncomfortable.

'I can see that you do. So long as we understand each other. Spend your money on her if you like. That's up to you. Take her to the theatre now and then, but that's all.'

Keir nodded, wishing the ground would swallow him up.

Mrs Wharton fixed him with a hard look. 'Now and then doesn't mean every week. Frequent meetings will not be encouraged. And keep your hands to yourself. You try to get into her knickers and I'll send someone after you with the garden shears.'

Blood rushed into Keir's face, making him suddenly so hot

and sweaty that he didn't know where to look – which was when Dawn walked into the room. Knowing she must have heard what was said, Keir expected her to be embarrassed, but instead she faced her mother with a cool look of disdain. 'Thank you, Mother, I'm sure Keir will remember his manners.'

'They only want one thing. I told you before –'

'I know what you told me. Anyway, we're going now –'

'And don't be late back,' Mrs Wharton snapped, suddenly agitated enough to spill her drink. 'You come straight home, you hear?'

'I hear,' Dawn answered in a tired voice. She smiled at Keir. 'Sorry I'm late, come on.' Linking her arm into his she turned so quickly that Keir had to crane his neck as he left the room. 'Goodnight, Mrs Wharton. It was . . . er, nice meeting you.'

Mrs Wharton was too busy drinking to answer.

During the journey Keir tried to discuss what had happened. Dawn's mother had shocked him. He would never have imagined a woman talking like that. His own mother would die sooner than say such things. But Dawn would only talk about the evening ahead. 'Isn't it exciting?' she said, hugging his arm. 'I can't wait to see Piccadilly.'

They were to see *South Pacific* again. 'I was too excited to take it all in the last time. Could we see it again? It will help my own performance so much . . .' So once again they found themselves swept away by the verve and the colour and the music of that spectacular show. And if, as they sipped Tio Pepe in the interval, they surveyed the bar with less innocent eyes, their enjoyment was enhanced by a sense of belonging.

Just as afterwards, when they plunged out into the street, anticipation was more pleasurable than surprise. Looking radiant, Dawn gloried in the sights, and he gloried at being with her, especially when they arrived at the restaurant. The Head Waiter rushed to greet them, smiling and bowing and kissing Dawn's hand, pausing to flash Keir a quick smile – 'Your usual table, of course, sir' – conducting them across the restaurant like visiting royalty, while Dawn's musical laugh attracted glances from every man there.

When they had ordered, Keir returned to the subject of her mother. Unable to get her out of his mind, he was both shocked and intrigued at the same time. He wanted to know about her, to *understand* her . . .

'What's to understand?' asked Dawn, resisting the direction of his conversation. 'I can guess what she said. She's said it to others in the past and no doubt she'll say it to others in the future.'

Keir winced. *Others in the past* was bad enough. He preferred not to think of more in the future.

'It's not so complicated.' Dawn shrugged. 'I told you before. There was a time when she might have had a career as an actress. Instead she got pregnant and had to get married.'

Keir was shocked again. *Had* to get married! He would have been ashamed. It could never be true of his own mother. Even if it were, which it couldn't be, but even if it were, he would never tell anyone. Never.

'Gran told me.' Dawn's glance was amused. 'I'm not supposed to know. I was, as they say, conceived out of wedlock. My real father ran away, leaving a long-time admirer to make an honest woman of her.'

'You mean your father isn't your real father? I mean, Mr Wharton is –'

'A meek little man who does what's he's told. He was a solicitor's clerk in Bristol. Thanks to Gran's money he gave it up. Now he spends his time in the conservatory, growing orchids.'

'You don't like him either?'

Dawn considered this. 'I don't *dislike* him. It's just that . . . well, he lives in a world of his own. They both do, I suppose. He grows orchids and she gets drunk.'

Keir tried to imagine what it was like never to know your real father and to grow up hating your mother.

'Don't look so sad.' She laughed. 'It's not the end of the world.'

'But the things your mother said –'

'About you wanting to get into my knickers? Well, don't you?' A wicked gleam lit her eye as she reached for his hand across the table.

Feeling guilty, his mind flew back to their rolling around in the back of the car. He had opened her blouse and fondled her breasts, and tried to slide his hand up under her skirt. *No, not that*, she had said, *We must never do that.* Afterwards she had done such wonderful things that all other thoughts had gone out of his head . . .

'Don't take life so seriously,' Dawn said, squeezing his hand.

'It's not only that,' he blurted out. 'She said I wasn't to see you so often –'

'Perhaps she was thinking of you.'

'Me? How –'

'Can you afford to take me to the theatre every week?' she asked gently, giving his hand another squeeze as she saw the look in his eye. 'I have a lovely time, Keir, really I do, but you must be realistic –'

'We could do other things.'

'I only like the theatre.'

'But it costs –' The protest fell from his lips before he could check the words. His flush deepened as he bit his tongue.

'Everything costs,' she said quietly, sounding so earnest that it might not have been her speaking at all. 'Everything costs, Keir. We spend our lives swapping something we have for something we want.'

He thought she was trying to soothe his injured pride until the words went round in his head. *We spend our lives swapping something we have for something we want.* He knew what he wanted. He wanted to be with this girl for the rest of his life. 'And what do you want?' he asked roughly.

Instead of answering, she slapped a hand to her forehead. Terror came into her face. She raised her left shoulder, then her right, then her left until she seemed to be hurrying along. Her eyes darted fearfully from side to side. She shivered. Clutching her dress, she drew it close to her shoulders, transforming herself into an old crone caught in a blizzard. 'Cossacks,' she whispered in a coarse voice. 'Quick, hide. The Cossacks are coming.'

As Keir gaped, the wicked gleam reappeared in her eyes. She burst out laughing. 'You see. What else can I be but an actress?'

Recovering, he found himself laughing as well, marvelling at her cameo sketch and her change of mood. She refused to be serious. Her laughter made their table the centre of attention. Hearing that she was in the restaurant, the chef emerged from the kitchen to instruct her personally in the art of making

51

zabaglione. Increasingly, the gypsy violinists played only for her, and by the end of the evening the entire restaurant revolved around the girl with the jet-black hair and brilliant dark eyes.

Missing the last train was inevitable. They travelled home by taxi, but Keir had ceased to care about money. He had spent half his savings. In the morning he would worry . . . Meanwhile he was with this beautiful, talented girl who would one day become a great actress.

Six

After the initial upheaval caused by Dawn bursting into his life, Keir's routine acquired a new shape. Life was different, even in the shop on the corner, where, for the first time, he asked for a wage.

'I dunno,' Joe Milford said doubtfully. 'I suppose it's only fair but –'

'Only for Saturdays, Dad. I'll work every Saturday from now on. And I do need the money –'

'To waste on that girl, I suppose,' said his mother, shaking her head. 'She's got her head stuffed full of fancy ideas. No good will come of it, you mark my words.'

His parents were unhappy about it, especially his mother, but from then on Keir drew a wage every week. Although not a fortune, added to the remains of his savings and supplemented by his earnings from delivering papers, it was enough to take Dawn up to town every third Saturday. They patronized the theatres, dined out in restaurants, returned home in taxis, and rolled around in the garage. The restricted meetings were echoed in the restrictions imposed upon Keir's passion, for never again did he thrust his hand up her skirts. Yet if the ultimate act was denied him, the immediate variations were so exciting that he never once left that garage feeling frustrated.

He knew he meant less to Dawn than her ambitions. He tried not to admit it, just as he pretended he was stronger than she. It was an idle pretence. In reality she was the most determined person he'd ever met. The unrelenting battle of attrition with her mother, and the everlasting lessons had developed a will-power of a quite exceptional strength. Keir consoled himself with the thought that, as much as she was anyone's, Dawn was his girl, and he clung to the hope that one day he would mean as much to her as she did to him.

Meanwhile, even Dusty appeared to accept the way of things. He made an effort to get on with Dawn and she responded, because the two of them squabbled less often. Occasionally, the long, lingering looks that passed between them filled Keir with disquiet, and their habit of finishing each other's sentences disturbed him, but they seemed to accept they were both part of his life and had to coexist if they wanted his friendship.

Life hurried past. October ended and November began. Trees lining the road to school shed their leaves which Keir kicked into new patterns of orange and gold every day. Some-times, especially if it were Friday and he was taking Dawn out the next night, he was like a puppy romping in the park. Dawn laughed and applauded and sometimes challenged Dusty to join in, but he never did. Instead, he watched with a wry smile and occasionally a wistful look lit his eye. The Team, if it still existed, had certainly changed. Keir was no longer playing second fiddle. Some said he was playing his own tune. Others said he was merely dancing to a new one, and that the fiddle had passed from Dusty to Dawn.

Finally, December came and the last week of term, and with it the school production of *South Pacific*. Rumours about squab-bles in rehearsals had been rife for weeks. Keir had spent hours placating Dawn as they had travelled home. 'They're such amateurs, Keir,' she would say, stamping her foot. 'If they won't do it properly, why do it at all?'

Nobody was as committed as Dawn. Once, when Keir asked what she did on Saturday nights when they didn't go out, she had said 'I stay in my room, rehearsing my part. I act it all out in front of the mirror, over and over again.' Her desperate craving for success made Keir nervous. He wanted her to have everything she wanted herself, yet sometimes the intensity of her ambition disturbed him. She had such hopes, such dreams. He dreamed too, but his were different. In his dreams five or six years had passed and they were married. He saw himself as a journalist in

Fleet Street by then, and imagined Dawn starring at Drury Lane around the corner. And each evening when they finished – he when the paper was put to bed and she when the curtain came down – they'd meet for supper at the Italian restaurant in Frith Street.

Dreams! Dawn's were about to be tested, for suddenly it was the end of December and time for the play. Four performances would be given. Tuesday through to Friday night, the last day of term. After the final performance, senior pupils would host a party for the cast before everyone disbanded for Christmas.

Keir was as nervous as Dawn on Tuesday morning. The train journey passed in relative silence, conversation limited to a discussion of the dress rehearsal which Keir already knew had gone badly. 'Don't worry,' he kept saying, 'It will come right tonight. Old Clemence seemed very confident yesterday . . .'

Dawn answered with a strained smile.

At lunchtime she was closeted away with the rest of the cast for a final rehearsal. It was the same at four o'clock. The whole cast was locked in the hall, preparing for the curtain to rise at seven-thirty.

Keir spent two hours biting his nails in the Golden Paradise with Dusty. 'Relax,' Dusty encouraged. 'She'll be fine.'

Keir found it hard to relax. He knew how Dawn had worked, knew what it meant to her. Suppose she gave a bad performance? Worse, suppose she lacked talent? Never having seen her on stage, he had no idea what to expect . . .

At seven o'clock the boys went back to the school to find the hall packed with staff, parents and pupils. Keir felt sick with nerves. The main body of the hall was reserved for guests, so he and Dusty had seats in the balcony. Craning his neck, he spotted Mrs Wharton's orange hair three rows from the front. Next to her was a thin, undistinguished, nervous-faced man who looked every inch a solicitor's clerk.

'Stop worrying,' Dusty whispered, 'she'll be fine.'

Good old Dusty. Keir felt a sudden sadness about the gap which had opened between them. Although they had both tried to close it, circumstances had defeated them.

Suddenly the orchestra struck up and plunged into a medley from the show. Feeling a stirring in his stomach, Keir began to pray that Dawn would do well. 'She'll be terrific,' Dusty insisted, 'I'll bet money on it.'

Good old Dusty!

The house lights dimmed. A thunderous fanfare blazed out from the orchestra. The curtain rose, and next moment the show burst into life.

An hour later, when the curtain fell for the interval, Keir slumped in his seat. He felt drained. His chest heaved. Sweat stuck his shirt to his skin. Unsure whether to laugh or to cry, tears prickled his eyelids. He could barely speak, let alone add to the shouts which arose on all sides. Dusty, face shining with excitement, dragged Keir to his feet. 'Wasn't she great? Fantastic? Wasn't she absolutely . . . bloody . . . fantastic!' And all around them people were saying the same thing.

Dawn's performance was even stronger in the second half. It wasn't just that she hit every note, or never put a foot wrong, or that every word was heard in the back row, although she did all of those things. It was more, much more. She brought the whole thing to life. When, in the play, she became anxious, the audience fretted. When all was lost and she wept, a wave of sympathy rolled up from the stalls. When her fortunes improved, the audience smiled at their neighbours. 'Isn't it wonderful?' they seemed to say. 'She's going to win through after all.' And when she was happy, they were ecstatic . . .

Keir cheered himself hoarse. The audience roared for an encore. The curtain rose again and there she was, alone in a spotlight, her dark eyes bigger and brighter than ever. She laughed and curtsied and waved with such joy that people's hearts warmed just to see her. Mr Clemence walked onto the stage to present her with a bouquet, and still the audience roared, 'Encore! Encore!' Clemence laughed and turned around, unsure what to do until Dawn did it for him. Running into the wings she drew the rest of the cast back onto the stage, a few at first, until others appeared and the entire company was assembled. Then Dawn blew the conductor a kiss and the whole orchestra struck up. With the cast behind her and the audience joining in every chorus, she sang again her three big numbers from the show.

Giddy when it was over, Keir's face shone as he basked in the praise which he heard on all sides. He felt so proud. Never again did he doubt she would be less than a great actress. Neither, it seemed, did anyone else, for Keir loitered in the foyer, eavesdropping shamelessly as people streamed past, all talking about Dawn.

In the taxi going home she listened wide-eyed as he described people's reactions. When he paused, she prompted him to go on. When he hesitated, she tugged at his sleeve. 'Did you see Jenkins? Was Gloria Manning there with her mother? Did the Bosworth twins like it?' Until finally, with a gleam in her eye, she asked, 'And Dusty? Did he really think I was good?'

'He was knocked out. We all were. Dusty said you were magnificent.'

'My word,' she mused, a satisfied smile on her lips. 'Even without taking my clothes off.'

Too happy to pay more than scant attention, Keir was as excited as Dawn with her triumph. In fact the whole week was a triumph. Dawn brought the house down with every performance, and at the party on the final night, she was unquestionably the belle of the ball.

And then came Christmas, when everything changed.

The first Keir heard about it was when he was serving in the shop on Christmas Eve. Christmas was the busiest time of year for the Milfords. The shop was crammed with customers and Keir was packing Mrs Green's basket when the telephone rang in the back room. 'It's for you,' said his mother, as surprised as he was, for he rarely received calls. Excusing himself from Mrs Green, Keir hurried off, wondering who it might be. His heart leapt at the sound of Dawn's voice. She sounded breathless with excitement. 'Keir? I must see you. I've got the most marvellous news. Can you meet me in the park in ten minutes?' He asked why. What was it all about? He asked her to tell him over the phone. He suggested that it wait until they met later, for their only date over Christmas. But to his dismay she said they wouldn't be meeting later after all. She had some marvellous news – 'Please, Keir, we must meet in ten minutes. It won't take long.'

Alarmed and disappointed, he returned to the shop where a queue of customers waited. 'Sorry,' he whispered to his mother, 'I must go. I'll be as quick as I can.' Ignoring his father's look of displeasure, he dashed upstairs to collect his coat and his

Christmas present for Dawn – three bars of scented soap and a tin of talcum powder in a fancy box – which he had intended to give her that evening. Now, even to wrap his gift in fancy paper demanded more time than he had. Throwing on his coat, he raced down the stairs and out into the street.

She was already at the park gates, pacing up and down, her face flushed, her dark eyes brilliant with excitement. As soon as she saw him she ran to meet him. Grabbing his arm she turned him into the park and skipped along at his side. Her words tumbled over each other. 'I'm going to Manchester this afternoon,' she said. 'I've got a part in a pantomime. Someone fell sick and an understudy broke her wrist, and – oh, all sorts of things. The point is I'm joining a repertory company. I'm not going back to school. Oh, Keir, isn't it exciting? It was only definite an hour ago. This is the most wonderful day of my life.'

It took Keir a while to gather the whole story. Apparently, a London theatrical agent had seen Dawn in the school production of *South Pacific*. 'Which was pretty marvellous in itself,' said Dawn breathlessly, 'but nothing much would have happened if this girl hadn't broken her wrist. They need someone immediately. Mr Maxwell – that's the agent – phoned last night and came down to see us this morning. Then he called Manchester and fixed everything up. My first performance is on Boxing Day. My first *professional* engagement! Isn't it fantastic?'

Keir struggled to take it all in. 'But what about school after Christmas?'

'That's the whole point. I've finished with school. I'm starting my career –'

'But you can't. What about exams?'

'Actresses don't need exams. And I *can* leave school. I'm old enough.'

'What about RADA?'

'Who needs it? It's just another school. Mr Maxwell says I'm ready for the theatre now. I'll learn far more in Rep than in RADA . . .'

He was still trying to cope with the idea of her going out of his life. 'What about your parents?' he asked weakly. 'Surely your mother –?'

'Can't wait to pack my bags. Come on, Keir, you know what

she's like. We hate the sight of each other. She wants to live in Spain, and I've always wanted to get away. This is my chance. Don't you understand what it means to me?'

She twirled away from him, coat billowing out above her knees, her hair flying out from her shoulders. Laughing she danced back and hugged him. 'I can only stay a minute, but I couldn't leave without seeing you. I'm catching a train at four from Euston or somewhere, I haven't even packed yet –'

Stupidly, he blurted out, 'But we were going out tonight.'

She laughed. 'Imagine, next time you go up to town it could be me on the stage.'

Blind to his bitter disappointment, nothing could quench her high spirits. She was laughing and jigging about, while he was reeling from shock. He had imagined the future a thousand times without foreseeing anything like this. Of course he knew they would leave school, but he had not expected it until next summer. He would have had another six months to establish their relationship, to put everything on a firm footing . . .

'When will I see you again?' he choked.

'Oh, soon, the contract's only for thirteen weeks. Mind you, after Manchester, who knows?'

Thirteen weeks was a lifetime! Keir struggled with his thoughts. 'After Manchester you'll come back home –'

'Huh, for a visit I might. I'll never live with them again. I'm leaving, Keir. Don't you understand what it means to me?'

Perhaps he hadn't properly? True, he had known she disliked her mother but . . .

'Be pleased for me,' she said, suddenly coming into his arms, 'and say you'll write. I'll send you my address as soon as I can.'

Still trying to adjust to the idea, Keir forgot his promise to return to the shop. 'I'll come to Euston with you –'

'No. They're taking me because of my luggage. There won't be room for you in the car.'

He could scarcely believe she was going away . . . now . . . like this. Suddenly he remembered the gift in his coat pocket. She giggled as she thanked him. 'My word, the audience can't say I stink after this lot.' She kissed him full on the lips. 'I was going to buy something for you this afternoon . . .'

He assured her he hadn't expected a present.

By now they had returned to the park gates and were back on

the road. 'Sorry to rush,' she said, tugging his arm, 'but I must do my packing.' A few moments later they reached her gate. 'I'll write as soon as I can,' she said, then laughed, as if struck by a sudden thought. 'I nearly forgot. Happy Christmas, Keir.'

As she ran down the drive he stared after her, wanting to shout, 'Stop! Don't go.'

She turned and blew him a kiss from the garage.

He waved, holding his breath, hoping against hope that she would run back and into his arms, but she lifted the latch and slipped inside without so much as a glance over her shoulder.

Dragging his feet, Keir walked back to the shop. A boy cycled past, whistling a Christmas carol. Illuminated Christmas trees glowed behind frosty windows, holly wreaths decorated front doors. Yesterday, Keir had glowed with the spirit of Christmas. His heart had been full of goodwill. Today life suddenly seemed totally empty.

'Happy Christmas, Keir,' said Mrs Hughes, emerging from the shop.

'Yes,' he said bleakly. 'Happy Christmas.'

Seven

Keir wrote every week, long letters of five or six pages. Dawn replied once a fortnight with hastily scribbled notes, often of only a few lines.

The excitement had gone from his life. He attended school, returned home, helped in the shop; but his heart was elsewhere. Dawn dominated his thoughts. He found himself wanting to talk about her – to his parents, to Dusty, to anyone who would listen – simply because talking seemed to bring her a bit closer.

His mother fretted. She told Joe, 'She sounds a flashy little madam if you ask me. I hope she stays in Manchester, that's what I hope. She's not the sort I want our Keir involved with.'

Joe was against girls altogether. 'The boy shouldn't be wasting his time. Another few months and he'll be working for that paper. They'll expect him to know more about life than girls with fancy ideas. It's time he took an interest in what's going on in the world,' was Joe's feeling.

Joe did all he could to interest Keir in what went on in the world. Politics were the love of his life and he wanted to share them with his son. His beloved Labour Party was still out of power and the Tories were running the country. 'Not running it,' Joe would say, 'ruining it, that's what they're doing.' He took some comfort from what was happening elsewhere. In Washington, General Eisenhower had become President Eisenhower, which Joe considered a good thing. 'I like Ike and Ike likes the British. He was a good friend in the war and he'll be a good friend in the future.' Britain was in dire need of friends according to Joe. The old Empire was breaking up and British influence was declining. 'Not that I believe in the Empire,' said Joe. 'People should be free to run their own affairs, unless they're Germans of course, and Germans are different.' He was like a dog with a bone about Germany. Twice in his lifetime, Germany had plunged the world into war. Joe said it could happen again. 'Those Jerries want watching,' he told Keir. 'Your generation will have to fight them next time.'

Which invariably led Joe to air his views on National Service. 'It's a blinking disgrace. Conscription's all right when there's a war on, but this is supposed to be peacetime. It's all wrong. The government will waste two years of Keir's life. National Service should be abolished.' Keir agreed about that, mainly because he was worried about being posted overseas and even farther from Dawn.

He treasured her letters. She wrote telling him that she lived '. . . *in theatrical digs, three minutes from the theatre . . . the landlady's as dotty as a dalmatian . . . the food's simply awful . . .*' Her pantomime role had been that of a butterfly – '. . . *don't you DARE laugh. And don't you tell anyone either. Most of the time I was strapped into a harness, swinging right out over the audience. I was terrified to begin with . . .*' But in February had come her first speaking part – '. . . *we're doing a new play called* After Eight. *It's a drawing-room comedy and I play a maid. My one line is –* "Yes, sir, thank you, will there be anything else?" *Which doesn't sound funny but it brings the house down every night because I wiggle my backside and say* "anything else" *to suggest the sort of things we used to do in the garage . . .'* God, how he missed her!

'She must be terribly lonely,' he confided to Dusty, 'stuck up there in a strange place, living in one room, without any friends –'

'It won't take her long to make friends,' Dusty said with that ironic look in his eye.

Unconvinced, Keir saved so hard that by the end of February he had enough money to visit Manchester for a weekend. After checking the timetable he found a train that would get him there to meet Dawn after her Friday evening performance. Joyfully he imagined the weekend, picturing them dining in restaurants, walking hand in hand through a park, and talking for hours about the future.

He would have gone without telling her, as a surprise, except he knew of nowhere to stay. So, bursting with excitement, he wrote asking her '. . . *to book me into a local boarding house. The train arrives too late for me to see the show but we could have supper after . . . it will be marvellous to see you again . . .'* He told his parents, he told Dusty, he told everyone. He was going to Manchester to see Dawn!

Her answer came as a blow. *'Manchester is terrible . . . you wouldn't like it . . . it's silly for you to spend so much to see me in such a small part . . . my contract ends at Easter . . . I'll be coming back to London . . . only another eight weeks.'*

Only another eight weeks! Keir was desolate. What did he care about her part? He wanted to see *her*, not some character in a play.

Having told so many people, he felt a fool. He might still have gone but for some words of his mother. 'It was a daft idea in the first place,' she said, 'spending all that for a weekend. You ought to be saving your money, that's what. Besides, what happens at Easter? I daresay you'll spend enough on her if she comes back here for good.'

Keir wondered about that. Dawn hadn't said she was returning for good, but if her contract ended where else would she go? He wished she wrote more in her letters. His own were full of questions – had she made any friends? Did she like the rest of the company? What did she do in her spare time? Her replies were so sketchy that he couldn't even begin to visualize her life. With his mother's words ringing in his ears and Dawn's letter burning a hole in his pocket, Keir tried to curb his impatience. *Only eight weeks*. He hung a calendar up in his bedroom and began to cross off the days.

Meanwhile, he was summoned to a formal interview with the local paper, a reminder that his own school-days were ending. He met the editor and a few of the staff, and was pleased to receive the official offer of employment. 'You'll get a good training when you start here,' the editor told him, 'and we'll keep your job open while you're doing National Service.'

His pay of three pounds, ten shillings a week as a trainee was only a few shillings more than he earned from delivering papers and working in the shop.

'It's the future that counts,' said his father. 'When you come out of the army they'll pay you ten pounds a week. You'll be making a thousand a year in no time.'

Keir hoped so. He and Dawn could set up home on a thousand a year.

March dragged on, bringing with it snow and ice, and finally another letter from Dawn. She was definitely returning at the end of the month '*but only for a weekend. The great news is they've extended my contract until June. I'll be travelling down a week on Saturday . . . we could go out in the evening if you like . . .*'

If he liked! It was what he lived for. He read the letter again, devouring the words, weighing the good and the bad. Her returning to Manchester was a blow, on the other hand it was only until June. He left school in June. Perhaps she'd join another repertory company closer to home? They'd be able to see each other on a regular basis. Meanwhile; at least – at *last*, she was coming home . . .

Keir planned that weekend like a general plotting a campaign. A new play called *The Mousetrap* had opened in the West End. He booked two of the best stalls for Saturday night, after which he began making plans for the Sunday.

Finally, the weekend arrived. Saturday dragged. In the shop, Keir pictured Dawn on the train, passing through town after town as she travelled down country. He checked the clock every five minutes until, at long last, it was closing time. Sighing with relief, he left his mother to lock up while he dashed to the bathroom and threw off his clothes.

Half an hour later he was ready. Never had he looked so smart, resplendent in new sports jacket, grey flannels, white shirt and striped tie. 'My word,' said his mother. 'You look just like that nice Dick Bogarde in the pictures.'

'So he should,' Joe said with dry humour. 'He's going out with an actress.'

Deaf to his father's gentle sarcasm, Keir was out of the door with a hurried goodbye and away up the street, to arrive at the Whartons' on the dot of seven as planned. Tingling with excitement, he was half-way up the drive when the door opened. Dawn stood framed in the opening with the lights of the hall behind her. He caught his breath. Instead of the top coat with which he was familiar she wore a fitted blue suit that hugged her figure, emphasizing the sweep of her legs. Her hair was arranged differently, shorter and cut in a style that added maturity to her face, banishing forever any hint of schoolgirl prettiness.

'Well?' She laughed, watching his eyes. 'Have I changed?'

It had not occurred to him that he would feel shy. His mouth went dry and opened only to utter the most hackneyed of words. 'You're beautiful,' he stammered. 'Lovelier than ever.'

Laughing, she coloured with pleasure as she closed the door behind her and ran down the steps into his arms. She clung to him for a moment, kissing his cheek before hugging his arm and turning to walk to the gate.

The reunion was exactly as he had imagined. Everything corresponded to his dreams, except the impossible had happened and Dawn was even more beautiful. As they walked to the station it was as if she had never been away. Keir felt ten feet tall until – and they had barely walked a hundred yards – Dawn groaned, 'I'd forgotten this routemarch and the long drag into town. God, what a bore. I hope you get a car as soon as you start work on the paper.'

A car? A car was out of the question on the money Keir would earn. Yet he knew what she meant as soon as they boarded the train. One look at other women in the carriage was enough. Dawn was strikingly different. Other women looked dowdy by comparison. Dawn was sparkling and smart. Her looks set her apart from people who travelled on trains. 'We'll come home by cab,' he promised, cursing himself for not planning both journeys by taxi. It was simply that he was a train person, and Dawn wasn't.

To his dismay, even walking through the West End was no longer a thrill for Dawn. Once, she had stopped to stare wide-eyed at shop windows, squealing with excitement – now she walked past with barely a glance.

Luckily, *The Mousetrap* lived up to expectations and Dawn was pleased with their seats in the stalls. But at the interval, when they went to the bar, she shook her head at his suggestion of sherry. 'No, let's have champagne cocktails, shall we? They're much more fun.' They were also much more expensive. It was the same at the restaurant later. The Italian waiters greeted her with delight, the food was superb, the ambience enchanting, but Dawn no longer liked chianti. 'It gives me a headache. Let's stick to champagne. After all, it is a celebration.'

There was no doubt about that. Keir's eyes shone as he looked at her. He listened entranced as she talked of her life in the theatre. Then came the first staggering revelation.

'Of course I'm still the lowest of the low,' Dawn admitted with a modest flutter of her eyelashes, 'but a few people are beginning to take notice.'

Some of them took her out to supper after the show, especially on Friday and Saturday nights. Keir was dumbfounded; so angry, so jealous, that he lost his voice for a moment. Suddenly, he suspected other reasons for her not wanting him to visit Manchester.

'Don't be silly,' she said, taking his hand, 'I'd much rather see you, but they're on the spot and can easily afford to buy me a good supper. It just didn't seem worth dragging you up to Manchester for a couple of days.'

He hated the thought of her going out with other men.

'Only now and then,' she protested. 'Don't look so disapproving. A girl's got to eat. The food at the digs would make you throw up. There's nothing to be alarmed about.'

It was hard not to be alarmed when she talked of the men who called for her at the stage door: Manchester businessmen with cars and money and the wherewithal to give her a good time.

'You give me a good time too,' she assured Keir with a

heart-stopping smile. 'They can afford it more than you, that's all. When I put you off from coming up to see me I was thinking of what it would cost. I was being considerate, really I was.' She was too, in a funny kind of way. 'They're only men, Keir. You're different. You're special.'

He hoped so. It was easier to believe when she talked about him. She made him feel special just by the look in her eyes. Steering the conversation away from Manchester, she encouraged him to tell her about school and the magazine, and about being interviewed for the job on the paper. Which was when another odd thing happened. Discussing the magazine, he suddenly realized she was telling him about an article he had written. He hadn't told her. Racking his brains he wondered if he'd mentioned it in one of his letters, but was sure that he hadn't.

'You must have.' She laughed.

'No, I'm certain I didn't. I wouldn't have bothered.'

'Oh well.' She shrugged. 'Dusty must have mentioned it.'

'*Dusty?*'

A pink flush spread across her cheeks. 'He . . . he dropped me a line. I thought you knew. He said you told him I was lonely. He wrote a note to cheer me up.' She smiled. 'It did too. It was very nice of him.'

'He didn't tell me,' Keir said blankly. An accusing look came into his eye. 'How did he get your address?'

'He wrote to the theatre. There's no need to look like that. It was only a couple of letters –'

'A couple? And you answered them?'

'Of course. Whatever's the matter? Dusty's your friend. He's *our* friend, isn't he?' Her dark eyes met his as her lips puckered into a smile of reassurance. 'You are silly at times. There's no need to look so . . . so hurt.'

Hurt? Certainly he was hurt. What hurt was that he hadn't known. It had taken from September to Christmas to get to know her. Now, in the space of sixteen weeks she was seeing men and writing to Dusty . . . he seemed not to know her at all. And what about Dusty? Dusty to whom he poured out his heart. Dusty should have told him . . .

'You are funny,' she said, squeezing his hand. 'Scowling like that. People will think we're having a row, not a reunion.' After regarding him solemnly for a moment her eyes brightened with an idea. 'I know, I'll buy you a brandy. No, no, I insist. My treat.' Releasing his hand, she beckoned to the head waiter. 'Antonio, be a darling and organize two large Remys. I want to pay for them separately. It's my treat –'

'No, *my* treat,' Antonio answered with a laugh. 'It's worth more than a brandy to see you again. We've missed you –' He broke off to pass the order for brandies to his wine waiter, then he turned back to Dawn. 'Where have you been . . . ?'

Reduced to an observer for the next five minutes, Keir thought, She's like a princess surrounded by courtiers, all anxious to please. Watching Antonio fall under her spell, he felt slightly contemptuous, only to realize he was as bad – he was *worse*, he would do anything to please her. Putty in her hands, and never more so than in the cab going home when she snuggled against him. 'Oh, Keir,' she sighed, 'I did enjoy tonight. I always have such a nice time with you.'

His earlier despondency was forgotten when her lips met his and her hand slid along his thigh.

Which typified the entire weekend. Alternating between bliss and despair, Keir was sure of her one moment and unsure the next. Sunday was a glorious day, almost as warm as midsummer. He had organized a trip to Maidenhead. They spent the day on the river, lunching at a riverside pub before drifting down stream to moor beneath the shelter of some willow trees. Sheltered from prying eyes, they kissed and embraced with even more passion than the previous night in the garage. She responded as never before, helping him unbutton her blouse, pulling his head down to suckle her breasts, while her nimble fingers aroused him, and teased him and, eventually, brought him to a climax.

At such moments Keir found it easy to believe she would be his for the rest of his life. It was only when she let slip a reference to a Manchester supper club, or said something about Dusty that he worried . . .

Too soon the day was over and it was time to say goodbye. On Monday, Dawn was meeting Mr Maxwell, her agent, at his London office before catching the lunchtime train to Manchester.

The hours had flown. Keir dragged his feet when they reached the end of the drive to her house. It was ten o'clock, not late but Dawn faced a long day. 'Let's say goodnight here,' she whispered, drawing him into the shelter of the yew hedge.

'I wish you weren't going.'

'It's only eight weeks,' she murmured, stroking his face.

'Yes,' he agreed bleakly. 'Only eight weeks.'

They clung to each other until she pushed him away. 'I must go. I'll write as soon as I get back.'

She took a step towards the house, but he caught her hand. 'Dawn,' he cried, without knowing what he was saying, simply trying to delay her. 'Er . . . have a good meeting with Mr Maxwell. Tell him to get you into a play in the West End.'

'I'll tell him!' She laughed, stepping towards the house, making him release her hand.

'Have a safe journey.' Keir's voice rose as the gap widened between them.

The smile she threw him over her shoulder was barely visible in the gloom of the night. 'Goodnight, Dawn,' he whispered, watching her shadowy form run down the drive.

'Eight weeks,' he grumbled as he walked home. Eight weeks of not seeing her. Eight weeks of men in flashy cars plying her with champagne, giving her a life to which he could only aspire. Eight weeks of writing long letters and receiving a few scribbled lines in reply . . .

By the time he reached home he was in the depths of depression. In his room he counted the money left in his pocket. In two days he had spent thirty pounds. *Thirty pounds*. A Manchester businessman would count it a pittance, but it was a fortune to Keir. It took him ten weeks to earn thirty pounds. Even in June, when he started on the paper, it would take nearly as long to earn thirty pounds.

The more he thought about it, the more hopeless his situation seemed. Dawn took the money he spent on her for granted. Why not, when men up in Manchester lavished a fortune on her. *I hope you get a car when you start on the paper*, she had said. A car! He had as much chance of owning an aeroplane . . .

Desperation verged on despair. He lay awake, tossing and turning, his mind full of worries. Three pounds ten would never be enough to hold Dawn. She would slip away from him . . .

He remembered her saying – *Everything costs. We spend our*

lives swapping something we have for something we want. He wanted Dawn more than anything. Exchanging didn't come into it. He would beg, borrow and steal to get the money to keep her . . .

Eight

'You're not joining the paper?' Keir's mother said in alarm. 'What do you mean? I've never heard such nonsense.'

Keir tried to explain. 'The paper won't pay me much more than I earn now. It doesn't make sense –'

'It will later on,' said Joe Milford, going red in the face. 'Reporters earn good money. When you come back from the army –'

'But that's years away. I want money now. *Proper* money.'

'You're only a trainee until you go into the army,' Joe said, stifling his temper. 'That's less than twelve months. And when you come out of the army –'

'It's no good, Dad, I've made up my mind.'

Everyone tried to make Keir see sense. At school, the Headmaster and Hugh Clemence begged him to reconsider. They said all the right things. They pointed out he was throwing away the chance of a worthwhile career. Sadly, no matter how attractive a future they painted, nothing could compensate for losing Dawn – and he was sure he would lose her unless he earned more than three pounds ten shillings a week.

Dusty and Keir had two bitter rows. The first was about the letters Dusty had written to Dawn. 'Why didn't you tell me?' Keir demanded. 'Why write behind my back?'

'I only wrote because you said she was lonely. I did it to cheer her up.'

Keir remained unconvinced, but Dusty argued so furiously about Keir not joining the paper that the matter of the letters got pushed into the background. 'It's madness,' said Dusty. 'Besides, what's the alternative? What will you do if you don't join the paper?'

'Get a job as a labourer on a building site. They're paying twenty pounds a week, more with overtime –'

'You can't be a labourer the rest of your life –'

'Only until I go into the army.'

'What about your future? What about your writing?'

Keir shrugged. 'Writers are supposed to know about life, aren't they? I'll learn more about life as a labourer than as a clerk in some cushy office –'

'That's not the reason,' said Dusty, losing his temper. 'Damn and blast it, you know it's not the reason! She's not worth it, Keir –'

Keir went white. He grabbed Dusty's arm. 'Don't *ever* say that. You don't understand. No one understands.'

No one did. Keir's parents were frantic with worry. 'It's not like our Keir to worship money,' said his mother. 'It's this girl's fault, her and her fancy ideas . . .'

The following week, Dusty made another effort. He had decided on his own future by then. As the most numerate boy in the school, everyone had expected him to become an accountant but, as usual, Dusty had chosen a less obvious course. He was going into advertising, a subject he had heard much of from his friends on the American Base.

'It's where the future is,' he told Keir. 'Advertising is wide-open for people with ideas . . .'

He knew a great deal about it. He talked about copywriters and account executives with the fluency of an expert. 'That's why it's perfect for us,' he said. 'You can write the copy and I'll deal with the clients. We could have our own agency in a few years.'

Keir doubted that American-style advertising agencies would catch on in conservative Britain, and the prospect of writing about cleaning powders and laxatives struck him as dull. Besides, even Dusty would begin as an office boy on very low wages . . .

'That's just for the start,' Dusty protested. 'It won't last forever.'

Keir refused to listen. Arguing was useless. No matter what Dusty said, irrespective of the wishes of his parents and the advice of his schoolmasters, Keir's mind was made up. So anxious was he to begin earning *proper* money that he almost left there and then, without waiting to take his examinations in June. Fortunately, on that one single issue, his mother's wishes prevailed – 'Please, Keir. It's not many more weeks and qualifications will come in handy no matter what you do with your life.'

So Keir stayed to complete his schooling, and what with playing cricket and swotting for exams, the weeks passed surprisingly quickly. If the Team was less than the sparkling partnership it once was, at least he and Dusty remained friends. In fact, without the distraction of Dawn, the two boys regained much of their former closeness.

'I wish you'd change your mind,' Dusty pleaded. 'Come into advertising with me, or join the paper. Don't mess up your whole future.'

But Keir refused to reconsider.

'Well,' Dusty sighed. 'Let's meet once a week. You never know, if you change your mind, I might be able to get you into the agency.'

Keir had no intention of changing his mind. A future without Dawn was no future at all.

'Five years,' Dusty mused, reminiscing over a coffee in the Golden Paradise. 'Do you remember me starting school in that second-hand blazer?'

Keir remembered. Five years! Now their boyhood was over and the real adventure of life was about to begin.

Keir found a job on a building site immediately. Britain was still rebuilding after the war and new structures were going up everywhere. Keir had only to walk onto a site locally and offer his services. The foreman took him on for a few weeks' trial, but not without expressing some doubts. 'Grammar-school boy, eh? No one 'ere went to any bloody grammar school. Give yourself airs and graces and you'll get a kick up the arse.'

The first few days nearly killed Keir. He mixed cement, carried bricks on a hod, off-loaded timber from lorries, while all the time the foreman yelled 'Get a move on, we ain't got all day. You ain't at no bloody grammar school now.'

The foreman, and some of his cronies, put Keir through the wringer. Convinced that he'd quit, they were amazed when he didn't. So, at times, was Keir. He knew he was being given the dirtiest jobs on the site but could do nothing about it – except tackle every task they gave him. Perversely, the foreman's attitude fuelled his determination. So many people had called him a fool that the foreman simply became another person to prove wrong. Even so, there were times when he envied former classmates their comfortable white-collar jobs. Neither was the work on the site Keir's only discomfort. The atmosphere at home had turned very sour. His father barely spoke, even though Keir still shifted the stock and re-stacked the shelves after work. 'A waste of a good education,' Joe grumbled. 'You had your chance and threw it away. All for the sake of a girl.'

Keir suffered his father's contempt. He endured his mother's disappointment. He dealt with the taunts of the foreman by working harder than ever. Nothing could break his belief that the most important thing in life was to have money to spend on Dawn Wharton.

The need to prove himself was not entirely a bad thing: after a month the foreman came to realize that Keir was the hardest-working labourer on the site. Bricklayers began asking for him, for the very good reason that the more bricks they laid the more money they earned. A good brickie developed a rhythm of working, trowel in one hand, brick in the other. Keeping him supplied with bricks and freshly mixed mortar was the job of a labourer. It made no difference that they were working four storeys up, bricks and mortar had to be there, and they were, when Keir was on site. He raced up and down ladders with a hod on his shoulder, barely pausing for breath. By the end of the month he was the only labourer there who could keep two brickies going at once. The highest paid brickies began asking for him – and his troubles with the foreman became a thing of the past. 'I might only be a labourer –' Keir grinned, pleased with himself – 'But I'll be the best in the business.'

Hard physical work developed his physique and the elements bronzed his skin to a deep tan. Even as a schoolboy he had been good-looking, and although it never occurred to him that women would find him attractive, the truth was that Keir fairly blossomed. The sun bleached his hair making his blue eyes a shade deeper in his tanned face. Being good at his job and having money in his pocket gave him an extra confidence, so that

71

many a girl turned her head to watch as he strode down the street. Not that he noticed. There was only one girl for Keir and he saw her every weekend.

Dawn was playing in summer season at Brighton by then, and every Saturday Keir took the train down to see her. True, he lacked the cars and real wealth of Manchester businessmen, but the money in his pocket was there to be spent and he was a dozen times better-looking. Dawn was envied by other girls in the company. 'He's more handsome than Eric Forbes,' said one of the girls, mentioning the company's leading man. And he was. He was often mistaken for an actor. 'Never,' he protested, blushing when Dawn told him. She giggled, delighted by his confusion and pleased that people should notice her escort. To be seen with a good-looking man helped her reputation, especially when he so obviously adored her.

It was a summer of enchantment for Keir. Having mastered his job, the rigours of life as a labourer ceased to bother him. Physically strong to start with, he grew even stronger, and the monotony of the work was a help not a hindrance, for he performed his tasks automatically, which left his mind free to dream about Dawn.

Weekends acquired a regular pattern. Keir finished work at noon on Saturday, went home to wash, change and pack an overnight bag, after which he took a train up to town and another down to Brighton, to arrive in time to meet Dawn for afternoon tea. He always arrived with a gift, sometimes flowers or a trinket, and quite often a book. Overnight he stayed at a boarding house close to her digs, cheap but convenient. They went out to supper after her show on a Saturday and spent most of Sunday together, sunbathing on the beach or walking along the Downs which rise behind Brighton.

Keir was never happier. Just being with Dawn was exciting, and watching her on stage was a joy. Although never playing the lead, she had graduated to more demanding parts and there was no doubt that she would become an important actress one day. He was so proud when the audience rose to her at the end of a performance.

Their private time together was satisfying too, because although she still refused to go all the way, Dawn was never slow to bring him comfort with her mouth and her hands.

72

Meanwhile, Keir was earning nearly thirty pounds a week and never hesitated to spend every penny on Dawn.

'Don't you save any?' Dusty asked when they met, as they did every week for a beer.

Keir smiled. 'We have so much fun spending it –'

'God Almighty,' said Dusty in disgust. 'You'll never understand women.' He might have said more but for the look in Keir's eye, so he shrugged and began to talk about advertising, which was closer to his heart than any girl would ever be. The other subject to interest Dusty was National Service, or rather how to avoid it. 'I'm buggered if I'll waste two years of my life,' he said. 'Did you know they don't call you up if you're working abroad?'

Keir didn't know. Neither did it seem relevant.

'It's relevant to me –' Dusty grinned – 'I'm trying to wangle a job in the States.'

The company he worked for was American owned. 'They'll employ me in New York if I go over there. That suits me fine. I'll learn all about advertising and skip National Service at the same time.'

'What happens when you come back?'

'They scrub round it if I stay there until I'm twenty-eight.'

'But that's ten years.'

'Don't look so horrified!' Dusty laughed. 'I reckon they'll abolish National Service before then. Besides, I'm not going into exile, I'm going to learn how to make a fortune.'

He wanted Keir to go with him. 'You could write better copy than some of the people in our office. Honestly. You'd be good at it. One day we could have our own firm, Miller and Milford, Practitioners in Advertising. How does that sound?'

The last thing Keir wanted was to leave the country. The most important thing in his life was to stay close to Dawn, and in September, something did happen to bring her even closer: Maxwell, her agent, got her a part in the West End. Dawn was beside herself with excitement. 'It's a good part in a good play. Keir, it could run forever!'

She was determined to get her own flat. She had always dreamt about having a flat of her own – theatrical digs had long since lost their charm. 'They're okay, I suppose, if you don't

73

mind living with other people's things. I just want my own place,' Dawn said.

Keir was all in favour. He reasoned that Dawn might not have gone out with Manchester businessmen if she'd had a place of her own. After all, eating bad food served by an ill-tempered landlady must have been awful. So he was delighted to help her search for a place.

The flat they found was the top floor of a Victorian terrace house in Belsize Park. It consisted of three rooms; two and a half really because the bathroom was little more than a door to an alcove housing a hip bath, WC, and a hand basin. The bedroom was about the same size. The largest room served as a living-room-cum-dining-room-cum-kitchen. Despite its limitations, Dawn fell in love with the place. She could afford the rent and, 'It's got its own telephone, and it's only five minutes from the West End. Keir, it's perfect. Once we've painted the woodwork and papered the walls . . .'

Keir did most of the work. He also paid for the materials and most of the second-hand furniture. He hung prints on the walls, built bookshelves into alcoves and fitted Venetian blinds at the windows. As a finishing touch he bought a huge Victorian vase and stocked it with fresh flowers once a week. And, as often as not, he paid for the groceries, for he never arrived at the flat without a gift of some kind. Incredibly, he was even happier than during the summer. He cared nothing for the fact that the darker evenings shortened his working day, making it necessary to toil all day Saturday to make the same money. It was a long week: six days of hard physical labour, working from first light until dark in all weathers, all endured cheerfully for the chance to see more of Dawn. They spent an hour or so together on Tuesdays and Thursdays before she left for the theatre. He took her out to supper after her show every Saturday, and they spent most of Sundays together. Although it was her flat he thought of it as theirs, something they had created together . . .

He never stayed overnight. No invitation was forthcoming and he would not force himself on her. They still did not make love properly and he accepted that they wouldn't until they were married. Not that Dawn was ready for marriage. 'Oh, Keir, there are so many things I want to do in the theatre. I'm not even established yet . . .'

But, as she never ruled marriage out of the question, he saw it merely as a matter of time.

'Perhaps I will marry you one day, but acting's what my life is really about,' Dawn once said, striking a pose and making him laugh. Despite her light-hearted manner, he knew she was serious. Even so, the importance she attached to her career never made him resentful. On the contrary, he was proud of her. Besides, even Keir had to accept that an immediate marriage was out of the question. 'Never mind,' he said cheerfully. 'You'll be established in the theatre by the time I come out of the army. I'll get a proper job, and *then* we'll get married.'

She always laughed, 'You'll be tired of me by then. Wait and see how you feel in two or three years' time.'

He could never believe he would feel any differently.

Meanwhile he was delighted with her new flat and did all he could to make it attractive. He visualized her there while he was away in the army. He saw her returning home from the theatre, opening a letter from him and sitting down to pen a reply . . .

Christmas came and went, such a different Christmas from the previous year when Keir had still been at school and Dawn was leaving home for the first time. She had been going away from him then. Now, every day brought her closer. Indeed, as the winter deepened, Keir began to see the future more clearly. Even National Service, looming up in the Spring, was less of a worry. He had heard of a way to get himself posted to the Woolwich Arsenal barracks, which would enable him to continue seeing Dawn on a regular basis.

So he bore life's discomforts with equanimity. He put up with his rough work and ignored the other labourers when they boasted of their girls. 'Hey, Keir, I gotta tell you about this bird I pulled Saturday night. You should 'ave seen her. Legs like a bleeding giraffe. Anyway, we goes straight from the dance to 'Arry's pub, where he lets me 'ave a room for the night. Except this bird don't 'ave to go 'ome Sunday, so I fucked her solid for twenty-hours. Christ, I'm too weak to piss this morning . . .'

Cheap tarts, Keir thought, not like Dawn. Dawn's beautiful and talented and she's got class. She's saving herself for when we get married. Similar thoughts helped him endure his mother's disappointment and his father's disapproval.

'I hope you're saving some money for when you're in the army,' said Joe. 'You'll be glad of an extra few bob then.'

How could he tell them that he spent every penny? They would never understand. They'd forgotten what it was like to be young.

He endured it all, even Dusty's nonstop talk about advertising. 'I tell you, Keir, advertising will boom in a few years. Come to New York when I go. My people will give you a job and in a few years we'll come home and clean up.' He tried to tell Dusty money was not the most important thing in his life. He tried to explain it would break his heart to leave London. He did *try* to make people understand, but no one would listen. Dusty was baffled, his parents were heartbroken, and men on the site wondered why someone like Keir would work as a labourer.

Yet, to Keir, it was crystal clear. He was building his life around Dawn. From where he stood the future looked golden. Furnishing her flat was merely a prelude to equipping a home of their own. The flat was a sort of practice run. It never occurred to him she would share it with someone else. It was *their* place, off-limits to the rest of the world. Naturally, Maxwell and people at the theatre had the phone number . . . but Keir could not visualize anyone in the flat except Dawn and himself. Until one Thursday in February.

Unexpectedly, Keir found himself with time on his hands. A week of continuous rain and a thunderstorm the previous night had waterlogged the site. The men persevered until ten that morning, but when conditions became dangerous the foreman abandoned work for the day.

Back home, washed and changed, Keir wondered what to do with himself. As always, his thoughts turned to Dawn. After giving a matinée and an evening performance every Wednesday, she often stayed in bed until noon on Thursdays. He would have phoned, but it seemed senseless to disturb her when she was sleeping, so he decided to surprise her instead. He could be there in time to treat her to lunch. It would make a change, be something different.

By eleven he was on the train, and outside Belsize Park Station by twelve-fifteen. Pleased with himself, he thought they might go to a restaurant in Hampstead, and then spend the afternoon shopping for things for the flat . . .

Reaching the house he took the stairs two at a time. Once up on her landing he straightened his tie and patted his hair before ringing the bell. When there was no answer he rang it again. Still no answer. He grew anxious. A frown creased his forehead. He glanced at his watch. Twelve twenty-five. Had she gone out? For a moment he wondered if she was meeting her agent for lunch. Feelings of pleasurable anticipation began to give way to disappointment. He rang the bell once more, keeping his hand on the button, hoping she simply needed rousing from sleep.

Suddenly the door opened and she peeped out, her face flushed and her hair tousled. 'Keir!' she exclaimed, alarm in her voice and shock in her eyes.

'Surprise!' He laughed. Then he caught her expression. 'Sorry, darling, did I startle you? You must have been in a deep sleep. I was beginning to think you were out.' Reaching for her, he drew her towards him, which was when he realized that she wore nothing beneath the silk robe.

'What are you doing here?' she gasped, retreating backwards across the threshold.

'Taking you out to lunch,' he said. Then, aroused by the warm softness of her body through the silk, he laughed. 'But I'd rather we went back to your bed –'

'No!' She flew across the room and stood against the bedroom door as if barring his way, her dark eyes huge in her face.

He looked at her in amazement. 'What on earth –'

'Sorry.' She shook her head in a nervous gesture. 'I wasn't expecting you, I was asleep –'

'I'll say. It took me ages to wake you –'

'Stay there. Make some coffee or something. I'll get dressed.' Opening the bedroom door a fraction, she squeezed through and closed it firmly behind her.

He stared. She had neither kissed him nor asked why he wasn't working. Her reaction had not been at all what he expected. Walking over to the sink, he filled the kettle to boil water for coffee. A dirty cup stood on the draining board, with another one next to it, and on the table was an empty bottle and two glasses.

It was such a regular occurrence to find dirty dishes in the sink that to wash up while waiting had become habit. He had no reason to be suspicious. Although jealous by nature he had heard her caustic opinions of actors often enough to discount them as rivals. And she scarcely had the chance to meet other men, what with Keir collecting her from the theatre every Saturday night and sometimes on Tuesday as well. He was always at the flat . . .

Putting the cups into the washing-up bowl, he was reaching for the glasses, when he noticed that only one had lipstick on the rim. Even then he was more curious than alarmed. 'Dawn?' he shouted. 'Did someone call round?'

No answer.

'Dawn –'

'What?' She half emerged from the bedroom in a sweater that was rucked up at the waist, exposing bare skin as she struggled with the clasp of her skirt. 'No one's been round, don't be silly. I won't be a second.'

The door closed before he could answer. He blinked and returned to his chores, collecting the empty bottle from the table. He stared, seeing it properly for the first time. Champagne? Moet and Chandon Black Label. Nobody drank champagne alone. Or drank from two glasses. Suddenly he was noticing all sorts of things. He picked up the ashtray, intending to empty it. Not every cigarette stub bore traces of lipstick. Frowning, he threw them into the waste bin under the sink, and he was straightening up when Dawn came out of the bedroom.

'I'll just pull a comb through my hair,' she said, closing the door and rushing past him to disappear into the tiny bathroom. He heard water splash into the sink as the kettle came to the boil. 'No hurry,' he said casually, turning to the stove. 'I'm still making the coffee.'

'Coffee?' Her head shot around the door. 'Oh, don't bother. We'll have some out.' Clutching her shoes in one hand and patting her hair with the other, she ran into the room. Collecting a handbag from a chair, she took two paces to the left and pulled down her coat from the peg on the door. 'Come on, let's go,' she said. 'You did say lunch, didn't you?'

She had taken less than five minutes. Getting ready usually took at least half an hour. Keir had known her spend ten minutes straightening the seams of her stockings. And she wore no make-up which, even at midday, was unusual.

'Shall we walk over the Heath before lunch?' She smiled,

reaching for his arm. 'I want to feel the wind in my face and get some air into my lungs.'

On the landing, she slammed the door with what seemed like a sigh of relief. Only then did she do the things he had expected, such as kissing him hello and asking why he was not working.

Once outside, they found the weather too blustery for a tramp on the Heath. The cold wind was laced with icy rain. The walk up to Hampstead was quite far enough to persuade Dawn to opt for the welcoming warmth of Le Bistro, a restaurant they had used before. Exchanging sallies with the *patron*, she cast her dark eyes from table to table, seeking that look of recognition which comes when people see even the slightly well-known.

Watching and listening over lunch, Keir sensed an extra excitement. He knew her every gesture by heart; everything about that lovely face was engraved on his memory. Today, she was different. A glow about her defied analysis. He was so used to seeing her in make-up that for a moment he thought her changed appearance was due to the lack of powder and rouge. Then he thought that walking in the wind might have brought the extra bloom to her cheeks, but when the bloom remained after half an hour in the restaurant, he knew he was wrong.

'It must be the champagne,' he said. 'What were you celebrating?'

'Celebrating?' Her blank expression conveyed bewilderment, until her eyes lit with a look of understanding. 'Oh, you mean the champagne in the flat? Maxwell brought me home from the theatre last night. It was his little treat.'

No one would have doubted her. Her dismissive way of saying 'his little treat' was superbly done. Anyone would have believed her, even Keir, and even Keir was uncertain.

'What was the celebration?' he asked, hoping for some marvellous news that would account for a man like Maxwell buying champagne.

'That was the silly thing!' She laughed. 'Nothing really. Simply that my contract has been extended for the run of the play. I mean, we knew that weeks ago. But when it was confirmed yesterday, Maxwell insisted on making a fuss. I was flabbergasted when he produced champagne. After all, you know Maxwell . . .'

Keir did. He had met him twice and been disappointed,

79

imagining theatrical agents as flamboyant, cigar-smoking figures. Maxwell was small, sober and almost scholarly. Suddenly, Keir was horribly sure that Dawn was not telling the truth.

Excusing himself, he went to the toilet and splashed cold water onto his face. His hands trembled and he felt slightly sick, unable to believe what was happening. For a moment, he was fearful of returning to the table, afraid of what he might say. Why was she telling lies? After all, she said she was flabbergasted, she herself said that it was out of character for Maxwell –

It took him a few minutes to pull himself together. Having always told her the truth, the thought of her lying to him filled him with misery. Seemingly, she had already forgotten the incident when he returned. Laughing and joking with the *patron*, she was in the highest of spirits. Once again Keir sensed an extra excitement. Her eyes flashed with extra brilliance, and the bloom never left her cheeks.

For the first time in weeks she declined to go shopping. 'I can't,' she said as they left the restaurant. 'I must be at the theatre early today. There's a part in the second act that's not working. I agreed to be there at three.' It was already two-thirty. 'Goodness,' she said. 'Let's walk up to the High Street and I'll catch a cab.'

A taxi came along almost immediately. 'Thanks for lunch, darling,' she said, kissing his cheek. 'It was lovely.' After hesitating a moment, she added, 'But, Keir, you know I hate surprises. It would have been better if you'd phoned. I could have been ready, and . . . well, I mean, look at us now, me rushing off like this. I feel awful about leaving you –' her expression softened into a beautiful smile – 'Promise me, if you get another day off, give me a buzz first.'

He felt like a small boy chastised by his teacher. After a hurried goodbye, he stood watching her cab jostle its way back into the traffic. Her hand fluttered at the rear window and he raised his arm in response. Then he walked to the station, depressed by a day that for some reason had turned into a total disaster.

Half-way home, he realized what had been at the back of his mind. His subconscious had told him her story was a lie. Suddenly it came to him. The ashtray, full of cigarette stubs, only half of which bore traces of lipstick. He remembered

Maxwell complaining that Dawn was smoking too many cigarettes. 'They're bad for your throat, my dear. You should have grown up in our family. My brother and I each got fifty pounds from my father for resisting the habit until we reached twenty-one. As a consequence, I've never smoked a cigarette in my life.'

Nine

Hating himself, he told himself he was being disloyal, that his suspicions were false . . . but the champagne bottle and the cigarette stubs played on his mind. They could only add up to one thing. Dawn was seeing someone else. The shock of that was followed by another when he remembered her behaviour when he arrived at the flat – so on edge, so anxious to leave, almost in panic. Realization struck with the force of a physical blow. The man had been there all the time! He must have hidden in the bedroom when Keir arrived – or been in the bedroom already . . .

He would have given anything for it not to be true. Dawn was his life. Money, career, possessions meant nothing to him. He had proved it by taking a job as a labourer, throwing away his chance with the paper.

After a sleepless night, he reported for work gaunt-eyed and listless.

Fortunately, the site was still waterlogged and no work was possible – for Keir was in such a state that he might have had an accident. Certainly he was in no condition for hard manual work.

'What's up?' asked a workmate. 'Been on the nest all night? By Christ, you gave her one for me too by the look of you.'

It was ironic that the very opposite was true.

Returning home, Keir went back to bed, but sleep eluded him. 'You'll not earn much this week,' said his father, knowing that labourers were paid only for the hours they worked.

'No,' Keir agreed bleakly.

Rather than sit around the house and risk an argument, he went out. He walked the streets, not knowing what to do with himself. Finally, at midday he went to a call box and phoned her, hoping that the sound of her voice would restore his lost faith. When she asked if he was working he said yes, simply because something in her voice made it clear that she *wanted* him to be working.

'Oh good. Then the site has dried out.'

'Yes,' he lied – the second lie he had told her in as many minutes.

'So you'll be working tomorrow afternoon?'

Her eagerness was like a knife. Pain caused him to close his eyes. Knowing she wanted him to say yes, he said, 'Everyone's working late tomorrow to recover the lost time.'

'Poor darling. You'll be exhausted. Why not get an early night tomorrow instead of coming up here?'

'All right,' he agreed in a hollow voice.

'So I won't see you until Sunday.' She sounded pleased, as if not seeing him were a treat.

He struggled to talk normally. 'That's right, I'll be up about twelve. We'll go to The Grapes for lunch if you like.'

'That will be marvellous.'

At the end of the conversation he said, 'I love you, Dawn.'

'I know you do, silly. I'll see you on Sunday. Oh, and Keir . . . you will phone won't you, I mean if there's any change in your plans?'

'Yes,' he said.

It was the last lie he would ever tell her.

Behind the terrace of Victorian houses in which Dawn had her flat was a row of single-storey garages. An eyesore, cheaply constructed from poor materials, they had already started to deteriorate. Keir had noticed them when he was fixing the Venetian blinds, although *fixing* is the wrong word because the blinds were his one failure as a handyman. The mechanism which raised and lowered them refused to function. Dawn either had to have them up or down. 'Oh, leave them up,' she had said at the time. 'The place will be too dark otherwise. We'll get them changed on Saturday.' But that Saturday and several others had passed without Keir remembering to fix the Venetian blinds. As a consequence Dawn's windows remained open to the world. Not that it mattered. The lane at the back was only used by people parking their cars, and their view was obscured by the brick wall at the end of the garden. It was only by climbing onto the roof of the garages that someone could see over the wall and into Dawn's flat.

Keir had been on the garage roof since five o'clock that Saturday afternoon. Before five he had loitered in the lane, waiting for darkness to fall. He had not slept in two nights, neither had he worked, even though normal working had resumed that morning. After leaving home at the usual time, he had walked to the site, intending to work, only for his ragged nerves to fail at the last minute. The thought of having to respond to cheerful banter defeated him. Instead, hollow-eyed and sick with worry, he had walked past the site and on towards Uxbridge. He walked without plan, merely to be alone, knowing if he went home he would only face questions. Dressed in a blue duffel jacket over a thick sweater, he was not physically cold. The cold was inside him.

He had travelled to Belsize Park simply because he was unable to stay away. Even then he had not formulated a plan, and only as he approached the terrace of houses had he remembered the garages around the back. It was still light at mid-afternoon, light enough to devise a way of climbing up onto the roof. He would have done so at once except for the fear of being seen. So he had skulked in the alley like a criminal, casting impatient looks up at the sky, waiting for darkness to fall. At five o'clock he had judged it safe.

Standing on a dustbin, he had hauled himself up a drainpipe and rolled over onto the flat roof.

Keir despised himself and self-disgust welled up within him. He would not have believed himself capable of spying. Yet there he was, crouched behind the mock façade which fronted the garages, peering up at Dawn's windows.

Although the flat was in darkness, he could remember spending many afternoons on the sofa, too busy talking to switch on the lights. Of course she could have gone out. She might be shopping or visiting friends. Except Dawn rarely went shopping unless he was there to pick up the bill, and as for friends, she didn't have friends the way most girls did. Even at school she had despised other girls, and in the theatre she saw other young actresses as rivals, never as friends.

Pride made him bitter. He despised her for reducing him to this – this *madness*, this caricature of a Peeping Tom. How was it possible to love her, knowing how selfish she was? Of all the people he knew – his parents, schoolmasters, Dusty – Dawn alone had not opposed his decision to throw up his chance on the paper. He knew she would never make a similar sacrifice for him. She rarely asked about the dangers of his work, or the hardship, or the lack of opportunity. And yet, whatever she did, however much he suffered, he would endure it as long as she stayed with him. She was something special and rare, he would work like a dog to provide her with whatever she wanted . . .

Crouched behind the parapet, shivering despite his thick coat, he prayed to be wrong. What a relief to be free of suspicions. After an hour of watching and seeing nothing, he wanted to rush round to the front of the buildings and run up the steps, to find her and beg her forgiveness, to tell her how stupid he had been to worry about a champagne bottle and a few cigarettes. She would tell him that Maxwell had taken up smoking . . . she would say he had misunderstood her on the phone . . . she would explain . . .

Suddenly a light went on in Dawn's living-room.

Taken by surprise, Keir strained his eyes, peering across the darkness. He glimpsed a figure emerge from the bedroom to pass beyond his line of vision. The view was more restricted than he had imagined. Changing position, he shifted his weight from one knee to another. Even craning his neck, he was unable to see the doors to the bathroom and the landing. Chairs and tables were invisible because of the elevation. Knowledge of the flat helped him visualize blind spots, and he was coming to terms with unfamiliar angles when Dawn appeared in the bedroom door. Keir blinked. He thought she had gone into the bathroom. Holding his breath, he hated himself, hated her, hated what was happening. She was talking to someone in the bathroom. Her robe gaped open to reveal her nakedness. She made no effort to cover herself. Suddenly, from the direction of the bathroom, a man appeared. His back was to Keir, he was shrugging into a raincoat, obviously about to depart. Keir cried out as the man took Dawn into his arms. She clung to him with her arms around his neck, pressing her nakedness against him, standing on the tips of her toes.

Overwhelmed, Keir buried his head in his hands, unable to watch. Even with his eyes closed the picture stayed in his mind. How could she do it? How could she!

Anger exploded, filling him with uncontrollable fury. He glanced up. Still embracing, the couple had moved towards the landing door, at the edge of his vision. Lurching to his feet on limbs clumsy with cramp, he staggered to the edge of the roof. The reality exceeded even his suspicions. He baulked at the picture of her exposing her body in a way she never had with him. It was so unjust! How could she? How could she treat him with such colossal contempt?

Cursing the cramp in his legs, he scrambled to the drainpipe and lowered himself over the roof, only to miss his foothold on the dustbin and to crash down into the lane. The fall winded him. He lay, sprawled across the tarmac, gasping for breath. Rising painfully, he limped into a run, forcing a response from his muscles. He lurched along the lane like a drunk, his breath rasping with every step. The lane was a hundred yards long but seemed longer. Eventually he reached the corner, where he turned left and left again at the next, out into the main road and along the front of the long terrace. Running past the first houses he lifted his head, squinting through a red mist of pain to the door of her house. Fifty yards . . . thirty . . . twenty. Taking the steps two at a time, he bunched his fists to attack the man coming down. But even as he reached the first landing he knew he was too late. The man had gone. He had missed him. The realization fuelled his anger. Throwing himself up the last flight of stairs, he pounded her door with his fists.

Dawn opened the door. 'You came back –' Her words died and her face froze as Keir launched himself over the threshold. Slamming the door, he grabbed her shoulder to force her backwards. Hearing shouting he was surprised to realize it was his own voice. Vile words sprang from his lips, expressing his pain and anger.

She twisted free. The silk robe came away in his hand. Naked, she threw herself into the bedroom, only to be knocked backwards onto the bed as he smashed into the room after her. Screaming, she scrambled up towards the headboard, drawing her legs under her, dark eyes wide with terror. He was onto her like an animal. 'Bitch!' he cried despairingly. 'How could you? How could you?' She struggled. He hit her. She tried to protest. 'How could we have told you –?' But her words ended in a scream as he hit her again. His hand, hardened by carrying bricks, fastened round her throat, pushing her down on the bed. She cried and beat his chest with soft hands. Aroused by her nakedness, he unbuckled his belt. Pulling down his trousers, he tore into her with unbridled ferocity. He had dreamt of this act a hundred times, but always with tenderness, always with love. Instead it was with hate, swearing throughout – 'Whore! Fucking whore! Fuck you, fuck you, fuck you . . .'

When it was over and she lay limp in his arms, with tears running down his face, he was engulfed by despair. Empty of passion, drained of hatred, he felt only the void of a life no longer worth living.

He dared not look at her. Her bruised face would have sent him down on his knees. He would have told her how much he loved her, and craved for the impossible all over again.

Instead, he rose from the bed and shuffled into the living-room, staring with unseeing eyes at the pictures he had bought, the shelves he had fitted, his flowers in the vase – before he stumbled out onto the landing and ran down the stairs to escape into the darkness.

Ten

Keir hardly spoke for a couple of weeks. People who talked to him were discouraged by his monosyllabic replies. Even on the site, where he had always been regarded as different, his brooding silences did not go unnoticed. He worked well enough – 'Like a bloody machine,' the foreman admitted. 'Trouble is, he acts like one too.' When the men took a break, Keir sat to one side and stared into space. 'Surly bastard,' someone said, which summed up the general opinion.

His behaviour was no different at home. Losing patience, Joe

Milford would have lost his temper as well, but for his wife. 'Hush, Joe, the boy's pining for that girl. Leave him to get over it. Cross your fingers that he's finished with her once and for all.'

Keir was haunted by what he had done. Rape! He wouldn't have believed himself capable of such violence. Rape was akin to murder in his book, and he had come close to committing both. Once or twice he considered going to the police and making a full confession.

He heard nothing from Dawn, and although he wrote letters of remorse and pleas for forgiveness every night, he tore them up every morning. He couldn't believe she would forgive him. She would never trust him again. Sickened by the knowledge that he had behaved like an animal, shocked to realize he had fallen short of the person he had thought himself to be, he could hardly live with himself . . .

The day after it happened, Dusty telephoned three times. Pretending to be out, Keir left his mother to answer the phone. 'You ought to speak to him,' she scolded. 'He sounded ever so disappointed. He leaves for America the day after tomorrow. You must see him before he goes. You've been ever such good friends. It might be years before you see him again.'

But Keir could not face him. Dusty was on the verge of a great career – going to America was the first step. Whereas Keir had made a complete mess of his life. Dawn had been all he needed. Dusty had his career, Keir had Dawn – the two had balanced out in his mind. Now he had nothing, and Dusty would give him that ironic look and know what had happened. Unable to face that, Keir needed time to adjust to his loss, and a life without Dawn.

So he avoided Dusty. He let him go to America without even saying goodbye. People who had known the Team for five years wouldn't have believed it possible.

The Milfords were at their wits' end to revive their son's spirits. Joe renewed his efforts to interest Keir in politics. 'Nye Bevan's speaking at the Labour Club next week. Why don't we go and hear him?' Keir declined. Edith Milford cooked her son's favourite dishes. She baked special cakes every Sunday. She and her husband made every effort. Keir's decision to work as a labourer had broken their hearts, but now was not the time to say 'I told you so' to their son.

At the end of the month, when Keir's army papers arrived,

Joe breathed a sigh of relief. 'I've always been against National Service,' he told Edith, 'but maybe it's what Keir needs. The army could give him a new outlook on life . . .'

Edith was less sure. In her opinion, soldiering was no better than labouring and she said so. However, National Service was compulsory and she steeled herself for Keir's departure. Eighteen years of her life had been devoted to raising him and it was hard to say which distressed her more – Keir's obvious unhappiness or the fact of his leaving home. Joe didn't help by saying 'He'll go in a boy and come back a man.' As if Edith cared! She had been pleased with the boy. The boy had been kind and considerate, someone she liked. The man might be a total stranger, someone she liked not at all.

'Don't be daft,' Joe said. 'The army won't change him that much. It will open his eyes to the world, that's all, give him something to think about apart from that damn girl.'

Joe proved to be right. The army did give Keir something to think about 'apart from that damn girl'. At training camp he was roused at five-thirty each morning to run six miles before breakfast. Every day, he was chased from pillar to post by demented NCOs who seemed determined to murder every conscript in their charge. He spent hours cleaning his kit, oiling his rifle, leaping to attention for barrack inspection. He endured routemarches and suffered assault courses. He was shouted at, humiliated, unfairly punished and, according to the ways of the army, generally knocked into shape. There was no time to mope. When awake he was running at the double . . . and when he collapsed into his bunk at night he was too exhausted to dream. Memories of Dawn, home, boyhood, friends began to fade until they seemed events which had occurred to somebody else a long time ago.

Basic training was hell for most recruits and Keir was no exception. Thinking processes became stifled by the needs of the body. Imagination dulled when every muscle ached, when stamina was stretched to the limit, when physical exhaustion was such that even to set one foot in front of the other was a triumph.

Yet, arduous though it was, Keir survived with flying colours. Carrying bricks and mixing cement had developed his strength. He was able to set an example. When a fellow recruit fell on the assault course, Keir was there to help him to his feet. When a comrade groaned at the impossibility of taking another step on routemarches, it was Keir who carried his pack, so that long before basic training ended, fellow recruits had learned to rely on Keir to help them survive. Unbeknown to him, he had become 'officer material', a prospect which became even more likely when it became known how well he played cricket.

'I've never thought about it, sir,' said Keir, ramrod straight in front of the CO.

'The army's got a lot to offer a young man like you,' said the CO. 'You could sign on for five years and get a short-service commission. You'd travel the world, serve your country, and get some valuable training for life in the process. Industry is crying out for men with a knowledge of man-management. What career were you planning in civvy street?'

Keir hadn't the faintest idea. He had thrown away his chance on the paper. His entire life had revolved around Dawn . . .

When he went home on five days' leave, his parents were pleased and excited. Joe resolved any conflict between socialist principles and his son becoming 'an officer and a gentleman' by being practical. 'It will give you a good start in life,' he said to his son. 'You'd make up for the lost time. I reckon your CO is right. A commission in the army *will* help you when you come out.'

Edith was overjoyed to have Keir home again and to see him looking so well.

Keir was fussed over and made much of, and at the end of his leave his mind was made up. He returned to the army and signed on for a short-service commission. After two weeks in barracks he was sent away for officer training, which was as arduous as basic except that NCOs called him 'sir' when they bawled him out.

Of course at times his heart ached for Dawn, but lack of any word from her confirmed his belief that she was lost forever. He felt an emptiness when he thought of what might have been. A sadness descended on his spirit. So badly had he wanted her that whatever he did with his life would seem second-best for a time. Even so, he did try to put her out of his mind. The army was a great help. Every day gave him something new and different to think about; constantly presenting him with a fresh challenge . . .

So that by September – what with the Passing Out Parade, a

89

new posting to Aldershot, adjusting to the privileges and penalties of rank – Second Lieutenant Keir Milford was beginning to congratulate himself on surviving the trauma of parting from Dawn.

Which was when he had a letter from her.

It was forwarded, unopened, by his mother.

Dear Keir,
What's past is past and cannot be undone. I don't want to talk about it but I would like to see you again. I phoned your home and your father said you were in the army. If you get this, please write or phone. Better still, come and see me. I miss you. Love, Dawn.

Reading the letter in the Mess over breakfast, Keir's blue eyes widened as he choked back a cry of elation. The words *I miss you* leapt off the page. He had an overwhelming urge to phone her at once. Immediately he began to plan ways of obtaining a weekend pass . . . he would go to London . . . they had so much to talk about . . .

Confused and excited, he read the letter again. It was more of a note than a letter, which brought the smiling admission that Dawn had never been one for writing.

Interrupted by a summons to the parade ground he swallowed his coffee and stuffed the letter into a pocket, so it was not until later that he had a chance to read it again. The urge to see her was as strong as ever. He pictured himself in his uniform, bounding up the stairs to her flat. So vividly did he imagine the scene that suddenly the pain was back in his heart. A bitter taste filled his mouth as he remembered the agony of his last visit, making him flinch at the thought of enduring such misery again.

Keir resisted doing anything about the letter that day and the day after, arguing back and forth, telling himself that this time would be different. Seven months had passed. He was no longer a love-sick boy. He was a serving officer in the British Army.

For a week he walked around with the letter in his pocket; making up his mind, changing it again, deciding to phone, then deciding against it. Looking back he could see the havoc she had caused. She had almost destroyed him. The army was a second chance. Dawn's life was the theatre. God knows she had told him often enough . . .

Finally, he tore the letter to shreds, vowing never to see her again. Dawn had written, *What's past is past . . . I don't want to talk about it.* Well neither did he! He didn't even want to think about it.

Luckily, he had enough to think about. His regiment had received embarkation orders for Germany. Keir's workload doubled as a thousand troops began to make ready to move out from Aldershot. *'We're not going until November,'* he wrote to his parents, *'but there are a million things to get organized.'*

Then, at the beginning of October, he received another letter from Dawn. Like the first, it came via his mother. He stared at the envelope, recognizing the writing. Guilt turned to anger. She had left him alone for months. He had endured days and nights of misery. Now, when he was getting her out of his system, she decided she missed him. 'Too bloody bad,' he muttered under his breath, tearing the letter up without even taking it from the envelope.

Had it not been for the army, he might have weakened. As it was, his mind was so full he scarcely had time to think about Dawn. The logistics of moving an entire regiment had captured his imagination. Although relatively minor, his duties were more complicated than he had anticipated, important enough to absorb him completely. Finally, at the end of the month, the Regiment was ready to move.

'Well done,' said the CO, addressing his junior officers. 'In fact we're so well organized that you can have a spot of embarkation leave. Seven full days . . .'

Keir returned home like the prodigal son.

Eleven

They made a great fuss of him. Joe's prophecy had come true – the army had changed Keir and all for the better. 'He looks so well,' Joe enthused to his wife. 'He got so hangdog moping about after that girl, I began to forget what he really looked like.

I'm so proud I could weep like a woman.' The pleasure the reunion gave the Milfords showed in their faces.

Mrs Milford did indeed weep, shedding tears of relief in the privacy of her bedroom. Like Joe, Edith had worried about Keir throwing his future away. Now, although not her choice, she was more pleased than she could say about the way he had adapted to life in the army. Customers in the shop were very impressed – 'I saw him in the street yesterday,' said Mrs Shaw. 'My word, he looks ever so dashing.'

And he did. Keir had recovered his former confidence and it showed in all manner of ways, not least in the way he chattered away about his new life in the army.

On the Sunday Joe's two oldest friends, Bob Cooper and Emlyn Hughes came to lunch. 'To give you some advice about all those Frauleins in Germany,' Bob Cooper told Keir with a laugh.

Keir had known them most of his life; they frequently dropped in to discuss politics with his father. Emlyn, the local librarian, was an erudite Welshman who seemed to have read every book ever written. A short man, with a crafty face, he had a deep and genuine fondness for Joe. 'Denied his chance,' he always said about Joe. 'If he hadn't had that accident, he'd be in the House of Commons by now.'

Joe dismissed it with a laugh. 'Bob's the one,' he would say, 'Bob's going to become an MP.'

Bob had been adopted as prospective candidate by a neighbouring constituency, so there seemed every chance. Taller than Emlyn, he was a well-built man who carried himself with an air of assurance. Never having married, he still lived in the area and often dropped in to chat with Joe and sample Edith's cooking.

'My word, that was splendid, Edith,' he said as they settled back in their chairs after lunch. 'Young Keir will miss all this home cooking.'

Which led to a discussion on Keir's impending departure for Germany. 'Of course we're pleased he's an officer,' said Edith, picking up her knitting, 'and I daresay Germany's all right, as long as those Russians behave. I know what Joe says, but that's not what they say in the papers. If the Russians turn nasty, our Keir's in the front line.'

'Don't believe all you read in the papers,' said Joe in a long-suffering voice. 'I told you –'

'It's you that's always reading them out to me –'

'Not the propaganda. I read out the little bits tucked away on the inside pages, the stuff they don't really want you to know.'

'Why do they print it then? It wouldn't be there if they didn't want you to know, would it?' Edith said sharply.

Bob burst out laughing. 'She's got you there, Joe.'

Keir felt a sudden wave of affection. This was how he always remembered home. This was how he had grown up, with his father's friends sitting around the fire, arguing politics.

'It's a matter of emphasis,' said Joe scornfully. 'The Russians couldn't do a thing wrong in the war. They were our glorious allies then. Now, according to the papers, it's all different. People ought to ask themselves *why* it's different, that's what. You listen to Bob about Potsdam. That's where all this trouble started. The world had a chance until Potsdam.'

The rest of the afternoon was spent discussing Potsdam. Edith sat knitting while Keir listened and put the occasional question. Pleased to be treated as an equal by these older men, he soon found himself caught up in Bob Cooper's story.

Potsdam, Keir learned, was a suburb of Berlin where the leaders of the Allied Powers had met at the end of the war. Bob Cooper had been a major in the Signals at the time, and his task had been to supervise a communications centre for the British contingent – 'We had about six weeks to set it all up before the top brass arrived,' Bob grinned, 'which sounds plenty of time, but Germany was in chaos and we were staging one of the most luxurious conferences the world's ever seen.'

Inevitably, Bob had got to know his opposite numbers, an American by the name of Ernie Kovacks and a Russian major, Serge Ovalaski from Stalingrad. 'The three of us became buddies. We swapped stories about the battles we'd fought and the sights we'd seen. There wasn't a scrap of difference between us, we were all soldiers who'd seen enough war to last us a lifetime. We all wanted the same things. To get back to our homes and get on with our lives. You could say we held our own summit conference. The way we saw it Potsdam was a chance for the world to start over again. The leaders of the three most powerful countries were going to sit down as friends and allies, to plan a world in which war would cease to exist.' He looked embarrassed. 'I suppose we were naive, but there was such enormous goodwill we believed Allied cooperation would last forever.'

The conference itself had lasted two or three weeks, during which time Bob continued to mix with his Russian and American counterparts – 'Churchill and Truman and Stalin used to give each other parties every night, so we did the same. One night I'd be the host in the British compound, then Ernie would take a turn, and then Serge. By God, we shifted some booze, I can tell you.'

The trouble arose when the conference was over. 'After the top brass had left, naturally we had to pack everything up. We'd more or less built a small town to accommodate everyone, so there was plenty to do before breaking camp.'

Four days after the leaders had left, Bob had been in his office when his Russian friend burst in – 'Serge was in a hell of a temper. White as a sheet and shaking all over. He got so excited that he forgot his English and started shouting at me in Russian. My sergeant ran in to see what was happening, and old Serge turned round and thumped him. I tell you, it's a hell of a thing for an officer to strike a man in the army. And a Russian major clouting a *British* sergeant would have caused uproar. Serge knew he was in trouble as soon as he'd thrown the punch. Luckily Thomo, my sergeant, wasn't the sort to make a fuss. Serge and I got him into a chair and I gave him a whisky while Serge apologized. Finally he told me why he was in such a temper. Apparently the Americans had just dropped a new weapon on Japan. It was the atomic bomb on Hiroshima.'

Keir returned Bob's stare, wondering if he had missed the point of the story.

'Don't you see?' said Bob. 'Truman knew about the atomic bomb all the time he was at Potsdam, but he didn't tell Stalin. In two weeks of talks and partying and all the rest of it, he didn't say a word. He even sent the order to use the bomb against Japan from Potsdam. Churchill knew as well. They both knew that America had developed the most powerful weapon in the world, but neither of them told the Russians. They kept it secret, and they were supposed to be allies.' Bob shrugged. 'Serge accused us all of knowing. Of course we hadn't. I think I convinced him in the end, but I don't think he cared much by then. As far as he was concerned, we were tarred with the same brush as Truman and Churchill. I tell you, I felt downright ashamed. Serge said all the Russians felt betrayed and I could see their point. They kept asking why their allies hadn't told them about this terrible new bomb? It made them suspicious.'

Edith returned from the kitchen at that moment, carrying a tray of tea cups and mince pies. 'I don't see that's any reason for your friend hitting that sergeant,' she sniffed.

Bob laughed. 'He did apologize, and he sent Thomo a crate of vodka next morning, so I don't think Thomo held a grudge. The point is, that was the start of the Arms Race. Serge told me exactly what would happen. It's got nothing to do with communism or capitalism. It's about people feeling safe. The Russians didn't feel safe after Potsdam. The Americans had atomic bombs, so the Russians felt threatened and had to have them too. Now we've got them as well. Everyone is building arsenals again, even though we all know that every arms race in history has led to a war.'

Bob accepted a cup of tea and sat stirring it absent-mindedly. 'I wonder what happened to old Serge. He was a lovely man. His wife and son were killed at Stalingrad, but some miracle had enabled his two daughters to survive. All he wanted was to get out of the army and back to his kids. I can remember him and Thomo and me, sitting in that office drinking whisky, as if it were yesterday. Serge was close to tears. This big man, who'd fought the Germans back all the way from Stalingrad to Berlin. "I won't get out of the army now," he said. "Not now the Americans have got this new bomb. Our leaders will want to keep a big army . . ."'

And so the talk droned on for the rest of the afternoon. Keir listened more than he joined in, interested especially because of his new career in the army. The world had moved on since Potsdam ten years before, and for the first time Keir was developing a taste to be part of it.

He went to bed that night feeling really pleased with his life. It was exciting to be a young officer about to be posted overseas. 'The world's your oyster,' Emlyn had said, wishing him luck. How well things had worked out! And how thankful he was to have got Dawn Wharton out of his system.

The following morning another letter arrived.

'Aren't you going to read it?' asked Edith, when her son left it unopened. 'It's the same writing as before. You got the others, didn't you? Who are they from anyway? Some school friend? It can't be Dusty because –'

'Dawn,' said Keir. 'Dawn Wharton.'

'Oh!' exclaimed his mother, unable to disguise her disappointment.

Joe looked up from his paper. 'I thought that was over and done with.'

'It is,' Keir answered, leaving no doubt.

Back at Aldershot with a million things to do, he might have destroyed that letter as he had the previous one, but he was embarrassed to tear it up with his parents looking on. The gesture would have looked melodramatic. So he opened it, feigning an air of casualness which quickly changed to one of concern.

Dear Keir,
I'm in such desperate trouble. I know you were fond of me once. Please phone me wherever you are. I don't know who else to turn to. So much has happened, far too much to put in this letter, but I know you'd help me if you could. I do hope I hear from you. Love Dawn.

Colour drained from Keir's face. Although he was used to the breathless quality of Dawn's notes, this one was different. There was no mistaking her panic.

'What's up?' asked Joe, his watchful eyes on Keir's face.

'I'm not sure. She's in some sort of trouble.'

'Hmph!' Edith exclaimed, tossing her head.

Staring at the letter, Keir reminded himself of his intention not to see her again. One look at his parents was enough to know their thoughts. They hoped he would stick to his vow. He *didn't* want to see her. Yet such was the plea for help in that letter that he couldn't ignore it completely.

'I'll phone her later,' he said, trying to keep his voice light and dismissive.

'You don't want to get mixed up with her again,' warned Edith quickly.

'Mum, I won't get mixed up with anyone. I'm going to Germany.'

It was ten o'clock when he phoned her, by which time his parents were busy in the shop. 'Dawn? This is Keir. I got your note. What's wrong?'

Instead of answering his question, she asked where he was.

'Home. I'm on embarkation leave. I'm going to Germany in a couple of days,' he replied.

'Oh God,' she groaned, 'I do so want to see you. Keir, it is urgent . . .' Sounding uncharacteristically tearful, she imparted such despair he found it impossible to refuse. He tried asking questions but she parried every attempt. 'No, Keir, I can't talk over the phone. I'll tell you when I see you. Can you come up this morning? *Please.*'

His parents were disappointed. They didn't say so, but he could tell from their expressions.

'I'll just see her for lunch,' he said casually. 'I had nothing planned for today anyway.'

Perversely wanting to look his best, Keir had dressed in his uniform, knowing it suited him, and an hour later he was on the train, mildly curious about why Dawn was upset. It had to be about her career, that was all she really cared about.

Belsize Park revived all the old memories. Approaching the terrace of houses he glimpsed the row of garages at the back and remembered climbing up there on that awful night. The memory disgusted him. 'I must have been mad,' he muttered.

Pausing to adjust his cap to a rakish angle, he took the stairs two at a time.

Dawn opened the door at once, as if she had been waiting. 'Oh, Keir, you look marvellous. So handsome,' she said, embracing him in the way he used to dream about.

His first thought was that she had put on weight. A lot of weight. Then he realized she was pregnant, heavily pregnant!

Shocked and confused, he heard himself saying, 'I didn't know, I didn't even know you were married.'

'I'm not married,' she said.

The next half-hour was bewildering. Since she did most of the talking, he was not called on to say much. As he listened he kept throwing her glances, inspecting her, shocked by her size. She wore a brown tent-like frock, which did little to disguise her

97

condition. When she crossed the room she put her feet down heavily, quite unlike the Dawn he remembered. Even her face was rounder, fleshier, disguising the slant-eyed, high cheek-boned look that was so attractive. Only her eyes were the same – deep and dark and full of expression.

'I've not been out much,' she said, noticing he was looking at her. 'Hardly at all in the last couple of months. Just to the shops on the corner.'

He tried to analyse what he felt for her. She was so *different* from how he remembered. In the old days she only had to look at him for his pulse to quicken. Now, she was different, and pregnant. Pregnant but not married. Where was the father? Who was the father? Shock waves began to reverberate in his head. It was almost nine months since that awful night in February. He went cold. Cotton wool clogged his brain. It was his child! Dawn was carrying *his* child!

Her voice was steady, lacking the hint of tears he had heard over the phone. Even so, Keir listened with horror.

She hadn't worked in four months. 'I stopped before it began to show. I couldn't risk it. My career would be ruined . . .'

Her and her bloody career!

'If any of the girls at the theatre had found out they'd have spread the story all round the West End. I told everyone I had to go up to Scotland to nurse a sick aunt. They all believed it, even Maxwell. I would have left here but it was cheaper to stay and I needed every penny to keep going . . .'

Keir stared, still numb with shock.

'You can imagine my mother,' said Dawn scornfully. 'I went to see her when I missed my second period.'

Keir blushed, not used to Dawn talking about her periods.

'We had a real screaming match,' continued Dawn. 'I told her I needed help, that I had nowhere to go, that I'd have to move back with them for a while. She went wild, lost control, called me every filthy name she could think of. After an hour of her screaming I couldn't stand any more. I'm not sure how it ended. I mean I don't know if she threw me out or if I just left. I can't remember to be honest. She got drunk and . . . well, it was hopeless.'

Dawn shrugged at the futility of it all. The week after seeing her mother she had tried to find an abortionist. 'A girl in our digs up in Manchester had had an abortion. It took her a year to get over it, if she ever did get over it – I don't think her insides were ever much good afterwards. She went into paralysing convulsions every month. She wouldn't go to a doctor in case they found out. Anyway, one night when she was in a lot of pain, she told me about it. She'd been to a place in Ladbroke Grove.'

Dawn had searched Ladbroke Grove every afternoon for ten days. Her face paled as she remembered. 'I didn't know where to start, and you can't go up to a policeman and ask directions.'

Eventually, she had obtained an address from a barmaid. 'I did go,' she said, shivering slightly. 'God, you hear about these back-street abortionists without really realizing that's what they are. You should have seen this place. I only got as far as the hall, which was filthy. And this old crone looked as ancient as Methuselah and twice as evil. There I was, with the fifty pounds in my purse and my knees shaking so badly I could hardly stand up. All I could think about was that girl up in Manchester . . .' Her voice faded and she closed her eyes to blot out the memory.

Overcoming his shock, Keir felt ashamed, more ashamed than ever in his life. He moved to sit beside her on the sofa and took her hand to comfort her.

Dawn swallowed hard. 'I might have stayed if someone had been with me, but I was so desperately frightened. I was three months gone by then. I knew it would be dangerous and, well, the truth is I lost my nerve. I ran away . . .'

Holding her hand, touching her again, stirred strange emotions in Keir. Even in his confusion, he felt the old magic. If her figure were no longer willowy, her skin was still flawless. Her hair was as glossy as ever. And although her smile was less quick it still had a quality that affected him like alcohol. Her dark eyes still reached him. He had thought himself cured of her . . . but he wasn't.

'People rang up for the first couple of months,' Dawn was saying. 'I pretended to be a cousin of mine who was using the flat while I was in Scotland. Everyone at the theatre was convinced, which shows what they know about acting.' She forced a smile but he sensed she was near the end of her tether. Her hand tightened on his as she continued. 'When I stopped work I paid the rent up six months ahead. I was doing okay until the last seven or eight weeks. I must admit they got me down. I haven't seen anyone except the doctor and the people in the shop on the corner. I don't want people to see me, or to know, and . . . oh, Keir, the thing is I've run out of money.'

His shame plunged to new depths as he remembered her letters. She had turned to him for help and he had ignored her.

She was weeping in his arms, great shuddering sobs of tears. He held her and stroked her hair, murmuring, 'It's all right, darling. It's all right. I'm here now, I'm here.'

They clung to each other, rocking back and forth, Keir as white as a sheet. Army training had prepared him for many emergencies, but not for this.

After a few minutes, Dawn stopped weeping. 'Sorry,' she said, drying her eyes. 'I didn't mean to cry. I despise people who cry. My mother was always crying, full of self-pity. It's just that I've had no one to talk to, and . . . I've hardly got any money left, and . . . Oh, Keir, it's such a relief to see you.'

Suddenly, the last nine months might not have existed. Keir's mind overflowed with memories of earlier days in the flat, reviving so many dreams of living happily ever. Before he could stop, he heard himself saying, 'We'll get married. Don't worry, I'll look after you. Everything will be all right, you'll see . . .'

She pushed him away, brushing a tear from her eye. 'You don't have to marry me. Don't talk like that. You'll start me bawling again –'

'I *want* to marry you –'

She stopped his words with a kiss. 'I'll think about it,' she said, teasing him and recovering enough of her old confidence to laugh. 'Oh, it's so good to see you again. I feel better already. I can't get over you being here, all dressed up in officer's uniform . . .'

He made some tea while they talked. He would have preferred something stronger, but tea was all she had in the flat. The larder was almost empty. Shuddering as he thought of her desperation, Keir asked, 'What on earth would you have done if I hadn't . . . ?'

'Oh, don't talk about it now.' She waved a hand dismissively, her spirits reviving by the minute. 'My prayers have been answered. You've come back. That's all that matters.'

The more of her story he heard, the more he admired her. She had coped amazingly well. The rent of the flat was paid up until

February. The doctor had arranged for her to have her baby at the local hospital.

'I'm booked in from tomorrow night. The baby's due in two or three days,' she said.

But the bad news began to stack up. After paying her rent so far in advance she had discovered a no-children clause in her lease. Desperate for help, she had telephoned her mother, prepared to beg if necessary. 'But they've moved to Spain. I knew they were going, she was packing things when I went there for the big argument. God, that argument! Know what she said? I'd ruined her life once, she wasn't going to let it happen again. Bitch! Anyway, they've gone . . .'

The other bad news was that Dawn had run out of money. The miracle was that she had managed so long. Keir was her only hope. 'If you could just find me another flat, and help out with some cash,' she pleaded, 'and be around to hold my hand for a while . . .'

The fear in her eyes broke his heart. He had no cash. He had spent it all on her before joining the army, and had since discovered that saving money on service pay was well nigh impossible. And he couldn't 'be around for a while'. He had to report to Aldershot in thirty-six hours. He was going to Germany . . .

Inevitably his thoughts turned to his parents. There was nowhere else to go. The Milfords were a close family. Keir had taken his problems to them most of his life . . .

Dawn argued for hours, persuaded eventually as much by the utter hopelessness of her situation as by Keir's persistence. If he was to help, it had to be with the cooperation of his parents.

Twelve

It was eight o'clock in the evening by the time the cab drew up outside the Milfords. The shop had scarcely been closed an hour. Keir watched Dawn glance nervously at the darkened windows, as she fretted about what his parents would say.

Similar thoughts were worrying him. Paying off the cab, Keir gave her a smile as he hoisted her suitcase. 'Don't worry. Mum and Dad will be all right, you'll see.'

Entering through the side door next to the shop, they were in the hall when Edith poked her head out of the kitchen. 'Keir? You're late. I thought you'd be home hours ago –' She broke off when she saw Dawn.

Introductions were a nightmare – awkward and stilted. 'Pleased to meet you, I'm sure,' said Edith, while conveying she was obviously not. Joe wasn't much better. He stared boggle-eyed at Dawn's stomach.

Keir draped Dawn's coat over a chair and sat her down by the fire, babbling nervously about it being cold and was sure to snow before Christmas. Then he talked solidly for at least half an hour.

His mother's face was tight with hostility. Joe looked sad and embarrassed. After listening in shocked silence to Keir's suggestion that Dawn stay with them until she went into hospital, they visibly flinched when he suggested she bring her baby back to the Milfords.

'Only for a couple of months,' he promised. 'I'll send part of my army pay home and Dawn will find a new flat. We've worked it all out. Dawn will get a job and what with the money I'll send home, she'll have enough to pay someone to look after the baby.'

It had sounded quite straightforward in the flat, but confronted by the frosty silence, the words stuck in Keir's throat. His heart ached as he looked at his mother who sat, dry-washing her hands, her head bowed like a prisoner in the dock.

Joe Milford, slumped in his invalid chair, seemed to age visibly as he listened. Yet it was Joe's dignity and good manners that finally brought Keir's nightmare of a recital to an end.

Taking a deep breath, Joe took the situation in hand. 'Questions can wait until later,' he said darkly to Keir. 'Meanwhile,' he said, turning to Dawn, 'you look tired. We must feed you and get you to bed. You need rest.'

Keir's was the only available bed. 'You'll have to sleep on the couch tonight,' Joe told his son, sending him up to put clean sheets on the bed.

Keir had done the talking. Dawn herself had said barely a

word. She sat at the fireside, mortified with embarrassment, looking exhausted. She seemed at the end of her strength. Refusing food, she accepted a glass of hot milk which Keir carried as he helped her up the stairs. She clutched his arm when he showed her his room. 'Oh, Keir, they don't want me here –'

'Shush, stop worrying. Get a good night's sleep. Everything will be all right, really.'

And then, after kissing her cheek, Keir went downstairs to make sure. His mother was blowing her nose noisily as he entered the room. She turned away quickly but not before he glimpsed the tears in her eyes. His father looked grave and unhappy.

'I'm sorry,' Keir began. 'I know it's a shock –'

'Being sorry won't help,' said his father. 'Sit down and listen to me.'

Keir did as he was told.

'There's only one question worth bothering about,' said Joe bluntly, staring at his son. 'This child. Is it yours?'

Forgetting what he had seen from the garage roof, forgetting the man in the raincoat, all Keir could see was Dawn falling naked across the bed and him standing over her. The scene was embedded in his memory. He reddened with shame. 'Yes,' he whispered, before clearing his throat. 'Yes,' he repeated, more loudly.

Edith stifled a sob and covered her face with her hands. Keir wanted to comfort her. Instead he remained in his chair, held by his father's eyes.

'I see.' Joe sighed heavily. He continued to stare at his son, 'There's only one thing to do then. You got the girl into trouble. You'll have to marry her –' he broke off with an impatient look at his wife – 'Be quiet, woman. You snivelling and Keir saying sorry won't change a thing. It's too late –'

Keir blurted out, 'I told her we'd get married.'

A look of resignation came into Joe's eyes. His head dropped for a moment, then he straightened up. 'Aye,' he said slowly, 'I knew you'd do the right thing.'

'She hasn't accepted. She said she'd think about it.'

'Think about it!' Edith snapped, bright spots of anger on her cheeks. 'That little hussy's got precious little time to think about anything.'

Neither her husband nor her son answered. They continued instead to stare at each other. Keir saw a glimmer of surprise in his father's eyes. 'Think about it, eh?' said Joe softly, and might have said more but changed his mind with a shrug of his shoulders. He looked desperately tired. 'We're all tired,' he said. 'No point in talking tonight. Likely we'll all say the wrong things. I reckon we've plenty to sleep on.'

Not that they slept. Keir was awake for hours, and as he tossed and turned on the living-room couch, the murmur of voices reached him from his parents' bedroom. His heart went out to them. How different from last night, when they had bid him goodnight with pride in their eyes. He was as shocked as they were. Once again Dawn Wharton had turned his life upside down.

The only one who slept was Dawn, and not simply from exhaustion. Some primeval instinct was at work. The primitive mechanisms which govern animals about to give birth had helped her survive and get to a refuge. And the Milfords was a safe place; despite the hostility with which she had been greeted, Dawn saw the word 'home' on every scuffed table and chair. There were no dangers here, only problems, and Keir had promised to deal with the problems. Feeling safe for the first time in weeks, Dawn slept soundly, so soundly that she slept until eleven the next morning – and the first contraction came at noon.

Having only just come downstairs, she was talking to Keir when a spasm convulsed her. She almost passed out with the pain. Grabbing his arm, she cried out.

Keir's mother ran in from the shop. 'Oh dear God! She's starting!'

Dawn sat panting like a beached whale, while Keir hopped from foot to foot, his face creased with worry.

'Phone that hospital,' said his mother. 'The one she's supposed to go to in London.'

Keir did, only to learn that an ambulance was out of the question. 'Hillingdon?' said the voice on the phone. 'That's miles outside our area. What's she doing there? You'll have to contact your local hospital.'

By the time Keir found the number and dialled again, Dawn was convulsed with another contraction. The response from the local hospital was positively unhelpful. 'We can't take her. Our maternity ward's full up. Besides, there's no point if she's started – the baby could arrive before she gets here. You'd best get onto Dr Farlow in Long Lane.'

Keir and his mother helped Dawn back up the stairs, then Keir rushed back to the telephone. Dr Farlow was out on his rounds, but the doctor's wife promised to get word to Mrs Cummings, the midwife.

Joe Milford propelled himself in from the shop. 'What's up, lad?'

'She's having it. There's no time to get her to hospital.'

'Bloody hell,' said Joe.

Mrs Cummings arrived half an hour later. 'Get some water on to boil,' she told Keir on the way past. Edith Milford was already at the stove, heating a saucepan.

There was a lot of toing and froing after that. Dr Farlow arrived within half an hour. The midwife went away and returned clutching a basket of knitting. 'Won't be long,' she told Keir brightly.

By now it was four o'clock. Soon Keir would have to leave for Aldershot.

He went out to the shop to talk it over with his father, breaking off whenever a customer came in.

'I can't just leave you to deal with everything,' Keir said desperately, 'but they'll go berserk if I'm not back tonight. We pull out at noon tomorrow. There's a hell of a lot to do –'

'You've *got* to go,' Joe said in a tone that defied argument. 'You start messing about now and you'll be finished with the army.'

Father and son stared at each other before Joe's stern look softened. 'We'll sort things out, don't worry. Try to phone us tomorrow, that's all, before you leave for Germany.'

Swallowing hard, Keir looked away, glancing at his watch. 'Thanks, Dad,' he said gruffly. 'I've still got a few hours. I don't have to leave until seven . . .'

The baby was born at ten minutes past six.

Joe had shut the shop, and he and his son were drinking tea in the kitchen when Edith came downstairs. 'It's a girl,' she announced and wore such a look of mingled pride and pleasure that Keir, who had been expecting cross words, felt a stab of surprise.

'All right?' Joe asked.

Edith nodded. 'She had an easy time really –' She turned, hearing steps on the stairs. 'That's the doctor, I'll see him out,' she said, leaving Joe and Keir in the kitchen.

Joe looked at his son. 'Well,' he said, 'I didn't think it would be like this, but congratulations are in order . . .'

Fortunately, perhaps, lack of time prevented further discussion. Keir had packed some of his things, but others were still in his room. 'Is it possible to collect some stuff from my wardrobe?' he asked Mrs Cummings when she joined them for a cup of tea in the kitchen.

'Don't stay long, she's tired and needs a good sleep.'

Dawn greeted him with a weary smile when he went up to his room. He sat on the edge of the narrow bed and held her hand. 'You're not to worry . . . just rest . . . I've got to go . . . I'll phone in the morning . . .'

'Her name's Elizabeth,' Dawn whispered. 'After my grandmother.'

Fifteen minutes later, after bidding goodbye to his misty-eyed parents, Second Lieutenant Keir Milford left the shop on the corner and set out for the station. It had all happened so quickly. Thirty-six hours earlier he had been sure that Dawn Wharton was no longer part of his life. Now they were to be married. Right at that moment he didn't know what he felt. *Now, for God's sake, he was a father!* He was so confused that even to walk in a straight line demanded attention. One thing was certain: whatever happened in the future, Dawn Wharton would be part of his life.

BOOK TWO

Dawn

One

Dawn had every reason to panic. Her career was ruined, she was living on the charity of Keir's parents, her own mother had disowned her, Christmas was but a few weeks away and she had very little money. On top of that she had a new-born baby to care for.

For four days and nights she was too confused to be fully aware of what she was doing. Disorientated by unfamiliar surroundings, she was prodded by the doctor, washed by the midwife, fed by Mrs Milford, wakened by the baby. Total strangers were running her life. It was hard to know what was happening. Even her own body felt alien, her breasts were the size of water melons and never stopped aching. She suffered nightmares of crushed hopes and ruined ambitions. Every time she closed her eyes she saw herself aged seven, or nine, or eleven . . . the year hardly mattered because she was always doing the same thing . . . she was forever attending lessons, while her mother never stopped screaming, 'You ruined my life. When I think of what I threw away when I had you.'

History was repeating itself. She could see herself living her mother's life all over again . . . Until, on the fifth night, she could worry no more. Her brain was exhausted. She fell into a deep, dreamless sleep and for a few blessed hours was unconscious of everything.

It was four in the morning when she awoke. Beside her, in a cradle fashioned from a dressing table drawer, Elizabeth slept so silently Dawn had to strain her hearing to catch each soft intake of breath. Outside the sky was pitch-black. Inside the house was peaceful and quiet.

'Stay calm,' she whispered into the darkness, and this time, when her heart began to pump and panic threatened to stifle her, she gathered her courage and clung on. She took deep breaths, sucking air down into her lungs, counting up to twenty and then to fifty, until she gradually recovered some of her strength.

'What a mess I've made of my life,' she groaned softly. The very words were a painful reminder of her mother. Like mother, like daughter. 'No,' Dawn cried angrily, 'I won't be like you. I *won't!'*

Reaching down into herself, she drew upon every ounce of determination. She closed her eyes, and pictured her mother; a sour, embittered woman, gorged on self-pity. 'How I hate you,' Dawn whispered aloud. 'You wouldn't have made the grade anyway. It takes more guts than you ever had. It's easy to talk but a darn sight harder to do something about it.'

But do what? Dawn refused to give up. Not now. She had survived other black times. Like when Gran died. That was the worst time of all. While she had been grief-stricken, her mother had remained dry-eyed and unmoved. Indeed at one stage she had been black with anger. The legacy for Dawn's lessons had reduced her to hysteria. Her face had twisted with fury as she had lashed into Gran's solicitor: 'I will not be dictated to from the grave,' she had shrieked. But the lessons had been part of the package; no lessons for Dawn, no money for her mother, and Gran's solicitor had safeguards to make sure the lessons took place.

The following six months had been the worst of Dawn's life. Her mother had ranted and raved from morning until night. 'We could have gone to Spain but for you. We'd be living in the sun this very minute. Instead we've got to stay for your precious lessons. You'd better make something of yourself, my girl. We're all making this sacrifice . . .' Nag, nag, nag. Day in, day out.

Dawn remembered one Saturday in particular. She'd had a bad cold; her nose was blocked and her eyes were streaming. Feeling wretched, she had asked to be excused lessons. Her mother had insisted. Dawn had begged. Her mother had screamed and shouted until, finally, Dawn had *refused* to go to her lessons. It was a weekend she would never forget; spent locked in a cupboard under the stairs, while her mother screamed, 'I'll teach you to show some gratitude, you spoilt little bitch.' Hour after hour in the dark, amid the cobwebs, with rats or mice scuffling in the corners, unable to stand upright without bumping her head, feeling ill and terrified at the same time. She

110

never refused to do her mother's bidding again, but from that day on she had ached to leave home.

How different life would have been had Gran lived. They could have shared a flat in town. Gran was always talking about that. 'We'll have such fun, and I'll be your dresser when you become famous. You'd like that, wouldn't you, with me helping you learn your lines and watching you from the wings? My word, I can't wait. But I'm not young anymore, so you'll have to grow up in a hurry.'

Seven-year-old Dawn had grown up as quick as she could, but Gran had still died. If Gran had lived they would have stayed in Bristol until Dawn joined RADA. Which meant she would never have come to Hillingdon. She would never have met Keir . . .

Meeting Keir had thrown her entire life into confusion. Everything had been cut and dried until then. Her plans had been made. She would leave home as soon as she could and become an actress. Every minute of every hour had been dedicated to that single objective. Keir's sincerity had confused her. She had been flattered at first. No other admirer had shown such devotion. Telling herself she could handle it had been one thing, remaining unaffected had been another. Her ambitions had been threatened in a way she had not expected. Dealing with her mother's harshness had been comparatively easy. It had honed her determination to a fine edge, but Keir's love could only weaken her will by making success less important. He wanted marriage. Perhaps she wanted it too . . . eventually . . . but only after she had taken her chance as an actress. She had grown up believing that to be an actress was what her life was all about. The dream had dominated her life, making her single-minded . . . She had tried to tell that to Keir so many times. If only he would realize it was as important for him as for her. If she was forced to live her mother's life all over again . . . frustrated ambition would poison their lives . . . she had seen it happen, and vowed never to let it happen to her.

Shame engulfed her. Dear, honest, reliable Keir. He was her first real friend, her only true friend – and she had betrayed him. The miracle was that he knew nothing of her involvement with Dusty. Beads of perspiration rose on her forehead as she remembered how he burst into her flat minutes after Dusty had

111

left. Convinced that somehow he had found out, she had even tried to explain. 'How could we have told you?' she had pleaded, but rage had deafened him to her words. The following day she had written a long letter, trying to explain to him what she could barely explain to herself. The task had defeated her. How could anyone justify an act of madness? She had destroyed her letter, convinced that Keir would never forgive her. The absence of any word from him had strengthened her conviction that she had lost him forever. Eventually her desperate predicament – the sheer impossibility of turning to anyone else – had compelled her to write, asking for his help. When she had heard his voice on the telephone she had braced herself, expecting him to launch into a bitter condemnation of her betrayal. But no such condemnation had been delivered. When he had arrived at her flat, she had braced herself again, expecting him to snarl and sneer about Dusty. But no such snarls had been uttered. And when the impossible had happened – when he had asked her to marry him – she had wanted to cleanse her conscience by explaining: and only then had she realized he knew nothing. The attempted explanation had died on her lips, not to protect herself but to protect him. She had hurt him already. Bad enough him knowing she had slept with another man, a hundred times worse if he knew it was Dusty. Now she could never tell him . . .

Restlessly, Dawn stirred in the bed, plagued by her conscience. Why, oh why, had she allowed it to happen? In all truthfulness, she *disliked* Dusty. She distrusted him. And yet, she had known what would happen.

He had turned up at the theatre one night, five weeks before he went to the States. For the first time in their lives they had not fought each other. For the first time Keir had not been there to confuse their emotions. They went out to supper and then back to her place, exchanging excited talk about their careers while their eyes spoke of a different excitement. It was as if they dared each other. She could still remember their first kiss; tasting the copper-penny taste of want in his open mouth. They had touched each other hotly, wetly, their bodies arching towards each other. Ridding themselves of their clothes had taken forever; she fumbling with his belt with trembling fingers while he unbuttoned her blouse. Shamelessly she had dragged him down onto the bed, her skirts flung backwards, unconsciously undulating her hips . . . Not until afterwards had they confronted their guilt. Dusty said they were two of a kind. Both ruled by ambition, both wanting to dominate. There was no talk of romance, no words of love. 'I want you,' Dusty had said, and she wanted him enough to rip the shirt from his back.

Five weeks of madness. Five weeks of making love, of arguing, of matching her will against one as strong as her own. They both knew it was fleeting. They *wanted* it to be fleeting, to get it over and done with, to be free of it, free to get on with the rest of their lives. Five weeks of being racked with guilt about Keir. Dusty too had been torn by conflicting emotions. Lust versus loyalty. Lust had won every time. They had behaved like animals. Sexual excitement had stifled all power of thought until their desires had been satisfied. Only then had they confronted their guilt.

Afterwards Dusty had accused her. 'We wouldn't feel so rotten if you'd chosen me in the first place.'

She could still feel her anger. 'Chosen you,' she had blazed. 'I'd *never* choose you. Besides, you were so full of Marcia, if she ever existed.'

'That's for me to know and you to find out,' he had laughed, teasing her.

'Huh! As if I cared –'

'As if I cared either. That's why we're here.'

Here meant both of them naked on her bed. Here meant lighting a cigarette while he watched with that mocking look in his eyes.

She had screamed at him. 'I don't even like you. You're selfish and conceited –'

'Unlike Keir –'

'Right –'

'Okay,' he had agreed, 'maybe Keir is more straightforward –'

'You think I don't know that? You think I'm not ashamed?'

'Of what? Making love?'

'Of letting him down!'

Yet she had been unable to stop herself. Now, in Keir's bed in the little room above the shop on the corner, she remembered the confusion of those five tempestuous weeks with feelings of shame. How was it possible to make love with someone and not even like him? How was it possible to like Keir so much and yet hold him at arms' length? The safety valve with Dusty had been his impending departure. The relationship had no future. Neither of them wanted it to have a future. The immediacy of sexual release had been enough. It was a comfort to know she need never see Dusty again . . .

As she turned in the narrow bed, feverish with worry, Dawn fretted about the old axiom, like mother, like daughter. Was history repeating itself all over again? Angrily she pushed the thought from her mind. 'I will *not* be like her,' she whispered savagely.

She saw Keir's anxious face in the darkness. Recalling his proposal of marriage, she could hear him apologizing. 'Sorry, Dawn, I must get back to Aldershot . . . the Regiment is leaving for Germany . . . I'll phone when I can . . .'

God, it was tempting! He would make a good husband. He would be her friend as well as her lover. If she were to marry anyone, she would want to marry Keir. But not yet . . . and not like this. She refused to take the same cheap way out as her mother. She owed Keir that much. Repeatedly she told herself that Keir was the father. Dusty had taken precautions . . . Elizabeth had to be Keir's baby, even if they had only done it the once . . .

Dawn wiped her hairline with the back of her hand. The pillow was damp with perspiration. 'Stay calm,' she whispered. 'Think. Make plans. Don't give up.'

Keir would crowd her. For the best of reasons – because he loved her, because he wanted to care for her and the child – he would persuade her to marry him. But he would deny her the dream she had cherished since childhood. 'I'm not ready to be his wife,' she whispered. 'I might be one day, if he still wants me, but not yet.'

Her hands clenched as she called on her courage. Concentrating she began to piece her life together again. She did it in her head, dealing with one worry at a time. It was as if she laid each problem out on a table and walked round it, studying it from different angles until she knew every detail. Taking one item at a time reduced its importance, making it more manageable, so that although the sky outside remained dark, Dawn began to see things more clearly. Keir's parents, for instance. They disliked her. Disapproval lay behind every word they spoke. It showed in their eyes. Who could blame them? They had raised a perfectly nice boy, only to find themselves landed with . . . Dawn searched for the right word . . . *only to be landed with a trollop*, she decided with a rueful smile. *I bet that's what they call me, a trollop!*

She was not ungrateful. She shuddered to think of what would have happened without them. What amazed her was their innocence. They had such trusting natures. Dawn's childhood had taught her to be wary. Yet the Milfords judged as they saw. They were forever making assumptions – about Elizabeth, for instance. 'The child is Keir's responsibility,' Keir's father had said. Joe Milford had said it, not Dawn. Without telling the truth, she had avoided telling them a lie. And yesterday she had heard Keir's mother say, 'Goodness knows what will happen. She'll have to help out in the shop. She'll have to do something. I can't run around after her all the time.'

Another assumption. Help out in the shop? That was the last thing Dawn intended – but yesterday she had been too muddled to think of the future.

Beside her, the baby stirred restlessly and began to cry. Dawn lifted her out of the drawer and brought her into the bed, cooing over her with an air almost of contentment until Elizabeth suckled at a breast. 'Ouch!' She winced. 'That hurts. Oh, baby, feeding you this way went out with the ark. I don't care what they say, I'll start you on a bottle tomorrow.'

Nonetheless it was a more confident mother who rocked her baby to sleep half an hour later. 'I'll make you a promise,' she whispered, nuzzling the tiny face with her nose, 'never to blame you for the life I could have had. I won't be able to. I'm still going to have it.'

She repeated that a dozen times over, just as she repeated, 'I will *not* be like my mother. I will not give up. Dammit, I won't!'

Then she lay back on the pillows and began to make plans.

Two

She put her plans into action half an hour later. When Edith Milford entered the bedroom bearing a jug of milk on a tray, Dawn greeted her with a confident smile. 'Good morning,' she said, 'I hope that's not for me.'

'Of course it's for you. You heard the midwife yesterday. Two quarts a day, to keep you on tap so to speak.'

Dawn groaned and shook her head. 'Not any more. I'm going to cut out the middle-man. From now on, Mrs Milford, Elizabeth can take her milk neat.'

Edith Milford was shocked. 'There's nothing wrong with you –?'

'There's nothing wrong with Elizabeth either. Bottle-fed babies are just as healthy as the other kind. It makes no difference to her, but it will make a big difference to me. I want to shed thirty pounds in a hurry –'

'You want?' Edith Milford turned pink with indignation. 'It's time you stopped thinking about what you want, my girl. Those days are over. What matters now is what's best for the baby.'

Dawn had no intention of arguing. Instead she set about winning Edith over.

'Do you know what I think?' she asked, cocking her head. 'What's best for a baby is to have a happy mother, and I know what would make this mother happy. A nice cup of tea and a cigarette.' Throwing her arms into the air, she gazed imploringly at the ceiling. 'A cigarette, a cigarette, my kingdom for a cigarette.' She curtsied as best as sitting in bed would allow and looked at Mrs Milford, her eyes bright with laughter. 'Be an angel, Mrs Milford. I do appreciate how kind you have been'.

Edith Milford was taken aback. She disliked this girl who looked like a gypsy. The girl was a trollop, Edith decided, disapproval written all over her face. 'You'll be in trouble with the doctor –'

'Dr Farlow? Never. He's a pet. He said I could have a bath

116

this morning. I can get up, wash my hair and have a bath.' Dawn laughed with sudden excitement. 'That will be heaven. Especially after a cigarette and a nice cup of tea.'

Disconcerted, Edith retreated to the door. 'Milk would do you more good –'

'Tea, *please*, Mrs Milford.'

Edith sighed and tried to reach a decision. 'Well,' she conceded grudgingly, 'I dare say there's one in the pot. Joe was just having a cup –'

'Bless you,' Dawn rewarded her with a smile. 'And a cigarette? Thank you, Mrs Milford, you're an angel. It's going to be a good day, I can feel it. Do you know something? Today is the start of the rest of my life.'

Edith Milford pondered that as she went down the stairs. Not until she was reaching for a clean cup in the kitchen did she exclaim, 'Well *of course* today's the start of the rest of her life! Daft thing. What's she on about?'

'Eh?' Joe grunted, looking up from his paper. 'What's that, love?'

His wife shook her head. 'I don't know. That girl's in a funny mood this morning. I thought she was ashamed of herself yesterday, goodness knows she's got reason to be, but she's as brazen as a brass monkey today. I can't make head nor tail of her. You never know where you are with someone like that.'

The Milfords did not have to wait long to find out.

So far as Dawn was concerned, starting the rest of her life meant resuming her career. Enlisting the doctor's support was easy. He was a shy young man, still in his twenties, with lank brown hair and a pimply complexion. By the time he arrived, Dawn had bathed and washed her hair and was glowing with health. Having a baby had not dimmed her charm. If her figure looked dumpy, her eyes still sparkled with brilliance. The doctor succumbed in a matter of minutes, agreeing that Elizabeth could be fed from a bottle. He even had a sample one with him, which he presented to Dawn as a gift. 'And yes, you can get up,' he agreed, 'if you take things easy for a few days.'

'Oh yes,' Dawn promised, 'I won't do too much.'

The Milfords were harder to charm. They were in the shop when Dawn went downstairs. Edith was soon back and forth to the living-room, doing her chores between serving customers.

117

Dawn could feel the older woman's disapproval. Ashamed to have an unmarried mother under her roof, Edith wore an expression of icy disdain. Even when Dawn offered to prepare the midday meal, Edith's manner remained frigid. The more Dawn sought to charm, the cooler Edith became, as if to say that Dawn was such a thoroughly bad lot no amount of good behaviour could atone for her sins. And at one o'clock, when Joe closed the shop and came in for his lunch, he too looked awkward and embarrassed.

Dawn tried to make conversation, but the Milfords were as responsive as stones. Finally, with the meal virtually over, she was glad to excuse herself and flee upstairs to answer the cries of her baby. Sitting on Keir's narrow bed, with her baby in her lap, she despaired. 'Oh God, it's even worse than I imagined.'

Her courage almost deserted her. Coping with the Milfords was sapping her strength. 'What will happen now?' she whispered. 'What will I do?'

The sound of her own voice saved her. It reminded her of her mother. Dawn heard the same, familiar, hated wail of self-pity. 'Oh no,' she said, pulling herself together, 'I'm not having that. Come on, Elizabeth, let's go down and get you some lunch.'

Which was how Dawn found a way to deal with the Milfords.

'I'll hold her while you heat the milk,' Edith offered, seeing Dawn with the baby on her arm and the bottle in her hand.

Hearing the nuance in Edith's voice, Dawn caught the look in her eyes. Edith's icy expression melted when she looked at the baby. 'Oh, thanks,' Dawn said, sounding suitably grateful. 'That would help a lot.'

Edith's face softened into a grandmother's smile as she took the baby onto her lap.

Dawn went into the kitchen and made the bottle. 'I'll wash up if you like,' she said when she returned, 'and then make the tea . . . if you could give Elizabeth her bottle.'

Edith needed no persuading.

Later, after washing the dishes and making tea, Dawn watched from the kitchen as Edith rocked the child in her arms while Joe looked up from his paper with an encouraging grin. And as Dawn watched, plans began to form in her mind.

During the afternoon, while the Milfords served in the shop, Dawn prepared the vegetables for the evening meal and tidied the kitchen. Then she took her baby back up to Keir's room and lay down to rest and think.

'They don't like me,' she told Elizabeth as she changed the baby's nappy, 'but they think you're smashing. So I'll be relying on you later.'

The baby burped her compliance.

The evening meal was eaten in the same hostile atmosphere as lunch. Conversation was awkward and stilted. Nobody mentioned the future; although it was uppermost in all their minds, they skirted the subject, as fearful as soldiers crossing a minefield. This time, however, Dawn did not flinch from the long silences. She was too busy making her plans.

When Edith began to clear the table, Dawn went upstairs and returned with Elizabeth. 'I'll wash up,' she suggested, 'if you keep an eye on the baby.'

Edith accepted the idea at once. She gave Elizabeth her bottle and rocked her to sleep.

Dawn deliberately took her time in the kitchen. Finally, when she could linger no longer, she emerged to say, 'Tea's made. I'll just take Elizabeth to bed before pouring it out.'

Upstairs, while tucking her infant into the makeshift crib, Dawn rehearsed what she would say. Then she drew a deep breath, kissed the baby goodnight, and returned to face the Milfords.

Hiding her nervousness behind a confident smile, she collected her tea from the kitchen and took a chair at the fireside. The room looked friendly and cosy in the firelight. The sideboard was decorated with pictures of Keir – Keir in blazer and cap, in football kit, in cricket flannels and, the latest, Keir in the uniform of a second lieutenant. Elsewhere in the room, deep shabby armchairs gave pride of place to Joe's wheelchair in front of the fire. He read his evening paper by the light of a table lamp, grumbling aloud as he did so. 'Listen to what it says here: "Herr Alfred Krupp, son of the man who armed Hitler, flew into London yesterday after an absence of seventeen years. Last night he dined at the Savoy with his beautiful American-born wife and was given the same suite in the hotel which he occupied in 1937."' Joe flung the paper aside in disgust. 'It makes me sick. There's Krupp at the Savoy while our Keir and thousands like him are over there looking after Germany. And the British taxpayer foots the bill. It's madness, sheer bloody madness, that's what it is.'

From past experience, Edith merely tutted and continued her knitting, but Dawn saw an opening. 'Talking of footing the bill,' she said carefully, 'I can't thank you enough for being so kind, but I ought to tell you that I'll be starting back at work as soon as I can.'

'We can manage,' sniffed Edith Milford with the air of a martyr.

'It's very nice of you, but –'

'And Keir promised to send some money at the end of the month.'

'That's just it,' Dawn protested. 'I don't want Keir's money.'

This was too much for Edith. Indignation got the better of her. Words fell from her lips before she could check them. 'Humph! You never hesitated before. You took every penny he had.' She flushed, embarrassed by her own outspokenness.

Dawn counted to five under her breath before she replied, and when she did her voice was softly persuasive. 'Keir spent money on *us*, Mrs Milford, him and me. I don't deny we had a good time –'

'I should think you don't. Well, good times have to be paid for, my girl.' Edith fairly bristled. She brushed a strand of grey hair back from her face.

Dawn was dismayed. The underlying tension threatened to erupt into a full-scale argument. She tried to reduce the temperature by agreeing. 'Exactly, and now I'm going to pay. Has it occurred to you that Keir won't be able to send money home?'

Edith almost dropped her knitting. Already agitated, she stared in surprise. 'What do you mean? Keir said he would –'

'That's right,' Joe agreed, 'and Keir always keeps his word.'

'I know,' Dawn said quickly, 'that's what worries me.'

They looked at her as if she had lost her senses.

'I don't know much about these things,' she confessed, 'but army officers have to live to a certain standard. Most of them have private incomes, don't they? Keir will have mess bills and goodness knows what else to pay. He won't be able to send money home if he's going to get on in the army.'

A flicker of alarm showed in Edith's eyes. Turning to her husband for reassurance, she found none was forthcoming.

Joe's brow furrowed into a frown. He concentrated for a minute, thinking over Dawn's words. It was easy to believe the girl might be right. Officers *would* have to live to a certain standard. It was a worry to think of Keir being embarrassed by lack of money . . .

A moment passed while the Milfords digested the idea. Finally, Joe broke the silence. 'That's all very well, but the boy must face up to his responsibilities.'

Dawn blessed the assumption that Elizabeth was Keir's responsibility. Without it all would be lost; with it all could be won. Meanwhile, she hardened her voice and pushed the point home. 'Keir can say goodbye to a career in the army if he's short of money. I think we should think about that.'

Joe's face grew shadowy with concern. It was easy to see what he was thinking. Keir had already abandoned one career. The army was a second chance to make something of his life . . .

But it was Edith, forcing the words from her lips, who dared put the biggest question of all. 'Are you going to marry our son?' she asked. 'That's what we want to know.'

Dawn was too good an actress to waste her best scene. This was her big speech and she knew it. Folding her hands in her lap, she adopted a faraway look and stared into the fire, as if seeking an answer amid the flickering flames. Her voice was soft and low when she spoke. 'I could use Elizabeth to trap Keir into marriage. Most girls would. They wouldn't care whether they loved him or if he loved them, all they'd care about would be getting a wedding band on their finger.' She raised her eyes to look Edith full in the face. 'You said Keir spent every penny on me. Perhaps he did in a way, but the money didn't matter then. If he hadn't spent it on me he'd have spent it on some other girl, or on a bike, or some piece of nonsense. Things are different now. He needs his money. He's got a career to worry about. He'll have to keep up appearances. At this moment I can't think of anything worse for him than to be saddled with a wife and child.'

They waited in silence, well aware that she hadn't answered the question. Even so, some of the strain went out of Joe's face. Warmed by Dawn's apparent concern for his son, he nodded slowly and waited for her to continue.

'Keir's a fine young man,' she said, 'but I'm not sure that he loves me, not now. Perhaps he did once. Perhaps he was infatuated. I was his first girl, but I think he's got me out of his system.' She paused to let them see the brave little smile at the edge of her lips. Sydney Carton's speech in *A Tale of Two Cities* came into her mind. She resisted the impulse to say, 'It's a far, far better thing that I do now . . .' and concluded instead by saying, 'If Keir marries now he'll throw away the chance of a lifetime. It might never come again. I can't have that on my conscience. So the answer is no, Mrs Milford, I'm not going to marry your son.'

Edith released a long sigh of relief, and even Joe failed to disguise his satisfaction although to his credit his expression quickly changed to one of concern. 'But what about the child? She won't have a name –'

'Yes she will,' Dawn interrupted confidently. 'Elizabeth Wharton. It's got a nice ring to it, don't you think?'

The atmosphere improved after that. The tension eased. Even Edith stifled her hostility, especially when it seemed that she might benefit from Dawn's plans. Details were still to be worked out, but Dawn set the main proposals out there and then. As soon as she had shed some weight and regained her strength, she would resume her career as an actress, 'most probably with a repertory company in the provinces'. Naturally she would prefer London, but even if she got a part in the West End, 'I'd have to live in my flat at Belsize Park. Travelling back here every night would be out of the question. I could come over on a Sunday, of course . . .' she told the Milfords.

Meanwhile she wanted them to look after Elizabeth, 'until I can afford a Nanny and a bigger flat'.

The Milfords listened with blank, unresponsive expressions.

'I'll pay you, of course,' Dawn added hurriedly. 'I could manage six pounds a week. Not immediately, but as soon as I start work.'

It was her top offer. She would be stretched to her financial limits. It would leave her broke, but it would get her started again, back in the theatre . . .

'I know six pounds isn't much,' she admitted, 'but it should be enough to pay an assistant for the shop, shouldn't it? Plus someone part-time? A young lad perhaps, strong enough to do all the heavy work, shifting the stock and so on.' Which would leave Edith free to devote her time to Elizabeth. Dawn watched them anxiously, waiting for a reaction.

Joe scratched his head and looked thoughtful, while a curious gleam lit Edith's eyes. The truth was that she had never taken to shopkeeping. The necessity of it had been forced on her by Joe's accident and although she had endured it with little complaint, she had always yearned to revert to the role of a housewife.

'I dunno,' said Joe doubtfully. 'It needs thinking about. A child's a big responsibility. I mean, how long do you think it would last?'

'It depends how I get on,' Dawn answered honestly. 'Months, a year, even a bit longer perhaps.'

'My word,' said Joe. He packed some fresh tobacco into his pipe and fumbled through his pockets for his matches. 'You can get your old job back, can you? Without any problems –?'

'Oh, I'll find work in the theatre,' Dawn said breezily. 'Give me a couple of weeks to slim down. I have an agent, you know. He'll find me a part. I'll be working by Christmas, no problem at all.'

Joe looked at his wife. 'What do you think?'

Edith sniffed with the air of someone being put upon. 'We don't have much choice, do we? We can't turn that baby out in the cold. We've *got* to help.'

Dawn saw through Edith's pretence. Quite sure the arrangement would suit Edith down to the ground, Dawn sensed a battle of wits and rose to the challenge. 'Of course,' she said, 'we must keep it hush-hush. I'd be finished if people found out about the baby. You wouldn't believe how narrow-minded they are in the theatre. But there'd be nothing to connect a baby in Hillingdon with an actress working in Manchester or somewhere like that, would there?'

For emphasis, she added, 'Of course if I can't work in the theatre, I suppose I'll *have* to get married.'

Edith's eyes widened. She saw the stick as well as the carrot. She had to agree. It was the only way to keep her son free from the clutches of this – this *trollop!*

Three

The arrangement soon acquired substance and, oddly enough, Edith was the moving force. She was terrified it would become known her son had got this girl into trouble. She knew she would never be able to lift her head in public again and had been fending off questions for days. The midwife lived in the next street – everyone knew her profession. She had delivered half the babies in the neighbourhood, and was far from being the soul of discretion. 'Oh yes,' Mrs Cummings had replied to enquiries. 'A lovely baby girl. Six pounds, four ounces.'

'But whose baby is it?' people had asked.

Martha Green, the biggest gossip in the street, had put that very question to Edith in the shop.

'She's a friend of ours,' Edith had lied. 'Well, the daughter of a friend actually. We're just helping out.'

'Fancy?' Martha had persisted, sensing scandal. 'Your friend's not from round here then? No one I'd know?'

'No, you wouldn't know her,' said Edith, feeling trapped until she suddenly remembered. 'As a matter of fact, she lives abroad these days.'

'Oh, nice for her, I'm sure. And you're helping her daughter?'

'That's right,' Edith had agreed. 'Just for the time being.'

Luckily, the man from the wholesalers had arrived at that moment, providing Edith with a chance to escape . . . but that incident had occurred three days before and every day since had been worse. So when Dawn had put her proposals that evening, Edith was already under a strain. She wanted to be shot of this girl . . . and yet, a chance to finish with the shop was hard to resist. Every year, Edith had promised herself 'This will be the last year I spend behind the counter.' What a joy it would be to give it all up.

Midnight found Edith making a cup of tea in the kitchen, unable to sleep. She had much to think about. There was the baby to consider. 'Poor little mite. She'll have a terrible life with that girl, dragged from one town to the next, growing up in furnished rooms, without a home of her own . . .' Edith whispered to herself. And Elizabeth wasn't just *any* baby. 'She's my granddaughter,' Edith continued, wringing her hands with the worry of it all.

Even when Edith did return to bed, sleep eluded her. She tossed and turned all night, and started the day feeling well below par. Consequently, she was at less than her brightest when old Mrs Bridges and Martha Green entered the shop.

'Morning, Edith,' said Martha, 'and how's the baby today?'

Edith answered without thinking. 'Fine. She's a dear little soul.'

'And the mother?' asked Martha, with a knowing edge to her voice. She waited until old Mrs Bridges had walked across to Joe at the other counter, before whispering, 'She's not married, then? This daughter of your friend?'

Edith blushed to the roots of her hair, fearful that the question would lead to Keir. 'Whoever told you that?' she asked sharply.

'Beryl Cummings said she doesn't wear a ring, so I thought –'

'There's a good reason for that,' said Edith, still red in the face.

'Oh?'

'Yes,' Edith nodded, improvising desperately. 'Her husband is . . . is dead.'

Joe was cutting cheese at that moment. He stopped and looked at his wife in amazement. Words fell from Edith's lips before she could stop them. 'He was killed,' she blurted out, 'six months ago, in an accident.' Feeling guilty about the lie, and angry at them for staring at her, Edith lost her temper. 'People shouldn't go around saying such things. You wait till I see Beryl Cummings. I'll give her a piece of my mind –'

'Oh, dear!' Martha exclaimed. 'It was an easy mistake. I mean, not wearing a ring –'

'She buried it with her husband,' said Edith recklessly, remembering a story she had read long ago. 'She put her wedding ring in the coffin. Haven't you heard of people doing that sort of thing?'

Martha shook her head, dumbfounded.

'Terrible,' old Mrs Bridges gasped, quite caught up in the drama.

'It *is* terrible,' said Edith, suddenly unable to stop talking. 'It's tragic. Joe and me have been thoroughly upset, I can tell you. As a matter of fact, we might foster Elizabeth. In fact we almost certainly will.'

'Really?' Martha exclaimed.

'We might.'

'Goodness,' said Martha, beginning to recover. 'She's not going to stay with you then? Your friend's daughter I mean?'

Edith began to flounder. Her nerves were a mess after her sleepless night. Swallowing hard, she said the first thing which came into her head. 'She travels. She works all over the place. Demonstrating things in stores. That's no life for a baby, is it? Elizabeth would be better off here.'

'Goodness,' Martha repeated, thoroughly overwhelmed by the whole story.

Drained and exhausted, Edith was frightened to look at Joe. She was also fearful of further questions, knowing that another one might push her over the brink. So she excused herself. 'I'm all behind this morning. I must get the orders written up. Joe, take care of Martha for me, will you?'

With that, Edith turned and fled into the back room.

Joe didn't like it. He hated lies.

'No more than I do,' said Edith, flushing pink with indignation, 'but I had to say something. Besides a few white lies never hurt. All I did was stop Martha from spreading goodness knows what kind of poison.'

But Edith had achieved far more than that and, having recovered, she was feeling quite proud of herself. What amazed her was how well her story knitted together. The words had spilled out before she could check them yet, thanks to the hours spent thinking during the night, not one part of the story contradicted another.

They sat at the table, eating the lunch Dawn had prepared, reviewing the morning's events like conspirators involved in a plot. 'I even kept your acting out of it,' Edith said triumphantly. 'So that's your story if you meet any of the neighbours. They'll all have heard it from Martha by now.'

Dawn nodded, staggered by the pace of events.

'And you're a widow don't forget,' Edith added, pleased with the touch of respectability.

Dawn smiled inwardly. Secretly, she was impressed by Edith's manoeuvre. She had never intended to blackmail Keir into marriage, but that possibility was removed once and for all by the story of a dead husband.

'It's only to stop folk talking,' said Joe, misreading her mind. 'Edith's right, she had to say something. The important thing now is to leave it alone. Don't embellish it. People will accept that's how things are and I doubt you'll face many questions.'

He gave her a long, disapproving look, as if reprimanding her for involving them in her lies. Then his face softened into an encouraging grin. 'It's over and done with, so don't worry. The point is you don't have to fret about Elizabeth. We'll take good care of her. All you've got to do is get yourself strong again and get on with your career as an actress.'

The words were so kindly meant Dawn felt an unexpected rush of affection. It was really quite touching that this man in a wheelchair should concern himself with her welfare. Dawn had coped by herself since Gran died. It was the way she had grown up. Re-assessing the Milfords, she began to understand how different Keir's upbringing had been. His parents had given him more love than she'd ever known. It gave her a warm feeling to think of Elizabeth being protected in the same way.

The value of Edith's protection was soon underlined. A story for the neighbours was one thing, coping with the law of the land was another. British law did not deal kindly with unmarried mothers. Dawn suffered her first humiliation two days later when she visited the Registrar of Births and Deaths. It was her first outing with Elizabeth, the first time she had pushed the pram the Milfords had bought her as a gift.

The Registrar was all smiles at the outset. A tall, thin, long-nosed man with receding grey hair, he peered into the pram and asked what the baby was called. 'Ah,' he said on being told, 'one of the new Elizabethans, eh?' And no doubt having made the same remark a dozen times over, he settled behind his desk and reached for a buff-coloured form. 'Now then, Mrs, er . . .?'

'Miss,' said Dawn, looking him straight in the eye. 'Miss Dawn Wharton.'

The smile died on his face. He sought an explanation. 'Are you here on behalf of a friend? I'm sorry, but I must see one of the actual parents . . .' His voice faded as he caught her eye. 'I mean, is the baby yours?'

'Yes.'

'Oh dear.' He gave her a look of stern disapproval. 'You mean it's illegitimate?'

Dawn remained silent, determined to keep her composure.

With a sigh, the Registrar picked up his pen. 'Very well, then,' he said. 'Let's begin with your full name and address.'

Dawn repeated her name and gave the Milford shop as her address.

He wrote the information on his form before asking, 'Name of the father?'

Dawn hesitated. 'That's a personal matter.'

The Registrar's eyebrows rose behind his glasses. 'It's an official matter, Miss Wharton. The father's name must appear on the birth certificate.'

She hesitated again, unsure of her ground. She wondered how he could enforce the requirement. Finally, she shook her head. 'I don't see that you need to know that –'

'To comply with the law. I need to know the father's name and occupation in order to complete the birth certificate.'

A faint flush coloured Dawn's cheeks. 'And if I refuse to tell you?'

'Then you will be behaving even more foolishly than you have already,' he said sharply.

Dawn's lips set into a determined line.

'Don't you *know* the name of the father?' asked the Registrar with a discernible sneer.

Dawn felt her flush deepen. She returned his stare in absolute silence.

'If you don't tell me, I'll complete these forms by writing Father Unknown,' he said, and to make sure she understood the implication, he added, 'I must warn you that people interpret that in a very unfortunate way.'

Dawn understood only too well. 'The father is known to me,' she blurted out angrily.

'Obviously.' The Registrar smirked. 'But I'm the person completing this certificate. If you refuse to divulge the man's name I must write "Father Unknown" –'

'Making me a whore in the process,' she said angrily, unable to control her temper.

A malicious gleam entered the Registrar's eyes. 'How people interpret the birth certificate is their business. What you tell me is your business. *My* business, Miss Wharton, is to complete the Register in accordance with the information given to me.'

Ten minutes later, Dawn left his office. Her face blazed. She felt so humiliated. In her purse she carried the birth certificate. Beneath the column headed 'Name of Father' was the damning indictment 'Father Unknown'.

'It's so unfair,' she cried under her breath, imagining the pain it would cause Elizabeth later in life. 'Never mind, baby,' she whispered to the tiny infant in the pram. 'By the time you're old enough to be embarrassed by that, I'll be so rich and famous it won't matter a damn!'

Four

Becoming rich and famous looked a lot harder the next morning. When Dawn telephoned her agent, Mr Maxwell was far from confident about finding her work. 'Nobody's casting at the moment,' he said.

Dawn wasn't ready at the moment. She had to shed at least twenty pounds. Glad that Maxwell couldn't see her dumpy shape, she invented a lie about having to return to her aunt in Scotland for two or three weeks. 'But after that, I'll be ready for anything.'

'I'll do what I can,' he said doubtfully, 'but there's not much about. You could be resting for three or four months.'

Three or four months! The Milfords had agreed to wait, but they would want paying before then. 'It doesn't have to be the West End. I'll take something in the provinces for the time being,' said Dawn.

'There's not much happening in the provinces,' Maxwell answered unhelpfully.

'There's always something, *somewhere*.'

'I said I'll do what I can,' Maxwell said impatiently. 'Leave it with me for a couple of weeks.'

'How can I leave it? I want to be working by Christmas.' Dawn was beginning to sound shrill. She took a deep breath. 'Please, Mr Maxwell, do your best. I'll call you on Monday.'

But the following Monday, Maxwell sounded more pessimistic than ever. 'You know what it's like at this time of the year,' he said. 'Everyone's fixed up. Things won't get going until March –'

'Come on, Mr Maxwell. You know I can act. Have you got copies of my notices? Shall I send you some more? Mr Maxwell, I *need* to get back into the theatre –'

'It's the time of year –'

'I'll call you on Wednesday . . .'

When Dawn telephoned on Wednesday, Mr Maxwell was out. He was out again when she called on the Thursday, and it took three calls to reach him on Friday.

'I told you before,' he said, very irritated. 'There's nothing at the moment . . .'

By now, Dawn was desperate. She had called three different theatre managements only to receive the same answer. It was no comfort to learn that Maxwell had already spoken to them on her behalf, even if it did reinforce his opinion.

Meanwhile, she continued to live with the Milfords, eating their food and accepting their shelter. She was terrified they would ask for their six pounds a week. Every day she expected them to ask when she was starting work . . .

To wait three or four months was out of the question; Christmas was coming, her purse was empty and the Milfords would want paying. Dawn was too proud to swallow her pride and take money from Keir. Or be even more despicable and accept his offer of marriage. She refused to take the same cheap way out as her mother. But she had very few options. Acting was her only skill. Besides, no other job would pay her enough to give the Milfords six pounds a week.

Then she remembered John Drayton.

She had met him only once: the summer before last, when she

130

had told him to go to hell. Looking back, she could only wince at her arrogance. She had been so pleased with life then. Her dream of becoming an actress had come true, and if her roles were minor at least she knew she was playing them well. She was sure of being offered better parts in time. Meanwhile, she was learning her craft. The outcome was never in doubt. One day she would star in the West End theatre. It was merely a matter of time . . .

Now time had run out. Now she was terrified of emulating her mother, scared stiff of spending her life crying about what might have been. So she telephoned Drayton.

They had met in Brighton. One night after the show, the stage-doorkeeper had handed her a business card, on the back of which was written 'Staying at the Metropole. Can see you noon tomorrow.' Turning the card over Dawn had read the name John Drayton above an address in Piccadilly. There had been no mention of his occupation.

'I'm not surprised,' said Celia Daniels, another member of the cast. 'Every girl trying to break into films has heard of John Drayton. That's why they all sleep with him. Not that the bastard doesn't deliver. He does. He got Mary October that part in *Columbus*, and Jilly Harris would still be kicking her legs in the air at the Palladium if it wasn't for him. Drayton and J. Arthur must be blood brothers . . .'

The J. Arthur Rank Organization was the most powerful film-maker in the business. For years past Rank had put young actresses under contract and groomed them for stardom. Dawn despised the whole process, thinking it attached more importance to charm than to acting. Biased in favour of the theatre, she was as contemptuous of starlets as of the films they appeared in. As for Mr Drayton, she thought he could do with a lesson in manners.

'Who does he think he is?' she asked Celia scornfully. '"Can see you at noon." Doesn't he ever say please?'

'He doesn't even say "*Please* take your knickers down." He just says "Get 'em off."'

Dawn wasn't the least interested. Apart from disliking the sound of Mr Drayton, she had no ambitions in films. She thought she might make one later, when her career was established, meanwhile she was learning her craft and the place to do that was the theatre. Nobody ever learned acting on a film lot.

Her indifference amazed Celia. 'I can't believe you won't go. I'd give my eye-teeth for the chance.'

'He wants your teeth too?' Dawn had asked drily.

Eventually, egged on by Celia and intrigued in spite of herself, she had walked round to the Metropole where, after being kept waiting in the lobby for five minutes, she had been shown upstairs and into Drayton's suite. She remembered thinking she'd scream the place down if he so much as laid a finger on her.

'Sit down,' he had said without looking up. 'I won't be a minute.'

It was a large sitting-room with a view of the sea. French doors opened onto a balcony and two other windows gave plenty of light. Period furnishings provided an air of elegance which would have made a good setting for anyone except John Drayton. He sat on a chesterfield in his shirt sleeves, leafing through the contents of one briefcase while another gaped open at his feet. From time to time he grunted into the telephone clamped between his chin and his shoulder. 'I got it here somewhere,' he rasped in a gravelly voice. 'It's a question of finding the fucking thing.' Without looking at Dawn, he said, 'Hey, do me a favour. See if you can find a red folder in there.'

She only knew he was talking to her because he kicked the briefcase at his feet, making it spill over in her direction. She rose from the chair, startled, and was down on her knees sorting through papers when she heard him say, 'Okay, Harvey, I got it. Now listen, look up clause twelve. That's right. See what it says? We get twenty per cent, not twelve and a half. So get back to Arnie and tell him to shove it. Okay? So what's the next problem?'

Dawn retreated to her chair, liking neither what she could see nor hear of John Drayton. He looked about fifty, balding, overweight and overbearing. Realizing that even to be there was a mistake, she was on the point of leaving when he slammed the telephone down. 'Fucking producers,' he snarled. 'I never met one who wasn't a crook.'

When he looked up she felt the full force of his eyes for the first time. They were as dark as her own and shone with the same

132

kind of intensity. He exuded energy. Even slumped on the sofa with his waistline bulging over his trousers he conveyed the aura of a powerfully active man. 'Hi,' he said, jumping up and bounding over to greet her. 'You're er . . . Dawn someone . . . the girl in this thing down the road.'

It was hard to say which offended her more: Drayton forgetting her name or referring to *Arsenic and Old Lace* as 'this thing down the road'. She rose, expecting him to shake hands, instead of which he gripped her shoulders and stared into her face from very close range.

'Beautiful,' he said, admiring her left profile. 'You ever see pictures of Swanson at your age?'

Dawn was too surprised to answer. Not that he gave her a chance. 'Sensational in close-up,' he said with embarrassing frankness. 'What's your name again? Dawn . . . er –?'

'Wharton,' she gasped, wishing he would let go of her shoulders.

'Right!' he exclaimed as if she'd made a lucky guess. 'That your real name?'

She would have retreated had the chair not been pressing the back of her knees. She nodded, feeling faintly alarmed.

'Smile,' he ordered.

She managed a surprised grimace.

'Good teeth,' he grunted.

'They're my own, too,' she answered and dropped into the chair as a means of escape.

He was quite unaware of the impression he was making. Later she realized he wouldn't have cared. He was too busy doing his job of 'inspecting the merchandise'.

Walking around the chair, he studied her from various angles. 'You can tell with some faces,' he said. 'The way the flesh sits on the bones, the planes and the angles. The camera will love you. You're wasting your time in the theatre.'

None of his compliments registered. He was so impersonal. He might have been discussing a piece of porcelain, or a lump of meat. What did register was the bit about her wasting her time. She boiled over at that. How dare he accuse her of wasting her time! It took her a moment to find the right words, and a moment longer to adopt the right icy tone.

'I'm an actress,' she said with all the chilling scorn she could muster. 'It may have escaped your notice, but actresses work in a place called the theatre.'

'Walk over to the window, will you?'

She might as well not have spoken for all the notice he took. His arrogance took her breath away. Lots of men treated actresses as idiots; Dawn had even grown used to bad manners, but Drayton was in a class of his own.

'Over there,' he said, pointing to the French doors.

She restrained an urge to spit in his eye. Inwardly she seethed, wanting nothing to do with this ill-mannered boor. She was furious. It wasn't even as if she was even the slightest bit interested in film work. But even as she fought her temper, something made her see the situation as a challenge. Why not walk over to the window? Why not see if he made her some sort of offer? Why not? Then she would have the satisfaction of turning him down. So she rose and walked to the French doors where she posed, looking out and picking delicately at the lace curtains with one hand so that he would notice her long fingers and beautifully shaped hands.

'That's good,' he said approvingly. 'I can't believe you're English. English girls walk like pregnant ducks. You move like an angel. Sit on the window ledge a minute. That's right. Fine, cross your legs . . .'

Incredibly, she found herself following his instructions for three or four minutes. Inwardly she burned. *Just let him make me an offer*, she told herself. *Boy, will I tell him!*

His instructions came thick and fast. '. . . Walk across the room . . . sit down . . . light a cigarette . . . go back to the window . . . cross the room . . . exit left.'

She stopped when 'exit left' took her through the door to his bedroom. Whirling around, she expected him to be a pace behind her, only to find he was still on the chesterfield, lighting a cigar.

'Terrific,' he said, admiringly, from behind a cloud of smoke. 'Come and sit down. Tell me something. Why haven't I heard of you? Why aren't you beating my door down to get into movies?'

That was her opening. *That* was when she told him what she thought of movies, and men like him, and so called screen stars who couldn't act their way out of a paper bag . . .

His face had been a picture. She had never seen anyone so

surprised. To say that someone's jaw dropped had always struck her as an exaggeration until then. The look in his eyes turned from shock to amazement and, finally, to anger.

'Okay, okay,' he had shouted against her flood of words. 'I hear what you say. It's a load of crap, but I hear it. Want to hear the other side of the record? Or are you going to run around with those crazy ideas for the rest of your life?'

Intending to leave after speaking her mind, she was half-way to the door when his words stopped her. 'Okay, stick to the theatre,' he shouted. 'That's as smart as a sculptor working only in clay. He should be using stone and marble and wood and bronze. Each one teaches him something. He's learning new techniques, meeting new challenges. Only a bigot closes his mind.'

She turned angrily. 'Are you calling me a bigot?'

Ignoring the question, he sneered, 'Of course it takes guts, meeting new challenges.'

His eyes held hers. He had a strong face, too fleshy perhaps, but pugnacious and stubborn. The face of a fighter.

'I can meet a challenge,' she said defiantly.

'Yeah? So why not sit down and talk about this? Quit now and you'll never know what you walked out on.'

An exit then would have left him with the last word. Which meant the last laugh from the sneer on his face. She wanted him to know that not all actresses were idiots. And, dammit, she wanted to pay him back for being so infernally rude.

'Very well,' she agreed. 'I've nothing better to do for half an hour.'

Their argument lasted longer than that. She was in his suite over an hour. No lunch was offered, but room service sent up a pot of coffee and some sandwiches. She had some coffee and he ate the sandwiches. She was frightened, amused, disgusted and fascinated by turn.

He had heard of her, despite his remarks at the outset. Someone had told him about her in *Arsenic and Old Lace* and he had travelled down to see her. The admission failed to mollify her. His dogmatic manner got under her skin. She found herself arguing with his every word. The certainty that she would never see him again made her recklessly outspoken. She just couldn't imagine ever bringing herself to work with such an arrogant man. And as for films – her career was too important to waste time on a film lot.

'Crap,' he said angrily. 'So what do you want? To play hick towns for another five years, living in cockroach-infested lodging houses, bumming a few decent meals from those old farts who hang round the stage door? And for what? Eight performances a week and your name in lights for a seven-week run? Big deal. How much money goes in the bank? Ever ask yourself that? Ever ask how many actresses get rich on the stage? So what do they do? They marry for money, they whore and they pimp. The smart ones get into movies.'

He drove his arguments home by jumping up from his chair, pacing the room, chomping on his cigar, swallowing coffee, chewing a sandwich, while talking, talking and talking. 'You think Vivien Leigh can't act? You think people like Swanson and Davis are dummies? Some little tramps off the street who don't know the first thing about acting? Or that they don't work at their art? Well, let me tell you . . .'

He did, for another half-hour, before returning to why he sent for her. 'You, I don't know about. Maybe you won't work on film. I think you will, but even JD gets it wrong one time in a hundred.'

He laughed, inviting her to join in, but she refrained. She disliked him more by the minute. He was the most obnoxious man she had ever met. The best she would say was that he was different. Energy alone made him different.

'I'm offering you a chance to earn a fortune,' he said. 'It's a whole –'

'Money, money, money. That's all people like you think about.'

'You wanna starve in a garret? Is that it? Suffer for your art? Christ, you'll suffer in technicolour if I take you on. You'll drop from exhaustion –'

'If *you* take me on? I already have an agent –'

'What you have is a limp prick. That's how effective he is. So don't tell me what you have. And don't confuse me with an agent. I'm a manager, not some skin-dealer who cares more about his ten per cent than his client.'

John Drayton took more than ten per cent. He took twenty-five per cent.

'And it's twenty-five per cent of a lot of dough because my people earn a lot of dough. But they get their affairs properly managed. They get looked after –'

Dawn had heard all she could take. She jumped up. 'You take twenty-five per cent of their money, then you make them sleep with you! They must be out of their minds –'

'Sleep with . . . !' He gaped. 'You think they get my body *as well*? Lady, I don't have the time. They'd be lucky to give me a quick blow-job.'

She was half-way to the door. This time there was no turning back. Instead she shouted over her shoulder. 'I wouldn't play Trilby to your Svengali for all the money in the world.'

'Svengali wouldn't waste his time with you. He'd have more sense.'

She had left, slamming the door behind her.

All of which, by that December, seemed to have happened a long, long time ago. Dawn wished it hadn't happened at all. But it had, and now she had to screw up enough courage to phone John Drayton . . .

Five

Fearful of being overheard at the Milfords, Dawn walked to the kiosk in the next street. If she had to plead, she preferred the Milfords not to know. She would be humiliated enough, without worrying about an audience . . .

'Yeah, this is Drayton. Who's this?'

She swallowed hard. The telephone in her hand was clammy with sweat. The strength drained out of her legs. She almost lost her nerve and hung up. Instead, she remembered her parting words and drew a deep breath. 'This is Trilby calling Svengali.'

He took so long to answer she was convinced he had forgotten. Finally, after an agonizing delay, he said, 'Don't tell me. Dawn Wharton, right? The theatre actress.'

Sighing with relief, she corrected him softly, 'No, Dawn Wharton, the would-be movie actress.'

She flinched, waiting for his sneer, ready for him to make her eat dirt, to humiliate her the way the Registrar had. Instead, he said, 'About bloody time. When are you coming to see me?'

Dawn travelled up to town on the Tuesday morning. Five weeks of rigid dieting and hard exercising had restored her figure to its former proportions. Nobody would have noticed an ounce of difference. Physically, none existed. She had slimmed down to her former weight. The difference was all in her mind, and perhaps in her purse, for the four pounds and six shillings it contained was the last of her money.

The flat was exactly as she had left it when Keir had taken her away. Wardrobe doors gaped open from where she had thrown things into a bag. God, what a nightmare that had been. Poor Keir, with his stricken face and his unfailing chivalry.

He had written such an anxious letter from Germany:

. . . *I wish we could have talked longer before I left, but everything happened so quickly. I got your letter about not marrying me. Mum's letter said much the same thing, so I guess it's official. I don't know what to say to make you change your mind. I can't see how you can possibly support yourself and the baby. Mum says you've worked something out with her and Dad, but that doesn't stop me worrying. After all, it's my responsibility* . . .

Reading it, she could see his anxious expression. His concern was a comfort. It was nice to know he cared. Even so, the letter was different from those he used to write. The earlier letters had been declarations of love, now he wrote of 'making ends meet', and although he repeated his offer of marriage, Dawn could sense his confusion.

'*Meanwhile,*' he had written, '*don't do anything rash.*'

Anything rash! Like meeting John Drayton for instance?

There was no time to tidy the flat. The clock said 10.30 and every minute was needed. What to wear? Did Drayton's office at noon mean lunch at a smart restaurant or a sandwich and coffee? She stripped off, and dipped in and out of the tiny bath so quickly she scarcely got wet. The towel was still grubby with mascara from when she had wept before leaving for the Milfords. The contents of her wardrobe looked hopeless.

Eventually, she decided on her tight, black gaberdine skirt with slits up the side, and a clinging botany wool black sweater, cinched in by a wide patent-leather black belt. The outfit had almost been her working uniform in the theatre and the idea of working again was a comforting thought. She added a splash of colour by slipping three red bangles onto one arm and two onto the other.

She was a bundle of nerves. Her hair took forever and her make-up even longer. Applying her eye-liner defeated her. Her hands were shaking too badly. She smoked a cigarette to calm herself. Eventually, fifty-five minutes and two cigarettes later, she was ready. Slipping into her pink duster coat, she twirled around in front of the mirror. Nobody would have taken her for the mother of a five-week-old baby. 'Nobody had better include John Drayton,' she muttered under her breath.

At the last moment she remembered her press cuttings. She rifled through her scrap book. There were two dozen notices in all, some of them very good. 'So what? He's not interested in the theatre,' she told herself glumly. 'He won't even look at them. He'll tell me where to put them and won't even say please.'

She recalled Celia Daniels. 'He doesn't even say '*Please* take your knickers down.' He just says "Get 'em off."'

'God help me,' Dawn groaned and made for the door.

The first surprise was Drayton's secretary. Instead of the glamorous young thing Dawn had expected, Pamela Parsons was about fifty and as prim as a school ma'am. She had grey marcelled hair, grey eyes, and peered out from tortoise-shell-rimmed glasses. Her severely straight nose was set above a neat little mouth, and she wore a Pringle twin set the colour of lavender. Charm enabled her to convey the impression of being both efficient and nice at the same time. Certainly, Dawn was made to feel welcome. 'Hello, Miss Wharton. I'm Pamela Parsons, I've heard so much about you. JD will see you at once.'

The next minute Dawn was shown into his office. He was exactly as she remembered, even to his rolled-up shirt sleeves and the loosened tie in his collar. His face was as craggy, his eyes as intense, he radiated the same energy. The only difference was that this time his scowl gave way to a smile, reminding Dawn of sunshine breaking through clouds.

Bounding out from his desk he held her at arm's length and looked her up and down, just as at Brighton. 'I gotta be right,' he muttered, more to himself than to her. Then he grinned. 'We won't go over old arguments, but I take it you've changed your mind. You've grown out of it, right?'

She nearly choked saying yes.

He took her to the Caprice for lunch. It was her first visit. Judging from the number of people who said hello, he virtually lived there. Later, Dawn found out that he was as well-known at the Ivy and Ciro's, and every other smart watering-hole in the West End.

When he began asking questions she had an insane urge to blurt out the whole story. To tell him about Elizabeth and the Milfords and all that had happened. She almost told him how desperate she was to find work. Thankfully, the moment passed. Sanity prevailed. She repeated the lie she had told Maxwell and people in the theatre – that she hadn't worked for some months because of nursing her sick aunt in Scotland. As far as she could tell, he believed her. When he asked about her parents she simply said they were living in Spain. And when he enquired about boyfriends, she said, 'Keir's a lieutenant in the army, serving in Germany. I spend most weekends with his parents.'

She had meant to convey a picture of a sensible, responsible life, but Drayton looked alarmed. 'You're not planning to get married?'

'Oh, no, not for a long time.'

'Five years at least,' he said, sounding very definite.

'Oh, at least,' she agreed. 'My career comes first.'

Her emphatic response seemed to satisfy him. She sensed he was pleased, especially about her boyfriend and parents being abroad. 'Families are best kept at arm's length,' he said. 'They can be a pain, poking their noses into things they know nothing about. This is a new life for you. Much better to be unencumbered.'

Unencumbered! Wondering what he would say to a five-week-old baby, she worked hard to conceal her nervousness, but too much was at stake for her to relax. Maxwell letting her down had come as a shock. His failure to find her work had knocked the bottom out of her plans. Maxwell had been the sheet anchor of her professional life . . .

140

To her surprise, Drayton did read the press notices. He studied them all at the end of the meal. Even more surprising was his admission that he had seen her in several performances, not just once down in Brighton.

He was surprised at her surprise. 'After all,' he explained, 'if I take you on I'll make a big investment in you. That's not something I do lightly.'

She was alarmed at the *if*. Christmas was little more than a week away and she had four pounds left in her purse. There were no other options. Without thinking, she blurted out, 'I thought you wanted me to join you. I thought –'

'Sure I do!' he laughed. 'But we've got some details to discuss first.'

He outlined some of them over coffee, which was when she got her first inkling of how Drayton Management worked. 'You don't just get me.' He grinned. 'You get a whole team.'

He mentioned some of them: 'Harvey Berlin, the best accountant in London. He'll take care of your banking and tax and everything like that.' There was also someone called Eric North: 'He'll buy your clothes, run your social diary, the lot. You'll love Eric. After a couple of months he'll be your best friend and Mother Confessor rolled into one.' And another man called Ray Cox: 'Ray's fantastic. He'll put you on the cover of every magazine in the country.'

It was breath-taking stuff, but Drayton left the real business until they returned to his office. 'Sit down, sit down,' he said, ushering her into an armchair while offering her a cigarette and organizing some coffee. When all that was done, he *really* got down to business.

'There're only three things worth talking about,' he began. 'What you get, what I get, and how we do it. Okay? I mean if we agree on them we cover everything, right?' He glanced at his watch. 'So here goes . . .'

For the next hour Dawn listened to him describe every dream she'd ever had – only bigger. A hundred times bigger. Her own ambitions were dwarfed. Where she had dreamt about starring in London's West End, Drayton took the whole world as his stage.

'You gotta think world box office,' he said at one point, 'I'll level with you. Properly handled you can be bigger than

141

Monroe. You can be to movies what Pickford and Swanson were in the old days. You got any idea of the sort of fame I'm talking about? Or the money?'

He prowled up and down his office, puffing his cigar, billowing smoke like a steam engine. 'I'm talking about you grossing maybe a million and upwards in a few years. You know what that buys? A mansion in Switzerland, an apartment in LA, a yacht at Antibes. That's the kind of life you'll be living . . .'

Dawn kept telling herself it was sales talk. She made a conscious effort to keep her feet on the ground, but Drayton was describing a lifestyle beyond her comprehension. The prospect made her dizzy. He talked of motion pictures she had seen and a thousand she hadn't. He talked of actresses past and present, the acclaim they enjoyed, the money they earned, the lives they led. He reeled it all off as if it were hers for the asking. She hadn't known what to expect, certainly nothing like this. Her purse was empty and he was talking in millions. The situation was more than absurd, it was madness. Was this the pitch he gave all his new clients? Make them so excited that they signed over twenty-five per cent of their income without thinking? Except that in her case it wouldn't be twenty-five per cent. It would be more.

'More?' she yelped. 'In Brighton you said –'

'I know what I said. That's how I usually work. You never asked how I'd work with you. You were too busy with all that Svengali crap.'

She coloured and lost her nerve.

'Look at it this way,' he said, 'I won't have time for new clients if I do what I want to with you. I may even have to let a few go. So to compensate it's got to be thirty per cent of every penny you make.' He softened his words by one of his smiles. 'But your seventy per cent will be more money than you can spend in a lifetime.'

Pulling open a drawer, he tossed a sheaf of bound papers onto the desk. 'That's the contract. Take it to a lawyer if you like, but I won't change a word. If we work together, those are my terms.'

She was confused. One minute he was praising her looks and her talent, the next minute he seemed to be threatening her.

'Not threatening,' he said, shaking his head. 'Bullying maybe, but not threatening. You've got to understand I'm taking a hell of a risk. You've got the looks, you've got the figure, you've got sex appeal and you can act. All of this I know. I can see it with my own eyes. What I don't know is *you*. I don't know if you'll screw around with every two-bit actor you meet. I don't know if you'll hit the booze, get into drugs, there're a million ways you could foul up. Sure it's a tough contract, but it's tough on me too. It commits me to backing you with a stack of money and our entire resources. That's fine, it's what I want to do, if you play straight with me. So for five years you don't screw around, you don't get married, you don't even miss a goddamn period without me knowing. Most of all you don't get a bun in the oven. Jesus! Can you imagine? Suddenly the big movie star is dropping little bastards all over the place. Even Bergman can't get away with that. She hasn't worked in two years and she'll be lucky to work ever again. So I'm flat on my arse without a return on my investment? No way. You do that to me and this piece of paper –' he scooped the contract up and waved it under her nose – 'will drag you into court so fast your feet won't touch the ground. And you won't come out with a penny.'

He returned to his side of the desk and slumped into his chair. 'It's not so tough really,' he said, smiling at her look of alarm, 'not if you play it right. Work hard and you've got nothing to worry about. Fame and fortune will be yours if you want them enough. Which brings me to the third point. How do we do it?'

It was a relief when he paused. She had time to collect her thoughts, except they were so contradictory that she simply couldn't. His next words took her breath away. 'Most of them fuck their way to the top,' he said bluntly. 'Take Monroe, that's how she got where she is now. Everyone in Hollywood's had her. Photographers, pressmen . . . You know Joe Schenck, the guy who runs Twentieth Century Fox?' He paused, surprised at her blank expression. 'I forgot, you don't know the business. Well, Joe's a hundred years old and she goes down on him once a week. Ben Lyon – you know him, the guy on the radio? He had her, and Johnny Hyde her agent, the list's a mile long . . .'

Giddiness turned to nausea. Dawn had been excited before. Now she was frightened. Her mind was in turmoil. She had read about Ingrid Bergman's illegitimate baby. The papers were full of the scandal. Listening to Drayton, Dawn's mind reeled from his stories about Marilyn Monroe to what would happen if he found out about Elizabeth.

'It's the same over here,' Drayton was saying. 'Every starlet in London puts out for the chance of a walk-on in a B movie. Managements want to sample the merchandise. Okay, that's good, we want them to want. But we don't want them to *have*. That's the difference and you're going to be different. You're good now and you'll be great when I finish with you. You're not some cheap little tramp. Get me? If we play it right you'll end up bigger than anyone . . .'

Totally confused, she held her breath, daring to hope.

'See what I mean?' He rose to his feet, unable to sit still for a minute. 'It will take money and work, blood, sweat and tears, but we'll build you up as Miss Untouchable. The girl everyone wants but nobody has. The unattainable. We'll have them crawling up the walls . . .'

He went on and on, throwing words over his shoulder as he paced up and down.

Dawn's relief was so intense she began to tremble.

'That's how we'll do it,' he concluded. 'Do it that way and I'll make you a promise. In the whole of five years I won't tell you to fuck more than four guys.'

Her smile froze. Words choked in her throat. 'You'll *tell* me . . . ?'

'I guarantee it,' he said over his shoulder. 'Three if we get lucky, four at the most.'

By the time he returned to his desk, Dawn's face was expressionless. She was numb. Images of big houses and yachts fled from her mind, replaced by the reality of the few pounds in her purse. The Milfords would want paying, Christmas was coming . . .

She cleared her throat. 'Mr Drayton,' she said shakily, 'when do you think I'd get my first part? I mean . . . if we were to go ahead –'

'Your first part?' His thick eyebrows rose in surprise. 'Oh, not for months. Maybe a year even. Who knows? We've got a lot of work to do before then.'

'But how do I live? I need to work –'

'You mean money?' Drayton's eyes widened in bewilderment. 'Harvey takes care of money. Didn't I cover that? That's on top of Eric of course. Eric will spend a fucking fortune on clothes –'

He broke off as Pamela Parsons opened the door. 'Sorry, JD,' she apologized, 'but your car is downstairs. You're due at Pinewood at six –'

'Shit!' He glanced at his watch. 'Is it four-thirty already? I must go. Sorry –' He stopped abruptly, struck by an idea. 'Pamela, organize some tea or something. I want you and Miss Wharton to have a long talk. Answer all her questions, okay? Get Harvey and Eric in on the meeting . . .'

He was already out from his desk and holding Dawn by her shoulders in what she was beginning to recognize as his version of a handshake. For a split second his smile reappeared, altering his whole personality. She felt differently about him when he smiled.

'I must go,' he said. 'They're got a crisis at Pinewood. Forgive me. Pamela will fill you in on anything I left out. Anyway, what else can I say? Except that we can give you a wonderful, wonderful future.'

With which he swept out of the office, leaving Dawn staring after him; hating him, intrigued by him, and totally and completely confused.

Six

'You look as if you could use this.' Pamela Parsons smiled as she poured tea into bone china cups. 'Has he been giving you a hard time?'

Dawn's answer was a bemused shake of her head. 'Like riding a switchback,' she said. 'Up one minute, down the next. I kept asking myself, is he real? Can he be trusted? Sorry, I know you work for him, but –'

'For ten years and the rest of my life if he lets me –' Pamela broke off as a man entered the room. 'Ah, Eric, I'd like you to meet Miss Wharton.'

Dawn turned in time to catch a fleeting glimpse of the man advancing from the door. He had a head of fine, very blond hair going grey at the temples, blue eyes and a delicate well-shaped

145

head which showed every bone. His slim frame was clad in eye-catching clothes; a big floppy pink tie fronted a crimson silk shirt worn beneath a midnight-blue corduroy jacket.

'Oh!' he exclaimed, fluttering his hands. 'I see what JD means. You're even more exquisite in close-up. And so sexy. Those eyes. So much sensuality . . . I'll adore dressing you.'

Meanwhile, Pamela was greeting the other man who followed Eric into the room. 'Harvey, come and meet Miss Wharton.'

Dawn turned to meet a dignified, silver-haired man in a charcoal-grey suit who actually shook hands in a conventional way. 'A pleasure to meet you, Miss Wharton.'

'Isn't her skin perfect?' Eric asked, peering at Dawn from one side of her chair. He turned to Harvey. 'Sensational colouring, don't you think? Not that you'd know; the only time you get excited about colours is if the figures turn red in your little black books.'

'Do sit down, Eric,' Pamela interrupted. 'I'm sure Miss Wharton wants to ask a whole host of questions. She hasn't said she's joining us yet.'

'Why ever not?' Eric asked with a look of surprise as he sat next to Harvey.

Why not, indeed. The three of them were quite different from the sort of people Dawn had imagined around Drayton. Harvey was quietly spoken and full of old-world charm, and although Eric's clothes were unusual the effect was attractive. Pamela Parsons had a beautiful speaking voice and was really rather elegant. They were all older than Dawn had expected. Middle-aged. She was puzzled. They seemed so civilized after Drayton, lacking his coarseness . . .

'We lack his balls too,' Eric chuckled, delighted when Dawn tried to put her thoughts into words. 'It's easy for us, sweetie. We don't fight the battles. JD deals with the sharp end. The poor man has to deal with all sorts of sharks. We could make you weep with stories about the film business.'

Pamela agreed. 'He has to be tough to do a good job for the clients, but there's another side to JD. He swears and curses about everyone on God's earth, but never about us or the people he represents. He's never even raised his voice to me in ten years . . .'

They obviously thought the world of Drayton and praised him

for ages. They even seemed fond of him. 'People let him down,' Pamela explained. 'I've never seen it happen in reverse. Even when some of our ex-clients have, shall I say, been less than honest, he's been more sorry than angry. He's simply told them to find someone else to run their affairs.'

Less than honest. Dawn thought, I've been less than honest already and I'm not yet a client . . .

'Quite simply, he's the best in the business,' said Eric. 'Ask around, sweetie. There's no one quite like him.'

Harvey Berlin nodded. 'I do assure you that whatever he promised –'

'That's the problem,' Dawn interrupted, 'I'm not sure what he did promise. I mean, we talked about a lot of things, but –'

'Here's the contract.' Pamela Parsons picked the document up from the desk and handed it to Harvey Berlin. 'Perhaps you could answer any queries Miss Wharton may have?'

He flicked through the pages, scanning clauses with an experienced eye. 'It's our standard contract, Miss Wharton. We manage you exclusively for five years and charge a fee for doing so. In your case the fee is –' he paused to turn back a page – 'thirty per cent of your total earnings, which is slightly more than usual but I'm sure JD explained –'

'He didn't explain when I *start* earning,' Dawn said earnestly. 'In fact he said it might be a year before he even got me a part –'

'I doubt it will be that long,' said Harvey with an encouraging smile.

'But what about the meantime? He said you'd take care of my money.'

'Naturally. You'll have a drawing account.' Harvey paused before adding an explanation: 'An advance against future earnings. Do you have a requirement at present?'

Did she have a requirement? Oh boy! Dawn thought of the cash in her purse. She thought of her promise to the Milfords. She thought of Christmas a week away and how nice it would be to buy a fluffy white rabbit for Elizabeth. Did she have a requirement! She tried to absorb what was happening. It was all so different from working with Mr Maxwell. Uncertain about how to reply, she wondered if she dared ask for an advance of fifty pounds?

Harvey Berlin cleared his throat. 'Shall I open your account at

147

two hundred and fifty pounds? Of course your wardrobe will be extra, but Eric has a separate account to look after that.'

Two hundred and fifty! Dawn had earned fifteen pounds a week in the theatre and thought herself well off, even after Maxwell had deducted his ten per cent. The Milfords had been delighted with her promise of six pounds a week. Two hundred and fifty pounds was a fortune!

Dawn looked at the contract. Drayton had said, 'Take it to a lawyer if you like, but I won't change a word.' So what was the point? It would only mean a delay. Probably until after Christmas. Besides Harvey had said it was the standard contract, which meant other people signed similar documents . . .

Half an hour later, Dawn returned in a cab to Belsize Park. She had signed the contract and a cheque for two hundred and fifty pounds was in her purse. Her head was swimming with pictures of mansions in Switzerland and yachts off Antibes. It was a different world. Drayton's world!

Arriving home, she had scarcely kicked off her shoes when the telephone rang. It was Pamela Parsons. 'Just to let you know JD's delighted. He'd have called himself, except he's still out at Pinewood. They want him to go to New York now. The poor man's leaving first thing in the morning. I'm still trying to make the arrangements. Anyway, he says to wish you a Happy Christmas and to say he knows you'll have a wonderful new year.' As for starting work, Pamela added, 'JD wants to begin immediately after the holiday. Will it be okay for Eric to call round at your place on the second?'

Dawn replaced the telephone and sat in a daze. In the space of a few hours her whole life had changed. She was rich and about to become richer. Instead of her career being over, it was about to begin. She was seized by a tremendous urge to make contact with Keir . . . to share her news, to celebrate . . . Suddenly she remembered what else Drayton had said. 'I promise you, I won't tell you to fuck more than four guys.' For Dawn the shock had worn off, dulled by a cheque for two hundred and fifty pounds and the beckoning prospect of stardom – 'But Keir will never understand,' she admitted aloud.

What else could she do? Drayton had painted such a glittering picture. Acting was what her life was all about. This was her chance. Besides she had to earn money to support Liz . . .

After she lit a cigarette, Dawn made some coffee, and her excitement faded as she confronted the consequences of joining John Drayton. She could no more turn her back on his offer than swim the Atlantic. Anyway, she had signed his contract. It was too late for second thoughts. 'And it might not even happen,' she told herself. 'After all, I never slept with anyone to get a part in the theatre.'

It was something to hope for. A way of preserving her own self-respect and of calming her conscience about Keir while allowing her to follow her dream. 'Even so,' she sighed, 'it will be like living on a tightrope.'

Seven

Dawn began to live her life on the tightrope the next morning. *Remember the money* she told herself firmly. Two hundred and fifty pounds was a lifeline. She had been close to being destroyed. The very thought was enough to bring her mother to mind. Dawn had grown up as a victim of frustrated ambition. So much bitterness. Drayton had saved her from that. She would be grateful forever. This was a second chance, not to be wasted. She had been dreading Christmas. Now, thanks to the cheque . . .

Dawn pushed her doubts aside, and plunged into the day. The branch of Lloyds Bank on the corner had barely opened by the time she arrived. Her account stood at twelve shillings and fivepence in credit; another reminder of how close disaster had been. 'I'll want to draw some cash later,' she told the clerk. 'Perhaps you could have this cheque especially cleared.'

She hurried home, leaving him to deal with the matter, and stopping on the way to buy milk, bread, a quarter pound of butter, half a pound of cheese and three rosy red apples. 'That's lunch,' she said, planning her day.

Half an hour later she was up to her elbows in suds as she started into a backlog of washing. Working hard, she scrubbed vigorously, her hands busy and her mind even busier. There was a lot to think about, and John Drayton was top of the list.

If girls form their ideas about men from their fathers, as some people say, then Dawn had little to work on. She had never known her real father. 'An actor', according to Gran. 'A bit erratic but very dashing.' So dashing that he had dashed off to America to make a name for himself, only to die early from an excess of drink. His substitute was a poor excuse for a man. Drayton would have included Bertram Henry Wharton among 'those old farts who hang around the stage door'. And Drayton would have been right. Wharton had admired Dawn's mother with dog-like devotion. No matter where she played, he had been there, adoring her from his seat in the stalls.

'He knew what he was getting when he married me,' Dawn's mother was fond of saying. True, he had known she was carrying another man's child, but he had expected his bride to reward him at least with affection. Sadly for him, he had been wrong. On good days she tolerated him, on bad days she treated him with contempt. Dawn had remarkably little to do with him, considering she had lived under the same roof. She had been too busy attending her lessons. The most he ever did for her was to remonstrate with her mother occasionally: 'Can't you leave the kid alone? I'm sick of hearing you nag,' he would complain, which was always met by the retort, 'The child's nothing to do with you, so kindly mind your own business.' And that always sent him back into his shell. Dawn's feelings about him were neutral. The fact that he had never shown her any affection was an advantage at times – after all, nobody missed what they never had. So to face problems alone was nothing new. Dawn had been doing it most of her life, *all* of her life since Gran died.

After hanging out the washing in the back yard, she set about cleaning the flat. The flurry of housework was almost symbolic. She was clearing up after one way of life to prepare for another.

She stopped at midday to make a pot of tea and eat her lunch. Sitting down at the table, she disposed of another task. Taking pen and paper, she wrote to Maxwell, thanking him for his help in the past and terminating his role as her agent. She read the letter through carefully, signed it, and sealed it into an envelope ready to post. After which she went down to the yard, collected

150

her washing, carried it back upstairs and began ironing. And all the time she was thinking and making her plans.

The rent was paid until February, so none of her precious money was needed for that, and although anxious to find a new home with room for Elizabeth, Dawn sensed it was safer to wait. Her caution stemmed from Pamela's request on the phone: 'Will it be okay for Eric to call round on the second?' Only after Dawn had agreed did she realize that sharing a flat with Elizabeth and a nanny was out of the question if Drayton's people were to call on a regular basis. 'Wait,' she told herself, 'and see how it goes.'

The same went for her wardrobe. She was tempted to buy at least a new frock, except that Drayton had said, 'Eric will spend a fucking fortune on clothes.' Dawn decided against buying even a skirt.

This was a second chance and she dared not waste it. Her mother's wasn't the only career ended by an unwanted pregnancy. Dawn knew of other examples. Actresses who'd had a child and the news had leaked out, others who'd had abortions about which people had learned. They'd all acquired bad reputations. *Easy lays.* They clung on, taking what parts they could get and doing anything to get them. And they *did* do anything, people made sure of that: men, mostly, but there were plenty of women around who encouraged such double standards. Dawn remembered reading in a magazine that scientists were experimenting with a contraceptive pill that was swallowed like an aspirin. It seemed unbelievable, but the magazine said it was true. Amazing, she thought, how women's lives will change if ever that comes about!

Even before her meeting with Drayton, Dawn had realized that Elizabeth was a hostage to fortune; something – someone – never to be spoken about in public. Any doubts were dispelled by the contract. There was even a clause on the subject. Not only had she vouched that she was unmarried, not only did she undertake not to marry for five years, but . . .

'. . . *in the event of Miss Wharton becoming pregnant and/or having a child, Drayton Management reserve the right to terminate the contract immediately, whereupon any advance not recovered from earnings will become repayable on demand . . .*'

Dawn had tried to joke about the wording to Harvey Berlin.

'That's silly. Becoming pregnant and/or having a child. How can anyone have a child without becoming pregnant?'

'It applies the other way round,' he had answered gravely. 'The pregnancy could be aborted. Apart from abortion being illegal, our investment could be jeopardized if the story got out. There would be a scandal. From our point of view an abortion would be as damaging as an illegitimate child. We must protect ourselves against both.'

It was called a Morals Clause. Dawn could only smile at the hypocrisy. The same man who had written this into a contract had told her, 'I promise you, I won't tell you to fuck more than four guys.'

It made one thing clear above everything else. Nobody, but *nobody* must know about Elizabeth. Dawn's thoughts turned to the Milfords. Edith worried her. Edith disliked her. The story about Dawn being a widow had been invented for Edith's sake, not Dawn's; and although it would suit her to look after the baby she would never admit it. At least not to me, Dawn thought wryly. She's too fond of acting the Mother Superior.

Then Dawn had an idea. If she was dependent on the Milfords, her best insurance was to make the Milfords dependent on her.

At ten minutes to three Dawn finished the ironing and hurried back to the bank. The cheque had been cleared. 'Just in time for your Christmas shopping,' grinned the clerk. Dawn smiled and left the bank feeling as rich as Rockefeller, but still with that voice at the back of her mind – *This is a second chance, Don't waste it.*

It was four-fifteen when she reached Oxford Street. Good-humoured crowds surged on all sides. Street vendors sold red-berried holly and white-berried mistletoe and long strands of ivy with no berries at all. A crocodile of small boys followed their parents, *en route* for Santa Claus in the Blue Grotto. The strains of Bing Crosby singing 'White Christmas' mingled with a school choir's rendition of 'Silent Night'. People smiled and laughed, imbued by the once-a-year spirit of Christmas.

Resolutely, Dawn resisted every temptation. She saw the most perfect little black dress in Selfridges and ignored it. She skirted the perfumery department for fear she would weaken, and instead made her way to the toy department where she

152

bought a fluffy white rabbit. In the baby-wear shop she bought six outfits for Elizabeth: two white, two lemon and two pink. Elsewhere she bought cot blankets and covers and three dozen nappies. Upstairs she purchased a fine leather handbag for Edith Milford and, on her way out, a briar pipe for Joe. All told she spent twenty-seven pounds, eight shillings and sixpence. 'And that,' she promised herself, 'is Christmas shopping for this year.' But all of her shopping did not include all of her gifts. She planned on giving one gift early.

Returning to Belsize Park, Dawn bought some fish and chips for her supper and walked home. A good, productive day, she thought, pleased with herself. Tiredness set in as she ate her meal. Physically it had been a hard day, her most strenuous since having the baby. Even so, she was pleased with her progress. Her clothes were washed and ironed. She had cleaned the flat and dealt with the Christmas shopping . . .

It was nine o'clock when she telephoned the Milfords. Joe answered. 'Hello,' he said. 'Do you want to speak to Edith about Elizabeth?'

'No, not at the moment. I wanted to talk to you. It's about our arrangement –'

'I told you, don't worry about the money. We can wait until you –'

'It's not that. It's just that I've worked out my sums.'

'Oh dear,' he joked, 'that's always bad news, working out sums –'

She interrupted his good-natured grumbling to put her proposal.

Joe Milford was astonished. He had been pleased with her offer of six pounds a week. 'Are you sure?' he kept asking. 'Are you *really* sure?'

'Absolutely. Eight pounds a week and three months in advance. I'll bring the cheque when I come down on Christmas Eve. I've worked it out. Including the last five weeks, it comes to a hundred and forty-four pounds.'

'Well, I never. That's a lot of money. Don't leave yourself short. We can wait you know –'

'I'd rather do it this way,' Dawn said, beginning to enjoy herself. 'I don't want Mrs Milford to worry.'

'Worry? She's delighted. Mind you,' he added hurriedly,

'we'd only want what's fair. Eight pounds a week might be too much, especially three months in advance. I'll have to think about it –'

Dawn insisted there was nothing to think about. She would pay him in advance every three months. 'So you can take your assistants on for the shop and get everything organized.'

Joe gradually yielded in the face of Dawn's determination. 'It would make life easier,' he admitted, 'knowing the money's coming in regular.' The truth was he could scarcely contain his excitement. 'I can plan if I can rely on it, can't I?' he said repeatedly.

Dawn felt very pleased when she replaced the phone. She was beginning to like Joe Milford and it was nice to be able to make a generous gesture. But it was more than that and she knew it. A hundred and forty-four pounds would keep Edith in her place nicely . . . and the Milfords would soon become used to the extra money.

Soon, Dawn thought, their whole way of life will depend on them keeping my secret.

Next morning, Christmas and the postal authorities of the United States, Germany and Britain combined to provide mail from Dusty and Keir by the same post.

'Well, well,' Dawn mused with a wry smile, 'my fan club.'

Dusty's Christmas card was predictable: 'Happy Christmas and a *Prosperous* New Year, Love Dusty.'

Prosperous was underlined three times. That was all. No message about what he was doing. Not that she needed telling. She could imagine him rushing from one meeting to the next, laying the foundations of his empire. She wondered what he would say if she wrote to him about Elizabeth. Deny she was his, she thought, or say I was trying to trap him into marriage. Not that she minded. She had no intention of telling him about the baby. Not ever.

Keir enclosed a long letter with his Christmas card. It was much on the lines as his previous letter. He wrote that he was still ready to marry her, and was worried about how she would cope. He asked if she thought she was acting wisely? She smiled fondly.

Meanwhile he had some news of his own. He had fallen on his

154

feet in Germany. At school he had always been top in modern languages, and his fluent German had been enough to get him transferred to the Army Information Office in Cologne.

'. . . *It's a really soft number. I'm excused parades and things like that. A dozen of us work here, writing announcements for the press and conducting VIPs around military bases . . . I'm meeting all sorts of interesting people . . . there's a party of MPs coming over next month . . . I might even get to meet Dad's idol, Nye Bevan . . .*'

Among the 'interesting people' he had met was Konrad Adenauer, Chancellor of the new Federal German Republic. '. . . *He looks a hundred years old but he's as sharp as a needle . . . of course he's far above my lowly station, but this work will involve a good deal of liaison with his officials . . .*' Keir seemed to admire most of them. '. . . *They work terrifically hard. You've got to take your hat off to them. Ten years after the war and they've got their country going again. Naturally things are different in East Germany, but the new Federal Republic is a bustling place . . .*'

Dawn was struck by his unusual enthusiasm. His lack of purpose had made him the odd one out before. While she had aspired to be an actress and Dusty had dreamt of a business career, Keir had never shown real determination about anything. 'Except me, and look where that got the poor boy,' she said with a wry smile.

Keir's letter pleased her. It justified everything she had said to the Milfords. He really was better off without a wife for the time being. A career demanded single-mindedness and the absence of distractions. After reading the letter again, she was delighted he was doing so well in the army. 'It should please Dad,' she mused, thinking of Joe Milford. Then she giggled, knowing that Joe would pull his hair out if his son became pro-German.

There was a PS to Keir's letter: '*I heard from the folks that you're spending Christmas with them . . . I don't suppose it will be much fun, but better than being alone in your flat . . .*'

Not much better, she thought. Christmas with the Milfords would be awful, but it had to be faced. In the new year she would have to do John Drayton's bidding and there was no telling where that would lead. Only one thing was certain, it wouldn't lead anywhere unless she covered her tracks with the Milfords.

Eight

In fact, Christmas wasn't so bad. Dawn's foresight got it off to the right start. The leather handbag and the briar pipe reduced the Milfords to embarrassed confusion.

'Oh dear,' said Edith, turning pink, 'I didn't expect this. I didn't expect anything. It's lovely, really lovely.'

'You shouldn't have spent money on us,' Joe scolded. 'It's right good of you, but we never thought to get something for you.'

Dawn had guessed they wouldn't and was glad, much preferring to watch their embarrassed pleasure. The expensive gifts, like the cheque in advance, helped put the relationship on the right footing. Edith was already beginning to sound like a grandmother. 'Elizabeth's ever so good,' she said proudly. 'She didn't cry at all in the night. Slept right through until seven this morning, as good as gold she is.'

Joe was equally pleased. Dawn's money had helped him employ three part-time assistants: Mrs Roberts who worked in the mornings, Mrs Davis who did afternoons, and her son Tommy who came every evening. Tommy did Keir's old job of stacking the shelves. 'He's a bit slap-dash so far,' Joe admitted, 'but he'll soon get the hang of it.'

All augured well for the secret arrangements. In fact, Edith took pains to be reassuring when they sat down at the table. 'There's no need to worry about that. None of the neighbours know you're an actress. They think your name is Mrs Wharton and you demonstrate kitchen gadgets in stores.'

Joe grinned sheepishly. 'We couldn't say different now if we wanted. Martha Green told the whole street, and she's got a reputation for unearthing the truth.'

Dawn went to bed knowing she had done all she could. The future lay in the lap of the gods. Even so, she made a mental note to avoid the neighbours as much as she could. 'With a bit of luck they'll forget I even exist,' she told herself.

156

However, not everyone could be avoided. On Boxing Day she was alarmed to hear that a friend of Joe's was coming to lunch. 'Don't worry about Bob,' Joe reassured her. 'We've told him the same as everyone else.'

'Besides,' Edith added, 'all Bob thinks about is politics. You can't get a word in edgeways when him and Joe get together.'

Which turned out to be true. Dawn found Bob Cooper to be a stocky, good-humoured man who barely said more than hello before engaging Joe in a long discussion.

'Them and their politics,' Edith sniffed when Dawn helped her to wash up. 'It's like the House of Commons in here at times.'

Boxing Day set the pattern for the rest of the week because Bob Cooper and Emlyn Hughes called several times. It quite suited Dawn in a way. When the men became engrossed in politics they forgot about her, especially as she kept so much in the background. When the weather permitted she went to the park, reviewing her plans as she pushed Elizabeth along in the pram.

So far, so good, she thought. She knew her baby would be well cared for, and that her secret was safe with the Milfords. So that, as the days passed, Christmas became a restful interlude, a chance to gather her strength for life with John Drayton.

Nine

As it happened, it was Eric North, more than John Drayton, who introduced Dawn to her new life, starting from the moment she opened the door to him several days later. Dawn had no idea what to expect. She had tidied the flat, dressed herself in sweater and slacks, put coffee on the stove and set pencils and paper out on the table.

'To take notes?' Eric exclaimed with amusement. 'Goodness. I came round for a gossip, not a board meeting.'

And they did gossip for a couple of hours. Eric took some

getting used to, less because of his colourful clothes – that day he wore a yellow shirt, white tie, fawn jacket and chocolate-brown trousers – than because of his manner. He had a way of looking at her that was disconcerting. One glance from Eric's blue eyes equalled fifty from anyone else. Without being the kind of stare that stripped her naked, she certainly felt she had been looked at.

'I know,' he admitted with a giggle. 'It is rude, isn't it? Never mind, you'll be glad of it later. It will give you confidence. JD boasts I can spot a hair out of place from fifty yards. Pass muster with me and you'll know you look good.'

Making her look good was part of his job. 'Your clothes, the way you live, everything about you must convey glamour,' he explained brightly. 'It's a matter of getting the public to notice you, then getting them to think of you in a certain way.'

He had a thin, intelligent face below greying blond hair and enough charm to make him easy to listen to. Once Dawn grew used to his watchful eyes she found him fascinating. In his time he had done just about everything, in the theatre as well as the film world – he had been dresser, set designer, stage-manager, publicist, and too many other things to mention. He knew everyone in the business and most of their secrets. Dawn could have listened to his stories for hours, except he wasn't there merely to talk about building an image, he was there to create one.

Although Drayton was still in the States, he had left firm instructions for Eric to evaluate her home, her wardrobe, in fact everything about her.

Eric's dismissal of the flat was uncharacteristically brutal. 'I can turn a gents' lav into Buckingham Palace, but this is too much,' he said, shuddering as he walked from the living-room to the bedroom. 'Gracious, I've gone goosey all over.'

His remark, and a certain air about him, made her wonder. Homosexuals were still prosecuted under the law in the fifties. They kept such a low profile she was not certain of having met one before. She wasn't even sure about Eric until he opened her wardrobe.

'Oh nice,' he said, taking a summer dress down from the rail. 'That might be fun. Slip it on and let's have a look at you.'

She changed in the bathroom and came out to find three other frocks thrown over the bed. Eric bobbed around her to view the back. 'I like it,' he said. 'We'll keep that. Now try the turquoise.'

Picking it up, she turned for the door when he stopped her. 'Sweetie, we'll be here all day if you do that. You and I will be in and out of changing rooms nonstop for the next couple of months. I can't turn my back every time you take your knickers down. I wouldn't if I could. It's my job to know about our basic equipment.'

She swallowed hard and stared speechlessly.

His face betrayed obvious amusement. 'Don't worry, I go for tall blondes. Usually someone who's served eight years in the navy with a schlong a foot long.'

She had never heard the word schlong before. It took her a second to realize what it meant. When she did she blushed to the roots of her hair. Days later she giggled about it, but to begin with it gave her an odd feeling, dressing and undressing while Eric watched from beneath his long eyelashes.

'Silly,' he teased. 'You'll soon get used to me.'

And she did. She and Eric spent all of January together. He found her a new flat, three times as large and seven times as expensive. She gasped when she saw it – 'Eric, it's fabulous, but I can't afford to live here.'

'Sweetie, you can't afford not to. It's a snip and we'll do the most marvellous things with it.'

They furnished it together, buying a bed and sofas at Heal's, and lots of bits and pieces in the Portobello Road. Dawn felt guilty when she remembered how hard Keir had worked to make Belsize Park cosy. 'Cosy' wasn't Eric's kind of word. Chic and style were Eric-type words and both were appropriate to Dawn's elegant new flat, with its sweeping views over Regent's Park. 'It's good enough for *House & Garden*,' she enthused, wildly excited.

It was the same with clothes. Eric had a wonderful eye. He knew exactly what would suit her, better than she did in some ways; she lacked the nerve to choose his more outrageous selections. She soon lost her shyness. Some of the changing rooms were the size of a matchbox, and with Eric unzipping her all the time there was no room for modesty. She lost count of the number of times he saw her naked and after a while it no longer mattered.

When they weren't buying clothes or things for the flat, they went to the movies. Eric chose the films and always with the purpose of making her study some particular actress. They saw Judy Garland in *A Star is Born*, Jane Wyman in *Magnificent Obsession*, Geraldine Page in *Hondo*, Katharine Hepburn in *African Queen* and Susan Hayward in *I'll Cry Tomorrow*. Sometimes Eric insisted on seeing the same film two nights running, three times if he felt that Dawn was missing some aspect of the performance; for afterwards they would discuss the film for hours, back at Dawn's elegant new flat.

The amazing thing was that she actually *owned* her new possessions. Everything belonged to her, paid for from an account Harvey had opened.

'Never forget we're spending your money,' warned Eric, who saved her a fortune, taking her to chain-stores and side-street boutiques as well as high fashion couturiers, where he used his influence to get her a discount.

She liked him. Indeed, he was such a fascinating companion that as January ended and February began, she began to look upon him as her 'best friend and Mother Confessor', exactly as John Drayton had forecast.

Not that she confessed everything. How could she with a secret like Elizabeth to guard? Fortunately most of Eric's questions were about her career, and what with the present being so busy and the future looking so exciting, they spent little time discussing the past.

While JD remained in America, Eric ran her whole life. He made appointments with a dentist who capped one of her teeth. He took her to a hairdresser who restyled her hair . . .

Dawn worried at times – 'We keep spending money. Spend, spend, spend. I love it, really I do, but I must owe a fortune. When do I start work?'

'All in good time,' said Eric.

It did make her wonder. She firmly believed what she had once said to Keir – *Nothing's for nothing . . . we spend our lives swapping something we have for something we want.*

'Eric,' she said pensively, one day. 'Is this what usually happens? With your other clients I mean?'

'You're joking. JD's never given anyone this kind of treatment.'

Her suspicions showed on her face, making him laugh. 'Forget it. This is strictly business. JD believes in you. You'd better start believing too. You're Dawn Wharton, goddess of the silver screen, superstar –'

'Don't be silly –'

'Sssh,' he put a finger to his lips, 'you will be, believe me. We know what we're doing.'

Believing was seductively easy. It seemed to Dawn that she was already beginning to live like a film star.

'Relax,' Eric soothed her.

It was hard to relax. She had never faced a motion picture camera in her life. The prospect began to play on her nerves. 'Suppose I don't come out well on the screen? Not everyone does –'

'Sweetie, the camera will love you. You'll be a sensation. Leave it to me.'

Dawn had no choice but to trust Eric. She partly succeeded in not worrying until seven o'clock one Friday morning in February. She was still asleep when he rang the doorbell. When she opened the door in a robe, he pushed past and went straight into her bedroom. Pulling an overnight bag from the wardrobe, he began packing some of her clothes. 'Screen test at 9.30,' he said. 'Come on, sweetie, today's the big day.'

The surprise announcement sent her into panic. Her hands flew to her mouth. 'Oh no! Why didn't you tell me?' Shivering, she was suddenly sick. There was barely enough time to reach the bathroom before she threw up. Eric was a step behind her, holding her over the WC, his arms around her waist to squeeze her straining muscles.

'You bastard,' she panted, 'I trusted you –'

'So? I should have told you? Would you have slept? Come on –'

'Won't I have lines? I need time to learn them. Oh, you – you sod!'

He bathed her face, made her gargle a mouth wash, fussed over her, calmed her and took her away in a taxi.

In fact there were no lines to learn. Eric explained the arrangements in the taxi. 'JD knows you can act. This isn't a test

161

for a part. It's just to give us something on film for JD to show around . . . you know, to producers and such like . . .'

The screen test was such a private affair it wasn't even held in a proper studio. Instead the taxi took them to a large building in Cricklewood, owned by a friend of Eric, Bernie Manning. 'He rents movie equipment out to all the film makers. He's got all the facilities we need. I hired in the other people. Bob Taylor's the best lighting man in the country, and Bill Simmonds is a hot young director . . .' Eric assured Dawn.

By the time they reached Cricklewood, she had regained control of her nerves, mainly because Eric insisted it would only amount to having her pictures taken. It proved to be rather more demanding than that.

She spent hours having her face made up and changing from one outfit to another. With her hair up she wore her most glamorous gown – an off-the-shoulder dress in midnight-blue silk. With her hair down she wore a black sweater and skirt, and no shoes. She spent as much time in the makeshift dressing room as on the set – an empty space save for a sofa, a table and a telephone, ringed by arc lamps, cameras and technicians. Taylor and Simmonds held endless consultations, sometimes with her but mostly with each other, and when they did go to work it was quite different from what she had expected.

Bill Simmonds gave her directions – 'That's right, Miss Wharton, sit on the couch. Fine, cross your legs, make yourself comfortable. Smoke if you like. Harry, trim that arc will you . . . and bring that dolly in a bit . . . that's better. Okay, Miss Wharton, here's what we're going to do. Improvise a few scenes. Put our imagination to work. I want you to pick up the phone and almost faint with relief. It's a call from your lover, a bomber pilot shot down over Germany. You thought he was dead. You can't believe it's his voice. You don't know whether to laugh or to cry. You get all choked up, trying to be brave. Make the words up as you go along. Get it . . .'

And later . . . 'That was marvellous. Take a break while you think of the next scene. I want to see some anguish in this. Imagine yourself in a hospital waiting room. Inside is someone you love dearly. The odds are he won't pull through. You're worried out of your mind. You can't sit still, you pace up and down, blame yourself . . .'

162

The session lasted seven hours. At the end of it Dawn was drained and exhausted, and more worried than ever. She complained to Eric all the way home. 'I wish I could do it again. I wasn't ready. That was a farce –'

'That was a *triumph*,' he insisted. 'Think about it, sweetie. You have now experienced the worst thing that can ever happen to you in the movie business. No script, no preparation, no rehearsal, no nothing. And you gave a performance. You were terrific. So imagine how easy it will be when you're working from a script, you'll be prepared, you'll have rehearsed –'

'But today –'

'Was great, believe me. It *worked*, sweetie, the footage will be sensational. JD will love it next week –'

'Next week?'

'That's when he gets back.' Eric grinned. 'We'll really start then.'

She had been vaguely aware that Eric was working to some kind of schedule, just as she guessed he reported on her progress. Pamela phoned him at the flat from time to time, obviously to put questions from JD.

Dawn fell to brooding on this latest information and they travelled in silence for the rest of the way. By the time they reached Regent's Park it was almost seven and Eric was hungry.

'Not ravenous, but I could eat an omelette or something. What about you?'

Dawn shook her head. 'My stomach's still in knots but I'll make you something if you like.'

It had become a habit to share a meal most evenings. Eric restricted his social life to weekends, which were spent in Bath with a boyfriend. Dawn overheard them on the phone once. The slight shock engendered by convention and inexperience had quickly given way to acceptance. Eric was Eric. She couldn't imagine him any other way. She never saw him as a limp-wristed old queen. He was her friend; gentle and knowledgeable, someone on whom she had learned to rely, she realized as she whisked eggs in a pan and talked about the screen test.

'Stop worrying,' Eric urged, sipping a glass of wine. 'JD needs something to show producers, that's all. Simmonds will cut all that footage down to five minutes. He'll show how you move, how your face expresses grief, sorrow, happiness . . . relax, you were beautiful.'

She looked at him, still wanting reassurance.

He grinned. 'It's my neck on the block. If Simmonds hadn't been totally happy, we'd be back there tomorrow, doing it all over again. Instead we can relax. Simmonds said JD will love it.'

Dawn knew it was the strongest commendation he could make. Everything was done to please JD. She began to gnaw on her next worry. 'What's he really like? I mean I owe him for all this –' she waved a hand at the gleaming kitchen – 'and I hardly know him.'

'JD? He's the best in the business. The most professional –'

'He's got a reputation with some people,' said Dawn, remembering what Celia had said in Brighton.

Eric laughed when she told him about Celia. 'Christ knows where she heard that. Maybe her agent said that because he was afraid of losing her. Everyone bad-mouths each other in this business. But it's wrong. JD's no saint, but he's too professional to play around with a client, especially someone he's got plans for, like you.'

Dawn blushed. 'I didn't really mean to imply . . . it's just I don't know the first thing about him,' she said weakly.

Over supper, Eric answered her questions. JD resided in Whittaker Road, Hampstead, locally known as Millionaires' Row. They all lived within a couple of miles of each other – Eric had a flat in Marylebone, Harvey had a house in St John's Wood and Pamela lived in Highgate. JD's mansion in Whittaker Road housed a collection of rare books in the library, a swimming pool in the grounds, a screening room in the basement, and a wife in one of the bedrooms.

'A wife? I didn't think of him as married,' said Dawn.

Eric smiled, a trifle sadly. 'They've been married for years. At least twelve to my knowledge. She's been an invalid most of that time. You name it and she's got it – I don't know what the sickness is. I'm not a doctor. She's looked after by a full-time nurse and what used to be called a lady's companion. I suppose they're still called ladies' companions. Anyway, the two of them look after her round the clock. I haven't seen her in ages but I'm told she gets progressively worse. If you want a clue to JD's character, think about his marriage. Most men would have rationalized a wife like that away years ago. They'd have said she was better off in a home, simply to get on with their own lives. Who'd blame them? But JD keeps her at home. We go out to his place to talk business, watch a film, have a few drinks, and we never see her. We never talk about her either, but she's there. Like I said, sweetie, JD's no saint, but he's quite something on loyalty.'

It was the last thing in the world Dawn expected to hear.

'Don't let his act fool you.' Eric smiled. 'He puts it on to frighten the world. It does too, but like the man said – you can fool some of the people all of the time and all of the people some of the time, but we've known him too long. We're family, the only real family he's got.'

Dawn sensed she was being given privileged information, something not usually shared with a client.

'I've never discussed it,' Eric admitted when she put it to him, 'but most people know. They must have heard the stories . . .'

She was grateful to him. It was like everything else; except for weekends, Eric had hardly left her side since the beginning of January. Whatever he did for other clients had gone by the board.

'Right,' he agreed cheerfully. 'You've got the number one spot, sweetie, exactly as JD ordered.'

'But why?' she wondered aloud.

He gave her a look of real surprise. 'Listen, sweetie, I'll tell you a secret. People think success comes to those who do something well. That's rubbish. Success comes to those who want it badly enough. And that's you.'

It was too. She had always been like that. Gran had sown the seeds of ambition, then to be an actress had become her means of escape. And she had escaped. Or she thought she had. Sometimes, in the small hours, she wondered whether she had simply jumped from the frying pan into the fire. JD would destroy her if he found out about Elizabeth. The new flat, the new clothes, the new prospects would be snatched away before she had a chance to enjoy them . . .

Meanwhile she coped with her new life as best as she could. On Sundays, with Eric safely in Bath, Dawn visited the Milfords. Elizabeth was fine; a healthy bouncing baby with brown hair and dark eyes, in whom Edith had managed to detect a likeness to Keir. Without passing comment, Dawn felt relieved. Edith's conviction that Keir was Elizabeth's father was another guarantee of her silence – not that the Milfords were likely to break their word. A promise given was a promise kept as far as they were concerned. Besides, the arrangement suited them. Edith had retired from the shop and Joe's new staff had settled in. People had adapted to the situation surprisingly quickly.

Even Keir had accepted Dawn's decision. In a long letter, he wrote:

> *'Dad sent me a screed about you being concerned about my career. He was very impressed with you. Me too I suppose, except I should tell you the Army would pay me a marriage allowance if we married. It wouldn't be much and you'd have to live with me over here in Married Quarters to get maximum benefits, but . . .'*

Dawn smiled while admitting that Keir's honesty was hardly romantic.

> *'. . . of course living here would scupper your acting career and I know how important that is to you. Perhaps we should leave things as they are for a while? After all, Elizabeth will be fine with Mum . . .'*

She wondered if he was secretly relieved. She wouldn't blame him. She was getting what she wanted, the Milfords were happy, it was a bonus for Keir to be happy too. He certainly sounded pleased with life in the army. The rest of his letter was full of talk about NATO and the Allied Forces in Europe.

> *'. . . there's talk of me being sent to NATO Headquarters in Paris for six months . . . it's only a rumour as yet, but the fact that I speak French quite well might help clinch it for me . . .'*

In the strangest of ways, Dawn was being introduced to family life. She had never known filial loyalties. After her grandmother's death, her childhood had been spent in alienation of her family, not in harmony. Mutual affection was something unknown. Whereas with the Milfords it was taken for granted. Joe never stopped moaning about NATO but he took great pride in Keir's career in the army. And while Edith was always grumbling about Joe and his politics, she obviously doted on her invalid husband.

In a way it was the same in the week. Eric said, 'We're family,' when he talked of JD. And Dawn saw constant examples. Sometimes Pamela called at the flat on her way home, and she and Eric were usually talking about JD. 'What's the news?' Eric always wanted to know. 'How's he doing in the States?' They were concerned, anxious and caring – and increasingly excited as his homecoming drew near.

'This time next week JD will be here,' Eric said with genuine pleasure, 'and we're exactly on schedule.'

In seven hectic weeks, Eric had set Dawn up in a new flat and restocked her wardrobe from underwear outwards. He had fixed the one less than perfect tooth in her head, restyled her hair and changed her ideas about make-up. He had got her image on film and taken her to at least twenty movies . . .

Now JD was coming home to inspect the results of his labours. Dawn couldn't help feeling apprehensive.

Ten

'You look fantastic,' JD purred, arms outstretched to hold her shoulders. 'I gotta tell you, I could have wept with joy when I saw that film clip this afternoon. You were *gorgeous*, even better than I dared hoped for, and believe me, I hoped for the moon.'

Dawn was pleased, even though some of what she felt was little more than old-fashioned relief. At the back of her mind had lurked the fear that once JD saw her on film he would change his mind and cancel everything. So his obvious approval dispelled at least some of her anxieties. But her feelings were not confined to relief. The devotion which JD engendered from all around him was beginning to rub off on her. She still thought him crass, vulgar and overbearing . . . but he was certainly a man of his word. She had lacked for nothing in his absence. On the contrary, Eric, on JD's instructions, had spent an absolute

167

fortune on her . . . so along with her feelings of relief were those of gratitude and the first glimmerings of a desire to sustain his approval.

She had spent the whole day getting ready, including two hours at the hairdresser's. On Eric's instructions she was wearing her little black Worth, the most expensive frock in her expensive new wardrobe, with a single rope of small pearls at her throat. Taking JD's arm, she led him into her sitting-room, while Pamela, Eric and Harvey followed behind.

'Hey, get a look at this.' JD waved an admiring hand round the room. 'This is really something. I like it. Dawn, darling, you've got marvellous taste.'

She felt absurdly flattered, and amazed herself by insisting on showing him the rest of the flat, protesting throughout about his extravagant compliments. 'No, no, Eric deserves all the credit, not me.'

'Nonsense,' Eric said as they returned to the sitting-room. 'Don't believe her, JD. All I did was to take her to the right places. Dawn chose everything when we got there. She's got flair, JD, genuine flair.'

Which wasn't true, even if Eric was nice to say so. It was an act of friendship. JD and the others had called in for a drink before taking her out to dinner. Perhaps that was why she felt so nervous? She was entertaining them in her new home, albeit briefly, being treated more as a friend than a client . . .

That was the mood later at the Ivy, five friends out for a meal. The warrior returned to the bosom of his family, Dawn thought, listening to the gossip. Not that she was excluded. They tried to make her feel part of them, but there was an obvious difference. The others had proved their loyalty in a dozen campaigns. Dawn was still to be tested. Some words of Eric's played on her mind. 'There's a golden rule with JD,' Eric had said. 'Always tell him the truth.' It was too late for that, Dawn knew. She had broken the golden rule even before they began.

Most of the talk was about JD's trip to the States and the panic gripping the film business. 'You wouldn't believe Hollywood since McCarthy started these Senate hearings,' said JD, sounding disgusted. 'The studios are hysterical about Communism. I went to see Zanuck about Morgan Fry. First thing Zanuck asks, is he a Commie? I say how the fuck do I know what

168

he thinks about politics? Zanuck says you'd better find out fast if you want to do business round here.'

Harvey shook his head sympathetically. 'I bumped into Wallowski the other day – you remember him? He did that wonderful job with *Fallen Angels*. He's blacklisted in Hollywood because his ex-wife is a Communist. His *ex-wife*! He hasn't seen her in five years. He's over here, looking for work. Can you believe it? A man with his talent.'

'Spineless lot of bastards,' JD growled. 'Ten years ago they were paying protection money to hoods, now they've gone weak at the knees about McCarthy. Guys like that don't deserve to be in business.'

And so the talk rolled on, gossip about a business to which Dawn was a newcomer. It was an education; listening to accounts of deals struck behind closed doors, and hearing about people whose names she had only seen in movie magazines. She began to realize what a Rough House it was, and how lucky she was to have JD on her side. His ripe language jarred less and less as the evening went on.

'So,' he said, looking at her fondly while they waited for their coats, 'soon it will be your turn.' He grinned. 'They don't know what's about to hit them, eh?'

Neither did Dawn. She was about to find out.

Dawn had considered her life to be busy before JD returned. 'That was a rest cure,' she wisecracked later to Eric.

Ray Cox, the man who ran the Drayton publicity machine, came into her life two days after JD arrived back in London. Ray was a neat little man of about forty who spent the whole of March rushing her from one photo-session to the next.

By the end of the month, Dawn had given picture sessions to every tabloid on Fleet Street. She had posed in bikinis, in short nighties, in lacy bras and black suspender belts. She was photographed in tennis shorts, plunging necklines, and pyjamas. She had been snapped in riding gear complete to the whip.

Ray Cox sold the same story all over the place – 'Dawn Wharton, acclaimed for her many roles in the theatre, soon to become an international star of the cinema screen.' The fact that she hadn't played even one lead in the theatre seemed not to matter. 'Why should it?' Ray countered when she queried a press release. 'You got good notices for what you did. It's not my fault nobody had the sense to play you in the lead. Dawn, honey, have faith in yourself.'

She did have faith. Lack of confidence had never let her down. It was just that she had dreamt of becoming a serious actress.

'You *are* a serious actress,' Ray Cox assured her, while blithely selling her as a sex symbol. *Reveille* heralded her as 'Britain's answer to Marilyn Monroe'.

The writer on the *Daily Mail* went even further. 'She has the come-hither eyes of Ava Gardner, the sultry allure of Lauren Bacall, Jane Russell's lush figure, and more sex appeal than any actress I've ever met.'

The *Express* said – 'She's beautiful, bountiful and BRITISH!'

By the end of April, Dawn's scantily clad figure had been gawped at by half the population. 'The male half,' Ray chuckled gleefully. On the last day of the month, the army adopted her as 'The Forces Pin-up of the Year'. Three hundred thousand eight-by-five glossies of Dawn in bikini were posted off, to take pride of place in soldiers' lockers from Aldershot to Aden.

Dawn knew what she was selling. She had been thirteen when she first overheard men talking about her. 'By Christ, I could fuck that. Look at the tits on her. She's built for it.' Men had been saying more or less the same thing ever since. Dawn accepted it as the way of the world. She was glad to have been born with her unusual looks, but sometimes men's salacious leers got her down. 'Is that all they ever think about?' she snapped at Eric one day.

'Don't let it get to you, sweetie. What does it matter if they jerk off over your picture? Let them have their hot little dreams. You can have dreams of your own.'

He was always there to smooth her brow. So was Pamela, who called at the flat increasingly often. And JD himself called once a week. Between them they were her social life, exclusively, until the beginning of May.

It was Eric who broke the news. 'Time for the next step,' he announced. 'You're attending your first opening night on Thursday.'

And after the first, the second came ten days later. Soon it became an established part of her life. In time, hardly a film première was to take place in London without Dawn being seen among the glittering mêlée. Cinema audiences began to notice her on newsreels, thanks to Ray Cox who bribed commentators to mention her name – 'British Show Biz gathers at Leicester Square's Odeon cinema for the opening of David Lean's *Goddess of Darkness* . . . here's Phyllis Calvert talking to Stewart Granger . . . Jack Hawkins and Margaret Lockwood . . . onlookers give a burst of applause to glamorous Dawn Wharton as she arrives on the arm of . . .'

She never chose her own escort. Eric arranged her dates from among those young actors likely to attract press attention; several of whom, to Dawn's surprise, were homosexuals, despite the heavy masculine roles they played on the screen.

'I know,' Eric chortled. 'Isn't it fun? We all get what we want. You lovely things get your pictures in the papers, and I get him in my bed at the end of the night.'

There was no danger of anyone getting into Dawn's bed. Eric, Ray Cox, even Pamela and JD were always on hand as chaperones. Dawn had no chance to form romantic attachments. She went out not to enjoy herself, but to be seen and to be seen at her best, which meant having her hair done beforehand and spending two hours on her make-up.

While all this was happening, JD was wheeling and dealing with Dawn's screen test. Several producers made offers. Rank even wanted to put her under contract. Drayton turned everyone down. He was searching for the right part in the right movie with the right billing . . .

The pace never let up. Increasingly Dawn was out late on a Saturday night, seeing a show or having supper in a smart restaurant with one of Eric's good-looking friends. Ray Cox never stopped pushing her photographs at the papers. Nothing pleased him more than to be able to pick up a tabloid and read about '. . . the stunning Dawn Wharton, seen here with . . .'

The hectic new life was more demanding than people imagined. Dawn's only rest days were Sundays. She would have loved to have spent them sleeping in bed . . . but Dawn lived her other life every Sunday.

'You will be here by twelve, won't you,' Edith Milford asked on the phone. 'Then you can spend a bit of time with Elizabeth before dinner.'

Lunch was always called dinner at the Milfords and was served at one o'clock prompt, which compelled Dawn to leave Regent's Park at ten because of the poor train service on a Sunday – not that she minded because it was always such a joy to see Elizabeth. Dawn cuddled her, cooed over her, and took her to the park in her pram.

Her secret life was sometimes a strain but she visited most Sundays, dressed in her dowdiest clothes to reduce the risk of being recognized, although there was not much chance of that in Hillingdon. Her mother had moved abroad, and more than two years had passed since she had lived there herself. Even so, Dawn never took risks. Nobody who saw her on the street would have taken her for the glamorous creature who appeared in the papers. Her cheap gaberdine coat came from a chain store, she dressed in her plainest frock and never wore make-up, her feet were shod in sensible shoes. She looked like a shop girl; clean and respectable, but so lacking in style that even Eric might have walked past her. 'I'm playing a part,' she told herself. 'It's good practice.' And it was, except that Dawn had little rest on a Sunday. Visiting sapped her strength, especially contending with Edith. The two seemed destined never to like each other. They had developed a mutual respect, less grudging on Dawn's part because she could see how well her child was looked after. Edith doted on Elizabeth, but her attitude towards Dawn was ambivalent. 'She keeps her word, I'll say that for her,' Edith admitted to her husband. 'But she's a scheming little madam if you ask me. If anything goes wrong with this fancy career of hers, she's quite capable of turning round and trying to marry our Keir.'

Joe spent his time keeping the peace.

'I thought you was supposed to be an actress,' Edith would sniff over lunch. 'I must say I don't care for these pin-ups. That one in the *Mirror* made me blush. Dressed only in your bra and panties. You wouldn't catch me showing off what I've got like that. Fair indecent, I call it.'

'Now, Edith,' Joe would say heavily, 'that's Dawn's business. I expect she has to do it. It's how actresses get known.'

'You don't see pictures of Jean Simmons in her undies. You can't say she's not known. Or that nice Anna Neagle . . .'

Dawn told them nothing of her professional life. She had

given them her new address and telephone number, for use in emergency, without mentioning a thing about JD or Eric. If Edith was baffled by pin-ups, she would never understand about Eric.

So, for the most part, conversation at the Milfords remained awkward and might have dried up entirely without Joe and his politics. It was what they talked about after Sunday lunch – or, rather, Joe talked, Edith knitted, and Dawn listened, putting the occasional question, less from interest than because she would have been embarrassed to sit there without saying a word. Even so, the mere act of listening brought her closer to Joe, and over the months, a curious bond began to develop between them. He's so like Keir, she thought, so honest and well meaning. The Milford men, Dawn decided, were the least selfish people she knew.

'No, no,' Joe argued. 'It's not a matter of being unselfish. If anything, the opposite. You've got to take an interest in what's going on in the world, because you never know when it will affect you.'

Dawn doubted that politics affected her at all. 'I'm an actress –'

'So? You're an actress. So what about this man McCarthy in the States? You think what he's doing to actors and writers and suchlike is right? He's conducting a witch hunt, all in the name of fighting Communism. People can't get a job after being called before his Committee, just because they went to a Communist meeting years ago. What if they did? Most of them have been too busy since earning a living even to think about politics, but McCarthy puts them on a blacklist and ruins their lives.'

Dawn knew that was true. She remembered JD talking about Hollywood when he returned from the States. Since then she had actually met a film director and an actor who were both banned from Hollywood because of McCarthy's smear tactics.

Watching her, Joe smiled. 'That rings a bell, eh? We don't want that sort of thing happening here. People like McCarthy are reason enough to keep an eye on the world.'

He was alarmed by events in America. 'McCarthy's a rabble rouser, stirring up fear and distrust among decent people. America's beginning to look like a lynch mob. The trouble is that sort of poison spreads. People get nervous, then whole countries get nervous. Take these H-bombs for instance. We're developing them to keep up with the Americans. So, of course, the Russians will want them too. Then what happens? France will want hydrogen bombs, to keep up with us. And some other country will want them to keep up with France. They've become a status symbol. People think a country is second-rate unless it's got hydrogen bombs . . .' Joe was beginning to develop his thoughts on the H-bomb. 'Britain should set an example by giving them up altogether. It's too late to stop America and Russia, but we could influence the rest of the world . . .'

And so, with Joe talking politics, another Sunday would draw to a close.

Dawn would escape after tea, pleading a two-hour journey and an early start the next morning. Back she would go in her drab clothes, back to her other life in London's West End. Sometimes it was hard to see where it was leading. She clung to a vision of living with Elizabeth and a Nanny under one roof, but where that roof would be and when it would happen were questions without any answers.

Meanwhile, Elizabeth was safe and well at the Milfords, and Dawn led her two separate lives . . . waiting for JD to find the right part in the right movie with the right billing.

And in June, he found *The Chrysalis*.

Eleven

It was the story of Sarah Brewster, an East End prostitute who after becoming a highly paid call-girl marries into the British aristocracy.

Eric joked at first. 'A cross between Nell Gwyn and *Pygmalion*.'

But the script provided a very strong story in which Sarah Brewster scorns her pimp and then fights for her life as he sets out to destroy her. The result was a taut, well-paced thriller with plenty of scope for fine acting.

'Nobody ever wrote a meatier part for a young actress,' JD

enthused when they gathered in his office. 'It's perfect to launch you into movies.'

Excited by the script, Dawn recognized the potential.

'So will every other actress in the country,' Eric warned with an anxious glance at JD. 'The competition will be –'

'I'll worry about the competition,' JD growled. 'You worry about getting Dawn ready for the part.'

So the campaign began to win the part of Sarah Brewster.

Life would have been easier if Ray eased up on the publicity campaign, but he continued to set a furious pace. Hardly a week passed without Dawn opening a fête or one of the new supermarkets that were springing up everywhere. And if she wasn't doing that she was being photographed for the papers or lunching at a charity bazaar. Ray was building her up as 'the most sought after young actress in the country'. Between public engagements she had her hair restyled again, gave interviews, and did everything Eric or Ray told her to do. Even a mild protest brought a lecture from Eric. 'Sweetie, be realistic. JD's breaking a gut to get you *Chrysalis*. He's got to have some ammunition.'

By the beginning of July, JD had plenty of ammunition. Dawn's file of press-clippings was more than a foot thick. She was a minor celebrity even before the public saw her in movies.

She would have been lost without Eric. The range of his accomplishments never ceased to amaze her. As the pace quickened, she ended most days stretched out on her bed, naked except for a towel, while Eric's sensitive fingers unknotted her tired muscles. He was masseur, confidant, and friend all rolled into one . . . but it was his role as her drama coach which turned out to be crucial.

One afternoon he took her to a smart house in Swiss Cottage where she met two girls who worked as 'hostesses' in a fashionable night club. Dawn was amused by the gentility of the chintz-covered sofas and by the fact that tea was served by a maid wearing a frilly white apron. Eric had met Angela and Veronica when he had taken some American film men to their club three years before. The Americans had become clients and Eric had put other business their way since, and as he never asked for a commission and his sexual preferences ruled him out as a punter, the two girls had become fond of him.

175

Quite honest about what he wanted, he told them about *Chrysalis*. '– And my dears, you sprang to mind the moment I read it. I said to Dawn, you must meet Angela and Veronica, what they don't know about Sarah Brewster won't be worth knowing.'

The girls were delighted to help. Dawn learned more from them in one afternoon than she could have found in an encyclopedia on sexual technique.

On another occasion, to help Dawn capture the flavour of Sarah's early life, Eric walked her around Soho at night, to watch the prostitutes ply their trade. He took her to a pub in Kentish Town where another friend introduced Dawn to a pimp. He made her talk in a cockney accent for hours. Gradually Sarah Brewster became more than a name in a script. She became a real person. Eric was always talking about her. 'Sarah wouldn't do that,' he would say, or 'What would Sarah do about this?' It became a game between them, the game of turning Dawn Wharton into Sarah Brewster.

At the beginning of August, Dawn gave a small dinner party at her flat. JD and Pamela were there, with Harvey and Ray – and Eric, of course. After the meal, the talk inevitably turned to Dawn's chances of getting the part.

JD had talked to Don Masters who was directing the film. 'According to him, it's between Ann Barclay, Olivia Fanning and Dawn. Barclay's got no chance. She's ten years too old. She's only in the running because Masters owes someone a favour. He's having his arm twisted. My guess is that he'll test her for the part, but that's as far as she'll get. The real competition is Fanning. She's box office, she can act, and –' JD paused – 'the word is that Butcher's got the hots for her and she's ready to put out.'

Dawn felt her flesh creep. Milton Butcher was the producer. She had met him at Churchill's one night – a bald man with a beak nose, bad breath and sweaty hands. The thought of a petite curvacious blonde like Olivia Fanning sleeping with someone like that was preposterous – except for the look on JD's face.

Glancing around the table, she wondered if they all knew what he had told her last December. She suspected they did, JD told them most things. The thought of them knowing made it worse. She still cringed at the thought of being compelled to

176

sleep with influential men, but it was the custom of the trade; she had heard enough stories from Eric to confirm that. She wondered if she could go through with it when the time came. She owed it to JD. He had kept his side of the bargain. She was obligated, but something about Butcher made her want to throw up. Please, God, she prayed, don't let it be Butcher.

'I've heard of living the part,' Harvey said drily, 'but isn't that taking it too far?'

'Sleeping with Butcher won't do Fanning any good,' Eric said firmly. 'All we want's a fair test for the part, JD. Get us that and sweetie will walk away with it.'

Dawn smiled gratefully, but the look on JD's face worried her. He had been in a good mood, laughing and joking and so attentive that, for the first time, she really did feel like 'one of the family'. But for an instant an anxious expression had come into his eyes. It was gone in a second, replaced by the smile that transformed his whole personality.

'Sure,' he said confidently. 'Dawn will walk away with the part.'

The next morning, Dawn asked Eric outright. 'Have we lost *Chrysalis* if Olivia Fanning starts sleeping with Butcher?'

'Forget it. It could make things harder, that's all. Ask yourself, what's the worst that can happen? Fanning buys Butcher, okay? So she's bought one vote. There're other people involved and Don Masters is one of them. He's our trump card. All Masters cares about is making great films. He'll be looking for one hell of a performance on the screen, not in bed. Give him that and it's all over.' Eric suddenly broke into a chuckle. 'Besides, once Butcher's had her, he's had her. She won't get a written guarantee.'

Dawn tried not to worry. Thankfully, with the part of Sarah Brewster to learn, there was no time to brood. Sarah Brewster was on her mind when she went to sleep and still there when she woke up. She invented little mannerisms, tricks to turn Sarah into a memorable character . . . but it was Eric, drawing on all his experience, who created the one single thing that was to etch Dawn's portrayal into the minds of audiences all over the world. His idea started with a simple question and culminated in a flash of sheer inspiration.

They were in Dawn's flat, discussing the script, a week before the test, when Eric said, 'You know that exit scene on page fifty? I wonder if we can steal it?'

She failed to see how. The scene belonged to Sarah's pimp, Eddie Bolton, played by Laurence Harvey in the film. Furious about Sarah spending the night with the Duke of Lincoln, Bolton ranted and raved and threatened. In the scene, Sarah, believing she could rely on the Duke's protection, finally walked out on Eddie Bolton.

'It's the *way* she walks out that's important,' said Eric, suddenly excited. 'She's got to do it in style. Think about it. The camera tracks you down that long corridor from Bolton's office. We only see you from the back. Bolton's insanely jealous. He wants you more than ever. The way you walk turns him on. As if you're flaunting it, underlining what he's going to lose . . .'

Wearing high heels and a tight skirt, Dawn walked up and down that apartment for an hour, swaying her hips as Eric directed.

'Again, sweetie,' he said, then, 'Again' . . . and, 'Again' after that.

By nine o'clock she had almost worn a furrow in the carpet in an unsuccessful effort to win Eric's approval.

'It would be brilliant on stage,' he admitted, 'but the body movement needs to be more subtle for the camera.'

The problem was that Dawn interpreted 'more subtle' as meaning she should sway her hips rather less.

'No, no, you're losing it,' Eric scolded. 'You've still got to be sexy.' After thinking for a moment, he had an idea. 'Take your skirt off. Maybe watching your leg movement will help.'

It would have been voyeurism with anyone else – watching her walk up and down wearing only pants and stockings and six-inch-high heels – but with Eric it was work, and Dawn knew it.

Ten minutes later he had another idea. *The* idea. He jumped up from his chair. 'I've got it. Give me your shoes.' Carrying them into the kitchen, he put the left shoe on the table and started hacking at the heel with the breadknife. The result lacked elegance. Slivers of leather made the heel look badly scuffed, but Eric had achieved his objective. The heel was a quarter of an inch shorter.

'Now try.'

'What about the other one?'

'No, no, that's the whole point.'

The effect was startling. Instead of swaying, her hips undulated. Instead of moving from side to side as she walked, her bottom gyrated in a circular movement. Tight little buttocks clenched and unclenched so seductively that Eric actually whimpered. 'Gorgeous,' he sighed. 'The most beautiful arse the screen's ever seen.'

Even with a skirt on, the languid, seductive roll had an appeal that was riveting.

Next morning, Eric took all her shoes to a shoemaker. A quarter of an inch was removed from every left heel. 'From now on, sweetie, you never wear them any other way. I can't wait to see Don Masters's face when he gets you on camera.'

A week later, Eric was proved right. Dawn was Sarah Brewster the moment she walked on the set. Rumours about Olivia Fanning sleeping with Butcher became irrelevant. Don Masters went into raptures. So did Laurence Harvey, who grinned wickedly to Eric on the way out. 'We both know who taught her that, don't we, darling?' he said.

Five days passed before it became official. Five days during which Dawn opened a supermarket, attended two garden fêtes, posed for a centre spread in the *Sunday Pictorial* . . . smiling graciously wherever she went, while all the time fretting about the outcome.

'What's holding things up?' she kept asking Eric.

He grinned. 'You hooked them, now JD's squeezing them dry. He's demanding equal billing with Laurence Harvey. Don't worry, sweetie, he'll get it.'

It seemed an awful gamble to Dawn. If they wanted her, why argue about the billing? But at the end of the five days, a triumphant JD came on the line. 'It's signed, sealed and settled. Dawnee Darling, you're on your way.'

They dined at the Ivy to celebrate; all of them: JD and Pamela, Eric and Harvey, and the irrepressible Ray Cox with the inevitable photographer. Dawn had no need to be told to smile, she beamed happily all evening. JD dragged people across to the table. 'I want you to meet Dawn Wharton. I tell you Harry, or Tom or Dick, this girl will cause a sensation with this picture . . .'

179

They went on to Churchill's afterwards, or at least JD, Pamela, Eric and Dawn went on. Harvey went home. So did Ray, but only after giving Dawn the next day off. 'I was trying to fix something with *Reveille*,' he said, 'but what the hell? Spend the whole day in bed. You deserve it.'

This was just as well because they made a night of it at Churchill's, dancing and talking, laughing and joking. Afterwards they shared a cab, and it was 3.30 when Dawn alighted outside her Regent's Park flat. She stood at the kerbside, holding JD's hands while Pamela and Eric grinned out from the cab. Words failed her for a moment, then they came tumbling out to express her gratitude, all spoken with so much affection that she choked up. Eight months ago she had despised this man. Now she looked upon him as a knight in shining armour.

'Don't forget,' he said, kissing her cheek with equal affection, 'this is just the start!'

After waving them goodbye from her front door, Dawn flopped into an armchair. Despite the late hour, she was wide awake. Her mind floated back over the evening, enjoying again all the fuss and attention. Poor Olivia Fanning. It was almost funny to think of a girl like that sleeping with a creep like Milton Butcher. For nothing! But Dawn's smile soon faded. She knew perfectly well she would have done the same thing. It was how the system worked . . . unless you had JD on your side.

Looking around the apartment was a reminder of what she owed him. The velvet drapes glowed a rich copper in the soft light cast by the table lamps. All this and more, thanks to JD . . .

Yawning, she kicked off her shoes and went into the bedroom, where she stepped out of her dress. She was inspecting it for damage when the telephone startled her. Wearing her slip she returned to the sitting-room, sure for some reason that it would be Eric or even JD, ringing up with a final word of congratulations. A smile of anticipation played on her lips as she reached for the phone.

'Hello,' said a voice. 'Is that London?'

Startled, Dawn gave her number and listened in amazement to a man speaking German. A moment later, Keir came on the line sounding breathless and worried. 'Dawn? Thank heavens. I've been ringing all night –'

'Keir? What on earth –'

'Listen, Dad's been arrested –'

'He's *what*?'

'Been arrested. He's up before Uxbridge Magistrates' Court in the morning.'

She sat down, her head swimming, trying to absorb what he was saying. It was all a bit garbled. The line crackled and hissed. Apparently Joe Milford had organized a public protest about the government's decision to make H-bombs.

'Only a local meeting,' Keir said, his voice fading in and out. 'Somehow the police got involved and Dad was arrested . . .'

Dawn listened, shocked, as Keir explained about taking a call from his mother. 'She was hysterical at first . . . I calmed her down, she's okay now . . . but I wonder if you could do something?'

'Do what?' Her imagination ran riot. In her mind's eye she saw Joe outside a prison, bouncing Elizabeth on his knee as he talked to reporters. 'This is Elizabeth. Her mother's Dawn Wharton, the actress, the one who's always in the papers . . .'

Keir was saying, 'I thought you might have a few contacts . . .'

Contacts? Sure, she had contacts. Like JD who would faint at the sight of an illegitimate baby. JD who was convinced she was as pure as the driven snow. JD who would tear up her contract . . . She groaned, imagining him talking to reporters. 'I'm as shocked as you are,' he was saying. 'I've asked Miss Wharton to find another manager, naturally . . .'

Naturally!

Twelve

Sleep was impossible after the phone call. Dawn didn't even bother to go to bed. Instead she made some coffee and sat down and worried. Her earlier euphoria was quite forgotten, replaced by fear of what Joe might say to the press. Imagining him being wheeled into court, surrounded by reporters, she could almost hear his too-honest answers to their questions. Why did it have to happen now, of all days? Just when contracts had been signed on the *Chrysalis*. Everything would be cancelled . . .

Finally, after fretting through the night, Dawn could wait no longer. At 6.15 she telephoned Edith.

The older woman sounded upset and frightened. 'Him and his politics,' she grumbled. 'Look where it's got him. He's always been so proud of his good name. He won't have a good name much longer, will he? Not with being in court and all that.'

The more Dawn probed, the more resentful, even angry Edith became. 'We're respectable people, we are. Never had trouble with the police. I don't know what things are coming to when someone like Joe gets arrested. Anyway, Keir had no business telling you. It's nothing to do with you . . .'

Dawn responded patiently, explaining that Keir had asked her to help. 'Though I'm not sure what I can do. What about your friend Bob?'

'He's away at some Trade Union Conference –'

'There must be someone who can help?'

'The Vicar came over last night, telling me not to worry –'

'What about a solicitor? Do you know one? Someone to represent Mr Milford in court?'

Edith didn't know a solicitor. Edith didn't know very much, only that Joe had organized a meeting in the British Legion Hall and had been arrested for threatening a policeman. 'I ask you, as if Joe would threaten anyone!'

Dawn knew she had to go to Uxbridge. She wouldn't rest otherwise. Edith was hopeless, likely to do more harm than good.

'Try not to worry,' Dawn told her. 'I'll find a solicitor. I'm sure it's all some stupid mistake. Meanwhile, don't talk to the press . . .'

Her single piece of luck was not having any appointments that morning. Even so, as soon as she had washed and dressed, she called Eric.

'Bloody hell, sweetie. Do you know what the time is?'

It was ten past seven. Apologizing, Dawn invented a story about being invited to spend the day with an old school friend.

'More celebrations, eh?' said Eric. 'Well, have a good time.'

A good time was the last thing she expected.

Uxbridge was new to her. She arrived at nine o'clock, not

knowing where to start. Opposite the station was a covered market, and behind that a narrow street choked with rush hour traffic. Hurrying along the thin ribbon of pavement, she searched the office doors for a solicitor's brass plate. The end of the street was in sight before she found one.

'I'd like to see a solicitor,' she told the receptionist. 'Er . . . a friend of mine is in the Magistrates' Court this morning.'

Pointedly the girl glanced at the clock on the wall. It was already 9.20. 'Oh dear,' she said. 'Please take a seat. I'll see if the young Mr Freeman is available.'

Only then did Dawn notice the firm was called Freeman, Moody and Freeman.

The *young* Mr Freeman emerged from an inner office almost immediately, 'Good morning,' he said, shaking her hand, 'Miss . . . er . . .'

She was reluctant to give her name. This business had nothing to do with her. She hesitated, weighing him up. A couple of years older than her, his healthy outdoor look would have done credit to a young farmer. He had fair hair and very blue eyes. Rather attractive, she thought, and realized he was thinking the same about her.

'My friend's name is Mr Milford. He's a cripple in a wheelchair. Somehow he got himself arrested at a political meeting last night.'

'I see,' said the young Mr Freeman, checking his watch. 'And you want us to represent him in court this morning?'

'Yes I do.'

'Then we'd better leave at once. You can tell me the rest in the car, Miss . . . ?' he trailed off, but this time his enquiring look demanded an answer.

Dawn had to say something. 'Green,' she lied, 'Pamela Green.' Why Green, she never knew, neither could she have explained her choice of Pamela. Her lies alarmed her. 'My name doesn't matter, does it?' she asked anxiously, wondering what she had let herself in for.

Freeman grinned as he opened the street door. 'We like to know who's instructing us. After all, you're not an existing client, or the daughter of a client, are you, Miss Green?'

'No,' she admitted.

'And I don't recognize the name Milford,' he said, guiding her to a car parked at the kerbside. 'So are you our client, or is he?'

Dawn stepped into the car and delayed her reply until he climbed into the driver's seat. 'I don't see the importance,' she said. 'I'll pay your bill if that's what you mean.'

He laughed. 'Not exactly, but it helps to know we'll be paid. Now then, tell me as much as you know about this business.'

The journey took less than twenty minutes and Dawn had finished her account long before then. After all, she had little to tell. However, even as they talked, something worried her. She had intended to engage a solicitor and do all she could to help Joe, but it had never occurred to her that she might have to go to court herself. She was reluctant to go within a mile of the place. Even if the risk of recognition was one in a million, it was a chance she was unwilling to take.

'What will happen when we get there?' she asked.

'That's simple. If you wait in the lobby, I'll pop down to the cells to see Mr Milford. Once I find out what he's charged with, and what he says happened, we can decide how to plead. You say he's an invalid in a wheelchair? How extraordinary. How on earth could he have threatened a policeman?'

The court-house loomed into view at that moment. One look at the steps was enough to alarm Dawn. 'Can I wait somewhere else?' she asked nervously as he pulled into the car park. 'A hotel, perhaps? I'll get a coffee or something.'

He looked at her in surprise. 'You'd better be in the public gallery. There's no telling what will happen, you know. The charge sounds ridiculous, but the police must have a reason –'

'No, I'm not going in. Is there a hotel? You could come there afterwards –' She broke off, realizing how stupid she had been to lie about her name. Freeman would go down to the cells to find Joe and say he had been sent by a Pamela Green. Joe would be baffled, he didn't know a Pamela Green.

'I really think you ought to come in,' Freeman said, staring at her.

She blushed bright red. 'Oh dear. Look . . . what I said earlier . . . I did say my name wasn't important, didn't I? It's not needed for anything official. The point is, I want to be kept out of it . . . for personal reasons.'

A glimmer of understanding came into his eyes. 'Your name isn't Pamela Green?' he said, accusingly.

She shook her head, humiliated to be found out in a lie, outside a court of all places. The words of the oath rushed into her mind. *I promise to tell the truth, the whole truth, and nothing but the truth; so help me God.* She swallowed again. 'If you tell Mr Milford that Dawn sent you, he'll understand.'

'Dawn who?' Freeman asked curtly.

'Dawn Wharton.'

He stared and repeated her name, as if vaguely recognizing it. For a second she thought he was going to demand a full explanation, or even worse, refuse to help, but after checking his watch he turned away. 'Very well. There's no time now, but I take it you'll tell me what this is all about later –'

'Oh yes, really I will. I promise. It's just that I don't want my name mentioned. I'd be grateful if you'd remind Mr Milford of that.'

Freeman was not pleased. Not knowing of a nearby hotel, the best he could think of was a restaurant called the Tudor Tea Rooms. 'Cross the road and it's about a hundred yards on the left.' He stood by the car, locking it, a frown on his face. 'This could take the whole morning you know. It depends when Mr Milford is called on the list. You will wait at the Tea Rooms, won't you, Miss Wharton? You will be there when I get back?'

'I've no intention of cheating you, Mr Freeman. I'll give you a cheque now if you like. Please . . . I really am very grateful.'

'No,' he said, 'I don't want a cheque. Just so long as you wait.'

She promised faithfully and watched him hurry away and up the steps of the Court. After which she went in search of the Tudor Tea Rooms.

It was an unprepossessing place with white-washed walls and a half-timbered ceiling. 'We don't start serving for another half-hour,' said a girl who was setting the tables.

'Oh? Do you mind if I wait? You see, I arranged to meet someone –'

The girl shrugged. 'Please yourself, but there's no service till 10.30.'

Dawn sat in a far corner, facing the door, away from the window. It was a gloomy spot and the table rocked slightly on uneven legs, but it became home for the rest of the morning. She ordered tea and toast at 10.30 and another pot of tea an hour later. Idly, she watched other customers come and go, while she fretted about what was happening in court. Her conscience plagued her. She knew she should be there to give Joe support. Keir had asked for her help and she'd given it, but more for her own sake, panicking about the damage it could do her. Keir would have been more generous. 'But he doesn't have my problems,' she told herself firmly, trying to stop worrying. Suppose Joe were sent to prison? The idea was absurd. Yet he had been arrested . . .

She was tired. Lack of sleep was beginning to take its toll.

At noon, the café began to fill up with the lunch trade. Dawn wondered about ordering a meal, less from hunger than to justify retaining a table. By half past twelve she began to fear the worst. Joe had been sent to prison . . .

Suddenly the door opened and Freeman came in, looking about him as if not really expecting to find her. Dawn recognized the man with him. She had met him at the Milfords. It was the Welsh librarian, Emlyn Hughes. Waving to her, he began to thread his way between the tables. She rose, alarmed by Joe's absence.

'It's okay,' he said, catching her expression, 'Joe's outside with the Vicar. There's a pub next door. We're going for a drink. Come on.'

Dawn hadn't bargained on Emlyn Hughes being there, let alone the Vicar. 'Oh,' she said, glancing at Freeman as he joined them at her table, 'very well. I'll just pay my bill. I'll catch you up.'

Freeman stood aside to let Emlyn Hughes return to the door. 'No problems,' he said reassuringly. 'Your name wasn't mentioned. Mr Milford was fined ten pounds and bound over. He's quite a character, isn't he?'

Dawn felt weak with relief. A ten pounds fine sounded very minor. 'What was it all about?' she asked as they crossed to the cash desk.

In a better mood than earlier, Freeman grinned. 'Apparently your Mr Milford and that fiery Welshman found two men making a note of the car registration numbers of people who were attending their meeting. None of the cars were improperly parked, so Mr Milford asked the men what they were doing. They turned out to be Special Branch detectives. Mr Milford tried to send them about their business, and an argument ensued –' He broke off as a waitress arrived to take Dawn's money.

Dawn paid her bill and turned for the door. 'Well?'

Freeman shrugged. 'The police have the right to note down almost anything. On the other hand, Mr Milford saw it as political persecution. He told them they were no better than Hitler's Gestapo. Hughes joined in and there was a hell of a row. Finally the detectives nicked them for abusive language and disturbing the peace.' He laughed, amused by the whole incident.

Dawn began to feel rather foolish. Keir's phone call in the small hours had caused her to panic. Nobody had told her about Emlyn Hughes. If she had known Joe wasn't alone she might have reacted differently. Of course, Edith had been useless . . .

Freeman said, 'Mr Milford's still very angry. I had my work cut out persuading him to pay the fine. He was ready to go to prison for the principle of the matter.'

Principle! Dawn flushed, suddenly angry. She'd been worried sick about Joe being sent to prison. Now, it seemed, he wanted to go!

'What intrigues me is how you fit into all this,' said Freeman cheerfully. 'You are Dawn Wharton the actress, aren't you?'

She froze, her hand on the door. Her dark eyes rounded in alarm. Denial would have been useless. She had already lied once and been found out. This whole episode was becoming a nightmare. What on earth was she doing? Talking to solicitors, worrying about Joe . . . suddenly other implications burst into her mind. 'Emlyn Hughes doesn't know,' she said quickly. 'You haven't told him who I am, have you?'

'I haven't said a word, but I'd like to know what's going on.'

As she stood aside to let other people get to the door, Dawn cursed Joe Milford for involving her in his matters of principle! Life was difficult enough without Joe causing complications.

'I'd rather you didn't say anything to the others. I'll . . . I'll explain afterwards,' she said, her dark eyes pleading with Freeman to trust her.

Shrugging good-naturedly, he accepted her assurance, and together they went to find Joe in the pub. Dawn was determined to escape. She would just make sure that Joe was all right. Then her duty was done. She would flee to the station. Of course, she'd have to tell Freeman *something* . . .

187

Joe was at a table in his wheelchair, eyes bright and a pugnacious look on his face. His scowl lifted when he saw her. 'Ah, Dawn. Come and have a drink and let me thank you. It was kind of you to engage Mr Freeman –'

'Wasn't it just,' Emlyn Hughes interrupted, joining them from the bar. 'Without Mr Freeman we'd be clapped in irons and half-way to Australia by now.' He grinned hugely as he stood aside to let a clergyman place two pints of beer on the table.

Straightening up, the Vicar smiled at Dawn and held out his hand. 'You must be Mrs Wharton. I'm Peter Williams,' he said. 'I'm along to provide moral support. It is nice to meet you at last. I'm a great fan of your daughter.'

Dawn could have murdered him. She managed a strained smile while wondering what Freeman was thinking. Now she would *have* to explain.

It took her forty minutes to escape. Under pressure, she stayed long enough to have one gin and tonic. Freeman was right about Joe, who was still very angry. He never stopped talking. 'This business has opened my eyes. I've found out a few things, I can tell you. I didn't know we had political police in this country until now. These Special Branch snoopers are just like the Gestapo. They collect all sorts of names and addresses. Anyone who opposes the government gets his name taken down in a little black book. What for, that's what I want to know? This is supposed to be a democracy . . .' He went on about what he called creeping McCarthyism and the threat to civil liberties. Emlyn Hughes and the Vicar were equally indignant. They talked about complaining to their MP, and Emlyn said Bob Cooper should involve the Trade Unions.

Finally, claiming an appointment elsewhere, Dawn managed to extricate herself. Joe wheeled himself to the door as she left to have a private word. 'It was very good of you, Dawn. Mr Freeman's sending his bill to us, so I don't want you paying that.' He cocked an eyebrow and gave her a stern look. 'You mustn't worry about Elizabeth, you know. You don't *ever* have to worry about that.'

Her exasperation faded. She knew what he meant. She should have known better than to doubt him. A promise given was a promise kept, whatever the circumstances.

Freeman drove her back to the station. Declining his offer of lunch, she insisted on going back to town. 'To sleep, if nothing else.' She laughed. 'I didn't get a wink last night worrying about this business.'

'Ah well,' he said, 'it's all over now. Even if the local paper reports the proceedings against Mr Milford, there won't be a word about you.'

'Thank goodness,' she sighed gratefully, giving him a sideways glance. 'I suppose you've guessed why I was so worried. The Vicar let the cat out of the bag, didn't he? You see, the Milfords look after my baby . . .'

She told him the truth. There was no avoiding it, and she was reassured by his explanation of the confidentiality of the solicitor-client relationship. In fact, he was very understanding. 'Look at it this way,' he said cheerfully. 'There might come a time when you need a lawyer again. When you do, you won't have to explain things to a total stranger.'

He was so pleasant that she felt guilty about her earlier attempts to deceive him. Thank goodness I found the young Mr Freeman, she thought, accepting his card as he walked her towards the ticket barrier.

'Don't forget,' he said, shaking hands. 'Give me a buzz if you need any legal help. From what I hear about your business, actresses are always being ripped off in the contracts they sign.'

Thanking him sincerely, she went off to board her train, never expecting to see him again. After all, she had only signed one contract, the one with JD. She hadn't needed a lawyer to help her with that.

Thirteen

The Chrysalis was shot in fourteen weeks. Work started at Pinewood half-way through September and continued until the second week of December. If Dawn thought herself well treated by Drayton Management before, her gratitude soared to new heights during the making of that film. JD and Eric left nothing to chance.

The weekend before work started, JD collected Dawn from her flat and drove her out to a country house he had hired from 'a friend of a friend'. Called Elm Tree Cottage, it far exceeded Dawn's idea of a cottage. Set in secluded grounds, it had eight bedrooms, a cook-housekeeper and a butler. A huge wisteria climbed along the front of the house, yew hedges flanked the drive and huge goldfish swam in the ornamental pool. Inside, Chinese rugs covered oak-boarded floors, period furniture graced every room and the scent of lavender clung to the air. Dawn's bedroom was full of exposed oak beams and the largest four-poster bed she had ever seen. JD dismissed such luxury as of little importance. 'The great thing,' he said airily, 'is it's quiet and only ten minutes from the studios. You and Eric will live here while you're filming and I'll get down whenever I can.'

After that, help and consideration arrived from every quarter. Dawn was a little in awe of Laurence Harvey at the outset. He was an established star; flamboyant, eccentric and gifted. Happily for Dawn he had known Eric for years and his first words were, 'You haven't a thing to worry about, little girl, I promised Eric I'd look after you, and I always keep my promises.'

And he did. He was very kind. So was Don Masters, the Director. He held a little conference on the set every morning, with Laurence Harvey and Dawn and the script girl, and whoever else might be in the scene. They sat in a circle of canvas chairs and read aloud from the script. When it sounded about right to Don, he asked an electrician for a work light – one light on the set – and they'd go through the scene to see how it felt. 'Move around,' Don encouraged. 'See where it feels most comfortable, take your time.' Only when everyone felt happy did he call the cameraman and talk about lighting and angles and camera set-ups. Eric said it was the perfect way for the movie actors to work. It certainly seemed perfect to Dawn.

Of course, there were tensions. Dawn was a mass of nerves at the outset. She was so desperate to please. If she had failed in the theatre, the only loser would have been her. Now, things were very different. JD and Eric, Harvey and the others had all invested so much. Now she would let them down. She *knew* she would the moment Don said he'd try for the first take. Her opening scene. Silence on the set. 'Quiet, we're rolling,' said the sound man. 'Action,' called Don. Dawn panicked. This was the real thing, this was for *real* audiences all over the world, for *real* people to see. The scene called for her to pick up a glass and propose a toast. Her hand was shaking so badly that the fake champagne slopped all over the place. She was mortified. The harder she tried to stop, the more she shook. She wondered what Don was thinking? Or Laurence Harvey? Or the crew? God, make it stop. She was petrified.

The first week was agonizing. In some scenes she had to look exquisite, which meant being combed, sprayed, kiss-curled, powdered and lip-glossed before every take. If a lock of hair fell out of place, Don shouted 'Cut' and the whole process began over again. If her smile became too broad – 'Cut! Dawn, don't smile so wide, you're showing your gums.' If she failed to hit her mark exactly the lighting would be off and her face not properly lit – 'Cut!' If her chest moved – 'Cut! Dawn, your bosom's heaving like you just ran upstairs . . .'

But gradually, helped by Don's early morning conferences and Eric's unswerving confidence, each day became a little less frightening. Dawn had only to believe in herself. After all, she knew the part of Sarah Brewster too well to give an indifferent performance.

JD telephoned every evening. She had begged him not to visit the set. 'Please JD, you'll make me even more nervous.' So he stayed away in the week and relied on Eric's daily reports.

Eric loved the whole business. He knew it all. He'd been there before and was aware of every pitfall. Even about how to behave with the crew – 'Be friendly, but don't overdo it. Some actresses fool around with the crew. It's silly. They don't like you any better for it. When you finish a scene, go back to your dressing room. Don't give it away, save it for when the cameras are rolling.'

He took charge of everything. Every morning he told the housekeeper what they would have for dinner, and every evening he coached Dawn in her scenes for the next day. And always with such encouragement. 'Sweetie, that's delightful. Masters will love you tomorrow.'

So embracing was his protection that, on the first Saturday at the cottage, Dawn was surprised to learn he was going to Bath. 'Don't worry, I'll be back tomorrow afternoon. You won't even

191

have time to miss me. JD's coming down to take you out to dinner tonight.'

'By himself?'

'Sure, by himself. Who else would he bring?'

Instinctively Dawn thought of Pamela who so obviously doted on JD that Dawn had long wondered about their relationship. Pamela had always joined them for dinner in the past. Not just Pamela, the whole crowd . . . somehow the thought of dining alone with JD was a worry.

But it was fine. She had a good evening. JD arrived and took her out to dinner. He grinned as they left the cottage. 'I figured you deserve one night out a week, otherwise you'll go stir crazy.'

He drove his black Bentley carefully through the narrow country lanes to a restaurant overlooking the river at Windsor, where they ate a fine meal and talked about *The Chrysalis*. 'You're doing great,' he told her, 'I got the word last night from Don Masters himself. He says you're delivering a fantastic performance.'

Dawn wondered how anyone could fail, given so much support and encouragement. When she realized he was staying overnight she grew slightly anxious, but even that passed without incident. After coffee and brandy back at the cottage, they went to their separate bedrooms and Dawn slept soundly until morning.

The first week set the pattern. At the studios, scene followed scene as day followed day. Up early, they left the cottage at 6.15 to arrive at Pinewood by half-past. Then Dawn would get into make-up and onto the set. Depart the studios at five-thirty to be home by six. Bath and rest for an hour. Dinner at seven-thirty. Discuss the next day's shooting with Eric, rehearse the tricky bits, and bed by ten or ten-thirty at the latest. No parties, little drink – a glass of wine with dinner and a brandy afterwards – no drugs, certainly no sex, Eric even cut down on her smoking – 'Think of yourself as an athlete in training,' he encouraged.

Dawn had already found out that the real professionals worked hard in the film business, and although her regime was harder than most she didn't mind in the least. She welcomed it. The grind of lessons endured in her childhood had developed self discipline. Ambition did the rest. Eager to learn, determined to succeed, Dawn followed Eric's instructions with such obedience that she conquered her fear within a couple of weeks. In fact in the third week, when Eric suggested an evening out as a reward for her dedication, she declined. 'No thanks, Eric, I'd rather stay in and talk about Sarah Brewster.'

She was really of the same mind on Saturdays when JD came down, so after the third week they stopped going out and ate at the cottage. JD liked the arrangement. 'Next week I'll bring a couple of sweaters, and we'll just sit around chewing the fat,' he said.

He enjoyed changing into casual clothes and sitting talking to her, and as the weeks passed he began to arrive earlier and stay longer. By the sixth week he had fallen into the habit of reaching the cottage in time for lunch on a Saturday and remaining until Monday morning, when he drove directly into his office.

Weekends became restful interludes amid weeks of concentrated work. If Dawn and JD ran out of conversation, they played canasta for a couple of hours, although cards were usually left until Sunday evenings when Eric was there to join them. Mostly they talked about the film and what would happen when it was finished.

With her every whim catered for, it was not surprising that she fell in love with life at the cottage. Her favourite times were Sunday mornings, when she and JD were at their most relaxed. Rested from their labours of the week, they ate a late breakfast and sat with their feet up reading the papers, looking for all the world like a contented married couple.

One particular Sunday the papers were full of Britain's 'other' young sex-symbol, Diana Dors. Every tabloid carried lurid tales of the drunken parties which had become a feature of her private life.

'What a waste,' JD growled, 'the girl's got talent. Properly handled she could really do something. Instead she's lumbered herself with a lot of bums who don't give a fuck about her future.'

Dawn shot him a quick glance of alarm. 'You're not thinking of taking her on?'

He lowered his paper and stared at her, a hurt look in his eyes. 'Are you kidding? Didn't I say I wouldn't take anyone else on if things worked out? Well, they are working out. You're a real pro, Princess. I always sensed it. Call it a gut feeling, call it what you like. Even Eric's never seen such dedication. Who needs new clients? I got the client I want. You've kept faith with me and I'll keep faith with you, forever and ever I hope.'

There was such sincerity in his voice that she had to believe him. She couldn't have asked for a bigger vote of confidence. Yet his talk about keeping faith was a painful reminder of the lie she was living.

His next words made her feel even more guilty. 'You wanna know what stinks about my business? Liars. I don't mean producers. Christ, I expect them to lie. I mean clients. You wouldn't believe the weeks, months sometimes, I can spend working on someone's career. Then they do something stupid and blow it. The whole fucking lot goes down the drain, and why? Because they told me a pack of lies at the outset.'

His scowl only brightened when he looked at her. 'That's why you're different, Princess. You I can trust. I know where I am with you. You won't let me down. I don't have to worry, understand?'

Nodding, she turned away to hide the guilt in her eyes. Once upon a time she had been a little afraid of JD. Now, thanks to their weekends at the cottage, she had come to see him as a rather lonely man who lived for his work. His abrasiveness was an act. With a start of surprise she was suddenly reminded of a big teddy bear. Chewed at the edges, but a teddy bear for all that. And she realized something else. She could *never* tell him about Elizabeth, for his sake as much as her own. Until then she had hoped that one day she might, but such hopes died when he said *You won't let me down*. He spoke with such total conviction. She couldn't add to the long list of clients who had failed him.

'Tell you what,' he said looking out of the window. 'It's not a bad day. Why don't we go for a walk?'

So when weather permitted they went for walks, and when it rained they stayed in front of the fire. Eric always arrived at teatime and they played cards in the evening. They became very close during those weeks, inevitably perhaps, considering they were all committed to the same thing; the business of turning Dawn into a star. JD was already talking about taking her to Hollywood in the New Year. 'We're going to the States anyway,' he said. 'You're appearing at the première in New York, it's part of the deal.'

194

Dawn hadn't known it was part of the deal. She hadn't even read the contract JD had negotiated for *Chrysalis*. She had just signed it. 'A première in New York! Goodness, what shall I wear?'

'Sackcloth and ashes unless your performance is brilliant,' Eric said sternly.

Few people doubted the quality of Dawn's performance. After a faltering start, she'd hit her stride. The mood at Pinewood was buoyant. Even the crew sensed a hit. When things go well on a film set, they go really well. When they go badly word goes around that the production is jinxed. People fall sick, accidents happen, actors have tantrums and directors walk out. Nothing of that sort happened on *Chrysalis*. As more and more film went into the can, the conviction grew that it would be a very good movie.

The single disaster to befall Dawn was a personal one. She forgot Elizabeth's first birthday. Appalled, she was furious with herself. She had remembered the previous week. *I knew it was Thursday!* She had been concentrating so hard, so immersed in her work that Thursday had slipped by without her doing anything about it. Not that she could do much with Eric living in the house. She had no privacy, no space for herself . . . As soon as he left on the Saturday morning, she rushed to the telephone.

'Oh, it's you,' said Edith, sniffily, as usual. 'We thought you'd forgotten where we live.'

'I did say I couldn't get down while I'm making this film. You did *know* –'

'You could have phoned surely? Joe got quite worried. He said you might have had an accident. After all, it's a funny kind of mother who forgets her own daughter's birthday.'

Dawn bit her tongue and let the criticism wash over her. It was a waste of breath to reply. Edith would never understand, Edith didn't *want* to understand. To make matters worse, when she finally got a chance to ask about Elizabeth, the words had scarcely left her mouth when she saw JD's Bentley sweep up the drive. 'Oh dear. I'm sorry, Mrs Milford, I've got to go. I'm glad she's all right. I'll be down in a few weeks.'

That was how it was left. How it *had* to be left. It was part of the price of success; living a life of secrets, always trying to keep things in their separate compartments. Keeping any hint of Elizabeth from JD and Eric. Keeping most of JD's plans secret from Keir and the Milfords. It was all part of living life on a tightrope.

The hurried phone conversation with Edith left Dawn edgy and tense, which was unfortunate because JD was in a similar mood for once. Usually he maintained a cheerful good humour. 'Anything to keep the star happy,' he would say grinning. But that day he was different. As always he began by asking about her week, and although responding in all the right places, he was less vibrant than usual. As she watched him, Dawn thought the teddy bear was even more chewed at the edges.

Even when they went for a walk, he seemed downcast. Dawn grew anxious in case his mood concerned her. She imagined him receiving a less than favourable report from Don Masters. Finally she could stand it no longer. 'JD, what's the matter? Is it something I've done?'

His surprise was obvious. 'You? Crazy. You're great. I've been waiting for you all my life.' He laughed, suddenly embarrassed. 'I mean as a client, professionally – shit, you know what I mean.' He laughed again, more awkward than ever. 'No, it's nothing. I'm tired that's all. Hell, this is terrible! I'm supposed to keep you happy, not get you in a state –'

'You're not. You just looked so . . . so miserable. Are you feeling all right? You're not ill –?'

'Me? I'm as strong as a horse.' His eyes searched hers for a moment, then he shrugged. 'No, I'm not ill. My wife is. Eric ever tell you about her?'

Instinctively, she hesitated, worried about breaking a confidence, but his look was so searching that she had to answer. 'Eric said she was an invalid. I'm . . . sorry.'

JD nodded. 'She's got Alzheimer's disease,' he said grimly.

Dawn had never heard of Alzheimer's disease, and was lost for a response.

He saw her blank face. 'It means she's not physically ill, she just forgets things. She always was a scatterbrain. In her case it got worse. People with Alzheimer's disease forget how to tie their shoe laces. They even forget where they live. After a while they can't remember anything; they can't remember how to use a knife and fork, how to dress themselves, how to go to the bathroom. Their entire memory goes. They sort of grow backwards into childhood and become babies.'

It was horrifyingly different from what she had imagined. When Eric talked of an invalid, she'd thought of someone in a wheelchair like Joe Milford.

'She hasn't recognized me in years,' said JD. 'She doesn't know who I am. She's not in pain or anything like that, it's just that she has to have everything done for her. She can't be left alone. She's *not* left alone. I have some very good people who look after her. It's just that . . .' He shrugged. 'It gets you down at times, that's all.'

Dawn asked the obvious questions about treatment and cures. Apparently, no cure was possible. He changed the subject, not wanting to talk about it. Yet she sensed he was glad that she knew, as if it was part of his rule about them not having secrets. He switched the conversation back to *Chrysalis* by asking questions about Laurence Harvey, and that was the last they spoke on the subject.

They did go out that night. Dawn insisted that he change back into his suit and take her out to dinner at the restaurant at Windsor. As always he donned his mask with his suit, the mask of a successful man without a care in the world. They had a good evening. She quizzed him about Hollywood and he responded with a fund of stories.

'The thing to remember,' he said, laughing, 'is that Hollywood is bounded on the north, and on the south, and the east and the west by the biggest bunch of crooks you ever met in your life.'

Back at the cottage, neither of them bothered with a nightcap. It was late and they went straight to their rooms. 'Goodnight, Princess,' he said, kissing her cheek.

As she undressed for bed, Dawn recognized that her life was about to become even more complicated. When she thought about it, she realized she had known for weeks without allowing herself to admit it. Every woman knows when a man wants her. The impossible had happened. Svengali had fallen for Trilby. Even more impossible was what she now felt for him. His language, his brashness and less endearing mannerisms no longer bothered her. She rarely noticed them. Instead she had come to see the man behind the mask – strong, loyal and desperately lonely. The realization left her shaken and more than a little confused. So much so that when she did fall asleep it was to dream of Keir fighting a huge teddy bear that looked somewhat frayed at the edges.

Next day, Eric arrived, and on Monday she was back at the studio. JD went off to his office in London. On the surface nothing had changed . . . yet underneath Dawn knew things were different.

Suddenly, abruptly it seemed, filming was over. Of course, really it was neither sudden, nor abrupt – Don Masters had been working towards his objective for weeks – but for Dawn it was like falling into a vacuum. For three months her life had been so tightly organized that every minute counted. Now it had ended. After a party on the set, at which people exchanged expensive presents and even more extravagant compliments, they were gone, like a band of gypsies breaking camp and moving on. Don Masters declared 'a wrap' on the Tuesday and the next morning Dawn left Elm Tree Cottage not for the studios, but to return to London with Eric.

'I feel I'm leaving part of myself behind,' she said.

'You are, it's on film, trapped for posterity.' He grinned. 'By the way, JD wants us to go straight to the Caprice. He's laying on a celebration lunch.'

As they drove into the West End, Dawn was startled by the street decorations. She had been in a time capsule for three months, locked away from the real world. In a vague way she had known it was December, but more time had passed than she realized. It was almost Christmas!

'Good Heavens,' she whispered.

Fourteen

It was hard to believe that a whole year had passed since signing that contract. She remembered returning to Belsize Park clutching that cheque, wondering if she'd done the right thing. Now who could doubt it? Her first film would be released in the Spring. JD was already searching for her next script . . .

'Sure,' Eric agreed, 'time flies. That's what people don't understand. When *Chrysalis* comes out they'll call you an overnight success. They'd never believe the years of work that go into making a star.'

'The whole of my life,' Dawn said softly, more to herself than to Eric.

Some of the material rewards for such dedication came over lunch. Harvey presented her with a folder containing pages of itemized figures. She was solvent. At least she was solvent on paper. Her earnings from *Chrysalis* just about cleared what she owed JD. There was no surplus. JD still had to bankroll her until her next film. Even so, Dawn was delighted to know he had recovered his initial investment. Meanwhile, she had bought the lease for her flat and everything in it. The whole lot was hers, all bought and paid for. She had met her bills for a year. She was an independent young woman on her way to a fortune.

'I don't know if I'm happier for you or me,' she laughed, clutching JD's hand.

'Be happy for all of us.' He waved a hand round the table. 'We're all happy for you.'

And so they celebrated. They would have made a day of it had JD not been leaving for the airport. 'I gotta go to Paris for a couple of days. Clementeau starts filming in four weeks.'

'Oh?' said Eric. 'Will you be back for Christmas?'

'Christmas?' He sounded flabbergasted. 'Jesus, I'll only be a couple of days. When's Christmas anyway?'

'End of next week. I was thinking of taking some time off.'

JD was shaking his head in bewilderment. 'Where does all the time go? Another year. Christmas already!' He checked his watch and pushed his chair back from the table. 'I gotta go. Sure, take some time off if you like. You know what's scheduled. I'll call you from Paris tonight, okay?'

They all stood up, everyone saying goodbye at once. Pamela rushed off to make sure a cab was waiting while JD kissed Dawn on the cheek. 'I'd forgotten all about Christmas,' he confessed. He grinned, as usual holding her by her shoulders. A year ago she would have seen only the confident mask. Now she saw the loneliness in his eyes and heard the anxious note in his voice when he asked, 'Are you going away to somewhere exciting?'

She shook her head. 'I'd forgotten Christmas too. There's been so much on my mind. I expect I'll just visit friends. What will you do?'

He shrugged. 'Same as usual. Sit with my feet up and read through some scripts. I got a whole pile in the office –'

Pamela returned at that moment. 'You'll miss that flight, JD,' she said urgently.

Next minute he was on his way out of the door, with Pamela one pace behind him. As she watched him go, Dawn caught herself wondering when she would see him again.

JD's departure broke up the party. After another coffee, Harvey went back to the office and Eric drove Dawn round to her flat.

'It feels like the end of term,' she said as he helped her in with her luggage. She disliked the feeling. Still wound-up from film making, she was still on a high of excitement. Everyone rushing off from her party had created an anti-climax. For the first time in a year, she felt alone. JD had gone off to Paris.

Eric was talking about going away not just for Christmas but for New Year as well. He was going to St Moritz with his boyfriend. 'Grab a rest while you can, that's my motto,' he said, following her from one room to another as they inspected the flat. 'You haven't had a break since we started. You'll learn. That's how it is in this business. Why not go to Spain to see your mother?'

Dawn tried to imagine it. What fun, to waltz in, the picture of elegance in her little black Worth, to talk airily of *Chrysalis*. To boast about going to Hollywood, to gloat and to name drop: *'As I was saying to Laurence Harvey only last week . . .'*

No, she wouldn't be going to Spain for Christmas. She had not heard from her mother. Not even a postcard. Once or twice she had been tempted to write, laying it on with a trowel – *'I'm thinking of buying a place in Switzerland . . . and a yacht at Antibes'* – but of course she had done nothing of the sort. She hadn't written at all. Much wiser, she had decided, to let a sleeping bitch lie.

'Take a holiday,' Eric urged. 'Go somewhere exciting for Christmas.'

Go where? With whom? In the course of the year she had met a lot of people without making many friends. JD and Eric were her friends. Harvey too. She would have included Pamela except Pamela had been very frosty over lunch, jealous because JD had stayed at the cottage. Silly cow, Dawn thought impatiently, I could have told her it was all perfectly innocent.

'You're not wasting Christmas with your friends in the suburbs,' said Eric accusingly.

She had told him a bit about the Milfords, a strictly edited version, enough to explain vaguely where she went most Sundays. Very vaguely. The version Eric had been given made the Milfords sound like an uncle and aunt.

He left shortly afterwards. Dawn suspected that he wanted to get back to his place to phone his boyfriend about St Moritz. His departure made her feel deserted, which she knew was unfair. Eric looked after her like a mother hen. He was entitled to a life of his own. Even so, knowing that didn't help. She still felt deserted. For once even her luxurious apartment failed to comfort her. Usually she could sit and purr like a cat, admiring her possessions. But Elm Tree cottage had altered her concept of luxury. Elm Tree cottage had a housekeeper and staff. More importantly she'd had company, she'd not been alone. The odd thing was that loneliness had not bothered her before. One way or another, she'd been alone most of her life . . .

Suddenly she was seized by an overwhelming desire to see Elizabeth. Waiting until Sunday was out of the question. Besides she had no need to wait. With Eric and JD away, she could go in the morning . . .

She left in a hurry, rushing from the flat to the shops, reminded of how carefully she had bought presents the previous year. She felt no such restraint this time. What was more, she

201

was shopping for Elizabeth's birthday present as well as for Christmas. Squeezing through the crush of late afternoon shoppers, Dawn went from store to store and from counter to counter. She bought the pink-cheeked, flaxen-haired doll in Harrods and the assistant was just placing the china figure in a blue and gold gift box when Dawn saw the teddy bear. Golden brown with eyes the colour of treacle, one of his ears was bent forward, giving him exactly the same bruised look that she had come to associate with JD. 'I'll take him as well,' she said, delighted.

The following morning, loaded with gifts, she caught an early train to Hillingdon.

Elizabeth was thriving. 'How you've grown,' Dawn enthused, picking her up, thoroughly excited about seeing her again.

The Milfords were also in a state of excitement. Keir was coming home on leave. 'He'll be here for Christmas,' Edith announced.

'That's right,' said Joe grinning happily. 'Are you coming too?'

Edith shot him a poisonous look. Despite Dawn's generous gifts, Edith still affected a coolness towards her. Looking forward to spending Christmas with Joe and Keir around the family hearth, Edith was hesitant about sharing it with Dawn. Feminine intuition warned her that there was no telling what would happen if her son started seeing a lot of Dawn. 'I'm not sure that you can stay here,' she said bluntly. 'There won't be the room.'

'Oh, I don't know,' Joe countered. 'Keir will have to sleep on the couch anyway. Dawn can sleep with the baby like last Christmas.'

Edith sniffed and gave a little shrug of feigned indifference.

All in all, it was an unsatisfactory visit. Dawn was delighted to find Elizabeth looking so well, but she had hoped for a warmer welcome from the Milfords. After having made *Chrysalis*, she was bursting with news. Joe listened to some of her stories, but Edith was as dismissive as ever. She even expressed a dislike of Laurence Harvey – 'He seems a bit smarmy to me. Not like Stewart Granger. Why don't you make a film with him, he's a *proper* film star he is.'

Even Joe was more interested in talking about a meeting he had attended. 'You should have seen the crowd. There must have been five hundred at least. I tell you, Dawn, a lot of people agree with me about these H-bombs . . .'

The truth was that they were busy with their own lives. Most of all, they were excited about Keir returning home: 'Won't it be good to see him again,' Joe kept saying.

Dawn agreed. It *would* be good to see Keir again. She was disappointed that he hadn't written to her. More than a month had passed since his last letter. Perhaps he had lost interest? Perhaps he had found someone else? A German girl perhaps?

After returning to her empty flat, Dawn was plagued by a fit of the blues. She had such big news and no one to talk to. Her feelings of isolation worsened when Eric telephoned. He had spoken to JD in Paris – 'Everything's fixed. Tony's coming up from Bath in the morning, and we're flying to St Moritz . . .' He was so full of his plans, so excited that Dawn couldn't help being pleased for him. She *was* pleased for him. Even so, she went to bed feeling depressed. Christmas gaped ahead like an undisguised yawn.

Luckily, things took a turn for the better next morning. A letter from Keir arrived. Mailed ten days before, it had been delayed in the Christmas post. Several pages long, it was full of news. He had been promoted and posted to Paris, specifically to SHAPE – which apparently stood for Supreme Headquarters, Allied Powers in Europe. Even in his letter, his excitement shone through: '. . . *the whole concept of NATO will be enlarged in the next couple of years . . . of course I'm only a small cog in a big wheel, this place is stuffed with top brass . . . even so it's a thrill to be involved . . . I see NATO as another step in the unification of Europe . . .'*

Dawn's spirits revived as she read the letter. Smiling, she wondered how many young men would think about politics when arriving in Paris. Thankfully his letter was not all about NATO.

'. . . *in Germany half the men in the unit had your picture pinned on their lockers . . . they wouldn't believe that I know you . . . now Dad says you're making a film. How fantastic! I always said you were a marvellous actress . . . I'm so proud of you . . .'*

He went on to write about his forthcoming leave:

'*I arrive on the seventeenth . . . I can't wait to see you again . . .*

203

so much has happened, we'll have a million things to tell each other . . .'

Reading the letter reminded her of how much she missed him. She wished he was there at that moment. She could tell him all about *Chrysalis*. He would *really* be interested. She could share her triumph with him as with no one else. He was always so pleased for her. Perhaps that's why she was so fond of him. Thinking about it, Keir, and of course Elizabeth, were more important to her than anyone in the world.

The telephone rang, interrupting her thoughts. She answered it with Keir's letter still in her hand and was amazed and delighted when he came on the line. 'Dawn? Hi, it's me. I'm home. I got in late last night, surprised everyone . . .'

He certainly surprised her. She had only just realized that today was the seventeenth.

'I'm only here for twelve days,' he was saying, 'so we've got to get things organized for Christmas. Can we have dinner tonight?'

She tried to imagine Edith's face. Edith would be furious, especially as he went on, 'Why don't I come up to your place at about seven? Tell me how to find it and I'll pick you up and we'll go on from there.'

Only when she put the phone down, five minutes later, did she realize she was breaking her rules. Determined to avoid any overlap in her two lives, she tried to keep people in their separate compartments. In her excitement she had forgotten the need to keep her two worlds apart.

She did not worry for long – after all, JD was in Paris, Eric would be on his way to St Moritz and Pamela was unlikely to call after her frosty manner on Wednesday.

Reassured, Dawn spent the rest of the day getting ready. There was a slightly musty smell about the flat from being shut up for so long. Opening windows, she turned up the heating, dusted and hoovered and polished.

In the afternoon she had her hair done and by early evening she was ready. Casting a last approving look around the sitting-room, she felt her rising excitement. Keir had saved Christmas, which had threatened to be perfectly awful. Now, with him home, they could do things together. He was right – they did have a million things to tell each other.

Ten minutes later, he rang the bell. She was at the fridge, filling the ice bucket. Wiping her hands, she hurried to the door, and there he was – taller than she remembered, and looking older and polished in his uniform. He'd even grown a smart military moustache that made him the image of Errol Flynn.

No two people were ever more pleased to see each other. After extricating themselves from each other's arms, he stood back to look at her – praising her hair and her dress and the way she looked. Then he stared round at the flat. Clearly impressed, he couldn't wait to be shown round. 'Fabulous,' he kept saying, admiring the sofas from Heal's and the paintings on the walls and the deep pile of the carpets. 'I didn't expect anything like this. It's just like the films!'

The grand tour lasted fully thirty minutes. He saw every room and admired every object; so it took her a while to get him settled with a drink in his hand.

'This place must have cost a fortune,' he said, an odd look in his eye.

She laughed, feeling unexpectedly embarrassed. 'Enough about me,' she said. 'Tell me about this new posting to Paris.'

He was his old self then. The odd look vanished and he was just like the Keir she knew, except that talking about the army made him sound very adult. *Lieutenant* Keir Milford. The serious, earnest-faced boy had grown up into a serious, earnest-faced man. It was easy to understand why he was doing so well. His qualities of reliability, responsibility and trustworthiness were tailormade for the army.

Light-hearted with happiness, Dawn was as pleased with his accomplishments as she was of her own. They were both making a success of their lives. 'Isn't it funny how things have worked out?' she said, replenishing his glass at the sideboard. 'I mean, neither of us thought we'd be doing what we're doing. You becoming an officer and me making films. It's not what we imagined –'

'It is for Dusty. I had a letter last week. He's still in New York in the advertising business.'

The blood rushed to her face. She cursed under her breath, knowing she should have been prepared for Dusty's name to crop up. It always did with Keir. He never could go five minutes without mentioning Dusty.

205

'He loves New York. He's making a pot of money by the sound of it.'

She had turned away to hide her flushed face. Suddenly, a frightening thought made her swing back. 'You haven't told him about Elizabeth?'

Keir looked startled. 'No, we've only written a couple of –'

'Well you mustn't. Not ever. Do you understand? I want you to promise.'

He stared, taken aback.

'Promise,' she insisted.

'Okay, but –'

All her fears returned. For a split-second she wondered if her own reaction had given her away. Her excuses came quickly, each word falling glibly from her lips. 'I'd be finished in the film business if people found out about Elizabeth. A breath of scandal now and everything I've worked for –'

'Dusty's not in the film business.'

'That doesn't matter. One word in the wrong place and some muck-raking reporter could get hold of it. You dealt with the press in Germany, you know what they're like . . .' She launched into an account of the way Ingrid Bergman was hounded after her affair with Rossellini; how the press pilloried her about her illegitimate baby, how the film-makers shunned her.

'Amazing,' he said.

She told him of other actresses who'd been denied work for similar reasons. She even said that JD would tear up her contract.

Surprised, he said he hadn't realized the extent of the problem. 'Naturally, I'll do whatever you want,' he promised. 'I won't say a word.'

Reassured, and not wanting to make too much of it, she went back to pouring his drink and was on the point of changing the subject when he said, 'Even so, aren't you getting over excited? After all, Dusty's in New York –'

'I'm going to New York,' she said quickly. 'In the spring,' she continued, handing him his glass. 'Isn't it exciting?'

Instead of looking excited, Keir looked distinctly alarmed. 'How long for?'

'I'm not sure, JD's still fixing everything up. But who knows?

We're going on to Hollywood. If we get a film it could be six months, maybe longer –'

'Six months!' he said, with undisguised dismay.

'It could be. Why, what's the matter?'

'Six months,' he repeated, looking very serious. 'I think we ought to talk about that.'

She stared, quite baffled.

'What about Elizabeth?' he asked.

'Oh, I see. Naturally I'll miss her like mad –'

'But you'd still go?' he said with mounting agitation. 'Sometimes I wonder if you miss her at all. You even forgot her birthday –'

'I was making a film –'

'Mum says you've hardly called since September.'

'I was at Pinewood. She knew while I was working –'

'Oh, we all know about your work,' he said with unmistakable sarcasm.

She would not have felt more hurt had he slapped her. Scarcely able to believe what she was hearing, her excited pleasure at seeing him began to evaporate.

He rose to his feet with sudden impatience and walked over to the window before turning to face her. 'It's just that, well . . . you're not behaving very responsibly, are you?'

She stared at him. His manner suggested that it was distasteful to find fault, but having done so he had to go on.

'This is all very well,' he said, waving a hand at the room. 'It's luxurious, I said so. And there's nothing wrong with you having a career, but surely the baby comes first? I mean you can't go gadding off to America for six months. You must see that?'

The only thing she could see at that moment was Keir, behaving like a pig, spoiling everything.

'After all,' he continued, 'you told me you'd return to the theatre. You said you'd see the baby every week –'

'It didn't work out.'

'Exactly.' He nodded, as if he understood and was about to explain. 'That's where it's all gone wrong. It's got out of hand. I come home to find that Mum's invented some cock and bull story about you being a widow. The neighbours think you go round the country demonstrating things in stores. No one knows who you really are –'

'I explained why things have to be kept quiet –'

'But where's it all leading?' he asked in a long-suffering voice. 'We must be sensible. Elizabeth will be two next year. Then three. Once she starts playing with other kids –'

'I'll have made other arrangements by then.'

'You said that before. A bigger flat and a Nanny, that's what you said. What's wrong with this place, it's big enough –'

'Your parents *like* having Elizabeth!' Dawn cried, beginning to wonder if she was having a bad dream. This couldn't really be happening.

'They do,' Keir agreed. 'They're potty about her. Me too, I think she's adorable, but you must be responsible about this. You're trying to have the impossible. Elizabeth *and* a career –'

Dawn's amazement gave way to temper. 'Oh! Isn't that just like a man! That's typical that is. For a woman it's always got to be one or the other. Why? Things work fine as they are. And don't you *dare* say I'm not responsible. I earn enough to support myself and my daughter –'

'But you're living a lie –'

'I'm living my life. In the real world. It's complicated and difficult and full of bloody problems, but I don't need your advice on how to run it!'

The words were out before she could stop them. She hadn't meant to be so brutal, hadn't meant to swear, but suddenly her excitement at seeing him vanished.

Flushed with temper, stung by her words, Keir lashed back. 'Whose advice do you take then? JD's, I suppose. All I've heard since I got here is JD this, JD that –'

'He's my manager. Of course I take his advice. He's done more for my career –'

'Oh, you and your blasted career. You're obsessed with it. Don't you ever think of anything else? Think about other people for a change. What about me? What about the baby? My parents do more for her –'

'I *pay* them –'

'They don't want your money,' he said, sounding shocked.

'They'd miss it. Thanks to my money your mother doesn't have to stand at that counter all day. They benefit as well you know. So don't you lecture me about my responsibilities.'

Colour drained from his face. He struggled to find his voice. 'Are you saying I neglect my parents?'

'I'm saying I support my own daughter –'

'Our daughter, not yours!' he shouted. 'Will you get that into your head? *Our* daughter. *Our* responsibility. It's bad enough me being away all the time without you going away too.'

'I'm living my life –'

'And how? Look at this flat. You must think I'm a complete fool. It's pretty obvious why you don't want her here. She'd get in your way –'

Her arm swept up and she slapped his face with all the force she could muster. 'How dare you!' she shrieked. 'How dare you come here –'

Rocked back on his heels, Keir recovered and took a step forward. The anger in his face triggered off a memory. She saw herself back at Belsize Park with him coming through the door. Suddenly she panicked. 'Get away from me!' she screamed. 'Get away! Don't you dare touch me!' Whirling round, she grabbed the table lighter and stood poised to throw it. 'Get away! Get out of my flat!'

He stared. The mark of her hand was livid on his white face. Then, shaking with temper he turned on his heel, snatching his cap from the chair.

'Get out!' she shrieked after him.

Next moment, the door crashed behind him.

Trembling uncontrollably, she hugged herself, trying to stop shaking. Her limbs refused to obey. Weeping without any idea of when the tears started, she struggled to believe what had happened. All day long she had looked forward to seeing him. She had been so pleased . . .

Crossing the room on wobbly legs, she flopped into a chair, her ears buzzing with the sounds of their argument, her cheeks wet and grubby from tears and mascara. *How could they have said such terrible things to each other?* Clutching herself, she rocked back and forward on the chair, unable to think.

It was fully ten minutes before she recovered enough to go to the bathroom. Dazed, she bathed her face and returned to the room, shaking her head, bewildered by what had gone wrong.

Temper set her going again. How *dare* he come in here, laying down the law . . . ! Then the tears started again.

When she had stopped weeping and was on her hands and knees, searching for the pack of cigarettes dropped during the row, feeling wretched and miserable, she was reminded, for some confused reason, of a press release written by Ray Cox – 'Dawn Wharton, Britain's most sought-after young actress.' 'Sought after,' she muttered bitterly. 'That's a laugh.' She felt more alone than at any time since Gran died.

The telephone rang. Too weary to rise, she dragged it down to the floor to answer.

'Hi, Princess!'

'JD!' Her eyes shone. She clung to the phone like a lifeline.

'I thought I'd call to say Happy Christmas in case you decided to go away after all.'

'I'm not going anywhere. I *hate* Christmas.'

He started to laugh. 'You too? Know something? Even as a kid I hated Christmas.'

She giggled, suddenly light-hearted. 'I did too. No, really. I stopped believing in Christmas when my Gran died . . .'

He was still in Paris. 'Are you really spending Christmas alone?' he wanted to know.

'Sure I'm alone,' she said, feeling like weeping again.

'You know the best time in Paris? Spring, when all the chestnut trees are out. We could pretend it was spring if you came over.'

She caught her breath.

'Correction,' he said. 'I wouldn't need to pretend; for me, it *would* be spring.'

'Really?' she said huskily, her eyes shining.

An hour later she was packing her bag.

210

BOOK THREE

—————◆—————

Keir and Joe

One

The argument with Dawn left Keir feeling shattered. He had been counting the hours to the reunion. A blazing row was the last thing he had expected. He would never have believed it possible, but Dawn's luxurious apartment had unsettled him, arousing suspicions. Her talk of JD was alarming. She was so obviously fond of the man, was it any wonder Keir had become jealous? On top of which was this business of going to Hollywood. She seemed to be excluding him from her life. Shutting him out. Her career had developed in a way he had not expected. If only she would stay in London, work on the West End stage, see the baby every week . . . in time she would adapt to the idea of motherhood and marriage. But *Hollywood*! Hollywood would take her away, make her more unattainable than ever!

After brooding for a day, Keir had telephoned Dawn. The lack of a reply had been yet another bitter disappointment. Where had she gone? He could do nothing except wait to hear from her. So he had spent a gloomy Christmas hoping that the phone would ring. It never did. His disappointment had turned to fury. Dawn's angry words festered at the back of his mind. Her assertions about *her* money wounded his pride, making him feel less of a man.

'I'll show her,' he vowed. 'Damn it, I've chased after her long enough.'

For the first time in his life he wanted success. Success with a capital S, success with power and influence, he wanted to be *someone*. He wanted people to look up to him . . . 'And then she'll come running to me!' As angry thoughts chased around his brain, Keir ached for a future in which Dawn would want to get married so much that she would ask him. 'By God,' he said, 'I'll make it happen.'

As Keir discussed Elizabeth with his parents, he told them, 'From now on, I'll pay for everything. You're not to take a penny from Dawn.'

213

They argued. It seemed senseless to them for their son to beggar himself to match what Dawn could so obviously afford. But Keir was adamant. Without explaining to his parents, he saw Elizabeth as the key to the future. If he kept Elizabeth, he would obtain Dawn. And after all, Dawn could not take Elizabeth away from the Milfords. Where would she take her? To Hollywood? That seemed unlikely. She was terrified that people might find out about the baby . . . and if she tried to find her another home, Keir could threaten to talk to the press. 'She wouldn't dare risk it,' was his eventual conclusion. Dawn had no option but to leave Elizabeth at the Milfords.

Joe had the good sense to take charge. Even before his son returned to Germany, Joe realized that although the heat created by the row would soon cool, to unravel their tangled lives would take longer. Confirmation came with Dawn's first visit after Christmas.

'However long will you be in Hollywood?' Edith asked Dawn.

'A year, possibly longer.'

Edith didn't mind in the least. More concerned about keeping Elizabeth, Edith cared nothing for Dawn. 'She can stay in Hollywood for good as far as I'm concerned,' she told Joe.

But Joe had taken a liking to Dawn. Her grit and determination appealed to him. So he wished her success and told her not to worry about Elizabeth, and he did something else – he made her promise to write to Keir. 'I know you had an argument,' he said, 'but if you write and say sorry, he'll say the same. You'll forget whose fault it was, and get on with your lives without harbouring bitterness.'

Consequently, Dawn wrote Keir the longest letter of her life, full of regrets about their silly quarrel, and he responded by return of post, exactly as Joe had predicted. The rift was mended again; not that Dawn or Keir changed their plans. She sailed for New York at the end of February and went from there on to Hollywood. Keir set about building a career in the army.

As for the financial arrangement, ignoring his promise to Keir, Joe said not a word to Dawn about money. Instead, he opened a bank account in Elizabeth's name and paid Dawn's money in there when it arrived every quarter. Meanwhile, Keir paid the bills, just as he had demanded he should.

'I don't like the idea of him going short,' said Edith.

'He can manage,' said Joe. 'He wrote and said so, didn't he. And it's right for a young man to face up to things, it builds character. Being a bit short never did anyone much harm. It's the only way to learn the value of money.'

Knowing the value of money made Joe realize how lucky he was. Trade in the shop had been increasing steadily. Fewer items were rationed. People were spending a bit extra. Better than paying its way, the shop was showing a nice little profit. Joe was really quite comfortably off. For the first time in his life, he didn't actually have to work for a living.

'Well, I'm blowed,' he said in wonder. 'Joe Milford, you're a bloody capitalist.'

The thought was so extraordinary it took a while to get used to the idea. But it was true. His staff could manage without his help. In fact, they managed *better*. Mrs Roberts was a natural shopkeeper. She loved the life. Where Joe was forever running out of some items, Mrs Roberts never ran out of anything.

A different man might have thought of expansion – get one shop going, then another, until a whole chain spanned the skyline – but such a thought never entered Joe's head. His need was for more time, not for more money.

Edith was alarmed. 'Retire? At your age? It wouldn't be right, you not working. Besides, I don't want you under my feet all day.'

Joe had no intention of getting under anyone's feet. Neither did he plan to retire, although as far as the shop was concerned 'an hour a day, that's all it needs from me. I'll offer Mrs Roberts a bit extra and ask her to become manager,' he decided.

Which was what happened, and after that, except for busy Bank Holidays, Joe was never in the shop for more than an hour a day.

'So what will you do with yourself?' Edith demanded.

'Read,' said Joe. 'I've got a lot of reading to do.'

Emlyn Hughes brought batches of books from the library and Joe read them one after the other.

'All that reading's bad for your eyes,' Edith grumbled. 'Anyway, who do you think you are? Some college professor or something?'

Impervious to her sarcasm, Joe gave her a good-natured grin.

'You don't have to be a professor to want to know what you're talking about.'

He read everything he could find about the bombs dropped on Hiroshima and Nagasaki at the end of the war. He studied photographs of the victims, those killed outright and others who died long, lingering deaths from radiation sickness. He read about the babies born to surviving mothers: deformed babies, mentally retarded babies, some already developing the cancers and leukaemia that would end their young lives. He waded through eyewitness accounts and medical reports, and was appalled at man's inhumanity to man. But what frightened him most was the realization that the bombs dropped on Japan had been superseded by weapons a hundred times worse.

In the evenings, he took his newly gained knowledge down to the pub. 'These H-bombs aren't weapons of war,' he told Bob Cooper during one of their discussions. 'They're weapons of mass destruction. They threaten mankind's very survival.'

In Joe's view, H-bombs were wicked. The slaughter of millions of innocent people could never be justified, no matter what the circumstances. Some people disagreed of course. They said Britain should have H-bombs as a deterrent. According to them, H-bombs made Britain as powerful as Russia.

'Nonsense,' said Joe. 'We haven't got huge spaces like Russia. We're a tiny island. Ten H-bombs would kill eighty per cent of our population and leave the rest injured and dying. Ten H-bombs on Russia would still leave vast areas untouched. The same applies to the States. They're big countries, with their populations spread across huge areas, not crammed into a little island. Having H-bombs doesn't make us equal. It makes us the easiest target in the world.'

Joe rarely stopped talking about the subject. While his main objection was on moral grounds, he was always ready to argue against the military case. 'There *isn't* a military case that makes sense,' he would say hotly. 'If a conventional war broke out, there would be a chance to halt the fighting, but not with these H-bombs. The first thing an enemy would do would be to stop us using them. Stands to reason. Experts say we could expect Russian planes overhead in four minutes. *Four minutes!* Remember the Blitz? The sky was black with planes and most of them reached their target. They only need to drop ten bombs this time and we're finished, finished for good . . .'

Wheeling himself around the streets close to the shop, he found many people as worried as he was. Especially when the British began testing H-bombs on Christmas Island in the Pacific. 'Christmas Island,' said Joe mournfully. 'What a terrible thing to do to a place called Christmas Island.'

Outrage prompted him to question things he had accepted before. He had always believed that Britain was the most democratic country in the world. It made him proud. His pride had been dented when he had been arrested by 'those little Hitlers in the Special Branch', but he had retained respect for the system. The British parliamentary system was the best there was. Everyone knew that. 'Kids are taught that at school,' he used to say proudly.

But when the government announced that American Thor missiles were to be sited in East Anglia, Joe began to wonder. The matter was not debated in Parliament. Opinion polls showed that most people were opposed to having nuclear missiles sited on their soil, yet the government went ahead just the same.

'What sort of democracy is that?' an enraged Joe asked in his letters to the papers.

He wrote to more than the papers. He wrote to Prime Minister Harold Macmillan, he wrote to his local MP, he wrote to the Archbishop of Canterbury and other church leaders.

'Someone's got to do something,' he said, wishing he could do more.

But the time was not ready for Joe. The day would come when he would do very much more, but that was still in the future. Meanwhile, months slipped past to become years, proving Keir right about one thing. Elizabeth remained at the Milfords. She lived with Grandad and Grandma, whom she grew to love very much. Everything had been explained to her. Mummy had to work a long way away in a place called America, and although too busy to write many letters, she never let a birthday or Christmas pass without sending some wonderful present. As did her Uncle Keir, who not only sent presents, but wrote once a month.

*

Keir applied himself as never before in the army. His self-discipline was awesome. His posting to Paris, to SHAPE – Supreme Headquarters, Allied Powers in Europe – put him at the centre of things. Every day he mixed with his foreign counterparts in NATO. With his quick ear for languages he soon added passable Italian and Greek to his fluent German and French. He worked hard and yet was liked well enough for people not to envy him his various promotions.

As for his father's views about H-bombs, they scarcely impinged on Keir's life. He rarely went home on leave and avoided the subject in his letters. Instead he asked about Edith and Liz, as Elizabeth was now called, and wrote of the places he was seeing.

Meanwhile, he followed Dawn's career from afar. *The Chrysalis* was a big success when it was released in 1957. In Britain it broke box-office records and without doing quite so well in the States, did well enough for Dawn to be nominated for an Oscar. She failed to win, it went that year to Joanne Woodward for *The Three Faces of Eve*, but the nomination itself was enough to make people sit up and take notice.

Yet Dawn's letters suggested she hated Hollywood:

'Everyone acts so scared, what with McCarthy's witch hunt and television affecting the number of people who go to the movies – you'd think they'd be happy with their super homes and gigantic swimming pools, but take it from me few of them are. And they're such snobs. Worse than in England. The studio's press agent is always telling me what to do and what not to do. I don't mean about acting. I mean who I can play tennis with, whose swimming pool I can be seen in, all that sort of thing. JD had a furious row with him and we haven't seen him for a while, but I guess he'll be back. JD says we've got to put up with it for the sake of good relations with the Studio . . .'

Keir had come to accept JD. Finding out that he was fifty-five helped. And Dawn's other friend, someone called Eric, was a bloody queer! Keir found it very reassuring, telling himself that 'she can't come to much harm with an old man and a poof'.

The other encouraging thing was that she never talked of settling in Hollywood. Her letters were full of references to 'when I come home'. All of this helped him accept the situation. Meanwhile, he worked flat-out on his own career, determined to become *someone*. He soon decided that the real NATO was different from the one portrayed in the papers. According to the press, the sole function of NATO was to counter any Russian aggression. Keir was quick to see other reasons. One was that the French were still nervous of the Germans, especially since the Germans had been allowed to re-arm. Quite simply, the French felt more secure with the British and American troops stationed in Europe. And the Germans relied on the Americans to tell the French to stop worrying. Whereas the British liked American troops on the spot so that if anything did happen America would be involved from the start. Meanwhile the Americans worked on the theory that trade follows the flag, and the presence of their troops was a help to their burgeoning commercial interests.

NATO suited them all. None of this bothered Keir. Far from making him cynical, the concept of mutual dependence appealed to his idealism. NATO was a 'Good Thing' he decided, just as the Common Market was another 'Good Thing'. He was disappointed when Britain failed to become one of the founder members. 'We must join as soon as possible,' he wrote to his father. 'Imagine the benefits. It's the first step towards a United States of Europe.'

He so obviously believed in what he was doing that he acquired a reputation for being pro-European among his colleagues at SHAPE. The French liked him because, unlike most Englishmen, he spoke French like a Frenchman. The Germans like him because he was always punctual and never went back on his word. The Americans liked the way he was forever praising their efforts in Europe.

By 1958, Captain Keir Milford was popular enough among his colleagues for them to overlook the fact that he was invariably hard-up. He rarely joined them for a night on the town. Supporting Liz left him short of cash, although he had quite enough for his needs. He was a non-smoker and only drank moderately, unlike some whose private incomes allowed them to drink a month's service pay in a week. As for women, he scarcely met any, what with being stationed in a foreign country and not mixing much with the civilian population. Besides, he was always working. If he wasn't studying a new language, he was standing in for a colleague, for Keir was always the first to be asked when someone wanted to get away for a weekend.

According to a senior officer who knew him well, 'Keir Milford really grew up at the end of the fifties. His duties compelled him to face issues and take decisions. He even became a bit of a diplomat.'

Diplomacy was essential to overcome outbursts of national pride. The French were the worst, forever going on about past glories. 'France is the light of the world,' a French colleague was fond of saying.

'Is that so?' would come a Texan drawl. 'So how come Edison was American?'

Keir would peg away, convinced that cooperation was in everyone's best interests. Too junior to be involved in policy, most of his work was liaison. It wasn't easy. Even in NATO, national pride was often at stake.

'Our way is best,' people would say. Even 'our equipment is best'. Keir was appalled to learn that NATO armies used fourteen different types of small-arms ammunition. The Russians used only one. 'It's crazy,' he argued. 'Combined operations would be much easier if we standardized.' But standardization meant the French adopting the British system, or vice versa, or both of them having to accept a new German idea. Arguments were unending, but Keir rarely lost patience.

He travelled to places that would have remained mere names on a map except for the army. His duties took him to Rome and Athens, and cities as far apart as Ankara and Reykjavik. In time he became more conversant with the streets of Brussels and Amsterdam than those of London – and wherever he went NATO colleagues were on hand to greet him. It was like a global freemasonry. Keir was introduced around one Officers' Club after another, in country after country, until eventually be began to think himself more as a European than merely British.

In May 1959, he was promoted to major. SHAPE was so full of colonels and brigadiers and oak-leafed generals that even major was small beer, but he was pleased with the extra rank and the money that went with it.

By the following January he was being encouraged to make the army his permanent career. It some ways the suggestion was tempting. After all, he did like the army. He had done well. He enjoyed the life. But one of the snags was that his next promotion would mean being posted. His gift for languages and the skill he showed in dealing with his European colleagues had already extended his tour of duty with NATO. Now it was a case of, 'We hate to lose you, old boy, but it's in your own interests to be posted.' Signing on for another five years would mean being sent beyond Europe to see service in Cyprus or some other outpost of Empire.

He didn't much believe in the Empire. India, Burma, Egypt had gone; the whole lot would go soon. It was 'the wind of change'. He didn't resent it. Like his father, he thought self-government a 'Good Thing' for the emerging nations. However, unlike his father, he did believe in NATO. In his opinion a strong NATO preserved the balance of power, a strong NATO helped maintain peace in the world. It was important, worth doing. By comparison, quelling rebellion in some sun-scorched outpost of Empire seemed a complete waste of time.

And then there was Dawn to consider. Her letters continued to suggest a yearning for home. Whether that also meant a yearning for him was hard to say. It was a tantalizing thought, and there was enough in her letters to encourage it. He sensed that she was sometimes confused about what she wanted most from life, but he did nothing to push the issue. Dawn was deep into what she called her 'Hollywood period' by then. *Gateway to Heaven* was followed by *The O'Brien Girl* in '58 and *The Wiseman Scandal* in '59. Keir saw them all and although he never said so, all three of them disappointed him. Not a patch on *The Chrysalis* which had been a much stronger story. Sarah Brewster was a determined young woman, just the sort Dawn could play well, whereas it seemed to him that Hollywood was trying to turn her into a vision of sweetness and light.

So he had much to consider when it was suggested that he stay on in the army . . . and he was turning it all over in his mind when he received a letter from Dusty. Usually Dusty sent a card every Christmas and little in between. Keir was more diligent, writing at least two letters a year, updating Dusty on how he was doing. He had learned little about Dusty's life except that he worked for an advertising agency called Owen Lacey. Now it became clear that Dusty had done well, very well indeed.

221

'. . . to begin with the big news. I'm coming back to London in March, to head up Owen Lacey's operation in Europe . . .'

There was a lot in the letter about Europe becoming '*a consumer market to equal the States*' and jargon like '*increased awareness of branded products*' most of which passed over Keir's head. It was the final page which gripped him.

'. . . *you wrote saying you'd probably sign on for another five years. Hold that decision until we meet. I always said we'd work together. Funny how things work out, but what with you in NATO and me doing my stint over here, we couldn't have prepared ourselves better for what I have in mind . . . it will earn us a fortune . . .*'

Dusty had added a postscript:

'*I arrive on March 19 aboard the SS* United States *and will stay at the Savoy until I find something permanent. Can you meet me in London that week? If not I'll try to get over to Paris. Either way DO NOT, repeat DO NOT, sign on for another term until we've had a chance to talk.*'

Keir read the letter three times. Although pleased and excited, he couldn't imagine what Dusty meant by them working together. He knew nothing about advertising. Even so, it would be a tonic to see Dusty again . . .

Two

To save money, Keir had used most of his leave passes to see Europe, so his return was quite an occasion. He arrived home like the prodigal son, bearing gifts of brandy for Joe, perfume for Edith and a dolls' house for Liz. Edith was so proud that she had to remind herself that this assured young man was really her son. He had made a success of his life. Boys along the street had grown up to be butchers and bakers and candlestick makers, but none had done as well as 'our Keir'.

For Keir, it was as if nothing had changed. Even the spicy smell in the shop was the same. True, the rooms seemed a shade smaller and his parents a bit older, but that was to be expected.

He had grown older himself. The one surprise was Liz, who had acquired charm as well as inches. Bowled over, Keir couldn't look at her without bursting with pride. He took her to the zoo one day and to a Walt Disney film on the next. 'Isn't she terrific?' he kept saying to Edith. 'I can't get over how she's grown.'

Edith laughed. 'She's been beside herself waiting for you. All week long it's been "How many days before Uncle Keir comes home?" Isn't that right, Joe?'

They got on famously. The family was back together again. Edith cooked Keir's favourite meals and every evening over supper he regaled them with stories of Europe.

Edith was wide-eyed. 'I've lost count of the different places you've seen. And fancy you knowing so many languages. Beats me how you remember them all.'

Naturally, they wanted to know if he was going to sign on for another five years. Keir had to admit he was undecided. Making up his mind would have been easier if he could stay at SHAPE. 'But that's out of the question,' he admitted. 'I'll be posted for sure.'

They discussed Dusty's letter. Edith was very impressed. 'Staying at the Savoy,' she said. 'My word, he must have made plenty of money. I wonder what he means about making a fortune with you. Sounds good whatever it is. Just as well you stayed in touch with him. He could be ever such a good friend.'

Keir couldn't help thinking that selling corn flakes and soap powder would be dull after SHAPE.

'It won't be dull if you make a lot of money,' Edith encouraged.

'When do you have to let the army know about signing on?' asked Joe.

'When I get back. That's why I thought I'd spend this week with you and next week with Dusty. Give me a chance to think before I commit myself,' Keir said.

'It's a big decision,' Joe agreed, puffing his pipe. He was careful not to advise his son either way. 'I reckon you know what's best for you. We'll be proud of you whatever you decide, you know that.'

Keir ...d and the knowledge gave him a warm feeling. He and his father had always been close, which was why the events of Thursday evening came as a shock. Neither Keir nor Joe saw them coming. Especially that evening, that evening of all evenings. Bob Cooper and Emlyn Hughes had called round and insisted on taking Milford father and son down to the pub for a drink.

Edith was the only one shrewd enough to envisage a problem. 'Don't get arguing politics,' she warned as they went out of the door. She had banned political discussions in the house for the duration of Keir's leave. 'I don't want you spoiling things with an argument,' she told Joe beforehand. 'It's bad enough when he's away, what with you always going on about banning the bomb. You want your cake and eat it, you do. You're ever so pleased about him being a major. He wouldn't be doing so well if there wasn't an army, would he? Stands to reason an army's got to have bombs and guns and things like that.'

Joe was in a cleft stick. He was as proud of his son as a father could be, but he could never abandon his principles. He had become a member of the Campaign for Nuclear Disarmament from its inception. Emlyn and he had been at the meeting where it all started, at Central Hall, Westminster; where so many people had gathered that extra halls had to be hired at the last minute, and the speakers had dashed like a relay team from one platform to another. With thousands of others, they had listened to historian Alan Taylor describe the results of nuclear blast – the hideous destruction, the scorched bodies, and the leukaemia transmitted to unborn generations. In a passionate speech, Taylor had challenged the vast crowd. 'Knowing all these horrors,' he had cried, 'who would push the button? Let him stand up.' No one had moved. Instead, at the end of the evening, emotionally charged by speeches, a thousand of them had set off to Downing Street with a petition.

Since then Joe had organized dozens of petitions. With the faithful Emlyn pushing his wheelchair, Joe had attended hundreds of meetings. He had met doctors and scientists, physicists and biologists, gathering facts in support of his arguments. He wasn't a pacifist and neither was Emlyn. Both had been in favour of the war against Hitler. Bob had fought in the war. But nuclear bombs were different. Nuclear bombs could destroy the whole of mankind. Even to test them was evil, poisoning the earth's atmosphere with radioactive dust, spreading cancers among unsuspecting populations.

224

Joe had avoided the subject since Keir had arrived home and in all fairness steered clear of it down at the pub – it was Emlyn who raised it. 'You being in the army don't make a scrap of difference,' Emlyn told Keir. 'We're all in this, soldiers and civilians alike. We all share the same world. We breathe the same air. Everyone's got a duty to speak out against nuclear tests. They're a crime against humanity . . .'

Given such fervour, the discussion inevitably became heated.

Keir did well for the first half-hour. Patience and diplomacy developed at NATO conference tables stood him in good stead. In fact, a really bad argument would have been avoided if Bob Cooper hadn't mentioned the march. The Campaign for Nuclear Disarmament was organizing a march from the Atomic Weapons Research Establishment at Aldermaston to London. It was to take place over the four days of Easter.

'Pity you won't be here,' Bob had said grinning. 'You could come with us.'

'Us?' Keir turned questioning eyes to his father. 'It must be forty or fifty miles. You're not serious?'

'Oh yes, I am. I'm going. So're Liz and your mother.'

Keir looked at him in amazement. The idea of a cripple on a march struck him as stupid, even eccentric, but to involve a child and a middle-aged housewife was downright irresponsible. 'You can't be serious,' he said, aghast. 'Liz and Mum?'

Joe failed to read the warning signals. If he had looked harder he might have seen the outrage in his son's face. Instead he chuckled. 'You know what your mother's like. She was up in arms about me taking Liz. "If you're taking that child, I'm coming too," she said, and there's been no changing her mind ever since.'

'So don't take Liz. You must be mad even to think –'

'She's what it's all about – kids of her age. Her generation is being put at risk –'

'That's not the point,' Keir said hotly. 'She's a child, not a political slogan. She can't possibly walk all that way –'

'I'll probably carry her most of the time,' Bob interrupted to set Keir's mind at rest.

But nothing would reassure Keir. He was horrified. It was an act of madness to make a little girl endure such a hardship. The weather was bound to be awful. Easter was always cold and wet and windy.

'She'll be well wrapped up,' Joe protested. 'She won't catch cold or anything –'

'There could be violence,' Keir argued. 'You know what these things are like. The crowd could get out of control. What chance would you stand . . . an old man in a wheelchair and a child . . . you could be trampled to death!'

Bob did his best to say nothing of that sort would happen. He had been on last year's march and that had passed off peacefully enough. 'Quite a lot of young couples carried their children –'

'I don't care about them,' Keir said, by now red-faced with temper. 'They must be bloody mad. Totally irresponsible. Come to think of it, I remember seeing some photographs of last year's march. Full of layabouts and Lefties and –'

'Layabouts and Lefties!' Joe erupted. 'I'll have you know some very clever people were on that march. Scientists and doctors –'

'Bugger them,' Keir shouted furiously. 'They can do what they like, Liz isn't going within a mile of that march and that's final.'

Joe went white. His hands tightened on the arms of his invalid chair as he pushed himself upright. 'Don't you give me orders. I'm not in your army. It's for me and your mother to decide –'

'Oh, is it? We'll see about that. And as for you –' Keir swung round on Bob and Emlyn – 'You should have more sense than to encourage such a damn silly idea –'

Next minute everyone was talking at once, shouting above each other to make themselves heard. Eventually, leaving an embarrassed Emlyn and Bob in the pub, Keir and Joe went home to finish the row. Keir fairly let rip in the living-room. His father slammed back, and to Keir's vast surprise, Edith joined in, making it clear that her right to criticize Joe did not extend to anyone else, least of all to her son. 'You're getting above yourself, my boy,' she said, becoming as heated as they were. 'If Joe says we're going, we're going. Who do you think you are anyway, laying down the law? You should be ashamed of yourself, insulting his friends . . .'

After that it was all over. Having had her say, Edith was in no mood to debate the issue. She packed Joe off to bed and took herself with him, leaving Keir to simmer. He had no bedroom to go to; the room above the shop in which he had grown up now belonged to Liz, relegating him to the living-room couch.

Next morning, the atmosphere was still brittle. No one apologized. Although regretting their harsh words, Keir and Joe both thought they were in the right. The Milford stubbornness was really on show. One black-faced scowl met another. In the confined space of that tiny living-room there was a danger that the row would break out all over again. The very air was oppressive and after breakfast Keir decided it would be wisest to move up to London. He had booked himself into the Army and Navy Club for the second week of his leave, so it was merely a matter of going a day early.

'Perhaps you're right,' Edith sighed. 'Everyone needs a chance to cool down. Like you say, you were going tomorrow anyway, so it won't make a great deal of difference.' Taking his hand, she held it for a moment, smiling a peace offering. 'We all said some daft things, but everything will be forgotten by the end of the week. Dad won't hold a grudge, you know that. He thinks the world of you really. So come and see us again before you go back to Paris, won't you?'

He promised he would, as anxious to heal the rift as she was.

Even so, he was in a sorry mood as he sat on the train. He thought himself badly treated, by the world in general and his parents in particular. Liz was in their care. He relied on them to act sensibly, to bring her up properly. 'Good God,' he grumbled. 'It's bad enough with Dawn being away all the time and the burden of responsibility falling on me . . .'

The sensible thing would be to send Liz away to a good boarding school as soon as she was old enough. That's what most of his fellow officers did with their children. But boarding schools cost money. Fellow officers either had private incomes or were properly married and in receipt of army marriage allowance. Keir had neither. 'It's all a question of cash,' he muttered as the train rolled on towards London.

Thoroughly unsettled, he looked forward to booking into the Club. He would have a bed of his own for a start, and a proper bedroom. But it was more than that and he knew it. Without liking to admit it, after five years in the army, he would feel more at home there than at the shop on the corner. He could have a drink at the bar, or play a game of snooker with like-minded men, or sit and read the papers in peace. And he would have a chance to think. With Dusty due to arrive the following evening, he could use the extra day to ponder his future.

Three

The five days spent with his parents in the suburbs had not prepared Keir for the capital. London, in the Spring of 1960, was vastly different from the city he remembered. Even the skyline had changed. What once had been horizontal was now vertical. Steel and glass cliffs had pushed up between old churches; big white office blocks had replaced rows of Victorian shops, St Paul's Cathedral was surrounded by skyscrapers. Lingering traces of wartime austerity had given way to a shining new world.

Wherever Keir looked he saw change, in the people as well as the buildings. Carnaby Street had been transformed from a scruffy back alley into a centre of fashion. The decaying King's Road had turned into a cat-walk, delighting male onlookers with a ceaseless parade of long-legged girls. Keir walked from one end to the other, openly staring. At lunchtime he had a beer in a pub, listening and watching, amazed by the sure talk and the money young people were spending.

Even at the Club, he met a surprise. Leafing through the evening papers before dinner, he began to notice the ages of the men making headlines. Young tycoons, some only thirty, were amassing fortunes. Every paper had a story about *young* Mr This or *young* Mr That who was doing so well.

For Keir, pondering his future in the army, it was all very unsettling, very unsettling indeed.

An incident the next morning seemed to sum it all up. He went for a walk after breakfast. It was a fine morning and he strolled quite a way – down Piccadilly and along Knightsbridge, as far as the Albert Hall before turning into Hyde Park. The park was ablaze with spring flowers: banks of red tulips, and golden daffodils. Yet girls, more than flowers, caught Keir's eye. They

228

were everywhere – in deck chairs, on the grass, basking in the sunshine. The mini-skirt had yet to reach Paris and Rome where Keir could walk through the streets without being distracted. London was different. Distractions abounded. As he sat drinking coffee in the open-air café near the Serpentine, he was reminded of the gaps in his life. Money and girls. The two seemed to go together. As if to underline the point, a bright red sports car squealed to a halt at the side of the road. He turned to watch a young man of his own age jump out and call to three girls on the grass. They looked up, waved and rose to their feet. Next minute they were all back at the car, the girls climbing in, their skirts riding up to reveal a flash of nylon-clad thighs. And a second later they drove off, the breeze catching their hair and carrying sounds of shrill excitement back to Keir as he watched. It all added to his restlessness. The sleek little car had been a Bristol. Handmade, or so he had heard. And not one girl, but three!

'Greedy bastard,' he grumbled as he walked back to his club.

It did make him wonder if he was wasting time. He had been pleased with his progress until then. To have made major in five years was no mean achievement. He had a fine career in the army . . . but it was hardly making him rich.

By lunchtime he was so restless that he wished he had gone to Southampton to meet Dusty's boat when it docked. But it was too late to do that. If he went now they would pass each other in trains travelling in opposite directions.

There was nothing for it but to wait for Dusty to arrive at the Savoy at about seven o'clock.

To kill time, he took himself to the cinema, to see a new film that everyone was talking about. *Room at the Top* was the last straw as far as Keir was concerned. It was all about a young man on the make who ends up with a bank full of money and a bed full of girls.

Emerging into the thin sunshine of the late afternoon, Keir felt punch drunk. Everyone seemed to be making a fortune except him. Not only that, they spent their lives going to bed with glamorous women . . .

Too keyed up to give thought to the luxious surroundings, he fairly bounced along the deeply carpeted corridor at the Savoy.

Excited as a schoolboy, he chuckled, thinking they had been little more than schoolboys last time they met. Five years! It seemed a lot longer. He wondered if Dusty had changed . . .

Reaching the door he paused to straighten his tie and adjust the rake of his cap, then, grinning broadly, he rapped hard on the woodwork.

The door was opened by a blonde. Five feet eight, with smoke-grey eyes, lightly tanned skin, perfectly white teeth and a welcoming smile. 'Hi,' she said.

Keir felt a complete fool to have knocked on the wrong door.

'You've got to be Keir,' she said smiling. 'Come in. It's great to meet you at last.'

The only familiar thing about her was her dress. White, with a plunging neckline, and very expensive-looking. Keir had seen one like it two hours before. Simone Signoret had been wearing it in *Room at the Top*.

The blonde laughed at his embarrassed confusion. 'Dusty's in the tub. He won't be a minute. I'm Amanda Lacey. I've heard so much about you.'

Taking Keir's hand, she led him into a beautifully appointed sitting-room, calling out as she did so, 'Dusty! The gallant Major has arrived.'

The words had scarcely left her lips when Dusty appeared, dripping wet, a towel knotted round his waist, black hair plastered over his skull, skin glistening and steam rising from his body. 'Keir! Hey – just look at that uniform!'

All was confusion after that as they stood shaking each other's hands, holding each other's shoulders and standing there laughing. 'I can't get over that uniform. *Major* Keir Milford. Hey, you really made it, old buddy. Isn't he terrific?' Dusty grinned at the blonde. 'Didn't I tell you he was a heart-breaker? Boy oh boy! It's just great to see you again . . .'

As his hand was pumped up and down, Keir tried to assess Dusty. The voice was deeper, still British with only a faint American twang. He looked older. There was a finished look to his face. The jawline was stronger, and lines around his eyes gave him the look of someone who worked and played hard and rarely got enough sleep. Even so, the eyes still mocked, the grin was as wide, the enthusiasm as infectious.

Dusty stopped pumping Keir's arm long enough to turn to the

blonde. 'Sorry, Mandy, I'm forgetting my manners. Allow me to introduce my oldest friend, *Major* Keir Milford –'

'We already met,' she said laughing, reaching and pushing his shoulder. 'Now how about you putting some clothes –'

'Right away, I won't be a minute.' Still grinning, he turned to go, then paused with an apologetic look on his face. 'Do you think you could –?'

'Fix us a drink? That's what I was doing when Keir arrived. Now will you go and –'

Dusty ran to the door, clutching the towel, throwing a final grin at Keir as he went. 'Great to see you again, old buddy, really great!'

'Fool,' laughed the blonde.

Keir wished he knew who she was. There had been no mention of her in Dusty's letters.

'Dusty boasts I mix the best martini in Manhattan,' she said, turning to the drinks trolley.

Too awkward to say he preferred scotch, lost for small talk, Keir stared around the luxurious room before being drawn to the panoramic view of the Thames from the window.

'Will you just look at that?' she said. 'I could never tire of that view. It's got to be the best in the world.'

Certainly the most expensive, Keir reflected. Questions fell over themselves in his mind. What did a suite like this cost? Was this willowy blonde sharing it with Dusty? Did everyone except him live like Joe Lampton in *Room at the Top*?

'I'm biased, of course,' she said. 'What with being English and –'

'English?' he exclaimed in surprise.

'Don't I sound it?' She laughed. 'Sure, Manhattan will wear off in a couple of days. I'd still be here except for my first husband. He took me to the States, and then . . .' She shrugged while unscrewing the cocktail shaker and pouring the drinks. 'One thing led to another and I stayed. I guess people are more important than places. Mind you, it's ages since I've been to Paris and I've never been to Rome. Dusty says you spend half your time in Rome. That must be exciting . . .' She launched into a description of the Rome she had seen in the movies, and was still talking when Dusty returned, tucking his shirt-tail into the waistband of his trousers.

'Thanks, Mandy,' he said, accepting a glass. 'Boy, can I use this!' He paused, his eyes going to Keir. 'Here's to you two,' he said, raising the glass with a flourish. 'To my best English pal and to my best American –'

'I'm not American!' Mandy laughed. 'I was just saying that –'

'I know,' he said, drinking greedily, smacking his lips, 'but you sure mix one fine American-style martini.'

'It's very nice,' said Keir awkwardly, still trying to reconcile himself to Amanda's presence. He had thought she was in her mid-twenties when she had opened the door, now he guessed she was older. Thirty maybe, even thirty-three or so. Very attractive. And what had she said about her *first* husband? How many husbands had she had, for God's sake? And where did Dusty fit in . . .

Catching Keir's eye, she smiled. 'I'm leaving in a minute, then you and Dusty can talk. I only stayed on to meet you –'

'Mandy's going to the theatre with some friends we met on the boat,' Dusty explained.

'That's right,' she said, 'so you two can gossip about old times.'

'Not old times, it's *new* times we want to talk about.' Dusty grinned before remembering something. 'But talking of old times, we saw a film on the boat . . . what was it called . . . ?'

'*The Italian Garden*,' said Amanda.

'That's right. Guess who was in it?' He turned to Keir. 'Dawn Wharton. She was pretty good too. Who'd have believed –?'

'She was *damn* good, not pretty good,' Amanda interrupted. 'And Keir, I don't blame you if you were as smitten as Dusty says.'

'Smitten!' Dusty hooted. 'I told you – he was poleaxed.'

'So were most of the men watching that film,' she said, smiling at Keir. 'You obviously have very good taste. Do you still know her?'

'We write occasionally,' he said cautiously, wondering what Dusty had told her.

'Really?' Her grey eyes speculated. She hesitated, as if about to add something, then changed her mind. 'I must go,' she said, setting her glass down. 'Unless I leave this minute the others will come barging in here looking for me. You'll never get rid of us if that happens.' She laughed as she crossed the room.

Keir realized she had an adjoining suite because she went to the door opposite the one Dusty had used, and returned a second later, patting her hair and twirling a silver fur cape over her shoulders.

'Nice meeting you, Keir,' she said, offering her hand. 'I'm sure I'll see you a lot in the future.'

Keir mumbled it was a pleasure to meet her and watched as Dusty escorted her to the door. 'Okay?' Dusty asked softly.

'Okay,' she nodded.

Dusty looked pleased and opened the door. 'See you later. Have a good time.'

'Bye,' she said, wiggling her fingers as she swept out.

Keir was fascinated by her looks and her aura of wealth – and about her relationship with Dusty.

'No, no.' Dusty grinned, as he returned from the door and caught Keir's eye. 'Nothing like that. I've known Mandy for years. She's a hell of a good friend. Truly a friend, I knew her husband. She was coming over to London anyway, and when she heard I would be looking for somewhere to live she offered to help find me the right place. So it's great. I can work in the salt mines all day while Mandy does my house hunting for me –'

'But who is she?'

'You could say she's my boss,' Dusty answered ruefully. 'She owns seventy-two per cent of Owen Lacey. Not that she's actively involved but nothing much happens without her knowing about it. Naturally I had to tell her about our deal. Not that I wouldn't want to. Mandy can punch holes in a bad idea faster than blinking. If ever she took business seriously, she'd end up owning America. Luckily for the rest of us she only dabbles at it between husbands, but don't let her act fool you. She's as shrewd as they come. That's why she was here when you arrived. To look you over. There's no such thing as an accidental meeting –'

'What deal?' Keir protested, 'Do you realize I don't know what you're talking about. Would you mind starting at the beginning?'

'Give me a chance,' Dusty said. 'There's so much to talk about I don't know where to start . . .' His voice faded as he peered out of the window. 'Tell you what, let's get some air. We'll go for a stroll before dinner. Hang on, I'll just get a jacket . . .' He was already half-way to the bedroom. 'I can't get over London,' he shouted, disappearing. 'We got off the boat train and I broke my neck over those mini-skirts. Wow! That's something New York could copy. I tell you what, old buddy, this town is buzzing. There's no doubt this is the place for the next few years . . .' he re-emerged, knotting his tie, the well-remembered grin on his face, 'I'm still getting used to that uniform. Ten-to-one I'll salute before the end of the evening . . .'

It was typical of Dusty to do at least two things at once. It saved time to go sightseeing while they talked. Outside the Savoy they turned left along the Strand, then left down Craven Street and out onto the Embankment. Dusty swivelled as he walked, twisting around for a view of the skyline, peering across the river, walking backwards to read the illuminated face of Big Ben. Words poured forth in an unstoppable expression of his energy. 'Going to the States was the right thing to do. No two ways about it. Just as you joining the army turned out to be right. But I'll tell you something. The Big Game of the sixties will be played in Europe. That's why I'm back. A lot of crap gets talked about guys being lucky to be in the right place at the right time. That's crap! They figure it out first, then they *put* themselves in the right place.'

Keir wished he was as confident about his own future. Dusty hadn't changed, he had always been sure of where he was going. He talked rapidly and with such conviction that to express doubt would have been futile. Keir felt invigorated just listening.

As for Amanda Lacey, 'she married my boss, Tommy Lacey,' said Dusty. 'When you get to know Mandy ask her about her first husband, she tells a hell of a good story. He was in real estate, and what Mandy doesn't know about property isn't worth knowing. Anyway, she divorced him and married Tommy about four years ago. Everyone says she married him for his money. *Mandy* says she married him for his money but that's crap, she likes to say what sounds outrageous, except if you play it through slowly you'll find most of it makes sense –'

'How old is your boss?'

'He's dead,' Dusty said, looking startled. 'Sorry, didn't I say that? Yeah, Tommy died last March, just over a year ago. He was seventy-three when he married Mandy.' He laughed. 'But Tommy was a *young* seventy-three. I was sort of his blue-eyed boy. Anyway I was always out at his house at Easthampton, so I spent a lot of time with them. They had enormous fun. You'd have loved Tommy, and Mandy was terrific for him –' He broke off as they approached Blackfriars Bridge. 'This is far enough. Let's head for home . . .'

Turning, they retraced their steps while Dusty talked about Mandy and embarked on other stories about his life in New York. By the time they reached the Savoy, five years seemed more like five months.

'Don't they just,' Dusty said lightheartedly as he led the way to the bar.

They sat talking in the bar for a long time with the easy familiarity that comes from long friendship. And if Dusty dominated the conversation to begin with, the talk evened out over the evening, for soon Keir was being bombarded with questions about NATO and his travels in Europe. In fact during dinner, it was Keir who hogged the conversation. Launched into his favourite subject, he was soon deep into explanations about the balance of power and the need to preserve unity within NATO. He made Dusty laugh with stories about the quarrelsome French, the mutable Germans and the volatile Italians.

'What about the Brits?' Dusty asked. 'Do you have a description for us?'

Keir answered without hesitating, 'Imperturbable. It makes us good at some things and bloody awful at others.'

Leaning back in his chair, Dusty chuckled, admiration in his eyes. 'You've sure been around. Rome, Paris, Athens –'

Keir shrugged. 'Europe's not such a big place –'

'But you know everyone who matters.'

'Oh, hardly –'

'I mean in NATO. The Defence Chiefs and so on –'

'I've *met* them, but I'm only a major, remember –'

'But you know them. You know the system. You know how decisions are made.'

Agreeing, Keir reflected on how much he would miss it. Whatever he decided about the future, his days at SHAPE were virtually over.

Dusty was far from reflective. His eyes sparkled with a secret. 'Come on,' he said, when they finished coffee, 'let's go upstairs.

We can have a drink in the room. I'm bursting to tell you about this new project.'

Years later, Keir traced everything back to that evening in Dusty's suite at the Savoy, where they sat drinking and talking while they watched the red and green lights of the tugs skim like fireflies over the dark surface of the river.

Keir was diffident at the outset. 'Before you get too excited, I ought to tell you I don't think I'd be much good in advertising –'

'Advertising? Who's talking about advertising? Did I even mention the word?'

'No, but I thought . . . isn't that why you're here? To run Owen Lacy in Europe.'

'That's reason number one. The other reason is to set up this new business with you. It's a completely new concept. A new kind of business. Something about which you're an expert.'

Startled, Keir laughed. 'You're not starting your own army?'

Dusty scowled. 'Come on, be serious. You don't spend much time soldiering. You said so over dinner. Most of your work is soothing troubled brows. Liaising between the – what did you call them – the mutable Germans and the volatile Italians and so on. Stopping them falling out. Right?'

'I suppose –'

'There you are. A soldier you may be, but first and foremost you're an expert in international relations.'

When Keir protested about the high-sounding job description, Dusty waved him down. 'Hear me out, will you. I've done a hell of a lot of work on this. So just sit there and listen, you see if it makes sense.'

Dusty always made sense when he talked about business. It was what he lived for. It was why he began at six every morning and worked at a pace that exhausted even his American colleagues. It was why clients relied on his judgement, why Owen Lacey entrusted him to run their affairs in Europe. There was no mystique about it. To Dusty it was like his beloved chess, a matter of finding an opening and planning six moves ahead. Business sounded very simple when Dusty explained things.

'It *is* simple,' he insisted, 'but like everything, timing is vital. So let's start by explaining why now is the right time for Europe. It follows on from why the forties and fifties were so good in the States. The troops came home from the war, there was a baby

236

boom, demand sky-rocketed for just about everything. People wanted houses, so houses got built. They wanted cars and ice-boxes and TV sets, so people made cars and ice-boxes and TV sets. But now most people have got them. Result, a slow down in growth. Question, how do you sustain growth? Answer, develop new products or find new markets. And when it comes to new markets, Europe's the best there is. What's more, suddenly it's a lot nearer. These new airliners will revolutionize travel in the next couple of years. Soon you'll be able to fly London–New York direct. And New York–Paris, or anywhere in Europe. Businessmen will travel more. They'll see new opportunities. At the same time, Europe's moving closer together. You were saying earlier NATO's just the start of it. There's this new Common Market. Britain must join soon. You agree?'

'I hope so. De Gaulle might be difficult –'

'Bound to come,' said Dusty firmly. 'Then Europe will be one big market place. Back in the States they can see all this about to happen and they want part of it. It's a chance to expand. America needs Europe and Europe needs America. But it's not easy. Take an American operating in the States. If he's any good he knows his Congressman, lawyers, the press, the radio people, everyone. Over here he's starting from scratch. Different laws, different procedures. Even incorporating a business is different. So just to get started is a problem. And when finally he does get going, he finds out the labour laws are different. Next thing he's got a strike on his hands. A strike puts his whole investment at risk –' he broke off and clutched his head, groaning theatrically – 'Oh boy, suddenly he wishes he'd stayed in Chicago.'

Keir laughed. 'I take the point, but a lot of American concerns are doing business –'

'You should hear the complaints. Horror stories like you wouldn't believe. Wanting to do business doesn't mean they want to foul up. Which is where we come in. I know the Americans, you know the Europeans. Between us –'

'Wait a minute,' Keir interrupted, 'I know nothing about business.'

'Will you let me *explain*! Go back to my American operating in the States. If he's worried about legislation, he calls his Congressman. Okay, so over here we'll have him advised by a

Member of Parliament. In Germany we'll have him advised by a – what do you call them in Germany?'

'Member of the Bundestag.'

'Right. And in France?'

'Préfet de la législature.'

'That's it. And in Italy?'

Keir had to think. 'Er, member of the Senate I suppose, but hang on, I don't know all these people –'

'You know some of them. You speak the languages. You've been around, mixed in the right circles. It's simply a matter of expanding your contacts.'

Keir swallowed, thinking Dusty was underestimating the difficulties. Dusty read his mind. 'You'll have help. We'll get the smartest tax advisers and the best lawyers in every capital in Europe. I've already started. We're seeing Owen Lacey's London lawyers tomorrow.'

'Tomorrow's Sunday.'

Dusty grinned. 'Don't I know it. The senior partners are coming to lunch. We can talk without being interrupted by secretaries and phones and the rest of the nonsense.'

Keir struggled to take it all in. Clearly, Dusty had already done a great deal of work on his idea.

'It's not an idea.' Dusty laughed. 'It's an entity. It exists. I've formed the Corporation. You'll love the name. I thought about the old Team getting together again, so I called it Team International. How about that? Fifty-fifty between us. I registered half the stock in your name.'

Keir was too overwhelmed to give thought to the name. Until then he had been drinking whisky, now the scotch and Dusty's excitement were making him light-headed. Resolutely he put his glass to one side. Stunned at the thought of investing in anything, he blurted out, 'I haven't money to buy stock –'

'Relax. Businesses aren't started by money. They're started by an idea.' Dusty was enjoying the look on Keir's face.

Silence prevailed for a moment. Eventually, Dusty asked, 'Well? What do you think?'

'I don't know what to think,' said Keir, shaking his head in bewilderment. 'I told you, I don't know the first thing about business –'

'And I told you, business is simple. The only people who

complicate it are amateurs. New York's full of Harvard management types impressing the hell out of each other. Most of them couldn't run a whelk stall. The real professionals keep it simple. Let me explain. There're really only two kinds of business, call them A and B. Business A sells a product at ten bucks a time, okay? To make money they calculate that they need an income of a million dollars. So simple arithmetic tells you at ten bucks a time they've got to persuade a hundred thousand people to buy the product. To get that many to say yes, they have to pitch to a lot who'll say no. One strike in five's about average. So they've got to pitch to half a million guys to find a hundred thousand customers, okay?'

Keir nodded.

'So it's obvious. Business A needs consumer advertising. That's where Owen Lacey comes in. Business A is my kind of client.'

'Okay.'

'On the other hand, Business B sells a product at a million dollars each. They only need to sell six to make a profit. This time only six guys need to say yes. Even at a one in five strike rate, they're only pitching to thirty guys. They don't need consumer advertising. No, sir –' Dusty shook his head – 'they don't need Owen Lacey. They need Team International. They need contacts. They need *your* contacts.'

For the first time, Keir began to realize where Dusty was going. He remembered Dusty's letter – '*What with you being in NATO and me doing my stint over here . . .*' He recalled Dusty's interest in NATO over dinner. Feeling as if a blindfold was slipping from his eyes, Keir asked, 'You mean my contacts in NATO?'

'Exactly. Europe's spending billions of dollars a year on defence and a good deal of that goes on American technology. Which is fine for outfits like Lockheed for instance, they've been established in Europe for years, but some of the others are having a hell of a fight. The result is NATO's not always getting the best equipment –'

'NATO doesn't buy anything,' Keir pointed out ruefully, remembering how often he had wished it was otherwise. The incompatibility of equipment was a constant headache on combined operations. He had spent months arguing for

239

standardization. 'Individual countries select their own equipment.'

Dusty brushed the objection aside. 'Okay, so what? You know the officials in every Defence Ministry in Europe. You know the Ministers –'

'I've *met* the Ministers,' Keir qualified. 'That's different. Naturally I know their officials, but that doesn't mean I'm involved in decisions –'

'But you'd like to be. You'd like NATO forces to get the best equipment. You were complaining over dinner about some of the crazy decisions. You said some of the Defence Ministers –'

'Don't make the right decisions. I know, but Ministers don't sign contracts without taking advice. They rely on their officials –'

'*Exactly*,' Dusty shouted triumphantly. 'And you *know* the officials. That's the whole point. Now, will you stop arguing for five minutes? I want to tell you about out first client.'

Keir gaped. He had arrived expecting to see Dusty by himself and discuss advertising. Instead he had met a beautiful blonde – a very wealthy blonde – and now Dusty was talking about NATO . . .

Dusty was enjoying himself hugely. 'Client number one is Beaumont Aviation. Pretty damn impressive, eh?'

Keir was lost for an answer. His knowledge of American plane-manufacturers was limited. Naturally he knew of Beaumont, just as he knew of Lockheed, Boeing and Northrop, they were all big outfits, but all he knew was that they made aircraft.

'Beaumont make damn fine aircraft,' said Dusty. 'I've got a whole case of stuff you can read later. Anyway, check them out with your own contacts. The point is they're breaking an arm and a leg to sell planes in Europe and getting nowhere. For instance, they thought they'd got the contract to supply the Germans with fighters, only to lose out to Lockheed.'

Keir nodded. He had heard about that. The German decision had surprised a lot of people.

'Beaumont are hopping mad.' Dusty scowled. 'They're hollering foul and God knows what else. The point is they're also trying to sell the Germans a transport plane, some sort of troop carrier, and they don't want to lose out again. This troop carrier

240

contract is pretty important. So they want you to open a few doors, get them next to the right people –'

'I'm not an aviation expert –'

'You don't need to be. Beaumont have got technical people chasing all over Europe, but they're not winning contracts. That's why Chuck Hayes is willing to give us a try –'

'Chuck Hayes?'

'Beaumont's President. He's appointed us. We get a fee of twenty-five thousand dollars a year plus expenses. Not a fortune, I grant you, but the big bucks are in the commission. One and a half per cent of all sales in Europe and that adds up to a hell of a lot.'

That was the deal. As simple as that. As Dusty said, business *was* simple, when he explained it. Team International – or more specifically, Keir Milford – was retained to advise Beaumont on their dealings in Europe.

'Starting just as soon as you can get out of the army,' said Dusty. 'Like I said, don't worry about technical matters. Our business is knowing people, not products . . .'

Dusty's surprise packet contained yet another element. There was one last item which he introduced with a broad grin. 'I haven't told you about our other client yet. It's Owen Lacy in case you're interested.'

'Owen Lacey?'

'Sure, they saw the sense straight away. Once you get going and widen your contacts, you'll come to know all sorts of people. Politicians, newspaper men, guys who can open a few doors. They might be useful to Owen Lacey's clients. So this is the deal. Team get free space and facilities in Owen Lacey's office in London, and France and Germany as soon as we open up there. In exchange, Team provide free counselling for Owen Lacey and charge a reduced rate for any of the agency's clients. That way the agency gets an edge over competitors by offering an additional service, and Team International gets off the ground. It's a trial arrangement for two years to see how things work out.'

Keir's mind was in turmoil. He could only shake his head in admiration.

Dusty continued. 'If you come down to Knightsbridge in the morning, I'll show you your office.'

Keir tried to sound calm. 'Is that everything?' he asked, absorbing it all. 'That's the whole deal, right?'

'Sure,' Dusty frowned, wondering if Keir was disappointed. 'That's what we start with. We'll have clients queuing up if you do a good job for Beaumont . . .' His voice trailed off as he watched Keir walk across to the drinks trolley. 'You do like it, don't you? You see what I mean about not needing money? You don't need to put any cash up for your share of the business. Beaumont and Owen Lacey fund it from the word go. There's only your salary and you can have the whole of Beaumont's twenty-five grand. I don't need any. Owen Lacey pay me.' He watched Keir pour a very large scotch. 'Keir? You do like it, don't you? Keir? Say something for fuck's sake!'

Unable to contain his excitement another moment, a huge grin spread over Keir's face. 'You're an absolute genius. It's terrific –'

Making Keir spill the scotch, Dusty grabbed him and went into a little Indian war dance of joy. Next minute they were shaking hands and slapping each other on the back, just as they had earlier. Which was the moment Amanda Lacey chose to return from the theatre. Opening the door, she stood watching them, round-eyed with surprise. It wasn't until she laughed that they were aware of her presence. 'Hey,' she said, advancing into the room, 'I've never seen two guys like you. Is this a private party or can anyone join in?'

Dusty hugged her. 'You're just in time to congratulate us. It's a deal. Team International is in business.'

Extricating herself, she ruffled his hair in a gesture of fondness. 'As if you ever doubted it,' she said, turning to Keir. 'Congratulations. I'm sure it will be a tremendous success. Do I get a hug from you too?'

Unable to remember the last time he had held a woman in his arms, Keir hugged her with such enthusiasm that she was breathless when he released her. 'Well,' she said laughing, 'I'll be sure to be around for your next deal.'

Then they all began talking and laughing at once. Dusty wanted to send down for champagne, but Amanda was going to a night club. 'I've got the crowd waiting downstairs. I only popped up to see if you'd finished your pow-wow. So come on, let's go out and celebrate.'

Dusty agreed like a shot, but Keir hesitated. The truth was he was still trying to assimilate their discussion. So much had been talked about, he wanted time to think, especially if he was meeting Dusty's lawyers tomorrow.

Amanda looked disappointed, 'Okay, take a rain check, but I'll be in town for a while. I'm sure we'll get to know each other better.'

Keir ignored the taxi rank outside the Savoy and walked back to the club. It was quite a long way, across Trafalgar Square, Pall Mall, up to St James's and into Piccadilly. He wouldn't have cared if it was twenty miles. It was only when he passed the RAC that he really noticed buildings and streets. His mind was full of his conversation with Dusty. Even when he reached the Army and Navy, he was too restless to sleep. After ordering a pot of coffee from the hall porter, he went into the deserted Writing Room, flopped down into an armchair, and cast his mind back over the evening.

The sheer unexpectedness of events left him breathless. He had imagined them discussing old times. Schooldays. It seemed laughable now to think of them wasting time talking about the past . . .

More soberly, he wondered if he could do it. Could he really help Beaumont? He knew nothing about aircraft. Against that Dusty's answer echoed in his mind – 'Team is about knowing *people*, not products.'

Rising from the armchair, he went across to a writing table and took a sheet of club notepaper from the rack. After a moment's thought, he began listing useful contacts, starting with the British – Members of Parliament, Defence Ministry officials, fellow officers at SHAPE. By the time the porter arrived with the coffee, Keir's pen was racing across the paper. Dusty had said, 'Even if you've only met them once it's a start . . . you'll be surprised how easy it is to get to know them better . . . take them out to lunch . . . they'll introduce you to their contacts . . . the whole thing snowballs . . .'

It was the chance of a lifetime. The best of all possible worlds, enabling him to stay in touch with his friends throughout NATO. Closing his eyes, he allowed himself to dream for a moment. Twenty-five thousand dollars a year! He'd be able to

243

send Liz to a good boarding school. He saw himself as a wealthy man, living in a big country house at the end of a long gravel drive, standing outside the front door, admiring a sleek red Bristol coupé parked at the foot of the steps. Liz waved to him from the back seat. Behind him the door opened and a woman emerged, casually dressed with a chiffon scarf over her black hair. Smiling, Dawn took his arm and they walked down the steps. He helped her into the Bristol, and a moment later they roared into the sunset . . .

'Starting just as soon as you can get out of the army,' Dusty had said. Keir began to reckon up all the leave due to him. Sometime in March, he thought, Easter at the latest.

Four

'I must be bonkers,' Edith complained. 'Stone blinking bonkers. Fancy letting you talk me into this. My feet are killing me and we haven't even started. How long do we have to wait here?'

It was the Falcon Field at Aldermaston, early on Good Friday morning. The great Easter march was about to begin. Edith was already having regrets despite the encouragement of those around her. Joe was in his element. So were Bob and Emlyn. All three were in high good humour, greeting old friends and acquaintances with the cheerfulness that imbues people who feel good about what they're doing. They were committed campaigners. Nothing would deter them; not the damp air nor the menacing grey clouds nor the prospect of facing trouble before they reached London. Bolt-upright in his invalid chair, Joe looked about him with bright eyes. 'There's only one place to be today and that's here with these people,' he said proudly. 'By golly, just look at them all.'

The multitude had been gathering for hours. Coachloads of people from all over Britain; a trickle at first, then more and more until the queue of coaches stretched a mile long, crawling to a halt outside the Falcon Inn to disgorge its wide-eyed passengers to the cheers of those already assembled.

Edith stood alongside one of the catering vans, sipping tea, while Bob, next to her, hoisted Liz high into the air and onto his shoulders. 'How's that?' he asked. 'Can you see better now?'

Squealing with excitement, Liz pointed first one way, then another. Nearby, six gigantic pantechnicons were being loaded with a mountain of luggage – rucksacks, duffel bags, suitcases, sacks, sleeping bags and bundles of blankets – each with its own coloured label to match the colour that hung from the van. 'Ours is blue,' Liz shouted. Edith responded with a faint smile and tried not to worry. She was already convinced they had seen the last of their suitcases.

'The whole thing's mad,' she muttered under her breath. She was tired of asking Joe what good it would do to march from Aldermaston to London. 'It's a waste of time,' she had wailed. 'The government won't take any notice.'

Joe had been unmoved. 'The whole world will take notice if enough people march!'

Now she wondered if he might be right; *someone* was taking notice judging by the number of press photographers and TV cameramen perched on top of cars. And the crowd grew bigger and bigger.

'However many people are here now, do you think?' Edith asked Bob.

'Hard to say. More than last year. Over a thousand. Nearly two thousand maybe.'

'Two thousand.' Edith shook her head, bewildered by the thought of two thousand people exchanging four days of Bank Holiday peace and quiet for the challenge of marching to London. Glancing away to her left to where the Elsan teams had erected rows of small tents to house portable toilets, she wondered whether to take Liz again before they set off.

'How long will it be before we start?' she asked Emlyn.

'Not long now. See –' he pointed – 'they're raising the banners.'

Indeed, as he spoke the huge black banner was raised at the head of the march. A sudden scuffle arose as people made ready. Up went other banners, scores of banners – 'Twickenham CND', 'Harrow Society of Friends', 'Gorbals Young Socialists', 'North London AUE'; a host of banners rising into the air, too many to count, most bearing the stark black and white emblem that was already becoming well known.

'It's sort of three things in one,' said Joe, explaining the emblem. 'First it's the semaphore signal for the initials ND, meaning Nuclear Disarmament. Then the broken cross means the death of man, and the circle around it stands for the unborn child. It tries to sum up that nuclear weapons are a threat to the whole of mankind –'

'We're off,' Bob interrupted with a shout.

Sure enough, people began to move forward. A jazz band struck up. A chorus of shouts arose as people exchanged encouraging grins and gathered their strength for the journey ahead.

'Liz!' Edith cried anxiously, glancing up at the child on Bob's shoulders. 'You all right?'

'She's fine,' Bob smiled reassuringly.

Liz certainly looked fine; rosy-cheeked under a woollen hat, and buttoned up into a yellow anorak, made bulky by the extra sweaters she wore underneath. Impatiently, she dug her heels into Bob's shoulders as she would to a horse. 'Gee up, Uncle Bob.'

And so they set off – the march uncoiling from the Falcon Field to move up to the gates of the 'Bomb Factory', with the little Co-op van leading the way, the great black banner bobbing behind and then the columns of people.

Edith felt a flutter of fear. She had never done anything like this in the whole of her life. 'Making an exhibition of myself at my age,' she grumbled under her breath. To her, marching seemed both un-English and undignified at the same time.

'There it is.' Joe pointed across the road to the Atomic Weapons Establishment.

Edith stared at the brick buildings behind the tall wire fences. The building seemed very ordinary. Aldermaston looked more like a big school or some government offices than a bomb factory. 'It doesn't look very sinister,' she complained.

'Camouflage,' said Emlyn as he pushed Joe along. 'Don't let it fool you, Edith.'

'Look at that barbed wire,' said Joe. 'I bet the fence round Auschwitz wasn't higher than that.'

His words made her shudder. He was right of course, a building was only a building, it was what went on inside it that mattered. Edith was thinking of that when she saw the blue-uniformed men behind the wire. They were looking at her. Watching her as she watched them. Some of them were using field-glasses. Several had cameras and were taking pictures. Photographs for official files . . .

Frightened, Edith glanced away. She looked ahead to where the head of the march was already turning onto the road for Burghfield. Unconsciously she quickened her pace, anxious to leave the Bomb Factory behind. The thought of losing a lifetime's respectability by being arrested was distressing enough but the thought of a closer encounter with those hard-eyed men behind the wire filled her with terror.

'Hang on, Edith,' Bob called cheerfully as a gap opened between them. 'We've a long way to go yet.'

Slowing her pace to allow them to catch up, she remained tense until they reached the corner, which she turned with a sense of relief. After that came a change of mood, not only for Edith but for so many others that she wondered if they'd all shared her moment of fear. Whatever the reason, people's spirits rose as they turned their backs on the Bomb Factory. Even the weather took heart, for the skies above them brightened as they set out for Burghfield. The jazz band, half a mile behind, began to blast away with 'As the Saints Go Marching In', playing with such verve and energy that even Edith felt herself responding to the rhythm. People laughed and talked as they walked, forgetting their shyness and talking to total strangers with whom they had little in common except this mad determination to walk all the way to London.

'I never thought I'd do anything like this,' a middle-aged woman said to Edith. 'To be honest, I feel a bit of a fool. My sister says I *am* a fool. She says I'm making a public spectacle of myself. I suppose she's right in a way. On the other hand, *someone's* got to speak out . . .'

Edith could scarcely believe her ears. Those were her feelings exactly, the fear of making a public spectacle of herself had haunted her for weeks. She had complained to Joe. 'They'll all be younger than I am,' she had told him, 'or more clever than I am.' She had not expected to find a kindred spirit.

'Oh, I am pleased to meet you,' she said. 'That's exactly how I feel.'

The woman's name was Ann and she lived at Ruislip. 'Oh,' said Edith, 'that's near where we live.' And minutes later they were swapping life-stories.

'I really don't know the first thing about politics,' Ann confessed. 'I didn't even vote in the last election. Politics is a man's thing in our family. Politics and football. That's all they ever talk about. We talk about the kids and the cost of things in the shops, and men talk about politics. I let them get on with it as a rule, but when it comes to these wicked nuclear weapons I want my say . . .'

Walking not far away, still with Liz on his shoulders, Bob was listening to a schoolteacher from Hull. 'I felt I had to do something,' the teacher was saying. 'Something's gone terribly wrong when a country spends more on weapons of mass destruction than on education . . .'

Joe was talking to a Frenchman. 'You came over specially? Well I never. Eh, Emlyn, listen to this. This feller – what's your name? Gérard? Gérard here came over specially from Paris to be on this march . . .'

'And there are others,' said Gérard, a young man in his twenties with a shock of dark hair. 'We are thirty all together, from Paris and Nice too, I think.' He smiled at Emlyn, a trifle shyly. 'I should be happy to push your friend for a while. We could take turns . . .'

And so they marched onto Burghfield, where the catering vans and the Elsan teams, who had passed them on the road, were already set up and waiting.

The marchers were resting on the village green, sipping hot tea and munching slab cake, when a clergyman arrived, ranting and shouting. There were so many clergymen among the marchers that Edith was surprised to find one in opposition. This one certainly was and she was alarmed when he made a bee-line for them. 'You're all a bunch of Communists,' he shouted, red-faced and waving a walking stick. 'You should be ashamed of yourselves –'

'I'm not a Communist,' Joe answered, 'and I never have been, but that don't mean I want to drop bombs on Russia –'

'Russia's a menace to the free world,' the clergyman shouted.

248

'People like you don't know what you're talking about. I don't suppose you've ever been to Russia, yet you pretend to know all about it.'

'Oh really,' Joe said grinning, 'I don't suppose you've been to Heaven but I bet you claim to know all about that.'

The roar of laughter from the onlookers drowned any response the clergyman might have made. After gaping for a moment, his face redder than ever, he stormed off, followed by good-humoured taunts from the crowd.

Edith felt pleased, especially when her new friend Ann laughed and complimented her on having such a quick-witted husband.

Joe's good-tempered retort set the mood for the rest of the day. Soon the marchers were on their way again, laughing and joking, and while the jazz band tooted merrily people sang or chanted slogans, or simply talked to a convivial companion.

'Come and join us,' Joe sang happily to the onlookers lining the pavements.

Liz skipped ahead. 'Come and join us,' she piped, handing out leaflets.

Liz soon exhausted herself and as the march approached Reading, she was picked up and carried by a tall blonde wearing a pair of black leather shorts. Bouncing behind in his chair, Joe admired the long shapely legs marching in front of him and wondered if the girl's face was as pretty as her figure. He was disappointed when she failed to turn round. Eventually, however, beginning to tire and anxious to be relieved of the sleeping infant, she glanced over her shoulder. 'Here,' said Bob, 'I'll take her.' The blonde gave him a beautiful smile. '*Danke*,' she said, handing Liz over. Bob was surprised. 'You're German?'

She nodded and smiled. 'Oh *ja*, there's about fifty of us somewhere. Now I go to find my brother.' And with another happy smile she melted back into the march, her blonde head bobbing as she disappeared into the crowd.

'Well, I'm blowed!' Joe exclaimed. He had always been prejudiced against Germans. The blonde was the first he'd actually met. And there were *fifty* of them. Fifty Germans, marching from Aldermaston to London.

'Makes you think, eh?' Bob grinned. 'There're some Italians too. I was talking to some a while back.'

'And some Swedes,' said Gérard the Frenchman who was pushing Joe's chair.

The teachers from Hull joined in. 'There're a lot of foreigners. I was talking to some Greeks earlier . . .'

French and Italians, Germans and Swedes, Danes and Japanese, Icelanders and Irish, Aussies and Kiwis, Cypriots and Greeks, Americans and Canadians . . . all marching from Aldermaston to London.

Edith limped into Reading. 'Oh dear,' she said to Ann Hillier from Ruislip. 'I promised Joe I'd go as far as Uxbridge, but I'm all in –'

'You'll feel better in the morning,' said Ann with an encouraging smile. 'A good night's sleep will work wonders.'

Edith was doubtful about sleeping at all. 'I've never used one of these sleeping-bag things . . .'

Everything worked out fine. They slept that night in a school at Reading; everyone jumbled up, men and women and children all sleeping together. Good humour triumphed over every discomfort. Those among the marchers who were doctors and nurses did what they could for blistered feet and aching limbs; the catering teams supplied hot food, the guitarists provided soft music. And in the morning they awoke refreshed, to tackle their chores like professionals who knew all about baggage wagons and colour-coded luggage. After breakfast, they used the toilets and washing facilities, 'cleaned the camp', and were ready in good time for the raising of the huge banner at the head of the march.

Off they went again, swinging through Reading High Street, bringing traffic to a standstill and shopkeepers to their doors, some applauding, others barracking, most simply looking overwhelmed by the sheer size of the march. It had grown overnight. The message had spread, carried by television and radio and pictures in the newspapers. That morning hundreds, *thousands* of new supporters arrived, like reinforcements coming to the aid of an army. 'Come and join us,' Liz sang as she skipped along handing out her leaflets. And come and join her they did.

'It must be twice the size of last year's march,' said Bob, craning his neck in an effort to see the column stretching for miles behind them.

'I know,' said Joe with a proud grin. 'The government must take notice of this.'

Ann and Edith had fallen into step with an Indian who told them he was a Hindu. 'Oh yes,' he said, twinkling eyes betraying his grave expression, 'even heathens like my humble Hindu self have joined your march. Mr Gandhi made many such marches to change your government's views in the past. Why shouldn't it work again? That's what I say.'

Edith, whose involvement in organized religion was limited to the jumble sale at her local church, was intrigued to discover how many other 'funny religions' were represented on the march.

The Indian chuckled. 'There are some Jews and some Catholics,' he said. 'Of course they might not be funny enough for you . . .'

Ann wanted to extend their count to include political as well as religious beliefs, so that it became a game between them, categorizing the Christians and the Atheists, the Quakers and Jews, the Moslems and Hindus, the Buddhists and Sikhs, the Tories and Socialists and Liberals, the Capitalists and Communists who marched side by side on the long road to London.

On they went, mile after mile, with the band playing lustily, never seeming to draw breath. Progress became more tiring as the day wore on. A strong headwind blew up, to buffet the marchers and the banners they carried. Squalls of rain soaked them, limbs ached and blisters burst. Good humour began to flag, and as they pushed on towards Slough many on the march were feeling the strain.

Now it was Edith's turn to encourage her friend Ann, who had developed a bad limp. It was Emlyn's turn to reassure Joe when he worried about Edith. It was the young Frenchman's turn to carry Liz, and he did it in style, wrapping her inside his raincoat so that only her woollen hat and her wide eyes peeped out. 'Frère Jacques,' he crooned. 'Frère Jacques,' she sang with him, her voice muffled inside his coat.

Bob Cooper's voice rang out with Harry Lauder's old song 'Keep right on to the end of the road'. Those walking with him joined in but, footsore and weary, many were beginning to doubt that they would.

'I don't think we'll ever reach Slough,' Edith muttered, aching with fatigue as she trudged on in sodden stockings and squelching shoes. Then she was revitalized by the most marvellous sight. Rounding a bend in the road, she caught her breath, scarcely able to believe her eyes. Coming towards them was another march. More people marching; hundreds of people, carrying at their head another huge banner – 'Slough welcomes the marchers!' Joe twisted around in his chair to point up a side road. Edith followed his gaze to see yet another march. 'Slough welcomes the marchers' proclaimed its huge banner. There were hundreds and hundreds more people . . .

A few minutes later the marches converged, like two tributaries flowing into a huge river, eddying and swirling around. People reached out and shook hands; slapped backs and embraced, and when the columns re-assembled behind the huge banner at the head of the march, the river took on the proportions of a flood. With the musicians blasting furiously on trumpet and trombones, people raised their voices in song. 'Oh when the saints,' they bellowed, 'come marching . . .'

And so into Slough, swaying and singing, came the march, by now swollen to a size far beyond that expected by the organizers, far more than the two thousand people for whom they had hoped. Far more than five thousand. More than seven, even more than eight thousand.

The two schools, booked to provide overnight accommodation, were swamped within thirty minutes. Most marchers faced a night with nowhere to sleep but the pavements.

Edith wilted. She began to talk of going home. 'Not so much for me,' she surprised herself by saying, 'but I can't have that child sleeping out all night. It's damp now. Goodness knows what it will be like later. It might rain again . . .'

It did rain again. The light drizzle worsened into a steady downpour. Huddled beneath umbrellas, Edith reminded Joe of the compromise they had reached before the march. She and Liz would go as far as Uxbridge, then they would go home. 'I was going home tomorrow anyway,' she said, 'and I think you've done enough. You've registered your protest, nobody would blame you if you came home with me.'

Similar conversations were taking place all around them. After two days on the march a bond had been established, friendships had been forged, nobody wanted to desert their companions, but to spend the entire night in the rain . . .

Yet even as they talked, the six o'clock television news was announcing their plight. 'Thousands of marchers are sitting on the pavements in Slough with nowhere to sleep . . .'

The response was immediate. Out from cosy vicarages and red brick rectories and grey stone manses came the clergymen. Nobody was going to sleep on the pavement if they could help it. A church hall was found for two hundred people. Along came the baggage wagons and off went the marchers. A hundred people could sleep here . . . off they went too. A hundred and fifty could sleep in the Methodist Hall . . .

Hard on the heels of the clergymen, came the town councillors. Another school opened its doors.

Finally, the Mayor himself arrived to offer the Town Hall.

Not since the worst nights of the Blitz had such scenes occurred in a civic building. The marchers slept everywhere. They slept in the Council Chamber. They slept in the corridors. They slept in the Rating Office, in the Parks Office, in every office they could find. They slept in the lobbies and on the stairs.

Next morning a very indignant Tory woman councillor arrived, her blue rinse standing on end as she inspected the Council Chamber. 'Someone,' she announced in shocked tones, 'has turned the Queen's portrait to the wall.'

Bob Cooper was the culprit. 'What else could I do?' he said grinning, 'I couldn't take my trousers down with *her* looking on.'

And so Edith Milford survived a second night away from the shop on the corner. Her feet were blistered and her legs ached, but the excitement of the march had reached out and touched her. She had been scornful before, scoffing at Joe. 'What chance have we got of changing the world? No one's going to listen to us.' Now she wasn't so sure. There were so many of them. So many people . . .

Indeed there were even *more* people that morning. The message was spreading.

'It seems a pity to give up at Uxbridge,' said Joe with an encouraging grin.

Edith sniffed. 'I'll make up my mind when we get there,' she said noncommittally. 'After all, I've got Liz to consider.'

'She'll march forever,' Joe laughed.

Certainly, Liz was in a marching mood that morning. She caught the eye of many a cameraman as the march wound its way out of Slough. Pictures of Liz dancing alongside Joe in his chair were to appear in most evening papers later. The march grew and grew. By the time it reached Uxbridge it was seven miles long and estimates of its strength had reached fifty thousand.

'Fifty thousand people!' Joe crowed as they rested on Uxbridge Common.

'Fifty thousand and one,' said a voice, and Joe turned to find a young man grinning at him. Baffled for a moment, Joe knew the face without being able to place it. Then he realized who the man was. It was the young Mr Freeman, the solicitor who had defended him in Uxbridge Magistrates' Court.

'Well, I'm blessed,' said Joe, who introduced Edith. 'Now we've got the law on our side.'

'And the Church,' joked the Reverend Peter Exeter as he emerged from the crowd. He was very apologetic. 'I can only march as far as Hounslow,' he explained. 'What with it being Easter Sunday, I must be back at the church by five.'

So, once more, they marched off – shopkeepers and solicitors, teachers and students, doctors and nurses, actors and musicians, librarians and philosophers, firemen and farmers, biologists and philatelists, old men and young men, mothers and fathers pushing babies in prams. Individuals lost their identities in the march. Homeless and faceless, it had become a community all of its own. Anyone could join. To belong all they had to do was step off the pavement.

There was no going home for Edith, not now. Not even when the heavens opened and the rain poured down once again. 'I've come this far,' she said, 'I'm jolly well going right into London.'

The following morning, *everyone* seemed to be going right into London. As the march rolled on through the suburbs, Londoners came out in their thousands, some to gawp, others to heckle, some to cheer and yet more to join in. No longer could it be compared to a river, the march was a tidal wave sweeping down on the capital. Growing all the time, it became fifty, then sixty, then seventy thousand strong. Instead of one jazz band, there were seven. Instead of a couple of Members of Parliament, a dozen now strode out beneath the leading banner. And the number of banners grew all the time – some stark, some funny, some banal, some witty – but all saying the same thing – Ban the Bomb! Ban the Bomb!

A hundred thousand people marched into Trafalgar Square. Even Trafalgar Square could not hold such a vast number. People clogged Whitehall and Pall Mall and the Strand, straining their ears to hear the speeches relayed by loudspeakers.

Edith had never felt so proud in her life. Her blistered feet throbbed, her ankles were swollen, her legs ached, her hair was a mess, her lips were chapped from the wind. She would have been the first to describe herself as just an ordinary woman; not clever or well-educated or possessing special talents. But she had met enough others among that huge crowd to have gained a new confidence in her own opinion. Ann felt the same. 'From now on,' she told Edith, 'men can talk about football as much as they like, but when it comes to politics I'm having my say.'

'Everyone's having their say,' said Joe. 'Just look at that crowd. It's a message from the people, that's what it is.'

All around them, people swapped addresses and promised to write. They wrung each other's hands, amazed at themselves and what they had started. And as they joined hands to sing 'Abide with me' before they went looking for trains and buses to take them home, Edith felt tears sting her eyes. If only Keir was here, she thought. If he could meet some of these people, he'd understand why it was right to bring Liz.

Five

So difficult was Keir finding it to understand so many things that he had completely forgotten the Aldermaston march. He was beset by more immediate problems. After that euphoric week with Dusty, he had returned to Paris, resigned his commission and set about pulling strings to obtain an early release. People had tried to dissuade him. He was popular, not just at SHAPE but in Ministries and Defence Agencies, Bureaux and Permanent Standing Committees all over Europe. Friends thought he was mad to turn his back on a promising career. Even so, when he insisted, they pushed and shoved his papers through Army channels to process his release in double-quick time.

On 10 April 1960, barely two weeks after Easter, Major Keir Milford became a civilian.

Returning to London he found Dusty still at the Savoy. Amanda Lacey had found him a spacious apartment in Chesterfield Place. 'But the decorators are in,' said Dusty. 'I'll be here for another two weeks.' With a shrug, he explained. 'Owen Lacey pick up the bill, it's not down to me.'

Keir, however, had to pay for his own accommodation and had no intention of splurging his new salary on a suite in the Savoy. Instead, he took a room in the Marchmount Private Hotel in Norfolk Street as a temporary measure until he could find a flat of his own. The Marchmount wasn't much of a place; cheap without being cheerful it possessed a gloomy bar, a dining-room reeking of boiled cabbage, worn carpets on the stairs and the ugliest receptionist in London. Keir was blind to its faults. Close to the Savoy for meetings with Dusty, it made a convenient base. He was more concerned about settling into his new office.

The truth was he had only the vaguest idea of what Beaumont would want from him. Dusty said it was 'to advise on their business in Europe', which sounded grand but was hardly specific. Keir had a shadowy picture of himself attending Air Shows and Military Exhibitions, receptions and cocktail parties, introducing his clients to old chums in NATO.

He was in for a shock.

Chuck Hayes and Sam Pickard, respectively President and Vice-President of Beaumont, were on a flying visit to London.

'We're joining them for dinner,' said Dusty with a confident grin.

Keir was eager to meet them. He had done his homework. He had read the material which Dusty had supplied and made his own enquiries before leaving SHAPE. With typical thoroughness he had asked all sorts of people about Beaumont and had received some very favourable answers.

'Be careful with Pickard,' Dusty warned on the way to the Dorchester, which was where Hayes and Pickard were staying. 'He wasn't too happy about your appointment. He said he didn't need anyone to introduce him to his customers. You can't blame him for being sensitive, but Chuck was so shaken about losing the fighter contract that he was ready to try anything. That's when I hooked him. But Pickard's a bit scratchy, he feels your appointment reflects badly on him.'

A bit scratchy proved to be an understatement. Pickard was hostile.

'So you're going to open doors for me,' he sneered as he shook hands. Short, dark, almost Italian-looking, he was expensively dressed in a black mohair suit. The hard look in his eyes was definitely unfriendly.

Keir was relieved to get a smile from Chuck Hayes, even though most of the warmth was directed at Dusty. Hayes and Dusty were old friends. They had met at the Lacey house on Long Island. Apparently the seeds of Dusty's idea had been sown there one night when Chuck had been grumbling about Beaumont's problems in Europe.

'Glad to know you, Keir,' he said, with a bone-crushing handshake. 'Any friend of Dusty's is a friend of mine.'

A big man, Hayes seemed even bigger next to Sam Pickard. Six feet four and heavily built, it was no surprise to learn that he had been a star footballer at college. Round-faced with receding fair hair, looking like an amiable athlete running to seed, he was so relaxed that he made no mention of business for half an hour. Instead he talked to Dusty about mutual friends in New York, especially 'the delectable Mandy. I hear she's over here. You see anything of her?'

Listening to Dusty explain how Mandy had found him an apartment, Keir was conscious of Pickard fidgeting and glaring, reminding him of a boxer at the outset of a fight.

The fight began over dinner, when Hayes finally turned the conversation to business. Even then he seemed reluctant to do so. 'What a girl that Mandy is,' he sighed. 'Know something, Dusty, I really envied old Tommy.'

Dusty smiled. 'Didn't we all?'

'Yeah, well, I guess we all dream now and then,' said Hayes with a sigh.

Sitting back in his chair he glanced casually around the restaurant, as if seeking a familiar face. Keir thought he was more likely making sure their conversation couldn't be over-heard, a hunch that was confirmed a moment later when Chuck grinned across the table. 'Well young man, I guess it's time to let Sam here loose on you. I know he's just busting with questions,' he said.

Instead of questioning, Pickard cross-examined. For the next hour and a half he quizzed Keir on his contacts in Europe – country by country, Ministry by Ministry, Defence Agency by Defence Agency. It was a gruelling examination which went on throughout the entire meal. Afterwards, Dusty said he counted the names of more than fifty officials. Unprepared, Keir grew flustered at times, but in the main gave a good account of himself. His credentials were so solid that eventually even Pickard had to accept them. 'Okay,' he said, turning to Chuck Hayes with a shrug. 'So he knows a few people in Europe.'

Hayes smiled. 'Dusty wouldn't hand me a lemon.'

Pickard scowled and spooned brown sugar into his coffee.

Relieved to have survived the unexpected examination, Keir caught Dusty's eye and was rewarded with a broad wink.

The tension eased slightly after that as Hayes talked about Beaumont's transport plane – the CX29 – and various negotiations going on around Europe. Much of what was said Keir had already discovered from his own sources, but he listened attentively, ready to learn more. Meanwhile, Pickard continued to fidget, as if impatient for Hayes to get to the point.

'The Germans are inching towards a decision,' said Hayes. 'We expect them to decide in the Fall. Sam here says we've a good chance. The CX29's a damn fine airplane. Trouble is we were in with a good chance with the Bullfighter and we lost out on that. We can't afford to lose out on this one.'

Until then his manner had been so relaxed that it made more noticeable the edge that came into his voice when he said *We can't afford to lose out on this one*.

Pickard looked up. 'We wouldn't have lost out in a fair fight. Let's lay it out on the line. Our only rival for the German fighter contract was Northrop with their Super Tiger. I wouldn't have been surprised if they got the business. I even spoke to their people on this. Know what they said? They wouldn't have been surprised if we got it. That's how close it was. Everyone said it was between us and them. But Lockheed! No one gave Lockheed a chance.'

Keir had already heard as much from his contacts. According

to *Luftwaffe* gossip, Northrop and Beaumont had been joint favourites. People were surprised when Defence Minister Strauss had announced that 'after evaluating nearly two dozen of the world's top fighter aircraft' the Federal German Republic had decided to buy the Lockheed Starfighter.

'Another thing,' Pickard added. 'The Starfighter will be a death trap for pilots. That plane's been modified so many times –'

'It must have something,' Keir said mildly, 'or the Germans wouldn't have bought it.' For a moment he pictured Kurt Schiller, Head of Procurement for the *Luftwaffe*. Without having met him, he knew Schiller's reputation. A former ace pilot himself, Schiller was a fanatic about safety.

'Crap,' Pickard said angrily. 'The Starfighter had nothing going for it. Lockheed have got something going for *them*. That's the point. If you find out what levers they're pulling you might be of some use around here.'

His words contained more than a challenge. Something else was implied, Keir could scarcely believe his ears. 'You're not suggesting –' he searched for the right word – 'something improper?'

'Improper? The fucking thing stinks,' Pickard hissed angrily. 'Someone authorized the spending of millions of dollars on a death trap. When that sort of thing happens there's only one reason.' Holding out his hand, he rubbed his thumb and forefinger together. 'I'll level with you. I didn't want you on the team, and I still don't but if you find out how Lockheed got that Starfighter contract I'll be the first to back off. But you'd better find out fast, before the bastards do the same on the CX29.'

Silence fell at the table. Pickard's face bore a look of angry defiance, Hayes stared impassively, Dusty blinked and Keir looked frankly incredulous. The shock of learning that his appointment was so vehemently opposed was equalled by disbelief at what Pickard was saying.

Eventually, it was Pickard who broke the silence. 'One last thing, then I'm going to bed, I got an early start in the morning. But losing the Bullfighter contract was a double blow. Someone's started a lot of talk in NATO about standardization. So the German decision will influence the Dutch and the Italians.

Winning in Germany gave Lockheed an edge big enough to push us out of the fighter business in Europe. If the same thing happens with the CX29 we're out of business, period. That's how serious this is.' With which he pushed back his chair, tossed his napkin onto the table, nodded goodnight to Hayes, and walked out.

Keir felt his entire future go with him. Team International's one and only fee-paying client was in trouble. If Beaumont went bust, that was it. Keir would have thrown away a career in the army for nothing.

'How could you do this to me?' Keir demanded bitterly. 'You must have known Pickard didn't want me.'

They were walking back to the Savoy after saying goodnight to Chuck Hayes. Keir had vetoed Dusty's suggestion of a cab, hoping that exercise might dispel his anger. He was furious. Any new business was a risk, even he knew that, but until then he had believed that Beaumont wanted him. Dusty had said, 'they want you to open a few doors for them.' Keir had seen himself writing press releases and dealing with journalists. Just as he had at the army Office of Information. That was work he could do. That was work he liked doing. He wouldn't even have a chance to do that with Beaumont. Pickard didn't want him involved!

'Calm down,' said Dusty, placating and soothing. 'Chuck Hayes is the boss –'

'But Pickard runs Europe.'

'I didn't know he was *that* hostile –'

'You suspected. You said so tonight. Why the hell didn't you tell me before?' Keir felt let down, betrayed. He had thrown up his prospects in the army, believing everything Dusty had said.

'There are bound to be a few difficulties –'

'Difficulties? Like them going bust unless they get this contract?'

'Pickard was exaggerating. You heard Chuck afterwards. Pickard's under a lot of strain –'

'Bollocks! Maybe he lost his temper, but I don't think he was lying.'

'They paid our fee without a murmur –'

'That's nothing and you know it. Twenty-five thousand is peanuts in their cash flow. They're dealing in millions. Come on,

Dusty, I don't pretend to be an expert in business but I know that much.'

They walked on in silence for a while, each busy with his own thoughts. Passing the Army and Navy Club was a bitter reminder to Keir of returning there in a state of excitement after their reunion.

'Be reasonable,' said Dusty, still using his soothing voice. 'No one's going to come to us unless they've got a problem. That's the business we're in. They won't pay a fat fee for sympathy. They want action.'

'Action?' Keir erupted, still boiling with temper. 'To listen to Pickard you'd think we were dealing with crooks. We're dealing with *governments* for Christ's sake. Pickard's talking a lot of rubbish. He's looking for excuses. Losing that contract made him look bad –'

'Sure,' Dusty agreed. 'That's right. So what are you going to do about it?'

Keir wished he knew. Most of all he wished he'd stayed in the army. He began to regret listening to Dusty. Why had he allowed himself to be carried away . . .

'There're always problems,' Dusty said as they crossed to the south side of Piccadilly. 'But you want to be rich, don't you?'

That's the answer, Keir thought, I did want to be rich. I wanted a red Bristol and a big house. I wanted to live in the same style as Dusty . . .

'Chuck's idea made a lot of sense,' said Dusty.

Hayes had suggested that Keir go to Germany and examine Beaumont's position in detail; meet their German agent and the technical staff, read the files, discuss the CX29 with the sales team and get a feel of how the negotiations were going. 'See if you can put your finger on what's wrong,' Hayes had said. 'Find out why we lost the fighter contract. Is Sam right about something funny going on, or is that an excuse? I'll keep Sam out of your hair. We'll be back in London in four weeks. That should give you enough time to produce an initial report.'

'Well?' Dusty persisted. 'What do you think?'

Keir frowned. Hayes had been very specific, he wanted a report in twenty-eight days. Without doubt the German contract was vital to Beaumont's future. 'Help pull this off,' Hayes had told Keir, 'and I'll be your client for life.'

261

He had omitted to say what would happen if Keir failed. He had no need, his expression was enough.

Dusty said, 'I reckon you should get the first plane out in the morning.'

Finding it impossible to concentrate and be angry at the same time Keir's temper had cooled. Even so he was still unhappy. Apart from disliking the idea of working behind Pickard's back, he realized Beaumont's agent in Germany had been appointed by Pickard. He reported to Pickard. He would be as hostile as Pickard himself.

'Pickard can be handled,' said Dusty. 'You want to know something? The answer to one question will solve your problems with Pickard.'

Keir shot him a look of surprise, 'What question?'

'Why did Beaumont lose the fighter contract? Answer that and your problems are over.'

'How do you figure that out?'

'If Pickard fouled up, Chuck will fire him. You won't even be working with Pickard. Chuck will appoint a new man who'll be pleased with all the help you can give him. Surely that makes sense?'

'Okay, but –'

'And if Pickard's right – well, you heard him tonight. What did he say? He'll be the first to back off. If something funny *is* going on, and you find out, he'll love you. He'll be your biggest fan. You'll have confirmed what he's said all along.'

Keir walked in silence, digesting Dusty's reasoning.

'See what I mean?' said Dusty cheerfully. 'Whatever answer you bring back makes you a winner. You can't lose. It's a perfect situation.'

Keir struggled to suppress a grudging smile. Dusty had a knack bordering on genius when it came to explaining problems. Perhaps that's why he was so good in business. Always anticipating difficulties, he never failed to find a way round them. Except that this time, Keir had to find a way . . .

'Just discover why Beaumont lost that fighter contract,' Dusty summed up.

Six

Twenty-four hours later, Keir booked into Cologne's Adler Hotel. He liked Cologne. Having spent a year there with the Army Information Office he had come to know the city well. Yet if he felt comfortable in Cologne he was thoroughly uncomfortable about everything else. *Find out why Beaumont lost the fighter contract*, Dusty had said. As if all Keir had to do was ask.

Knowing when to start was a problem. He saw no point in calling on Beaumont's German agents. 'Their technical people will blind me with science.' He was tempted to go on to Bonn, where he had contacts, government officials who might be of help. But Bonn was a small town dominated by the Bundestag; full of politicians and civil servants. Nobody stayed there unless on government business or to do business with the government. It was a gossipy town, a one-topic-of-conversation town. If people found out he was working with Beaumont, everyone would know in five minutes. Commonsense told him to remain close-mouthed. 'Just for a couple of weeks,' he told himself, 'until I see how the land lies.'

Thankfully, he had told friends at SHAPE in Paris very little about his plans, just that 'an old pal has asked me to go into business with him . . . sort of public relations'. And although he disliked the thought of deceiving former colleagues, he invented a story about being on holiday. 'I'm taking a last look at Germany before starting in Civvy Street.'

Unable to think of a better plan, he went down to the desk and hired a car. 'Nothing too big,' he told the clerk. 'Just something to tour around in for a couple of weeks.' He ended up with an NSU from Avis which suited him fine.

To start with he had no luck at all. Perhaps he got what he deserved because, without any clear plan, he floundered around hopelessly – telephoning friends he had made during his years in the service. To begin with he concentrated on his contacts in BAOR – the British Army of the Rhine. His release was so recent that some of them thought he was still in the army. They were amazed. 'You packed it in? Good Lord. You were heading for full Colonel. Come and have a drink if you're in the area.'

For the next seven days, Keir did the rounds of the officers' clubs. It felt strange, dressed in civilian clothes, to walk into an officers' mess as a guest. Startled to realize how much he missed it, he was grateful still to be included as one of them. Several said he would re-enlist. 'You won't *like* Civvy Street, old boy. Of course we all get pissed off now and then, but you can't beat army life. I said to Tommy, "Keir will be back. I give him six months . . ."'

Keir was beginning to doubt he would last six months.

His SHAPE background was so well known that it was easy to drift in and out of military circles, which included the RAF as well as the army, and it was a RAF wing commander who got talking about the Lockheed Starfighter one night. 'I'm damn glad we're not getting it. The *Luftwaffe* boys are hopping mad and I can't say I blame them . . .'

As he was more interested in technical performance than commercial matters, it took Keir a while to shift the conversation to how the deal came about.

'God knows, old boy,' came the answer. 'From what I hear the contract was signed like a blank cheque. No firm delivery dates, not even a fixed price. Complete shambles if you want my opinion. The *Luftwaffe* made it perfectly clear they wanted either the Northrop or the Beaumont.'

Keir began to hear the same story from other sources. All the gossip supported Sam Pickard's views. So why, to use Defence Minister Strauss's own words 'after evaluating nearly two dozen of the world's top fighter aircraft', had the Germans plumped for the Starfighter?

Refusing to believe Pickard's wild talk about corruption, Keir thought someone had blundered. While he was prepared to believe there had been a monumental balls-up, to talk of corruption was simply absurd.

Even so he grew increasingly anxious. The twenty-eight days given him by Chuck Hayes were slipping away. Gathering gossip was getting him nowhere, it was just making him miserable, for the one thing becoming clear was that Beaumont were well respected in Europe. RAF pilots had heard good reports of the

CX29. Those men who knew him even praised Sam Pickard. Beaumont's German agent was highly regarded. On the face of it, Beaumont was doing everything right. It was only too easy to understand Pickard's resentment – they simply had no need of Keir Milford.

'I can't open doors for Pickard,' Keir concluded gloomily. 'He's been through them already.'

By the tenth day he was desperate enough to consider a change of tactics. Apart from anything else, his story about a holiday was wearing thin, especially when his questions caused an ex-colleague to exclaim, 'Are you *sure* you've resigned your commission? You haven't transferred to the cloak and dagger boys, have you?'

Keir laughed but it made for an awkward moment. It also made him realize he'd gone as far as he dared with the British, without finding out anything of importance. The obvious next step was to try for a meeting with Kurt Schiller, Head of Evaluation and Procurement for the *Luftwaffe*. Keir hesitated. Schiller had a formidable reputation; he was hardly the sort to answer questions easily. 'He might even refuse to see me,' Keir admitted, casting around for someone who might arrange an introduction. Sam Bartleman's name came to mind. Sam was a major in the US Army who was rumoured to know just about everyone.

'Sure, I know old Iron Pants,' Sam said on the phone. 'What's it to you? Someone told me you'd quit. What the hell are you up to, you limey bastard?'

Even before making the phone call, Keir had accepted that Sam would insist on knowing the truth. 'I'll tell you when we meet. I was thinking of driving down to Frankfurt tomorrow –'

'Make it the next day. Friday evening. We'll have dinner at Schmidt's. You ever meet Max, the guy who owns it? You can't have, you'd have remembered. Nobody forgets Max . . .'

After making the arrangement, Keir's spirits improved. Sam would insist on knowing chapter and verse, but in a way it would be a relief to tell someone. 'I'm getting nowhere by myself,' he admitted, 'and Sam might come up with some other ideas.'

The only other idea Keir had was to call in at Koblenz on the way to Frankfurt. NATO had an office there, mostly staffed by German nationals, some of whom he knew, notably Holst

Libberman who was delighted when he phoned – 'Keir. You could do me a favour. My wife and I go for the first time on holiday to England next month. You will tell us where to go and what to see, *ja*? Stay over and have dinner . . .'

Keir might have declined except that someone had told him the NATO office in Koblenz was processing the Starfighter contract. Lockheed had opened a liaison office in the town.

'*Ja*, that's right, it's a big project,' Libberman confirmed.

So the next day Keir drove to Koblenz, booked into a hotel, and met Libberman for dinner. In fact he met both Libbermans, for Holst brought his wife, complete with travel brochures and guide books.

They were an unspectacular couple; quiet, neatly turned out, slim and fair-haired, looking more like brother and sister than husband and wife. Holst resembled what Keir knew him to be – a conscientious civil servant who was strong on detail but weak on policy. His wife was equally earnest, especially about planning their holiday. Consequently, while eating *sauerbraten* and quaffing good German beer in a beer cellar, the talk was more of places to stay in the Lake District than of NATO. Keir probed away but was reconciling himself to a wasted evening when they were interrupted. They had virtually finished their meal when a man stopped at their table and put a heavy hand on Libberman's shoulder.

'Ah, Holst, you old bastard. Caught in the act. This fraulein can't be your wife, she's too pretty for you.' Laughing loudly, the man staggered slightly, obviously feeling the effects of good German beer. Libberman stood up and, with an embarrassed grin, invited the man to join them – unnecessarily, since the man had already slumped into the empty chair next to Keir. 'Name's Ruark,' he said in English, offering Frau Libberman his hand. 'Harry Ruark.'

Frau Libberman looked to her husband for an explanation. In German, Libberman explained that until recently Ruark worked for Lockheed as one of the liaison team based in the town. Unimpressed, Frau Libberman's face bore a look of disdain, but Keir's interest picked up as Libberman introduced him to Ruark. The American was about forty years old, flush-faced from his consumption of beer, heavily built without quite being fat.

Conversation was strained after his arrival. Ruark's German was tortuous and Frau Libberman spoke no English at all, but Keir gathered that Ruark had joined an American engineering company after resigning from Lockheed in a huff. Libberman, who clearly disliked Ruark, seemed to take malicious pleasure in reminding the American about Lockheed. 'All because of Herr Hausser, eh, Harry?'

Ruark reacted with a furious scowl. 'He's an arsehole,' he glowered, then remembered Libberman's wife. 'Sorry –'

'It's all right,' Libberman said mildly, 'she doesn't speak English.'

'Oh yeah.' Ruark's scowl brightened to a smile. 'That's okay, then. In that case, Hausser is a *fucking* arsehole.'

While Ruark spluttered into his beer, Libberman explained that Lockheed had flown a man called Hausser in from the States to take charge of public relations at the Koblenz office. 'And he fell out with our friend here,' he said, indicating Ruark.

'Not just me. Everyone hates his guts,' said Ruark, becoming angry.

Frau Libberman had had enough at this point. Even without knowing what Ruark was saying it was obvious he was swearing and cursing about someone. Thanking Keir for his help with their holiday, she told Libberman to finish his drink and rose to go.

Keir stood up too, but Ruark caught his arm. 'Stay an' have another one.'

Keir hesitated. The prospect of drinking with Ruark held little appeal, on the other hand he saw an outside chance of learning something about Lockheed and the Starfighter contract. Having gleaned nothing from Libberman, Keir was desperate. 'All right,' he agreed. 'Order them and I'll pay when I get back.'

He walked the Libbermans to the entrance, thanking them for the evening and wishing them a good holiday in England. Frau Libberman said, 'I think that is not a nice man. Are you sure you won't leave with us?'

Keir had his own doubts, especially when he returned to find Ruark leering hungrily after a waitress. 'Kraut bitch,' he grumbled as she walked off with her nose in the air. 'You think they'd teach 'em all English.'

For the next hour, Keir sat drinking with Ruark, but to his

disappointment he learned little about Lockheed. Probe though he did, he failed to draw Ruark out on any part of their business except for the arrival in Germany of Ernest F. Hausser.

'Ernest F. Hausser,' said Ruark, dwelling on every syllable. He hated the man, and the more he had to drink the more intense became his hatred. 'You know the biggest lie in the world?' he asked Keir at one point. 'All that shit about the American dream. Hard work don't count for anything. Influence is the thing to have . . . influence . . . like Ernest Hausser.'

Apparently, Hausser had been appointed by no less a person than Robert Gross, President of Lockheed. And had arrived in Koblenz within months of Lockheed winning the Starfighter contract. Throwing discretion to the wind, Keir asked direct questions about the Starfighter and how Lockheed had won the contract, but all Ruark wanted to talk about was Hausser. He had the drunk's knack of converting any subject into an excuse to talk about his obsession. And it was an obsession. It seemed that he had hated Hausser even before setting eyes on the man.

'They even sent me to the airport to meet him. Me! Like some office boy . . .'

The plane had been late and Ruark had stood at the barrier for an hour, smouldering with resentment and holding a placard marked 'Ernest F. Hausser'. To make matters even worse a courier had arrived with a huge bouquet for Hausser, after which Ruark had found himself with the placard in one hand and the bouquet in the other, standing there 'like a spare prick at a wedding'.

Ruark's bloated face suddenly brightened. 'Show you the sort he is. Know what the card with the flowers said? "Welcome! FJS." That's all. Just FJS. Any dame sends me flowers she'd say Frieda . . . or Frances . . . or whatever her fucking name was. Not some sneaky set of initials . . .'

It was then they were asked to leave. Ruark's voice had been getting steadily louder and his language progressively worse, but the possibility of being thrown out had not occurred to Keir until that minute.

'I ain't going,' said Ruark belligerently, 'I want another beer.'

Keir made the only suggestion he could think of, which was that they adjourn to his hotel for a nightcap. He wanted neither another drink nor any more to do with Ruark, but unless they left there would be trouble for sure, so he sighed with relief when Ruark accepted.

'I've had enough of this crumby joint anyway,' said Ruark, weaving up the stairs on india rubber legs, one arm flung over Keir's shoulder in an affectionate embrace. 'You're a good old boy, you are, a real pleasure to know you.'

Outside, fresh air felled him like an assailant coming out of the dark. He was retching and spewing into the gutter before they had walked twenty yards. Dizzy himself, Keir could only stand and watch, praying that a prowling police car wouldn't cart them off to the cells for the night. 'Let's get you home and leave the nightcap for another time.'

Too ill to protest, Ruark said he lived only two blocks away and, tightening his grip around Keir's shoulder, led the way at a stagger. Even then he couldn't stop talking about Hausser. 'Promise me something. You met me for the first time tonight, right? You got no axe to grind. You be my witness, that okay with you . . . ?' He stumbled and would have fallen without Keir to heave him upright. Grabbing Keir's lapels, a confused, almost frightened look came into his face. 'They're moving money around. Hausser's doing it, but Gross gives the orders. Some tax racket . . .'

Keir wished he'd never met him. 'Come on, let's get you home. You'll feel better in the morning.'

He got them walking again, with Ruark still protesting. 'I had no part of it. Anything happens you'll be my witness . . . Harry Ruark's hands are clean –'

'How much further –'

Ruark lurched into a side turning, dragging Keir with him. 'The Merck Finck Bank in Munich. Can you remember that name?'

'Of course –'

'Say it.'

'The Merck Finck Bank, Munich. Are we nearly there?'

'That's where the money's going. Anything happens, you tell 'em I said so. You'll be my witness . . .'

Even when they reached the apartment building, Ruark still clung to Keir's arm, imploring him to listen. 'They'll skim ten million dollars off the Starfighter contract at this rate.'

'Sure, Harry,' said Keir, leading him up the steps. 'You'll be okay from here.' Eventually he shoved Harry through the door. Ruark's last words were 'Hausser's mixed up in some sort of racket.'

Keir hurried away without a backward glance. Muzzy-headed himself, he cursed the evening as a complete waste of time. First Libberman had been useless, then he had wasted hours listening to the ramblings of a lunatic drunk. The final straw came when he found the door of the hotel locked against him. He hammered away for twenty minutes before being admitted by a sleepy-eyed porter. After an argument, Keir went to bed wishing with all his heart that he was back in the army.

Nearly twenty-four hours were to pass before he realized that meeting Ruark was one of the most important moments of his life.

Seven

Keir woke late, hung over, with a foul taste in his mouth. Memories of Ruark lingered like a bad dream.

After breakfasting on two cups of black coffee, he collected the NSU from the garage and set out for Frankfurt. A mood of depression descended like a black fog with every mile. Never, at any time in his life, had he felt such a sense of failure. It was his twelfth day in Germany and he had nothing to show for it except a handful of bills and a hangover. Bitterly regretting resigning his commission, he was beginning to loathe the world of commerce. If messing about like this can be called commerce, he reflected, deciding that the most useful service he could perform for Beaumont would be to resign.

Such was his mood when he arrived in Frankfurt that afternoon. Booking into a hotel, he sat in his room nursing his worries. I'm an idiot on a fool's errand, he concluded, angry with himself, Dusty and the whole wretched business. Making up his mind to resign as soon as he returned to London, he regretted arranging to meet Sam Bartleman. He'll laugh when he hears what a fool I've made of myself.

Although not meeting Sam until eight, an hour of being cooped in that bedroom, stewing over his worries, was the most Keir could stand, and at six o'clock he set out to find Schmidt's.

Schmidt's had become an institution in Frankfurt. More than a bar, more than a restaurant, it was a little piece of home for every American soldier serving in Germany. Its owner was an American, Max Smith, who had been in the US Army during the war. When the war was finished he had stayed where he was, seeing in the ruins of Frankfurt a chance to get rich. The way Max Smith figured it was that American GIs would be in Europe for a long time to come. So in 1946 he had opened 'Max's American Bar – Home from Home – All the Comforts of States Side'. In time the bar had become a restaurant, and by the time Germans could afford to dine out again it had become Schmidt's, comprising two bars, two restaurants, and a private room upstairs where the rich and the powerful of the two countries could meet. Outside the Stars and Stripes and the Tricolour of the Federal Republic were intertwined over the main entrance, and every inch of wall space inside was devoted to photographs. According to *Die Welt*, Germany's entire post-war history was recorded on the walls of Schmidt's. There were big photographs, small photographs, signed photographs, framed photographs, coloured photographs, black and white photographs . . .

Walking through the main restaurant, Keir saw every top face in NATO, past and present. Dwight Eisenhower's famous grin beamed across the table to General Speidee, CIC of NATO Ground Forces, the only general in history to command the forces of the nation that defeated him. German politicians abounded: Keir recognized Adenauer, Erhard, Strauss, Brandt. Everyone had eaten at Schmidt's. So had half the American government – Truman, Stevenson, Harriman, Foster Dulles . . .

Obeying the instructions Sam Bartleman had given him on the phone, Keir climbed the staircase at the far side of the restaurant and crossed a wide landing to where a blonde sat at a reception desk. She watched with puzzled eyes as he approached.

'I'm looking for a Major Bartleman –'

'Ah,' she smiled, recognition showing in her face. 'Major Milford. I was expecting you in uniform. Welcome to Schmidt's.' She explained that Major Bartleman was running late and had phoned to ask that Keir be 'looked after'.

'Herr Schmidt is expecting you,' said the blonde, 'I'll take you through, shall I?'

Keir followed her into Schmidt's famous private room, oblong in shape with a dozen tables at the far end and a comfortable bar just inside the door. Apart from a dozen waiters wandering between the tables to polish a glass here and some silver there, the place was deserted. As elsewhere, photographs covered every inch of wall space, even the door next to the bar, which opened at that moment to reveal Max Smith himself. Since his picture was everywhere – Max Smith with Chancellor Adenauer, Max Smith with Vice-President Nixon, Max Smith with Defence Minister Strauss – Keir recognized Max Smith immediately.

'You gotta be Keir Milford,' Smith said, offering his hand. 'I'm Max Smith. Welcome to my humble establishment.'

There was nothing humble about the establishment or the owner. Wearing a beautifully cut dinner jacket and a heavy tan, Smith looked every inch the successful businessman. Keir could understand why Bartleman and Smith were such good friends; Smith looked like Sam's older brother – the same expansive grin, the identical firm handshake and shrewd appraising look. Dusty too, Keir guessed, would feel instantly at home in the private room at Schmidt's.

'You're early,' said Smith, glancing at his gold watch. 'Sam said to expect you at eight, it's only a little after seven.'

Not wanting to admit leaving the hotel to escape a fit of the blues, Keir said, 'This is my first time here. I thought I'd have trouble finding it.'

'In Frankfurt? Everyone knows Schmidt's,' Smith admonished with a look of reproval while clicking his fingers at a waiter. 'Drink?'

Keir ordered a scotch and soda and listened to Smith explain about Sam's phone call. 'He won't be here until about nine, so what with you early and him late . . .' He shrugged and flashed Keir a quick smile. 'Don't worry, we'll entertain you, but you'll have to give me a minute. Come nine o'clock and this place will be jumping. There's a few things I gotta check on. Be back shortly, okay?'

Settled in a leather armchair, Keir decided that the room had the atmosphere of a club, except that the folded copies of the *New York Times*, *Der Spiegel*, *The Washington Post* and *Die Welt* made clear it wasn't an Englishman's club. The German–American theme was everywhere. Tiny replicas of the intertwined flags decorated every table. Even the photographs were exclusively of Germans and Americans. In vain, Keir scanned the walls for an English face, or a French face, or a Dutch or Italian face. There were none. No pictures of Churchill or Montgomery, or Attlee or Mountbatten; none of De Gaulle or Gasperi or Schuman. Just Germans and Americans. Keir recognized people he knew; staff officers he had met at SHAPE, colonels and majors as well as generals. Carrying his drink over to the far wall, he began to count the number of familiar faces. Twenty minutes later, having started on the second wall, he was still counting when Smith returned.

'Started as a hobby and ended up as a trade mark,' Smith laughed, waving a hand at the photographs. 'It's cheaper than having the place decorated.'

'They go back a long way –'

'Sure, from when I opened the place.' Smith surveyed the room with obvious pride. 'Those days were different. I dunno, maybe it was just this place that was different. Less well-known. The early fifties were the best years. Ten years ago they'd kick shit out of each other in public, then fix up a deal here the same evening. No one knew except me and I wasn't telling.'

He grinned. 'Can't do that no more. Schmidt's is too well known. I succeeded to fail.' He laughed. 'Hey, I just thought of that. Make a good epitaph, don't you think?'

A waiter arrived with another drink and Smith laughed as Keir drowned the scotch with soda. 'Pacing yourself, eh? Wise man. Sam said you were wise. He tells me you were a big noise at SHAPE.'

'As a major?' Keir shook his head. 'No one makes *any* noise below the rank of colonel.'

'I guess,' Smith nodded. 'Still, Sam said you were pretty good. Said you know all the angles. Like those guys.' He gestured at the photographs.

Keir grinned. 'I don't know many angles, but I know most of them. I was just counting how many –'

'Yeah?' Smith's interest quickened. 'Really? Who do you know?'

Smith loved his photographs. Within minutes he was beaming with pleasure. 'Fancy you knowing old Frank. He was in here last week with Joe Brewer. You know Joe too? Shit! Who'd have believed –' He broke off from time to time to deal with interruptions from his staff. He answered their whispered questions and sent them away quickly, to plunge happily back into conversation with Keir. Knowing people was a hobby with Max Smith. He prided himself on knowing everyone, and although by 'everyone' he meant mostly the famous, he was ready to tell a story about dozens of Keir's American and German contemporaries at SHAPE. He even knew where they were on his walls. Confronted by a name, his eyes narrowed for a moment, then widened in triumph. 'I got Bill over here somewhere. Yeah, here he is. See, here's Bill and me with General Bradley . . .'

Obviously it was a game he had played many times and which he still enjoyed, for once he had started he was reluctant to stop. He had dozens of anecdotes. 'Good job you came early!' He grinned. 'Another hour and there'll be too many people to see properly.'

They were talking about Alan Prentice, an American major, when Smith mentioned Defence Minister Strauss. He could hardly not mention him since Strauss was in the photograph – his fat, jovial face grinning out from between the thinner faces of Prentice and Smith. 'There's someone who's done well for himself,' said Smith. 'Good old Franz Josef. You ever meet him?'

Keir had met the German Minister of Defence twice, briefly.

'Hell of a guy,' said Smith. 'Franz Josef and I go back to the end of the war. In fact, this'll shake you – first time I met Franz Josef he was still a prisoner of war. If you'd seen him then, you wouldn't recognize him. You know how fat he is? Well, I tell you, in those days he was thin as a rake. Here, come and look over here. I got a picture somewhere . . .'

It took him less than a minute to find it. The photograph was among those pinned on the door. Peering at the faded picture, Keir agreed it was hard to recognize the rotund figure of the

274

Minister of Defence. He shrugged and turned to Smith with a grin. 'You've kept in better shape than he has.'

'You bet. That must have been taken in '45 or '46. Hell of a long time ago.'

Keir stared at the old print, in which a young Max Smith stood with his arms draped around the shoulders of two other figures. Identifying initials were written in white ink at the foot of the photograph – FJS, MS, EFH.

'Good old Franz Josef,' said Smith, shaking his head. 'We had some fun, us three. Ernie Hausser, Franz Josef and me.'

Hairs rose on the back of Keir's neck. A tiny shiver ran up his spine. Hausser? He could hear Ruark spitting the name – *Ernest F. Hausser*. Riveted, Keir's eyes went to the initials. EFH. He blinked and took another long look. It had to be a coincidence. Hausser was a common German name.

'German, was he? Your friend Ernie Hausser.'

'Christ, no. We were Intelligence Officers together. That's how we met Franz Joseph. He was a POW. He spoke good English, so we yanked him out of prison camp and made him an interpreter.'

Still staring at the photograph, Keir could hear Ruark talking about the bouquet of flowers at the airport. *'Know what the card with the flowers said? "Welcome! FJS." Just FJS. That's all. Any dame sends me flowers she'd say Frieda . . . or Frances . . .'*

FJS wasn't a woman. It was there in the photograph. FJS. FJS stood for Franz Josef Strauss.

'Ernie really helped him,' Smith was saying, 'Franz Josef wouldn't be where he is today if it wasn't for Ernie. He owes him a lot.'

Unable to move, Keir was rooted to the spot, staring at the photograph. *Find out why Beaumont lost the fighter contract*, Dusty had said.

Scarcely believing his ears or his eyes, Keir said, 'Ernie Hausser and Strauss are friends?'

'Sure, thick as thieves in the old days. Like I said, Franz Josef wouldn't be where he is today if it wasn't for Ernie's help at the end of the forties. Just shows how the world's changed.'

And how, thought Keir. Franz Josef Strauss had changed from Prisoner of War Strauss to Defence Minister Strauss. Ernie Hausser had changed from an Intelligence Officer to a

Lockheed employee. Strauss signs a controversial contract with Lockheed and Hausser returns to Germany in charge of liaison.

Keir closed his eyes and squeezed his eyelids tightly together. When he opened them again he saw not the photograph, but Sam Pickard rubbing his thumb and forefinger together in the Dorchester. *Someone authorized millions of dollars on a death trap. When that sort of thing happens, there's only one reason.*

Keir stared, seeing the reason less than two feet from his face.

For the following four days, Keir lived on his nerves, telling no one of his suspicions. All ideas of asking Sam Bartleman's advice died before Sam arrived at Schmidt's that night. Their meal together turned into no more than a pleasant reunion. The following morning Keir drove back to Cologne, pushing the rented NSU to its limits in his hurry. In Cologne he called on newspaper men, friends from his days with the Army Office of Information. The next day he went on to Bavaria to trace the roots of Franz Josef Strauss's political career back to their beginnings. The third day he flew to Paris, where he broke the law by persuading a friend in SHAPE to disclose certain records belonging to the United States Army. Gleaning a fragment here, another there, Keir worked on until he pieced the story together and although still incomplete when he flew back to London, the notes in his briefcase added up to a lot more than conjecture.

Poor, drunken, misguided Harry Ruark was wrong to suppose Lockheed were moving money around to avoid tax. They were playing an even more dangerous game. They were paying out millions of dollars in bribes.

Lockheed, one of the largest aircraft companies in the world, had bought itself a government!

Hausser was the key. Hausser and Strauss. At the end of the war, Franz Josef Strauss, slim and unknown then, was released from a prison camp to work as an interpreter – exactly as Max Smith had remembered, except that he had exaggerated his own role. Max had his picture taken with too many people to be close friends with them all. Hausser and Strauss were the real friends. The son of Austrian parents, Hausser soon found that he and Strauss had much in common, and when the prisoner cooperated so willingly, it was Hausser who had arranged for him to move from the stark prison to more luxurious quarters in the American camp. After that, Hausser helped his new friend in many ways, not least by recommending that he be given the post of deputy to the ageing county commissioner, 'Landrat' Bauer. Strauss was to use the appointment as the first stepping stone to a political career.

In 1948, when Hausser divorced his wife in America and married a local German girl, Strauss was best man at the wedding, and the close friendship continued until Hausser was transferred back to the States in 1950.

Meanwhile, in Germany, Franz Josef Strauss built a political career. Decidedly right wing, he moved from local to national politics by winning control of the Bavarian-based Christian Social Union – the CSU. Chancellor Adenauer, leader of the Christian Democrats (CDU), grew alarmed that his majority in the Bundestag would be threatened if Strauss split the conservative vote in Bavaria. So Adenaeur did a deal. His Christian Democrats would not compete in elections in Bavaria, if Strauss supported him in the Bundestag. The result was the CDU-CSU coalition which transformed Strauss from the boss of a provincial party into a national politician with the plum post of Minister of Defence.

All of these facts were in the public record. Also on record was that shortly after signing the contract with Lockheed, Strauss made an official visit to the USA. But it was not generally known that during his visit Strauss sought out his old friend Ernie Hausser, who had left the army and was struggling to establish a career in civilian life. Within weeks, Hausser joined Lockheed, and after an absence of ten years returned to Germany, to be met at Frankfurt Airport by an enraged Henry Ruark holding a bouquet of flowers bearing a card saying 'Welcome! FJS'.

Keir had no doubt that 'FJS' was Franz Josef Strauss. Just as he had no doubts about Hausser's *real* job at Lockheed. *He's supposed to be in public relations*, Ruark had sneered. *Private relations would be more like it.*

The answer lay in the Merck Finck Bank at Munich. As far as Keir could find out, Lockheed did not maintain an account with the Merck Finck Bank. Neither, to Keir's knowledge, did Franz Josef Strauss. But the Christian Social Union did. That's where the funds were going. Without paying Strauss directly, Lockheed were boosting the funds of his political party.

Harry Ruark, drunk and frightened, had said, 'They'll skim ten million dollars off the Starfighter contract at this rate . . .'

And Keir believed him.

Eight

'So Pickard was right,' said Dusty when Keir finished. 'Something fishy is going on.'

'Worse than fishy. All Pickard had was a gut feeling that something was wrong. This is a Minister of State for God's sake. And we're talking millions of dollars.'

They were in Dusty's office. Large and rectangular, with walls adorned by Picassos loaned from the collection of the late Mr Lacey, the office was high enough up for Hyde Park's green acres to be visible above the rooftops. The desk and conference table were of rosewood, the chairs upholstered in black hide. Greenery trailed from white earthenware pots onto a rich amber carpet. It was a room designed to impress, and Keir had been impressed seeing it for the first time but at that moment, he was too worried to notice. Unable to sit still, too agitated to remain at the table, he pushed back his chair and paced up and down.

Watching him, Dusty said, 'If Lockheed are in bed with the Minister of Defence, it looks curtains for the CX29.'

'Forget the CX29,' Keir said hotly. 'This is much more important. Don't you see what it means? It will be the biggest political scandal since the war. It will destroy the German government. God knows what it will do to NATO. The repercussions will be enormous –'

'Steady on. You can't prove anything. Most of what you've told me is conjecture. Especially about Strauss and Lockheed. It all sounds possible, even probable –'

'We can call for a Public Enquiry. A proper investigation would expose everything –'

'We can't do that!" Dusty sounded horrified.

278

'Why not? I'm going back to Germany –'

'To do what? Charge around making wild accusations based on the ramblings of a drunk – a disgruntled ex-employee? Be sensible, Keir. Anyway, what did Strauss do? He found a job for an old buddy. So what? That's not a crime –'

'There's more to it than that. You're forgetting the bank account –'

'There might be another explanation. Slow down, Keir. You're getting carried away.'

Keir looked at him in amazement. 'I don't understand you. Find out why Beaumont lost the fighter contract, that's what you said. Well I did. I'm telling you that there's collusion between Lockheed and the German Minister of Defence.'

'And I'm not saying you're wrong,' said Dusty, 'I'm saying you can't *prove* it –'

'That's why we need a Public Enquiry.'

Dusty shook his head. 'Think about your friends for a minute. You've spent the last two weeks pumping them for information. They won't thank you to involve them in a scandal, not with powerful politicians involved. Screw up their careers and they'll never speak to you again. Once that happens you've lost your connection –'

'This is more important –'

'To whom? To you? To friends you'll drop in the shit? To Chuck Hayes?'

Dusty's reaction was not what Keir had expected. He tried to explain. 'This affects everyone. Europe. NATO –'

'You don't work for NATO any longer.'

'What's that got to do with it?' Keir demanded, taken aback. 'If the Starfighter is as bad as Pickard claims, there won't be an effective Fighter Command left in Europe –'

'Right,' Dusty agreed, 'I buy the importance of NATO having the best aircraft. Which brings us back to the CX29. What's the word on that?'

'You're missing the point –'

'No, I'm not. You want to strike a blow for NATO. Make sure they get the CX29 –'

'It's a totally different issue.'

'It's the issue that concerns us. Stop thinking about NATO and think about Beaumont. We're Beaumont and Lockheed is the enemy. That's the way you've got to think. It won't do any good to start shouting about Public Enquiries. Like I said before, slow down. This needs careful thinking about . . .'

But Dusty was up to his eyes in work. People were queuing up to see him. He could spare little time for meetings with Keir. Owen Lacey's London office fell well below Dusty's standards and he was on an all-out blitz to bring things up to scratch. Even before Keir went to Germany Dusty had said, 'I've got to get London right before I can open offices in Paris and Rome.' And to get London right he started at 6.30 and worked like the devil all day; holding breakfast meetings at the Savoy, meeting clients for lunch and yet more for dinner.

To underline the point, his secretary poked her head round the door at that moment and announced the arrival of his next visitor.

Dusty groaned. 'I won't be a minute.' He turned back to Keir. 'Sorry, I must go. Look, why not go and see Smart and discuss it with him?'

Disappointed, Keir asked, 'What about lunch? Perhaps we could talk –'

'Sorry, I've got a meeting –'

'Tonight?'

'No good, I'm taking some people to the Colony. Go and see Smart. Discuss it with him, then see what you think.'

Deflated, Keir walked along the corridor to his office. Team International was a grand-sounding name, but he was coming to realize it consisted solely of him. He had his own plush office in the Owen Lacey building, a telephone, a secretary when he needed one, and most important of all a real client in Beaumont. It wasn't quite as he had imagined, but it was hard to blame Dusty. After all, Dusty had delivered what he had promised. Now it was up to Keir.

He phoned Smart. He had met the lawyer over lunch at the Savoy some weeks before. On that occasion, Dusty had done most of the talking. Now it was Keir's turn and he suspected he was about to say something that wouldn't find favour with Dusty at all. Dusty's reaction worried him. A knowing look had crept into Dusty's eyes. Instead of being shocked about corruption in high places, Dusty's first concern had been for Beaumont. It seemed an odd sense of priorities to Keir.

The earliest Smart could see him was three o'clock and after confirming that he knew the whereabouts of Lincoln's Inn, Keir hung up and set to work on his notes. So shaken was he by Dusty's reaction that he was determined to present his case more effectively to Smart. 'At least a lawyer will understand the importance of a Public Enquiry,' he muttered, thinking that Dusty's background in advertising was a disadvantage at times.

After working on his notes for an hour, he had lunch at the pub on the corner and arrived at Smart's office in plenty of time.

'And how is Mr Miller?' the lawyer enquired as he led the way into his office.

'Fine,' Keir answered, looking around the book-lined room.

Aged about fifty, Toby Smart had the red-cheeked, broken-veined face of a man who ate and drank more than was good for him. Only the superb cut of his suit saved him from looking fat. His plump hands were soft and he had the most beautifully manicured finger nails, shaped and polished, that Keir had ever seen on a man's hands.

After his secretary had served tea and biscuits, Smart settled himself behind his desk and beamed amiably at Keir. 'Now then, what brings you to see me?'

This time, Keir told the story in exact detail, omitting nothing and dwelling heavily on the essential points.

Smart listened with an expressionless face. He remained silent until Keir finished, when he nodded gravely and said, 'I see. I hope you haven't told this to anyone else?'

'Only to Dusty – That is, Mr Miller.'

'Very wise. Keep it to yourself. I'm not even sure why you've told me.'

'Because we must do something about it. We've got to expose what's going on,' Keir said earnestly, surprised by Smart's bland reaction. He went through the story again, fearing he had left something out, and only when he had repeated his accusations in full did he suspect that Smart had understood perfectly well the first time.

'There's nothing wrong with my hearing,' said the lawyer. 'It's just that I can't see what's in this for you.'

Wondering how any intelligent man could fail to grasp the

issues at stake, Keir set about explaining the consequences for Germany and NATO. He talked of the decision to re-arm Germany five years before, and the opposition it had aroused in England and France.

'It was the most controversial political decision since the end of the war,' he said. 'A lot of people were opposed to it, even in Germany . . .'

Describing the need for a democratic Germany to be part of a unified Europe, he admitted, 'Some people are still sceptical about Germany's ability to adapt to democracy. Something like this – a scandal – could do untold damage.'

Smart remained unimpressed. 'I hear what you say,' he said, 'but I question why you're saying it. My function is not to advise Germany, nor is it to advise NATO. My function is to advise you.'

'Very well, and I say we've got to expose what's going on –'

There was nothing flabby about Smart's mind, despite his appearance. Even his voice took on a hard edge. 'Now listen to me, Mr Milford. You're playing with fire. What you've told me is mostly conjecture. It's all based on gossip. Keep one thing in mind. Large commercial enterprises and powerful politicians have one thing in common. Anyone who threatens their reputations gets hit and hit hard. I shouldn't like to defend you in an action for slander. Quite frankly, you wouldn't stand a chance. And consider the consequences. You will have thrown away a fine career in the army for nothing. You will be ruined. Your new enterprise will be finished before it even starts, and you'll have let down your friend Mr Miller very badly . . .'

He went on at some length, alarming Keir more by the minute. Finally, Smart said, 'Quite apart from which, even if you are right, I can't see that any law has been broken.'

Keir gasped. 'Lockheed are making payments –'

'It's not illegal for a commercial enterprise to make donations to a political party, either here or in Germany. Consequently even if – and I stress the "if" – your suspicions are correct and Lockheed have contributed to CSU funds, they haven't broken any law in the process.'

When Keir said it was a bribe, Smart refused even to consider the word. He said it was a matter of interpretation. 'For instance,' he said smiling, 'my firm contributes rather generously to the Conservative Party. I hope you're not suggesting there's anything improper in that.'

'But you don't do it in expectation of gain.'

Smart's eyes gleamed. 'We do make our donations via certain Tory MPs, most of whom ask us to act for them from time to time, but of course you're quite right – *naturally* we don't contribute in expectation of gain.'

Keir felt a fool. He realized that Smart thought him naive. The wisest response would have been to end the meeting there and then. Instead, perversely, he hammered away, making things even worse. Smart won every argument hands down. By the end of an hour, Keir felt miserable and humiliated.

Leaning back in his chair, Smart gazed up at the ceiling. 'I'm reminded of my father,' he said. 'He founded this firm. Shrewd old bird, he was. He gave me some advice when I started. "Toby, me boy," he said. "Who decides if a lawyer's any good? Answer, the client. It's no good telling a client that justice was done if a case isn't settled to his satisfaction. He won't think you're much of a lawyer. But *win* the case, and that's different. He'll think you're a hell of a feller."' Smart chuckled. 'I think you're in the same business, Mr Milford. Your client won't thank you to go around shouting about Public Enquiries. But if you find a way to turn what these people are doing to your client's advantage, I think you'll find my father was right. Your client will think you're a hell of a feller.'

'You mean we let them get away with it?' Keir asked, scarcely believing his own ears. 'Instead of taking what we've got to the authorities?'

'What have we got? Hearsay and suspicion. And who are the authorities? The government? You say they're involved –'

'The point is –'

'The point is what's best for your client,' Smart interrupted. 'My experience is that scandals hurt everyone. Mud sticks to the innocent as well as the guilty. Public Enquiries take months to convene, a year to pontificate, and nine times out of ten come up with a whitewash. Didn't you say Beaumont were expecting a decision on their transport plane this autumn?'

'They were hoping –'

'They can kiss that goodbye for a start. I've seen Enquiries at work. Everything stops. With something like that going on Ministry officials won't buy as much as a paper clip.'

Keir continued to argue, without budging Smart by an inch. Finally, at six o'clock, he called it a day.

'Remember my old father,' said Smart as he led the way to the door. 'Find a way to turn what these people are doing to your client's advantage.'

'That's condoning bribery and corruption –'

'Certainly not,' Smart said sharply. He paused, searching for words, his annoyance changing to a look of perplexity. 'I'm trying to give you good advice,' he said with a sigh. 'You're moving into a different world, Mr Milford. It's like buying a car from a dealer. If you don't ask whether there's an engine or a steering wheel, he won't bring it up.'

Keir departed, perplexed and angry, with his head buzzing from the long argument. First Dusty, then Smart. Neither had reacted as he'd expected. Of course proof was needed. He knew that. He didn't need some pompous fool of a lawyer to point out the obvious.

Steaming with temper and frustration, he walked down Chancery Lane, heading for the Marchmount Hotel. If only Dusty could spare more time. If only there was someone he could talk to, someone who would listen, someone who would *understand*. While packing up in Paris he had written a long letter to Dawn, full of enthusiasm about his new career with Dusty, pages and pages about the money they would make. Writing had led to dreaming, tempting him to raise the subject of marriage again. Now, with his future so uncertain, he was glad to have left the subject alone. 'Anyway –' he shrugged – 'she still hasn't answered my letter.'

No letter awaited him when he collected his key at the Marchmount, but there was a note saying his mother had telephoned two days before. It was a reminder that another part of his life had not developed as expected. Leaving the army should have enabled him to see more of the family, instead he had seen them scarcely at all.

Even so, he brightened as he stepped into the telephone booth in the lobby. Liz would cheer him up. A few words with her were exactly what he needed. She would giggle and thank him for the doll he had sent her from Germany . . .

But Liz wasn't there.

'She's in Norfolk with Joe,' said Edith, sounding almost surprised that he didn't know.

'Norfolk? What are they doing in Norfolk?'

'Protesting of course. Don't you ever read the papers? There's a Thor missile site near a place called Thetford. Oh, hold on –' She broke off and sneezed loudly, returning a moment later, still snuffling – 'This wretched cold won't go away. That's why I had to stay behind. Otherwise I'd be with them –'

'I can't believe it. Aldermaston was bad enough –'

'The only bad thing about Aldermaston was setting it up in the first place.'

'Oh, for God's sake!' Keir exclaimed. Another argument was the last thing he wanted. One way and another, he had been arguing all day.

He took himself off to the bar, and from there to the dining-room, where a thoroughly bad meal added to his state of dejection. And finally he went to bed, hoping that his problems would look less daunting in the morning.

But he was wrong, for even as he slept a letter was on its way containing even more bad news.

Nine

The letter from Dawn had been redirected twice. She had written to his SHAPE address, the army had sent it to Hillingdon and his mother had sent it on from there. The date surprised him. It was over a month old. And it came not from Hollywood but from Sydney, Australia.

'*JD is dead*,' Dawn wrote on the opening line. There was no preamble – no 'Dear Keir, how are you' or anything like that. Just '*JD is dead*.'

Keir stared, not feeling anything much. He had not met JD, not known him, been jealous of him often and had finally accepted his importance in Dawn's life, none of which was enough to stir Keir's feelings. But it was clear that Dawn's feelings were stirred. She was heartbroken. Pain and grief leapt from every line and from every one of the many pages. It was a long, rambling letter in which she poured out her heart.

The first three pages were so choked with emotion that Keir had to read them several times to understand them. JD had suffered a heart attack, that much was clear from the opening paragraphs, but the circumstances of his death and what they were doing in Australia took a while to establish. Eventually it became clear that JD had arranged for Dawn to work on a movie on a co-production basis: *'which means we put up some of the money and I don't get a penny until the cost of the negative has been recovered . . . after which we split fifty-fifty with the co-producers . . .'*

Apparently a lot of things had gone wrong. Shooting the film in Australia had proved more expensive than planned, freakish bad weather had added weeks to the schedule, finally the production was so over budget that JD and the co-producers had fallen out about money: *'JD did it for me. Everything was for me. They wanted to cut corners to save cost and he wouldn't let them. He didn't care if we spent a whole week on one scene if it produced the effect he wanted . . .'*

Keir's impression was of JD working round the clock, supervising filming while dashing back and forth between bankers to raise more and more money:

'He was winning too. Another couple of weeks and I'm sure he'd have tied everything up . . .'

But then: *'he came into my dressing-room the other afternoon, saying he didn't feel well . . . I was only a minute, I went to fetch a glass of water . . .'*

The rest of the page was blotchy with tears.

Although feeling nothing for JD, Keir's heart ached for Dawn. Reading on only fuelled his misery for there was no mistaking her sense of loss.

'. . . he did so much for me. I don't expect you to understand . . . no one could . . .'

Skipping the rest of the page, Keir wished the words were not there, wished they had never been written. Dawn revealed more than he wanted to know. After making himself believe that JD was her manager not her lover, he had no wish to believe anything else. Besides, the man was dead. JD was dead.

286

Her financial affairs were in a mess. Most of her savings were locked up in the film. '. . . *it will be ages before I see any money back. The film is more or less finished, except for cutting and editing . . . I won't see a penny until it's released . . .*'

Apparently someone called Harvey had flown out from London to help straighten things out. '. . . *and Eric's with me of course. God knows what I'd have done without Eric . . .*'

She expected to return to Hollywood at the end of the month. Glancing at the date, Keir calculated she had already left Australia. '. . . *Harvey and Eric say I'll have to sign with one of the studios to earn some money . . . I don't know, I don't much care at the moment . . .*'

All she cared about was Liz. '. . . *it's hard to explain . . . all this time without telling JD about her, I've felt so disloyal and neglectful. After the mother I had I ought to have done better . . . the trouble was I could never admit to JD that I'd lied to him. So many people betrayed him in his life, I couldn't add to that number. He spent so much time singing my praises, always so sure that I'd never let him down . . . I just couldn't do it . . . but I told Eric and Harvey last night. Naturally they were shocked, but we're all so broken up and weepy about JD that maybe the shock was less than it would have been . . . I don't know, all I know is I couldn't exist another day without telling them . . .*'

Keir read on, vaguely pleased that at last she had told someone.

Then he stiffened. Startled, he knocked his cup as he turned a page, sending coffee all over the table. The Marchmount's only other guests, two commercial travellers and an elderly spinster, looked up from their breakfasts. A waitress poked her head out from the kitchen, to emerge a moment later carrying a cloth. Cursing his clumsiness, Keir pushed his chair back from the table. Absorbed in the letter he had forgotten his breakfast which had long since congealed on the plate. With a look of disgust at the debris, he rose, the letter firmly clutched in his hand. 'Bit of a mess, I'm afraid,' he said to the waitress on his way to the door.

Upstairs in his room, he spread Dawn's letter on the bed, rifling through pages to find the one he wanted.

'. . . *so I told Eric I want Liz to live with us in Hollywood . . . we can avoid bad publicity by saying I adopted her . . . I really*

*don't care what we say, I'll say anything they want . . . but she's
my child and she should be with me . . .'*

'Oh no!' Keir exclaimed. 'That's not on.'

*'. . . it can't be until things get sorted out . . . I'm in such a mess
at the moment . . . but in a few months . . .'*

'No,' Keir repeated aloud, 'you can forget that idea.'

*'. . . I know you'll understand. You always do, that's what's so
marvellous about you. Dear, reliable Keir . . .'*

'Here we go,' he said bitterly. 'Good old Keir. Buckets of soft
soap for dear, reliable Mug of the Month Keir!'

His letter about leaving the army clearly hadn't reached her.
*'. . . you've done so well in the army, I don't suppose you have
much chance to see Liz . . . and suddenly my life seems quite
empty without her . . .'*

'Bloody bad luck!' he shouted, suddenly boiling over with
rage.

He ripped the page in half. Then he started on the others,
tearing every page into shreds, tossing the confetti into the
waste-paper basket.

'A bloody mug,' he said, grabbing his coat from the wardrobe,
'that's what they take me for. They're all the same – Dusty,
Smart, Sam Pickard! Okay then, I'll show them who's a mug!'

He slammed out of his room and set out for the office.

Ten

Howard Street to Knightsbridge by cab took no more than
fifteen minutes. Never did Keir use time to better effect. He
took stock of his life, fuming with temper. Even before Dawn's
letter he had been in a bad mood. He had woken in a bad mood,
still angry about his meeting with Smart. 'Patronizing old sod,'
Keir grumbled under his breath. He had been patronized before, in his early days in the army. More than one fellow officer
had been amused by Keir's grammar school background. He
knew what had saved him. The Germans, Americans, French
and every nationality in NATO, who were deaf and blind to the

nuances of English snobbery. His quick ear for languages had saved him. Given a different posting, the British class system would have been a bar to his progress. But at SHAPE he had shone, being promoted to major when those who had patronized him were still struggling to make captain.

Serve them right too, he thought. They're living in yesterday's world, not the world of today.

The thought reminded him of his father. 'Silly old fool,' he said in exasperation. Nuclear bombs *existed*. You couldn't make them go away by marching up and down waving a banner. The Russians had nuclear bombs, so we must have nuclear bombs. The balance of power kept peace in the world. Surely anyone could see that? 'Wasting his time tilting at windmills . . .' Keir grumbled, before laughing aloud at the thought of Sam Pickard. Sam Pickard thought he was a waste of time. 'He'll have to eat his words about that,' Keir concluded with some satisfaction.

Even so, he was having second thoughts about a Public Enquiry. Dusty and Smart were dead set against it, seeing it as a side issue to the business of making money. Maybe they were right, after all they both made more than he did. And he needed money, especially now with this letter from Dawn – he needed to prove he could give Liz a better future in England . . .

Round and round went the thought in Keir's head – the need for money reminding him of his mission to Germany. Meeting Harry Ruark had been a stroke of luck. Even so, the full story was bound to come out. It always did. Someone else would discover what he had found out. Perhaps it's best to leave it to them, he decided, and get on with earning a living.

Find a way to turn this to your client's advantage, Smart had said. *Do that and you'll find my father was right. Your client will think you're a hell of a feller*.

'And you'll get the shock of your life,' said Keir, sick and tired of being taken for the Mug of the Month.

Keir gambled everything on one meeting with Kurt Schiller.

Schiller had a formidable reputation. Twenty years earlier *Oberleutnant* Schiller had been the darling of Goering's *Luftwaffe*. Tall, slim, aristocratic, fair-haired and blue-eyed, his looks had been perfect for all the propaganda magazines. During the *Kanalkampf*, as the *Luftwaffe* named the early period of the Battle of Britain, he had destroyed three Spitfires, two Defiants and a Hurricane. By the end of the war, forty-nine fallen Allied aircraft were credited to his account. After the war when Germany was denied any armed forces, he had lived the life of a recluse – a proud, aloof figure, descendant of a family who had supplied Prussia with soldiers for three hundred years. Everything changed when Germany was elected to NATO. Schiller was back, not as leader of the *Luftwaffe* as many had predicted, but in charge of Evaluation and Procurement of Aircraft. The rumour was that his low-profile job was in deference to British sensibilities. The legend was that he was as tough as ever and determined to build the best airforce in Europe. The fact was that he had opposed the Starfighter contract.

Even without having met him, Keir knew a good deal about him. Only that month *Time* magazine had described Schiller as 'Father of the modern Luftwaffe'. He lived for the *Luftwaffe*, something Keir kept in mind when he telephoned him. 'No sir, I can't explain on the phone, but the matter is of vital importance to the *Luftwaffe*.'

Cautious and suspicious, the German resisted Keir's request for a private meeting. Schiller lived by the book, and private meetings in hotels were definitely not recommended in the manuals.

This reaction was no more than Keir had expected. Mentioning Sam Bartleman and a dozen other acquaintances in common, he said, 'If I could ask you to check with any of them, I'm sure they'll give me a reference . . .'

At Schiller's request, he telephoned him again two hours later. Sounding a little less frosty, the German said, 'I am told you are pro-NATO, pro-Europe, and favourably inclined towards Germany. Most important of all, they tell me you were a trustworthy young officer. That being the case, I find it all the more surprising that you won't tell me your business on the telephone.'

'Sorry, sir, all I can say is that it is of vital importance to the *Luftwaffe*.'

Ten minutes later, Keir was granted his meeting, and the following day he flew to Cologne where he again booked into the Adler Hotel – this time into a suite.

That evening, indeed that night and most of the next morning, were among the most worrying hours of Keir's life. His whole future depended on his meeting with Schiller. Time and again he rehearsed his arguments, trying to make every word count. By noon, still in his shirtsleeves and fretting about the extent of his gamble, he walked from the bedroom into the sitting-room where waiters were setting the table in the window. For something to do he checked the bottles on the sideboard: vodka, gin, scotch, schnapps, mineral waters. Nearby lay three packs of cigarettes, one pack open with two cigarettes protruding from the rest.

'I'll put the coffee here, sir,' said a waiter, carrying a percolator over to the sideboard. Switching it on, he turned to a colleague who was setting an ice bucket next to the table. 'Two bottles of Moselle, sir,' he said, displaying the labels to Keir before plunging both bottles into the ice.

Keir returned to the bedroom where he brushed his jacket and straightened his tie. 'Don't look so bloody anxious,' he told his reflection in the mirror.

Back in the sitting-room the waiters set the food on the table – landleberwurst, cold chicken, Westphalian ham, Coburg ham, big bowls of salad. Keir examined the cheese board and the selection of fruit. It was all as he had ordered. Anxious that the meeting should be totally private, the cold buffet ensured that he and Schiller could serve themselves, undisturbed even by waiters.

With everything completed and the staff departed, Keir went down to the front lobby, concerned to greet Schiller at the door. 'Take charge from the start,' he told himself, peering out into the street.

Schiller arrived exactly on time, removing his brown trilby as he came through the door. The once famous fair hair had long since turned grey, but the eyes were as blue and just as intense. In his late forties, of medium height, he had the lithe frame and suntanned face of the excellent tennis player he was reputed to be. The well-cut grey suit was worn with the stiff correctness of a man who had spent a lifetime in uniform and who would never dream of leaving a button undone.

When Keir introduced himself, Schiller's manner was cool and reserved, although not unfriendly, as if he was prepared to give Keir the benefit of the doubt. He only expressed surprise on seeing the suite. Looking around the good-sized room with its superb view of the Rhine, a quizzical look came into his eye. 'Am I to be seduced?'

Disguising nervousness with a laugh, Keir said, 'Nothing like that, sir. May I offer you a drink? Or I could open the wine if you prefer?'

Schiller did prefer, and while Keir uncorked the Moselle, the German strolled around the room with his hands clasped behind his back in the manner of an inspecting officer. 'This must be a very private matter,' he said, his voice cool and dry, 'for you to go to so much trouble.'

Keir had guessed it would be like this. There would be no small talk, no fooling Schiller. According to his men he could detect a lie as it formed on a man's lips, a story Keir was prepared to believe as he handed him his wine.

Accepting the glass with a faint smile, Schiller said, 'I'll leave you to propose a toast. It might give me a clue as to why I'm here.'

'The *Luftwaffe*,' said Keir, raising his glass.

Schiller's eyebrows twitched a fraction. 'The *Luftwaffe*,' he echoed, drinking deeply. Pausing to enjoy the wine, he said, 'Excellent. Now I must propose a toast, but I have a difficulty. I would like to drink to my host, if I knew who he was. After all, surely you are not paying for this out of your own pocket?'

Keir managed a rueful smile. 'I'm not sure, sir. I might be. It depends on the outcome of our meeting.'

The answer appealed to Schiller. It amused him. 'Ha!' He threw back his head. 'A speculative venture, is it? In that case I suggest we sit down at once. You might change your mind and cancel my lunch.' Drawing a chair back from the table, he smiled. 'You agree? Then let us begin.'

The words 'let us begin' were spoken with authority, leaving Keir in no doubt that any further delay would incur Schiller's displeasure. The moment had arrived, there was no going back. Keir delayed a fraction while serving food onto his plate, then took a deep breath and launched into his presentation. Beginning by saying that the *Luftwaffe*'s decision to buy the Starfighter had surprised many people, he edged into his well-rehearsed assertions about bribes, avoiding names, merely saying he could prove involvement of 'a high-ranking politician'.

Schiller glared fiercely from under his eyebrows, but the impression he gave was less of being startled by the allegations than hearing them from Keir. Several times he seemed about to interrupt, and each time checked himself. Instead he chewed solidly, wiping his lips with a napkin, sipping his wine, waiting for Keir to finish.

'So,' he said eventually, indicating the room, 'all this to tell me some scandalous nonsense. I'm disappointed –'

'Not nonsense, sir. I can prove it –'

'I doubt it.'

'If you'll just hear me out –'

'Why should I?' demanded Schiller with the first signs of temper. 'What's your interest in this anyway? I don't even know who you represent.'

There was no avoiding it. Keir would have preferred to leave it until later, but Schiller tossed his napkin onto the table and began to show signs of leaving. Keir had to tell him about Beaumont.

The German's eyes lit with understanding. 'Ah! So that's it. You're out to create a scandal are you? I get the picture. Lockheed are discredited and Beaumont come up smelling of roses . . .' Pushing his unfinished meal away, he rose from the table. 'Keep your lunch,' he said angrily, the tan of his face deepening. 'I wouldn't have come –'

Keir jumped up. 'No, sir. That's not my intention at all. I'm trying to *avoid* a scandal.'

Remaining on his feet, Schiller hesitated, surprise mingling with anger in his eyes.

Swallowing hard, Keir said, 'A scandal would be bad for everyone. It would damage the *Luftwaffe* –'

'You *dare* to suggest the *Luftwaffe* is involved?'

'No, sir. I said it will *damage* the *Luftwaffe*. That's what I believe. Just as it will damage Germany's reputation.'

'Who do you think you are? Talking about the *Luftwaffe* and Germany?'

'A scandal will bring down the government –'

'Rubbish! Some petty official –'

'This man is *not* a petty official.'

Again Schiller hesitated. Meeting those angry eyes convinced Keir that the German had suspicions of his own. Keir tried to push the point home. 'Sir, I repeat, this man is not a petty official and the bribes amount to millions of dollars. No government could survive such a scandal.'

This time, Schiller was visibly shaken.

'Please, sir,' said Keir earnestly, 'won't you sit down? Hear me out. Believe me, I am not trying to make trouble.'

Bristling with hostility, Schiller resumed his seat, checking his watch as he did so. 'I'll give you five minutes,' he said with evident distaste, clearly wishing he was elsewhere.

It was enough. The fact that he had sat down was enough to convince Keir that Schiller had suspicions of his own. He might even have proof, Keir thought while marshalling his thoughts. He talked steadily, and for more than five minutes; at least twelve passed as he outlined his experience at SHAPE and his convictions about NATO. 'The world needs a strong and unified Europe,' he said more than once. He talked respectfully about Germany. The Federal Republic was only seven years old. If Adenauer's government fell, what would replace it? Democracy was still fragile. Finally he talked of the *Luftwaffe*, the youngest airforce in Europe, still regarded with suspicion by some of the Allies. 'A scandal now would do untold damage,' he concluded.

If some of Schiller's hostility faded, his suspicion remained. 'My impression was that Beaumont –'

'Are in the business of making aircraft, not making news,' Keir interrupted.

'What does that mean?'

'They'd rather be supplying CX29s to the *Luftwaffe* than be shouting about a Public Enquiry into the Starfighter.'

Schiller's startled look turned to disbelief. 'Blackmail? I can't believe what I'm hearing. You wouldn't dare –'

'It's not blackmail,' Keir protested. 'Sir, I'm pointing out our common interest. A Public Enquiry would blacken the name of the *Luftwaffe*. Everything that is important to you –'

Anger flooded back into Schiller's face. 'I work with clean hands, no-one ever bought Kurt Schiller. I've never been part of a deal. Not ever –'

Cursing his clumsiness, Keir was quick to apologize for any wrong impression. 'I would never insult you by suggesting anything of the sort. Your reputation for integrity is known all over the world.'

Choosing his words with great care, Keir went over his arguments again, stressing their common interest in averting a scandal. 'Aren't you recommending the CX29 anyway?' he asked at one point.

'My recommendations are confidential,' the German said stiffly.

Although it was like stroking a hedgehog, Keir knew his arguments had got home. A Public Enquiry *would* damage Germany and the *Luftwaffe*. Schiller would go to the ends of the earth to protect both.

Finally, without liking it, the German said, 'Very well. What exactly are you suggesting?'

'We need your help on the CX29 contract.'

'I'm not so important. I opposed the Starfighter and look what happened.'

'Yes, sir, I never understood about that.'

'So?' Schiller's eyebrows rose. 'An admission of ignorance. How refreshing,' he said with undisguised sarcasm. Then, he seemed to relent because after taking a cigarette from a gun-metal case, he shrugged. 'It does no harm to tell you. Quite simply, we weren't unanimous. The *Luftwaffe* report left no room for doubt, but other people write reports too, you know. Minor officials at the Ministry, some of whom were very taken with the Starfighter's technical specification.' Avoiding Keir's eye, he continued. 'Controversial though it was, the Minister could point to *some* support for his decision.'

The inflection in his voice gave him away. *He knows*, Keir thought, *he's known all along but can't say a word.*

'Beaumont overlooked human nature.' The German shrugged. 'They forgot to make a fuss of a few minor officials. Such people are short on knowledge but long on self-importance. Beaumont left a door open –'

'They won't this time. If you could tell me which people . . . if Beaumont go at them from one way and you from the other . . . then the report to the Minister would be unanimous. Isn't that what you meant?'

'Ministers rarely resist a unanimous report,' Schiller said drily. 'It could be politically dangerous. With one controversial decision already, it could be political suicide.'

Keir took out his pen. 'The names, sir?'

Schiller got up and went over to the window. 'I don't like this,' he said, gazing out at the view, 'but you're right, we have common interests. My report in favour of the CX29 has already been submitted. That's why I didn't walk out half an hour ago. We've already got a bad fighter, I don't want a bad transport plane to go with it.'

Keir breathed a sigh of relief. 'Thank you, sir. I know we both –'

'The ends justify the means?' Schiller laughed deeply. 'I once worked for a man who believed that. I flew in his airforce. He came to a sticky end, my young friend. We could finish up the same way.'

Turning from the window, he dictated four names. 'Make sure they support Beaumont and you'll get your contract,' he said, collecting his trilby from the sideboard. 'Now I must go. Don't come downstairs, the less we are seen together the better.' A thin smile touched his lips. 'I'm not sure how our alliance will work, but I suggest we make that a rule for the future.'

Eleven

A week later, when Keir met Hayes and Pickard for the second time, the atmosphere was very different from when they had dined at the Dorchester.

'You've done an incredible job,' said a beaming Chuck Hayes.

Even Sam Pickard was full of compliments. The little man's face fairly shone with relief. At the Dorchester he had felt angry and threatened. His very future had been in question. Now he was proved right and his reputation was enhanced. Keir made sure it was enhanced, because after telling Chuck Hayes about his meeting with Schiller, he admitted something quite frankly. 'I can't open any doors for Sam. He's doing a marvellous job. Everyone speaks well of him. And although I didn't call on your agent, he's got a good reputation too. Quite honestly, I think our original idea of me going around with your people is a waste of time. I don't think it will help you win any contracts.'

Chuck Hayes burst out laughing. 'Jesus, you're some salesman. You come back in triumph and tell me I should fire you. I don't get it.'

But Sam Pickard got it. Exactly as Dusty had predicted, Sam was to become Keir's staunchest ally. 'Keir's right,' he said, 'and he was right to keep quiet about working with us when he was going round seeing people. They'd have clammed up. I think we should re-define Keir's role. What we need, and what he can provide, is better market intelligence.'

Sam really hit his stride after that, putting into words conclusions Keir had been struggling towards for more than a week. 'The way I see it,' he said, 'is we've got good agents all over Europe. Name a country and we've got a good agent, believe me. So why aren't getting the business? Because we're new, that's why. Lockheed were here before World War Two. Same goes for some of the others. Over the years they've built up two organizations. One we can see – that's their agents and salesmen and technical people – but behind that there's a hidden organization of string-pullers and fixers. It's a grease machine.' He paused to rub his thumb and forefinger together. 'I don't know how extensive it is, but shit, it's effective . . .'

He talked about his suspicions for a long time. 'It's not just Germany,' he insisted. 'It's all over.'

Gradually, his ideas evolved, many of them vague thoughts being expressed for the first time. 'I know it's vague,' he agreed, 'but how can I be specific? I don't know how big it is, how deep it goes, but take this thing Keir uncovered in Germany. Lockheed bought the government, for Christ's sake. Who have they bought in Italy? Or Holland? I'll tell you something –' he hesitated, looking slightly embarrassed – 'now this is something I wasn't going to mention, okay? I was going to keep it to myself. It's so wild, so unbelievable that you're going to laugh. You know whose name cropped up in Amsterdam some weeks back? Someone said he was on the take. You ready for this? Prince Bernhard. That's right, Prince Bernhard of the Netherlands. So it's crazy . . .'

Hayes exclaimed in surprise and Keir was shocked. In Holland the Dutch Royal Family's popularity equalled that of the Royal Family in Britain. Keir's shock would have been no greater if Sam had offered proof of the Duke of Edinburgh taking bribes.

'I'm not saying it's true,' Sam admitted. 'All I'm saying is someone told me he could be bought.'

Chuck Hayes remained sceptical. 'In South America you expect that sort of thing, but in Europe –'

'Look at Germany,' said Sam. 'I tell you, it's happening all over. We'll keep losing contracts until we find out what's going on. That's why Keir should stay behind the scenes. If he can find out about the grease machines in Italy and Holland and other countries in NATO . . .'

It was Keir who hesitated. He knew how lucky he had been in Germany. It was unrealistic to expect to be so lucky again. Besides he could no more pretend to be on permanent holiday than continue to mislead his friends.

'Sure, I understand,' Sam nodded. 'Why not say you're doing research work for a client? You don't have to say who, but you should tell people something. Another idea,' he said, turning to Chuck. 'At times, Keir might have to promise people their names won't be mentioned. They'll talk more freely if they know it's confidential. And it *must* be in confidence, Chuck. Keir can give us the information without revealing sources. I don't see why we should worry, so long as we get the information . . .'

The meeting lasted six hours.

Without his being fully aware of it at the time, it was to change the course of Keir's life.

Sam produced a fund of ideas. 'Keir can't do this on his own. We need a string of people, all asking questions and feeding answers back to Keir. He recruits them, coordinates them, pays them, sifts the information, he runs it. We keep out of it . . .'

Chuck bought the entire package. Germany had proved something for Chuck. Keir's strong impression was that the big man would have found it hard to fire Sam. After working together for six years, he and Sam had become friends. Now Chuck was feeling guilty about doubting Sam's abilities and wanted to make it up to him. Not only that, but they were both excited about the CX29's prospects in Germany. Thanks to Keir, that contract was beginning to look a lot closer.

As for Keir, after admitting that he couldn't help Beaumont in more obvious ways, Sam's ideas were an obvious solution. Besides, he was beginning to get a taste for the work. He *wanted* to know what was going on . . .

The weeks flew past after that. While Sam followed up Schiller's list of names in Germany, Keir was busy elsewhere in Europe. Wherever he went – Paris, Rome, Amsterdam, Brussels – he appointed agents; lawyers mostly, who in turn engaged private investigators with the brief of uncovering more about the grease machine in Europe.

Keir was as busy as Dusty, so much so that for two people supposedly working together, they rarely met, for Dusty's world of advertising was a far remove from Keir's business on the fringes of NATO. For the most part their meetings were a hurried exchange at the office, or at a party at Dusty's new apartment.

It was at a party of Dusty's that Keir found himself talking to Amanda Lacey. He was not alone, every man in the room was talking to Amanda Lacey, particularly Chuck Hayes, over on another visit, and Lord Kirby who that day had shown her round the House of Lords. 'The sense of power in that place really turns me on,' Mandy was saying with a wicked look in her eye.

Watching the sixty-eight-year-old peer almost swoon brought a faint smile to Keir's lips. From his brief encounters with her, he liked Mandy. She was attractive, vibrant and amusing. She was also, he had to admit, a bit overpowering. At the back of his mind was always the memory of Dusty saying 'She works at that Dizzy Blonde act, don't let it fool you.' She also, Keir remembered, owned seventy-two per cent of Owen Lacey, which made her more or less a client. Although he was as polite as any man there, Keir retreated behind a shield of reserve.

So he was surprised a few days later when Mandy telephoned him at the office. 'Hi,' she said breathlessly, 'I just spoke with Dusty. He said you were in. I want to ask a favour.'

'Anything,' he said, startled.

She giggled. 'Are you always so obliging? You might regret what you've let yourself in for.'

'What have I let myself in for?' Keir asked.

'I want you to live in my house.'

'You what?'

'I've just bought a house. London prices are crazy. I couldn't resist it.'

'I didn't know you were buying property in London.'

She giggled again. 'Neither did I until I went house hunting for Dusty, but prices over here are plain ridiculous. If you weren't going to make so much money with Chuck, I'd tell you to get into real estate. Prices will double in the next six or seven years.'

Wondering how much she knew of his arrangements with Chuck Hayes, Keir also remembered Dusty saying 'If ever she took business seriously, she'd end up owning America.'

She chattered on at a furious rate. 'I'll be away so often it would worry me to have it stand empty. Besides the staff will go bananas without someone to look after. And there's acres of space. Even when I'm there we could go days without bumping into each other . . .'

He gathered that the house was in Westminster.

'. . . if I'd thought of it before I'd have asked Dusty, but he's fixed up now, thanks to me I might add. Really you'd be doing me an enormous favour. I'd feel better with you keeping an eye on things. You haven't found a place yet I hope? Don't say I've left it too late?'

'No.'

Keir's frequent absences had left no time to find something permanent and he was still living in the Marchmount.

'That's a relief. Tell you what, why don't I show you the house? What are you doing at the moment?'

His hesitation was enough.

'I'll get a cab,' she said, 'and pick you up in ten minutes. I'll show you the house, then you can take me to lunch. How does that sound?'

After that it was merely a matter of waiting for her to choose a restaurant.

Finally, she said, 'Why don't you call Peter at the Twenty-One and book us a table for one o'clock.'

Five minutes later, peering out into the street from the lobby downstairs, Keir wondered what on earth he was doing. He felt sure he would dislike living in the same house as Mandy Lacey.

'You look worried to death,' she said, when her cab drew up at the kerb. 'Does the prospect of lunching with me depress you so much?'

Wrong-footed by her directness, he managed an embarrassed grin while trying to decide whether to treat her as a client or a friend.

She was too busy talking to notice his confusion. 'It's in Lord North Street, round the corner from the Palace of Westminster. I've been digging back into its history. The house was built in 1782 . . .'

Her zest was enough to overcome his misgivings, especially when they arrived in Lord North Street.

'Look at this,' she said, leading the way up the wide staircase to a drawing-room on the first floor. 'Isn't this rather grand?'

The whole house was rather grand. Built on four floors in the way that town houses were in the days of George III, every room was spacious and elegant.

He expressed suitable admiration.

'And guess what?' she said laughing. 'It's wired into the House of Commons. The division bell rings here when there's a vote in the Chamber, so you can pop over and join the Ayes or the Nays or whatever they do. Isn't that fun? I shall keep it for when the neighbours come to dinner . . . There're at least two Ministers . . .'

They toured the entire house, including the staff flat in the sub-basement. 'I've found exactly the right couple. The Westwoods. I interviewed them yesterday . . .'

Keir thought the house magnificent and he said so. 'But I hadn't realized you intended to live in England.'

'I don't. Not all the time, I'd miss New York too much. Besides my tax position only allows me to be here ninety days a year. But that's okay, ninety days is about right. I can have the best of both worlds. And my accountants adore the idea. Buying this house will save a fortune . . .'

He listened to her compare the cost of the house with ninety days a year at the Savoy.

'Even including staff this place will save money. It will appreciate like mad and I'll have my own home in London, somewhere permanent where I can entertain when I'm in town.'

The need for somewhere to entertain became apparent at lunch. Mandy held court in the Twenty-One. Seated in the big armchair in the bar, she bobbed her blonde head in constant acknowledgement. 'Hello,' she would say smiling, offering her cheek. 'Lovely to see you again. I don't think you know Keir Milford . . .'

In the space of forty minutes in the bar Keir was introduced to a film producer, a Tory MP, the Financial Director of the *Evening Standard* and a man who had made a million pounds selling potato crisps.

'Now you see why I need a house!' Mandy said when they sat down in the dining-room.

She refused to take no for an answer about Keir moving into Lord North Street. 'You'll be doing me a favour. Besides you're one of the family now. You and Dusty and Chuck. Everything's working out fine.'

Even when he pointed out he was likely to be away three or four nights a week, Mandy was unperturbed. 'You'll be there enough for the place to feel lived in. I can't stand a house that doesn't feel lived in.'

Six days later, mildly surprised and still wondering if he was doing the right thing, Keir moved out of the Marchmount and into Mandy Lacey's house on Lord North Street. In addition to a splendidly furnished bedroom, with a dressing-room and bath-room *en suite*, he had the run of the place, particularly the library on the ground floor. 'Use it for meetings,' Mandy told him. 'I know Chuck would prefer to discuss his business here than at Dusty's advertising office.'

Keir was introduced to the Westwoods – John and Barbara – an efficient, pleasant couple whom he liked immediately. John Westwood was an ex-regular soldier, so he and Keir were destined to get on. A man in his late forties, he was tall and well-built and conveyed that air of general competence that often comes to men after a successful career in the army. A gentle giant, he towered over his wife who was as round and wholesome-looking as a pat of butter. A Devon burr touched her speech and she had the merriest brown eyes Keir had ever seen.

'Aren't they darlings?' Mandy said afterwards. 'They'll run this place like a Swiss watch, but a *homely* Swiss watch if you know what I mean.'

Keir thought he did.

The arrangement worked out very well. Mandy was quite right about them not bumping into each other, for she was frequently away herself, most of June in fact and even more of July, because she left for St Tropez on the tenth to stay with friends. 'Until October when I really must get back to New York or they'll forget what I look like.'

Keir doubted that. Mandy was a force of nature, once met never forgotten. Although he was growing used to her, there were times when he found her a bit daunting – an admission which Dusty found highly amusing. 'Treat her like a sister,' he advised. 'I do. That's how she sees us anyway, as younger brothers I mean. It comes from being married twice to older men. I'm not smart enough to figure it out, but that's my theory. One thing's for sure, don't make a pass at her. Not if you want to keep her as a friend. And you're a fool if you don't. Mandy knows everyone.'

She certainly knew a lot of people. Away so often in Europe, Keir missed most of the parties she gave before she left for St Tropez, but he was there for the last one. The first-floor drawing-room fairly overflowed with businessmen, media people and politicans. Of course, Dusty was there, picking up clients, and at some point Toby Smart emerged from the throng to take Keir by the arm. 'I hear your clients think you're a hell of a feller,' he whispered and went away with a smile on his face.

Kirby was there too, totally smitten with Mandy. Dusty murmured, 'He's her next unless I'm mistaken. She rather fancies a title and he's loaded, someone said he's the third richest man in Britain.'

Later that year, when Kirby followed Mandy first to St Tropez and then to New York, Keir remembered Dusty's words. Mandy had obviously landed her fish by then but at the party in June she was still casting the bait with provocative glances and her own wicked humour.

Before she left for St Tropez, she allowed Keir to buy her lunch again at her favourite Twenty-One Club. It was then that she asked about Dawn.

'Are you still carrying a torch for that actress?' she asked in her usual blunt way.

Keir was uncertain. He had written to Dawn, resisting her

303

plans for Liz and telling her of the new life he was making. Dawn had sent a note in reply, saying she would be in London in October and would discuss Liz with him then. Her letter had been too short for him to gauge her mood and although he read it several times, excited at the prospect of seeing her again, it had left him feeling vaguely uneasy.

'I nearly became an actress,' said Mandy, laughing at his expression. 'Don't look so surprised, it's a phase lots of girls go through. All women become actresses anyway,' she said with a shrug. 'It's just a question of where they ply their craft. You could say I chose life instead of the stage. Still I did have my chances.'

When he asked why she had decided against it, she said, 'It's an awful investment. Only one girl in a hundred makes money at it. Meanwhile, she's risking her looks and her youth. Those assets depreciate fast after thirty. Did you ever think about that? Usually a man's assets increase, whatever he's doing with his life, he's getting better at it by then. He's on his way up. A woman's on her way down. I didn't think odds of a hundred to one were attractive.'

Her smile portrayed such cool amusement that she might have been joking, but Keir knew her well enough to know she was perfectly serious. It was the closest he ever came to hearing her philosophy, if it could be called a philosophy. Never as mercenary as she sounded, his own experience proved that Mandy simply wanted a good life for herself, and the same for her friends to whom she was unfailingly generous.

He enjoyed that lunch, and not solely because he was beginning to feel at ease in her company. He was coming to terms with every aspect of his new life – buying his suits in Savile Row, having his hair cut at Trumpers and dining out in fashionable restaurants. It was a style to which he was becoming accustomed and living at Lord North Street was a colossal bonus because of the people he met.

'And when I'm away,' said Mandy, 'treat the place as your home. You invite them, you give the dinner parties, I shan't mind in the least. Especially if you do good work for Chuck.'

Sometimes Keir wondered if Chuck was the reason she had invited him to live there. She was clearly fond of Chuck Hayes. Even later, when it became clear that she would marry Lord

Kirby, Mandy never failed to lend Chuck a helping hand whenever she could.

Keir saw little of his family during those summer months, for Sam Pickard kept him hectically busy. Time was a constant problem for Keir. The most he could find was an occasional Sunday, when he took the train out to Hillingdon to lunch with the family. Sadly such days rarely relaxed him.

'No politics,' Edith would lecture Joe before every visit, which so inhibited conversation that often father and son found little to say to each other. Liz filled the vacuum – Keir played with her, took her to the park, listened to her describe her first days at school. Her education caused Keir some concern. 'I don't want her going to the local school,' he told Edith, 'you must find something better. I'll pay for it, money's no problem.'

'The local school was good enough for you at her age,' said his mother. Eventually Edith complied with his wishes and found a small private school near the park, where she took Liz every day.

Money was certainly not a problem for Keir, who was beginning to realize the full value of the contract Dusty had negotiated with Beaumont. The fee of twenty-five thousand dollars a year had blinded him initially, but as the German order for CX29s began to edge closer, the extent of his commission grew large in his mind. Previously he had attributed little importance to the one and a half per cent of all sales in Europe. Now it transpired that the seemingly tiny percentage was really a fortune. If Sam was successful, the *Luftwaffe* would place a contract for eighteen CX29s at almost two million dollars each. Team International would earn three hundred thousand dollars, tax free in a Swiss bank account, half each for Dusty and him.

'Do you really think Sam's going to get it?' Dusty asked eagerly.

'There's a very good chance. Everything's changed since my meeting with Schiller.'

'Three hundred thousand in one hit,' Dusty whooped. 'A couple more of those will put us in clover.'

But winning even one more was not easy. Up to his neck in what he called 'the battle for Europe', Sam left Keir in no doubt that it was a life or death struggle for Beaumont. 'Trouble is,' Sam admitted, 'every time I sit down to do business, I wonder how many guys across the table are on Lockheed's payroll. It scares the hell out of me. I want to give them my best pitch, but there's this nag at the back of my mind that as soon as I leave someone's going to phone Lockheed and give them our bottom line. It's the weirdest feeling I ever had in my life but I got a strong instinct . . .'

Keir was developing a healthy respect for Sam's instincts. Sam's hunch had been right in Germany, and it was proving right elsewhere for Keir's investigators were beginning to unearth a mass of suspicious-looking data. Even before the end of that summer Keir was getting the measure of the grease machine which spread like a cancer through public life, linking politicians and officials all over Europe. And one name cropped up again and again – the name of Bernhard, Prince of the Netherlands.

Keir was so worried by some of his discoveries that he kept them even from Dusty. Instead of working in the office at Knightsbridge he spent his time when in London in the house on Lord North Street. With Mandy's permission he installed a safe in the library which became his office from then on. He had his mail directed there, he made his telephone calls there; Lord North Street became his centre of business as well as his home. When his agents were in London they called at Lord North Street, never at Knightsbridge – and increasingly they brought him the most perplexing reports on Prince Bernhard of the Netherlands.

Keir resisted the idea of a link between Bernhard and Lockheed. It simply made no sense for one of the most influential men in Europe to be involved. True, the Prince had commercial interests, but he declared them. He was a director of three hundred companies, spread over a cross-section of Dutch industry. The Prince was founder and sponsor of the Bilderberg conferences, at which gathered politicians from all over the Western world. He had married into one of the richest families in Europe.

'Quite frankly,' Keir told himself, 'it would be difficult to think of anyone more respected.'

Yet the rumours persisted. Keir's Dutch agents were so convinced of a link with Lockheed that they asked him to approve the expense of putting the Prince under continuous surveillance. Alarmed by the idea of investigating one of

Europe's royal families, and afraid of the consequences if the news ever leaked out, Keir went to Sam for a decision.

'Do it,' said Sam. 'I don't care what it costs, just do it. We're dead unless we get to the bottom of this.'

The following day, Keir flew to Amsterdam and gave his approval.

After that not a week passed without a memo arriving at Lord North Street from Amsterdam, and every week the evidence mounted. July ended, then September, bringing fresh revelations in every post. But the most damning indictment arrived on 10 October.

SUBJECT – BERNHARD Leopold Frederic Everhard
Julius Coert Karal Godfried Peter, Prinz der
Netherlands.

Reliable informants confirm that Fred Meuser (see reports 5, 9, 14 and 15) suggested that Lockheed make B a gift of new Jetstar. This proposal was put to Robert Gross, President of Lockheed, last year. The idea was eventually scrapped; perhaps because B flying around in a Lockheed Jetstar would make his connection with the company too obvious. However, B indicated he would take the money instead – one million dollars.

After a meeting between B and Gross in Rome on September 2 (see reports 11 and 13), Lockheed's legal counsel, Roger Bixby-Smith (see reports 6 and 8), called at the Royal Palace at Soestdijk on September 30, at which meeting we believe Bixby-Smith received instructions about how to pay over the money.

Bixby-Smith was put under surveillance. On 3 October he went to Zurich and called at the Hotel Dolder where he asked for a 'Mr Pantchoulidzew'. Pantchoulidzew handed Smith a piece of paper bearing his own name and a number. We believe the number to refer to a bank account in Switzerland.

We followed up on Pantchoulidzew. He is in fact Colonel A. E. Pantchoulidzew, a white Russian émigré who had been a house guest at B's family home since before the war. (In making enquiries at Reckenwalde in Germany, the location of B's family home, one shopkeeper repeated local gossip which suggests that Pantchoulidzew secretly married B's mother some time ago – in which case, of course, he is B's stepfather.)

We cannot confirm whether the entire million dollars have now been transferred to this bank account, but it seems logical to believe so.

Thus, you would be safe to assume that B is now on Lockheed's payroll.

A thin sheen of sweat gathered at Keir's hairline as he read the memo. Alone in the library at Lord North Street, a shiver ran up his spine. Sam had been negotiating with the Royal Dutch Airforce for the past six months and was growing ever more hopeful of progress.

'I've had eight meetings,' Sam had said. 'Each one takes me another step up the ladder.'

'Bloody hell,' Keir cursed, looking at the memo, 'now we come to the snake.'

Twelve

With so much going on in his life, it was not surprising that Keir paid little attention to the passing of time, so it was almost a shock the following week to realize October had almost come to an end.

What brought it home to him was another letter from Dawn. This time she wrote at some length:

'. . . I've just about put my life together again. Work is the biggest cure. Portraying other people's emotions leaves you too exhausted to feel your own . . .'

Keir skipped the opening pages. He was as reluctant as ever to acknowledge her feelings for JD. Regretting that the man had ever entered her life, he felt no inclination to shed tears about his departure.

'. . . I've signed a seven-year contract with the studio. JD wouldn't have approved, but Eric and Harvey say it's for the best . . .'

That was a shock. Seven years in Hollywood. With JD dead, Keir had hoped she might come home. Vaguely, at the back of his mind, he had seen himself buying a house like the one in which he had become so comfortable in Lord North Street. He could picture himself introducing Dawn to his new friends . . .

A worse shock was to follow:

'. . . I think I've talked Eric and Harvey into letting me have Liz. I shall tell people that she's my adopted daughter and they can think what they like . . .'

There was nothing about his letter of protest. Nothing at all. He might never have written it. Dawn had simply ignored it. The closest reference was: '. . . honestly, Keir, I do need Liz with me now and it's the right thing for her, a child and a mother should be together . . . of course I'm more grateful to Joe and Edith than words can ever express . . .'

'What about me?' he asked angrily. 'I beggared myself to provide for Liz while I was in the army. I went without . . .' Words failed him, until finally he said, 'It's not on. She's my daughter and she's staying in England.'

Of course it was a selfish reaction. He knew it was selfish. Sometimes weeks would pass without him getting down to see Liz. But damn and blast it, he *did* get down to see her every so often. He *did* take her to the zoo. He *did* take her on outings. What's more, he enjoyed it. So did Liz. She had a settled, happy life. It would be monstrous to uproot her and take her to the States. Keir returned to the letter scowling furiously.

'. . . the British première for *Burning Obsession* takes place at the end of the month at the Leicester Square Odeon . . . I'll be over for a week, doing personal appearances and so on. Eric says the studio has booked us into Claridge's . . . I'm so looking forward to seeing you again . . . and I can't wait to see Liz . . .'

According to Nigel Hawthorne, film critic of the *Evening News* – 'Dawn Wharton returned to London yesterday – happy, successful, famous and wealthy . . . two and a half years of Hollywood have added a graceful maturity to the glossy sheen of the highly successful . . .'

This was certainly the impression she conveyed when interviewed in her suite at Claridge's.

'Rubbish,' she snorted, reading it over breakfast in bed. 'If anything proves I can act it's interviews like that.'

The truth was that she was far from happy. Emotionally drained by JD's death, subsequent events had given her no chance to recover. After a mixed reception in the States, *Burning Obsession* had fared little better in London.

'Like the Curate's egg,' said the *Daily Mail*, 'the film is good in parts.'

'. . . only memorable for the scenery, in which I include the delectable Miss Wharton . . .' said the *Observer*.

The best review appeared in the *Daily Express* – '. . . a good old-fashioned weepie in which Dawn Wharton shows her talent as well as her body . . . should do well in suburbia.'

'They could have been worse, sweetie,' said Eric. 'No one actually knocked it –'

'They condemn it with faint praise.'

'Nobody condemned you. Everyone praised your performance.'

'Let's hope it's enough,' she said drily.

Every penny she had and a lot that she hadn't was invested in the film. Worse, JD had also sunk everything into the project. After his death, the John Drayton Agency would have collapsed if Dawn had not signed with the studio for seven years. Leaving Australia she had flown directly to Hollywood, signed the contract and been working within three days; sustained by Eric who consoled her, encouraged her, put her to bed, woke her and generally dealt with the world. Her function was simply to be on the set on time, line perfect and ready to work. Her earnings now paid the salaries of everyone on Drayton Agency's payroll, including the medical staff at JD's Hampstead home for nursing a widow who long ago had forgotten that JD even existed.

'It's only until we get our money back from *Burning Obsession*,' Harvey had assured her. 'We're locked in for nine months, a year, it's hard to say, it depends on the box office.'

Dawn had agreed without a moment's hesitation. They had all done so much for her. The agency was only in trouble because of JD's faith in her. It was a debt she paid willingly, eagerly even.

'But as for being wealthy,' she tossed the *Evening News* onto the floor, 'Nigel Hawthorne should know the half of it.'

It was Saturday; her third day in London and the ordeal of the première and most of the gruelling press interviews were behind her.

'I've run your bath,' said Eric, 'and Harvey will be here at eleven.'

Instantly defensive, Dawn set the tray aside and swung her legs out of bed. 'I won't see him. He'll only start lecturing me about Liz. I'll have trouble enough with Keir over lunch.'

As he followed her into the bathroom, Eric accepted her nightgown from her and settled himself into the wicker chair. 'Sweetie, you know we'll do whatever you want –'

'You know what I want,' she said truculently, stepping into the bath.

They had discussed Liz for hours. Eventually, reluctantly, Eric and Harvey had agreed to her demand that she be allowed to take Liz back to Hollywood.

Eric shrugged. 'Harvey's still unhappy –'

'So are you, so's Keir, so are Edith and Joe. But what about me? Don't I deserve some consideration?' Angrily she splashed into the scented water. 'I didn't want to be tied down for seven years, playing whatever garbage they give me –'

'We do have artistic approval –'

'They'll drive a coach and horses through that and you know it!' A desperate note entered her voice. 'I'm not blaming you or Harvey or anyone. We had to sign that contract. But I didn't spend all that time with JD without learning –'

'Okay,' he soothed, afraid that mention of JD's name would make her tearful.

Predictably, there was a catch in her voice when she spoke. 'Be fair. That's all I ask. I deserve *something* for seven years in the salt mines –'

'You'll get it, sweetie, if only you'll be patient.'

'Liz is nearly five years old!'

'A few more months. That's all we're asking,' pleaded Eric.

'Next year –'

'Next spring. It's October now. This film will be finished by March, at the latest by April.'

Immersed in warm water up to her shoulders, Dawn lay back

and listened. She had heard it all before. Her work would prevent her from seeing much of Liz even in Hollywood. She left for the studio at six and it would be the child's bedtime by the time she returned.

'We'll engage a Nanny,' she said. 'Liz will be looked after –'

'She's looked after now. We're only thinking of you. Sweetie, you'll tear yourself in half –'

'I'll have the weekends with her.'

'You sleep most of Saturday,' Eric pointed out.

'There's Sunday.'

'You learn your lines and go to bed early to be ready for Monday.'

'That's what I do now. I won't be like that if Liz comes to live with us.'

Eric sighed and began all over again. 'If we could leave it until next Spring, it's only a few months. With the film finished you could come to London for a holiday. See Liz –'

'Big deal.'

'– for three months. It's in the contract. After the first two films you have three months' rest. And from then after every film. Just think, from next Spring you can spend three months of every year with your daughter. Take her on holiday, have fun with her, enjoy her. You'll be able to spend time with her instead of snatching a few hours when you should be resting or learning your lines.'

Feeling wretched, Dawn knew it was true. In her heart she knew Eric's arguments made sense, so did Harvey's. But she had felt so alone and guilty and mixed-up.

'I've already let her down,' she said, choking up. 'What kind of mother leaves her baby?'

'You didn't *leave* her. Sweetie, you had to provide for her. You did the right thing. She'll be proud of you when she grows up.'

Eric continued for the next couple of minutes, soothing her with gentle words of reassurance.

Partly recovered, she tried to explain. 'It's just that I want to give Liz a good start in life. Something better than growing up over a corner shop and going to the local school.'

Eric listened patiently, a sympathetic look on his face. No longer new to him, he had heard the story several times over since JD's death in Australia. His biggest surprise had been that she had borne a baby at all. He knew Dawn's body almost as well as his own. 'It took work,' she had answered, remembering how grimly she had exercised at the Milfords.

Finally, Eric asked, 'What about Keir? What did he say in his letter?'

'He's dead set against Liz coming to Hollywood.'

'But just then you mentioned the local school. What would he think about a better school, for instance?'

'Oh that. You mean paying fees –'

'I'll pay the fees if it helps. You can stop them out of what you pay me –'

'Oh, Eric,' Dawn said, shaking her head, and smiling her thanks. 'I couldn't do that –'

'Of course you could. We will if we have to. Now you'd better tell me more about your mysterious lover. I want to understand him. You never know, I might be interested myself!'

'You fool,' she shrieked before being convulsed by giggles. 'Don't you dare . . . you'd frighten him to death!'

Talking about Keir improved her humour. 'I suppose he's a bit square,' she conceded, emerging from the bath, her body a lacework of foam. 'He's full of old-fashioned virtues like honesty and integrity, always eager to do the right thing. Which makes him nice and safe –'

'And dull.' Eric pulled a face as he opened a towel for her.

'Not as dull as you'd think.' Her eyes gleamed at old memories.

'Ah ha! Which means other women –'

'Oh no.'

'How do you know?'

'I . . . I just do. I can tell from his letters. Besides, he's always so busy.'

Having dried herself, she spread another towel on the bed and prepared herself for her massage. Once, as a joke, she had told Eric he was worth his weight in gold as a masseur. There were times when she believed it. His knowing fingers always relaxed her, and talking about Keir helped. 'It will be so good to see him again,' she said into the pillow, wriggling with anticipation as Eric poured warm oil down her back.

By eleven o'clock the stress and anxiety of the past few days

313

had been reduced to tolerable proportions, and for the first time since JD's death she felt almost light-hearted. Clad in underwear and slip, she sat at the dressing table, applying her make-up.

'Harvey's arrived,' said Eric, opening the door from the sitting-room.

'Did you warn him not to bully me?'

'Better than that. I dropped a Mickey Finn into his coffee. He'll be putty in your hands,' Eric said, grinning.

Unfair really, she thought, slipping into her robe. Harvey never bullied her. He was as careful about her money as Eric was with the rest of her life. Only last year, Harvey had done as she asked and sold the flat in Regent's Park for a good profit then invested her money at a good rate of interest. Poor Harvey had tried to persuade JD not to plunge so heavily into *Burning Obsession*; if his advice had been taken most of the current mess would have been avoided. As it was, only Harvey had the skill to pick up the pieces – and Dawn was sure he would, in the fullness of time.

'Harvey, darling,' she said, offering him her cheek. 'I hope you're not here to give me another lecture.'

A lecture would have been the wrong tactics. Harvey was too skilful to commit such a blunder, especially when Eric had primed him; they both wanted the same thing, which was for Dawn to return to Hollywood without Liz. And with Dawn seeing Keir today and her daughter tomorrow, Harvey was gathering his arguments for an eleventh-hour stand.

He was playing for time – in a year, fifteen months, he could see their money back from *Burning Obsession*. Even without a profit they would be back on an even keel. But the next fifteen months were crucial. The studio was demanding two films without a hitch, without Dawn missing so much as an hour when shooting started, without a scandal or rumours about a child – they wanted Dawn at the peak of her form. Taking Liz to Hollywood was too great a risk.

'The last thing we want is a fight with anyone at the moment,' he said as they sipped coffee together. 'Even Keir worries me. If he's so opposed to you taking Liz, he might go to the press with his version of the story. Imagine the scandal.'

Having hammered that argument home, he returned to the

idea Eric had already floated. 'Time's on your side, Dawn. Suppose for the next couple of years you spend three months a year with your daughter? Take her on holidays and have fun. What's going to happen? She'll want to spend time with you. She'll *want* to go to Hollywood. That's the difference. Once that happens I'll risk problems with the press, or even the studio. Besides Keir sounds the sort who wouldn't cause hassle, not if Liz *wants* to live with you. Don't you see, this will work itself out in a couple of years.'

Bitterly disappointed though she was, Dawn had to accept that she would see little of Liz while she was working.

'So the child will be miserable,' said Eric, 'uprooted from familiar surroundings, left with a nurse all day –'

'She might even resent you for that,' Harvey interrupted. 'Things will work out the exact opposite of how you want.'

Dawn was no match for the pair of them. It wasn't as if they were discussing the subject for the first time. Harvey and Eric had been sniping for days, filling her mind with doubt and confusion.

'If you can sell Keir the idea,' Harvey concluded, 'I don't see you've got a problem.'

'Sell him the idea?'

'Sure, he might not like you spending so much time with –'

'Oh no.' Dawn shook her head. 'He isn't like that. He only wants Liz to be happy. That's what we all want.'

Harvey looked doubtful.

Unable to remember a time when she couldn't twist Keir round her little finger, Dawn regarded Harvey with astonishment. Then she realized what he had done. The idea of taking Liz back to Hollywood immediately had been supplanted by another idea, his idea. She would have been angry if his arguments hadn't taken root, but they had, especially the possibility that Liz might resent her. She remembered her own childhood as an unceasing war between her and her mother. She couldn't bear that.

'What time are you seeing him?' asked Harvey, breaking the silence.

'Keir?' Dawn glanced at her watch, surprised to see that it was almost noon. 'Oh, my goodness. He'll be here at half past. He's coming for lunch.'

315

Rising to her feet, she said, 'You crafty old devils. Don't think you put one over on me. You didn't. It's just that –'

'You know we're on your side,' Harvey said smiling.

'Sweetie, you know there's nothing we wouldn't –'

'Come on, Judas, you can help me to dress.' She told Eric before turning to Harvey, 'Very well, we'll do it your way. To be honest I've had a few worries. But from now on I take Liz on holiday every year –'

Harvey smiled with relief. 'Of course, that's understood. Really, Dawn, it will work for the best.'

Eric opened the door to the bedroom. 'But first of all, sweetie, you must convince your old flame.'

Full of confidence, Dawn smiled. 'That,' she said, 'is the least of my problems.'

Thirteen

It was. Talking to Keir was a reunion overflowing with warmth. After introducing Harvey and Eric, she sent them downstairs and entertained him to lunch in her suite. Almost to her surprise, instead of being awed by the surroundings, he made himself immediately at home. She was simultaneously disappointed and delighted. He was the same and yet different. The biggest difference was that any similarity to a love-sick boy had been banished forever. There was a man-of-the-world look about him which puzzled her – identifying it was difficult until she realized it was the sum-total of many parts. The stylish haircut, the well-tailored suit, his easy manner with the waiters over lunch, his familiarity with the wine, even the determined glint which lit his eye when they started to talk about Liz.

She let him talk her round about Liz, knowing exactly what she was doing and happily surprised to learn that some of the things worrying her had also been worrying him. He had already taken steps to find Liz a good school – so when he began to list objections to Liz going to America, Dawn could restrain herself no longer, she plunged in with her suggestion about coming to London every year to take Liz on holiday.

'Marvellous,' he said, reverting to schoolboy enthusiasm for a moment. 'That's terrific. That's the best news I've heard since . . . I can't remember . . .'

After that they talked most of the afternoon away. It was almost four when he asked what she wanted to do that evening. Sunday had already been planned – he was to collect her at ten for their visit to Hillingdon.

'Tonight?' she said. 'I don't know. I've had enough of people and making public appearances. I thought we'd stay here. What do you think?'

Half inclined to suggest they went in search of their little Italian restaurant in Soho, suddenly he had a better idea. 'Why don't we have dinner at my place?'

'Have you learned to cook as well?'

'Nothing like that, but you'd like the house.'

Curious to see where he lived, Dawn accepted the invitation, and shortly afterwards he left saying he ought to have a word about dinner with someone called Barbara. She let him go, thinking it was a give-away sign, a more assured man would have picked up the phone instead of rushing home. Not that she minded. His anxiety to please was a touching confirmation of her assessment that she remained the only woman in his life.

Eric and Harvey returned like curious infants. 'How did it go? We sat downstairs until he left.'

They were delighted with the outcome.

At eight o'clock she was troubled by what to wear. All Keir had said about where he lived was that it was an old house owned by a widow, 'probably full of the frumpish furniture they put in theatrical digs. I can't be too dressy. Keir lives there. I don't want to embarrass him,' said Dawn.

As usual, Eric took over, dressing her in a plain black cocktail dress that relied on cut alone for its elegance.

'Shall I wait up?' he asked with a wicked grin as he took her downstairs to her cab.

'Fool!' she muttered as she drove off.

Keir was manageable in this mood. It was a joy to see him again, but she couldn't be crowded. Bruised about JD, worried about the studios, fretting as to whether she was doing the right thing with Liz, concerned about money – the last thing she wanted was Keir to start planning their future again. His loyalty was enough . . .

Three hours later she was having second thoughts. Lord North Street had a graciousness and elegance that was totally unexpected. After dining – superbly – she was comfortably ensconced in the drawing-room, sipping brandy and coffee, listening to Keir talk about winning contracts in Europe, and still trying to collect her thoughts. At Claridge's the talk had been mostly about her and their plans to see Liz tomorrow. She had commanded the situation. But here, seeing Keir so at home, with a butler to open his door and a cook to prepare his meals . . .

'I work here a good deal of the time,' he explained, 'in the library. You must see it before you go.'

Her existence had always been the more glamorous. Keir had been a soldier. Casting a glance around the room, she began to wonder if their positions had been reversed.

'That's when I'm in London,' he was saying. 'I'm away half the time. Nowhere exotic like Hollywood, just Paris, Amsterdam, Oslo, places like that . . .'

Making herself comfortable, she kicked off her shoes and put her legs up on the sofa, smoothing her frock over her knees, carefully revealing a frothy inch of lacy black slip.

Watching him lean against the mantelpiece, listening to him talk in this elegant room, she thought, This is what he always wanted. He used to talk about a house like this, with him working in Fleet Street and me at Drury Lane.

'You must give lots of parties,' she said, indicating the room with her hand.

'Me? No.'

'But you must have *some* social life?' she coaxed, a faintly flirtatious note in her voice.

Listening to him explain that dashing around Europe kept him too busy filled Dawn with quiet satisfaction. Dear, faithful Keir, she thought, her heart warming to him more by the minute.

Suddenly, the door behind her opened and she heard a woman's voice. 'Keir, honey, thank Heavens you're home. Boy, am I glad to see you. You wouldn't believe the hassle

I've had. Is that brandy you're drinking? Oh, pour me a large one.'

Next moment a stunning blonde came into view who kissed Keir on the lips before flopping into the armchair next to the hearth. 'I'm whacked,' she sighed, then her eyes widened as she caught sight of Dawn. 'Oops! I didn't see you there all snuggled down on the couch.' She cast a glance at Keir. 'Sorry, honey, I didn't know you had company.'

Raising herself upright on the sofa, Dawn stifled her incredulity. This was the widow? She had imagined some white-haired old lady, or at least someone in her fifties with hair soaked in blue rinse. This – this baby-eyed, bouncing blonde, showing off her golden tanned skin in a chic little white dress, was no more than thirty.

Mandy smiled when Keir introduced them. 'Of course, Dawn Wharton. Sorry, I didn't recognize you for a minute.'

Dawn cursed her simple black frock. The blonde was wearing a white silk which had cost at least twice as much. I should have dressed up, not down, Dawn thought bitterly, yearning for the glamorous gowns back at Claridge's.

'Don't bother putting your shoes on,' Mandy assured her. 'I curl up on the couch myself when it's just me and Keir.'

I bet you do, Dawn thought furiously.

For the next five minutes she concentrated on nodding in the right places while Mandy explained that a strike at Paris airport had cancelled all flights to New York. 'Orly's in chaos. I grabbed the first plane to London . . .'

What a fool I've been, Dawn scolded herself, to have imagined Keir leading the life of a monk when all the time he's been living with her. She refused his offer of another drink. 'Thanks, but I really must go. The last few days have been exhausting –'

'Of course,' Mandy said brightly, 'you're in London for your new film. *Enduring Passion* or something –'

'*Burning Obsession*,' Dawn corrected her, acidly.

'Right, I read the review in the *Sunday Times*.'

Smiling sweetly, Dawn thought, You bitch. The *Sunday Times* had hated the film.

The butler had called a taxi by the time Keir folded the wrap over her shoulders. 'See you in the morning,' he said.

She drove off as the blonde joined Keir on the doorstep, both waving goodbye. The sight of them together filled her with fury.

How dare he humiliate me like that!

'What on earth's the matter?' Eric asked, taking one look at her face.

'If you must know,' she snapped, hurling her wrap into a chair, 'I made a bloody fool of myself –'

'Sweetie –'

'Don't Sweetie me! I hate this place. I want us on the first flight back to the States –'

'But –'

'Do it, Eric! Do it. Don't argue.'

'But your daughter –'

'How on earth can I see her now? I can't face Keir tomorrow. How he must be laughing – he and his blonde, sugar-coated bowl of lard. I feel such a fool! I played everything wrong, the whole scene. All I can do now is give him an exit he won't forget in a long time.'

BOOK FOUR

Dawn and Liz

One

'Another glass of port, Gerald?' Keir pushed the decanter towards his guest. 'And help yourself to more cheese.'

Replenishing his glass, Fairbrother declined a further attack on the cheese board. 'I'd have to visit my tailor if I lunched here every day,' he said laughing. 'That was splendid, Keir.'

'Tell Barbara before you go. She'll be pleased you enjoyed it. Now if you're really sure about the cheese . . . ?'

'Positive.'

'In that case, let's take our glasses across the hall,' said Keir, pushing his chair back from the table. 'It will give John a chance to clear up in here.'

Fairbrother extracted a gold hunter from his waistcoat as he rose. 'Two-fifteen. That's good timing. I have to be in the House at three –'

'Oh easily.' Keir opened the door and ushered him into the hall. 'I wish we could get together more often –' He broke off as John approached from the direction of the kitchen. 'Ah, John, we'll have coffee in the library.'

'Very good, sir,' said John, stepping nimbly around Fairbrother to open the library door.

The annual salary of a Member of Parliament was £3,250 in 1968, which was less than a fortune even then. It was peanuts to Keir. Since the first German contract seven years before, his income had risen steadily and never failed to reach two hundred thousand. In '66 and '67 it had exceeded a quarter of a million. He had become wealthy; wealthy enough to buy the house from Lady Kirby (as Mandy had become on her marriage in '62). True to form, she had asked twice what she had paid for it. He had met her price, for even at that it was a good buy. Mandy had spent lavishly on improvements and property values had risen as rapidly as she had predicted. The transaction seemed fair to them both, especially as it had become important to Keir to have a base close to the House of Commons.

323

With its 2 miles of corridors, 100 staircases, 13 quadrangles and 1,100 rooms, the House of Commons was a confusion for most people. Awed by the policemen and uniformed attendants, many of the tourists who passed through its doors felt a thrill to be in 'The Mother of Parliaments'. Keir had been thrilled himself in the early days. By 1968, however, such feelings had long passed. By 1968 he knew that power, real power, the power to get things done, bypassed the House of Commons completely. Experience had taught him that Members of Parliament were of limited value. Even to be an MP, in Keir's opinion, was to belong to an odd profession which did business at odd hours. From 2.30 p.m. until 10.30 p.m. from Mondays to Thursdays, and 11 a.m. until 4.30 p.m. on Fridays were hours more suited to a gentleman's club. The House of Commons was a leftover from the days when governing the nation was a part-time occupation for the wealthy. Even now MPs pompously congratulated themselves on belonging to the 'Best Club in Europe'. They ran it as a club. Not for them the licensing laws they saw fit to impose on the rest of the land – the seven bars in the House of Commons were open at all hours. Easy access to alcohol was one of the perks, like the long holidays, for Parliament was shut for a third of the year, and any Member who ran a bit short of cash had plenty of chances to make more on the side.

Sir Gerald Fairbrother, for instance, made nearly ten thousand a year. The extra came partly from journalism but mostly from Keir, a fact that would have shocked Fairbrother's constituents, who thought he was in Parliament to represent them. The reality was rather different. Once, to amuse himself, Fairbrother had divided his parliamentary salary by the number of people who had voted for him. 'They can't expect much for that,' he concluded on calculating that each vote was worth sixpence a year. Consequently he devoted a good deal of time to serving Keir's interests, which he was convinced had something to do with ship-building. Prodded by Keir, Fairbrother gave speech after speech in the House, arguing the case for a strong navy.

'We're an island race,' he would bellow at the government benches, 'with a history established by maritime power. We neglect the navy at our peril . . . if we can no longer afford the world's *biggest* navy, we must afford the world's *best*. The navy needs more ships . . .' As a bonus, Fairbrother expressed the same sentiments in his regular articles for the *Evening Standard*.

He looked rather pleased with himself, seated in a leather armchair in the library. 'I've got a little bonus coming your way,' he said, accepting a cigar. 'The *Sunday Times* asked me to write fifteen hundred words next month. I'll have another go at the navy estimates then.'

Keir's smile conveyed exactly the right amount of grateful appreciation. 'That's very good of you, Gerald. Every bit helps at this time of the year.'

This time of the year was early in February. In Downing Street, the Chancellor of the Exchequer was putting his budget together. Of the huge sum raised every year by taxation, almost a third was spent on defence. The army, the navy, and the Royal Air Force competed for every penny. Keir's interest was not in the navy, as Fairbrother suspected, but in the RAF. He wanted them kept short of money. Keir was close to the biggest deal of his life – a deal with the RAF. He knew they would prefer to buy British, but the British aircraft industry was in a state of flux. Hampered by government interference, British manufacturers were lagging behind American competitors on price and performance. Helped by big orders from their own armed services, American plane-makers could spread their costs over great numbers. Plane for plane they were cheaper. This year Beaumont had a chance to supply the RAF with their C-199s, and while the competition had the advantage of being British, they suffered the disadvantage of being more expensive. Keir's reasoning was simple. The less in the RAF kitty, the more likely they were to buy Beaumont. And *that* was why he paid Fairbrother to make speeches for the navy.

Half an hour later, as he showed his guest out, Keir said, 'I will try to get over to the House later. Forgive me if I don't. I've a million things to do before leaving for Geneva tonight . . .'

It was the polite thing to say. He hadn't the slightest intention of squeezing into the public gallery to listen to the debate on the defence estimates. His will would be done without him wasting time on such things.

Disappointment showed in Fairbrother's eyes. 'Not to worry,' he said gamely as he shook hands, 'you can rely on me to give them hell.'

Returning to the library, Keir had forgotten Fairbrother even before he sat down. There was no more to think about. The Tory MP would do his stuff. So would Harry Llewellyn, Keir's other 'tame MP'. Llewellyn, the Labour Member for a mining constituency in South Wales, would hammer away at his favourite topic. 'Every penny on defence is a penny less for education,' he would say. As he closed his eyes, Keir could see the thin, bespectacled figure as he leapt to his feet. 'Point of order, Mr Speaker . . . Britain's future depends on today's *children*, not today's army . . .'

On the face of it, Fairbrother and Llewellyn were arguing against each other. In fact, both arguments suited Keir. More money for education or more for the navy meant less for the RAF – and that added up to a contract for Beaumont, their first ever with the RAF. Which was why Keir paid two MPs a retainer, and although their noise was rarely of vital importance, their speeches did help shape public opinion. Besides, Fairbrother and Llewellyn had a usefulness beyond making speeches. They were Keir's ears and eyes in the House. Between them they picked up all the gossip. Keir had known that Defence Secretary John Profumo was sleeping with a call-girl named Christine Keeler months before the scandal broke. Macmillan's government had collapsed as a result, Profumo had resigned in disgrace, and after that ceased to be of interest to Keir. He had files and dossiers on every defence minister in Europe. It was part of his job.

The telephone rang. From an extension down the hall, John announced that Sam Pickard was calling.

Sam came on the line, as breezy as ever. 'Hi, old buddy. I caught you at home. It's easier getting the Pope these days. How's it going?'

'No complaints, Sam. How about you?'

'In good shape. I'm in Munich. We just put on a show for von Hassel. It went like a dream . . .'

Keir smiled as he listened. He and Sam had become very good friends since they had re-defined his role way back in 1960. Since then he had kept in the background, working behind the scenes while Sam barged through all sorts of front doors. So well did they work together that Beaumont had forged ahead of Grumman and Northrop to rival even Lockheed in Europe. Now, once again, Sam was trying to sell fighters to the *Luftwaffe*. His chances had improved since the demise of Franz Josef, and although Strauss's resignation had mystified some, others had glimpsed the tip of the iceberg. *Der Spiegel* had published an attack on Strauss's competence as Minister of Defence, singling out the Starfighter contracts for particular mention. As a result two reporters and an editor had been arrested on a secret's charge but the resulting uproar had forced Strauss to resign amid scenes of bitter acrimony.

'I think we're in with a real chance this time,' Sam was saying, unable to contain his excitement. 'You should have seen those Bullfighter Mark Twos. Christ, what a show! Von Hassel's eyes damn near popped out of his skull . . .'

Inevitably the talk moved on to the Starfighter. The worrying thing was that von Hassel was as staunch in his public defence of the aircraft as Strauss had been before him, which was inexplicable in view of its performance. The Starfighter had been a disaster for the *Luftwaffe*. One crashed every ten days in 1965. Hating to fly them, some pilots even sedated themselves with alcohol or drugs before take-off.

Within the *Luftwaffe*, the aircraft had become known as 'the flying coffin'. Its record was an ongoing disaster.

'I heard a story today,' said Sam, breaking into a laugh. 'You'll love this. Ready? What's the definition of an optimist?'

'I don't know.'

'A Starfighter pilot who quits smoking because he's afraid of dying of cancer,' Sam spluttered, bursting into laughter.

Even as he chuckled, Keir couldn't help picturing Kurt Schiller, bleak-faced as he attended all those funerals of *Luftwaffe* pilots.

'. . . So I'm going home tomorrow,' Sam was saying, 'I'm seeing Chuck on Friday. Anything special you want me to pass on?'

Keir couldn't think of anything. He and Chuck had already spoken last week.

'Anything new on B?' Sam asked.

B was Prince Bernhard, Holland's wheeler-dealer Prince whose influence never stopped growing. In addition to the

Bilderberg conferences, the Prince had founded another grand-sounding organization, the World Wildlife Fund, with support from international big names and tycoons, among them his old friend Fred Meuser and Courtland Gross of Lockheed. The irony was that while Bernhard won headlines as the protector of the world's wildlife, speculation grew about his interest in wild life of a quite different kind. Increasingly the Dutch press hinted at 'Royal Liaisons', especially Bernhard's relationship with Helen 'Pussy' Grinda, the glamorous jetsetting sister of an international tennis star. Those in the know were convinced that the Prince was supporting at least one illegitimate family, all of which cost a great deal of money, and perhaps explained why the Prince was no longer working only for Lockheed. Keir had recently obtained proof that the Prince was drawing a hundred and twenty-five thousand dollars a year from Northrop, Lockheed's archrivals. Quite certain that Lockheed were ignorant of Bernhard's arrangements, Keir and Sam Pickard were following the situation with great interest.

'Nothing new to report,' said Keir.

'What about Italy?' Sam asked, changing the subject.

'I'm going there after Switzerland. I'm meeting Barzini in Geneva, then we're flying to Rome.'

'How long for?'

'Rome? A couple of weeks. Then I'll return to Geneva, collect the parcels and fly to the States. I'll check with you next week, maybe we can get together at the end of the month.'

They met every ten weeks, sometimes in London, sometimes in New York, occasionally elsewhere if more convenient.

'End of the month looks good to me. I'll check with Chuck.' Sam laughed. 'You take good care of those parcels.'

Keir fidgeted. The parcels made him uneasy, even though Sam assured him, 'Everyone does it. Hell, it's been going on for years, ever since Old Man Kennedy came up with the idea.' Old Man Kennedy was Joseph Kennedy; one-time company lawyer, ambassador to London, and father of John Fitzgerald Kennedy, the assassinated President. According to Sam, 'the Kennedy plan is as American as apple pie'. It was also simple, ingenious and foolproof. Beaumont paid sums of money to a dummy company in Geneva, supposedly for 'advice on the European market'. Once the transaction had passed through Beaumont's books, Sam or Keir collected the money from Geneva in hundred-dollar bills and took it back to the States. The cash was then available to grease palms in Washington. Chuck was a great believer in charity beginning at home. When Keir flew to New York at the end of the month, forty thousand dollars would be divided up in his coat pockets. Last year he had made four such trips and Sam had made twice as many.

'. . . It's all looking good,' Sam was saying, 'especially the deal with the RAF. That's the big one, old buddy. By the way, you give any more thought to Japan? You know, what we talked about?'

They were losing out in Japan. As in Europe, Lockheed and some of the others had got in first and were hanging onto the market. Sam wanted Keir to take a long hard look at Japan.

Keir said, 'I can't leave Europe for a few months. Too much is happening. The earliest I could go would be September. I know it's way off –'

'September's fine. Aim at September and try to allow two or three months for the trip. It's a long time but I've a feeling it will be worth it. Look, I gotta go now. Good luck in Rome. See you in New York around the end of the month . . .'

Keir was left wondering whether he could be away from Europe for as long as three months. Even in the Autumn it would be difficult. Leafing through his desk diary, he calculated that he would have to return at least once to Europe.

Team International had developed in a way no one had expected. Dusty had envisaged glossy front offices all over the place – London, Paris, Rome, Frankfurt – all of which would have been quite wrong for the work Keir found himself doing. Even the name Team International was misleading. Keir was virtually a one-man band, running the lowest of low-profile operations, not from bright advertising offices in Knightsbridge but from his discreet house in Lord North Street – when he was there. Mostly he wasn't. Mostly he was in Brussels or Bonn, Oslo or Ankara, Madrid or Lisbon, or somewhere *en route* from one to another. He maintained no office and employed no secretary. His only staff were John and Barbara, who had become invaluable because both possessed natural discretion. They took all the messages and knew what to say on the phone.

They called him 'sir' when people were about, but otherwise had become almost like family.

Unusual though Keir's work was, it was quite legal, or at least it was for the most part. He simply advised Beaumont on their business in Europe, and did so by keeping his ear close to the ground. By 1968 he had an army of contacts – newspapermen, politicians, lawyers, MPs like Fairbrother and Llewellyn, Members of the Bundestag, of the French Assembly, the Dutch Parliament – Keir had at least one representative in every parliament of the thirteen NATO countries in Europe. Some of them were on the payroll. And beyond them were his contacts in the Defence Ministries – clerks, officials, bureaucrats, most of whom cost him virtually nothing. It all *looked* very casual, just as his continued contact with old NATO military friends looked casual, but it was a casualness that Keir worked hard to maintain. Less casual was the work he paid lawyers and detectives to do – digging into the affairs of people like Bernhard. It was not a career in the true sense of the word, yet it fascinated Keir. Those years at SHAPE had given him a taste for being on the inside, for knowing what went on behind locked doors. It was a taste which his new life allowed him to indulge to the full.

The telephone rang again. 'It's Mr Miller,' said John.

'Dusty!'

Keir and Dusty were in danger of becoming strangers. Keir saw far more of Sam. Dusty's plans for them to work together had never really materialized. True, Dusty still owned part of Keir's business, but his percentage had been reduced in light of events and his involvement had become rare.

'Hi, Dusty. What's up? Run out of clients to talk to?'

'Clients,' Dusty groaned. 'Don't pollute the airwaves. This would be a great business if it weren't for clients. We had lunch with this schmuck today . . .'

Keir sat back in his chair, grinning, and hoisted his feet onto the desk. Dusty was in Paris, calling from the offices of Owen, Lacey & Miller, as the agency had now become. If Keir had grown wealthy, Dusty had become rich, using his early profits from Keir's business to buy stock options in Owen Lacey. The name change had occurred two years before when he had become European President.

'This guy at lunch today. He's talking about a big campaign,

330

right? A new perfume. The thing is he's got a mistress. So, okay, who hasn't? Now here comes the rub. This schmuck wants to plaster her all over France. Every bill-board, every ad, carries her picture, right? He insists. Like he makes it a condition. A million dollars' worth of advertising. Can you believe the way some people behave? So, okay, we say let's have a look at her, and this you'll never believe. Keir, she's a dog! I swear in the whole of your life you never saw an uglier woman . . .'

Dusty had become an expert on women: twice married, twice divorced, and twice cited in paternity suits. Now he lived in Paris with a model. 'This month's model,' was Dusty's joke. 'Next month I trade her in for a new one.' He did too. Either that or they got fed up and left of their own accord. Most of them were beautiful girls, some of whom Keir had met. All were attracted by Dusty's nonstop energy, the frenetic pace at which he lived, the aura he created by action and money.

'. . . So we sell him the idea of a mystery campaign. Reveal her slowly. Like a striptease in reverse. Thank Christ, her figure's all right. In fact, I gotta admit, she's beautiful with her clothes off. Really stacked. Terrific. It's only her face that's so awful. Anyway, the first month you see her from the back. Nude. Who's the mystery woman wearing Cleo perfume? Get the angle? Second month you see just her torso. A really good close-up of these magnificent tits. Third month you see her easing a silk stocking onto one shapely leg. And so on. We run the campaign for twelve months, with a different ad every month. You don't get to see her face till the last month. Then the shit hits the fan, but so what? He'll have spent his budget by then . . . we'll have made our money . . .'

Keir laughed at first then started to cough.

Dusty bellowed, 'Is she with you now? I can hear barking.'

He missed Dusty. By a quirk of fate, France was the one country that Keir no longer visited on a regular basis. General de Gaulle had asserted French independence and had withdrawn France from NATO. In 1966, NATO Headquarters had moved lock, stock and barrel from Paris to Brussels. While Keir now visited Brussels, Dusty spent more and more time in Paris, establishing Owen, Lacey & Miller in France. It was another reason why they saw little of each other, and a pity because Keir really did miss him. No one could make him laugh quite like

Dusty. Sam was all right – once you got to know him he had a dry New York sense of humour that was really funny; and a few others were good company – Bruno Barzini, a lawyer in Rome; Buddy Johnson, an American ex-pat in Oslo; Ossie Bessault in Amsterdam – but too many were like Gerald Fairbrother, stuffy and pompous, with an exaggerated idea of their own importance.

'. . . So I figured it was time for a break,' Dusty was saying. 'Maybe a long weekend in Nice or somewhere. What do you say? I can arrange some very nice company . . .'

Flicking through his diary, Keir reviewed his commitments. Geneva then Rome, and the States by the end of the month. Maybe the weekend before flying to New York? Really, he owed that to Liz. It was ages since they last spent a weekend together . . .

Dusty said, 'I was thinking around the end of the month. Something like that. How you fixed?'

Keir had told Dusty about Liz. Not the truth, not who she was, just 'a young cousin of mine who lives with my parents'. Dusty hadn't shown a scrap of interest. Girls of less than nineteen didn't exist for him. His only reaction had been surprise:

'That's how you spend your spare time? Taking a kid to the pictures? What are you, some kind of monk?'

'I don't know about that weekend,' Keir said doubtfully. 'Let me call you from Rome. If I can tie things up in a week, who knows, maybe we'll fix something up . . .'

Time. There was never enough. Sometimes he wondered where it all went. His eye fell upon the framed photograph of Liz on his desk. Thirteen years old. It didn't seem possible. He could remember picking her up and throwing her high into the air. She had loved it. Now the very suggestion would strike her as undignified.

Finishing the conversation with Dusty, he hung up and began to gather papers together for his trip. A knock announced John as he put his head round the door. 'You've a visitor,' he said, grinning broadly.

'Oh no, we need to leave in an hour –'

'Oh yes,' Liz cried, springing out from behind John. 'That's not a nice welcome.'

332

'Liz!' He came out from the desk, arms outstretched. 'What are you doing here? Why aren't you at school?'

'Half-term,' she said, clutching his hands, pulling away from him and rocking back on her heels. 'John says you're going away?'

'Only for a couple of weeks.'

'You're always away when I need you,' she scolded, pulling a face.

'Ah-ha! Hear that, John? She wants something. Wouldn't you believe it? The only time we see her is when –'

'That's not true!' Rising to the bait, Liz swung round to confront John. 'That's not true, John, and you know it –' She broke off as Barbara appeared at her husband's side. 'Barbara!' she shrieked, rushing to greet her.

Lord North Street had become a second home for Liz. There was even a bedroom upstairs with a notice on the door proclaiming 'Liz's room. Private. Keep Out.'

For the past five years she had been a constant visitor, delighting John and Barbara as much as Keir. Like Edith and Joe, the Westwoods had become another set of surrogate parents, two more adults to lavish love and affection on her. They were forever entertaining her in their sitting-room, or more accurately, she entertained them while waiting for Keir to finish with a visitor or a phone call.

At thirteen, Liz lacked her mother's curious beauty. Her jaw was more square and her nose a shade broader. Her mouth was firmer and wider. The resemblance was strong – the thick black hair and huge dark eyes marked her indelibly as Dawn Wharton's daughter, but the latent sexuality which had been Dawn's all her life was missing from Liz. Where Dawn used her eyes to tease, Liz gazed with a solemn intensity. There was an earnestness about her that, if it existed in her mother at all, only showed itself when Dawn talked about the theatre. With Liz it was there all the time. 'Don't look so serious,' Edith told her constantly. So did Dawn, and Barbara and her teachers at school. Joe never did. Neither did Keir, nor even John. Men saw her serious demeanour as a challenge. Joe clowned around, Keir teased her, John was forever making up funny stories. All three of them were delighted if they could make her collapse into giggles.

She had called everyone by their Christian names since she was eight, which was when Dawn had told her that Grandad and Grandma were not her Grandad and Grandma, and that 'Uncle' Keir was not really her uncle. 'They're our friends,' Dawn had told her. 'Very special friends who look after you while Mummy's working abroad.'

Joe had been startled when Liz had used his name for the first time – 'Blimey, I've been sacked,' he complained to Edith. 'I thought I made a jolly good grandad.' In teasing retaliation he had called Liz 'Miss Wharton' until the joke had worn thin. 'Dawn had to say something,' he admitted to Edith, 'the child's been asking all sorts of questions. She's promised to explain everything when Liz is old enough to understand.'

Edith's only response had been to sniff, 'That should be interesting.' Keir hadn't minded. He had never been happy with 'Uncle'. If he couldn't be called Dad he'd settle for Keir.

'Have you heard from your mother?' he asked, as Liz turned to face him, still holding Barbara by the hand.

Liz rolled her eyes at John. 'There he goes. That's always his first question. And guess what? Hers is always "How's Keir?" The pair of them use me as a postbox –'

'Oh dear. Stand by, John. We're in for a lecture.'

John grinned. 'Usual procedure. Softening-up tactics –'

'Don't you gang up to Liz,' Barbara interrupted, 'I'm on her side, remember.'

'I had a letter this morning,' Liz blurted out. 'She wants me to go and live with her in the summer.' Her dark eyes pleaded with Keir. 'She's making all sorts of arrangements. You've got to stop her . . .'

'There, there,' Barbara soothed, 'don't go upsetting yourself –'

'But she means it. I'm to go over in the summer and stay for good.'

'That's no reason for getting upset,' said Barbara, casting an anxious look at Keir. 'Let's go and make a nice cup of tea. You can tell me all about it.'

The girl hesitated, her eyes on Keir.

'Good idea,' he said. 'Give me time to finish packing. Then we'll talk about it, eh?'

With a doubtful look, Liz allowed herself to be led away.

'Blast!' Keir muttered, throwing papers into the briefcase. 'Dawn might have waited.'

He had known it was on her mind – she had written to him, full of plans for the future. 'If only she'd waited until we'd had a chance to talk . . .' But instead of waiting, Dawn had forged ahead, as strong-willed as ever. 'Talk about like mother, like daughter,' Keir grumbled. Liz would give him hell. The whole situation would create problems.

Keir and Liz had become very close. His only regret about the past couple of years was that the hectic pace had prevented regular weekends with Liz at Lord North Street. Once upon a time she had arrived straight from school every Friday to stay overnight, sometimes to stay until Sunday. His work pattern had been more predictable then. Most Fridays had found him winging in from somewhere. Friday nights had become special, and Saturdays – Saturdays had been devoted to outings – trips to Windsor Castle, Whipsnade Zoo, Brighton in the summer and around town in the winter – days spent together, enjoying each other.

Then the routine had been interrupted, partly by work, partly by Jennifer Hollis. Keir had met her at a party, given by Mandy, of course. Jennifer was one of Mandy's New York friends; a curvaceous, quick-witted blonde newly arrived from the States. Looking for somewhere to live, Keir had invited her to stay, 'until you sort something out'. After that, one thing had led to another. Three weeks later she had moved across the landing and into his bedroom. The single complication had been Liz. Inevitably, things had changed, even though the pattern had remained constant. On Friday evenings they went to the pictures or played Scrabble in front of the fire, and Saturdays continued to be the day for exploring. But slowly little jealousies and resentments had built up, more than Keir realized. In bed one night, Jennifer had pushed him away – 'I'm sick of that child trailing around all the time. She spies on us, did you know? I bet she's outside the door listening now. It's bad enough that I have to suffer dirty looks from John and Barbara all the time, I'm damned if I'll be censured by an eleven-year-old child . . .'

When he had tried to reason with her, saying he wanted Liz to look upon Lord North Street as her home, Jennifer had interrupted. 'What about *us*? You're away all week. I only see you at weekends. We never have time for ourselves . . .' A month later he had returned to find Jennifer had moved out. She had left a note, giving an address in Bayswater.

'Come up and see me sometime. *Without* that bloody child!'

He had never bothered. Since then other girlfriends had stayed overnight, but never when Liz was in the house.

In all truthfulness, there had been precious few girlfriends. His life was deficient in women, sometimes achingly so. Not through choice, more because he rarely met any. There were none in his business, and it was hard to nurture a relationship while rushing around all the time. He could never be tied. He could never guarantee to be in London on a particular day. If something cropped up in Brussels or Athens, if one of his agents wanted to see him, if Sam was in trouble, Keir was there, on the spot, sorting it out. He and Sam had sorted out a lot in eight years. With Keir pulling the strings in the background, Sam had clinched deals all over Europe – fighters in Belgium, anti-submarine planes in Holland and Norway, transporters in Greece, a toe-hold in Italy – and soon the huge RAF contract for C-199s.

Jennifer's departure had delighted Liz, although she had admitted to liking her at the outset. 'She was all right until she got all soppy. I couldn't stand all that business of her hanging on your arm and nibbling your ear. Ugh! I don't know how you put up with it. Edith didn't like her either. Neither did Joe –'

'They only met her once –'

'Once was enough,' Liz had said darkly. 'Sometimes it was nice having her around – you know, to make three of us, like a proper family.' Her face had brightened. 'Like when Mummy was over last year. That was marvellous. That was the best time of all. Everyone likes Mummy. Barbara and John said she was wonderful. "A real lady," Barbara calls her . . .'

It was true about it being the best time. They had spent three magical days together last summer.

Dawn had 'served out her time' on her contract with the studio. That was how she referred to it, like a prison sentence – 'chalking off the days until my release'. In seven years she had made eleven films which, in her judgement, included 'one good one, four that were nearly right, and six absolute stinkers'. Luckily the one good film had been very good. *A Night to Remember* was a smash hit at the box office. If it had not coincided with a resurgence of Hollywood's love of the musical, it would have won an Oscar. As it was, *My Fair Lady* won the Best Film and Julie Andrews walked off with the Best Actress Award for *Mary Poppins*. Dawn had written to Keir saying, 'I console myself with the money. The good news is the accountants tell me I'm solvent again.'

The bad news was that she had never quite made it in Hollywood. Some people blamed JD. 'He was such an awkward son of a bitch, he put everyone's back up, cursing and swearing and calling them all crooks. Sure they're crooks, but telling them doesn't help. The aggravation rubbed off on Dawn.'

Dawn refused to believe that. She believed JD was a film genius, a bit like Mike Todd, and that if the money hadn't run out, *Burning Obsession* would have established him as a top-flight producer, and would have done for her what *Gone With the Wind* did for Vivien Leigh. Her faith in JD never wavered, not even after his death. '*He was a wonderful man,*' she once wrote to Keir. '*You and he might not have got on, but I wish you had known him.*' Another time she wrote: '*I wish I'd told JD about Liz. I'm sure he would have understood really.*'

As for *Burning Obsession*, as if to prove JD right, the public liked it more than the critics. It played and played. Distributors revived it and audiences packed in to see it again and again. Dawn recovered her money. 'The film showed a good profit at the end of the day,' she said wryly. 'The only problem was that the end of the day took so long to come.'

By 1967 she was solvent and free – free also in that she was unmarried. Her name was linked with various actors; there was a lot of talk about her and Peter Finch in '64, but to read the papers was to believe that Finch was in bed with every actress in Hollywood. 'Just newspaper talk,' Keir told himself, searching Dawn's letters for clues. There were none. Names were mentioned all the time – actors with whom she was working, directors, writers – but the only name to crop up on a regular basis was Eric's, and he didn't count.

Dawn hadn't found what she was looking for in Hollywood. No one could say she had failed. She had become moderately successful, fairly well-known, reasonably well-off – enough to satisfy most people, but not enough to satisfy her. Keir had detected signs of dissatisfaction even in 1960, when they had dined at Lord North Street and Mandy had returned so unexpectedly. Dawn's letters themselves were a sign of her restlessness. Prior to 1960 she had written occasionally, then she started writing to Liz as well as to Keir on a regular basis. Far from weakening the links between them she had made them grow stronger. These days she visited London at least once a year to spend time with Liz and Keir too if he was around, and he did *try* to be around. Sadly, only too often Sam needed him in Rome or Brussels or Athens, so his meetings with Dawn were fleeting – dinner here, lunch there. 'You and I never seem to be in the same spot for more than five minutes,' she had once said laughing.

But last summer they were. Last summer they had been in the same spot for three glorious days. Keir had insisted that Dawn stay at Lord North Street. Barbara filled the guest suite with flowers – she was more impressed by Dawn than by any staid politician. 'Dawn Wharton is *someone*,' she had said breathlessly. 'I've seen all her films.' In her forties, Barbara had been as excited as a teenager. Liz, on the brink of becoming a teenager, had been even more excited. Naturally she stayed as well, causing Barbara to blurt out that it was 'like looking after a proper family'. Her incautious words had stayed in Liz's mind, to be trotted out on countless occasions. The uncanny thing was how like a proper family they had behaved. For the three of them to be together seemed the most natural thing in the world, and if the naturalness stopped short of Keir and Dawn sharing a bed it extended to everything else. A warm feeling of togetherness touched every moment.

Afterwards, Dawn's letters had been full of returning to Europe. Free of the studio contract at last, she was available for independent productions. Her chance came in the autumn, when she was offered the female lead in *The Troubles*, a drama to be shot entirely on location in Ireland.

In the first week of December, she had written saying:

'I've found the most marvellous house. There's a quality of enchantment about it. For a start it's set in the most beautiful grounds, acres and acres of lawns and old trees, with a tennis

338

court and a stable block and goodness knows what. And it overlooks the sea, there's a path down the cliffs to its own private beach. The house itself is magnificent – original Georgian, full of marble fireplaces and lofty ceilings and tall gracious windows . . .'

To buy a house in Ireland was less reckless than it seemed.

'There are all sorts of tax benefits. I was talking to Peter Sellers, he's just bought a house here . . . there's quite a colony of actors and directors. John Huston and Bob Shaw have been here for ages and they love it. London's only an hour away by plane and I'm inundated with offers of work . . . there's more for me in England and Ireland than in the States . . .'

Most important of all was the personal angle. *'I've been so restless . . . it will be lovely to put down roots . . . to have a place of my own where Liz and I can be together . . .'*

Keir imagined she meant for holidays, especially as the letter continued:

'Christmas here will be fantastic, big log fires roaring in all the fireplaces . . . I intend to fill the house with people . . . you really must come over and stay . . . the summers will be marvellous for Liz, she can ride and swim and play tennis . . .'

But last week had come another letter.

'I tried to reach you but Barbara said you were in Oslo or Munich or somewhere . . . I've got the most exciting news. I clinched the deal on the house today! I'm a landowner, with fields and trees and a beach and some cliffs. There's an enormous amount of work to be done to the house, installing central heating and extra bathrooms and so on, but the builders promise everything will be ready for the summer. You MUST come and visit. And guess what? I've found the most perfect school for Liz. I thought I'd have trouble, the schools here are so heavily Catholic, but the British Embassy put me in touch with one the Embassy people use for their kids . . . an international school . . . and when I spoke to them they said they could take Liz after next summer . . . so everything's working out fine. . .'

Rooting around in the desk drawer, Keir found Barzini's report which he added to the papers in his briefcase. He paused a moment, checking everything was there that he needed before closing the case with a click. The noise coincided with the sound of a knock as John opened the door and stood aside to make way for Liz carrying a tray with the tea things. Frowning with concentration, she advanced towards the coffee table as John withdrew.

Watching Liz set the cups out on the table, Keir was struck by how tall she was growing. There had been times when he had come close to telling her that she was his little girl, that he was her father, that she should come and live permanently at Lord North Street. He never had. How could he? He was abroad too often to play the role of permanent parent. Besides, it would have caused trouble with Dawn. It would have breached their agreement. And Joe and Edith would have been up in arms about Liz leaving them. Now they would be up in arms anyway . . .

'She says you know about it,' Liz commenced abruptly, fixing him with a look of reproach. 'She says she wrote and told you about it –'

'I had a letter last week,' he admitted, crossing the room to join her on the sofa. 'I haven't had a chance to –'

'I won't go. If she makes me go, I'll run away.'

Close to tears, the scrubbed look beneath Liz's eyes suggested she had been weeping already. Keir imagined her clinging to Barbara in the kitchen, with Barbara uttering soft words of comfort. Now it was his turn to search for the right words. Taking her hand, he said, 'It's only natural for Dawn to want you with her. She is your mother –'

'When it suits her,' said Liz with such bitterness that he was startled.

'Liz?' His eyebrows rose. 'That's not like you. You're always saying what fun we have when she visits –'

'Not because of her. Because of you! And Barbara and John. And because Edith and Joe are at home waiting. It's like a holiday when she comes. It *is* a holiday. We do things together . . .' her voice broke, and she gulped, catching her breath. 'You should have told me!'

'I only just got her letter –'

'Last week, you said. A whole week!'

How could he explain that a week was no time at all? That for five of the past seven days he hadn't even been in London, that he had been flying from meeting to meeting . . .

'Liz,' he said, his voice gentle and persuasive, 'you're making

340

a mountain out of a molehill. After all, you always have such a good time –'

'I just *told* you,' she said angrily, staring at him, willing him to understand.

'Like a holiday, you said. So your whole life will be like a holiday –'

'Not without everyone else. How can it be? It's us being *together*, not me being stuck in Ireland.'

'You might like it –'

'I *won't* like it. She told me about it in her letter, all fields and things, stuck out in the middle of nowhere. It will be awful. Boring, boring, boring –'

'You won't be by yourself.'

'You won't be there.'

'I'll visit.'

'When? You'll never have time, you know you won't. And what about Joe and Edith? I *can't* leave them. What about my friends at school . . . ?'

Her arguments came nonstop, she flailed him with words in a passionate outpouring. Her hands clenched in her lap, and the hurt, angry look in her eyes filled him with guilt. *You can't abandon me*, she seemed to be saying, *I'm relying on you.*

'Please talk to her,' she begged. 'She'll listen to you. You know she will.'

He wondered. Perhaps Dawn would listen to him. She had listened before when it came to Liz. Between them and Edith and Joe, they had done their best for the child. They had always put her first. He hoped, he believed, that despite differences with Joe about taking Liz on demonstrations, they had given her a happy childhood. Now it was in danger . . .

'Please, Keir. You *can't* let her take me away.'

And he couldn't. Not just like that, not after thirteen years – there was too much between them, too many memories. Absent he may have been, far too often, but he had been to her school on Open Days, taken her on outings, sent her for a seaside holiday every year with Joe and Edith. He had snatched time; half days, a few hours . . . he had done what he could. Yet a fight with Dawn was the last thing he wanted. He no longer knew what he felt for her, he didn't see her often enough to be sure, but that time last summer had been full of such warmth and affection that there had to be *something* between them. With an unconscious gesture of frustration, he glanced at his watch.

'You're always looking at your watch,' said Liz.

'Only when I've got a plane to catch.'

'You've always got a plane to catch,' she said wistfully.

He sighed, recognizing the truth.

'Can I come to the airport with you? John can take me home afterwards. Please, it will give us longer to talk.'

How often had he heard that? Usually he teased her, saying, 'Oh, I don't know, John might have something better to do . . .' And she would flee, shrieking down the hall, to return pulling John, with Barbara on his heels, scolding her husband for 'teasing that child'. It was a game. They never went too far, Barbara made sure of that, but today Keir sensed it was wiser not to tease her at all.

'Sure,' he said, tousling her hair. 'Phone Edith first, though, to let her know where you are.'

She rose, wanting to run and tell John, but she hesitated, her worried eyes searching his face. 'Oh, what are we going to do?'

He hugged her. 'I'll think of something,' he said with more hope than conviction.

Twenty minutes later they were on their way to the airport, Keir and Liz in the back of the Daimler while John circumvented the traffic. Keir's blood-red Bristol had long been discarded. It had taken about eighteen months for him to realize it was an expensive toy. The truth was he had very little need to drive. In London he conducted most of his business within a five-minute walk of the house. Apart from expeditions with Liz, and visiting Joe and Edith, his sole use for a car was to go back and forth to Heathrow – and to have John collect his visitors from the airport. Chuck Hayes had been the one to persuade him that a blood-red Bristol was the wrong sort of car. 'It's like a fucking fire engine. Couldn't you have got one with spots on? You know, something really flashy?'

The black Daimler had replaced the red Bristol the following week.

'What are we going to do, Keir?' Liz repeated, desperately worried.

He tried to sound positive. 'Perhaps we're getting into a

muddle about this. You know, it will be great to have Dawn living in Ireland. We'll see her much more often.'

Liz listened with her usual grave expression, anxiety still in her face, but so too was a glimmer of hope. Keir had solved her problems before. She crossed her fingers in an unspoken plea to the gods.

'After all,' Keir continued, 'she'll be making films in England, so she'll be over a lot. Flying back and forth all the time –'

'Like you,' said Liz, sounding hopeful.

'That's right. So when it comes to next summer, I think you should go –'

'No,' Liz interrupted, her hand tightening on his arm.

'Just for the holidays. See if you like it. Take it a step at a time –'

'But her letter says for always –'

'I know. We'll talk about that. I'll try to persuade her. No promises, mind . . .' He gave her a hug, laughing to reassure her. 'The thing is, we all want to see more of you. You're a very popular young lady. And you really do like to spend holidays with Dawn, you said so –'

'Will you come with me?'

'I can't for the whole summer –'

'For part of it. For a couple of weeks. Surely you can come for two weeks?'

He sighed. Sam wanted him to go to Japan. The Farnborough Air Show was in August. June and July were thick with meetings. But he had to do something. Liz looked sick with worry. Dammit, he deserved some time off! And it would be good to spend time with Dawn . . .

'Okay,' he said, reaching a decision. 'Here's what we'll do. I'll come over with you and stay for two weeks.'

'You will? Honestly?' She grabbed his hands, her dark eyes shining. Next moment she flung her arms round his neck and smothered him with kisses. 'John,' she shrieked, throwing herself forward over the front passenger seat. 'Did you hear that, John? Two whole weeks in the summer!' She swung back to Keir. 'Promise? You really promise? Cross your heart and hope to die?'

So he promised. They even fixed the date. Liz insisted on writing it in his pocket diary, crossing out several engagements in the process. On 15 July, one week after she broke up from school, they would go to Ireland together.

She was full of it on the way home from the airport. Riding in the front next to John, she scarcely stopped talking. 'You'll remind him won't you, John? Don't let him forget. Put it in the other diary when you get back,' she said, knowing that Keir's schedule was duplicated in the leather-bound diary on his desk.

The problem was solved. Her mother never disagreed with Keir, there would be no more talk of living permanently in Ireland, Keir would see to that.

'By golly,' John chuckled, 'you'll have three homes to go to. You are posh. I'll have to start calling you m'lady.'

Liz was so happy that she giggled.

Home for Joe and Edith was no longer the shop in Hillingdon, but a four-bedroomed bungalow in Ealing to which they moved in 1962, largely because of Liz, although she was unaware of the fact. Following a promise to Dawn, Keir had made the effort to see more of Liz, but the journey out to Hillingdon was tiresome and time-consuming. Also, the area lacked a good school for girls, a consideration of increasing importance. So in 1962, Joe had sold his shop and moved closer to the West End of London.

'It's hardly a sacrifice,' Edith said at the time, delighted with the amenities of her new home.

And of course, a bungalow was ideal for Joe. He still saw his friends. Bob and Emlyn were constant visitors, along with a whole host of people. Number fifty-eight Arcadia Gardens was rarely empty.

'More people go through this house than through Paddington Station,' claimed Edith. All sorts of people, from doctors to dustmen, sharing only one thing in common – their opposition to nuclear weapons.

Joe devoted his life to what had become known as the Peace Movement. He served on committees, wrote letters, raised funds, gave speeches and went on marches. By 1968 he was a veteran of countless campaigns. Joe Milford had been among the 826 people arrested in 1961 for marching down Whitehall to protest about Britain's testing of nuclear weapons. On that occasion he had merely been fined.

Later the same year, arrested again, he had been hauled up in Bow Street Magistrates' Court with Lord Russell and thirty-five others. Liz had been seven years old at the time. Her most vivid memory was standing outside the court watching the frail, elderly figures of Lord and Lady Russell, and Joe and the others being taken from the court to begin two months in prison. She had wept, clinging to Edith for comfort. Edith had wept too, silent tears trickling down her cheeks as she watched policemen lift Joe and his chair into the back of a Black Maria.

'What can we do?' Liz had cried.

'Be proud,' Edith had choked back. 'Be proud.'

Liz was proud. More proud of Joe than she could put into words. Not that she tried to express her feelings often, and never to Keir. Keir was so disapproving. She was afraid of saying the wrong thing and causing trouble for Joe. Once before she had heard Keir shouting, 'I won't have Liz involved in this bloody nonsense!' It had been the only time she had heard him swear.

John glanced at her, aware that the chatterbox of a few minutes before had fallen suddenly silent. 'Penny for them?'

She shrugged. 'Just thinking.' She liked John. John was calm. That was her word for him. So was Barbara. They were both calm. She had words for them all. Keir was busy, her mother was beautiful, and Joe and Edith were brave. Sometimes she wondered which was best – to be calm, busy, beautiful or brave? She would never be beautiful like her mother. Not that it mattered. She would hate to be an actress. It seemed a waste of a life, forever pretending to be somebody else – an unreal life.

'What was that?' John cocked his head, making her wonder if she had spoken aloud.

'I was thinking . . . Mummy's life must be very peculiar. Being someone one day and somebody different the next. Do you think she ever forgets who she is?'

He laughed. 'What an odd thing to say.'

Liz didn't think it was odd. The thought was clear, even if it was hard to express. To be an actress was a pretend sort of life.

'I don't want a pretend life,' she said. 'I want a real life when I grow up.'

'Don't you think your mother has a real life?'

Liz thought about that and concluded the answer was no. How could you have a real life if you spent your time pretending to be somebody else? 'See what I mean?' she asked, trying to explain. 'You'd be living in a sort of imaginary world all the time, wouldn't you? Not the real world at all.'

'Oh dear,' said John solemnly. 'If that's what you think, it's a good job you've got your Uncle Keir to balance things up. He lives in the real world all right.'

Liz even wondered about that. She could hear Edith saying 'people believe what they want to believe . . . and close their minds to everything else'. Keir closed his mind about some things. Telephone tapping for example. Joe knew his phone was tapped. Edith knew it was tapped. Liz knew it was tapped. But when Joe happened to mention it one day, Keir threw his hands in the air. 'People's phones aren't tapped in this country. Good Heavens, it's not Russia you know. Where on earth do you get these extraordinary ideas?' he had said.

After suspecting for years that his phone was tapped, Joe had set out to prove it. By word of mouth he had arranged to picket the USAAF base at Ruislip, beginning at 7 a.m. on a particular Monday. However, over the telephone to Bob and Emlyn and others, he had arranged for the demonstration to take place at 7 a.m. on the Wednesday. When the demonstrators turned up on the Monday, the police were so surprised that a young inspector confessed, 'We weren't expecting you until Wednesday.'

Joe could quote twenty or thirty other examples, but most people preferred to agree with Keir. 'People's phones aren't tapped in this country.'

'People believe what they want to believe,' said Liz with a shrug.

John took his eyes off the road to give her a quizzical look. 'I don't follow?'

'It doesn't matter,' said Liz, feigning indifference. But it did. Some things made her blazing mad. Like the people in Arcadia Gardens who wouldn't speak to Joe because he had been arrested so often. (Twenty-eight times by 1968.) Where Joe could accept it with a grin – 'I'm not considered respectable' – Liz was filled with furious outrage. Like at school, where Miss Chambers was forever going on about nuclear power being the answer to the world's energy needs. Once, Liz had written an essay, using Joe's vast library of material, to point out that scientists had calculated that all the uranium in the world would be used up long before nuclear power could

346

supply even ten per cent of the world's energy needs. The essay had been marked three out of ten for 'the use of unproven theories'.

When Liz had pursued the matter in the classroom, Miss Chambers had snapped, 'I will not allow politics into this school.'

John persisted, 'What do you mean? "People believe what they want to believe." I don't understand.'

Liz looked at him. No, she thought, you don't. People like you close your eyes to what's going on in the world. The Arms Race, the war in Vietnam . . .

'It's no good you frowning like that,' said John, 'I'm not frightened of you.'

Liz grinned. John had his good points.

'Very well,' he said, pausing to concentrate as he negotiated the traffic. 'Talk in riddles, see if I care.'

'You're my holiday people,' she announced. 'You and Barbara, Keir and my mother. I do like it when I see you –'

'And we like it when we see you,' he interrupted, smiling at her.

She returned his smile before looking out of the window. They were nearly home. Soon she would be back in the real world, leaving her holiday people behind. That was what she had been about to say. Luckily, she had stopped herself in time. John would be hurt by something like that.

'How's Mr Milford?' he asked. 'And Mrs Milford? Are they well?'

'Fine,' she answered, wondering if the Swedish lady would still be at home. The Swedish lady was from the Peace Movement in Stockholm, staying with the Milfords while she was in London, as so many others had done before her. Liz had met Germans and Belgians, Australians and New Zealanders, Canadians and Americans . . . the bungalow was rarely without a guest from somewhere or other. 'The army of the good,' Joe called them, his cheerful good humour containing, as usual, a hint of self-mockery.

Liz loved listening to them talk about their campaigns, thousands of people marching in city after city, adding up to millions of people all over the world. They were the people who lived in the *real* world.

347

'Here we are then,' said John, as they turned into Arcadia Gardens. 'Home Sweet Home.'

After declining Liz's invitation to go in for a cup of tea, John listened with mock solemnity while she instructed him about making a note in the desk diary.

'Don't forget, John. Promise. Two weeks starting from the fifteenth of July. Write it in red and don't let anything get written over it. It's very, very, very important.'

Driving off afterwards, he raised his hand in salute as she waved to him from the kerbside. What a nice kid, he thought, not for the first time. He and Barbara often discussed her. They worried about her. It wasn't right for kids to grow up with old people. The kids got too solemn. Look at Liz. Sometimes you'd think she'd got the worries of the world on her shoulders. Was it any wonder with Old Man Milford forever predicting a nuclear holocaust . . .

'One thing's for sure,' John muttered under his breath, 'Keir's got to make those two weeks in the summer. If he doesn't, she'll never forgive him.'

Two

The rash promise to take Liz to Ireland was to cause Keir a great deal of heartache. He regretted his words as soon as he met Barzini in Geneva. The news from Rome could not have been worse. Where Lockheed had bought themselves a Defence Minister in Germany, and a Royal Prince in the Netherlands, they seemed set to buy an entire republic in Italy.

Keir told Chuck Hayes what he had found out when they met in New York at the end of the month. The big man took the news badly. 'Let's get this straight. You're telling me that the Prime Minister, and this guy Fanali – and this other general, what's his name, Nicolo? – are all rooting for Lockheed?'

'I'm afraid so.' Keir nodded. 'And there're a few others as well.'

'Holy Christ! Go through the list again. There's gotta be a way round these guys.'

'I don't see how. After all, Rumor *is* the Prime Minister.'

'Don't they come and go in Italy? Maybe he won't last long.'

Keir shrugged. 'I suppose we can hope for that, but –'

'This General Nicolo. What does he do again?'

'Deputy Head of the Air Force Procurement Agency.'

'Brilliant,' said Hayes bitterly. 'And Fanali?'

'Chief of Staff of the Air Force.'

'Real cosy.' Hayes sounded disgusted. He scowled at Sam Pickard before rising from his armchair to walk to the window.

They were meeting in the Waldorf Astoria, two hours after Keir had touched down in New York. Tired after the long flight from Rome, his nerves were still recovering from his brush with Immigration. On previous trips he had scarcely been asked to open his briefcase. This time even his suitcase was examined. The cursory search, in fact less than eight minutes, had seemed an hour long. Keir had stood there in a sweat, waiting to be told to empty his pockets. Luckily, no such request had been made and, after fleeing from the Arrivals Hall, he had leapt into a cab, rushed into the hotel and delivered the forty thousand dollars with a sigh of relief. Sam had fallen about laughing. 'I told you it would be okay. They never make you turn out your pockets.'

Even Chuck, who had seemed worried when Keir arrived, raised a wry smile. 'It's our money, Keir, and forty thousand don't last five minutes in Washington. Guys there don't come cheap. There're a lot of them, that's the headache. Know how many retired officers on Lockheed's payroll? Over two hundred, and not one retired below the rank of colonel. And every day they're on the phone to their old buddies wanting a favour.'

Nobody sells military aircraft by handing out leaflets. Keir had become part of a very tough business. He estimated that Chuck had employed the Kennedy plan to launder at least a million dollars – money which was then used to open doors in Washington. 'I didn't invent the system,' was the way Chuck summed it up. Keir knew it was true. No longer shocked, he was merely thankful not to be involved in that end of the business. He had changed his mind about a lot of things since that day in Smart's office when he had erupted with outrage. Smart had been right. Like battles in court, orders for aircraft weren't won by being outraged. Chuck did what he had to – there were a lot of people to satisfy – stockholders, customers, bankers, employees, and people who could influence important decisions.

Scratching his head, Chuck turned from the window. These days he combed his hair carefully across his scalp to disguise his advancing baldness. His large frame still gave him the look of a retired athlete, and the pugnacious gleam in his eye gave him the look of a fighter. 'Know what really gets me?' he asked, returning across the room and dropping lifelessly into his chair. 'The thought of the Italians buying the Hercules. They've got to be dumb.' He looked at Keir. 'Honestly, if you were running things over there, which plane would you pick?'

Keir answered at once. 'I'd make it a three-horse race. The Franco-German Transvall, the Fiat G-222, and us. All medium-range transporters. That's what the Italians need, not a Goliath like the Hercules. It's madness for a country that size. Twice the initial cost, higher operating costs, everything about it is wrong.'

'Thank Christ, I thought I was beginning to lose my marbles. I always figured it would be between us and Fiat. I gave them the edge because I guessed the Italians would look after their own.'

'I don't think Fiat are in with a chance,' Keir said flatly.

'Madness.' Chuck rubbed his jaw reflectively. 'Economically it's madness. From a military point of view it's madness. From NATO's point of view it's madness. Yet that's what they're going to do. Sometimes I think the whole world has gone crazy.'

As he watched and listened, Keir thought Chuck looked tired. Even before hearing the bad news about Italy, he had seemed out of sorts. Something was troubling him.

The big man shrugged. 'Give me a run down on these guys,' he said. 'Let's see if we can come up with something. What about this Fanali, Chief of the Air Force?'

'General Diulo Fanali,' Keir answered without bothering to consult his notes. 'He was a war-time pilot for Mussolini –'

'Naturally,' Chuck interrupted sarcastically, 'and, of course, he's a good anti-Communist.'

Keir grinned. 'He's been linked with the MSI. Very right wing. He'd be labelled a fascist in England.'

'Oh, our people don't give a shit about that. You ought to

know that by now. He can be a fascist, a sadist, a rapist, anything he fucking well likes, so long as he's anti-Communist. Or so long as he *says* he's anti-Communist. I suppose we helped get him his job?'

'You mean the US government?'

'Who else?' Chuck raised an eyebrow. 'Specifically those arseholes in the State Department.'

Keir shrugged. 'I think there was American pressure.'

'You bet there was,' said Chuck, shaking his head. 'They won't learn. They think they're so smart, shoving and pushing to get the right guy in the right place. Pro-American and anti-Communist. What they don't realize is most of these guys don't give a shit about Communism. Or Americans. They just like ripping us off. But State don't know a thing about that. Oh no. They're in the clear. We're the jerks who get shafted!' His face flushed angrily and he fell into a rasping sort of silence. After a moment he looked round the room, his eyes lighting on the bottles set out on the side table. 'Get me a bourbon, will you, Sam?'

'Sure.' Sam rose to his feet. 'Want something, Keir?'

It was 11 a.m. Keir's flight had landed at 8.40. Alcohol was the last thing he wanted and he had never known Chuck drink during the day.

'Just coffee, please,' Keir said turning to Chuck with a look of concern. 'What's wrong, Chuck? We knew Italy wouldn't be easy –'

'It's not that.' Chuck shrugged, sounding depressed. 'It's just that sometimes you wonder where it will end. If these deals ever leak out, we'll be the ones to get crucified. Not the politicians or those creeps over at State. It'll be us. Greedy American businessmen, always handing out bribes. Like the system was invented by us, instead of these political bandits who've always got their hands out. And I'll tell you who'll crucify us – self-righteous politicians, that's who.' He paused to take a glass from Sam. 'Cheers,' he said, without looking the least cheerful. Even after a drink, his expression remained mournful. 'Sam and I got to talking last night. He tells me you're planning a trip to Japan?'

Surprised by the change of subject, Keir looked at Sam. It had been Sam's idea that he should go there.

Chuck sniffed and took out a large handkerchief to blow his

351

nose. 'Goddamn cold. I can't seem to shake it off.' After blowing his nose again, he put the handkerchief away.

Sam said, 'I told Chuck I'd asked you to look at the situation.'

'Japan's just like Italy,' said Chuck. 'Another pile of horse shit. You ever hear of Genda?'

Keir shook his head.

'You will when you go to Japan,' said Chuck with unmistakable bitterness.

He talked about Japan for the next ten minutes, sketching out a potted history of events since 1945. According to Chuck, it was planned to transform Japan into 'the Switzerland of the Far East' after the war. The country was given a 'peace constitution' which prohibited the establishment of an army, a navy or an airforce.

'Then came the war in Korea,' said Chuck, 'and everything changed. Before you know it they've got a thing called the National Police Reserve which gets turned into the Japanese Self-Defence Force and soon they've got an army, a navy and an airforce again. Instead of the Switzerland of the Far East, Japan becomes the eastern bastion of the US alliance. It's an instrument of our foreign policy. So what do we do? Just like in Italy, we push and shove to get the right men into power. Who are the right men? Anyone who's anti-Communist. Don't matter if they're in prison for war crimes. Forget all that. Get 'em out of jail and put 'em in power.'

Finishing his drink at a gulp, he said, 'So I'll tell you about Genda. By now it's about 1959, okay? Fourteen whole years since World War Two. So Genda gets "rehabilitated" and is appointed Chief of the Japanese Air Staff. First thing he does is come to the States, leading a purchasing mission. Soon he's in California, being wined and dined by Lockheed, flying a Starfighter and calling it the best fighter the world's ever seen. Next thing you know, Japan buys the Starfighter. Three months after that, General Genda gets awarded the US Legion of Merit by the US Air Force.'

It seemed an unremarkable story to Keir, so he sat blank-faced, waiting for Chuck to continue.

Chuck scowled from beneath furrowed brows. 'That's Genda for you. He's the man we'll be dealing with. His other claim to fame is that he planned and led the raid on Pearl Harbor. At the time we called it the biggest act of treachery ever perpetrated. Nineteen years later we give him the US Legion of Merit.'

Chuck's bitterness suddenly made sense. Keir remembered Mandy talking about Chuck. Mandy knew his whole history. In 1941, Chuck Hayes had been a twenty-three-year-old lieutenant in the US Air Corps, stationed in Hawaii. It was an idyllic posting, much coveted among officers with young families. Chuck had only managed it after some judicious string-pulling. His family had a strong military tradition. His father and older brother were already there, both in the navy. Captain James Hayes was captain of a J Class cruiser and Chuck's brother Ben was executive officer aboard a destroyer. Chuck was the only flyer in the family. He had been married two years and his wife was pregnant with their first child. By the time the Japs finished bombing Pearl Harbor, Chuck was the only member of the Hayes family left alive.

'I'd hang Genda by the neck,' said Chuck gloomily, 'but that's me talking, the private citizen as opposed to Chuck Hayes, President of Beaumont. Wearing my corporation hat, I'm supposed to shake hands with the bastard. Maybe I will, I dunno, but I sure as hell won't like it.'

Keir could think of nothing to say. He had come to like Chuck. He wondered if Chuck's odd mood owed more to last night's talk about Japan with Sam than about Beaumont's prospects in Italy. After all, they had known business would be difficult in Italy.

Chuck stirred himself. 'Let's forget Japan for a while. We'll talk more about it over dinner tonight. Finish telling me about Italy. Who's riding herd on this prize bunch of villains?'

'Carl Kotchian's been over a lot,' said Keir, naming Lockheed's Vice-President, 'and Roger Bixby-Smith has been seen around.'

'Ah.' Chuck's eyes narrowed. 'That's a sure sign money's changing hands. Wasn't he the guy who met with Bernhard's White Russian?'

'The very same.'

'Hmmm. Who's the local muscle? Anyone we know?'

Keir recited what he knew about Ovidio Lefebvre, the flamboyant Rome lawyer hired by Kotchian as the go-between between Lockheed and Italian high-government officials.

As Chuck listened, his old attentiveness came back to his eyes. Whatever had been troubling him before seemed forgotten as he concentrated. Finally, he nodded. 'You gotta give Lockheed credit. Lefebvre's got the right connections so what's your guess about the deal?'

'We know some of it. Lockheed have submitted a written offer to supply twenty Hercules C-130s at 2.7 million dollars each. My guess is that the Italians will haggle for five per cent compensation.'

'Compensation,' Chuck snorted, 'I love that word.'

'Five per cent?' Sam whistled as he worked it out. 'Shit, that's more than five million dollars in bribes.'

Keir nodded. 'Barzini thinks it will go even higher. His guess is eight per cent.'

'Holy Christ,' said Sam, sounding awed.

Chuck stared at Keir. 'How's it to be paid?'

'Usual way. Added onto the price. The Italian taxpayer will pick up the bill.'

Chuck's expression remained impassive. Keir had spoken no more than the truth. It was the usual way. He knew of countless deals where the price was raised to accommodate the high cost of pay-offs. It was always the taxpayer who picked up the bill.

'Okay, leave it with me,' said Chuck. 'I'll try and think of something, but this one is rough, really rough.'

The door opened at that moment and Billy Sachs came in. Sachs was Beaumont's treasurer and he and Chuck were lunching with Beaumont's bankers. The prospect did little to improve Chuck's temper. 'They're ass-holes,' he said dismissively. 'Billy meets with them every quarter. I only get wheeled on now and then to keep them in line.' He rose, grinning at Keir. 'You and Sam keep pegging away. I'll be back by three. You can fill me in then.'

As soon as the door had closed, Keir turned to Sam. 'What's eating Chuck? He looks half-dead and I've never heard him like that. Was it this talk about me going to Japan?'

'Not really,' Sam sighed and shook his head. 'Mind you, he can never discuss Japan rationally. He always sounds off about Genda. He refused to meet him when he came to the States. Snubbed him in public. That's partly why we're having such a

354

hard time. I can understand how he feels, but –' he shot Keir a questioning look – 'You know about his family at Pearl?'

'That's why I thought –'

'No, it's not that. Chuck's been in this mood for a couple of weeks. We've got problems, Keir. You may as well hear the bad news now . . .'

Three

The bad news was very bad. Over a discreet corner table in the dining-room, Sam explained the problem. It was really quite simple. Beaumont, racing Lockheed and Boeing and others to develop the next generation of aircraft, had run out of technical staff. Keir already knew the background. The problem had been worsening for years. Draughtsmen, stressmen, main-frame engineers, specialists in aerodynamics were in short supply. America's aviation industry – a boom-or-bust business in the past – had experienced ten years of continued expansion. Fuelled by conflicts in the Middle East and the Vietnam war, demand for new aircraft continued unabated. Even working flat out, design teams were unable to cope. Change was occurring at an unprecedented rate. Aircraft were flying higher, faster and carrying bigger payloads. Most of the plane-makers had formed aero-space divisions. Development of guided missiles was racing forward. As a result, the skilled labour market had run dry. Competing against each other, the plane-makers were offering ever higher inducements, but there were simply not enough skilled people to go round.

'We're snapping up anyone who can hold a pencil,' Sam growled.

Three weeks earlier, Ike Stevens, Beaumont's Director of Personnel, had come up with a brilliant idea. The faltering British aviation industry had an abundance of such men. Why not hire them? British aero-engineers were technically among the best in the world. Rates of pay in Britain were half the American rates.

'So Ike argued that we can offer them a big pay rise, a better standard of living and a more settled future. The Board jumped at the idea,' Sam continued.

By the time Sam returned from Europe, the 'Recruit British' policy had become firmly adopted. Owen, Lacey & Miller had even been instructed to prepare full-page recruitment advertisements for the British newspapers. Ike, and a whole team of selection people, had booked flights to London. Hotel suites had been reserved for conducting interviews. A firm of international removals experts was standing by in Britain to transport the personal effects of entire families . . .

Aghast, Keir said, 'I don't believe it. When is this supposed to happen?'

'Next week, unless we can persuade Chuck to change his mind.'

'How many people are being recruited?'

'About fifteen hundred. Assuming each has a wife and couple of kids, we're looking to bring six thousand Brits into the States. Ike wants them all here and working by the end of the summer. It's a big operation.'

'It's an act of madness.'

'You think I didn't tell them? I went bananas. That's all I've been doing for days, bending Chuck's ear. That's why he's in a sore mood.'

'It will kill the contract with the RAF. It might finish Beaumont in Britain –'

'You know that. I know that. Even Chuck is afraid it might happen. But what can he do? He's got the future of the entire corporation to worry about. With these people, we might forge ahead of the competition. Without them, we won't. Even worse, we might drop behind. Ike says we *will* drop behind. And if we do, we're out of business. These people can't be recruited anywhere else. If we've got to lose the RAF contract to get them, Chuck says it's a risk we've got to take.'

'It's not a risk,' Keir said angrily, 'it's suicide.' He thought of all the work he had put into that contract. They were so close. One of the biggest contracts of all time. Beaumont's first chance to supply the RAF . . .

Suddenly, Keir felt exhausted. Raw-eyed from jet-lag and lack of sleep, he longed for his bed. The smell of food nauseated him. Unsure whether he was eating breakfast or lunch, the truth was that he fancied neither. All thoughts of discussing other business in Europe went out of his head. The RAF contract was the big one, and they were about to throw it away. Keir's only positive thought at that moment was to call a break.

'Sam, I'm going to crash out for an hour. Sorry, my brain just seized up. Chuck's not back until three –'

Instantly sympathetic, Sam said, 'Sure, I should have suggested it. You're probably not hungry anyway. I'll stop by your room just before three.'

Keir was already on his feet. 'We've got to stop this, Sam. It's crazy.'

He walked back to the lobby and took the elevator up to his room, his mind already assessing the damage. Britain, in political and economic decline, had been losing its brightest citizens for years. The British press had labelled it 'The Brain Drain' – that exodus of talent which increased every year. Doctors, nurses, scientists, engineers were all finding better futures abroad. Harold Wilson, the British Prime Minister, had been swept to power on a promise to end the Brain Drain. He had painted a picture of a new future, forged 'in the white heat of technology'. He had described a better, more prosperous Britain, which would not only produce more scientists but 'would be a great deal more successful in keeping them here'. More than any government in Britain's history, the Labour government was committed to bringing about 'a technological revolution'. Now Beaumont was about to take a full page in every national newspaper to tell British aero-engineers that 'there's a better future in America'.

Kicking off his shoes, Keir fell onto his bed. There could be only one outcome. Minister of Defence, Denis Healey, would kill the talks about the C-19s. Beaumont would become a dirty word with the Labour government. Sam Pickard would become a leper. The contract would either stay in Britain or be broken up around Europe.

He dozed for an hour, neither properly asleep nor fully awake, tossing and turning. Finally at 2.15, he took a shower, first running it hot, then cold, letting the freezing water beat down on him like icy needles.

By the time Chuck returned, Keir and Sam had resumed. They were not making progress.

'I broke the bad news,' said Sam in a dispirited voice.

Chuck sat down heavily, looking like a man who had escaped one set of problems only to be confronted by others. Keir's impression was that lunch with the bankers had gone badly, an impression which Chuck soon confirmed. 'There's a buzz going round that we're falling behind, technically I mean. It's a lot of crap. For my money we're up there with everyone else, but it's the sort of talk that's doing us damage. It's creating a loss of confidence. I gotta have those people from England, Keir. I need them like yesterday.'

'Then you can tell Sam not to show his face in London!'

'Now then, Keir. Calm down. I guess it was a bit of a shock –'

'A shock!'

The defiance in Chuck's eyes gave him the look of someone who knows the odds are against him, but who is steeling himself for the fight of his life. Next minute he proved it. 'Keir,' he said quietly, 'we *need* those technicians, and we need that British contract. There's not an order that size anywhere in the world this year, maybe not next year either. We've *got* to get that contract.'

Scarcely believing what was happening, Keir repeated what he had told Sam – that it was impossible to kick the British government in the teeth and expect them to give you an order.

Sam agreed. 'I've been saying that for the last ten days.'

Chuck's only answer was to repeat again and again, 'We must have them both, the people and the contract.'

The impossibility of what he was asking caused them to grow angry with each other. Tempers shortened. Poor Sam was caught in the middle, agreeing with Keir, but bound to Chuck by ties of friendship and loyalty.

As the afternoon wore on, suggestions, solutions, ideas to resolve the difficulty became increasingly wild, each proposal more bizarre than the last. At one point, Chuck, speculating aloud, said, 'Do you think it would help if we threw some money about? You know, Italian-style money?'

Keir shuddered. He imagined Healey's face, big bushy eyebrows bristling with anger. What made things worse, as if things *could* be worse, was that he regarded Healey as the best

Minister of defence in Europe. Unlike most politicians, Healey had made himself an expert on defence. He understood the strategy, the need for a fully coordinated policy within NATO, the detail and the nitty-gritty of what was involved . . .

As patiently as he could, Keir explained that Beaumont's full-page advertisements would send Healey into a rage. 'Let's not add insult to injury. England's not Italy,' he said coldly.

'Yeah, well . . . it was just an idea.' Chuck scowled. 'The thing is, it's no good you and Sam sitting there belly-aching. Let's hear you come up with something.'

It was five o'clock when Keir did come up with something. It was so simple that, like most brilliant ideas, it seemed obvious, and was conceived partly by accident. Chuck was talking about the logistics of the recruiting operation, air-lifting six thousand people out of England and transferring them to the States. 'Ike's working on it round the clock. The cost is colossal. I don't even know where we're going to put them. We're organizing temporary office space all over the place. You know, fifty here, a hundred there, that sort of thing –'

'Aren't they going to one plant?'

'There's no point. Ninety per cent of these people are draughtsmen. They can work anywhere.'

'Don't they have to be near the airstrip? You know, for test flights and things?'

A look of amusement crossed Chuck's face. Having spent his entire life in aviation, he was sometimes taken aback by Keir's lack of technical knowledge. In eight years, Keir still had to visit one of the Beaumont plants. Every now and then Chuck promised to lay on 'a royal tour' but invariably something more important cropped up. Nobody attached any urgency to showing Keir how aircraft were made. It was simply not his end of the business.

Grinning, Chuck said, 'Keir, I'll let you into a secret. Draughtsmen work on a drawing board, not an airstrip. Our main design shop is six miles from the strip. Most of the draughtsmen never go anywhere near it. Draughtsmen make technical drawings. They can work anywhere you like.'

Keir stared before saying quietly, 'I'd like them to work in England.'

Laughing at the joke, Chuck would have gone on to change

the subject except for the look on Keir's face. 'In England?' he echoed blankly.

Keir continued to stare.

'You mean . . .' A glimmer of understanding crept into Chuck's eyes. 'You mean we employ them, and *leave them in England*?'

'You said they can work anywhere.'

'I know, but I meant –'

'Is it possible?'

'Christ, I don't know. It's something I hadn't thought about.'

'Think about it now. It would slash the costs to a fraction of the sum Ike is talking about.' Keir's excitement grew as the idea took hold. 'You wouldn't be involved in uprooting families –'

'It's a terrific idea!' Sam leapt up from his chair. 'We employ them in England!'

Chuck spent the next couple of hours on the phone to his technical experts. There were snags, but surprisingly few. The British group would have to stay as one unit and not be assimilated into Beaumont's overall work force. 'But that doesn't matter,' said Chuck, adapting the idea as he went along. 'We want to release people to work on specific projects. So, okay, we'll put specific projects into England. Each project gets headed up by a Project Engineer sent over from here . . .'

By 6.30 it was confirmed that the British GPO could provide as many links as were necessary from London to Beaumont's computers. By seven o'clock, Ike Stevens was on the phone to Chuck, agreeing that eight senior engineers from Beaumont would be enough to provide technical leadership. By eight o'clock it was clear that Keir's idea was not only practical, but would save a million dollars in the first year of operation.

'Wage costs alone will lower. Even if we pay more than the British rate, we don't need to pay 'em double . . .' said Chuck. He forgot about his cold.

Keir forgot how tired he was. Refinements of the idea, extra benefits, further bonuses kept occurring to him.

'It's brilliant,' Sam enthused, pacing up and down with excitement. 'We employ them in England.'

'No,' Keir said suddenly. '*We* don't employ them at all. Let's keep Beaumont's name out of this. We'll form a company. Call it . . . anything you like . . . Technical Drawing Services, or something like that, okay? A British company that works on a contract basis for different clients. So to begin with it's only got one client, Beaumont. So what? Maybe it ends up with only one client. Who cares? We don't give a damn, but the publicity value will be tremendous.'

The benefits of the idea grew and grew. 'To the public at large Beaumont are not operating in England. The name won't appear anywhere, not on the building, not on the stationery, nowhere. It's this other company – whatever we call it – that runs everything, employs people, pays the wages and does everything.' Keir grinned. 'Mind you, I think a whisper ought to reach the Prime Minister and the Minister of Defence. They might be very grateful to learn that Beaumont are investing in a British design company, and working flat out to help stop the Brain Drain!'

Sam was at the bar, pouring them a drink. They only had the one. The truth was they were already intoxicated, consumed by the excitement which grips businessmen when they come across a truly viable idea.

Chuck kept saying, 'It makes such colossal sense. Why the hell didn't we see it before?'

'Because Keir wasn't here,' said Sam with undisguised admiration. 'That's what makes him our secret weapon in Europe!'

Over dinner, Keir should have been ravenous, but he was too excited. He only pecked at his food, enough to take the edge off his appetite while he talked. They all talked. It was eleven o'clock when they left the dining-room, and even then they returned to Chuck's suite to talk some more.

So much was decided that night. So many decisions were made. Keir would call Smart and tell him to have a company incorporated by the end of the week . . . Keir would become the company's chairman . . . He would find an office building near to Heathrow, convenient for the Project Engineers as they flew back and forth . . . Ike and his team from Personnel would delay their departure for a couple of weeks . . . Lacey, Owen Miller would be told to hold the advertising . . .

Finally, at one o'clock, they had talked themselves out. Excitement gave way to exhaustion. Bone-tired, Keir staggered off to his room, weariness descending in waves as he fell into

361

bed. Ahead lay the busiest year of his life. And the richest –
Chuck had promised a bonus of two hundred thousand dollars if
'the British group' was operating by September. Not that Keir
could neglect his other responsibilities in Europe, and somehow
he had to get to Japan . . .

As he fell asleep, Keir forgot the promise he had made to a
young girl at Heathrow Airport, and had no idea that in chasing
one prize he was likely to forfeit another.

Four

From January to June of that year an army of carpenters and
stonemasons, painters and decorators, gardeners and contractors laboured to renovate the buildings and grounds which
together made up Carrickfergus. For most of that time, Dawn
was busy film-making on location in Nice and Marseilles. Every
second weekend she flew back to Dublin, staying at the Shelbourne by night and going out to Killiney each day. Progress on
the house delighted her. Ireland delighted her, especially after
her Hollywood years. The unhurried way of life, the lush, green
countryside, the good humour of Dublin reached out to capti-
vate her. She felt so at ease, so at home. In Hollywood she had
been an actress among many; neither top of the heap nor bottom
of the pile, not everyone's first choice as female lead but good
enough to steal the picture if the part was a strong one. That was
her Hollywood 'slot' and the categorization had caused her
frustration. It made for an unsatisfying life, both professional
and personal – since the two went together in Hollywood.

Even the love affairs were unsatisfactory. There was always
an element of business about them. Everyone was in the business. Who could say, in the blissful afterglow of lovemaking,
whether a remark about a part or a script was the casual talk of
lovers or the premeditated words of one party using another?
She had caught herself at it once. Her affair with Jack Ransome,
the director, had lasted three months. One morning, waking in
his bed, sunlight flooding in through the windows, feeling

relaxed and happy, she had asked for a part in his next film. The request had sprung from all the right reasons. She admired his work, had read the script, knew she could play the part and thought it would be fun.

But she had reeled from the look in his eyes. So that's what all this is about, he had thought. Without waiting for him to speak, she had taken her clothes to the bathroom to dress. ''Bye Jack,' she said, sweeping out of the apartment. He had phoned but she had been out from then on. And there had been nobody since . . .

Ireland was a fresh start. A new life. In Dublin she was a big fish in a small pond. A celebrity. Ever since the Irish *Independent* had revealed the identity of the new owner of Carrickfergus House, she had caused a buzz of attention. Newspaper photographers were on hand at Dublin Airport when she arrived on her regular visits. The Shelbourne was besieged by admirers. And in March came another development. A letter from the director of Dublin's famous Abbey Theatre. Would she consider a summer season of eight weeks, in two plays of her choice with her in the lead?

'Eric, Ireland's so *right* for me,' she had exclaimed in excitement. 'Don't you just feel it?'

Whether he did or not, Eric had also been ready to quit Hollywood, for himself as much as for Dawn. Age was taking a toll that not even his dyed yellow hair could disguise. He was considered 'old meat' in Hollywood's homosexual underworld, and although his desires were beginning to fade he had suffered some painful rejections. Perhaps in Europe – an older continent, more tolerant of the weaknesses of the flesh – he would find another companion? And he did. Within a month of filming in Marseilles, Eric returned to the hotel with a honey-skinned Algerian called Mahoud Mamoud. Dawn turned a blind eye. She didn't mind, she never begrudged Eric his pleasures. She was glad for him. No secrets existed between her and Eric. Their intimate knowledge of each other's lives had cemented a friendship that was truly unique.

From being Dawn's teacher, Eric had become her dresser, her principal press agent, her buffer against the outside world, on occasion her housekeeper and forever her friend. Always there when she wanted him, discreetly absent when she did not, he understood her better than she knew herself. Nobody appreciated more the importance of Carrickfergus than Eric. It was much more than a status symbol, the great rambling house would be home, the first Dawn had had since she had lived with her grandmother as a child. And since in Dawn's mind, a home had to have a child, Carrickfergus would be incomplete without Liz.

'She's thirteen, Eric. All those years . . . God, where did they go? Every time I see her in London, I tell myself, Next year we'll be living together. Next year. Like the Jews. You know that saying of theirs? Next year Jerusalem. I'm like that about Liz. Well this is it. This is the year.'

Carrickfergus was to be their home. Liz would have more than a bedroom, she would have an entire suite – a bedroom, a dressing-room, a bathroom, and a sitting-room all of her own. 'Somewhere she can do her homework, entertain girlfriends from school. Space is very important to a girl of that age.'

Space was hardly a problem. Carrickfergus possessed fifteen bedrooms and umpteen reception rooms, quite apart from the ballroom – 'marvellous for Liz in a few years. She'll be able to give the most enormous parties.' Quite apart from the conservatory – 'so romantic, don't you think? I always wanted a house with a conservatory.' Quite apart from the vast principal drawing-room – 'now this, Eric, is where we put on the style.'

The house was huge and the grounds were vast.

'It's ideal,' Dawn exulted on every visit. 'Liz will love it. I can't wait for her to see it. The only reason not to send for her now is that I want everything perfect when she sees it for the first time.'

By the time shooting on *Royal Feud* finished in April, enough of the house was habitable for Dawn and Eric to take up residence. The structural alterations were complete, and the decorators were hard at work, while outside in the grounds the fine Spring weather enabled the gardeners to quicken their progress.

'At this rate we'll be finished by June,' Dawn said proudly.

Early July was the deadline. Early July was when Liz would arrive. Everything had to be ready by then.

Dawn felt in control of her life, perhaps for the first time since JD died. She had high hopes that *Royal Feud* would be a success when it was released in the Autumn. There were a number of scripts to be read, several offers to consider. Meanwhile she could look forward to her summer season at the Abbey. Her return to the stage, her first and her best love, and in one of the world's most famous theatres! Everything was turning out right. She decided her engagement at the Abbey was the only work she would commit herself to for the rest of the year.

'I want to spend time with Liz, get her settled in. There's so much time to make up. And Keir might come to stay – he said he would try. Wouldn't that be marvellous? That would made everything perfect.'

Sadly, Keir telephoned in May to say he was too busy. 'It will be a bloody miracle if I get a weekend off. Sorry, Dawn, I was looking forward to it, but this year is an absolute cow. I do want to see you about Liz though. Could I fly over on Monday? We could have lunch. There's an Aer Lingus flight out to Amsterdam in the evening. I can just about fit everything in if I catch that . . .'

Immediately anxious, Dawn was alarmed by the ominous mention of a talk about Liz.

'No need to worry,' he reassured her. 'She's fine, really.'

Yet Dawn did worry. Keir had talked her out of taking Liz to America. Perhaps he had been right then, she wasn't complaining, but this time he would be wrong. Carrickfergus would make a marvellous home. He would see for himself . . .

Still nervous on the day of his visit, Dawn decided against going to the airport to meet him. Mrs Daley the cook, only engaged that week, was relatively untested, as indeed were the housemaids. So Dawn stayed behind to supervise the arrangements, and Eric – in the temporary absence of a chauffeur – drove the new Rolls to the airport.

The weather was marvellous, the best May for years, warm enough for summer dresses, warm enough for the hardy to take a dip in the sea. The orchard was a blaze of apple blossom. The gardens were vibrant with flowers, and the elegant freshly painted façade of Carrickfergus stood tall and proud under the massive slate roof.

Keir was enchanted by the house and his hostess.

Taking his hand, Dawn led him from room to room, upstairs and downstairs, and then out across the gardens, through the orchard to the path which zigzagged along the cliff before descending to the beach.

Afterwards, they lunched on the terrace, just the two of them, Eric tactfully busy elsewhere. 'I'm overwhelmed,' Keir chuckled. 'I can see what you meant. It's . . . paradise.'

'Won't Liz be wild about it? Did you see the tennis court? And the stable block? We'll get some horses and go riding. Oh, Keir, you really *must* take a couple of weeks off this summer.'

Regrettably, that seemed out of the question. She listened, vastly impressed as he talked of having to attend meetings all over Europe. His success rather awed her. Forgetting what she accomplished herself, she listened wide-eyed as he spoke of his work as the chairman of an aircraft design company in England, and of his need to spend at least a month in Japan. Yet she also felt sadness. How strange, she thought, once I was the one who never had time. My career was all important. Now I've got some time and he hasn't . . .

As for Liz, Keir fidgeted with the sleeve of his jacket. 'She's a bit worried about changing schools and leaving her friends.'

'Children adapt,' Dawn said. 'She'll make new friends. And the school will be perfect. Just think, an international school, with the daughters of ambassadors. It's only half an hour away in the car. Some of the ambassadors have residences in Killiney. They're neighbours. Liz will have friends all over the world by the time she's finished. So useful later on –'

'And there's Edith and Joe, of course,' said Keir, realizing that he had not called them Mum and Dad since Liz started using their names.

'They can visit. Everything will work out fine. I've thought it all out. Really, Keir, I'm not completely selfish you know. That's why Ireland's so perfect. It's not six thousand miles away. You must come over as often as you can, and when I come to London I'll bring Liz with me, school permitting of course, and we'll stay at Lord North Street . . .'

Keir seemed anxious that Liz should see the change as her choice.

'Of course,' Dawn agreed, somewhat startled, unable to imagine anyone *not* choosing Carrickfergus. How could anyone prefer a tiny house in the London suburbs to a mansion?

'And it goes further than that,' said Dawn, 'it's the whole

quality of her life. Once Carrickfergus is totally finished, I shall invite all sorts of interesting people to stay. Living here will bring her out of herself. She's such a serious girl –'

'So I can tell her that it will be her choice?' said Keir, anxiously. 'Suppose I say you've invited her for the summer holidays, and if she likes it she can stay on? After all, that's what it amounts to, isn't it?'

'It's an odd way of putting it –'

'I don't want her to feel she's being forced.'

'Forced?'

Keir squirmed. Dawn was setting such store by this. She had gone to such trouble. The whole house was being geared up to please Liz. He could see that, and it was a magnificent house, he could see that too. Liz couldn't help but be enchanted.

'Forced?' Dawn repeated, sounding distinctly unhappy.

'It's just that Liz can have very definite ideas at times. She is her mother's daughter, you know,' he said with a smile, 'and I'm told thirteen is a difficult age.'

'Oh, she'll love it here. Any child would.'

Dawn's face lit up with an encouraging smile, full of reassurance, her megawatt smile, her film star smile, the smile she always used when she wanted agreement. Few men could harden their hearts against it, and Keir, of all men, had never been able to resist it. Privately, Dawn thought that Edith might be being troublesome, and that poor Keir was trying to be tactful. Either way, she decided they had discussed it enough.

'Be an angel, darling, and open the other bottle of wine in the cooler. And you didn't say whether you liked this dress? I wore it especially for you . . .'

So they finished their lunch, warmed by the sun and feelings of mutual affection. As he drank straw-coloured wine on a dove-grey terrace, under a cloudless blue sky, surrounded by flowers, Keir would not have been the only man to use the word paradise.

'I really will come across with Liz,' he promised, 'even if it's only for a few days.'

She reached for his hand. 'I can't wait. Do you remember those days we had together last summer? I often remember them. I don't think I've ever been happier.'

Like mother, like daughter.

All too soon, he was glancing at his watch and enquiring about the time to get to the airport. 'See you in July,' he said when he kissed her goodbye, 'when I come over with Liz.'

Keir did everything possible to set at least four days aside for the summer. He and John blocked them out in the diary and worked round them. July 15 to 18 were regarded as sacred. Four days were not the fourteen promised to Liz, but even four required a triumph of planning. The confidential nature of Keir's business ruled out the possibility of employing an assistant. Where MPs and Members of the Bundestag would talk freely to Keir, they would clam up if he sent a deputy. Worse, some would feel insulted. They would say Keir was getting too big for his boots. Besides, an assistant wouldn't even know what questions to ask.

Thankfully there were some tasks he could delegate. As soon as an office block had been leased in Hayes, Ike Stevens and his personnel experts arrived to take on the business of recruitment. Smart took care of all the legal work. Owen, Lacey & Miller revamped the advertising, removing Beaumont's name from everything and substituting the innocuous CDD Limited. For those who asked, CDD stood for Contract Design and Development. Luckily few people asked and those who did were really no wiser.

By June, Ike's Project Engineers were already instructing the first intake of draughtsmen. Chuck's target of September looked attainable and with it Keir's bonus of two hundred thousand. However, even that bonus would be dwarfed by his commission on the RAF contract, and the prospects for that looked remarkably good. Rumour had it that Defence Minister Healey would announce the contract at the Farnborough Air Show in August . . .

At the beginning of July, he was on target for everything, even including his four days in Ireland with Dawn and Liz. 'We're going to make it,' was his cheerful prediction to John.

Then, on the twelfth of the month, he flew to Ankara for two days. 'If there's time I'll stop off in Athens on the way back to see Papadouris, if not he'll have to wait until next month. Whatever happens I'll be back here p.m. on the fourteenth.'

Sadly, he wasn't. In Ankara, Sam called him from Rome. Unbelievably – despite a vast increase in price to cover the bribes – Lockheed were edging closer to the Hercules contract.

'Finish up in Ankara and get the first flight to Rome,' Sam pleaded. 'Barzini's out of his depth. Keir, if we lose this, it could mean laying off a thousand men back in the States. You know what that will do to our image. I think we gotta find a replacement for Barzini. Three or four days here could be crucial . . .'

After those three or four days Keir and Sam were due to meet Chuck in Bonn, to brief him on a meeting with Defence Minister von Hassel. And after Bonn, Keir was expected at the new CDD offices in London. Then there was Japan.

'You can go to Ireland anytime,' said Sam. 'Hell, it's only an hour out of London. Keir, we just *can't* lose out on this Italian contract!'

Keir telephoned John and told him to make his excuses . . .

Five

Liz arrived in Dublin three days after her mother opened at the Abbey. The newspapers were full of Dawn Wharton. 'A night to remember,' ran the headline in the Irish *Independent*, punning the title of Dawn's famous film. 'A dazzling performance,' said *The Irish Press*. 'Memorable,' enthused *The Irish Times*.

Dubliners had fallen in love with their new resident celebrity. Apart from devoting endless columns to her beauty and talent, the papers lavished praise on her new home. 'Killiney mansion transformed,' praised the *Independent*, with a complete page of pictures. Dawn Wharton was news. In Grafton Street, she had only to step out of her car to be swamped by autograph hunters.

Beside herself with excitement, Dawn was a star of the theatre. Her dreams had come true. In the days immediately after opening at the Abbey, she gave scores of interviews. Inevitably, her appearance at the airport to greet her daughter brought reporters and cameramen into the Arrivals Lounge by the bus-load. The interviews and the photo-session were almost obligatory. 'One more shot, Miss Wharton,' they chorused, while Dawn obliged and encouraged her daughter to do likewise.

'Smile, darling. Don't scowl. You always look so serious,' she encouraged Liz.

Naturally, the story came out. It was too good a story not to come out. Complete with pictures of Dawn, looking elegant and beautiful, with Liz scowling at her side, it was all there in the evening papers. 'Together at Last!' screamed the headline.

Actress Dawn Wharton talked frankly of the sacrifices made for her career when she greeted her daughter Elizabeth at Dublin Airport. 'I've waited thirteen years for this day,' said Miss Wharton, overcome with emotion as she told of how she had left her baby in England with friends while she sought fame and fortune in Hollywood. 'My dreams were always to make a home for Liz and myself,' said the actress. To prove that dreams sometimes come true, at the turn of the year Miss Wharton acquired Carrickfergus House. Now, completely modernized with the latest in American plumbing, the Killiney mansion will truly be the home of their dreams . . .

'You'll love it,' Dawn promised Liz as the Rolls purred out of the airport. 'The decorators only finished last week. I've been so busy, what with the house and starting this new play. I wrote you about that didn't I? Darling, the notices were out of this world! I know it's not Broadway or the West End, but the Abbey is a very distinguished theatre . . .' She paused, a look of surprise showing in her eyes. 'Darling? What's the matter? You look quite pale. You're not feeling sick?'

'What you said to the reporters about it being my home.'

'Well? It *is* your home. Darling, it's *our* home –'

'But Keir said . . .' Liz broke off as the most awful suspicions began to form in her mind.

'I can't wait for you to see it. Liz, it's a dream! *House & Garden* are coming to photograph it next week –'

'But . . .' Liz gulped. 'It's only for holidays, isn't it?'

'Goodness, I hope not. Once you see it, you won't want to leave. I promise you. Oh, darling, we'll have such fun –'

'I only brought things for the holidays.'

Dawn laughed. 'You do say the funniest things. As if we need worry about that? We can send for anything you want, though I can't think what it would be. As for clothes, darling, you're really too tall for that coat. Honestly, poor Edith hasn't the foggiest. As soon as we've got you settled in, we'll get you a new wardrobe.'

She broke off, peering over the chauffeur's shoulder at the splashes of rain falling on the windscreen. 'Oh dear, I did hope we'd have a nice day. The weather's been brilliant for weeks. I did want your first sight of the house to be in sunshine. What a nuisance. Never mind, nothing can spoil Carrickfergus really. What a shame Keir isn't here. John telephoned to say he'll be over as soon as he can . . .'

Dawn was aware she was burbling, but she was unnerved by the look on her daughter's face. There was a truculent set to her mouth that was most unattractive. So to avoid travelling in silence, Dawn burbled – about the Abbey, the play, and the fact of her working in the evenings.

'But we'll have the days together. We can swim and play tennis. Do you play tennis? Isn't it terrible, I really ought to know things like that. I played quite often in California. And we must buy some ponies . . . Which reminds me . . . Did I ever tell you who taught me to ride? Dear Gary Cooper. Well, he didn't actually *teach* me –'

'I'm only here for five weeks,' Liz interrupted.

Disappointment brought a tiny gasp from Dawn's lips. Deeply hurt that her enthusiasm was not shared by her daughter, several moments passed before she recovered enough to respond. 'You could change your mind, you know,' she said with a shaky laugh. 'Honestly, darling, you've only just arrived. You're still tensed up from flying I expect. Give us a chance, darling.' She threw an arm around Liz's shoulders and hugged her. 'Wait until you see the house.'

Sadly, the earlier drizzle turned to a cloudburst as they reached Killiney. The sky darkened so much that Keiran, the chauffeur, had to switch on the headlamps. The Rolls crept through the deep gloom until Carrickfergus loomed out of the mist looking more like a prison than a fairytale castle.

'Is that it?' Liz asked, sounding appalled.

The rest of the day was a catalogue of disasters. After showing Liz her rooms ('Aren't those silk wall coverings just something? The decorators had to go to Paris to find them. They couldn't even get them in London . . .'), Dawn had planned to lunch on the terrace, just as she had with Keir, but so torrential was the rain that the meal was served in the dining-room. Liz shrank amid the grand formality of the room. And Eric – dear, well-intentioned, faithful Eric – made things a hundred times worse by gushing over Liz in a way that clearly unnerved her. Unused to children, he thought the way to treat them was as if they were slightly deaf and a little bit dim.

'Liz!' he shrieked on entering the room. 'Hello. What a joy to meet you at last. Welcome to your new home. Oh, my, just look at you. The image of your mother. Beauty runs in the family, doesn't it? Did you enjoy your airplane ride? You weren't sick or anything, then?'

Dawn had intended to spend the afternoon touring the grounds. Instead they spent it going round the house, inspecting one room after another while peering out of the windows in the hope that the rain had stopped. It hadn't and didn't.

At four o'clock, Dawn went for her rest. She had planned to do without it, thinking they'd be on the beach and she'd stretch out in the sun, but there was no sun, and finding things to say to Liz was becoming a strain. She felt her nerves tightening up like piano wires. God knows what it will do to my performance tonight, she thought. Oh why couldn't Keir be here? Things would be so much easier. Liz was bound to feel a bit shy to begin with . . .

She explained her routine to Liz. 'When I'm working in the theatre, I always rest from four until five. Eric and I have worked out a routine . . .' She laughed, inexplicably nervous. 'It's nothing really. I go to bed for an hour, then Eric gives me a massage. We leave for the theatre at 6.15, I like to get there an hour before the curtain. Some people dash in at the last minute, but that would destroy me. I have to have plenty of time to gather myself.' She smiled brightly and looked at Eric for confirmation.

'Oh, absolutely, sweetie. The point is when we're resting, we're getting ready for our performance. Work starts in the afternoon in this house. All arse –' Eric checked himself – 'All back to front.'

'Come and have tea with us in my dressing-room later,' Dawn interrupted, 'and if you'd like to see the play, Keiran will bring you into town. You can come out to supper afterwards if you like, or Keiran can bring you home, whichever you'd rather. Meanwhile, make yourself at home, darling. And don't look so *serious*. You're on holiday, remember?'

Upstairs, undressing while Eric pulled the drapes against what was left of the grey afternoon, she thought, At least we've broken the ice. Things will get better . . .

But they didn't.

Liz arrived at the dressing-room door promptly at five and sat, solemn-faced, watching Eric massage her mother on the massage table. She said she would like to see the play, which encouraged Dawn enormously.

'My word, I shall have a very special audience tonight, won't I?' she said, giving her daughter a beautiful smile.

They left in the Rolls with Eric driving. Liz waved from the front door. Keiran would bring her in later in the Land-Rover. Dawn felt horribly guilty. 'I suppose she could have come with us, except what would we do with her? You know I can't stand anyone fussing me before I go on. Do you think she understood?'

'Stop worrying, sweetie. Put her out of your mind and start thinking about your performance.'

'I hope she finds a prettier frock if she's coming out to supper. I never thought to ask what clothes she brought. Really, Edith's got no idea . . .'

At supper afterwards, Liz looked like a refugee among the dozen people in their party. Awkward and ill at ease, she offered no congratulations on Dawn's performance, merely agreeing when someone said, 'Your mother was wonderful, wasn't she? You must be very proud of her . . .'

Usually voracious after a performance, Dawn scarcely touched her supper. She couldn't wait to leave.

'We'll go shopping tomorrow,' she said in the car. 'Dublin has some very nice shops. I was surprised. If we go into town at about eleven we can have lunch out. You'd enjoy that, wouldn't you? And we'll buy you some really nice things . . .'

One of her happiest memories was of being taken around Bristol's department stores by her gran. She could even remember the blue frock they had bought. Poor Gran had saved hard to buy her a few decent dresses. Thankfully money wasn't a problem. Tomorrow she'd take Liz into Dublin and they'd have a really good spend. Really enjoy themselves.

But they didn't.

The weather was awful again. Rain fell steadily from an asphalt-grey sky. 'Never mind,' said Dawn brightly, making the best of it. 'If it was a nice day we wouldn't want to go shopping, would we?'

As soon as she crossed the threshold of Brown Thomas, she was recognized. Shop assistants and customers alike stopped and stared, people smiled and came up to ask for her autograph. Many wanted to chat, to tell her how much they enjoyed her performance. They wouldn't do that in London. They'd blink and take a second look before hurrying off. In Dublin, people liked to talk and they expected their idols to talk back to them. And Dawn did. She enjoyed it. This was her public. But Liz slouched and fidgeted, and looked bored and embarrassed. Even when she tried on dresses she did so with such indifference that Dawn felt an urge to shake her.

'Enjoy yourself,' she pleaded, before adding more sharply, 'That frock would look twice as pretty if you smiled.'

It was another difficult day. So was the next and the one after that.

If only the sun would shine, Dawn told herself. But the sun failed to shine. After weeks of glorious weather, perversely the rains had set in. Solid rain that fell from a leaden sky with scarcely a break. At Carrickfergus the atmosphere deepened into a miserable gloom. Dawn took to sleeping in late, despite her promise to herself to be up early to entertain Liz. The difficulty was to know *how* to entertain her. Eric, bless him, did his best. He had a repertoire of show-business stories that entertained most people for hours. Sadly, they failed to entertain Liz. She listened politely, but found few of his anecdotes amusing. They went out for walks, cocooned in mackintoshes and wellington boots.

'What *would* you like to do?' asked Dawn, bereft of ideas.

Liz answered with a shrug of her shoulders.

On Sunday, they invited a crowd of people to lunch. Sunday lunch at Carrickfergus was becoming the 'in thing'. Invitations were much sought after. In compliance with Dawn's wish to 'fill the house with interesting people', Eric had organized the first even before the house was finished. Organizing such events was exactly the sort of thing he was good at and he couldn't fail in Ireland, where talking and drinking are national pastimes.

'Just mingle,' Dawn told Liz beforehand. 'They'll like you if you give them a chance.'

They were a mixed crowd, mostly from the theatre and the arts, but Eric had included one or two well-heeled neighbours. Some arrived at about 12.30 and would stay all afternoon, helping themselves to food from the buffet and drinking as much as they wanted. About thirty people in all were usually present, delighted to be all guests of Killiney's famous new resident, who wafted graciously among them, drawing admiring looks from the men and uncertain ones from the ladies. As the drink flowed, the conversation flowed with it, rising with bursts of laughter, falling to a beehive-like drone, and once – at about three o'clock – for a split second stopping completely, which was how everyone came to hear Liz say, 'That's the most stupid thing I ever heard. No wonder people say the Irish are thick!'

Afterwards, Dawn admitted it could have been worse. Laughing with nervous embarrassment, people made allowances, but all, without exception, wanted to know what had caused the remark.

'We were talking about nuclear weapons,' explained a pink-faced Arts Editor. 'I was saying that Ireland is neutral, and this young lady . . . er, Liz . . . said that if H-bombs go off in England we'll all be killed by the fall-out whether we're neutral or not.'

Later that evening, Dawn said to Liz, 'There are two things you never talk about. Politics and religion. Especially in Ireland. Goodness, you should know that at your age.'

'How can you *not* talk about politics?' Liz demanded, red-faced and indignant. 'Everyone's affected by politics. They're much more important than all this boring stuff you and Eric go on about all the time.'

Dawn went to bed thinking she had left it too late. We've grown too far apart, she thought despairingly. My own daughter and I can't reach her. She cursed Joe and his politics. She blamed Edith for allowing the child to be brain-washed. And Keir! He was also to blame, yet Liz was different when he was around.

They had fun. Look at last summer, they'd had a marvellous time . . .

The following morning she sent Keiran into town to buy some indoor games. He returned with Scrabble and Monopoly, dominoes and cards, Cluedo and Racetrack.

The games helped. They passed the time. Blue skies and sunshine would have been better, but they remained as elusive as ever. Meanwhile, playing games did get a response out of Liz. She did talk, even if she chose to talk about Joe and his politics at every excuse.

The second week began. Liz stopped coming to the theatre. 'What's the point? I've seen it four times.' Dawn remembered when she was thirteen: I'd have gone every night of my life. I'd have done anything to spend more time in the theatre . . .

Mannerisms began to irritate. Shocked to see Liz biting her nails, Dawn said, 'Liz! That's a disgusting habit. Stop it at once.'

The way Liz walked bothered her: such a graceless, awkward, gawky sort of walk. 'Really, Liz, deportment is very important. I remember when I was your age – no, younger, much younger now I think of it – my Gran made me walk up and down with a book on my head. We did it for hours . . .'

What with staying in bed late every morning and going for her rest promptly at four, Dawn saw her daughter for only five hours a day. But five hours were enough to realize that things were not working out. Give it time, she told herself, things will get better.

But things did not get better. They got progressively worse.

Six

Fourteen days! The longest fourteen days of my life, Liz moaned. She wondered if the rain ever stopped. Standing at the tall windows, she looked out over the lawns, watching trees bend in the wind as rain lashed down from an angry grey sky. In vain she searched for a patch of blue, a sign of a break in the weather. Instead, grey clouds, hung low enough to brush the tops of the trees. Gulls dived in and out of the mist, screaming complaints about the sea which, unseen from the house, crashed onto the beach at the foot of the cliffs. The garden, the lawn and flower beds were sodden. Pools of water filled every dip. Puddles a yard wide spread themselves up and down the long gravel drive.

And this was summer! Liz shuddered to think of the winters, week after week, month after month in this great mausoleum of a house. She thought Carrickfergus was grotesque. It belonged in a bad Hollywood movie. There was an unreality about it, like a stage set. It was so huge. She couldn't imagine why anyone would want a house with fourteen bedrooms and a ballroom and goodness knows what. It was as ostentatious and vulgar as the white Rolls-Royce in the garage. Brought up in the thin air of Labour Party egalitarianism, Liz felt uncomfortable amid such trappings of wealth. At Lord North Street she never regarded John and Barbara as servants. They worked for Keir, she recognized that, but they were friends . . . not servants. Whereas at Carrickfergus, servants were undoubtedly servants.

Oh, where was Keir? He had promised. She would never forgive him. She could cope, when he was around. He would make her mother understand that she couldn't possibly live here. Just the holidays. That had been the compromise. The *promise*. 'Spend the holidays there,' Keir had said after his visit in May. 'It's a marvellous place. You'll love it. And you can decide, not me or Dawn or Joe or Edith, *you* can decide if you stay there.'

But the Famous Film Star had different ideas.

Liz had taken to thinking of her mother as the Famous Film Star ever since she had faced the flash-bulbs and reporters at Dublin Airport. That had been awful. Humiliating. Watching the Famous Film Star brush a tear from her eye as she said 'I've waited thirteen years for this day.' Liz had wanted to scream, 'That's not true! It's not been like that at all!'

She had cringed, wanting to hide, not smile, as her mother had urged, 'Smile, darling, smile . . .'

Then there was Eric with his awful dyed hair and coloured clothes and mincing walk. She had never met anyone like him. There was something . . . she couldn't put her finger on it . . . something dirty about him. She had thought that the moment she met him, and had been convinced in the dressing-room later.

377

She would never forget her mother casually discarding her robe, to stretch out nude on the massage table, uttering a sigh of contentment as Eric slid his hands over her body. Liz hadn't known where to look. She had tried not to look, but her eyes had been drawn as Eric's hands worked their way up the naked thighs, stroking and squeezing and smoothing and patting. She had wanted to scream, 'Stop touching my mother!' Instead she had choked with embarrassment.

The whole thing was so awful. They were awful, the pair of them. All they talked about was the theatre. They never discussed the real world; important things like the Bomb and Vietnam and politics . . .

'Ah, there you are, darling.'

Liz turned as the Famous Film Star entered the room, looking elegant in a dress of green wool. Liz knew she would never look like that. Not that she cared. She'd hardly thought about her appearance until her mother started telling her to stand up straight and smile all the time. She had wanted to say, 'I'm not like you. I'm me. We're different . . .'

'Guess what? Some marvellous news. I've just had a call from Miss Murgatroyd. You know, Headmistress of the school I told you about. The International School.'

Liz flinched, instantly wary.

'She's offered to give us a private tour of inspection. Isn't that nice? Of course, the school is closed at the moment, but she'll open up especially. I said we'd be there at about twelve –'

'No.' Liz shook her head and took a pace backwards.

'What do you mean, "No"?'

'I'm not going. I don't want to go.'

'Oh, darling, please don't be tiresome. I've only this minute arranged it –'

'No,' Liz repeated, panic rising within her.

'It won't do any harm to have a look at it.'

'What's the point if –'

'You might like it. Just give it a chance. Let's look at it, that's all I'm asking.'

Shrinking back against the window, Liz suddenly felt unable to stand the situation a moment longer. 'I told you. I don't want to go. I want to go home.'

'This is your home –'

'Keir said I could go. He *promised*!'

Mother and daughter stared, each wishing Keir was there to defuse the anger they saw in the other. Then frustration. erupted. The storm, brewing for days, suddenly broke.

'He had no right to promise. And you've no right to be –' Dawn searched for words – 'so downright difficult. You've sulked and shown off ever since you got here. I can't think what's got into you. You weren't like this in London –'

'Neither were you!'

'Don't shout!' Dawn shook with fury. 'Don't you *dare* shout at me. I've spent months getting this house ready for you. I've done everything I can think of –'

'For you, not for me. I hate it. It's awful.'

'Awful? How can you say such a thing? This beautiful house . . . I've worked all my life to give you something like this, ever since you were born –'

'When you ran off and left me.'

Dawn jerked as if from a blow. 'How dare you say that! I never ran off. You don't understand –'

'No, I don't. How could you do it? You promised to tell me –'

'I promised to tell you when you were old enough to understand –'

'I'm old enough now!'

'No, you're not. Look at the way you're behaving. Is this what Joe and Edith taught you?'

'I love Joe and Edith. That's where my home is . . . and my friends . . .' Liz could no longer hold back her tears. 'And my school,' she sobbed, 'my whole life. I hate this place . . . and I hate you. I'm going home –'

'You'll go where I tell you!'

'I'll run away,' Liz cried, white-faced, her cheeks wet with tears. 'You can't keep me here in this awful place with these awful people. I'm just another role to you. The Famous Film Star plays Mother!'

'Stop screaming!' Covering her ears, Dawn realized she was screaming herself. Her shaking legs carried her to a chair. She sank down, unable to believe what was happening. *Another moment and I'd have hit her. How could I? My own child . . .*

'Go on, then,' she heard herself saying. 'Go! I can't do anything with you. If you want to go, go!'

Liz rushed past blindly, her hands at her face, sobbing and choking.

Dawn called after her. 'I tried. My God, I tried, no one can say I didn't –'

The door crashed as Liz left the room.

An hour later, still shaking and feeling totally drained, Dawn tried to reach Keir on the phone. He was in Tokyo. She arranged with John that he would meet Liz at Heathrow. 'The four o'clock flight,' she said. Her voice was so lifeless that he asked if she was feeling all right.

'I feel empty. Totally empty,' she said and put down the phone.

Liz took one look at Joe, flung her arms around his neck and burst into tears. Falling to her knees, she collapsed in a heap next to his chair. He embraced her; comforted her, and stroked her hair as he cradled her head to his chest. Out in the hall, Edith, anxious and fluttery, thanked John Westwood for bringing Liz home. 'Stop for a cup of tea,' she invited out of politeness, relieved to see that he was already shaking his head.

'Thanks, but I'd better go,' he said, turning towards the front door. 'Let me know if there's anything I can do, won't you?' There was pain in his eyes, guilt too, as if it was his fault that Liz was upset.

Joe let Liz talk herself out. As she made the tea, Edith listened from the kitchen, concern and worry written all over her face. With a glance Joe warned her to keep quiet, otherwise she would have interrupted to air views of her own. As it was she bit her tongue, knowing she would have her say later. Back and forth to the kitchen she went, bringing tea and cups and slices of Liz's favourite Battenberg cake.

It took Joe an hour to get the full story. With little nods and encouraging smiles, sometimes a chuckle and always with patience, he listened until he pieced it together.

Eventually the tension in the girl worked itself out. Half ashamed, half embarrassed, a glimmer of a smile lit her face. Taking his hand, she rubbed it against her tearstained cheek. 'Oh,' she cried from the heart, 'I can't tell you how glad I am to be home.'

They talked a while longer, Joe full of soft comforting words,

380

drawing Liz out until he was sure that the panic had gone. And Liz was growing more tired by the minute. Exhausted by travelling and drained by emotion, she was soon ready for sleep.

'Come on,' said Edith, 'I'll unpack your things while you get into bed.'

Ten minutes later, Edith returned to the sitting-room. 'She was asleep before her head touched the pillow.'

Joe smiled, a thoughtful look in his eyes. 'Poor Dawn,' he said softly.

Edith's head came up with a jerk. 'Poor Dawn, my foot! She ought to be ashamed of herself, upsetting the child like that . . .'

But Joe saw things differently. Unlike Edith, who blew hot and cold, praising Dawn sometimes and condemning her at others, Joe had been steadfast in his admiration. To his mind, Dawn had courage. She met her obligations. If she made mistakes, she paid for them, all of which counted for a great deal in his book. Even when listening to Liz, he couldn't help thinking of how upset Dawn would be. Clearly she had tried very hard indeed . . . only to have her efforts thrown in her face.

The following morning, he telephoned her. Edith was at the shops, Liz had gone joyously to call on a schoolfriend, and Joe, the perennial peace-maker, telephoned Dawn.

She was cautious at first, as if expecting criticism, but when she heard the sympathy in his voice, she was quick to respond. 'Is she all right? Oh, Joe, it all went so horribly wrong. If only Keir had been here. God knows what happened at the theatre last night. My mind was a blank. Eric said the performance was fine, but I don't remember a thing. All I could think about was that terrible row with Liz . . .'

Joe calmed her much as he had her daughter the previous evening. 'Sometimes,' he said, 'we rush our fences when we want something badly. I think that was the trouble. Give Liz a couple of days and she'll feel ashamed of the way she behaved. Then she'll feel guilty and want to make it up to you.'

'Do you think so? Really? Oh, Joe, I said some terrible things . . .'

He assured her that all parents said terrible things to their children at times. 'They could bite their tongues out afterwards.' He chuckled. 'Don't worry, I've never known it cause permanent damage.'

He gave her hope.

'Won't you be in London more often?' he asked. 'That will give you the chance to see more of her. Take it a step at a time. Don't worry, things will work out fine in the end. I think it was just a case of too much too soon . . .'

By the time the conversation ended, Dawn had taken fresh heart. Sounding brighter, she said, 'That's what was so baffling. We had such fun last year. I really think it would have worked . . . if only Keir had been here.'

Joe sat thinking about that afterwards. *If only Keir had been here.* It saddened him to think of how distant he had become from his son. They had been close once. Such a united family, the Milfords. Then Keir had gone into the army and that had been that. 'Kids grow up,' he told himself, 'it's only natural they move on.' There was no doubting that Keir had done well for himself – one look at the house in Lord North Street was enough to know that. Edith was always saying, 'Our Keir must be worth pots of money.' All from something to do with public relations.

Joe knew little about it. Keir kept his business to himself. They met so infrequently that the subject rarely cropped up, and then only in connection with Keir's travels. Liz had dolls from every country in Europe. No doubt Keir would bring her a doll back from Japan. 'He'd have done better taking her to Ireland,' Joe muttered, his anger rising. Odd, but lately whenever Keir came to mind, a touch of anger came with it. Perhaps it all stemmed from politics? Joe shrugged. He and his son hadn't seen eye to eye about politics for years . . .

Sighing heavily, Joe searched his pockets for his pipe. 'Even so,' he said, 'Keir should have taken Liz to Ireland.'

Edith returned at that moment. 'Talking to yourself?' she said, puffling slightly from the exertion of carrying the shopping. 'Who are you grumbling about now? Harold Wilson again?'

Joe grinned, slightly shamefaced. 'I was thinking about our Keir. He should have taken Liz to Ireland, you know. He did promise.'

'Yes, well . . .' Edith said, taking off her coat and sitting down. 'It's no good you going on about it. Talking won't make any difference. He didn't go and that's that. How about you making me a nice cup of tea? I'm fair worn out, carrying that shopping.'

If the truth was known, Keir was a disappointment to them both. Neither liked to admit it, Edith even less than Joe. Funny really, she thought, why be disappointed? He's made a success of his life. He's very good about money. The allowance he gave them for Liz was more than enough. And yet . . . he had grown up differently from her expectations. Being generous with money didn't make him generous in spirit. Taking Liz to Ireland was an example. Joe would never have let her down like that. A promise was a promise to Joe, even to a child – especially to a child. They hardly ever saw Keir these days, he was always off somewhere, making money. And when they did see him, she was on edge in case he and Joe argued about politics.

It fair wears me out keeping the peace, she thought, and then sat bolt upright, struck by a dark premonition. The day will come when I *can't* keep the peace. Then what will happen?

Seven

The day Edith failed to keep the peace drew a little closer in October.

Joe was 'on the march' again, though this time not a CND march. In fact, some people said that the Campaign for Nuclear Disarmament had run out of steam. Joe would have argued of course. He had been involved in hundreds of marches by then, a familiar figure in his wheelchair – from Aldermaston to London, from the enormous American base at Lakenheath to the NATO base at Loch Lomond, from Flyingdales on the Yorkshire moors to the Polaris base on the Clyde. He had given dozens of speeches and written thousands of words . . .

Yet the tide of events was running against him. When he had first campaigned only the United States, the Soviet Union and Britain had the Bomb. The hope then had been that if Britain renounced atomic weapons, other nations might follow. Alas, neither hope had been fulfilled. Britain had kept its 'independent deterrent' and the number of countries possessing the Bomb had multiplied.

Other defeats pained Joe almost as much. His beloved Labour Party had forsaken the cause. Victory through the Labour Party had been basic strategy – 'Get Labour In and the Bomb Out' – and for twelve glorious months the Labour Party had adopted the pledge to ban the Bomb. Sadly the Party had reversed its decision. Now, with Labour in power, Joe saw no difference between the arms policy of Prime Minister Wilson and his Tory predecessor. All this despite the risks of war and the huge waste of money. In one year alone three hundred million pounds of taxpayer's money was written off when the government cancelled the British-designed Blue Streak and other items of military hardware. Three hundred million pounds! Enough to build twenty badly needed hospitals . . . enough for ten new universities. It seemed madness to Joe.

At times, even he might have retired from the struggle had it not been for Edith, whose opinions had developed in a quite remarkable way. Once upon a time Edith had dismissed politics as 'stuff and nonsense'. But that had been before her first march, before meeting her friend Ann from Ruislip and hearing her say 'We talk about the kids and the cost of things in the shops, and men talk about politics . . . I let them get on with it as a rule, but I wanted my say about these wicked nuclear weapons . . .' One thing had led to another. Edith and Ann had never lost touch. Since then she had met other 'Anns' who believed it was downright silly to say that 'politics is a man's thing.' It affected the way Edith had brought up Liz. 'When I was a girl,' she would say to the child, 'we were taught that our job was to get married and have babies. We left the running of the country to the men. Well a fine mess they made of it. You've got a brain and a tongue in your head. Learn to use them, my girl.'

The political system as much as contact with Ann and like-minded women had changed Edith. Once upon a time when someone said, 'It's a free country,' Edith had taken it for granted. Not any more. It wasn't 'free' to those who protested. She had seen her husband arrested in the street for carrying a placard, and seen him imprisoned for refusing to promise not to protest in future. She had watched Special Branch detectives search every room in her house, and heard Joe swear down the telephone at those who listened in. A combination of such things had changed Edith.

She had hated that shop. In those days she had literally spent her life talking about the cost of things in the shops. It had been a stultifying existence. Once free of that counter, a new world had opened before her. 'It's opened my eyes, I can tell you,' she was fond of saying. It had opened Joe's too. There had been a time, during the war and immediately after, when he had believed 'the only good German is a dead German'. By 1968 he was ashamed of ever having had such a thought. By 1968 he had met Germans who were as committed to the Peace Movement as he was, and not only Germans – Americans, Poles, Czechs, Swedes, Japanese, every nationality under the sun. 'It's not the people,' he would say, 'it's governments. The people would be sick if they knew the things done in their name.'

He felt like that now, in October, the month of the march that was to cause all the trouble. It was the reason he was worried. 'If we're not careful,' he said to Edith, 'this march could end up a blood bath.'

It was the season for blood baths. On television, the ongoing blood bath in Vietnam was depicted night after night. In the States, black civil rights marchers were clubbed to their knees by troopers. In Paris, students fought pitched battles with the police. In Chicago, police used tear gas and bullets against protestors at the Democratic Party Convention. Out of step with the aspirations of their people, governments scented a whiff of revolution and began to clamp down.

Joe despaired sometimes. What had been achieved after eight years of campaigning? More countries than ever had the Bomb. The blood-letting in Vietnam showed no signs of abating. The arms race gathered pace . . .

. . . and yet . . .

The strange emblem designed by Gerald Holtom – the broken cross meaning the death of man, the circle for the unborn child, the semaphore initials ND – had swept round the world. People everywhere saw it as a symbol of protest, of defiance, of resistance. In East Anglia it decorated the wire fences encircling American bases. In Greece, a million people carried it behind the coffin of the murdered leader of the Peace Movement, Grigoris Lambtakis. In Prague, when the Russian tanks moved in, there was the symbol again, as defiant as ever.

If the world's arsenal of nuclear weapons had multiplied, so too had the protestors, for the Aldermaston March had swept round the globe. In the early days they had come to join it; French and Germans and Italians and Scandinavians and all sorts of Africans. Then the march spread to Denmark, to Sweden, to Germany, to Athens, to Washington, to Selma. By 1968 eighty other countries had marched in its wake – all with the same mass refusal to conform, the same determination to change the world. They demonstrated against nuclear weapons. They demonstrated against the war in Vietnam. Which was why Joe was on the march again in October.

He was concerned about Liz. In one sense she had grown up on the march, yet this one promised to be very different.

Even before the march, the papers were spreading rumours: 'Militant Plot Feared in London' screamed *The Times* with a story about 'militant extremists' planning to use the march as a cover for attacks on the police. Identifying the plotters as anarchists and American students, *The Times* predicted a level of violence equal to that seen in Chicago and Paris.

Joe dismissed the story as propaganda. 'We're being set up,' he said, even more convinced when the *Guardian* published the same story.

'So do we go or don't we?' Emlyn wanted to know.

It wasn't their march. They weren't even on the committee. The mass demonstration against the war in Vietnam was being organized by a coalition of various student, trade-union, religious, peace and anti-war groups.

'Too many of our friends will be on that march,' Joe concluded. 'We must lend our support.'

What a triumph was that march – a well-organized demonstration which wound its way through London to culminate in Hyde Park. A triumph for those who preached non-violence. Of course it was noisy – they chanted as they marched; seventy thousand people expressing their revulsion of war – but they protested without violence. Joe was there, Bob Cooper was there, Emlyn was there – and Liz was there too.

'You try telling her she can't come,' Joe said grinning as he bounced along in his wheelchair. 'She's got a will of iron has young Liz. If Edith hadn't got a cold, she'd be here too.'

Never had he seen so many policemen lining the route. 'By God, they're out in force today.'

'They're looking for trouble,' Emlyn said darkly.

'They won't get it from us,' said Bob Cooper, breaking off from discussing the Labour Party with a man who marched beside him. Bob had resigned from the Labour Party, disgusted with its policy on arms, disgusted with Prime Minister Wilson's about-turn on Vietnam. Before taking office, Wilson had argued forcefully that people in Indo-China should be allowed to decide their own future. Once in office, Wilson had changed his tune. 'Bloody turncoat,' Bob growled. Over his shoulder he carried a placard, an enlarged cartoon from *Private Eye* picturing Wilson with his tongue hanging out in order to lick President Johnson's backside. The caption read 'Vietnam – Wilson right behind Johnson'.

On went the march, the older men discussing the issues while the younger element chanted 'Hey! Hey! LBJ! How many kids did you kill today? Hey! Hey! LBJ! How many kids did you kill today? Hey! Hey . . .'

Soon they were in Hyde Park – without a brick being thrown, without one policeman having his helmet knocked awry.

'So much for *The Times*,' was Emlyn's wry comment. 'Won't they be disappointed?'

'It's not over yet,' said Joe with the caution born of a hundred campaigns.

Indeed not, for while the vast body of the march remained to listen to political speeches in the park, a delegation of three hundred was despatched to deliver a petition to the American Embassy in Grosvenor Square.

'Bloody hell. I don't like the look of this,' Emlyn muttered as they marched up Grosvenor Street.

Even Joe, who had seen police in action from Aldermaston to Holy Loch, from Fylingdales to Lakenheath, had never seen the like of the police assembled that day. Neither had he seen them in that sort of mood. Normally good-humoured banter was swapped by the marchers and the uniformed police. The right to march peacefully was a proud British tradition. The police played their part with tolerance and goodwill. But there was no goodwill that day. Instead, an air of menace prevailed. Looking above the serried uniformed ranks, Joe searched their eyes.

Hard eyes. The eyes of men who were waiting for conflict and ready to provoke it. Emlyn's earlier words rang in his mind. *They're looking for trouble.* One glance was enough to know that Emlyn was right.

Unafraid for himself, Joe was afraid for Liz. If Edith had been there, she and the girl could have retreated to a safe place, but Edith was not there . . .

By now they were half-way along Upper Grosvenor Street. The police were densely congregated in the side streets. Joe saw hundreds of them, clambering down from trucks and buses, while behind even more were visible, mounted on horses.

Ahead, the leading marchers pressed on into Grosvenor Square. Behind, the rest of the three hundred entered the street from Park Lane.

'Hey! Hey! LBJ! How many kids did you kill today? Hey! Hey! LBJ! How many . . . ?'

The chants and noise doubled in volume as the shouts reverberated back from the fronts of the tall houses in that narrow street. Sensing danger, Joe made up his mind. 'Emlyn!' he shouted to make himself heard. 'Get Liz. Let's get out of this.'

The same thought occurred to Bob Cooper. Separated by the crowd, Liz had been pushed twenty yards ahead as people surged on towards the Square. 'I'll get her,' Bob shouted to Emlyn. 'You take Joe back now.'

Without waiting for an answer, Bob dropped his placard and began to shoulder his way between those who separated him from the girl. 'Liz! Liz!'

The level of noise rose all the time. In defiance of the vast police presence, the marchers yelled at the top of their lungs –

'Hey! Hey! LBJ! How many kids did you kill today? Hey! Hey! LBJ! How many . . . ?'

Emlyn was struggling to turn the wheelchair. The crowd behind was pressing forward, anxious to get into the Square, shouting and chanting, bellowing furiously –

'Hey! Hey! LBJ! How many kids did you kill today? Hey! Hey! LBJ! How many . . . ?'

'Liz!' Bob roared, closing the gap but still ten yards behind her.

Turning the wheelchair, Emlyn and Joe were fighting against the oncoming tide of people.

'Liz!' shouted Bob, reaching out to catch her arm.

Suddenly, shouts of anger could be heard in the square ahead. Chants gave way to cries of alarm. People turned, some began running back towards Park Lane. Bob heard a girl scream. 'Come on,' he shouted to Liz, pulling her round to face him. Over her shoulder he saw mounted police, dozens of them unexpectedly filling the road at the head of the march. 'Come on,' he bellowed at Liz.

Then the police charged.

Screams filled the air. Bob glimpsed a mounted policeman flailing with a truncheon. He heard the clatter of hooves as horses mounted the pavement. Jostled by the crowd, he tightened his grip on the girl's arm. He and Liz were caught in a cross-current as people surged up from Park Lane and met those running back from the Square. Staggering as a man barged past, Bob yelled as he took a kick on the ankle. The crowd eddied, then swirled as people fled from the advancing horses. Liz tripped and would have fallen had Bob not yanked her upright. He lost sight of Emlyn and Joe. Using his bulk, he shouldered his way through the crowd, dragging Liz with him. Fighting for every yard, he struggled from the centre of the road to the pavement. Behind him came shouts and screams and the noise of horses.

'Come on, Liz!' he cried, reaching the kerb and pulling her after him. Directly ahead he saw a short flight of steps – a refuge from the mêlée around them. Suddenly, he was knocked backwards as a huge chestnut horse mounted the pavement and reared on its hind legs. A man clung to the horse, fighting the mounted policeman, dragging him down from the saddle. Rolling its eyes, the horse was out of control as the rider lashed and whacked with his truncheon. Liz threw herself forward, escaping flying hooves by a whisker. Almost unseated, the policeman hit out wildly in every direction. Just in time, Bob saw the truncheon arching down on Liz's head. Throwing an arm up to shield her, he cried out as the club smashed down onto his knuckles, leaving him feeling giddy and sick. Bucking wildly, the horse lurched off towards the centre of the street, the rider still raining blows down on his assailant. Gasping with pain, Bob staggered up the steps, half protecting Liz with his body, half crushing her under his weight.

Upper Grosvenor Street looked like a battlefield.

From the vantage point of the steps, dizzy with pain, sucking his broken hand, Bob surveyed the scene with shocked eyes. Trembling violently, Liz clung to his side, gasping and choking. A terrifying drama unfolded before them. Liz screamed, wide-eyed, pointing, her hand shaking. Bob followed her gaze.

Joe was sprawled in the road, helpless, with his wheelchair yards away, knocked on its side, one wheel still spinning. Liz screamed again as the line of horses clattered past. Joe lay in their path, unable to move.

'Holy Christ!' Bob gasped and started down the steps.

Suddenly, a young man, sheltering as they were on some steps, leapt down into the road. He flew to Joe, covering the ground in seconds, reaching him in six or seven strides. Joe was a big man; heavy, deep-chested with strong shoulders. The young man was slim; tall but slightly built. To carry Joe seemed out of the question. Swooping he got Joe's arms over his shoulders, jerking upwards, throwing Joe's weight over his back. The horses were twenty yards away. The young man's legs buckled. Turning, he staggered, making for the pavement and beyond that the safety of the steps. Bent double, he took tiny steps, much shorter than before. The horses were almost on top of him. Reaching the pavement, his legs buckled again. With a final despairing lunge he threw Joe and himself forward onto the steps, at exactly the moment the horses charged past.

Screaming, Liz broke from Bob's grasp and scrambled down the steps into the momentarily empty road. Limping after her, Bob hobbled painfully on his aching ankle, with his damaged right hand tucked up under his left armpit. He saw Emlyn, staggering like a drunk, both hands clasped to his head, blood running down his fingers.

'Bob!' Emlyn cried. 'Where's Joe –?'

'Over here. What happened?' Using his left hand, Bob grabbed Emlyn's arm.

'Some bastard policeman clubbed me. I let go of Joe's chair, and . . . oh, Christ, there's Joe now.'

Joe was upright on the steps, looking dazed, an angry black bruise already rising on his forehead. Liz was in his arms, sobbing with relief, while the young man sat next to them, grimacing and rubbing his ankle.

The noise from the Square rose to a roar. Bob guessed that some of the protestors had got through. In confirmation, more policemen ran past, heading towards the Square. Sirens wailed in the distance. Sensing more trouble, Bob was anxious to move off. His car was parked round the corner. It was always at the end of a march, part of the system he and Emlyn had developed over the years. One car at the starting point and one at the finish. It was the only way they could move Joe about.

'Let's get to the car,' Bob said, watching the young man stand up and gingerly put some weight on his foot. As soon as the foot touched the ground, his face contorted with pain. Watching him, Bob guessed he was about twenty; tall, with long fair hair, almost touching his shoulders. 'That was a hell of a thing you did. We can't thank you enough.'

The boy made light of it with a deprecatory shrug of his shoulders. Turning to Joe, he apologized. 'Sorry about the bumpy landing, sir. I didn't think we'd make it. How are you feeling?'

Hearing the American accent, Bob looked again at the boy's long hair. A student? An American student? After the newspaper publicity, the police would be looking for 'American students and foreign agitators'.

'You won't get far on that foot,' said Bob, interrupting Joe, who was trying to express his thanks.

Propped against the wall, the boy grimaced as he tested his foot again. 'I took a kick from that horse –'

'Are you with anyone?' Bob asked urgently.

The shouting and sounds of battle from the Square grew louder all the time. More police ran past. When the boy said he was alone, Bob grabbed his arm. 'Come with us.'

Emlyn recovered the wheelchair, battered and scratched but still functioning, and once Joe was in it they set off, Emlyn nursing his cut head, the boy hopping along, supporting himself with an arm over Bob's shoulder. Thankfully they had only a short distance to go. Within minutes they were lifting Joe into the back of the car and folding his wheelchair into the boot. Emlyn and Liz scrambled into the back, and the boy was next to Bob in the front. Then they were off – looking like the survivors of some ghastly traffic accident.

391

'Heck, I only just got here,' said the young man with a wry smile. 'Is it always like this in England?'

Eight

The headlines next morning were predictable. 'The day the police were wonderful', crowed the *Daily Mirror*, while *The Times* preferred 'Police win battle of Grosvenor Square'. The *Daily Express* gave it as 'Fringe fanatics foiled'.

'Typical unbiased reporting,' said Joe in a sour voice.

Edith snorted with indignation. 'They should have seen you last night.'

Thankfully, their injuries had been more apparent than lasting. Emlyn's head wound had only required two stitches, and although Bob's fingers were swollen and bruised, none were actually broken. As for Joe, miraculously, he had escaped with only a bruise on his forehead. Most incapacitated was their young American guest, whose ankle had swollen so badly he was unable to get his foot into his shoe.

'A very bad sprain,' diagnosed Dr Cooper when he had called round. After applying a cold compress, he had warned, 'You won't be able to walk on that for three or four days.'

Edith had taken to Nick Grant from the moment he limped through her door, and by the time Bob and Liz had described his heroic dash to save her husband, admiration shone from her eyes. Liz was the same. While Edith and Joe were trying to persuade Nick to stay she was putting fresh linen onto the bed in the guest room.

'It's all organized,' she had announced, 'you're staying with us until your foot gets better.'

The young man was too incapacitated to argue.

Liz was equally attentive the next morning, when she learned Edith had run out of coffee. She dashed to the shops, firmly convinced that no young American would willingly drink tea with his breakfast.

So they spent the whole of the next day together – Joe with his bruised head and the young man with his swollen foot – like two injured soldiers home from the war.

Nick was shy at the outset – painfully shy in some ways. It took him most of the day to stop calling Joe 'sir', and only his swollen foot restrained him from rising whenever Edith entered the room. Although impressed by his good manners, Joe was adamant. 'We want you to feel at home. If you keep on with this "sir" business, *we* won't feel at home.'

Nick gave them one of his shy smiles and apologized for being a nuisance.

'A *nuisance*?' Joe yelped. 'I'd be in hospital if it wasn't for you. I thought I was done for when I saw those horses . . .'

Gradually, never pushing, Joe probed away until he discovered what Nick was doing in London. Joe's liking for people made him a natural interviewer. They enjoyed talking to him and many ended a conversation revealing more than they had intended. And Nick was at a disadvantage; propped up on the sofa, with Liz bringing him coffee, Edith serving him cake, and Joe asking gentle questions. So although it took the best part of the day, by the time they sat down to supper that evening, Joe knew a good deal of Nick's story.

Joe thought it was the most fascinating story he had heard in his life.

Nick's reasons for being in England had really started two years earlier when, against his will, he had registered for the draft. At the time he hadn't given it much thought. What with leaving high school and starting at university, he was so busy that the horrors of Vietnam seemed a long way away. He had been required to show his draft card upon entering university, but he looked upon that merely as an entrance formality. A whole year passed before he gave the matter serious thought.

'That was when I heard from the draft board again,' he remembered ruefully.

Even then he had no reason to worry. The draft board merely informed him that he was exempt from military service while at the university. They sent him a new card to show to college officials and left him to get on with his life. 'Provided I didn't flunk out,' he explained. 'The army grabs you real fast if you flunk out.'

A friend of Nick's did flunk out. 'I guess that's when I first started to think,' said Nick. His friend Arnie, a fat, amiable boy had a knack with funny stories but no ability to memorize anything of academic importance. 'Maybe he shouldn't have been in college,' Nick admitted, 'but sure as heck he shouldn't have been sent into the army. The rest of us thought it was criminal to make someone a soldier just because he's dumb.'

It went deeper than that. Nick and his friends began to question the morality of a system which permitted college to serve as an exemption from a service which was compulsory for everyone else. 'It's unfair when you think about it,' he said simply.

Questioning the morality of the system was like lifting rocks to see what slithered out. Blacks were drafted, white men were not. The poor went to Vietnam, the rich stayed at home. The dumb guys got shot at, smart boys found a way out. Most important of all, Nick and his friends decided it was immoral for the United States to wage an undeclared war that had never been authorized by Congress.

'Everything about Vietnam bypasses our democracy. It makes a mockery of the constitution,' said Nick, becoming heated. 'We're supposed to be the greatest democracy on earth. That's what we tell ourselves . . .' He broke off, becoming embarrassed. 'Sorry sir, I didn't mean to imply anything derogatory about the system in Great Britain.'

Embarrassed by what he saw as a chauvinistic gaffe, it took a while to get Nick going again. Finally, after explaining that there were many flaws in the British system, Joe coaxed him to continue.

Another friend of Nick's, an articulate philosophy major called Harry Shaw, had given Nick even more to think about. If the war in Vietnam was immoral, which it was, and if college exemption was immoral, which it was, 'Harry maintained that no one can live with immorality without becoming tainted himself.' Nick began to see countless examples. Young men took education courses at college, not because they wanted to teach but because teachers were exempt from the draft. Boys got girls pregnant and had to get married, not because they cared for the girls but simply to escape the draft.

'Even without going to Vietnam, the war was distorting our

lives. We weren't doing what we really wanted, we were doing things simply to stay out of the army.'

Some people were speaking out against the system. Nick remembered a lecture given by one of the younger professors in his college. 'According to him, the United States is the most military minded country in the world. This professor quoted all sorts of examples, proving that the newspapers, television, even the churches are dedicated to war. They rubbish any opposition. They discredit it. I saw what he meant. Newspapers sneer at those who speak out against the war, they get labelled "peaceniks" and lunatics. On TV they never get a fair hearing, commentators call them rioters and scum, as if anyone talking about peace is some sort of threat. I suppose they *are* a threat in a country geared up for war. This military thing, this violence, goes so deep. Take our college. We had an orchestra, a really excellent conservatory. But the college couldn't get it funded. The only way for the music department to get its budget was to have a military band. You know, a hundred and fifty guys all dressed up in uniforms, swinging out onto the football field playing John Philip Sousa. That's what people want. They've been conditioned to want it. There are so many other examples. Anyway, listening to that professor, I knew he was right.'

Undecided about what to do with his future, the moment of truth for Nick came with a peace demonstration. It had been organized by students opposed to the war. 'It was nothing on the scale of that one yesterday,' Nick said. 'That was vast. Ours was just a local college affair.' However, even before proceedings got underway, marchers arrived from the town, waving placards. One said 'Support our Brave Men in Vietnam'. Another said 'Love America or Leave it'. For a while the men from the town stood at the edge of the crowd, then the police arrived and they too stood at the edge of the crowd, just observing. Nothing very dramatic happened to begin with, some students and one professor made anti-war speeches. Then eight students filed up onto the platform and solemnly took out their draft cards which they held in the air. Some of the audience began to sing 'Blowing in the Wind', the song which was becoming symbolic with the anti-war movement in America. Slowly and with due ceremony, the students on the platform took out pocket lighters and set light to their draft cards. It was as if a signal had been given. The men from the town went berserk, rushing the platform and trying to haul the protestors down to the ground. Next moment, the police joined in. Nick expected them to restore order. Instead, to his astonishment, the police went not for the rioters but for the students on the platform. As soon as Nick saw the way the police were treating his friends, he went to their aid.

'I wasn't really involved until then,' he explained. 'You know, I wasn't one of the guys burning draft cards or anything.' So he tried to explain that the crowd from town were causing the trouble. Sadly the police took him for another long-haired troublemaker and lashed into him. For the next half-hour, the quadrangle was the scene of a pitched battle. The police were ferocious, clubbing students to the pavement, smashing their way through the crowd to arrest the card burners. Nick's last memory was being doubled up by a blow to the stomach, then oblivion as a police club smashed down onto his skull.

Some days later, he decided to drop out. It was a very hard decision. 'I knew I'd be called a coward and things like that. I don't know if I'm a coward or not. I don't think I am. I mean if we were fighting someone like Hitler, someone massacring millions of people in gas chambers, that would be different. If the United States was invaded, that would be different. But Vietnam? I don't even think we should be there.'

He had a choice, go to jail or leave the country. Through a friend of a friend, he was introduced to the wife of a law professor. At a private meeting, she had said to him, 'Young man, through no fault of your own, you face an impossible dilemma. Since no war has been declared, the government's position is, to say the least, contradictory, certainly immoral, arguably illegal and without doubt unconstitutional. Any action they may take against you can have no real basis in law. On the other hand, they certainly *will* act against you for refusing to be part of the system. You want my advice? Get the hell out of America.'

Nick was astonished to discover that an underground network had long been in existence. Good people all over America were willing to hide young men like him . . . to feed them, clothe them and help find them jobs. However, there were snags. To comply with the law, personnel managers asked job applicants for their draft cards. No draft card, no job. Consequently young men like Nick who remained in America found themselves either working at a variety of menial jobs or working for the underground – and always with the fear that some day someone might turn them in.

Nick chose to leave America. In effect he chose to become a political refugee. The wife of the law professor was quite specific about what was involved. 'The decision you are about to make will affect the rest of your life. If ever you return to the States, you will be liable for immediate arrest. If arrested, you will certainly be convicted and sentenced to a term in penitentiary. This will apply even if you become a naturalized citizen of another country. America is very vengeful. Don't kid yourself that there'll be an amnesty. Your hopes will be dashed. At the end of World War II, President Truman initiated the only amnesty board we ever had. After reviewing over a hundred thousand cases of draft dodging and desertion, pardons were granted to only five thousand. If you do go, resign yourself to the fact that you'll be sent to jail for a very long time if the authorities ever catch up with you.'

Two weeks after listening to those stern words, Nick, helped by the underground, skipped the country for Canada. For three months he worked in a garage in Quebec, then he got a job on a tanker, sailing first to Rotterdam and then to England. He signed off at Southampton and took the train to London. 'I always wanted to see London,' he said. 'We had a professor at college who was always talking about it.'

After booking into a cheap hostel, he went out for a walk. 'Just to see some of the sights and to try to get a feel of the place. I'd heard about Hyde Park so that's where I went. Then this huge demonstration against the war in Vietnam came along, so I sort of got involved.'

He grinned at Joe over the dinner table. 'I guess that's about it. You know the rest, sir . . . er, Joe.'

'What about your parents?' Edith asked, her maternal feelings aroused.

'I haven't seen my father in years. He and Mom split while I was still at high school. She's re-married now, and . . . my stepfather and I don't exactly get on.' Nick shrugged, 'I told Mom about Canada though. She said to do what I thought was best.'

Liz sat watching him, her dark eyes huge in her face, full of mute admiration. Edith, too, could hardly find enough words. 'Fancy,' she said shaking her head. 'To have taken so many big decisions, to have done so much by yourself.'

Nick coloured slightly. 'I am twenty, ma'am,' he said defensively.

Joe had never met a young man who impressed him more. Few people of any age had impressed him as much. Nick's story reinforced Joe's belief that America was gripped by a terrible sickness – a sickness that could be terminal for the rest of the world. On the other hand, there could be little wrong with the United States when it produced young men like this. Nick's fumbling explanation of his moral dilemma, his heart-searching to do the right thing, his fearless acceptance of the consequences of his own acts stirred deep feelings in Joe. He had always hoped his own son would develop similar instincts, yet, of late, there were signs that Keir had taken a wrong turning. His priorities had become confused . . . rushing around the world in pursuit of money when he should have been in Ireland with Liz was merely an example. Something about this rangy young American suggested he had the strength to order his priorities differently.

'What are your plans?' Joe asked, easing his wheelchair back from the table and fumbling through his pockets for his pipe. 'Will you stay in London?'

Nick hesitated, awkward for a moment, as if ashamed of being indecisive. The truth was that he still making up his mind about what he wanted from life. At college he had read law. 'I guess I saw myself as some hot-shot Perry Mason,' he said ruefully, shaking his head. 'Anyway, I'm off that idea. I mean, if the government acts outside the law, what's the point of being a lawyer?'

Joe coaxed him to continue, encouraging the boy to express his thoughts, unworried by the occasional contradiction. Clearly influenced by his old college professor, Nick wanted to stay in London. But there were problems. Anxious to further his education, he was worried about finding a job to pay for it all. In vague terms, he talked about enquiring at colleges and asked Joe about the prospects of finding part-time work.

Joe was thinking furiously. Over the years, he had made hundreds of friends in the Peace Movement. No fortune was to be made in serving in the army of the good, but making money did not seem to be this young man's immediate goal. 'I dunno,' Nick said at one stage. 'Seeing all those people in that demonstration made me think. If they're willing to take all that trouble . . . I can't just turn my back on it. I wondered if I could do something here? Then I thought, what the heck can I do? I'm no public speaker or anything, you know? But I figured if I could get into some sort of college and get myself a part-time job . . .'

Inevitably, Joe's thoughts were imprecise but before they were ready for bed he had formulated a few ideas of his own. He talked of the need to find out about student grants, and spoke about people who might offer Nick work. 'Meanwhile, stay here,' he said, receiving a look of agreement from Edith. 'Seriously. We'd be pleased. Make it your base . . .'

Edith was equally adamant, refusing to take no for an answer. 'You'll be doing me a favour,' she said. 'People come and go all the time here. That guest room is always in use. It will be really nice to have someone permanent . . .'

Later, in the privacy of their bedroom, Edith said, 'I do hope he stays. I've really taken a shine to young Nick.'

So had Liz. She had stars in her eyes as she sat brushing her hair in front of her mirror. For the first time in her life she wished she looked more like her mother. And she wished she was older. Twenty was grown-up. Sighing, she went to bed, comforting herself with the knowledge that soon she would be fourteen . . . and that meanwhile this heroic young American was sleeping in the next room.

Nine

The pattern of life at Arcadia Gardens changed with the arrival of Nick Grant. Slowly and surely his presence altered the routine of their lives. As always the impetus for change came from Joe who said that Nick's bravery in Grosvenor Square was equalled by his courage in leaving his country. To have turned his back on everything, knowing he could never return, knowing that some would despise him – and to decide, not in anger, but after weeks of soul-searching – seemed to Joe to be the actions of a very special young man, someone deserving of help. Luckily Nick proved an easy person to help. He was quiet, intelligent, well-mannered and competent. Odd jobs around the house – things Joe had been meaning to pay someone to do – were so casually dealt with that they were done before most people noticed. But Edith noticed and was suitably grateful. 'It's just like having a grown-up son around the place,' she told Joe.

Nick soon obtained a grant to attend the Regent Street Polytechnic, where he abandoned his study of law in favour of a course on economics. And as for earning money, two opportunities arose within a week. First the local garage engaged him to work every Saturday, for he was a skilful mechanic, and then Tom Bradford, a journalist friend of Joe's, rang up. Joe had spoken to him about Nick, and Tom telephoned to ask Nick to do some research work for a book he was writing. Nick seized the chance. The work involved combing through journals and reference books, many of which were in the Polytechnic library, so Nick added an hour or so onto each day and did research work for Tom Bradford. The subject of Bradford's book fascinated him. It was a study of the Arms Race since the Second World War. Blaming both sides, Bradford claimed that the Communist rulers were the ideological lookalikes of their opposite numbers. 'There's nothing to choose between them,' he argued, 'both sets of leaders are the puppets of men who profit from the Arms Race. In the West they grow rich and live in big houses, and in Russia they're awarded Ziv limousines and daches in the country . . .'

Joe had been saying that for years. 'Maybe Tom's book will show the public the true face of the enemy,' he said, ever hopeful.

Once Nick started, few evenings passed without him rushing home from the library, anxious to share his new information with Joe. And Joe helped out, culling through his own reference books and calling up people he knew.

A blind man could have seen the bond growing between them.

For a while, the flow of other guests of Arcadia Gardens lessened, as it did every winter. Spring and summer are the best

400

times for campaigning. However, some old friends, active in the peace movements stopped over on visits to London – the indefatigable Olga Bjord from Oslo, Gunter Hess from West Berlin, and Olaf Peterson from Copenhagen each spent a night with the Milfords in November. The fourth bedroom – hitherto used as an untidy office for Joe – was pressed into service and that strand of life continued much as before, except that now a rangy, young American joined in the political discussions.

As for Liz, she was growing up as fast as she could. She now wore a bra which, although not essential, did wonders for her morale. She was quite pleased with her breasts, which was more than she could feel for the rest of her body. Her legs seemed too long and her feet the wrong size, her elbows were awkward and her hands were all thumbs – all of which had come about since Nick moved into the house. So changed were her views that she even wished she had listened to her mother's strictures on deportment. Certainly she stopped biting her nails. Nick didn't notice, she was lucky if he noticed her at all. Most of the time he had his nose in a book, or was working at the garage, or discussing the state of the world with Edith and Joe. Yet she did capture his attention at times. Having been in the Peace Movement all of her life she had met all sorts of people and knew things which Nick, coming to it for the first time, found absorbing. 'Heck,' he would say, grey eyes shining with admiration, 'did you really do that? You and Joe actually marched up to Scotland to protest about Polaris? Well, what do you know!'

Girls from school who called at the house cast admiring glances at the young American. Angela Duxbury sighed dreamily. 'With him in the next room, I'd get up in the middle of the night and go sleepwalking.'

Such comments encouraged Liz to stake her claim. 'Nick and I are going out again on Sunday,' she would say airily to the girls, quite prepared to lie when they begged to be told what happened. In fact, nothing happened, or at least what happened was nothing like the lurid tales which fell from her lips. But she and Nick did go out together on Sundays. She took him sightseeing, showing him London, revisiting places she had seen with Keir in earlier years.

In a way, Nick compensated for Keir's absence. Keir was in Japan for the whole of the Autumn – absent longer than Liz

401

could ever remember. Without Nick, she would have missed Keir desperately. Even with Nick, she missed Keir. Inevitably. Staying at Lord North Street and the Saturday expeditions had been part of her life, and although such expeditions had become less frequent they had still happened until the start of that year. The abrupt cessation left a gap – a gap which Edith and Joe filled as best they could, but they could only do so with more of the same love and care they had given her all her life. She loved them for it; Joe was the bravest person in the world, closely followed by Nick, since the riots of Grosvenor Square, and Edith was the kindest; but Keir was holidays, he was fun, he was her extravagance, her favourite treat. Keir was her prince among men. And she missed him. It was as well that Nick was around, filling her with new and unexpected sensations. Proudly she took him to Lord North Street, showing him off to the Westwoods. Barbara gave them tea and John talked about the time he went to the States.

Nick was intrigued by the house and the obvious wealth of its owner. It was very different from what he had imagined. Where Arcadia Gardens was comfortable, Lord North Street was grand and imposing. But he was beginning to expect the unexpected from the Milfords. After all, Liz *was* the daughter of Dawn Wharton, the film star. Altogether, Nick decided, they were a truly remarkable family. Even Liz herself, although only a kid, knew more about politics than he did.

By the time November ended and December began, Nick had become part of the fabric of life at Arcadia Gardens. He and Joe spent many an evening working on the research for Tom Bradford's book, and on Sundays he was happy to trail round London with Liz. As for Joe, he presided over the family, enjoying the obvious harmony. Thanks to his careful fence-mending even the trauma of the summer between Liz and her mother was a thing of the past, for he had encouraged Dawn to write and Liz to respond, so that the bitterness of their quarrel was now only a bad memory.

Then, on the seventh of December, a letter arrived from Japan. It was from Keir, full of his plans to spend Christmas at Carrickfergus. *'I don't care what happens,'* he wrote, *'I'm going to Ireland for Christmas. I've hardly had a day off in the last year. It would be nice if Liz came with me. I know everything went wrong in the summer, but things will be different at Christmas. I spoke to Dawn and she's desperate to try again. If you could help persuade Liz, I'd be really grateful. I promise not to let her down this time. I finish here on the tenth, then I'm flying to the States . . . I'll be back in London some time during the week before Christmas . . . I can't think when I was more ready for a holiday . . .'*

Joe was pleased. 'It shows his heart's in the right place,' he said to Edith.

'Why can't he spend Christmas in London?' she grumbled. 'Then we'd all be together.'

Joe shrugged. 'It's only natural for Dawn to want them at her new house. It will be her first Christmas at home.'

Edith continued with a token show of resistance while in her heart she knew he was right, Dawn should have her daughter with her for Christmas.

And a day or two later, Dawn telephoned. Joe took the call and as he listened he was struck by her loneliness. She disguised it, chattering away about her four-week stay in Durban where she had been filming. 'Only a cameo part, but I think it comes off . . . and Durban was marvellous, miles of golden beaches . . . but it's so good to be home.'

Yet listening to her describe the homecoming party given her by her new Dublin friends, Joe detected an anxious note in her voice. Christmas was coming and she was afraid of spending it alone. 'Even Eric is going away to stay with a friend. I was so pleased when Keir called to say he was definitely coming . . .'

Joe grew hot and angry at the thought of his son breaking his promise again.

As for Liz, Dawn showed every consideration. 'I know she usually spends Christmas with you, but could we make an exception this once? Perhaps you could all come over and stay in the summer . . . but I think if it were just Keir, Liz and me for Christmas it would give us time to get used to each other again . . .'

Every word revealed her anxiety.

Afterwards, Joe muttered, 'If Keir lets them down this time, I'll break his bloody neck.'

Liz expressed the same doubts. 'Will Keir *really* be there?' she asked anxiously.

'Of course he will. He and Dawn have planned everything. You'll have a marvellous time.'

In fairness, Keir showed every sign of keeping his word. On the eighteenth, he actually telephoned Joe from New York. 'I'll be back in a couple of days,' he promised. 'Guess what? The people I work with have put a private plane at my disposal. Liz and I will fly over to Dublin in style. I've spoken to Dawn and she can't wait for Christmas . . .'

Everything was arranged. Privately, Liz grappled with conflicting emotions. She would miss Joe and Edith over Christmas. And Nick. No doubt he would be involved in a round of parties with friends at the Polytechnic, parties at which there would be girls of nineteen and twenty. Liz comforted herself with the knowledge that she would soon be a year older. She was growing up as fast as she could. Besides, Nick saw girls of nineteen and twenty every day at the Poly and took no more notice of them than of her . . .

Teetering between childhood and womanhood, part of Liz *wanted* to spend Christmas with Keir and her mother. And this year they were to have two Christmases, because Keir was coming to lunch the day before Christmas Eve. They would exchange presents and have their own little party before flying to Ireland in Keir's very own plane.

'You'll love Keir when you meet him,' she told Nick as he helped decorate the Christmas tree.

As days passed, Liz looked forward to the reunion with ever mounting excitement. And on the twentieth, her mother telephoned. 'Hello darling, I just couldn't wait a moment longer. I'm so looking forward to seeing you again.'

That conversation, which lasted an hour, finally healed the wounds of the summer. The pain was gone, replaced by joyous anticipation. Reading his paper in front of the fire, Joe pretended not to listen. He pretended to be deaf to the catch in Liz's voice, and blind to the tears in her eyes when she replaced the receiver.

'Are you all right?' he asked gently, and scarcely had time to take the pipe from his mouth as she rushed to embrace him. 'Oh, Joe,' she cried, clinging to him. 'Everything's marvellous. It's all going to work out. I can't wait for Keir to arrive in the morning.'

Ten

It happened over breakfast. They were all there. Edith was pouring the tea, Nick was buttering toast, and Liz was on her way in from the kitchen with a fresh pot of marmalade. One moment Joe was looking perfectly well, then his face went grey and darkened to the colour of ash. The newspaper shook in his hands. A tinge of blue marked his lips. 'No,' he choked. 'No, I don't believe it . . .'

Edith cried out in alarm. 'Whatever is it?'

Without answering, he stared at the paper.

Liz ran to the side of his chair. 'What's the matter?'

Nick leaped up, fearing Joe was having a heart attack.

For a split second everyone froze like a frame in a film, the only movement being the newspaper shaking in Joe's hands. Then he plunged forward, thumping the paper down on the table, making cups rattle and milk slop from the jug. 'I can't believe it,' he gasped, swivelling his chair abruptly round from the table to sit with his back to them, facing out of the window.

'What's the matter?' Liz repeated.

Nick was relieved to see some normal colour return to Joe's face, although he looked very shaken.

They were all shaken.

'My goodness,' said Edith, coming round the table to take Joe's hand, 'you gave us a start. Whatever's the matter?'

Liz saw it first. Reassured that Joe was beginning to recover, she turned her attention to the newspaper. Her eyes went straight to the picture of Keir.

Beaumont's Mr Fix-It back in London

Mr Keir Milford, one of the highest paid businessmen in Britain, returned to London last night after a successful trip to Japan and the USA. After his Beaumont Executive jet aircraft landed at Heathrow, Mr Milford refused to confirm rumours that CDD Ltd, a British company of which he is chairman, is in fact no more than a front for the Beaumont Corporation of America. Investigations into the tightly knit world of defence contracts reveal that Mr Milford has been Beaumont's Mr Fix-it in Europe for years. His behind-the-scenes activities have helped persuade many NATO governments to buy war planes from Beaumont. In the cloak and dagger world of the arms salesmen, Keir Milford has few equals . . .

Liz went white, green-white, sick-white. Clutching the table for support, she sank into a chair.

'My own son,' Joe choked, hoarse-voiced. 'Few equals . . . as an arms salesman.'

Edith too was reading the paper. 'Oh, dear God. Not Keir, surely they can't mean our Keir.'

Liz began to weep, silently at first, then with great shuddering sobs she ran from the room. They heard her bedroom door slam behind her.

Nick read enough of the story to understand its importance. One look at Joe and Edith was enough to see its effect upon them. Quietly, without fuss, he went to the kitchen and opened the carton of bottles delivered the previous day. It was a moment's work to find the brandy. He poured two generous measures and returned to the room.

After that it was Nick who took charge. He cleared away the breakfast things, washed up, and brewed some hot coffee which he served, laced with brandy. Tapping on Liz's bedroom door, he pleaded with her to come out, only to be told tearfully to go away and leave her alone.

It was as if a death had occurred in the family. A death might have been easier to bear.

Joe remembered Tom Bradford's book, *The Face of the Enemy*, which described the armaments manufacturers who grew fat on the world's misery . . . All the money and research devoted to building even deadlier arms . . . While part of the world starved and the rest lived in fear . . .

'My own son,' he said, over and over again.

He and Edith slowly recovered. They sat in the living-room amidst the trappings of celebration. In one corner, the Christmas tree was aglow with lights. The mantelpiece was adorned with cards. Beneath her apron, Edith was already wearing her best frock. She had dressed that morning to welcome her son home. Now she was unsure if she could bring herself to look into his face.

Pulling herself together, she said, 'I must go to that child, poor little thing. She's sobbing her heart out, she thinks the world of him. How could he *do* this to her?'

Watching her shuffle from the room, Joe smouldered with rage. The shock had passed, leaving him full of a furious anger. 'All these years,' he muttered. 'I knew he disagreed . . . but to be on the other side, actually to be selling arms . . .'

'Didn't you have the faintest idea?' Nick asked when Edith emerged from Liz's bedroom and joined him in the kitchen.

'No, none.' She sat down, looking ten years older. 'Years ago . . . I forget . . . when he came out of the army I suppose, he said he was starting some sort of public relations business with Dusty. Dusty is a friend, they went to school together –' the words choked as, to Nick's vast embarrassment, she began to weep.

It was a nightmare of a morning. Liz refused to leave her room. Her bags were packed, everything was ready for her visit to Ireland. 'But she won't even see him when he gets here,' said Edith.

The ingredients for the festive lunch lay untouched in the kitchen. Nothing was prepared. The turkey remained un-cooked, potatoes unpeeled, sprouts unsoaked and parsnips unscraped . . . And at 11.30, Keir arrived.

After opening the front door, Nick fled to his room.

'Who was that?' Keir asked, entering the living-room where Joe and Edith were waiting.

Never had Keir looked more prosperous. Dressed in a melton navy-blue overcoat, over a Savile Row suit, he came through the door laden with presents. And behind him came John West-wood, clutching even more of the gaily coloured boxes.

'Happy Christmas everyone!' Keir's voice rose with high spirits. 'Where's Liz? John wants to give her his present before he goes –'

'Never mind that,' Joe interrupted. 'I want an explanation of this.'

'Of what?' Keir asked, looking with astonishment from Joe's angry face to the newspaper in his lap.

'Is it true?'

For the first time, Keir sensed the hostile atmosphere. He saw clearly his mother's pinched, white, tear-stained face and the black anger in his father's eyes.

'Oh, that,' he said dismissively, setting his parcels down on the table. 'You're not upset about something in the paper –?'

'Is it true?' Joe demanded, his voice rising. 'These people you work for . . . they make arms –'

'They make aircraft.'

'Military aircraft?'

'Not exclusively. We make civil planes too. Wait until you see this executive jet. It's the most beautiful thing you ever saw. After Christmas we'll all go –'

'And ballistic missiles?' Joe trembled with temper. 'You make them too?'

'Everyone makes missiles. It's how things have developed –'

'And gas chambers? You'd make those if that's how things develop?'

Keir flushed. 'For goodness' sake! It's Christmas. I didn't come here to argue politics.'

'Answer my question!' Joe shouted.

Keir turned a beseeching look to his mother. 'What's up with him? I arrive looking forward to seeing you all, loaded down with presents –'

'We don't want your presents. All these years, you never told us.'

'I don't know what you're talking about. You want to know what I do? Okay, I advise Beaumont on their business in Europe. That's all. I don't actually *sell* anything –'

'Oh no, people like you never do. They never pull the trigger or drop the bombs –'

'This is ridiculous!' Keir shouted, losing his temper. 'I'm not a criminal. You're the one who gets arrested. You don't live in the real world –'

'And you do? You pollute it with missiles and –'

'We sell weapons for defence, to keep the peace.'

'You sell weapons for profit, to make money for yourselves.'

'That's the most stupid –'

Edith cried, 'Don't you dare shout at your father!'

'Stupid?' Joe snarled. 'I'm stupid and you're smart, I suppose? By God, the face of the enemy, the face of my own son!'

Liz ran into the room at that moment and threw herself into Joe's arms. Edith cried out and tried to calm him. But Joe was consumed by an anger so fierce that he shook with uncontrollable rage. 'You make me ashamed!' he roared. 'Get out of my house. Get out! I never want to see you again.'

Eleven

Keir was still shaking four hours later. Holding out his hand he could detect a tremor which owed nothing to the aircraft. In flight, the Beaumont Bluebird was steadier than anything in the sky. The maroon leather seats in the cabin were deeply upholstered, the woodwork shone with a rich mahogany glow, the gold-plated fittings sparkled with self-satisfaction. A million dollars' worth of aircraft. The ultimate status symbol. A bonus from Chuck for Keir's work in Japan.

He had returned to London like a hero, only to be treated as a criminal. 'First by those bloody reporters,' he muttered, 'then by my own father. He's a fanatic. He's mad. Anyone else would be proud of me . . .'

Closing his eyes, he tried to blot out the memory. He had argued with his parents before, but never so bitterly. Opening his eyes, he stared at the empty seat opposite. Liz should have been there. All the way home from the States he had imagined her excitement. Instead, she had refused to come with him. Clinging to Joe, she had screamed, 'I'm staying with Grandad!' Not Joe, Keir suddenly realized, but Grandad. 'It's five years since she called him that.' He shook his head, baffled as he searched for the significance.

Christmas! He had been looking forward to it for months. It was to be their Christmas; the three of them together, like the days of summer eighteen months ago. Dawn's letters were full of those days – What fools we were not to hang onto them, she had written longingly. Do you realize she'll soon be fifteen? We'll lose her completely in another few years. Oh Keir, what did we do with the time?

Dawn had written of *them*, the three of them. It was a constant theme in her letters, and always on her lips when they spoke on the phone . . .

Reaching into his pocket, he drew out the velvet-covered box. The gold ring inside was set with diamonds and pearls. It had seemed so right when he was in Tiffany's. Even last night it had seemed right. He and Dawn had spent an hour on the phone. 'I can't wait to see you both . . .' had been her closing words.

But now . . . without Liz . . .

At Carrickfergus, Dawn's opening question was 'Where's Liz?' She peered over Keir's shoulder as he mounted the steps, expecting her daughter to emerge from the Rolls.

Initially stunned, it took her a moment to react to the news. 'But I only spoke to Liz two days ago. She was as excited as I was. She was really looking forward to spending Christmas with us . . .'

The first hour was harrowing.

Describing the angry scene at Arcadia Gardens, Keir expected her to blame him, to be furious about spoiling the longed-for reunion.

In fact, Dawn was less angry than shocked. She was incredulous. 'I can't believe it. Not Liz. She adores you. She never stops talking about you . . .'

More wretched than at any time in his life, Keir's mind was still full of the scene in his parent's sitting-room, with Liz clinging to Joe, tears streaming down her face. 'I won't go with you!' she had screamed. 'I hate you, I hate you . . . I'm staying with Grandad.'

Dawn calmed him and tried to make him see the quarrel in perspective. 'Liz was upset. She lost her temper. Really, darling, you should have heard her scream at me last summer. She'll get over it, really she will.'

'I don't know,' he said, shaking his head. 'I've made a right mess of Christmas.'

They were sitting in front of a blazing log fire; he dejected and

410

long-faced, she, comforting and holding his hand. 'Of course I'm disappointed about Liz,' she admitted, 'but you mustn't blame yourself. It wasn't your fault. What else could you do?'

'That's it, honestly, what else *could* I do?' he asked, brightening with relief. 'He's got this bee in his bonnet –'

'And you had a row. Darling, it wasn't your fault. Stop blaming yourself. He attacked you as soon as you stepped through the door –'

'Exactly! He was sitting there, boiling over, just waiting –'

'Well, it won't spoil our Christmas. You're here. We're together, aren't we?'

Only then did he properly look at the room, and at her. Impressions had registered earlier – the huge Christmas tree in the hall, the decorated room, the warmth and comfort of her luxurious home – but in his misery he hadn't taken it all in, hadn't even thanked her when she poured him a whisky while he was talking, he had been so tense and hangdog and upset. Yet when she said 'We're together, aren't we?' he was so relieved that he laughed.

Dawn laughed with him . . . and after that the evening got better and better. Far from being a disaster, it turned into one of the most memorable of their lives.

They would have been inhibited with Liz there. The holiday would have started on a different footing. Inevitably, they would have made her the centre of attention. Without her they could concentrate on each other.

Christmas had become vitally important to Dawn. Their first Christmas at Carrickfergus. Only recently had she realized that was why she had bought the place. Without being broody for a baby (Heaven forbid!) she had visualized the three of them in the house from the moment she saw it. Carrickfergus needed a family. It was what she wanted most from life and although the realization was a shock as soon as she admitted it she knew it was true. Just as she knew Keir wanted to marry her. He always had. She had encouraged his calls from Japan and New York, hearing the warmth in his voice and responding with warmth of her own. Talking to him so often was a reminder of how much she liked him. Liking was important. She had liked JD and Keir inspired the same feelings of trust, of knowing she was safe in his hands. Passion was something she distrusted; perhaps portraying it on the scene had led her to see it as an illusion, something transitory. Certainly it had not lasted on her location romances, most of which had ended on the last day of shooting. She had made love with men who had flattered her, amused her, attracted her – but in truth she had liked very few of them. Liking someone was much more important . . .

They had so much to tell each other. Keir talked of his trip to Japan, Dawn told him about Durban. Suddenly it felt so right to be there together, drinking champagne and eating supper in front of the fire.

'My God,' Keir said at one point. 'The years we've wasted. I can't believe we allowed it to happen.'

'It's past. We've got the future to think about now.'

He knew from her voice that she would marry him. It was in her eyes too. She even teased him. 'I sent Eric away for the holiday,' she said laughing, 'and this is my house. Your rich widow won't disturb us tonight . . .'

She liked the ring.

It was all she wore in bed later.

They remained in bed most of the next day, only rising in the evening, ravenous from their lovemaking. 'From now on,' Dawn decided, 'that's how we'll spend every Christmas Eve.'

She changed her mind after supper when they made love in front of the fire. 'I was wrong!' She laughed, holding out her glass for more champagne. 'This is how we'll spend next Christmas Eve.'

Blissfully happy, it was inevitable that their talk turned to the future. 'Together at last,' Dawn sighed, never doubting that together would include Liz. Her comment was a statement, not a question, and when Keir hesitated, she laughed. 'Darling, you're not still worrying about that silly argument, are you? Liz will get over it. As for Joe, he'll be so excited about our wedding that he'll forget everything else.'

Reluctant to let memories of the quarrel impinge on his happiness, Keir took her into his arms. 'I refuse even to think about it,' he said.

But Dawn found herself thinking about it when she awoke the next morning. It was Christmas Day. For a moment she stroked Keir's face, enjoying waking with him beside her. She felt so happy that the thought of him at loggerheads with his father was unbearable. She left Keir asleep, and slipped downstairs to telephone Joe, fully confident of the outcome. Edith was one thing, Joe was another; she had always been able to charm Joe.

'Joe?' she said, 'it's Dawn.' Careful to choose the right words, she scolded him gently about spoiling her Christmas, before saying '– but I'll forgive you if you congratulate me. Your son and I are getting married.'

Her smile froze at his reply.

'I don't have a son,' he said bitterly, 'and I pity you if you marry a man in the arms business –'

'Joe, please, this is ridiculous –'

'. . . and if you take my advice, you won't tell Liz for a while . . .'

There was no changing his mind. She was on the phone for half an hour, but he was adamant, unyielding, impervious to her coaxing.

Eventually she accepted his advice and did not speak to Liz. 'Just wish her a happy Christmas from me,' she concluded bleakly.

Afterwards, she sat by the telephone, shaking her head in shocked amazement. Joe sounded so bitter. The situation was worse than she'd imagined. Even so, it was inconceivable that the quarrel would last. He's always been so proud of Keir, she told herself, thinking back over the years.

Keir was angry about her speaking to Joe. 'It was time he heard the truth about his half-baked ideas. I hope you didn't say I was sorry.'

'Of course I didn't. What sort of wife would I be to say something like that?'

Her answer pleased him. The thought of her as his wife pleased him.

Forgetting the quarrel for a moment, they began to talk of the future, yet – and there was no avoiding it – everything about the future brought them back to the quarrel. 'We'll have to leave the wedding for a while,' Dawn said, 'until the pair of you calm down.'

'Why? He doesn't have to come –'

'Keir! He's your father. And what about Edith and Liz? Especially Liz.'

At that moment he would have married without them, but it

413

was more complex for Dawn, even sifting her thoughts was more complex, cluttered as they were with the memory of promises made to herself long ago.

'It's important that Liz understands . . .' she said, searching for the right words.

He listened, watching her with quizzical eyes.

'It's hard to explain. Your quarrel with your father reminds me of the row Liz and I had last summer. She got so angry, so furious . . . and, Keir, it was *my* fault. I promised I'd explain –'

'About what?'

'Darling, she doesn't know who she is. That you're her father. I was going to tell her. She *needs* to be told. I would have if you had been here. I wanted us to tell her together, to explain –'

'I didn't know you planned to do that.'

'Planned isn't the right word, except that I promised to tell her one day and I thought, with the three of us here, enjoying ourselves . . . I don't know, I'm not sure what I thought. Anyway, everything went wrong and I couldn't do it. I imagined trying to explain and making it sound like the Middle Ages.' She laughed. 'I know it sounds stupid, but so much has changed. Freedoms we take for granted now didn't exist then. Attitudes have changed. It's understandable for Liz to pass judgement on me, but she's judging by today's standards. That's not fair. It was so different then . . .'

Keir's mind went back to finding her in that flat all those years ago, when she was trying to cope without money and the baby due any day. The painful memories made him uncomfortable.

'I want Liz to know that I couldn't have taken her with me,' Dawn said, wistfully. 'If it hadn't been JD it would have been some other manager, wanting to hush everything up, frightened of a possible scandal . . .'

Over the next hour she edged closer to defining her thoughts. 'I vowed that I'd tell Liz the whole story one day. I owe her that much, and –' she reached for his hand – 'I don't know . . . perhaps it goes deeper. I think I always saw us together. Eventually. Like the end of a film. The three of us together. That's what I want to tell Liz, that I never abandoned her, I always came back for her. Last summer when we had that awful row, I thought I'd lost her forever. I might have if it hadn't been for Joe. You've no idea how much he helped. I want to sit down with Liz and tell her everything. We must both do it, tell her that you are her father . . . that we both love her . . . and . . . and that we'll be a proper family from now on . . .'

She choked up then and when he took her into his arms he thought that she had expressed exactly what he wanted himself. A moment passed before he realized she had also imposed a condition . . . that she wouldn't marry without her daughter's consent.

'I didn't say that,' she protested when he put it to her. 'That sounds much too formal. I want her to *understand*, that's all. Darling, what's the matter? You know she worships you. She always has. Telling her you're her father will be a bonus, not an obstacle.'

But Keir was hesitant and gloomy. 'I'm not sure I can reach her, not now. She's so on Joe's side, and he won't even let me in the house. He said he never wants to see me again. He's obsessed . . .'

Patiently, she calmed him and listened to the story of the quarrel all over again.

'Joe will get over it,' she assured him.

Keir remained worried. 'You'll have to be the one who talks Liz round, not me. She's dead set against me at the moment. It would be better to get her to accept the idea of us getting married, before you tell her I'm her father. Don't spring everything on her at once . . . let her adapt to one idea at a time.'

'Very well,' Dawn agreed, confident of a reconciliation. 'Everyone needs time to cool down,' was her conclusion as she busied herself with plans for the future.

Their life together would be perfect. 'We'll live in Lord North Street Mondays to Fridays,' she said, hugging his arm, 'and Carrickfergus will be for weekends and holidays . . .'

They had it all. Everything. Success, wealth, health, and years ahead to enjoy them.

'Perhaps I'll be offered a part in the West End,' she said with mounting excitement.

With the future all settled, they gave themselves over to enjoying Christmas; finding endless things to discuss, walking arm in arm through the grounds, before returning to make love in front of the fire.

'Don't worry about your father,' she assured him. 'If he healed the rift between me and my daughter, I can end this quarrel between him and his son.'

Dawn was never more wrong in her life.

BOOK FIVE

Liz

One

Shocks fell one after the other for Liz. She was still recovering from the bitter argument with Keir when she learned he was to marry her mother. It was in the papers. Even without a formal announcement, the press had very quickly got hold of the story. The papers gave it the prominence they thought it deserved, which meant headlines in Dublin, feature articles in London, and four column inches in L.A. It was understandable for the Irish papers to give it top billing, for once Peter Sellers had sold up, Dawn Wharton was the most famous celebrity remaining in Dublin. Besides a headline like 'Famous Actress to Wed Childhood Sweetheart' was guaranteed to win readers in Ireland. Not that a wedding was announced, but Dawn was photographed too often for the diamond ring to escape notice. Added to which, she was living with Keir. 'If I didn't,' she was quoted as saying, 'we'd never see each other. Keir spends so much time flying around Europe and back and forth to the States.'

Crushed by the news, Liz felt her whole life disintegrating. Once, after their marvellous time together that summer, her dearest wish had been for Keir and her mother to marry. 'Then we'll be a *proper* family,' she had said at the time. Now everything was cock-eyed and different.

Three days after the news appeared in the papers, her mother arrived at Arcadia Gardens. Liz had only that day started back at school after the Christmas break and she returned home to find John waiting outside in the Daimler, something he never usually did because Edith always asked him in for a cup of tea.

'John?' said Liz, approaching the car window. 'What are you doing? Is Keir indoors?'

She was startled to hear that the caller was her mother.

Entering the front door, Liz could hear them in the sitting-room. Her mother seemed to be pleading. 'I can't believe you're behaving like this. It's so unlike you. You care about people,

419

Joe, you always have. So care about Keir. You can't turn your back on your own son.'

'I won't go to any wedding and that's final. Not while he's mixed up in that business.'

In the hall, Liz stopped and drew back from the door.

Her mother cried, 'Is it me? Do you still disapprove?'

'Don't be daft. You know it's not that.'

Liz had never heard Joe speak in such a gruff voice.

Her mother muffled a sob. 'Please, Joe, for my sake, for Liz's sake . . . we've waited all these years.'

At that moment Edith emerged from the kitchen to catch Liz eavesdropping. 'Liz?' she said, raising her eyebrows.

After that they all sat down together – Joe, stubborn-eyed; Edith, tight-lipped; Liz, confused, and her mother, emotional.

Emotional or not, Dawn did her best to be persuasive. 'Keir has loved you all your life,' she said to her daughter. 'You know he has, and you love him really. Now we're to be married we want you to live with us, at Lord North Street as well as Carrickfergus . . .'

She painted pictures with her words, joyful pictures of them all together.

Feeling wretched, Liz looked at Joe. His expression broke her heart. He sat rigid in his chair, as motionless as a statue, with a face like granite. Liz knew he was hurting inside. She just knew. He hadn't stopped hurting since before Christmas. Poor Joe, he was so good and kind . . . it was awful for someone to talk of being happy while he sat bleak and silent and crying inside.

Liz felt tears spring to her eyes. Words burst from her lips. 'No! It's wrong what Keir's doing. I don't love him, I don't . . .' Gulping for breath, she ran from the room, rushing to fling herself down on her bed sobbing and choking.

Her mother left half an hour later. Joe's chair creaked down the hall as he showed her out. Listening to the murmur of voices, Liz heard her mother say – 'I do want you to come to my wedding. We've waited this long, I suppose we can wait a bit longer. You and Keir must end this quarrel soon.'

But as the weeks passed, there seemed no likelihood of that. Keir never called at the house and Joe wouldn't so much as telephone him. The rift grew deeper and deeper.

It was a bad start to 1969 and, to make matters worse, another blow fell a month later. Nick moved out.

'Don't think I'm ungrateful,' he said, explaining his plans over supper, 'but I can't impose on you forever. If I'm still welcome, I'd sure like to visit a lot.'

He and Pete Grimshaw, a Canadian fellow student, had found a seedy flat on the fringes of Soho, overlooking Berwick Street market. 'It's only five minutes from college,' said Nick, 'and Bob's set up a deal for us to work in the market every Saturday.'

Liz was plunged into dismay; lurid pictures filled her mind as she listened. She imagined Nick throwing wild parties and bedding every twenty-year-old girl in the West End.

The young American's departure that weekend was one of the most depressing days of Liz's life. Now she had to exist not only without Keir, but also without Nick. 'Men,' she grumbled to Edith. 'You can't rely on any of them.' A rueful smile touched her lips as she relented. 'Except Joe, of course.'

It was a grey time for Liz, and while her grades at school were above average, she never claimed the same for her looks. One glance around the classroom was enough to remind her of her shortcomings.

'No wonder Nick moved out,' was her gloomy conclusion.

Joe too was having a bad time of it. He was as unhappy as Liz. 1969 was proving to be a thoroughly bad year. The world, and Britain in particular, was learning to live with the Bomb. Because Europe had been spared war for twenty-four years, some people claimed it was due to the deterrence provided by Britain's nuclear bombs.

'Rubbish!' Joe would exclaim. 'That's as daft as saying drinking whisky every day keeps toothache away. If you don't get toothache, that's not *proof* it's because of the whisky. But two things are certain. Drink enough whisky and you'll fall over drunk. Make enough H-bombs and some lunatic will use them.'

Even so, the truth was that the Campaign for Nuclear Disarmament had run out of steam. 'Is that CND business still going?' people would ask on the street. They were more worried about the war in Vietnam. 'There seems no way of ending it,' they would say.

'It will end if enough people demonstrate against it,' said Joe, exasperated by their apathy. There was nothing apathetic about Joe. He attended rallies and delivered open-air speeches. 'Stop the arms race,' he roared at his audiences, 'before it stops the world.' Quoting from Tom Bradford's book, he gave them facts and figures. 'The manufacturers of weapons are making fortunes . . . selling arms and ammunitions is the most profitable business in the world . . .'

He could never utter those words without boiling with rage about Keir. His own son! He searched his memory, and blamed himself for not doing a better job of raising the boy. Yet Keir had always seemed so sensible as a lad. 'I brought him up always to do the right thing,' Joe grumbled to himself and to Edith when she would listen. But mostly she wouldn't. Although heartbroken, she had a mother's reluctance to criticize her own son, even to her husband. So for the most part Keir's name went unmentioned in Arcadia Gardens.

Meanwhile, the first days of Spring warmed the land. Fresh green leaves appeared in the hedgerows and blossom came to the trees. No wedding was announced. It seemed that Keir and Dawn were waiting for Joe to relent. Dawn called every two or three weeks to see Liz; taking her shopping, buying her clothes, seeking to persuade her to make up with Keir. The girl remained resolute, refusing even to visit Lord North Street.

It distressed Joe to see her caught in the middle. His conscience troubled him, especially when Dawn called one day to say she was going to Spain to make a film. 'I shall be there most of the summer,' she said. 'Keir's flying out in July for a couple of weeks. Why not come with him?'

Without giving any definite answer, Liz made it clear that she was opposed to the idea.

Joe tried to persuade her afterwards. 'I think you should go,' he said. 'It would make Dawn happy and you'll have a good time –'

'No.' Liz shook her head. 'I don't want to go.'

Joe coaxed her. 'Liz,' he said, taking her hands into his, 'my quarrel with Keir has nothing to do with you and your mother. She tries so hard. I feel bad about you and her. Come to that, I feel bad about you and Keir. You used to get so excited about seeing him –'

'No,' she repeated, her face turning pale. 'I don't want to see him.'

'He does love you, you know.'

Liz studied her feet in silence.

Releasing her hands, Joe reached forward and gently lifted her chin. He chose his words carefully. 'It makes me very unhappy to see my argument with Keir coming between you and him.'

She looked at him with her solemn eyes. 'But I feel the same as you about the Bomb and the war in Vietnam. If you're against Keir, I'm against him too.'

The following day when Liz was at school, Joe confessed to Edith, 'I didn't know how to answer her. Sometimes I think we're doing a terrible thing, depriving Dawn of her daughter –'

'We're not depriving anyone,' Edith said sharply. 'Besides, I daresay she could get a court order compelling Liz to live with them.'

He was shocked. 'Oh no, Dawn would never do that. Nobody wants to make Liz unhappy –'

'Really? All this fuss started when Dawn got that fancy house in Ireland. Ever since then she's been after Liz –'

'She is her mother,' he protested gently. 'They're a family. It's only natural for Dawn to want them together.'

Edith snorted and set her knitting aside. 'If you feel that strongly about it, why don't you go to this wedding?'

'I can't do that. I'm not even speaking to Keir –'

'Then speak to him!' Edith's eyes blazed then softened into a look of appeal.

A clenched look came into Joe's face. 'No,' he said, 'I'll have nothing to do with him while he's selling weapons of death.'

Silence prevailed for a moment, while he struggled for the right words. 'But that doesn't mean I like to see Liz caught in the middle. Or you come to that. If you wanted to go to his wedding –'

'I see,' Edith sniffed indignantly and rose to her feet. 'You're the only one with principles are you? Liz and I can go to the wedding. It doesn't matter if we disapprove. You won't compromise your principles, but you'd feel better if we compromised ours. That's what it amounts to and don't you deny it.'

Joe did not deny it. Recognizing the truth of her words, he

retreated into silence and never raised the matter again. But he grieved over the consequences of his actions. He knew he was right. Opposed to anyone who played a part in the Arms Race, he had to include his own son, even if it tore the family apart. He knew that Edith was desperately upset, more than she would admit, about the rift between them and their son. He had seen the heartbreak on Dawn's face when Liz refused to meet Keir at Lord North Street. But Joe knew he could never back down. He would not back down . . .

So the family feud developed. As if to justify his actions, Joe became more active than ever in the Peace Movement. Scarcely a meeting took place in London without him being there. He was often in some personal danger. More than once, when thugs broke up demonstrations, his invalid chair was overturned. He was arrested twice in 1969, once for protesting outside the Russian Embassy, and again in October for demonstrating against the war in Vietnam.

Protests about Vietnam were world-wide. All over Europe people petitioned their governments to condemn what they saw as American imperialism. In Australia, tens of thousands marched on state capitals, demanding the withdrawal of all foreign forces from Vietnam. Unrest erupted in America itself. Americans were horrified to learn that their troops had committed massacres equal in barbarism if not in scale to the atrocities perpetrated by the Nazis in World War II. Students, first at the University of California, then at Kent State, protested against the escalation of the war. More than two hundred colleges were closed by student strikes and walkouts . . .

Paradoxically, though, the Vietnam war which divided so many people also brought two young people together. Protesting against the war had brought Nick Grant and Liz into contact in the first place, and it continued to hold them together for Nick attended every demonstration against the war, and where Nick was, Liz was never far behind.

So far as Liz was concerned, something akin to a small miracle occurred in the autumn of 1969. She was wolf-whistled on the way home from school. It had never happened before. She turned, expecting to see Gloria Hastings or one of the other girls attracting attention, only to see men on the building site waving to her. Blushing, she hurried away, to reach home out of breath and inordinately pleased.

'My word,' said Edith, 'you looked just like your mother as you came up the path.'

Of course, it wasn't true. Her mother was beautiful. Liz wasn't beautiful and she knew it. Yet, when she inspected herself in her mirror, the blemishes were less obvious. She was no longer gawky. Her bust had filled out and her waist remained trim. Her long legs were well shaped. Her teeth were straight and a glossy sheen drew attention to her black hair.

'Well. . . .' she mused doubtfully, 'I'll pass in a crowd on a dark night.'

Luckily, boys rated her more highly and by the end of the year she was getting her fair share of dates. Only her fair share . . . she did not blossom into a raving beauty overnight, but she blossomed enough for Nick to stop treating her as a kid sister.

He visited most weeks, although Liz found it depressingly obvious that he came to see Joe and Edith as much as to see her. But things took a turn for the better the following summer. Nick had bought his motor-bike by then; a battered, second-hand machine that needed his skill as a mechanic to keep going. He roared into Arcadia Gardens most Friday evenings with Pete on the back.

Pete took to the Milfords from the first meeting, especially to Joe, but then most young men took to Joe Milford. They enjoyed talking to him, perhaps because he never talked down to them and was always interested in their opinions. 'What do *you* think?' he would ask, sitting forward in his chair, his keen eyes searching their face.

In Pete's case it helped that his views and Joe's coincided. More politically aware than Nick, Pete had been a member of the CND in Canada. 'I know Vietnam is the hot issue,' he would say to Joe, 'but CND must get back to basic principles. That's what is turning people off. They see CND banners against Vietnam, against apartheid in South Africa, against political persecution in Russia . . . it's too much. CND has got to get back to being a single-issue campaign . . .'

They talked for hours. Pete was earnest and fresh-faced under a mop of ginger hair, and usually more vocal than Nick, while Liz fetched and carried coffee from the kitchen, adding her comments when she got a chance. Her political knowledge made her seem older and that, together with her ripening body, diminished the age gap between them. So much so that as the months passed Nick began to watch her with a quickening interest.

It was an age before he made his first move. Even then he was prompted by Pete, talking about their antiques stall in Berwick Street market. 'It's good fun,' he said to Liz. 'Why don't you come up on Saturday? A pretty girl will draw the crowd while Nick and I give 'em them the spiel. Wear a tight sweater and a mini-skirt. We'll make a fortune with you there.'

Flattered, Liz wanted to go, but held back for fear of making a fool of herself. 'I don't know the first thing about antiques.'

'Neither did we when we started. All we know is what we've picked up from Sammy.'

Nick grinned. 'And I wouldn't guarantee that as being totally accurate.'

Sammy Solomon supplied their stock. He owned three shops selling antiques, and the stall in the market was another outlet.

'Sammy's okay,' said Pete. 'He's very fair with us. He lets us keep a third of the takings.'

Liz lived for Saturdays from then on. She took the tube into town in the morning and Nick brought her home on his motor-bike at night . . . and if the hour of their return became gradually later, Edith comforted herself with the knowledge that Liz was with Nick. Joe agreed. 'He's a steady lad. She'll not come to harm with young Nick.'

To begin with, Liz was just one of the gang, helping out in the same way that Nick and Pete's other student friends helped out. In the evenings they went to a disco or all piled into Nick's flat, to sit around drinking cheap wine and arguing politics. Liz was thrilled. Sometimes there was a demonstration on the Sunday and she saw Nick again, so that eventually they became a couple whom people always expected to see together.

The first time they made love was on a wet September evening in Nick's flat, eight weeks or so before Liz's seventeenth birth-day. Two days later she put herself on the pill. From then on it became common knowledge among their crowd that she was 'Nick's girl', and it seemed to Liz she had obtained everything she wanted from life.

During this period she continued to see her mother on a more or less regular basis, although Dawn was often away making films – *The Talisman* (1969), *Elephant Walk* and *Sunday's Child* (1970), and *Manhattan Adventure* in the Spring of 1971. When she was in London, however, Dawn tried unceasingly to heal the rift in the family.

Joe remained resolute. 'I'll have no truck with a merchant of death,' he declared. And it became obvious that what went for Joe went also for Edith and Liz.

Few people knew it, but Dawn Wharton was living through one of the most testing times of her life.

Two

To the gossip columnists, nobody conveyed the essence of womanhood in the Slick Seventies better than Dawn Wharton. If Women's Lib meant anything, it was the right to follow a career and live with a rich lover. Housewives in suburbia sighed enviously over photographs of Dawn arriving at the Cannes film festival – flown there in Keir's private jet – to mix as an equal with the rich and the beautiful.

Yet Dawn wanted more. She wanted Keir as her husband and Liz as their daughter to live together happily ever after, just like in the films. Sadly, after two years, a tension was growing between her and Keir.

No outsider threatened to part them. There were no other women in Keir's life. Dusty once called him 'the only guy in the world hooked on monogamy'. If there were other such men, Dusty never met them. 'It's unnatural. There's a million women out there waiting to be screwed. You let the side down when you pass up your share.'

Dawn was Keir's share. He never envied Dusty his way of life. The constant parade of bed partners simply bemused him. And since Dawn showed a strong aversion to spending even an hour in Dusty's company, the old boyhood friendship fell away. They spoke on the phone now and then, but by that autumn – the autumn of 1971 when events were to reshape their lives so dramatically – an entire year had passed without Keir and Dusty setting eyes on each other.

So it wasn't women or Dusty which caused the tension between Keir and Dawn. Instead it was a series of pinpricks, most of which were an inevitable consequence of their respective careers. Evenings alone were rare at Lord North Street – mostly Chuck was there, or Sam, or some politician . . . or Eric, or a producer, or Dawn's show-business friends. When Keir was in London, Dawn gave dinner parties, and when he went away she often went with him – dining with his clients all over the globe. In a competitive business she gave him an edge – an amazing number of elderly Cabinet Ministers perked up at the thought of dining with 'Dawn Wharton, the film star'. Yet pinpricks could scratch even there, for what was acceptable to glossy magazines was less so at formal gatherings where the couple were announced as 'Mr Keir Milford and guest', never as Mr and Mrs. It was an irritant to Keir, in much the same way as he was nettled when he saw himself described as Mr Dawn Wharton' in the tabloids.

But the worst irritant of all, the most painful pinprick was Liz. Two years had passed since it became clear that she was unwilling to make up. 'Is it any wonder,' Keir would rant, 'with Joe filling her head with this CND nonsense?' Left to Keir, his marriage to Dawn would have taken place at the outset, and he would have applied to the courts for custody of Liz. 'If we do that we'll lose her forever,' Dawn had protested. 'She'll never forgive us. Please Keir, trust me in this. We must be patient . . . wait until I talk them round . . .'

It was that which caused the tension. Not always of course. They had fun together. He was as dazzled by the sparkle of her show-business friends as she was impressed by his world of big business. They made a handsome couple. Their lives were rich and exciting, full of reward and interest. They were good in bed together. Similar things amused them. They danced to the same music. It was only when they discussed Liz that friction arose.

Inevitably it had become Dawn's fault. 'We should have done things my way,' had become Keir's familiar cry. 'We'd be married by now. All the unpleasantness would be over. Liz would be here, everything else would be forgotten. But, oh no, we have to wait for you to talk Joe round. We'll wait forever at this rate!'

But by that autumn Dawn could wait no longer. Even she had to admit that her efforts had failed so she finally set the date for her wedding.

'Some time in the Spring,' Dawn said over tea at the Milfords. 'We've waited two and a half years as it is. I can't see the point of waiting any longer.' Gathering her strength and her powers of persuasion, she made one final effort to coax Joe. 'Please come, for my sake if not for Keir's. You're my family too you know. Apart from Keir, all the family I have or will ever want is in this room.' She looked first at Liz and then at Edith before returning to Joe. 'Keir's not a monster. How could he be when he's your son? He's so like you in so many ways. Just as stubborn. But although he won't say so, he *wants* you there as much as I do . . .'

She went on at length, using her charm, sometimes making Joe squirm in his seat. In his own way he had become one of Dawn's devoted fans. He knew nothing about acting or the theatre or the cinema, but he knew a good deal about people. The truth was that he admired her tremendously.

Even Edith, always so grudging about Dawn, had to admit that she had tried to reconcile the family. 'You've been more patient than I would have been, I'll say that for you,' she said, coming as close as she ever had to paying Dawn a compliment.

Dawn responded at once. 'Oh, Edith, if only you could be there . . . I'd give anything to persuade you . . .'

Watching the look Edith passed to Joe gave Dawn fresh heart. She redoubled her efforts. Turning to Liz, she reached for her hand. 'Please, darling, for my sake. There's so much I still want to tell you. I've never forgotten my promise that one day we'll sit down and have a long chat, just the two of us . . .' She paused, struck by a sudden idea. 'I know. Let's make it my wedding day. Isn't that a wonderful idea? That would make it just perfect. What do you say?'

Liz cast a quick glance at Joe, seeking guidance. As solid as a gnarled oak, Joe sat wrestling with his conscience. Edith reached out and placed her hand on his arm. Liz felt herself willing him to say yes.

Joe's brow creased in a frown. 'I'll not go to my son's wedding,' he said, shaking his head. 'I'll not go anywhere as the guest of my son.'

Having delivered his judgement he avoided their eyes by staring at the floor.

Crushed, Dawn almost missed the nuance in his voice. It took her a moment to understand the message contained in his words. Leaving her chair she knelt before him, the better to see into his face. 'Joe?' she said softly. 'Will you come to *my* wedding? Will you come as *my* guest?'

Raising his head, he regarded her for a long moment. There was no doubt of the importance she attached to his answer. Her eyes pleaded. Turning slightly, Joe looked at his wife, and beyond her to Liz, seeing in their faces the same look of hope. He sighed heavily, hesitated, and turned back to Dawn, the stiffness in his face giving way to an awkward, shamefaced little smile. 'If I was to come,' he began hesitantly, 'I want it clearly understood that it would only be for your sake –'

'Oh, of course,' cried Dawn, laughing with sudden relief. 'Forget the monster I'm marrying. He doesn't count. But for my sake. Please. Oh, Joe, you'll make me so happy –'

'Very well, for your sake –'

Dawn flung her arms around him and kissed him full on the mouth. Using his chair to pull herself up from the floor, she turned to hug Edith, who even hugged her back, and everyone took it into their heads to hug Liz. For the next ten minutes the scene was of flush-faced excitement, with Dawn several times close to tears. Finally she clutched both of Liz's hands. 'Now, darling, it's going to be your day too, remember. I want you to invite whoever you like, all of your friends . . .' She paused, her dark eyes gleaming. 'It will be our day, Liz, really it will be, our day. So you invite anyone. What about this young American boy you were telling me about? What's his name . . . Nick? What about him?'

430

Three

Liz mentioned the wedding to Nick at the first opportunity, which was the following Saturday evening when they were on picket duty outside the French Embassy. Nick carried a large placard proclaiming 'End Nuclear Tests Now' and Liz was wearing a sandwich board which repeated the message on her back and her chest. Pete Grimshaw, his curly ginger hair jammed under a woollen cap, paced up and down some yards away, thrusting leaflets at passers-by. In all, four hundred protestors milled around outside the Embassy gates, chanting occasionally to relieve the boredom and stamping their feet to keep warm in the chill evening air.

They were mounting a ninety-six-hour vigil, demonstrating against French plans to conduct more nuclear tests in the atmosphere. For years the French had exploded their bombs in the Sahara desert, ignoring protests about the fall-out which contaminated southern Europe as well as North Africa. Eventually, thrown out of Africa by the Algerian upheaval, the French had moved their test site to their colonies in the South Pacific, indifferent to the fact that the explosions swept radioactive dust across the Southern Hemisphere, dusting the shores of the South Seas from Tahiti to Peru. Harried and pilloried by CND pressure, the governments of the United States, Russia and Britain had signed a Test Ban Treaty prohibiting tests in the atmosphere. France and China now stood alone as the only countries prepared to ignore world public opinion.

'Sure,' Nick agreed when he heard about the wedding, 'we'll go if you want. Tell you what,' he said grinning, 'the press are bound to turn out in force for your mother, we'll hold a Ban the Bomb demo in the church –'

'No!' she shrieked before realizing he was teasing. 'Swine! I'll pay you back for that later –'

'Promises, promises.' He grinned, checking his watch. It was almost eight o'clock. They finished at eight when other members

431

of CND would relieve them to prolong the vigil through the night. 'I'm glad our two hours are nearly up,' Nick grumbled. 'The poor devils on the night watch will freeze –'

'It's freezing now,' said Pete, flapping his arms as he joined them.

'I thought lumberjacks were impervious to cold,' Liz grinned, ducking behind Nick's back as Pete pretended to punch her.

'Lumberjacks,' said the Canadian loftily, 'don't respond to words like impervious. We respond to words like crispy fried bacon and mushrooms and eggs –'

'Okay, I'm doing the cooking, Nick already told me –'

'And we've got company,' Pete interrupted. 'Harry's coming back to supper, and Angie and Dennis –'

'Oh, no,' she groaned with mock horror. 'How many does that make?'

It made ten altogether, all crammed into the tiny living-room, spilling over from the inadequate chairs to sprawl onto the floor, eating food from their laps and drinking cheap wine. 'Any more for any more?' Liz bellowed, emerging pink-faced from the tiny kitchen. By unanimous agreement she was the best cook. Nick was the best washer-up, Pete the best spud-basher, Eric made the best coffee, and Angie – who worked for a wine merchant – the best provider of wines and liqueurs. Between them they were an embryonic United Nations: one American, one Canadian, two Aussies, a Kiwi, three Brits, an Indian, and an ex-South African – ex because he dared not return after the *New Statesman* published his views on apartheid. Liz was the youngest and Eric Searle, the New Zealander, at twenty-five, the oldest.

Later with the food finished and her share of the chores completed, Liz sat on the arm of Nick's chair before wriggling into a more comfortable position on his lap. She held out an empty glass as Angie, a bottle of Algerian red in one hand and a much better hock in the other, stepped carefully over the figures reclining on the floor.

'Sometimes I think we're wasting our time,' Pete was saying. 'I mean, look at tonight. We all stood around outside the French Embassy for a couple of hours. So what? Do you really think the French took a blind bit of notice?'

'Perhaps not,' admitted Arthur Jones, a tall, bespectacled LSE student, 'but the effect on British public opinion –'

'Is worth bugger-all,' interrupted Harry Oldcastle. 'Were any reporters there tonight? Did you see even one curious cameraman? Did you hell. So what will make the papers tomorrow? More tit and bum and garbage about the Royal Family –'

'We can't stop because we don't get newspaper coverage –'

'Then stop talking about public opinion. Without media coverage you can forget it.'

'So you're saying it's pointless?' Arthur challenged.

Harry shrugged. 'No, not pointless. At least we're expressing our own outrage, and maybe a few of the people who passed the French Embassy went home and thought about it –'

'That's a start,' said Liz, trying to be positive.

'If it is we'll all die of old age before the message gets across –'

The conversation rolled on. It was a familiar subject. Everyone in the room had occasional doubts about the value of demonstrations. A lot of commitment was needed to withstand being harassed by the police, spat upon by onlookers, talked down to by politicians, and vilified by the press – when, as Harry pointed out, the press took any notice at all.

'Pete's right,' said Nick, catching the gloomy mood. 'I mean, take Joe for instance.' Everyone knew Joe. Most of them had pushed his wheelchair at one time or another. 'Don't misunderstand,' Nick continued, 'he's great. I never met anyone like him. He's got all the guts in the world and he's devoted his life to this, but he's losing. People switch off when he talks about the Arms Race. I've seen it happen. They can't relate to it. They're so busy living their own lives, buying a house, bringing up kids, paying bills . . . I'm not knocking them, that's how it is, that's life. They're too busy to notice the world's getting more dangerous by the minute. Joe's got all the arguments, he knows the facts inside out, but he's preaching to the converted most of the time –'

Liz kissed his ear. He had expressed her own feelings exactly. There were times when she grieved for Joe. She had grown up watching him wear himself out, fighting in the army of the good.

Nodding his agreement about Joe, Pete switched the talk back to the French tests in the Pacific. 'What gets me is why other countries don't stop them. The French haven't the right to cordon off a hundred square miles of the Pacific. It's not theirs. No country has a right to do that. It's clearly in violation of international law, yet the Yanks and the Brits and everyone else just stand around sucking their thumbs.'

Eric took the point up at once. He was convinced that the French were breaking the international law of the sea. Liz had forgotten he was a sailor. The walls of his tiny flat round the corner were covered with photographs of yachts and pictures of deep-sea fishermen standing proudly next to their catch. Eric was in some of them, white cap pushed back on his dark hair as he grinned into the camera. Shorter than Nick, he was broader and more powerfully built. He had spent that summer delivering yachts to the Mediterranean, earning enough in seven weeks to keep himself until he returned to New Zealand at Christmas. Pete had also sailed a good deal and he and Eric were special friends, always talking about boats, swapping yarns like a pair of old salts.

Angie said, 'I don't know the first thing about international law, but the French get away with it every time. Next year will be the seventh they've carried out tests in the Pacific –'

'And they'll go on testing.' Pete scowled. 'They won't stop because we march up and down outside their Embassy in London –'

'Not just London,' Liz pointed out. 'People are protesting all over the world –'

'That's the point,' Harry interrupted, 'they can march up and down forever. The French won't take a blind bit of notice.'

'So what else can we do?' Liz demanded.

'Some Canadians stopped the Yanks testing at Amchitka,' said Pete with a touch of national pride.

'Where the hell's that?' asked Harry.

'Hang on,' Nick interrupted, shaking his head, 'that's not quite right. The tests still went ahead. Afterwards the Atomic Energy Commission said they won't test there again. They're turning the island back into a game reserve.'

'That's still a victory,' Pete insisted.

Only Pete and Nick knew about the US atomic test site on the remote Aleutian island of Amchitka, so it was left to Pete to tell the story of how protestors set out from Vancouver in two small boats in an attempt to reach the island. Neither vessel succeeded but the brave effort had captured the imagination of so many Canadians that thousands marched down to the US border and blocked it with their bodies, closing the world's longest undefended frontier for the first time in over a hundred years. Shaken by the strength of public opinion, Canadian Prime Minister Pierre Trudeau had been forced to protest to the US government who grudgingly agreed to abandon the island as a test site.

Liz listened with shining eyes. 'How marvellous!' she exclaimed, turning to Nick. 'I wish I'd been there. Just imagine, thousands of people linking hands right across Canada –'

'The boats did it,' Harry insisted. 'They caught the public's attention in the first place.'

'So why doesn't someone get on a boat and go down to the Pacific?' she asked.

Everyone laughed except Pete. He stared at Liz as if she had sprouted wings. 'Bloody hell fire,' he whispered. 'That's it! Of course, that's it exactly.'

Embarrassed by the way he was looking at her, Liz stared back, wondering what on earth she had said.

'That's it,' Pete repeated, turning to Eric. 'Remember what you were saying about international waters? Suppose you sailed into the danger zone? You know, this huge chunk of the ocean the French have cordoned off? They're carrying their tests out on an island. So suppose you set sail for the island and stopped just outside the twelve-mile limit? You just sat there. What could they do?'

Eric's eyes gleamed. Pete's words clearly intrigued him. 'You mean just sail up and down, protesting, twelve miles off the island? What a brilliant idea.'

'Twelve miles sounds a long way,' said Angie. 'Would the French know you were there?'

Pete laughed. 'They'd know all right.'

Angie tossed her head. 'Then I can't see the point. They'd just board you and tow you away –'

'That is the point,' Eric interrupted. 'That's why you'd stay twelve miles out. Twelve miles is the legal extent of territorial waters. Beyond that and you're in open sea. International waters. They can't touch you. If they boarded you it would be an act of piracy. The law is very clear about that.'

'Absolutely.' Pete nodded. 'It would definitely be piracy.'

Nick said quietly, 'And detonating the bomb, knowing you were there, would be murder.'

A shiver ran up Liz's spine. Complete silence fell in the room. Pete stared first at Nick, then at Eric, before saying in an awed whisper, 'It's a magnificent idea. So simple. The ultimate protest.'

That too was digested in silence, until Eric laughed. 'That's all very well,' he said, 'but you're talking about one hell of a voyage. You North Americans are always boasting about the Atlantic. The Pacific is five times as big and ten times as dangerous.'

'Could you do it in *The Dove?*' Pete asked bluntly.

Liz remembered seeing a photograph on Eric's wall, showing him in a small boat, waving a bottle of champagne in one hand and some kind of trophy in the other. She had asked him about it. 'That's my boat,' he had said proudly. '*The Dove.* Ain't she a beauty? Thirty-six feet of sheer magic.'

Eric shrugged. '*The Dove* could do it if any vessel could. She's not as pretty as those gin palaces I've been delivering all summer, but she'd lose them on the open sea.'

'So what about it?' asked Pete, adding a note of challenge to his voice.

Eric appeared to consider it for a moment. Then he laughed. 'Forget it, I'm going home in a few weeks, remember? I start work in Christchurch in the New Year. They sent me a letter confirming my appointment, everything's fixed –'

'Write back and postpone it. They'll wait for the right man.'

'You're mad. You haven't the slightest idea what's involved. I read a bit about the French test site. It's on an island, an atoll really, called Mururoa, eight hundred miles south of Tahiti –'

'What's the distance from New Zealand?' asked Pete.

'About three thousand miles. Maybe more –'

'Whew,' Nick whistled. 'That would make a round trip of over six thousand miles –'

'Exactly. Four or five months at sea, out of sight of land most of the time –'

'One hell of a trip,' said Pete, grinning broadly.

Eric stared at him. 'Forget it. It's not on –'

'It's worth thinking about,' Pete countered.

436

'No it's not. Even to get the boat ready would take three months –'

'So there's time,' said Pete. 'The French don't start testing until June –'

'I just told you. The voyage would take about two months.'

'And three months to get the boat ready. That's five altogether. That means there's still time –'

'God Almighty! Apart from anything else, it would cost a fortune. I couldn't afford it –'

'If we raised the money?' Pete persisted.

Eric gave him a long, searching look. 'I believe you're really serious.' ·

'You bet I'm serious. It's what we need. Everyone agrees that marching up and down outside the French Embassy won't shift the buggers. But this might. It would arouse public attention. Like those people who sailed to Amchitka. That voyage got thousands of Canadians up off their backsides. Just think what this could achieve.'

Apart from Pete and Eric, no one had spoken for some minutes. The others were listening with mounting excitement. Particularly Liz. She could feel her heart pounding. Her casual remark had been a joke, she had never imagined it would lead to a conversation like this.

Nick was the first to express support. 'I think it's a fantastic idea. It might stop the French, if it attracted enough public attention . . .'

Suddenly everyone started talking at once. The tiny room became a hubbub of noise and excitement. Everyone took it upon themselves to persuade Eric, drowning his every objection with a chorus of enthusiastic voices. No one was more enthusiastic than Pete. Launched upon the idea, he seemed determined to match the achievements of his countrymen at Amchitka. 'It's such a perfect plan,' he kept saying. 'We just sail up and down twelve miles offshore. They can't touch us. It really would be the ultimate protest.'

Eric's eyes betrayed him. Intrigued from the first moment, his arguments against the idea never quite matched the look on his face. Eventually, under pressure from Pete, he began listing the things to be done to his boat – the engine had to be overhauled, a new propeller fitted – he began to itemize a hundred and one things. 'Even so, if I started immediately after Christmas . . .' he mused, forgetting the job that awaited him in New Zealand.

Half an hour later they were trying to estimate the cost of the voyage. 'What's the total?' Pete wanted to know. 'The maximum, the worst possible figure.'

Eric shook his head. 'It will take days to work out –'

'Roughly,' Pete pleaded.

Between them they produced what Eric called 'the roughest estimate anyone ever came up with'. It was a great deal of money, but even that failed to quell Pete's enthusiasm.

'We'll raise it somehow,' he said, looking around at the others, 'won't we?'

'Yes!' they roared, quite carried away.

It was hot in the room; stuffy with cigarette smoke and charged with excitement. The pressure on Eric was relentless. He was clearly very taken by the idea, attracted by the challenge of the voyage as much as by Pete's arguments. At one point he even answered some of his own objections, proving how smitten he was. Eventually after much discussion, he said a lot would depend on raising the money. 'And it would have to be guaranteed before I go home,' he said apologetically. 'I mean, be fair. I can't chuck up this job on some pipe dream . . .'

No one argued with that. They all saw his point of view even though it left only four weeks to find a sponsor. At that moment raising the money seemed less important than hearing him say yes.

'Very well,' he said finally, looking at Pete. 'If I take the voyage on, will you sail with me?'

'Like a shot.'

'And me,' said Nick.

'Me too,' said Liz, her pulse racing.

Startled eyes focused on her face. Eric was the most startled of all. 'Wait a minute, we're talking about a dangerous voyage –'

'No more dangerous for me than for you,' she shot back at him.

Their evident hostility dismayed her. It hadn't occurred to her that they would exclude her. She had never crossed the English Channel on a ferry, let alone sailed a yacht, but the thought of not going never entered her head.

'It would be too dangerous,' Eric said emphatically.

She regarded him coldly. She had been campaigning all her life. She had been on the Aldermaston March as a four-year-old. She'd grown up in CND and knew more about the Arms Race than all of them put together.

'Honey.' Nick squeezed her hand. 'Imagine, we'll be at sea for months. Life on board will be primitive. There's no privacy, you'd hate it.'

She hated him at that moment. Her eyes blazed and her face went red. All because she was a girl, that's all it was. It was so unfair!

'Besides,' Nick coaxed, 'Joe and Edith would never allow it. You know they –'

'They couldn't stop me,' she answered, boiling with temper.

'They'd have a bloody good try. And what about your mother? She'd go spare. And Keir? Can you imagine his reaction –'

'I don't care about Keir!'

An embarrassed silence reigned for a moment, broken by Liz. 'I know what you're thinking,' she said to Nick, her face glowing. 'I've never been on a boat in my life. So what? You know all about engines, and Eric and Pete are expert sailors, but not one of you can boil a kettle. You'll give yourselves food poisoning in five minutes –'

'Nonsense!'

'No, it's not. This voyage was my idea and I'm coming as ship's cook.'

Nick looked abashed, Eric was astonished, but Angie shouted 'Bravo!' and clapped her hands. 'Fantastic. You tell 'em, Liz. You're right, it *was* your idea.'

Eric turned to her. 'Don't tell me you want to come too?' he said, sounding appalled.

'Not me. I know my limitations. But Liz should go. She's right about your cooking. You lot will end up poisoning each other.'

Everyone laughed and Harry began talking about ways of raising the money, so that what with one thing and another whether Liz would go or not was momentarily forgotten. It was not until later – when most of the crowd had left, still buzzing with excitement about the possible voyage – that Nick raised the matter. He and Liz were on the landing, donning leathers and helmets for the ride out to Ealing. 'You can't be serious,' he

439

said, 'Joe and Edith would never allow it, and you know you wouldn't do anything to hurt them.'

She looked at him sharply, wondering if he was being sarcastic. It was true that she took care not to hurt Joe and Edith. They were very precious to her, more than ever since her estrangement from Keir. She considered their feelings in all sorts of ways, not least by not staying at Nick's every Saturday night. They had often discussed it, it was what they both wanted and it would save Nick the journey to Ealing and back. To make matters worse, Angie slept with Pete most Saturday nights. But Angie was eighteen and lived with her sister. Liz was younger and lived with Edith and Joe. She and Nick had few opportunities to make love. Saturday afternoons had become their lovemaking times. After working until three at the stall, they left Pete and Angie to run things while they slipped back to the flat for a couple of hours. Everyone knew where they went – and why – which had caused Liz some embarrassment at the outset, but she preferred that to an upset with Edith and Joe.

'I didn't mean that,' Nick said quickly, seeing the look on her face.

'I know.' She smiled gratefully. 'I don't want to upset them, but if this voyage ever takes place I'm going to be part of it.'

'Oh, are you?' he said grinning. 'And what about me? Imagine, five months on a boat. I can't be around you five minutes without wanting to undress you. You know that. And that wouldn't be fair to the other guys, would it?'

Giggling, she dodged away as he lunged at her. 'You'll have to learn self-control then, won't you?'

Five minutes later they were roaring through the night on his motor-bike. Liz clung to him, huddled into his back, the cold air stinging her face and bringing tears to her eyes. Tearful was the last thing she was. She felt exhilarated. 'We're going to change the world,' she sang, suddenly deliriously happy. Never had she felt more alive. The ultimate protest . . .

She knew everyone would try to stop her going. 'I don't care,' she vowed. She knew there would be arguments, several probably . . . with Edith and Joe . . . most of all with her mother. 'She'll go spare,' Nick had said.

Liz knew he was right.

Four

Dawn had felt relief more than triumph when Joe had agreed to attend her wedding. The tears in her eyes had been genuine, needing none of her skill as an actress. Few people knew the strain she was under. Had Keir been in Lord North Street she would have rushed home to tell him, but Keir was in Tel Aviv with Sam, selling B-20 missiles to the Israelis. Resisting the urge to telephone him, she waited until he returned on the Sunday. His plane touched down at eleven o'clock and she was at Heathrow to greet him, hoping desperately that Sam wasn't with him.

'No, Sam's still there, combing through the small print.' Keir chuckled. 'He'll be lucky to finish by Wednesday.'

All the way into town she hugged the news to herself, resisting the urge to blurt it out, content instead to listen to his account of his trip.

Not until Keir came downstairs, washed and changed for a drink before lunch, did Dawn tell him. As usual his face darkened when she mentioned his father. Undeterred, she rushed on, the words fairly tumbling over each other as they fell from her lips. 'They are coming. Joe gave his word. He won't go back on it now.'

Keir's scowl changed to a look of disbelief. 'He's coming to the wedding without making any conditions? No nonsense about –?'

'No conditions at all.' Dawn had already decided not to tell him the full story.

A moment passed while Keir assimilated the news. 'I suppose your famous charm got through to him at last.'

If there was a touch of sarcasm in his words she chose to ignore it. 'The old Chinese torture would be nearer the truth,' she admitted. 'You know, drip, drip, drip.'

'What was Liz's reaction?'

'She was on our side. Honestly, darling, she helped to

441

persuade him. So did Edith. Can you believe Edith helping to persuade Joe? But she did, she was wonderful. She really misses you, you know. She's desperate to come to the wedding. And Liz was tremendously excited –'

'Will she come and live with us?' Keir asked, raising the issue that mattered to him most.

Dawn hesitated. 'Steady on, darling. One miracle for one day –'

'Did you discuss it?'

'Oh, Keir, darling, there was so much to discuss. The important thing is that she's delighted. She wants to come. I told her, it will be her day as much as mine. I said we'd have our little chat . . . you know –'

'But did you discuss her living here?'

Reluctantly, Dawn admitted, 'Not in so many words –'

'The longer she lives there the more she gets poisoned by his damn fool ideas,' said Keir, his temper rising. 'I should have thought it was perfectly obvious that living under his roof –'

'Not necessarily. She's growing up. She's not a child anymore. Naturally she's influenced by Joe, but these days she's got friends of her own age. Believe me, darling, girls take far more notice of friends than anyone else. That's what will wean her from Joe. I told her to invite her friends to the wedding –'

'And will she?'

'Of course she will. Now do you see what I'm driving at? Once she and her friends start coming here, everything changes. We can offer to fly them across to Carrickfergus for weekends, they'll love that, we'll spend holidays together. It will happen naturally. She'll *want* to live with us because she'll have so much more fun . . .'

The frown faded from Keir's face. Listening to Dawn describe the future cheered him enormously. It had been a trying week. Negotiating with the Israelis was like eating melted butter with a fork. Still, Sam had got his order, he was happy. Chuck would be pleased. Another bonus would soon be on its way to the bank in Zurich.

'Okay,' he said grinning, 'You did a great job. Sorry, I should have said so before. It's just that whenever I think of Liz being indoctrinated by Joe's rubbish –'

'I told you. She has friends of her own age. I'm sure they've got better things to talk about than nuclear weapons and the Arms Race.'

'You mean boyfriends and things? I hadn't even thought of that. Do you realize it's two years since I last saw her?'

'Calm down,' she said gently, 'don't blow your stack again. I missed more of her childhood than you did, remember? The way I look at it is that I lost out on the child, but tread carefully now and we've got Liz for the rest of our lives.'

Over lunch they discussed the date for the wedding.

'Why wait?' Keir wanted to know. 'Why don't we have it now?'

'Darling, we're going to Japan next month. Everything's arranged.'

The arrangements had been settled months before. Keir had to go to Japan on business and she would go with him, spending two weeks there before going on to Sydney to begin filming *Resting Point*, the long-awaited sequel to *Burning Obsession*. She had mixed feelings about returning to Australia and might have rejected the idea if Keir had not been planning a three-month-long trip to Japan. The fact that he would fly in from Tokyo every weekend was an antidote to old memories. *Resting Point* was to be her last film, she had made up her mind to that. After that, she would concentrate solely on the theatre. Really it was what she had always wanted. To star in London's West End . . .

'We don't leave until half-way through the month,' Keir persisted. 'There's still time.'

'Not if you want your VIPs to be there. You know how much notice they need. Meeting them for a drink requires a week's advance warning.'

Of course, she was right. Invitations would have to be sent out months before.

After lunch they settled down happily to making lists and fixing the date. As he looked at her on the sofa, for some reason Keir was reminded of the first day he set eyes on her – in the school corridor, so long ago.

'Heavens above!' Dawn laughed. 'You've got a memory like an elephant's. Don't say you wanted to marry me then?'

If not then it was only a week later. He had wanted to marry her for as long as he could remember. Now, at last, the date was set. They would marry on 12 March, 1972.

Dawn reached for Keir's hand. 'And believe me, darling, our daughter is almost as excited as we are.'

Liz had forgotten all about the wedding. The proposed voyage to the Pacific occupied her thoughts morning, noon and night. Countless times it was on the tip of her tongue when talking to Joe. Wanting to tell him, imagining his excitement, she checked herself every time, fearful he would argue against her involvement.

'You'll have to tell him some time,' said Angie the following Saturday.

'I might not need to.' Liz shrugged gloomily. 'Eric's still against me being one of the crew.'

It was true. After working on the idea all week, Eric had stiffened his resistance to her being a member of the crew. 'It's nothing personal, Liz, but Pete and Nick agree with me. We'll have enough to worry about as it is. Suppose you fell ill?'

'I never get ill,' she answered furiously.

Later she had called Nick 'a treacherous rat'.

'That's not fair,' he had said hotly, 'I would spend all my time worrying about you.'

The irony was that they needed her help. Eric and Pete had spent hours pouring over charts at the British Maritime Museum, calculating distances and sailing times, then they had retired to Eric's tiny flat and worked on the budget. By Saturday, Eric had sheets of calculations to prove how much money was needed – all they had to do now was raise it. It was Nick who suggested they should discuss it with Joe. 'He knows so many people. He might be able to send us to someone who can help.'

Time was pressing, mainly because of Eric's impending departure for New Zealand. Liz could hardly say no. She had to help. Besides, the thought occurred to her that if she helped raise the money they might reconsider taking her. It was a last lingering hope. So they descended on the Milfords – Liz and Nick, Eric, Angie and Pete.

Edith was delighted. She liked nothing more than for Liz to bring her friends home. Her first question was, 'Have you all eaten?' quickly followed by, 'There's cake in the cupboard, and biscuits . . . come on, Angie, you can give me a hand.'

Five

Joe was enthralled. He sat with Eric's large atlas on his lap, open at a map of the Pacific. Names leapt up at him – Samoa, Tonga, Tahiti – faraway places with strange-sounding names, all dominated by the vastness of the blue ocean. Listening to Eric and Pete filled him with admiration. He wondered if he'd had as much self-confidence at their age. It was so long ago that he could hardly remember, but dimly, in the distant past, he could still see himself on the footplate of a Hudson-class engine. Straining his memory he could still feel the heat from the firebox and smell the acrid steam in his nostrils; he could still hear the thunder of wheels on the rails as they raced through the inky black night. King's Cross to Edinburgh in six and a half hours! What a feeling. He had been alive then, properly alive, a complete man, as vigorous then as these young men were now.

'Everything would have to be ready by the middle of March,' Eric was saying. 'Naturally I'll start work on the boat as soon as I get home.'

'What do you think?' Nick asked eagerly.

Packing his pipe, Joe took his time to answer. Inwardly, he seethed with excitement. What a marvellous scheme. What incredible young men. Eric had a job waiting for him in New Zealand. Nick and Pete faced final examinations. They would throw all that away and give up nearly a year of their lives to fight for their beliefs. It was as much as Joe could do not to applaud.

'Well?' Nick persisted impatiently.

Joe smiled. He regarded Nick as a son and Pete as a nephew, but Eric was a comparative newcomer.

'Eric's very experienced,' said Nick, reading Joe's mind. 'He's delivered big yachts to Bermuda from New Zealand, as well as smaller ones from Southampton to Monte Carlo. Isn't that right, Eric?'

Eric nodded. 'But that's not to say it's a one-man show, Mr Milford. Pete's an experienced sailor too, and Nick's a fine engineer. He's a genius with engines. He even knows something about radio –'

'I'll know a lot more by the time we set sail in April,' said Nick.

'Sorry about the short notice,' Eric apologized. 'You see I leave for home in a few weeks. I'll need to order things for the boat as soon as I get there. The money wouldn't all be needed at once, twenty per cent would get me started, as long as I could rely on the rest by next March.'

Joe nodded. Although none of them would draw any wages and Eric would do most of the work on the boat, it was still a great deal of money. Raising it at all would be difficult, raising it in a few weeks sounded downright impossible. Joe frowned and began to rack his brains.

'Well, Mr Milford?' Pete asked. 'What do you think?'

Joe could delay no longer. Puffing on his pipe, he glanced at their faces – Liz anxious, his wife shaking her head in wonder at it all, Angie looking hopeful and the three young men looking very determined. It occurred to him at that moment that they were of different nationalities – an American, a Canadian, and a New Zealander. Wonderful ambassadors, he thought, wishing that there was a British representative.

'It's a magnificent idea,' he pronounced. 'You'd be taking the fight to the enemy. By God, the times I've longed to do that.' He had, too. Demonstrations and marches were all very well, they helped spread the message, but a project like this stirred the blood.

'Then you'll help?' Nick asked eagerly.

'Of course I'll help. I'll do everything I can.' Joe laughed as exclamations arose on all sides. 'Steady on,' he protested, 'my help's not worth much. It doesn't guarantee you the money. Frankly, we'll need a miracle to raise thirty thousand pounds.'

They spent the next half-hour discussing the budget, with Eric working out sums on a pocket calculator and producing his sheets of notes. It was while Joe was studying the notes that a query arose. Seeing that the cost of provisions had been calculated by working out the requirements of one person for six months and then multiplying by five, Joe asked, 'How many of you are going on this voyage?'

Nick and Pete exchanged guilty glances, while Eric tried to avoid the question by saying, '*The Dove*'s got six berths. We could make the voyage three-handed if we have to, but two more would spread the load and give us insurance. With only three of us, if one fell sick or something, the others might be hard pushed to manage –'

'So who else is going?' asked Joe.

Eric glanced at Nick, who looked helplessly at Liz.

Swallowing hard, Liz said, 'Me. I'm going as ship's cook.'

Joe's astonishment was almost comical. He stared open-mouthed at Liz.

Edith found her voice first. Her hands flew to her face to catch the words 'Oh, my God,' as they fell from her lips. 'You can't possibly go. I never heard such –'

'I am going,' said Liz, white-faced and defiant. 'Please Edith, don't try to stop me –'

Joe recovered to say, 'It's not just Edith. There's your mother to consider –'

'She can't stop me. I'll be seventeen –'

'It's out of the question,' said Joe firmly, his face darkening as he looked at Nick. 'You should know better. I'm surprised at you –'

'Don't blame him,' Liz interrupted. 'He's being as difficult as you are about it.'

Edith's eyes lit with relief. 'I should think so. Thank goodness Nick's got some sense –'

'Oh?' Liz exclaimed. 'It's all right for him, I suppose? Just because he's a man –' she bit her tongue, regretting her outburst. 'Sorry, I didn't mean to be rude.'

Joe seized the olive branch. 'We know you didn't,' he said, laughing to reduce the tension. Turning to Angie, he asked, 'You want to go too, I suppose?'

'Not likely. I get sea-sick in the bath. But the boys would take good care of Liz, really they would, Mr Milford.'

Joe laughed again, trying to turn the idea into a joke. 'Five months on a boat,' he said. 'My word, I'd have to go along too as a chaperone.'

Amid the general laughter, Joe was suddenly gripped by the most astonishing idea. *Why not go?* The palms of his hands started to sweat with excitement. His heart thumped. 'What about that?' he asked, looking at Eric.

'Yes.' Eric laughed, somewhat embarrassed.

'Seriously,' said Joe, 'that's a fantastic idea.'

Eric's eyes betrayed his dismay. 'Seriously?' he echoed. 'Hold on, sir, I mean . . . well, have you ever done any sailing?'

'Of course he hasn't,' Edith said quickly, laughing nervously, her face expressing her alarm. She began to think that everyone had gone stark, staring mad. 'It was a joke,' she said. 'Wishful thinking, that's what it was, wasn't it, Joe?'

'No,' he said, in flat contradiction.

Never had Joe wanted anything more. Suddenly he ached to be part of this voyage. For fifteen years he had campaigned up and down the country in all weathers, without ever having a chance to take the fight to the enemy.

The others reacted in various ways. Pete caught his breath. Liz's dark eyes rounded, making them larger than ever. Alone among them, Nick betrayed the least sign of alarm. Surprise certainly, but there was no mistaking the respect that shone from his level grey eyes.

Eric groaned. 'Oh Lord, perhaps I gave the wrong impression before. There could be great dangers –'

'Not least,' Pete interrupted, 'of being killed in a nuclear explosion.'

'All the more reason for me to be there,' said Joe. 'How d'you think I'd feel if I helped raise the money and something happened to you? I couldn't live with that on my conscience.'

Eric, floundering with embarrassment, appealed to Nick. 'You explain. Any incapacity . . . I mean . . . there are times when agility is essential.'

'What Eric means,' Nick said, looking directly at Joe, 'is that you're a cripple.'

No one else could have said it. Even Edith, in all the years of living with Joe in a wheelchair, had never called him a cripple. Liz couldn't bear the word. They avoided it, as did all of Joe's friends. It was an ugly, spiteful sort of a word, an insult to a man as active as Joe. Yet when Nick said it – lightly, calmly, looking Joe in the eye – it was a million miles from an insult. It sounded more like a tribute.

Joe nodded, a faint smile touching his lips. 'Good boy, Nick, this is too important for mealy-mouthed words.' He turned back to Eric. 'How big is your boat?'

'Thirty-six foot.'

'You won't be walking far then?' said Joe, his smile broadening.

'It's not a matter of walking. It's a question of balance, bracing yourself –'

'I understand,' Joe agreed, 'except in all the photographs I've seen, yachtsmen brace themselves sitting down. I've had a heck of a lot of experience of that.'

Eric shook his head. 'It's not only that, Mr Milford. There are hatches, steps down to the cabin –'

'How many steps?'

'Er . . . four, five –'

'I'll do those on my backside before you can say "Jack Robinson".'

Eric retreated into an embarrassed silence, but Joe kept after him. 'Of course,' he said, 'you'd have to be strong, I can understand that. For instance, you need very strong arms I imagine?'

'Absolutely,' Eric agreed. 'I've seen waves forty feet high in the Pacific. With seas like that you need every ounce of strength to hang onto the tiller. After half an hour you think your arms are being wrenched out of their sockets. That's when it's exhausting. That's when it counts, Mr Milford – someone really fit can make all the difference.'

Joe's eyes gleamed. 'If I prove I'd be better than you at one job on your boat, will you consider taking me as one of your crew?'

Eric shook his head in bewilderment. 'I can't think what it could be. How could you prove it?'

'Come over here, Liz,' said Joe. 'Bring that side chair with you.'

Suddenly, Edith guessed his intentions. 'No, Joe, that's enough. This has gone too far. Stop now before . . .' Words failed her as she met the steely look in his eye, a look that said more clearly than speech, *Don't shame me in my own house, not in front of these young men.* Edith choked on her words, and clenched her hands so tightly that the knuckles shone white. She knew the strength of Joe's arms. He hoisted himself out of his chair often enough – in the lavatory, in the bath. He dressed himself, bathed himself, he did everything, all without help. In the shop he often lifted heavy cartons from one spot to another.

He could easily lift his own weight. Ever since the accident, Joe had lived on his arms.

Liz also knew Joe's intentions. He used to do it when she was a child. But she was smaller then, and lighter. As she crossed the room, her mind was in turmoil. If Joe went, surely he would take her? Without more argument . . . Setting the upright chair down beside him, close enough for him to reach, she sat down with her back to him.

Joe locked the wheels of his chair. 'Did you ever think a cripple might have an advantage?' he asked Eric. 'You know – the way blind people develop other senses more than sighted people?'

Edith could stand it no longer. 'I've had enough of this nonsense,' she sniffed, distress in her eyes. 'I'm going to put the kettle on.'

She had scarcely left the room when Joe turned, gripped the underside of Liz's chair and lifted. His face mottling with effort, a vein bulging in his neck, he held her a foot off the ground.

Liz began to count. 'One . . . two . . . three . . .'

Arms fully extended, Joe lifted her a few inches higher.

'. . . Eight . . . nine . . . ten . . .'

Eric stared boggle-eyed, feeling his stomach muscles clench as he imagined the strain. Proud of his own fitness, he knew Joe's feat of strength would defeat him.

'. . . Fourteen . . . fifteen . . .'

'Bloody hell,' Pete swore in a soft whisper, 'I couldn't do that to save my life.'

'. . . Nineteen . . . twenty.'

Beads of sweat broke out over his forehead, he gritted his teeth with the strain, and as his arms shuddered slightly, Joe lowered the chair to the floor.

'Terrific!' Nick whooped, jumping up. 'I think Joe's proved his point. What do you say, Pete?'

Pete was taking proper note for the first time of Joe's barrel chest and strong shoulders. 'It's fine with me,' he said, 'if it's okay with the skipper.'

Everyone looked at Eric. Joe wiped the sweat from his forehead with the back of his sleeve, willing him to say yes.

A rueful grin spread across Eric's face. 'I think you've the makings of a first-class helmsman, Mr Milford.'

Liz flung her arms round his neck and kissed him. 'He's coming as my chaperone, remember.'

Amid the laughter and excitement which followed, no one actually said yes or no about Liz, perhaps because Joe remained the centre of attention. The tension which had developed during his exhibition of strength was transformed into a lot of excited chatter, centred around Joe who sat, red-faced from his exertions, with a huge grin on his face.

'I feel like Nelson,' he laughed, 'sailing out against the French at Trafalgar.'

Liz rushed out to the kitchen in search of Edith, and when she didn't find her there, went along the hall to her bedroom. Edith was sitting on her bed, knotting and unknotting her handkerchief, a defeated look on her face. She looked up as Liz entered the room. 'He's going isn't he? The stubborn old fool. He's fifty-six you know. Hasn't he done enough without going to the other side of the world . . . ?' Her face crumpled and she began to weep. Liz was at her side in an instant, taking her into her arms, reversing a situation she had known all her life.

A great howl of laughter reached them from the living-room. 'Listen to that,' Edith sniffed. 'He thinks he's twenty again. What can you do with someone like that?'

Liz rocked her in her arms and remembered a scene from her childhood, standing outside a court as Joe and Lord and Lady Russell were led off to jail. 'Be proud of him,' she whispered, 'that's what you told me once. I've never stopped being proud of him. I'll be proud of him for the rest of my life.'

Everything that followed could be traced back to that night at the Milfords. Decisions made then were to change the rest of their lives. And not merely theirs, but Dawn's and Keir's too, changed beyond recognition by the following summer.

The voyage to the French nuclear test site in the Pacific captured their imagination completely. It was all they talked about morning, noon and night. Most evenings found them gathered at Arcadia Gardens – discussing, planning and dreaming. Eric, however, was no dreamer, neither was he reckless. He dealt with his reservations about taking Joe and Liz by lecturing them politely but firmly on their conduct at sea. Once aboard his boat they would take orders from him. 'It's not a matter of ego,' he said, 'it's the age-old rule about there being only one skipper. A squabble in a time of crisis could spell doom for the whole crew.' Neither Joe nor Liz argued, they were quite willing to do as they were told. Joe also accepted that he would wear a safety harness at all times except when he went below. 'That way,' said Eric, 'you'll be perfectly safe.'

Eric's competent manner was a comfort to Edith. She still had reservations. Left to her she would have vetoed the involvement not only of Joe but also of Liz. 'Leave it to young men who know what they're doing,' was her familiar cry. But faced with Joe's massive determination her surrender was inevitable, and she had to admit that Eric's matter-of-fact manner was reassuring. 'After all,' she told herself, 'it's nothing new for him. He's sailed every ocean in the world, has young Eric.'

Bob Cooper and Emlyn Hughes were summoned within days, first to be thrilled by the concept, then to be dismayed by the need to raise the money before Eric left for New Zealand. 'We'll have to launch a national appeal,' said Bob. 'It will take time. You can't expect us to do much this side of Christmas.'

'I must have something,' said Eric. 'I'll have to start work as soon as I get home if we're to be ready in time. The money won't all be needed immediately, but I'll have to spend three or four thousand in the first week.'

The problem seemed massive. Without the cash their dreams would be over before they began. Liz was the only one to gain an advantage from the problem. She still had her mother to face. Joe had said, 'I'll do what I can to persuade her, but you must tell her yourself.'

Liz knew she was walking a tightrope. Everyone had opposed her involvement – first Eric and Nick, then Joe and Edith. There was no doubt in her mind about her mother's reaction. Playing for time, she insisted, 'There's no point in telling her until we raise the money. Why have a row about something that might never happen?'

Joe was willing to accept that. The argument was strong enough for him to convince himself they were not being totally deceitful. 'It does make sense,' he told Edith. 'I wouldn't want to upset Dawn unnecessarily.'

So nothing was said about the proposed voyage when Dawn called to say goodbye before leaving for Japan. Instead, most of her visit was taken up with her plans for the wedding. 'I won't be back until the end of February,' she said, 'and that will only leave a couple of weeks.'

The wedding itself was to be a simple Registry Office ceremony with only the family and Eric in attendance. Dawn smiled. 'The world and his brother will be at the reception, but I wanted it to be just us at the wedding.'

Her happiness was so obvious that Edith was surprised to feel a lump in her throat. She coughed, telling herself she was a ridiculous old woman. Casting her mind back over the years, she remembered her first meeting with Dawn, when Dawn was heavily pregnant, very frightened and almost at the end of her tether. *I called her a trollop. I was afraid she'd be bad for Keir. Now look at us. She's the one working to bring the family together again, not me or Joe . . .*

Afterwards, Edith walked Dawn out to the car, to where John Westwood stood ready to open the door. 'Take care of yourself in Australia,' she said, 'and you can tell Keir from me, he's very lucky to be marrying you.' With that, to Dawn's pleased astonishment and somewhat to her own surprise, Edith kissed Dawn on the cheek and gave her a hug before putting her into the Daimler.

Returning misty-eyed to the house, she caught the grin on Joe's face. 'I know,' she snapped. 'I'm a silly old fool, but I'd be a bigger one not to admit I was wrong. I thought that girl was just a pretty face. It's taken me all these years to admit she's got brains and courage to go with it.' This was quite an admission for Edith. Joe reached out and patted her hand, but very wisely remained silent. Thinking that Liz also had brains and courage, he was worrying about the inevitable clash between mother and daughter.

Liz proved her cleverness a few days later when everyone had once again gathered at Arcadia Gardens. Bob and Emlyn were there to report on their failure to raise the money before Eric's departure. 'I'm sure we'll succeed in the end,' Bob said. 'We've been beaten by time. If we could have until the Spring . . .'

But *The Dove* was to set sail in the Spring.

It was into that gloomy silence that Liz produced her trump card. The idea had come to her weeks before, from the very first moment the voyage had been thought of in Nick's flat. Nursing it carefully, she had bided her time and now – with her mother safely in far-off Japan – the moment had come.

'I've got the money,' she said. 'Pay me back later if you like, but I've enough to fund the entire voyage.' And she had. Ever since Keir had insisted on paying for Liz's upkeep, Dawn's money had been paid into the bank. Over the years it had mounted up. Interest had accumulated. It had now grown to the staggering total of thirty-two thousand, eight hundred and twenty-eight pounds.

Of course, there were protests. Edith especially was against the idea. 'That's every penny you've got in the world,' she said, staring at the bank book in Liz's hands.

'And I'm giving it to Eric,' said Liz.

Eric might have refused had Bob Cooper not been there. 'We *will* raise the money,' Bob said. 'Honestly, Edith, we'll pay Liz back every penny if she'll wait until the spring.'

In a strange way it made everyone even more determined. Nick's were not the only eyes which shone with admiration. Without saying a word, everyone seemed to say the same thing. *We can't back out now. We can't let Liz down.* Nobody was prouder than Joe, who was struck by the irony that in a sense Keir's money was making the voyage possible – money earned from armaments would be used against the makers of arms. The humour of the situation brought a grin to Joe's face.

The evening turned into a celebration after that. Emlyn disappeared for half an hour and returned clutching a magnum of champagne. 'I want to propose a toast,' he said filling their glasses, 'to the voyage of *The Dove.*'

The concept of the voyage became a little more definite and less of a dream, and a week later, when Eric left for New Zealand, they all went to see him off from Heathrow – including Joe and Edith, driven there in Bob's car. 'I'm relying on you to take good care of my family next summer,' said Edith as she kissed him goodbye.

Edith saw the sea, not the French, as the danger. Having tried to imagine three thousand miles of ocean she had found the concept beyond her, but the French were the French. Despite the callous disregard with which they conducted their nuclear tests, they were a civilized people. If *The Dove* succeeded in reaching Mururoa Edith was sure they would stop testing. After all, as Nick had said, to do otherwise would be murder. And the French would never commit murder . . .

'Not with the rest of the world looking on,' was Joe's only qualification.

So, naively or otherwise, they all believed the same thing. The sea, not the French, was the biggest danger. If they had thought differently they might not have gone. In due course they were to find out they were wrong. But by then it was too late to turn back.

Six

Even Christmas Day that year was devoted to discussing the voyage. By two o'clock lunch was over at the Milfords and pencils and paper were out as lists were made of letters to write and jobs to be done. Everyone had gathered at Arcadia Gardens – Nick and Pete, Angie and Betty, her sister, Emlyn and Bob.

'It's growing so big,' said Angie, her eyes shining with the wonder of it all. 'I never expected anything like this.'

The project was certainly growing. Joe had written to people all over the world, telling them of the voyage and seeking their support – not financial support, for by now Bob had that in hand and expected to raise the full amount in England – but support was needed in other ways.

'What we want,' Joe said, 'are simultaneous protests taking place all over the world.'

The signs were encouraging. Public concern about the tests was growing in many countries, especially those with shorelines on the Pacific. Even governments were becoming alarmed. The government of Peru, for instance, was talking of sponsoring a similar protest voyage into the test zone.

'That would be fantastic,' said Pete, imagining a whole armada of boats.

It was Edith who made the suggestion of leading a march to

Paris. 'I can't twiddle my thumbs,' she said indignantly. 'I want to do something too.'

Emlyn fell in love with the idea. 'If we went to Belgium first, we could link up with more marchers from there . . .'

Very shortly, in the same way that the idea of the voyage had grown, so did the concept of staging a march upon Paris. 'It could be colossal,' said Bob, glowing with enthusiasm. 'Just imagine, a march going from country to country, crossing national frontiers.'

'The army of the good,' Joe whispered. He could see them in his mind's eye, he could hear them singing and the sounds of their feet on the road, a column stretching for miles; pilgrims in search of peace.

'Who shall I write to about that?' Angie asked eagerly, pencil poised over her pad.

Names were suggested and Joe's filing cabinets were emptied for appropriate addresses. Every idea they had was with the intention of providing *extra* support for the voyage. They could do little about the voyage itself until they heard from Eric. Nick had already enrolled at night school to learn more about radio, Joe had started exercising every morning to strengthen further his arms, and Liz generally fretted. 'What else can I do? I can cook now, there's no point in me going to cookery classes.'

They spent New Year's eve together. 'To *The Dove*,' said Emlyn, raising his glass, 'and all who sail in her.'

'To 1972,' Joe added. 'May it bring us a great victory.'

One thing was sure. The new year promised to be the most eventful of their lives. No one thought then that they might not live through it. New Year's eve was a time of hope and optimism. The dark thoughts were to come later.

The first hint of the forces ranged against them came with Eric's first letter. It had been sent to Nick's flat, and was meant for them all. That evening, Nick roared into Arcadia Gardens like a despatch rider bringing news from the front. The opening pages were full of good news. With meticulous thoroughness Eric detailed the work he had put in hand on the boat, beginning with an overhaul of the engine and continuing with such items as installing auxiliary water tanks and the fitting of a new propeller. Although he was doing a good deal of the work himself, inevitably his list of purchases was extensive – a new barometer,

456

a spare sextant, spare warps, extra rigging, a portable twelve-volt generator for emergency standby, binoculars, extra tools for the tool kit, and so on. Receipts were enclosed for every item.

'Goodness,' said Liz, 'that makes me feel awful. Doesn't he think we trust him?'

'It's just Eric's way,' Pete reassured her. 'Everything ship-shape and above board.'

'Quite right,' said Joe, even more impressed with his skipper.

Further good news was that Eric had made contact with CND in New Zealand. 'I've been overwhelmed with offers of help,' he wrote. All sorts of people have called round to lend a hand, so to say I'm doing a lot of work myself isn't quite true. Really I'm just the foreman and the volunteers have taken over . . .'

The bad news came in a few paragraphs on the last page. 'I'm getting a lot of flak from government departments – it's hard to explain but every official I come up against seems determined to make complications. I've sailed a dozen boats out of New Zealand and never had any trouble before. This time is definitely different. Officials keep finding reasons to double-check this and that, or to confer with a colleague, anything to delay me. It's happening too often to be coincidence. I don't want to sound paranoid, but I'm beginning to think the government would like to stop this voyage if they could. Dad agrees with me. Before he retired he was a civil servant so he's got some idea of how the government goes about getting its own way. He says it's like being stopped by a bad-tempered traffic cop, if he wants to book you he'll book you for something even if he has to tear your car apart . . .'

'Blinking bureaucrats,' Edith snorted.

'– Dad's advice is to make sure I get every form filled in, in triplicate, so as not to give them any excuse. That's what I'm doing. I don't want you to worry but I'm beginning to think our voyage may have blown up into a political storm by the time you arrive . . .'

Eric's final paragraphs were more reassuring. '. . . Most of the press are on our side . . . local CND people are bombarding the papers with letters protesting about the French tests . . . if they keep this up I don't think the government will dare stop us from sailing.'

'Thank goodness for that,' said Joe. Even so, he was left wondering why the New Zealand government should even contemplate stopping them. 'I thought they'd be on our side.'

It was a worry to contemplate making the long journey down to New Zealand only to be refused permission to sail.

January and February flew past. More letters arrived from Eric, full of reports of excellent progress, but all with the underlying worry that the government might intervene in some way at the last moment. In one letter he enclosed a press clipping culled from an Auckland paper:

They Sail at Own Risk – says Prime Minister

. . . the arrest of people who sail into the French nuclear test zone was a 'hypothetical question at this point' said Prime Minister Marshall today. He said any person who sailed into international waters was free to do so but if anyone sailed into the French test area he would do so at some risk . . .

'Some risk!' Nick exploded. 'His government should be doing something to stop it.'

Joe scratched his head. 'What does it mean about arresting people who sail into the French test zone? Who's going to arrest us? The government of New Zealand? For what? Apparently even the Prime Minister agrees that anyone is allowed to sail into international waters.'

Pete was frowning over Eric's letter. 'There's a bit here I don't understand. I think the strain's getting to Eric.'

Eric had written: '. . . regarding the arrangements for you to come down on the twentieth of April, perhaps you could make it a week earlier and spend a few days getting used to the boat. If you discuss this with Joe I'm sure he'll understand.'

Nick looked at Joe. 'What's that supposed to mean? We're due there on the third. We were going to spend a week on the boat anyway. We sail on the tenth.'

Pete shrugged. 'He just got muddled up. Write back and tell him to buy a new calendar.'

Everyone laughed except Joe who had taken the letter from Pete and was staring at it with a puzzled frown. 'From what I've seen of Eric,' he said, 'he's not the type to get muddled up. Especially about the date we're due in New Zealand. And why

458

discuss it with me in particular? He's never said anything like that before?'

As he looked up he caught the look on Liz's face and realized they shared the same thought. Liz coloured slightly. 'We told him about the time you gave a wrong date on the phone. Remember, for the demonstration at Ruislip?'

Even Joe was shocked. His voice fell to a whisper. 'He doesn't trust the post. That's what he's telling us. He thinks they're opening his mail.'

'Dear God!' Edith exclaimed.

'I can see what he's doing,' said Joe with rising excitement. 'He's telling us to get there a week early and making them believe we don't plan to sail until after the twentieth.'

'Who's "them"?' Pete demanded.

'The New Zealand government,' said Liz.

Joe was thinking about that. 'Or the British government,' he said. 'They've intercepted my mail before.'

'But Eric wrote to my address, not here,' said Nick.

They stared at each other, trying to fathom the implications. Finally, they decided that Nick had been on so many anti-Vietnam and CND demonstrations that Special Branch were almost certain to have his address. 'And you've phoned here often enough,' Joe pointed out with a wry grin. 'No doubt even your voice is on tape somewhere in New Scotland Yard.'

Apart from being worrying, none of their speculations helped them to understand Eric's letter. The only thing they agreed upon was that Joe was right and that Eric would never make a mistake about their departure date for Mururoa. His reference to the twentieth must have been a deliberate attempt to mislead.

Eventually, Joe dictated the answer to Nick. 'Write and say we'll be there seven days early, and point out that seven days early will make it the thirteenth of April –'

'Whereas,' Liz pointed out, 'seven days early actually means we'll get there on the twenty-seventh of March.'

Joe nodded. 'If we've got this all wrong, we can rely on Eric to send us a cable asking if we've gone off our heads.'

Nick said, 'I take it you don't expect a cable?'

'Do you?'

Nick thought for a moment, then shook his head.

'Bloody hell,' muttered Pete, 'you'd think we were the

criminals. The French are the ones breaking international law, not us.'

After a final cup of coffee, Nick and Pete donned their leathers and set off on Nick's bike to the West End, leaving the Milfords and Liz to worry and wonder. Edith, especially, was in a fretful mood as she washed up the supper things. Dark thoughts piled up in her head like heavy rain clouds on the horizon. Her worries about the sea were being held at bay by her faith in Eric's skill as a sailor – but now he was sending letters in code and hinting that political forces were massing against them.

Later, in bed, she made a final attempt to dissuade Joe from embarking on the voyage. 'Why not march to Paris with me? I'm sure Eric will find plenty of volunteers in New Zealand. You'll still be making a protest –'

Even as she spoke she knew she was wasting her time.

Joe put down the navigation manual that had become his bedtime reading and gave her a smile. 'Stop worrying. We've been through all this before –'

'Then at least let Liz stay behind. She'll listen to you. It's not just the voyage, though goodness knows that's worry enough, but what about her and Dawn? We're behaving deceitfully, Joe. We've never done it before. It's getting me down, especially with Dawn working so hard to bring the family together . . .'

Joe weakened. He knew it was true. They *were* behaving deceitfully and his conscience was badly troubled about Dawn. Yet if anyone had a right to sail on *The Dove* it was Liz – her money had made everything possible.

He sighed. 'Whatever we do we'll let one of them down. The truth is I don't know what to do for the best.'

'Do what your conscience tells you. You feel as bad as I do about this . . .' Edith went on at some length, pressing her arguments until finally Joe promised to talk to Liz in the morning.

'But I don't look forward to it,' he grumbled as he switched out the light.

Talking to a brick wall would have been more profitable than talking to Liz. 'It's my life, my money, and it was my idea in the first place,' she said. 'I don't know why we keep discussing it. I'm going.'

Even so, behind the show of bravado she knew she was still walking her tightrope. Her every action was designed to buy time. She had delayed offering to finance the voyage until her mother had left London, and now she used the excuse of not wanting to upset Dawn by writing to her in Australia. 'She's in the middle of a film,' Liz said. 'She'll only worry. Let's wait until she comes home, I can explain properly when I see her.'

Letters had arrived nonstop from Dawn, first from Japan, then from Australia. Letters, photographs, Christmas cards, presents – Dawn was making sure she was not forgotten during her absence.

'I'm happy for her,' Liz said to Joe, 'really I am. And I'm pleased she's marrying Keir . . .'

Mention of Keir's name was still rare in Arcadia Gardens. It could bring a scowl to Joe's face, though since he had agreed to go to the wedding, Edith had risked his wrath increasingly often. Determined to end the family feud, she was now of the same opinion as Dawn. The quarrel had lasted too long. 'Life's too short to harbour bad feelings,' she said, 'especially against your own son.' Liz also wanted an end to the quarrel. She missed Keir more than anyone, something she had tried explaining to Nick, not that Nick understood. Nick was like Joe. 'People are either with you or against you,' was Nick's view. There were no in-betweens.

'You can still *love* someone,' Liz had argued, 'without approving of everything they do.'

'. . . and I'm glad we're going to the wedding,' Liz continued to Joe. 'I want us all to be friends.'

'Right,' Edith agreed quickly, 'which is why we're so worried about you and your mother.'

'I know,' said Liz, taking her hand, 'and I'm worried too. I don't want to quarrel with her. But I was thinking . . . She must have started on the stage at my age. She was only a year or so older when she had me –'

As always, Edith shied away from the subject. 'That's got nothing to do with it.'

'What I'm trying to say,' Liz persisted, 'is she did what she wanted to do. She wanted to be an actress and that was it as far as I can make out. Nothing ever stopped her from doing what she wanted.'

Edith protested, 'This is different –'

'This is a lot more important,' said Liz hotly.

She was unyielding. Her only concession was that she would tell her mother, 'When she gets back. We'll have an awful scene, but it won't make any difference. I'm still going.'

Afterwards, alone with Edith, Joe laughed. 'You've got yourself to blame. You bought her up to think for herself –'

'And you didn't, I suppose? You know what will happen? Keir will blame us –'

'Oh, will he?' Joe went red in the face. 'In that case I'll tell you something. I don't mind being blamed for Liz. I'd be *proud* to be blamed for Liz. It's being blamed for him that would upset me.'

In a sense they were all walking a tightrope, especially when Dawn returned to London on 2 March. Every day they expected her to visit. Every day they expected a confrontation between her and her daughter in which they would be trapped in the middle.

Luckily, no such visit and no such confrontation occurred. Instead, Dawn telephoned to say she was going to Carrickfergus until the day before the wedding. 'I'm on my knees after making that film, and that flight from Australia is perfectly awful. If I don't rest for a few days I shall positively keel over. And there's no way I can rest here. Eric's getting the place ready for the reception. He seems determined to knock down every wall in the house . . .'

Only as she replaced the telephone did Edith realize that the single chance remaining to tell Dawn about the voyage would be on the day of her wedding. 'They'll be off on their honeymoon immediately after, and you'll be gone by the time they get back,' she said to Liz, horrified at the way things had worked out.

Joe said, 'You must tell her. I'm sorry, Liz, but you did promise.'

'You'll have to tell her at the reception,' said Edith.

Seven

And so they were married: Keir Hardie Milford to Dawn Mary Wharton.

No one doubted their happiness as they stood receiving their guests at Lord North Street. Keir had won the prize he had always wanted, and if Dawn had been hesitant in times past she was hesitant no longer. The new Mrs Milford, to quote the *Evening News*, 'looked even more radiant as a real-life bride than when she played Alice Black in *The Passage of Time*.

The *Evening News* story continued –

. . . rarely in recent years has such a diverse and cosmopolitan group gathered at a London wedding. Seen entering the couple's elegant Westminster home for the reception were Cabinet Ministers, Members of Parliament, senior civil servants and serving officers of Her Majesty's Forces. Most embassies in London were represented, while from the world of show business came stars too numerous to mention . . .

The house on Lord North Street fairly bulged at the seams. The upstairs drawing-room, large enough for fifty guests to drink cocktails in comfort, was no match for the two hundred and twenty invited. Eric, organizer of everything down to the last canapé, had longed for the open spaces of the ballroom at Carrickfergus. 'Fly them over in a Jumbo,' had been his suggestion, but he had set to work with a will when his idea was rejected.

Every room on the ground floor had been pressed into service. The double doors to the dining-room had been removed, as had those of the library opposite, to form a space double the size of the drawing-room above, with the hall in the middle and the staircase rising out of that. John's pantry-cum-office further down the hall had been turned into a bar, and a three-piece ensemble played music from hit musicals in the space under the staircase. Pink and white flowers decorated every niche, nook and cranny. Baskets of pink fuschias and creamy white stephanotis were suspended from the first-floor ceiling to hang over the hall like a false ceiling made entirely from flowers.

Waiters flitted back and forth with trays loaded with glasses of champagne . . .

Into this gathering came seventeen-year-old Liz Wharton, arriving by taxi with Joe, Edith and Nick.

'I promised to go to the wedding,' Joe grumbled as the taxi drew to a halt. 'No one said anything about any reception –'

'You can't go to one without the other,' said Edith. 'Besides it was a lovely wedding –' She broke off, catching sight of John Westwood on the step. 'Oh, there's John now. And don't forget,' she gave her husband a warning glance. 'No politics.'

John opened the door and helped Edith alight. 'Good afternoon, Mrs Milford. It's been a lovely day for the wedding.'

'Hasn't it, John? We've been lucky, considering it's still March.'

John's eyes twinkled as Liz stepped onto the pavement. 'May I say you look very pretty today, Miss Wharton?'

All at once it came back to her; John and this house and all they had meant to her. She had spent her 'growing-up years' climbing the three steps to the front door and waiting for John to answer the bell. 'Oh, John, I have missed you. How's Barbara?'

He grinned. 'In for the biggest shock of her life. She's expecting that schoolgirl. You know, the one with pigtails –'

'I *never* wore pigtails,' she exclaimed, as always rising to the bait of his teasing.

By then Nick had helped Joe into his chair and they were ready to move into the house. John Westwood lent a hand and he and Nick lifted Joe in his chair up the three steps and into the hall.

Liz's eyes rounded with wonder at the scene inside the front door. This was the house as she had never seen it before. The scent of stephanotis filled the air and elegantly dressed people filled the floor and the stairs and the landing above.

The happy couple had greeted their other guests in the drawing-room, but they came downstairs to greet Joe. Father and son shook hands for the second time that day – for the second time in more than three years.

'You're a very lucky man to have Dawn for your wife,' said Joe gravely. He had said the same at the wedding earlier; congratulating his son, but not his daughter-in-law, Joe was not ready to go that far.

Edith was and so was Liz. Edith had wept at the wedding and hugged them both. 'Look after each other,' she had choked, with tears streaming down her face.

Liz had shed a tear too, overwhelmed at seeing Keir again. Keir had clung to her, telling her how grown-up she looked and that they would always be friends in the future.

'It's a new start,' Dawn had said, her eyes shining, 'a new start for the whole family.'

Now, standing just inside the library, surrounded by people, seeing the happiness on her mother's face, Liz wondered whether she could go through with it. 'I can't tell her,' she whispered in panic to Edith, 'I can't spoil today for her, it would be awful.'

Dawn was with them before Edith could reply. 'Edith, darling,' she said, taking her mother-in-law into her arms, 'I didn't have a chance to tell you before, but that hat looks absolutely perfect.'

Watching them, Joe smiled, pleased that after all these years his wife and Dawn had become friends. Dawn deserves it, he thought, raising his face as she turned to kiss him.

As she hugged her daughter, Dawn whispered, 'Keir and I have something very special to tell you later. We'll slip away by ourselves in an hour.' Standing back, she smiled. 'Oh, darling, I'm so happy. I'll see you again in a minute. I must circulate for a while longer.'

Liz felt like Judas in the gardens at Gethsemane. She gave no thought to what her mother would tell her. Whatever it was would be swamped by her own news. The next half-hour was an agony of anticipation. Whenever she saw her mother across the room, her heart leapt, fearing that the time had come for them to slip away. Joe talked to her, Edith chattered, Nick squeezed her arm. Liz scarcely noticed. Thoughts went round and round in her head. *I should have written to her in Australia. Edith was right. I can't break the news now.* Every time a waiter passed with a tray, she helped herself to a glass of champagne, drinking absent-mindedly, thinking only of what she would say to her mother.

An hour passed. Other people spoke to her. She said yes and no and laughed a lot. She drank more champagne. Her mother was nowhere to be seen. A waiter offered her some canapés but the thought of food made her gag. She drank some more champagne. Her mother still hadn't come for her. Any minute now, she told herself. And when a hand fell on her shoulder, she nearly jumped out of her skin.

'Hey, little lady, I didn't mean to startle you.'

Turning, she saw a big man with a beaming smile. Releasing her shoulder, he held out his hand. 'Name's Chuck Hayes,' he said, 'Beaumont Aviation. I just had to come across and say hello.'

'Hello,' she said as he took her hand.

'Who'd have believed it?' he asked, shaking his head. 'Who'd have *believed* it?' Still holding her hand, he half-turned as he caught sight of a short, dark man. 'Sam! Come over here, Sam. You got to meet this little lady. Ain't she just something?'

The short man took her hand away from the big man and shook it, while staring hard into her face.

The big man laughed. 'You don't know who she is, do you? Go on, Sam, admit it.'

'I'm afraid not,' said the little man, still staring.

'She's Dawn's daughter. Can you believe that?'

'Dawn's daughter?' Sam looked astonished. 'You mean Keir's Dawn?'

'That's right. Can you believe it? Eighteen next birthday. Right, little lady?'

Every time he called her 'little lady' she winced. 'My name's Liz,' she said.

'I know.' The big man nodded genially. 'Dawn's been – I mean, your mother's been telling me all about you.'

'Pleased to meet you,' said the small man. 'I'm Sam Pickard. Keir and I work together. You could say we're Beaumont Aviation everywhere outside the States.'

The name registered properly then. Beaumont Aviation, makers of guided missiles. The cause of her estrangement from Keir.

466

'Eighteen,' said the big man, shaking his head, 'with your whole life ahead of you, eh? What you going to do with it, little lady? Become an actress like your mother?'

The last 'little lady' did it. The previous ones had set her teeth on edge. The previous ones had stoked up her mounting hysteria about facing her mother. The last 'little lady' turned the screw until it snapped.

'I might never see eighteen,' she said. 'I might be killed by a nuclear bomb.'

The big man gaped.

The small man choked on his champagne.

'That's what I'm doing in June,' Liz blurted out, unable to stop once she had started, 'sailing into the French nuclear tests in the Pacific. Trying to keep the world safe from people like you.'

'Oh, my God,' Edith groaned, clutching her arm. Joe and Nick, a few yards away, swivelled towards her. As she turned, Liz saw Dawn and Keir bearing down on her, their smiles frozen in shock, Keir's face already darkening with anger.

Dawn dealt with the situation. Taking a firm grip on Keir's left arm, she swivelled him around in his tracks, directing him towards the staircase to where Marcel Lappière, the Belgium Air Attaché, was talking to his French opposite number. 'Marcel! Darling!' Dawn gave him her cheek while slipping her other arm through his and guiding him onto the staircase. Not for a second did she release Keir's left arm. 'We were just talking about you, weren't we, darling? Keir was saying he hadn't seen you in ages . . .' It took her ten minutes – smiling all the time, saying hello to other guests they passed on the stairs – to steer Keir and Marcel to a corner of the drawing-room. It took her another ten minutes to satisfy herself that he would remain there. Then, excusing herself, she hurried downstairs, only to find that Liz and the others had gone . . .

Edith had acted quickly. She had seen the murderous look on Keir's face. 'Excuse us,' she said to Chuck Hayes, gripping Liz by the arm and propelling her towards the front door. 'Joe! Nick!' She delivered the names like bullets, without reason, for Nick had reacted equally swiftly and was already easing Joe's chair through the throng.

'Going so soon?' asked John at the door.

Once in the taxi, Liz burst into tears.

Back at the house, Keir escaped Marcel Lappière and went in search of his wife. Not finding her downstairs, he retraced his steps to the drawing-room, and thence upstairs to the bedrooms. His anger dissolved at the sight of her tears. 'Darling,' he cried. Crossing the room to where she sat at the dressing table, he took her into his arms.

'The guests,' she sobbed. 'Oh, Keir, you must get back to our guests.'

Ten minutes later, they both returned to their guests, and if Dawn's eyes were a shade brighter and her cheeks a shade paler, no one was the wiser for that.

Luckily – or otherwise – they could only mingle another half-hour, for they were due at Heathrow at five, where their pilot and co-pilot awaited, their flight plan to Marrakesh already logged. Two days to explore Marrakesh, then on to Kenya for the honeymoon proper – a seventeen-day safari, seventeen nights under an African moon.

Even so, Keir almost diverted the car on the way to the airport. He wanted to go to Ealing, 'to deal with this nonsense once and for all.'

It was Dawn who protested. One setback on her wedding day was one too many. She had rehearsed what she would say to Liz a dozen times over, although, 'Keir is your father' didn't need rehearsing. It was everything that went with it that needed words.

'Please, Keir, leave it until we get back, I've had enough, I don't want to argue today.'

His hands clenched into fists. 'Will we ever get that child away from my father? I'm sick of him poisoning her mind.'

'Keir, *please* –'

'Insulting Chuck –'

'I saw Chuck. I calmed him down and apologized.'

'What was that nonsense about the French tests in the Pacific?'

'In June. Liz said June. Darling, that's months away. Please. I promise we'll sort it out when we get back.'

Keir slumped back into his seat with a sigh. 'You're right. Sorry. It's just that –'

'I know,' she said, taking his hand, 'but let's forget it for now. Just think, in a few hours we'll be in Marrakesh.'

Being transported in secluded luxury to a different world was a big help. They made love on the plane and were in a quite different mood that evening when they arrived in the ancient red-walled city.

'Forget everything for a few days,' Dawn had entreated her husband. And forgetting was easy in the oasis city, with the snow-capped peaks of the High Atlas towering above the gardens and the palm trees. Forgetting became even easier as they soaked up the sun, exploring the souks by day and being entertained every evening by whirling dancers and acrobats and snake charmers. And forgetting became yet easier still when they flew on to Nairobi, where their white guide and black servants took them over dusty roads and sun-scorched grasslands to show them impala and zebras, and elephants and lions, and how to make camp in the evening and break camp every morning . . .

It was a different life under the African sun: less complicated, less damaged by the follies of man. The nights too were different: relaxing by the camp fire under a sky glittering with stars, listening to strange sounds carried on the soft air.

Dawn had expressed doubts about a safari. It was so beyond their experience – 'Darling, it's just not us. We're city people, used to the bright lights,' she had said when Keir had first floated the idea. 'How wrong I was,' she admitted on the third day . . . and the fourth day . . . and the fifth . . .

Eight

But even as Dawn and Keir relaxed and made love, fell in love with each other all over again, and fell in love with Africa for the first time, a sleek airliner cut through the blue skies above them.

After an emotional farewell at Heathrow, where they were seen off by Edith and a host of supporters, Joe and Liz, Nick and Pete were making the first leg of their journey. London to Muscat, and thence on to Singapore, then Sydney, until finally –

thirty-one hours after leaving London – they would land at Christchurch International Airport.

They were all nervous, especially Liz. She had to pinch herself to remember it was really happening. Until then she had feared the idea would fall through, or that someone would stop her at the last moment. Once on the aircraft she knew it was true; they were really going, travelling half-way round the world to fight the enemy.

Tired after being cramped for hours in their seats, it was Joe who revived their spirits. At one point Pete said to Nick, 'Sitting down all the time wears you out, doesn't it?'

'I've often thought that,' replied Joe.

One look at his deadpan expression sent them into howls of uncontrollable laughter. So although they arrived in Christchurch weary, they were in good humour and looking forward to seeing Eric.

It was something of a shock to meet him at the airport. He looked wan and haggard, weighed down by worry. Nick jumped to the conclusion that something had happened to the boat.

'No, the boat's fine,' Eric answered, 'it's the bloody government that's a pain in the arse.'

He recounted some of his worries as he drove them to his home. 'Thank goodness you had the sense to read between the lines in my letters,' he said. 'I don't know whether my mail's being opened or my telephone's bugged, but the government's been breathing down my neck ever since they got wind of this voyage.'

At his home in the Christchurch suburbs, they met Eric's father – a widower, tall and sprightly in his mid-sixties, white-haired and lean. Mr Searle was an enthusiastic weekend sailor who had passed on to his son a love of the sea.

Liz liked him instantly. He showed her to her room. 'I expect you're whacked out after your journey,' he said. 'We figured all you'd want tonight was a wash, some supper and bed.'

'Bless you,' Liz said smiling, 'I think I could sleep the clock round –'

'Scrub round supper if you like.'

'Oh no,' she protested, not wanting to appear rude. 'Give me twenty minutes to freshen up and I'll be down.' Later, tired though she was, she was glad she had gone down for supper. Once they were all round the table, Eric embarked on a council-of-war. 'I could only hint at things in my letters,' he said, 'but the government's been pulling every trick in the book to scupper this voyage, right, Dad?'

Mr Searle agreed. Looking at Joe, he said, 'I'm afraid I still think they'll find a way to stop you, even now. Your voyage is an embarrassment, especially at the moment.'

'Why now especially?' asked Joe.

Instead of answering, Mr Searle got up and went to the sideboard to fetch a copy of that morning's newspaper. 'Read it for yourself,' he said, passing it to Joe. An article on the front page had been circled in red.

France Organizes Loan for New Zealand

It was confirmed in Paris yesterday that a consortium of international banks have finalized arrangements to provide New Zealand with a loan of seventy-five million francs. This will be the first loan that New Zealand has ever raised in France and is an indication of the close financial and trading links now being forged between Wellington and Paris . . .

Joe swore when he read it. From his inside pocket he pulled another piece of newsprint torn from one of the London papers the day they left Heathrow. 'Read that,' he said, passing it to Mr Searle. Mr Searle read it aloud.

Paris Buys Peru's Silence on Tests?

In a shrewd move to quell mounting Peruvian unease about the forthcoming French nuclear tests in the Pacific, an announcement was made in Paris today that credits of sixty million US dollars will be made available to the Lima government . . .

'They're paying people off,' Joe said grimly, 'buying silence with blood money.'

'Crafty bastards,' Eric muttered viciously.

His father shook his head sadly. 'They must think they can buy everyone in the world.'

471

It was a gloomy meeting, made worse for the new arrivals by feeling so tired. Liz was grateful to get to her bed.

Her spirits revived the following day when she met some of the people who refused to be bought. Down on the jetty, taking her first look at *The Dove*, she was amazed by the number of people helping to get the boat ready.

'This is nothing,' Mr Searle told her, 'you should have been here when the real work was going on. Dozens of people turned up, all wanting to help, and they did. Everyone pitched in. They did a marvellous job.'

And still they came, every day, a steady stream of people bearing food and provisions and all sorts of gifts. Housewives and bank-clerks, typists and managers, whole families, some bringing their children, just to look at the boat that would sail out to face the Bomb. Sailors and yachtsmen came, furious that the French should illegally cordon off 100,000 square miles of international waters. All types of New Zealanders came, many ashamed that their own government thought raising loans and selling butter was more important than causing genetic damage to the next generation. And as they talked about the petitions they were raising, Liz felt the same love around her that she had first sensed on the road from Aldermaston, feelings never forgotten and re-experienced many times since.

The Dove was tiny. Even though Liz had seen photographs on Eric's wall, she had imagined the boat to be bigger. It seemed impossible to believe that this tiny wooden craft would carry them three thousand miles – and three thousand miles back again if they survived the nuclear blast.

Eric took them out that day, and the next, sailing up and down gentle coastal waters to get them used to the boat. It took Liz all of that time to learn to duck her head in the saloon to avoid the beams, and to protect her shins from the heavily gimballed table. When she counted the berths she found only four, not the six Eric had talked of in London. 'There are six,' he confirmed, 'but the forward cabin is full of stores.'

It was, too. The tiny space was packed tight with potatoes and onions and canned food. 'So where do we all sleep?' asked Liz.

Eric grinned. 'One of us will be on watch, so we only need four berths. You'll learn,' he said. 'After a few days at sea you'll just

472

fall into the nearest empty bunk and be grateful for a chance to get your head down.'

Eric only relaxed when on the boat. On land he was nervy and tense, every hour expecting more trouble from the government. On the third day, again out on the boat, he made his announcement. Calling them together, he said, 'We're sailing tomorrow night.'

Everyone voiced surprise. Even though the dates had been moved forward, the plan had always allowed for a week's familiarization on the boat. Their official sailing date was still eight days away. The local CND were planning a big send-off.

'I know,' said Eric, 'and I feel bad about misleading the CND people, but you heard Dad the other night. He used to work for the government and he's bloody certain they'll step in at the last minute. And so am I. So far we've had hassle from the Marine Department, the police, customs, and just about every official with the right to ask questions and a good many who haven't. They even sent people from the marine radio department for a radio inspection. There's no such thing as a radio inspection. There never has been. I don't know what they'll come up with next, but they'll think of something. Especially now you've arrived. They know we've got a full crew. They might even suspect we'll slip away early.'

A shiver ran up Liz's spine. Courage had come easily back home in Arcadia Gardens. The plan was simplicity itself. To sail to Mururoa and position *The Dove* in the direct line of fall-out from the nuclear blast. *The ultimate protest*. Looking at the others, she could see they were scared. Nick bit his lip and Pete chewed a finger nail. It was the moment of truth for them all. Only Eric seemed confident that to set sail as soon as possible was the right thing to do. Liz knew that everything was ready. Pete had been full of praise about the advanced state of preparations ever since he had arrived. Nick had checked over the diesel engine and pronounced himself satisfied with the radios. Every spare inch on *The Dove* was crammed with food and provisions. If the government was preparing itself to intervene at the last moment, Liz had to admit that the new plan made sense.

Eric looked at Joe. 'Sorry, Mr Milford, it's a bit unfair on you and Liz. You both deserve more time. No one would blame you if you decided to drop out.'

They all looked at Joe. Over the three days he had adapted amazingly well. His biggest embarrassment was at the quayside where Nick and Pete had to carry him aboard under the eyes of the onlookers, most of whom expressed sympathy or shock that a man with his disability should be allowed to embark on such a voyage. Once out of the harbour, however, Joe was already proving himself capable of everything required of him.

'Thank you, Eric,' he said with simple dignity, 'but I'd count it an honour to serve as one of your crew.'

Liz flinched when they all turned to her. She laughed and raised her face to the sky to avoid them seeing the fear in her eyes.

'Liz.' Joe reached out for her hand. 'You've got your whole life in front of you –'

'No,' she stopped him and recovered control of her nerves, 'I'm coming too. Please, Joe, let's not even discuss it.'

Nick came over and put his hand on her shoulder. 'That's it then, Skipper,' he said to Eric. 'We sail tomorrow night. You've got your full crew.'

It was a subdued supper at Eric's home that evening, and when Mr Searle raised his glass to toast 'The Dove and all who sail in her,' Liz thought the words sounded more sombre than when Emlyn had expressed exactly the same wish in Arcadia Gardens.

As always, Joe raised everyone's spirits. He produced the draft of a cable he wanted Mr Searle to send as soon as they set sail. It consisted of only a few words. Addressed to Edward Heath, Prime Minister of Great Britain and Northern Ireland, it read SAILING FOR MURUROA AS NUCLEAR PROTEST. ASSUME YOU WILL UPHOLD OUR RIGHTS AS BRITISH CITIZENS TO SAIL IN INTERNATIONAL WATERS. WE APPEAL FOR YOUR PERSONAL SUPPORT. LIZ WHARTON AND JOE MILFORD ON BOARD THE DOVE.

As he grinned across the table at Mr Searle, Joe said – 'I'd be grateful if you'd send a similar cable on behalf of your son to the Prime Minister of New Zealand, another one to the President of the United States for Nick, and one to Prime Minister Trudeau in Canada for Pete.'

Everyone thought it was a marvellous idea.

'Sort of balances up the odds, don't you think?' Joe concluded. 'And after all, the governments of America, Britain, Canada and New Zealand have a *duty* to protect their citizens.'

It was a perfect note on which to go to bed.

The following afternoon Liz almost gave the game away. Eric had gone off to fuel the boat with Nick and Pete, leaving her at the house with Joe and Mr Searle, when three of the CND crowd called round with the news that more than 100,000 people had signed their petition protesting about the French tests. 'That deserves a glass of wine to celebrate,' said Mr Searle, 'sit yourselves down while I open a bottle.'

They sat down with the easy familiarity of friends, delighted with the success of their petition and hoping to obtain many more signatures. 'The target is twenty thousand more before you sail,' said Mabel Flint. 'Of course that's assuming you don't sail until next week.' Something in her voice alerted Liz to a hidden message.

'If you left before our little party we wouldn't mind, you know,' Mabel continued. 'We'll give you an even bigger one when you get back.'

Feeling obliged to respond, Liz laughed. 'That's nice of you, but we'll be there, don't worry.'

Mabel gave her a shrewd look, 'Well, of course you know best, my dear. It was just that some of us are worried about the government stepping in.'

Liz blushed. That was all she did. She flushed with embarrassment. Luckily Mr Searle returned with the wine at that moment and he commanded the conversation until Mabel and her friends left twenty minutes later.

Liz told Eric and Nick as soon as they returned. Eric exonerated her of any blame. 'Even so,' he said thoughtfully, 'Mabel's a shrewd old pussy with her ear to the ground. She knows the government are playing cat and mouse, it might have been a warning.'

Liz said, 'I got the strong impression that she *wanted* us to go early.'

Eric grinned. 'We won't disappoint her then, will we?'

When it was dusk they said goodbye to Mr Searle. Joe gave him a long letter to post to Edith. Liz kissed him goodbye, for it had been decided that it would be wiser for him to remain in the

475

house. Then Eric phoned the Customs, asking them to send someone down to clear *The Dove* in half an hour. 'They can't refuse,' he said when he replaced the phone. 'It's a risk of course. The news will get out. We'll just have to hope that all the civil servants are at home tucking into their dinner.'

When they reached the jetty they saw the usual crowd of people looking down at *The Dove*.She was riding heavily in the water, weighed down by the extra stores and provisions. The people of Christchurch had taken it upon themselves to watch over the boat at all hours, for Liz never boarded her without being cheered by a group of onlookers.

'What's up, Eric?' someone called as Eric clambered aboard.

'No problems,' he answered. 'We're just off for some night practice.'

His answer was unlikely to have fooled them, but when the Customs van drew up at that moment, all doubts disappeared. A hubbub of excitement arose on all sides. About to board, Liz felt a hand grip her arm. As she turned she met the shrewd grey eyes of Mabel Flint. 'Good luck, my dear,' she whispered, thrusting something into Liz's hand. 'It's a St Christopher that belonged to my father. It kept him safe through a lifetime at sea.' She gave Liz a quick hug before surprising her further by hurrying off.

Liz called after her, 'Thank you!' But suddenly Mabel Flint seemed in a great hurry for she was already getting into a car some twenty yards away.

'Liz,' shouted Nick, holding out his hand from *The Dove*.

Next moment she was aboard, to other cries of 'Good Luck' from the crowd.

The gold St Christopher on its chain in her hand brought them instant luck for the Customs official turned out to be a friend of Eric's father. He checked and cleared the bonded goods within ten minutes. He too wished them luck and Liz could see by his eyes that he meant it.

Everything was happening too quickly for her to feel nervous. With the mooring ropes away, a breeze filled the sail and the figures on the quay began to fade into the gloom.

'Course east north-west,' Eric called to Pete in the cockpit.

The harbour lights winked and distant shouts carried over the water. 'Goodbye,' Liz whispered back under her breath.

Half an hour later an amazing thing happened. With Pete at

the helm, everyone else was in the saloon where Eric was opening a bottle of wine. The portable radio, tuned into a local station, was playing quietly in the background, when Pete shouted, 'Hey! Come and get a look at this.'

Liz had only just become aware of lights sweeping across the portholes. Once on deck she saw the reason. All along the shoreline, headlights of cars were being flashed on and off. Faintly she heard the sounds of horns being honked.

Last up on deck, clipping his harness on as he emerged, Joe shouted, 'The radio just announced our departure. People are phoning the station, asking for messages of good luck to be relayed.'

As Joe took over at the helm, the others stood on deck and waved. Liz waved until her arms ached. In response – for mile after mile – the shoreline blazed with the headlights of thousands of cars. Horns blared, creating a cacophony of sound which reached out across the water. Mabel Flint had organized her send-off after all.

Christchurch was saying goodbye.

Nine

Too agitated to sit down, Keir paced up and down the small room, fairly spitting with temper. 'How could you be so deceitful? To have planned all this and not told us. Doing it behind our backs –'

'We wanted to tell you,' Edith countered, spots of red marking her cheeks. 'Joe and I worried ourselves sick –'

'And remained silent,' Keir said in disgust.

They were in Joe's study – the fourth bedroom – at the bungalow. Edith had retreated behind the cheap wooden desk and trembled slightly while doing her utmost to put on a show of defiance. Dawn ignored the other chair and sank onto the convertible divan. She stared at the map of the Pacific Ocean pinned to the wall. 'You could have told me, Edith,' she said in a voice full of reproach. 'Surely you could have told me?'

Edith answered with an anguished look. 'We wanted to. Liz wanted to. She was screwing up her courage to tell you at your wedding –'

'Great!' Keir shouted. 'As if she didn't cause enough havoc.'

'Don't shout at me!' Edith said, shouting herself, clenching her hands into fists on the desk in an effort to stop shaking. Drawing a deep breath to recover, she turned her attention to Dawn. 'Liz would have told you. Then there was that awful scene and we left. Liz wept all the way home. By the time we got here and I made a cup of tea and calmed her down, Joe had decided to tell you himself. He did telephone, but by then you had left –'

'What a shame,' said Keir with heavy sarcasm, slumping into the chair.

It was Keir and Dawn's second day back in London. Keir had returned to a dozen messages from Sam Pickard. 'And now this,' he said, with his head in his hands. 'I still don't believe it.'

'What I don't understand,' Dawn said, 'is why Liz said June. She definitely said something about –'

'June 1 is when the French begin testing,' Edith explained. 'It will take them seven or eight weeks to get there –'

'Where are they staying in Christchurch?' Keir interrupted.

'With Eric's father –'

'Another lunatic parent,' Keir said angrily. 'No wonder the world's in a mess when –'

'You should be proud of her! And you should be proud of your father –' Edith broke off as Angie poked her head round the door.

'Betty's just made some tea,' said Angie. 'Do you want it in here or –'

'We'll have it in the living-room,' said Edith, feeling recovered enough to come out from behind the desk. 'Thanks, Angie.'

Arcadia Gardens had become General Headquarters. CND stickers adorned every window and leaflets about *The Dove*'s voyage could be seen in every room, awaiting collection by volunteers who would hand them out in shops and pubs and outside cinemas and along busy high streets. Angie and Betty had moved into the bungalow 'for the duration', partly to provide company for Edith, but mainly to answer the telephone and to make themselves generally useful.

'What the hell's that?' asked Keir, looking at the large map of western Europe spread over the living-room floor.

'You'll have to excuse the mess,' said Edith, lifting some leaflets out of a chair in order to sit down. 'We were working on the map when you arrived. It's for our march on Paris –'

'Dear God!' Keir exclaimed, turning to Dawn. 'It's an asylum. I tell you, this house is a bloody asylum!'

'Is it mad to want peace in the world?' Edith asked sharply.

'Don't start that again,' he said angrily, pointing to the map. 'Are you going on this march?'

Edith shook her head. 'I wanted to. It was my idea, but we agreed my best place was here taking messages and passing them on –'

'Thank Christ for that,' said Keir, sitting down heavily next to Dawn on the sofa. 'I'll tell you something now, for your own good –' He stopped as Angie and Betty entered the room, both carrying cups in each hand.

They contrasted oddly with Dawn's expensive elegance. Neither of the girls wore make-up; Betty's pony tail was held by an elastic band, Angie's feet were bare and her shirt and jeans were no match for Dawn's tailored chic. 'Is this private?' asked Betty, looking at Edith. Most meetings at Arcadia Gardens were communal affairs, with everyone joining in. Usually the meetings were between like minded-people. In the face of Keir's obvious anger, Betty was anxious to demonstrate solidarity with Edith.

'I was just saying,' Keir said icily, 'that anyone who's seen the French riot police in action would know better than to go anywhere near Paris –'

'Funny kind of democracy where they beat people up for carrying a placard.'

'More than beat you up. They'll half murder you.'

'It's my daughter I'm worried about,' Dawn blurted. Until then she had said very little. Still trying to absorb what had happened, her imagination stalled at the thought of Liz setting out in a small beat to sail half-way across the Pacific. 'I just can't get over it. Three thousand miles –'

'Eric's a very experienced sailor,' said Edith.

'And Pete knows what he's doing,' Angie added loyally.

Keir's face, bronzed by the African sun, went a deep shade of red. 'None of you know what you're doing. Can't you imagine the sort of operation the French are involved in? The investment is enormous, in time and money and national prestige. Do you think they'll take any notice of one little boat? I saw what the French did in Algeria. By Christ, their military don't go in for niceties. They won't be stopped by a senile old man, a girl and three other lunatics. They'll chop them into pieces and feed them to the sharks –'

'No!' Dawn cried. 'Don't even say something like that.'

Keir jumped up. 'I don't want any tea. I haven't time to drink it. Just give me this address in New Zealand.'

'Why?' asked Edith.

'Because I want it, that's why. I can find it for myself anyway. Searle, you said his name was, Eric Searle from Christchurch, New Zealand.'

Edith's lips compressed into a determined line.

'Very well,' said Keir decisively. 'Come on, Dawn, we've wasted enough time as it is.'

Outside in the car, Dawn clutched Keir's arm. 'You said that to frighten them, didn't you? The French wouldn't really do them any harm –'

'The French won't be stopped,' he said grimly. 'They've got too much riding on this.' Leaning forward, he tapped John on the shoulder. 'Get us to Toby Smart's office in Lincoln's Inn as quick as you can.'

Dawn asked in surprise, 'Why Smart's office?'

'To do what we should have done a long time ago. I want Liz in our custody with a court order barring my father from having anything to do with her –'

'You can't do that –'

'Let Smart be the judge of that. If we'd done this years ago –'

'Liz would never have forgiven us. She'd have hated us. We'll lose her.'

'We'll lose her anyway. Can't you get that into your head? If she's anywhere near that test area when the bomb goes off, Liz is dead!'

The savagery of his words brought a cry from Dawn's lips. Pulling away from him, she stared out of the window, struggling

480

to hold back her tears. New Zealand was so far away. Her inclination was to get the plane and fly down there, not waste time talking about court orders and things. She wanted to be with her daughter.

When she arrived at Smart's office, Dawn's legs shook and her strength seemed to desert her. 'This is not the right way,' she kept saying to Keir.

After listening carefully to what Keir had to say, Smart shook his head. 'It's not as easy as you seem to think. In effect, your father, with the mother's consent, has been the child's guardian for the whole of her life –'

'We're withdrawing that consent,' Keir interrupted. 'Liz is only seventeen. She's still a minor.'

'I understand, but you're not suggesting she was taken to New Zealand against her will, are you? She hasn't been kidnapped.'

Dawn cried, 'No, no, nothing like that!'

'That's what it amounts to,' said Keir angrily. 'She's been duped. Brainwashed if you like –'

'Oh Keir, stop it!' Dawn rose and went to the window, where she stood, desperate with worry, staring out into the spring sunshine.

The lawyer said, 'Everything gets more complicated when it's outside our jurisdiction. Of course, the law in New Zealand is very similar . . .' He sighed and paused for a long moment before saying, 'Sometimes the court can be persuaded to move quickly, for example if the child is at risk –'

'At risk!' Keir exclaimed. 'If taking her within range of a nuclear explosion isn't a risk –'

'Quite.' Smart nodded. 'I think what we have to do is apply for her to be made a ward of court –'

'What does that involve?' Dawn whirled round from the window.

Smart shrugged. 'In simple terms it means the court decides what happens to her. They'll listen to your side of the case, and to Mr Milford senior, but the principal consideration is what's best for the child.'

'That's what we want,' Keir said quickly.

Dawn imagined herself facing Joe across a courtroom and shuddered.

'Even that won't be easy,' said Smart, checking his watch. 'I

481

need to take advice from our associate in New Zealand to see if he agrees. It's almost midnight down there at the moment if I remember right. I think they're twelve hours behind –'

'Can you reach him at home?' Keir asked urgently.

Finally, Keir accepted Smart's suggestion to leave the problem with him for an hour. 'Go and have an early lunch,' said Smart.

They went to the pub on the corner, not to eat ('I'd throw up,' said Dawn), but to make short work of two very large brandies. By the time Keir returned to the table with more of the same, Dawn had made up her mind. 'Can Martin fly me down there?' she asked. 'I'd like to leave this evening if possible.'

Keir was about to reply when he saw Smart come through the door, obviously looking for them. One look at Smart's face was enough to know the news was not good. 'It's very bad,' he said. 'Our man wasn't too pleased to be woken up as you can imagine, but he knew all about your daughter. She left three days ago. I'm afraid *The Dove* has already sailed. It was in all the papers down there.'

Ten

The boat was really flying. Three days out from Christchurch, *The Dove* had made nearly five hundred miles, far in excess of Eric's estimated seventy miles a day. Liz found herself hanging on for dear life. Cruising in the gentle waters of Pelican Bay had not prepared her for this. She felt she was on the back of a runaway horse, racing at full gallop and out of control. Her shins were a mass of bruises and her arms were only marginally better.

It was cold on deck. Winter was in residence in the southerly latitudes. The steady force seven filled the sails with a chill wind that never stopped blowing. At the helm, Eric and Joe were clad in thick sweaters and oilskins. Eric whooped with excitement, a totally changed person since escaping the political tentacles of the New Zealand government on land. At sea, he was free. So was Joe. Clamped into the cockpit, he had discovered a freedom unknown since he lost the use of his legs. Not only was he quickly becoming a good helmsman but, under Eric's expert tutelage, he was learning the ancient skill of night navigation, which was just as well, for until Eric judged Joe to be ready the others were taking exhausting four-hour watches. Still heavy, *The Dove* wallowed in the troughs like a sea turtle before cresting fifteen-foot waves. The wind screamed through the rigging as the boat wallowed again, rolling now, her bow crashing through the waves, rising slowly, decks awash. The water had changed colour, no longer green, blue pyramids erupted, with the wind skimming the foam into blizzard-like plumes.

Liz was in a state of abject depression. Unable to keep her food down, she spent half her time in the head being violently sick. The head had become her sanctuary. The tiny space offered the only privacy on the boat. She spent more time there than the rest of the crew put together, most of it on her knees, huddled over the lavatory, her face down the pan, throwing up. When she had finished, she would roll over, gagging her tears, determined not to let them hear her weeping. Finally, feeling utterly drained, she would stagger upright to wash her face in the basin. She needed all her courage to try again. They had been right. She should never have come. Every fibre of her body ached to be back at Arcadia Gardens with Edith. The motion of the boat was endless. It never stopped. She felt her muscles bracing themselves all the time.

Cooking was impossible. How could anyone cook when the stove kept rising and falling and cupboards were constantly moving? On the second day she had spent four hours making a casserole, only to open the oven door as *The Dove* crested a wave. The casserole flew out to crash upside down on the floor. Joe had never heard her swear until then. Nick had only ever heard her say bloody, not the torrent of foul language that had poured from her lips. But it was either that or bursting into tears, and she was determined her tears would remain private. Everyone was very nice to her, very sympathetic, especially Nick. She was beastly to him. 'Leave me alone,' she had screamed when he tried to clean up the casserole from the floor. 'It's my job. Leave it to me!'

Afterwards, she told herself she was a cow. Poor Nick. She would make it up to him . . . if she lived . . . which seemed

483

increasingly unlikely. What upset her most was letting them down. Four hours at the helm, fighting that sea, was exhausting. They fell into the saloon, lines of tiredness etched on their faces. They needed hot food to keep up their strength. The very smell turned her stomach. Yet she kept at it, spending two hours to cook a single meal, resigned to the fact that when the sea was like this she could cook for only one person at a time.

There was no bedtime. Day or night made no difference. They slept when they could, including Liz who crawled into the nearest berth to curl up into a ball, and even then she didn't sleep properly: she merely rested. At least being wedged into a bunk stopped her from smashing her shins on the table. If only everything would stop, just for an hour, just for a few minutes . . .

But *The Dove* went on, crashing through the seas, closing the gap between them and Mururoa.

'They'll never reach Mururoa,' said Keir, jabbing his finger at the atlas, 'Henri says the entire French South Pacific Fleet is patrolling the zone. They've put everything within a hundred miles of the island under quarantine. The cordon's so tight not even a mouse could get through.'

He had spent the afternoon on the telephone, calling his contacts in Paris. Dawn had pleaded on the way back from Smart's office. 'Keir, you know these people. They're friends of yours. Surely you can do something?'

'I damn well intend to,' he had answered, going straight into the library and reaching for the phone.

Now, at six o'clock, Dawn was more in control of herself. Hysteria had receded. She had abandoned her plan to fly down to New Zealand. The urgency had evaporated with the knowledge that *The Dove* had put to sea. There was no point. Besides, with Keir's contacts, they could learn more in London.

'Drink?' he asked, coming out from his desk and going to the sideboard.

'Just a small one.'

Dawn had not eaten all day. Her entire afternoon had been spent in the library, listening to Keir's rapid-fire French, following his conversations more from watching his expression than

484

understanding his words. Now perhaps she could eat an omelette.

'Naturally the French are being very tight-lipped,' Keir said, pouring their whiskies. 'There's a big security clampdown. Henri was a bit coy on the phone but he'll open up in Paris tomorrow –'

'I'll come too,' she said quickly.

Keir looked surprised. Carrying the glasses over to the sofa, he sat down beside her. 'They won't let you in. Darling, you know what the French are like. They've been a law unto themselves ever since they pulled out of NATO. Henri's only seeing me because of the old pals' act.'

Taking her drink, Dawn shrugged. 'I'll wait at an hotel if you like. I can't stay here. I'd go mad, worrying about what's going on.'

'Relax.' Keir patted her knee and left his hand on her skirt, stroking her leg.

'Is he very important – your friend Henri?'

'Middling. The thing is he can open doors to people who are really important. Not that I think we need bother –'

'Of course we must.' She pushed his hand away angrily, too tense to accept his easy reassurance. 'Keir, that's our daughter out there. And your father. In a tiny boat half-way across the Pacific –'

'With at least six weeks to go before the first test,' he interrupted. 'Darling, that's what you must remember. Time's on our side. The French will find them –'

'Then what?'

'I suppose they'll tow them off to some safe place.'

'Didn't Edith say that was piracy? Something about international waters?'

'Don't take any notice of her. She's as mad as he is. How can it be piracy? The French aren't going to plunder their boat or anything. They'll simply make sure they are perfectly safe –'

'If they find them.'

'Darling,' he said, laughing, 'of course they'll find them. I told you what Henri said. Not even a mouse could get through that cordon.'

485

Eleven

Eric was tracing two lines on his charts, one *The Dove*'s true position, and the other the false position which Nick broadcast every night. Eric increased the deviation a little further every day. 'Our actual position will be two hundred miles to the south by the time we cross into the zone,' he forecast. Joe chuckled at the thought of French warships being sent on a wild goose chase. Of course there was a risk. Every plan carried a risk. Broadcasting false positions nullified any chance of being rescued if disaster overtook *The Dove*.

Such dangers seemed less likely that day. The wind had dropped considerably. The sea was easier. At mid-morning an excited Nick called Liz up on deck. 'Look,' he pointed as a school of porpoises appeared off the starboard bow. Close to the boat they left the water like projectiles, curving effortlessly into the sunshine before dipping back under the water with scarcely a splash. Liz was enthralled, fascinated by their dark and mysterious eyes, not at all the eyes of a fish.

Snuggling up to Nick in the cockpit, she was feeling stronger. The reduced motion of the boat, together with the sea-sick pills, had enabled her to eat a good breakfast. Nick hugged her. 'We'll make a sailor of you yet!'

Liz doubted that, but felt sufficiently well to want to try her hand at the tiller. Nick was delighted and for the next hour they remained in the cockpit, watching the porpoises and admiring the sea. Twelve hours earlier, Liz would have denied there was anything to admire, yet now she was compelled to marvel at the constantly changing ocean. Even the colour had changed. Leaving New Zealand the water had been a deep emerald green, here it was cobalt blue, with waves marching in white-spumed rows. Shafts of light fell from a sky streaked with clouds. Craning her neck, Liz looked at a sky bigger than she had ever seen, reminding her of a vast archless cathedral. 'It's so vast,' she said breathlessly. 'On land you've got something to measure yourself by: a house, a tree, buildings. But out here –' she laughed for the first time in days – 'I didn't know there was so much empty space in the world.'

For an instant she was happy. There was a timeless quality about that moment. Cuddled up to Nick, with the spray glistening on his face and his arm round her waist, they could have been any couple from any age, going back hundreds of years. A shadow came into her eyes as she thought of the mushroom-shaped cloud that would rise over Mururoa. Fear, not the wind, made her shiver. No one had ever sailed into a nuclear test zone before. No one could survive a nuclear explosion. Suddenly she was angry with the porpoises for being so trusting. *Go back*, she wanted to scream, *don't come with us, go back, go back* . . .

Her mood changed, she kissed Nick on the cheek and returned to her galley.

Later, they heard from Radio Australia that Paris had announced the tests would start on schedule. Wedged into his bunk, Joe put down his book and looked at the anxious faces around him. 'What else did you expect them to say?' he asked. 'Cheer up, my hearties. We'll win in the end.'

His grin warmed Liz to the marrow. There was something indomitable about Joe. Sailing out of Pelican Bay, with those thousands of headlights flashing and horns honking had given Joe the thrill of his life. 'See,' he had cried, pointing, 'there they are. You'll find them all over the world. The army of the good!'

Indeed, Radio Australia followed with an announcement that seemed to strengthen Joe's argument: 'Dock workers in Australia joined their counterparts in New Zealand today by blacking all French ships. No cargoes will be unloaded from any French ship from midnight on Sunday –'

'Oh ho!' Joe shouted. 'See how they like that in Paris!'

They spent hours listening to the radio, twiddling dials in an effort to find out what was happening elsewhere in the world. The snippets of good news began to mount up. The United Conference on the Environment was due to start in Stockholm in June.

'That's another thing to worry the French,' said Joe. 'They won't like that going on while they're polluting the world's atmosphere with radioactive dust.'

He was a source of constant encouragement. 'See those

porpoises today, Liz. They're a sign of good luck. All of us old sailors know that.'

Joe was quite sure of the outcome. Four or five days before the first test, the French would come looking for them. 'They'll warn us to get out, and when we refuse they'll tow us out of harm's way.'

They had already agreed on a policy of no cooperation. The French would have to take over *The Dove*. No one in the crew would lift a finger to help them.

'But first,' Nick said, grinning as he prepared to broadcast another false position, 'they'll have to find us.'

Having flown to Paris that morning, Dawn had spent the day cooped up in a suite at the Orly Hilton, adjacent to the airport. She had failed to persuade Keir to take her to his meetings, and eventually agreed that Henri Berguet might be more forth-coming without her, even though it meant condemning herself to hours of waiting.

'I'll try to be back for lunch,' were Keir's last words as he left the hotel.

At lunchtime she had sent down for sandwiches and coffee. At three o'clock she sent for more coffee and began to grow cross. 'At least he might have phoned me. He knows how worried I am . . .' At four o'clock, when he returned, she saw at once that he was as worried as she was. 'Darling,' she said, rising from the sofa, 'you look exhausted.'

Keir did look very tired. It was less his face, which was still tanned from the African sun, than the way he moved: sluggishly, with no spring in his step, and the way he slumped into an armchair.

Dawn put a hand on the coffee pot. 'It's still warm. Do you want –'

'Not likely. I've spent the day being fed coffee by secretaries whose bosses have done their best to avoid me. Most of them succeeded too,' he said bitterly, his eyes going to the bar in the corner. 'Fix me a drink, will you?'

As she curbed her impatience, Dawn went to the bar and poured a stiff whisky.

'What a bloody day,' he said, taking the glass.

'What happened?' she asked, sitting down opposite.

He swallowed a third of the whisky before he replied, 'The main thing is they're all right –'

'You mean Liz –?'

'That's right. This boat, *The Dove*, is sending out false information.' He broke off and shook his head. 'The bloody fools. Apparently they're saying they're in one place when they're in another. The idea is to throw the French off the scent. What they don't realize is the French have two of the most powerful tracking stations in the Pacific in Tahiti and New Caledonia. They've known the whereabouts of that boat ever since it left New Zealand.'

'Thank God!' Dawn declared. Her nightmare was that someone would declare the boat 'missing'. She looked at Keir. 'That's all right then, isn't it? They can simply turn it back, or tow it away, or whatever they do.'

He took another pull on his drink. 'Yes,' he said noncommittally, 'they could do that.'

The tone of his voice alerted her. 'There's more, isn't there? What else did they say? Tell me what happened.'

Keir had endured a day of utter frustration. His friend Henri had known little about the nuclear tests, and most of his attempts to push Keir up the line had failed. 'You'd have thought I had the plague. No one, but no one, wanted to see me.' Henri had persevered and at 2.30 Keir had been taken to see a rear admiral involved with the test programme – at the headquarters of the Centre des Expérimentations Nucléaires du Pacifique.

Keir's face darkened to a scowl. 'This rear admiral fairly roasted me. He said a man with my background should be able to control my own family. How did he know I wasn't another anti-nuclear nut, snooping around for restricted information? All that sort of stuff. He went on for about fifteen minutes without giving me chance to get a word in edgeways.' He paused to finish his drink. 'One thing became very clear. The French are absolutely furious about this boat. They've been conducting tests in the Pacific for seven years and no one's ever tried to stop them. There's no doubt *The Dove* is a source of acute embarrassment. This admiral fairly bristled with hostility. He told me about *The Dove* laying a false trail. Then he said something else. He said accidents happen at sea. Naturally, he said, when *The*

489

Dove enters the test zone, his ships will watch out for it. But if *The Dove*'s not where it claims to be, it could easily be run down in the night. He said no one would blame them. They've got big warships steaming up and down on legitimate business. His ships can't be expected to know *The Dove*'s three or four hundred miles out of position –'

'But they do know. You just said –'

'They'll deny it.' Keir ran a hand through his hair. '*The Dove*'s played right into their hands. The French will record its broadcasts about their position, then play 'em back to the world when an accident happens three or four hundred miles away. They'll have a perfect excuse –'

'Accident!'

'That's what the French will call it,' he said, going to the bar for another drink. Without having to ask, Keir poured one for Dawn. 'Of course, the bastard was trying to frighten me. I don't think they'd really do it.'

She took her glass from him, and searched his face. Her eyes met his. 'Don't lie to me, Keir. And don't treat me as the little woman.'

'Dawn –'

'You believed him, didn't you?'

'I believed him, yes. He was so hopping mad –'

'That he'd do it. He'd run that boat down in the night. Drown them. Murder them.'

'I can't really believe the French would commit murder –'

'That man would. You just said so.'

'People say all sorts of things when they're angry. The important thing is for us to stay calm. Time's still on our side. It will be a couple of weeks before *The Dove* gets anywhere near the actual test zone –'

'You mean we just wait?' she asked in horror. 'After what you heard –?'

'No, we don't just wait. As soon as we get back I'm going round to the Foreign Office. Joe and Liz are British citizens. They're entitled to support and protection. And I had an idea in the cab coming back. This Eric Searle, he's a New Zealander. And Nick what's-his-name, he's an American. The other boy's Canadian. By this time tomorrow I intend to have called on all of their embassies. We'll see if the French are so high and mighty

490

when half the governments of NATO are breathing down their necks!'

Twelve

Liz wrote in her diary:

Today is our thirty-first day at sea. It seems more like thirty-one weeks. I shall never get used to it, even though I'm not sick as I was at the outset. I was so ill then that I thought I was going to die. I think I even *wanted* to die. Eric says I'll never be as bad again. Apparently lots of people have one bad bout, then it's over, like chicken-pox or the measles. Even so I'm not taking any chances, I still take a sea-sick pill every day. My legs remain very bruised. They ache most of the time. The biggest problem is that the boat sails on twenty-four hours a day. I suppose I imagined everything would stop at night and we'd all go to sleep. Instead nothing stops and we sleep when we can. Anyone who's not actually doing something is resting in one of the bunks. The constant motion means I'm always on edge, bracing my muscles ready for the next wave. We all get very tired, even Eric and Pete. I hardly slept at all to begin with, but I do now, or at least I doze, because I'm so tired I suppose, and because I no longer wait until nightfall.

We've lost a lot of time over the last seven days. The wind fell away last week and only picked up again last night. Consequently we covered less than twenty miles on some days. I thought we'd use the engine but apparently that's impractical, we only run the engine for half an hour a day to charge up the batteries and haven't the fuel to do more. Eric says that thanks to our flying start we're still roughly on schedule, which means we should reach the test zone in five or six days.

They've all grown beards. Joe's is iron grey, making him look like a stern Father Christmas. Nick's is darker than his hair which has been bleached almost white by the sun. I

491

spent two hours of his watch with him yesterday, it's the only chance we have to talk by ourselves. Neither of us feels sexy, which is just as well, I suppose, since we couldn't do much about it. I suppose we're both tired and I look a mess, sticky with salt and my hair is all knotted. Still, it's nice to spend an hour at the helm, snuggled up to each other, just talking. There's a surprising amount to look at, the sea and the sky change all the time and some of the sunsets are achingly beautiful. I saw an albatross two days ago and Nick says he saw a shark. It's quite a lot warmer than when we left Christchurch.

The big radio has been playing up for the past few days. We're not receiving anyone. Nick still sends out the false position every evening. The radio howls and screeches, and sometimes we think we hear something identifiable as a human voice, but I'm beginning to think it's just wishful thinking on our part. The truth is we can't hear anyone and I'm left wondering whether anyone can hear us, which is a bit worrying. The small radio will only transmit five or six hundred miles and although Nick also tries that, all he gets for his efforts is more ear-shattering static. We've still got the portable for listening to ordinary short-wave news broadcasts, and we leave it on for most of the time. Nick is hoping to fix the big set before we get to Mururoa.

We talk a lot about what it will be like. If the French do try to board us the plan is for Nick to broadcast the fact on the big radio (if it's fixed), while Joe and I take pictures of their boarding party with the cameras. Eric and Pete will negotiate. (Let's hope the French speak English.) Eric has a document prepared by some lawyers which states quite clearly that no nation has the right to stop or search a ship of another state on the high seas except in time of war. In peace it is illegal for a warship of one state to interfere with a foreign vessel when on the high seas. Therefore, international law is clearly on our side. Not that we really think that will stop the French, but Eric intends to hand them the document rather like a process-server serving a writ. After that, we can only wait to see what happens.

Our biggest worry (although we all keep it to ourselves) is that we've been forgotten. Pete's idea was that the voyage might stir up public opinion in the way those Canadian boats did at Amchitka. So far there's no sign of that. We keep tuning into Radio Australia and the BBC World Service (which we can't always hear), but the only thing they seem interested in is the Stockholm Conference on the Environment. Apparently Australia has put down a motion to ban all nuclear tests, which is encouraging. It's to be debated next week so we can only hope for the best. Meanwhile we managed to pick up a faint and garbled transmission from the BBC this morning saying despite mounting world pressure, the French will still go ahead with their tests. Very depressing, as is the fact that there's nothing about us, or Edith's march upon Paris, or any other protests. The lack of news is getting us down. Joe (as always) remains confident. He keeps reminding us about that wonderful send-off from Christchurch. I must admit it's hard to believe that people like that will just quit, but I can't think of a time when I so badly wanted Joe's army of the good to stand up and be counted . . .

Cramped and uncomfortable, Keir sat in the gallery at the House of Commons and watched intently as the Labour Member for Swansea South rose to his feet.

'Mr Speaker, can my Right Honourable friend, the Under-Secretary of State for Foreign Affairs, assure this House that the government has protested in the strongest terms possible to the government of France about their proposed nuclear tests in the Pacific, and if such a protest has not been lodged, will the honourable gentleman please tell the House why?'

Growls of support rumbled from the Opposition benches as the Under-Secretary rose to make his reply. 'Mr Speaker, such a protest would represent unwarranted interference in the internal affairs of a good friend and ally –'

'Internal affairs with external consequences, Mr Speaker. France's "internal affairs" will spread death and destruction over half the Pacific. Radioactive fall-out, causing genetic damage to future generations –'

'Mr Speaker,' the Under-Secretary held his ground. 'The Honourable Member opposite has no proof –'

'Rubbish!' came shouts from the Opposition benches, while

493

the government's benches rallied behind their man with shouts of 'Hear, hear.' By the time the Speaker had restored order, the Member for Swansea South was back on his feet.

'Mr Speaker, further to my question of last Monday, I wish to ask the Under-Secretary whether the government has any information of the whereabouts of *The Dove* and its fine, public-spirited crew?'

The Under-Secretary began to look visibly bored. 'As I said on Monday, Mr Speaker, this . . . er, sailing ketch, *The Dove*, is not a British vessel. It is not registered here and does not fly our flag. The Honourable Member really must understand, as I'm sure does the rest of the House, that it is impossible to keep track of a ship sailing under any flag other than our own.'

'And as I said on Monday, *The Dove* is sailing on a British-sponsored mission with two British citizens aboard. Mr Speaker, may I ask the Under-Secretary of State what steps he has taken to ensure the safety of British subjects sailing in international waters in the area of the French nuclear tests?'

Rising again, the Under-Secretary answered with a voice edged with irritation, 'Mr Speaker, our information is that the sailing ketch in question was last reported to be well *outside* the French test zone. Under the circumstances, my honourable friend's question is totally hypothetical and it is neither my practice nor my intention to waste the time of this House dealing with hypothetical questions.'

Mounting cries of 'Hear, hear,' from the government benches signalled the end of the exchange. Resuming his seat, the Member for Swansea cast an apologetic glance up at the gallery. Keir managed a glum nod in response and edged his way along the bench to the door.

As he crossed Parliament Square, Keir wondered how to explain another failure to Dawn. In the three weeks since their return from Paris, they had suffered so many setbacks that he was beginning to fear for her health. They had scrapped all of their plans. Dawn was due to start rehearsals for a new play in the West End. She had cancelled that. She had cancelled *all* engagements. Her life revolved around the telephone and visits to Edith. She had told Edith what had happened in Paris. Keir's conversation with the Admiral had been recounted exactly. Edith had tried to send a message to *The Dove*. So had Dawn.

She had telephoned Mr Searle in New Zealand, only to be told that *The Dove*'s radio was malfunctioning. 'We keep trying,' Searle had said, 'but they don't seem to be receiving us.'

Meanwhile the French were planning to murder them.

Keir swore under his breath. The Foreign Office had refused to become involved. His allegation that the French planned to sink *The Dove* was greeted with derision. 'My dear chap, you're overwrought. We can understand your concern. Naturally, you are worried, with your father and daughter aboard, but the French don't go around sinking yachts. The suggestion is simply preposterous . . .'

The memory made Keir hot with temper. The truth was Britain's application to join the Common Market was once again on the table in Brussels. The French had kept Britain out of Europe for years. This time they might – they just might – condescend to allow Britain to join. This year, 1972, was the year of the big push. 'If we don't upset them, old boy. Quite frankly, your father and daughter are doing us no good at all. The last thing we want is a diplomatic incident with the French. The Prime Minister has staked his reputation on taking us into Europe . . .'

Keir had called at the New Zealand High Commission.

'We're not quite sure how we can help you, Mr Milford. We're aware of this vessel and our government is dealing with the matter in Wellington. Perhaps if you contacted them there . . .'

The Canadian High Commission had been equally pathetic. They had no record of a boy called Peter Grimshaw. 'We don't know if he even exists. If you could give us his place and date of birth . . .' The truth was, the Canadians were earning millions of dollars selling uranium to the French for their nuclear programme. The last thing they wanted was to upset the French.

At least the Americans knew of Nick Grant. 'Frankly, Mr Milford, they say every barrel contains a few rotten apples – well, he's one of ours. You know he's a draft dodger from Vietnam? The kid's a Commie. Ever since he came to London he's been mixed up with Commie politics. If he's somewhere out in the Pacific, at least he's out of our hair . . .'

The only people who had believed Keir's story were his contacts in the Ministry of Defence. Old friends, stretching back to his days at SHAPE, had listened intently to his account of the meeting in Paris. 'You are right, Keir, your father and his friends have played into their hands. The French will stage an accident. Look at it from their point of view. If this boat holds them up for even a day, they'll have to contend with a whole bloody armada next year. They can't possibly have that. They'll hit this boat hard. We would. You can't have idiotic civilians messing up military operations . . .' They could offer no help, except express sympathy and suggest he asked the Foreign Office 'to do something on the quiet'.

'Fat bloody chance,' Keir grumbled as he walked up Lord North Street. But with the French planning to sink *The Dove* when it reached the test zone, he knew he had to keep trying.

Thirteen

The gale struck at noon. The waves had been building steadily all morning and the barometer had fallen alarmingly. At the helm, Joe looked over his shoulder and saw what looked like a small tidal wave almost on top of him. Next moment, *The Dove* was tossed high onto a crest of foam before being pitched forward at alarming speed. Emerging from the cabin, Eric could see nothing but a vast wall of grey water as high as the side of a mountain. Seconds later, Pete scrambled up onto the deck just as the avalanche of water engulfed them. After that they were fighting for their lives. 'Slow her down,' yelled Eric. 'Use the nylon warp for a sea anchor.'

Pete and Nick struggled with the warp, hurling it over the stern. It made no difference. *The Dove* was lifted again before plummeting at terrifying speed into a cavernous trough. While Joe clung to the tiller, the others hauled in every inch of canvas. Within minutes *The Dove* was running on bare poles. Below, Liz clung to the sides of the bunk to avoid being smashed against the wall of the cabin. Everything in the galley broke loose. A deep rumbling came from outside, then advanced steadily to become a deafening roar which filled the cabin with ear-splitting noise until it receded with the hissing sound of a thousand sea-serpents. Water poured down the hatch and through every vent.

Joe was a pathetic sight in the cockpit. His grey hair was plastered over his skull, his eyes were red, blue hollows showed under his cheekbones. Gripping the tiller for dear life, his hands were as white as bone. Fear showed in every line in his face. The swells were the size of mountain ranges. From the top of one to the top of the next was at least a couple of miles. So great was the distance that even though *The Dove* was flying, she took twenty minutes to descend each slope to the valley below. The wind howled and shrieked like a chorus of demented lunatics, adding another eerie dimension to their terror. Eric clung to the cockpit, and gasped as they rose to the crest of the next wave. 'How far can you see? Sixty miles, seventy, a hundred?' For a heart-pounding second, as *The Dove* tilted on the edge of the precipice, they surveyed a seascape that stretched to eternity. Then they plunged down, down and down . . . Liz was sure they were sinking. Ankle deep in water, she salvaged books and items of clothing by throwing them onto the top bunks. Fighting for her balance, she struggled to remain upright and throttled the scream in her throat.

On deck, Eric was weighing their chances of survival. Gusting at seventy knots, winds lashed them furiously as they rose to each peak, only to fall away in the troughs, cut off by the next mountainous wave rising behind them. Eric had never seen such huge seas. *The Dove* seemed to have shrunk. They had all shrunk. They were ants on a matchbox in the midst of a flood. It was useless to try to steer a course. They had to go where the wind and the waves took them. If the boat rolled they would be swamped within minutes. Keeping the boat upright would test Eric's skill to the limit. He relieved Joe at the helm and sent him below with Nick to help in the cabin . . .

All afternoon, all through the night, they ran with the storm. By daybreak they had been blown a hundred miles south. By midday they were even further off course. Eric clung to the tiller, coaxing *The Dove* with an unceasing flow of encouraging words. 'Come on, darling, you can do it . . . keep it up . . . come on, darling, keep it up . . . you can do it . . .' Only Pete shared the helm with him during those desperate hours. Two hours on, two hours off; two hours lashed into the cockpit, two hours of uneasy rest below.

The first hopeful sign came at mid-afternoon. 'It's easing,' Eric whispered, afraid to tempt fate by saying it out loud. Indeed, the ponderous rhythm was slower. The swells over which *The Dove* crawled like some soaked and injured insect were a little less threatening. The wind was dropping; it still gusted and buffeted at the peak of a crest, but fell away in the hollows. Indeed by the time *The Dove* had made the long, long descent into the trough, the wind could be heard only as a faint whistle far above. Even though the swells were still mountainous, making Eric feel like a midget adrift in a toy boat, he sensed that the worst was over. In the troughs, cut off from the wind, *The Dove* slowed almost to a halt. An age seemed to pass until the next crest. Eric let it happen twice then, taking a chance with the fuel reserves, he started the engine and puttered across the flat bottom of the valley. When the sea caught up and began to carry *The Dove* to the crest of the next wave, he cut the engine. Once over the top and after the long descent, he started the engine again.

Later, Liz wrote in her diary:

It took us three or four days to recover from the gale. Everyone was completely exhausted, Eric most of all. He was utterly drained, mentally and physically. We owe him our lives. The others showed their gratitude by sharing his watch between them and making him take a complete rest for forty-eight hours. He was too tired to protest. I expressed my thanks by cooking him his favourite meal (my version of shepherd's pie) for several days in a row. Luckily the weather improved afterwards and settled into a calm spell which, with the exception of a couple of days, has prevailed ever since.

Eric said that the gale surpassed anything he's ever known, so it was really quite something. I'm very proud of myself for not getting sea-sick. I was sick with fear but that doesn't count. I kept remembering the shark Nick had seen and my mind was filled with nightmarish thoughts . . .

After the gale we were well off course and behind schedule, but we've made steady time since. As I write this, Mururoa is less than five hundred miles away. We should enter the test zone in the morning. I thought the zone would be a circle around Mururoa until I saw how Eric has drawn it on the chart. It's the shape of the keyhole, with the long end running towards South America. Not that the shape matters to us. It has no legal significance. International law permits us to sail to within twelve miles of Mururoa, which is what we will do, to take up a position directly in line with the main fall-out from the Bomb. The next move will be up to the French.

Our radio is still on the blink. Nick broadcasts – if that's the right word for shouting 'This is *The Dove*. This is *The Dove*. Do you receive? Do you receive? Over?' for forty-five minutes every evening. The only response is high-pitched squeals and crackles, and a lot of manic shrieks and whistles. We all listen like bats. Now and then someone – usually Pete – insists he can hear a human voice in reply. I never hear anything that sounds even remotely human.

The sense of isolation becomes very oppressive. We have each other, and that's it. The rest of the world's forgotten we exist. Thank goodness we get on reasonably well. We have Joe to thank for that. He knows who is feeling blue or scratchy before they know it themselves, and makes a special fuss of whoever it is until they recover their spirits. I would have gone off my head without Joe. God knows where he finds the strength. His constant good humour is all the more remarkable because I know he's fretting about Edith. He knows Angie and Betty are with her, and that Bob and Emlyn and all sorts of people will watch over her, but it gives him little comfort. It's another reason to curse the loss of the radio. Mr Searle had planned to act as a sort of post-box, passing messages back and forth. A message from Edith would brighten Joe's life.

Every morning we listen eagerly to Radio Australia for some word about us, or about other protests. We're always disappointed. Reception varies a lot. You get an ear-splitting burst of 'Waltzing Matilda', followed by the announcer wishing good morning to all the islanders of the South Pacific, then the news – with the announcer's voice fading in and out all the time amid crackles of static.

One piece of news came through loud and clear. The result of the vote at the Stockholm conference on the environment. The Australian resolution to ban nuclear tests was passed fifty-six in favour, with twenty-nine abstentions and three against. Those against were France, China, and the African state of Gabon, who were presumably bribed by the French. We expected the French to vote against, but the news that the United States, Britain and Russia all abstained was very depressing . . .

The following morning Liz wrote:

May 23   We crossed into the forbidden zone early this morning. As there was no reception committee, we thought the French must have been misled by Nick's broadcasts after all. We shook hands rather solemnly with each other, which gave us an excuse to hide our true feelings. A sort of creepy feeling came over me even then. The very words 'forbidden zone' make me shudder. The morning was beautiful, the sun was shining, the sea calm, yet I had the strongest premonition that we had just entered some terrible place and something awful was about to happen. And half an hour ago it did. Radio Australia say the French have announced that as the test zone is completely clear, they may take advantage of the good weather to bring their tests forward. They may start any day.

Nick immediately broadcast our true position, again without knowing if it was heard by anyone. Eric tried to reassure me by saying the French will have radar on Mururoa and on their ships, so they'll see us on that. I don't know anything about radar. All I know is I feel frightened by us being here without anyone knowing. There was no word about us on the radio again. Neither was there anything about the march upon Paris, or any other protests.

Meanwhile we're sailing straight for Mururoa, straight for the Bomb.

Fourteen

Dawn knew all about the march upon Paris. She had been at Arcadia Gardens when Edith took a call from Bob Cooper. Edith was with her now, in the drawing-room at Lord North Street. Eric and Harvey were there, her two staunchest friends, as supportive as ever in her time of trouble. They looked as worried as Edith who sat dry-washing her hands, stern-faced, defiant, proud, but suddenly old. The past five weeks had aged her ten years.

It was Harvey, trying to divert their minds for a moment from the plight of *The Dove*, who had enquired about the march upon Paris. Dawn told the story of how, after gaining strength and supporters all across Belgium, the march had been stopped on the French border. Hundreds of French sympathizers were waiting to greet them at the frontier, but the guards kept them apart, refusing to let either side cross.

'So what happened?'

'They camped by the side of the wire. They made shelters from sheets of plastic and sang protest songs. Some even gave flowers to the guards. Apparently several New Zealanders and Australians asked for asylum in France on the grounds that the French nuclear tests will make their own countries uninhabitable.'

Eric whooped with delight. 'They never give up, do they? So then what happened?'

Sadness darkened Dawn's face. 'French riot police arrived by the wagonload. They charged into the crowd and laid into them with batons. A lot of the protestors ended up in hospital. Others were carted off to jail. Many were women. Bob Cooper said one was clubbed in the face. Her jaw was broken and she will lose her teeth.' Dawn shook her head. 'A few weeks ago I'd have been shocked. Now it's what I've come to expect.'

Edith raised her head and regarded her daughter-in-law fondly. How wrong I was about you, she thought. It was my fault, wasting all those years, keeping you at arm's length . . .

Dawn said, 'Something's gone terribly wrong with the world when a woman who offers flowers gets smashed in the face.'

Harvey sighed. 'I never realized. We don't, do we?' He looked at Eric for confirmation. 'I mean, ordinary members of the public –'

'My God,' Dawn interrupted bitterly, rising and going over to the window. 'I'll tell you one thing,' she said, looking down into a street bathed in late afternoon sunshine. She checked her watch. Ten past six. Keir must be home soon. She returned to her chair. 'The one thing I've learned in the last five weeks is that the public would be sick to their stomach if they knew half the things done in their name.'

While Harvey nodded gravely, Eric said, 'That's a strong line. Are you going to say that at the press conference?'

'I don't know.' She ran a hand through hair which although still thick and glossy now contained a few silver threads. 'I keep telling myself there won't be a press conference, that we'll hear from them and they'll be safe.'

'They won't turn back,' Edith said quietly, 'even if we could get a message to them. They won't turn back. You know Joe, and the others are the same –'

'They'll be *killed*! How can you sit there . . . ?' Dawn broke off, recovering a grip on her nerves. She was flying to New Zealand in three days' time. CND supporters were planning a march out to Heathrow to see her off. Eric had had the idea of a press conference. He was going with her. So was Edith. Keir was less sure, still hoping to achieve something in London. Poor Keir. He had been so convinced it would never come to this, so sure his friends in high places would come to his aid. Dawn had believed him at first. Why not, she had seen half the Cabinet troop through this house. She had given dinner to politicians and civil servants from all over Europe. Keir knew so many people. Yet door after door had closed against him. Enemies had moved in, seeing something almost humorous in the situation of Beaumont's Mr Fix-it becoming involved with the CND. Friends had begun to distance themselves. Some had been embarrassed, others had been genuinely sorry. 'Rotten luck,' they had said. 'Hell of a thing to happen to someone like you. Never mind, a man can't be blamed for the misdeeds of his family . . .' Yet they did blame him, and slowly but surely they distanced themselves . . .

Dawn had watched him tear himself to shreds. Keir had defended his friends, seen their points of view, and reserved his anger for Joe. Until – Dawn wasn't sure when – a week ago, ten days ago, he had begun to change. He and Sam had argued bitterly. Apparently a deal with Israel for missiles had fallen through and Sam wanted Keir to fly to Tel Aviv to sort it out. Keir had refused. He had neglected his work anyway; ever since they had returned from Africa he had been preoccupied with the fate of *The Dove*. Dawn sighed. Africa seemed light-years away. They had been so light-hearted then, so full of plans . . .

'Ray asked me if Keir will speak out at the press conference' Eric asked.

'What?' Deep in thought, Dawn had forgotten them for a moment.

'The press conference, sweetie,' said Eric patiently. 'It would help if Keir gave them chapter and verse about this admiral in Paris. Ray was saying –'

'Keir won't be at the press conference,' she said quickly. She had kept it from him. He would be dead set against it. Even though he had agreed that she should fly to New Zealand, any mention of the press put Keir on his guard. Despite setback after setback, he was convinced that pressure through what he called 'his channels' would yield results. Even now, at this eleventh hour, he was still trying. Meanwhile the date for the first nuclear test drew ever closer.

'He is coming to New Zealand with us?'

'I don't know, Eric. We'll see –'

'We are using the Beaumont, aren't we?'

'What? Yes, I mean I suppose so, I hadn't really thought . . .' She pulled herself together. 'Sorry, I'm not concentrating. I keep thinking the phone will ring to say they're all right. Your press conference went right out of my head.'

Eric looked anxious. 'You can't change your mind, sweetie. Ray's winding it up now. You know what Ray's like. He's already out beating the bushes.'

'Is he?' she said blankly. 'Oh, listen! That sounds like a cab.' She jumped up and hurried to the window to look down into the street. 'Yes, here's Keir now. Thank goodness. He might have some news.'

As he watched her leave the room, Harvey asked, 'Where's Keir been?'

'The French Embassy. He's been there all afternoon.' Eric sighed. 'Poor Dawn, she doesn't know whether she's coming or going.'

'I don't suppose she does,' said Harvey, glancing at his watch as he rose to his feet. 'Or you, Mrs Milford,' he said sympathetically to Edith.

'I'll survive if that boat does,' Edith said fiercely.

'Yes, of course,' agreed Harvey. 'I must be going. I'll just see if Keir has any news.'

Keir burst into the room at that moment, with Dawn on his heels. 'Why wasn't I told about this?' he said furiously, thrusting a rolled-up newspaper at Eric.

Startled, Eric unrolled the paper. Dawn's photograph and a picture of the Beaumont Executive Jet appeared side by side on the front page.

Film Star Says France will Sink Peace Boat

Actress Dawn Wharton fuelled speculation today that the tiny yacht carrying her daughter and four others into the nuclear test zone will be sunk on sight by the French Navy. That the French will run the yacht down and fake an accident has been rumoured in London for the past ten days. Miss Wharton now reveals the source of those rumours to be no less than her husband, millionaire arms-salesman Keir Milford who, she says, received the information from a senior French officer in Paris two weeks ago. Miss Wharton is preparing to fly to New Zealand on Saturday in her husband's private jet . . .

'Oh, lovely stuff,' Eric whooped. 'Good old Ray –'

'I'm glad you think so,' Keir said angrily. 'It's taken two weeks of arm-twisting and string-pulling to get a meeting with the French Ambassador. What happens? I walk in and he hits me with this. Who the devil gave you permission to interfere in my – ?'

'Steady on,' said Eric, backing away. 'There's nothing there that's not true. You said yourself –'

'I know what I said. But not to the press. Not while I had a chance to sort this out. This kind of publicity is thoroughly irresponsible –'

'No,' Edith interrupted, taking the paper from Eric's hands. 'It might save their lives. The French will have second thoughts about sinking them –'

'The French won't sink them,' said Keir, 'the boat's nowhere near the test zone. A French aircraft sighted *The Dove* this morning. Fifteen hundred miles west of Mururoa and sailing back to New Zealand.'

'Oh, thank God!' Dawn sank into the nearest chair. 'Thank God!'

'Exactly.' Keir nodded grimly. 'Now you can imagine how I felt with the Ambassador. In response to diplomatic pressure – which I started, I might add – the French have been conducting a massive aerial search covering thousands of square miles of ocean. A huge exercise, mounted at colossal cost. The Ambassador received news of the sighting from Paris only ten minutes before I arrived at the Embassy. Unfortunately the early editions of the evening papers reached him at the same time –'

Dawn was weeping. Her body heaved with great shuddering sobs.

'Darling.' Keir was on his knees at her chair in an instant. 'Darling, it's all right. It's all over. They're safe.'

Eric also sat down. 'What a relief,' he said softly. 'What a relief.'

'Fantastic news!' Harvey beamed. 'Absolutely fantastic. Keir, we're all so pleased for you both. Oh, what *wonderful* news!'

Keir looked up, cradling his wife in his arms, and managed an apology. 'Sorry, Eric, I know you meant well –'

'Sorry nothing. Don't be silly. They're safe. That's all that matters –'

'Right.' Keir nodded wearily. 'They're safe.' Suddenly a grin lit his face, his first grin in weeks. He turned back to Dawn. 'Come on, darling. It's all over. They're safe –'

'I'll get some champagne,' Eric exclaimed, springing up.

'Absolutely,' Keir agreed. 'Tell John to serve it in here. Bring Barbara up too. They've been as worried as we have.'

In all the excitement no one except Eric noticed Edith leave the room. He waved her through the door with a flourish. 'Isn't it wonderful? You must be so happy.' Only as he closed the door did he see the look on her face. 'Hold the champagne, Eric, and don't say anything to John for the moment.'

Eric followed Edith downstairs and into the library where she picked up the phone. About to dial, she said, 'I don't believe it. They would never turn back.'

'But if the Ambassador –'

'Fetch my son for me, would you, Eric? Make some excuse. Don't let on to Dawn if you can help it.'

Eric had never seen such a bleak look on anyone's face in the whole of his life. He found it easy to fetch Keir. Dawn had gone to her room to repair her make-up.

'What's up?' Keir asked on the way downstairs.

Eric shook his head in bewilderment. Edith was talking into the telephone when they entered the library. If anything, she looked even older. Her face was grave. 'Hold on please,' she said. Upright, bracing herself against the desk, she turned and offered the telephone to Keir. 'It's Mr Searle,' she said, 'in New Zealand. I told him what the Ambassador said –'

Keir took the phone with a confident smile and said, 'Hello, Mr Searle. It's good news, isn't it?'

'It's a pack of lies,' came the voice on the other end of the telephone. 'A radio ham in Auckland picked up a message from *The Dove* last night. It said they crossed the line into the zone yesterday morning. They had a good following wind and expected to reach Mururoa by nightfall. By my reckoning they've been off Mururoa for twelve hours.'

Afterwards, slumped into the chair behind his desk, his face white and his voice scarcely audible, Keir looked a broken man. 'The lying bastard. I was so relieved, and so embarrassed by that bloody newspaper –'

'But what does it mean?' asked Eric.

'They didn't need an air search. The whole thing's a lie. They've always known *The Dove*'s location. They've been tracking it from their radar stations in Tahiti and New Caledonia.' With a look of horror, he buried his head in his hands. 'Christ!'

'You mean *The Dove*'s not on its way back to New Zealand?' Eric was dumbfounded.

'Of course not.' Keir raised his head, and stared at his mother. 'That's what the French want us to believe. They were releasing the story when I left. If everyone believes *The Dove*'s fifteen hundred miles away . . .' The words died on his lips. 'Dear God, it doesn't bear thinking about.'

Fifteen

The Dove lay sixteen miles north-west of Mururoa, her sails reefed and water slopping gently against her hull. She had been hove-to for twelve hours, having come to rest the previous evening for the first time since leaving New Zealand. Three thousand miles of ocean lay behind her and her crew. Six weeks of gales, calms, storms, tempests, sharks and sunsets; six weeks of bruising movement and continuous effort. Now, at last, *The Dove* was at rest.

Strangely, none of the crew had slept well. Anxiety played a part. Deep in the forbidden zone, they were close to the Bomb. The evening before the sight of Mururoa coming up over the horizon had caused Liz to shudder. And later another factor had deprived her of sleep. When they had finally lowered the sails, the motion of *The Dove* had changed. Under sail on the open sea, she had pitched laterally along her length. Overnight, hove-to, she had rolled from side to side. Unaccustomed to the new movement, tired bodies needed time to adjust. After the pounding they had taken, more than one night was needed to come to terms with the unfamiliar motion.

Morning therefore found them raw-eyed and nervous, quite unprepared for the first shock of the day which came only too quickly. The announcement was on the early morning news from Radio Australia. They all heard it. Reception was unhindered by static for once. There was no possibility of a mistake.

'. . . It was announced in Paris last night that in response to public concern, a large-scale aerial search has been carried out for the yacht which was to have sailed into the French nuclear test zone. *The Dove*, a thirty-six-foot ketch, has now been sighted by French military aircraft, fifteen hundred miles west of the test zone and sailing towards New Zealand. Consequently there is no possibility that the yacht or its crew will be harmed by the nuclear explosions which are now imminent on the French test site at Mururoa . . .'

'What the hell?' Nick exclaimed, staring at the portable in disbelief.

'The lying bastards!' Eric erupted.

'What does it mean?' asked Liz, clutching Joe's arm.

Badly shaken, they all spent the next half-hour trying to answer her question. The possibility of the French mistaking another vessel for *The Dove* was considered, only to be rejected. 'That's beyond belief,' Pete said flatly. 'They're not incompetent, whatever else they are.' Only one conclusion was left: that the French had deliberately lied about *The Dove*'s location.

Eric went up on deck. He feared the radar reflector might have been damaged in some way by the storm, and climbed the mast to inspect it. 'Perfectly all right,' he announced when he came down. 'The French *must* know we're here.'

By now, they were all on deck. Initial disbelief gave way to frowns and looks of dismay as they grappled with the implications of the French statement. Across the sunlit water, Mururoa sat squat and brooding, verification in itself of the French lie. 'Perhaps they're testing our nerve,' Pete suggested. 'They think we'll hear that broadcast and turn tail and run.'

Eric was still staring up at the reflector on the mast, a baffled look on his face. 'Believe me,' he said, 'they must know we're here. You could pick that up with a radar set costing a few quid. They must have a million pounds' worth of radar on that island.'

Nick laughed, a nervous, dispirited sound on the morning air. 'Perhaps they hope we'll go in closer to give them physical sight of us –'

'So they can snatch us,' Pete interrupted. 'Not bloody likely.'

Joe, as always the last on deck, had shuffled crab-like to sit with his back against the cockpit. The voyage had weathered his face and tanned his arms, giving him the look of a disreputable beachcomber. As he packed his pipe, his shrewd eyes studied the faces around him. They were clearly frightened, depressed, unsure of what to do next. Even the storm had failed to shake them as much. Joe's eyes settled on Liz. Standing at the rails, she looked close to tears. He cleared his throat, not wanting to startle her. 'Penny for your thoughts, Liz?'

She swallowed hard. 'I was just thinking about all those wonderful people in Christchurch. Do you remember? The night we left. They must feel horribly let down.'

'Bloody right,' Pete agreed.

Liz gulped. 'It's not fair. We made it through that terrible storm and everything else, and –'

'Hey.' Joe reached out for her hand. 'You're forgetting the most important part of that broadcast.'

She brushed her eyes with the back of her hand, and looked at him in astonishment.

'Sit down here.' He patted the deck next to him, and waited until she was beside him. 'Think about it,' he said, putting his arm around her shoulders. 'The French were forced to tell a big lie to combat a big truth. Without the truth, they never would have issued that statement. That's where they gave themselves away. You seized on the lie. We all did. Knowing it was a lie made us so furious and upset that we overlooked what they were forced to admit in the process.'

Pete turned from the rail. 'I didn't hear them admit any-thing –'

'Oh?' Joe cocked his head and squinted up at him. 'I re-member it word for word.'

Eric, staring at Mururoa through binoculars, lowered the glasses and gave Joe a quizzical look. 'I didn't hear them admit anything either.'

Joe grinned. 'There were some magic words in that broadcast. Know what they were? In response to public concern they mounted a search. "In response to public concern." Liz is getting upset about those people in Christchurch. They haven't given up on us. Not by a long way. "In response to public concern." You know what that means? I bet every French embassy in the world is under siege at the minute. I bet switch-boards are jammed. They haven't given up on us, and they *won't* give up –'

Liz interrupted. 'But if they think we're sailing back?'

'Rubbish! Who's going to believe that? Will Edith believe it?

Will Bob believe it? Will Emlyn? What about your father, Eric? Will he believe it?'

'Well,' Eric said doubtfully, 'he'll be surprised –'

'Surprised! He'll be bloody flabbergasted.' Joe turned to Pete. 'What about Angie? Will she believe it? Surely she's got a better opinion of you than that?'

Pete answered with a shamefaced grin.

'That's the admission the French had to make,' said Joe triumphantly, giving Liz a squeeze. '"In response to public concern." Just you remember that. No one's forgotten us, darling. They're out there rooting for us. Don't you worry about letting those people in Christchurch down. You haven't and they know it. They'll be asking for verification. If the French sighted us, why has no one else seen us? They'll be kicking up such a clamour that the French will be forced to issue another statement, then another one, getting deeper in the mire all the time with their lies. There's only one way the French can make us win now, and that's to *make* us turn back.'

Suddenly, everyone felt very much better. Even Eric laughed. 'We can't turn back. Our provisions won't last more than another five weeks. I planned to put into Tahiti first –'

'Right.' Joe nodded. 'Meanwhile we stay here, eh? And give the bastards a run for their money.'

Assent came now with smiling faces and determined grins.

'That's the stuff,' said Joe, turning to Nick as if with a sudden idea. 'Why not get broadcasting again? Keep hammering away. My hunch is you're getting through to someone, even if they can't reach us in return.'

Filled with fresh heart, Nick went below. Liz gave Joe a kiss. 'Do you know what I'm going to do now?' she asked. 'Wash my hair over the side. Then I'll feel ready for anything.' She leapt to her feet and bent to kiss him again before disappearing down the hatch after Nick. Joe smiled, thinking any second now, Nick too would be in receipt of a kiss.

'Thanks, Joe,' said Eric, stooping to touch him briefly on the shoulder.

That was all he said. Next minute he and Pete were busy with sextant and stop-watch, trying to get a sun-sight to calculate how far *The Dove* had drifted during the night. Shortly afterwards, Nick could be heard below trying to raise Tahiti or Rarotonga or

510

Pitcairn. As usual, his words were interspersed with howls of static every time he sought a response. Then Nick again: 'Hello, Pitcairn. Do you receive me? Hello, Pitcairn. Do you receive me . . . ?'

Joe settled back against the cockpit and cast a defiant glance at Mururoa over the water. In his heart he was far from sure about the public clamour he had described. 'We can only hope,' he whispered. And he did, he hoped desperately with the whole of his being. Meanwhile, he thought, we sit here and await the enemy's next move.

It came with frightening swiftness. Liz was climbing out of the cabin, shampoo in hand, when a tremendous clap of sound rocked *The Dove*, causing them to duck instinctively as a four-engine aircraft came swooping down less than three hundred feet over their heads. Sprawling sideways, Joe turned just in time to see the aircraft bank and level out, heading straight back towards *The Dove* as if on a strafing run.

'Dear God!' yelled Eric. He stood frozen, fighting the urge to leap over the rail before bullets tore him apart. The plane dived straight for *The Dove*, its pilot lifting the nose only at the very last second. It screamed over their heads. They turned fearful eyes to watch it climb high into the sky, dreading the next run. Thankfully, this time it headed back to Mururoa.

Pete picked himself up from the deck and examined the stop-watch which he had dropped. He held it to his ear, unable to hear a thing because his ears were still ringing. 'Bloody maniac,' he muttered furiously.

Joe recovered enough to prop himself back up against the cockpit. He too had been frightened, but as he looked at the others, a rueful grin came to his face. 'Well, they know we're here now,' he said.

Half an hour later, the aircraft returned. Again it roared in so low that sound hit the sea like an explosion. *The Dove* rocked furiously. Back came the plane, screaming down on them, like an angry eagle driving interlopers away from its nest. Climbing, it turned again . . . and again . . . and again . . .

For ninety nerve-shattering minutes, the crew of *The Dove* endured pass upon pass as the aircraft dived, banked and dived again. The noise was torture. Even in the cabin, it was terrifying.

Finally the pilot gave up and returned to Mururoa, leaving them white-faced and trembling, exhausted and deafened.

'Every dirty trick in the book,' muttered Nick in disgust.

They spent the afternoon screwing up their nerves in preparation for the aircraft's return, but it remained absent. Indeed, the French remained absent. There was no sign of any of their ships, although a BBC broadcast had said the French navy had at least fifteen warships in the area. Eric stood with binoculars to his eyes, sweeping a horizon which remained ominously empty. Then, at 3.30, he turned his gaze back to Mururoa. 'Holy Christ,' he whispered. Lowering the glasses, he adjusted them, and looked again. 'Oh Christ! Joe, take a look at Mururoa. Do you see what I see?'

Joe raised the other pair of binoculars. His eyes were older and weaker. At first he thought he saw a helicopter hovering over the atoll. Then, with an awful sinking feeling, he knew what it was. 'It's the balloon,' he said, his voice shaking. 'It's the bloody balloon.'

They knew how the French planned to explode their bomb. It would be lifted over the atoll with a dirigible balloon.

'They're going to do it,' Eric said in disbelief. 'The bastards are going to set the thing off knowing full well where we are.'

The Dove sat directly in line of the fall-out.

Liz and the others came up on deck. After handing the glasses to Nick, Joe turned away. Never once had he thought it would come to this. He had been clear what would happen. The French would board them. Eric would hand over the legal protest. The French would take control of *The Dove*. In effect, the crew would become prisoners of war, to be led off to some island before being released.

'Joe?' Liz touched his arm.

Joe couldn't bring himself to look at her. How had he brought her to this? His cherished granddaughter of whom he was so proud, with her life ahead of her. Whom he loved so dearly. How could he protect her from this?

Nick came to him. 'It's another bluff, Joe. They're trying to scare us.'

Joe wondered. If it was a bluff, why had they not seen even one ship? Why did the horizon remain empty? Where was the aeroplane? Had the French removed all personnel from the scene of the crime? He tried to imagine what would happen. First, the fireball with its blinding flash of light, then the scorching heat blast, then the huge thunderous roar; shock waves coming across the water, bringing heat-cracked rocks to fall on them like molten lava.

Eric came to him. 'Nick's right. They'd never do it. They know where we are.'

Joe was still wary. The French had put themselves in the clear with that broadcast. They would claim *The Dove* was far, far away. When the boat failed to reach New Zealand, they would say it had been lost at sea, as it so nearly had been lost in that terrible storm.

'Joe?' said Liz again.

'I don't know,' he confessed, taking her hand. 'Nick might be right. They could be bluffing.'

'On the other hand?' she said softly.

They saw the fear in each other's eyes. In a day of shocks, the balloon was the worst of them all.

Joe pulled himself together. 'On the other hand,' he said, raising a grin, 'let's not get caught with our trousers down.'

Later, Liz wrote in her diary:

> Even Joe faltered when we saw the balloon. He quickly recovered, but for a moment he was as scared as the rest of us. Perhaps shocked is a better word. Shocked that the French would be so barbaric, although after that dive-bomber I wouldn't put anything past them. Anyway, shocked is a more accurate word than scared to describe Joe, who really is the bravest, most wonderful man in the world. I remember thinking the other day if this turns out to be a battle of wills, the French will lose hands down when they come up against Joe. He's like a rock about some things. Like this afternoon. Within an hour of seeing the balloon everything was decided upon. If anything does happen, we will seal the interior of the cabin by blocking up all the vents. After that, only Joe will be allowed on deck, wrapped in oilskins to protect him as much as possible from radioactive dust. He will start the engine and try to motor us out of the danger zone. None of us know if escape is really possible. There's a chance that *The Dove* (which is all

wood) might ignite from the heat blast. Joe says we're far enough out to avoid that, but I don't think he really knows. Anyway, if Joe gets us clear, one of the others will go up and douse the boat down with sea water, pumped up from a depth of about thirty feet which Joe says will be uncontaminated from fall-out. I won't be allowed on deck at all. Joe made me promise to stay below whatever happens. Even though it's terribly unfair, the others all sided with Joe and will draw lots to see who goes up to man the pump.

I don't know what to think. I can't really believe it will happen. Perhaps I'm too frightened to think straight. This evening lasted forever. I did hamburgers for dinner. Standing over the stove, I looked out through the porthole. It was a marvellous evening – another breathtaking sunset, with lots of scarlet splashes and streaks across a sky that turns purple as the sun goes down – then I saw the balloon, hanging there, ugly and menacing. I began to giggle. It just seemed so crazy. Imagine being asked what you were doing when the world came to an end, and saying you were making hamburgers. I couldn't stop giggling. I tried to explain but no one else thought it was funny. And when Eric opened our last bottle of wine, I asked if it was the Last Supper and started giggling again. I said the Last Supper demanded something more dignified than tinned hamburgers. I fell about. The others looked at me as if I'd gone mad. Then I started to cry. I couldn't help myself. When I've wept before it's always been in the head where no one could see me. Tonight I just sat at the table and howled my eyes out. Nick got me to my bunk where with my face to the wall I finally stopped blubbering. I shall have to apologize tomorrow – if there is a tomorrow. The odd thing is I feel very calm now. Drained and empty, but calm. I've spent the last hour thinking about Edith and Keir and my mother, wondering if I shall ever see them again. Not feeling sorry for myself. Just thinking about them. I wish I'd had the courage to tell Keir and Mother about coming down here. They wouldn't have understood, but I should have told them. They deserve that. They deserve a lot really. I was wondering what my mother wanted to tell me on her wedding day. Funny, but I think I know. She was going to tell me Keir is my father. At least, that's my guess. Deep down I've sensed it for a long time. It was what I wanted most when I was a kid. For Keir to be my father, my *real* father, and not the pretend one he'd become in my mind . . .

Sixteen

The strain was showing. Not merely by the bluish skin under Keir's eyes, but the eyes themselves betrayed his inner conflict. He had the bruised look of a man who has lost faith in something of which he was once certain. He was in the library at Lord North Street. Forty-eight hours had passed since he sat in the same chair talking to Eric Searle's father in New Zealand. Forty-eight hours of which he had slept about seven, which was no more than Dawn who sat in the adjacent armchair, her wan face devoid of make-up, her eyes huge as she looked up at Chuck Hayes.

Still in his overcoat, the big man stood the other side of the desk, his round face flushed and contorted by anger. 'No one can say I haven't been patient!' he exclaimed. 'For Christ's sake! Sam's been onto me for weeks. We've got deals coming apart all over Europe. Now I fly into London and that's the first thing I see.' He flung the newspaper on Keir's desk.

Keir glanced at the headline.

Peace Plane to Join Peace Boat in Pacific

In a desperate bid to locate the missing Peace boat, actress Dawn Wharton and her businessman husband, Keir Milford, are to fly to Mururoa . . .

Chuck struggled to control his temper. 'I know what you're going through. You have my every sympathy. You have everyone's sympathy. I can understand, it's a personal tragedy for you. For both of you. Your entire lives have been screwed up by this thing –'

'Our daughter's life is being more than screwed up,' said Dawn coldly, 'it's being brought to an end.'

'You don't know that,' said Chuck sharply. Placing his hands on the edge of the desk, he leant forward to Keir. 'So it's terrible about your daughter. I'm sorry, believe me, I'm sorry. But do you have to destroy yourself as well? Is that the answer? Throw away everything you've worked so hard to build up? That's what you're doing –'

'What have I built up, Chuck?'

A look of astonishment passed over Chuck's face. 'You need to ask?' he said, waving a hand at the room. 'Look around you. Look at the life you lead. The people you meet –'

'You mean bent politicians?'

'Oh, come on, you know better than that. People do what they have to –'

'Well I don't. Not any more. Not after this.'

'Come on,' Chuck entreated Keir. 'You're upset. You're not thinking straight –'

'Wrong. For the first time in years, I *am* thinking straight. When this nightmare is over you and I will sit down and have a long talk.'

'What about?' Chuck responded. 'We don't have anything to say to each other after this circus tomorrow.'

'Circus?'

'You know what I mean. This public rally in Trafalgar Square.'

Events had moved fast since Ray Cox had taken a hand. Seventeen years before he had put a then unknown actress onto the cover of every magazine in the country. Now he had dropped everything to tell the world about the plight of *The Dove*. And Ray was succeeding, although he would have been the first to admit he was not working alone. An army had come forward, different people from all walks of life. Political activists found themselves joined by people who had never attended a public meeting. Shoulder to shoulder they were protesting outside the French Embassy. With linked hands, they were picketing the House of Commons. With raised voices, they were chanting and baying beneath the windows at the Foreign Office. The march out to Heathrow had been cancelled. Instead, there was to be a mass rally in Trafalgar Square.

'If you get involved with that, you're dead,' Chuck said angrily, 'and not only with Beaumont. No one in the defence industry will touch you –'

'The defence industry!' Keir jumped up from his chair and walked across to the filing cabinets. He leant against them, and turned to face Chuck. 'Don't talk to me about the defence industry. It all made sense once. I believed in it, I really did. Then it got out of hand. I don't know when, some time in the sixties, who knows? Everyone got greedy. That's where it went wrong. Making arms was highly profitable, so we kept on making arms. What did it matter that the world had enough arms to blow itself up a hundred times over? That was their problem, not ours. Our problem was to sell them more. If they hesitated we plied them with money. They could have as much as they wanted. Why not? It didn't cost us. It didn't cost them. They just added a few noughts to the paperwork and raised it in taxes –'

'That's enough!' Chuck shouted.

'Why? That's how it works. We both know it. Why kid each other?'

'I'm going.' Chuck picked his hat up from the table. 'You're through, Keir. I'm sorry, but I can't work with you like this. I came here to make one last effort –'

'Make an effort to tell the truth. Face up to it for once. Call things what they are. All this stuff about the defence industry is crap. We're in the arms business. We don't give a shit if weapons are used for defence, offence, or if they get broken up into pieces, just so long as the orders keep coming in. That's all we care about. Because that's how we stay rich –'

'I'm going,' Chuck repeated. 'By the way, is that story true about you flying to Mururoa –?'

'Of course it's true.'

'Not in our plane you're not. It's no longer available for your use. I've already given instructions. Martin is flying it to Frankfurt in the morning.'

'Oh, Chuck.' Dawn rose from her chair. 'We're leaving tomorrow. We need the plane –'

'Sorry,' Chuck said as he walked to the door, 'I can't afford to get mixed up in what you're doing. It's caused us enough damage. I've already got the Pentagon asking me what the hell our man in Europe is doing with the Peace Movement –'

'Okay, Chuck,' Keir interrupted. 'You've had your say. Now listen to this.'

The big man stopped with his hand on the door.

517

Keir patted the filing cabinets. 'Here's how you help me and help yourself at the same time. We both know what's in here. Enough dirt to bring down every government in Europe and then some. If anything happens to our daughter or my father, or anyone else on that boat, I'm going public with this lot.'

Chuck froze. He searched Keir's face for a sign of weakness and saw only desperation.

Keir continued. 'They'll listen to you. They've stopped taking my calls. I'm being frozen out. I can't get through to them, but you can.'

'Don't be a fool –'

'Save it. Someone has got to lean on the French and lean hard.'

Chuck shook his head. 'There's no guarantee that they'll listen to me –'

'If they don't, this lot goes public. A lot of people will be embarrassed. Here, Washington, Bonn, Rome – all over. Get them to help you persuade the French. I want them to start twisting arms in Paris, and you can tell them I mean it.'

They stared at each other across the abyss of a dead friendship.

Keir said, 'You haven't got long. Every hour counts, maybe every minute, I don't know.'

Chuck licked his lips. 'What do you want me to tell them?' He nodded at the filing cabinets. 'The first question is going to be what happens to them –'

'They can have them. You can have them. I don't care as long as those people aboard *The Dove* survive.'

'And you'll keep quiet?'

Keir smiled thinly. 'We both know what will happen to me if I don't.'

Chuck looked down at his feet. 'Christ,' he said miserably, 'I never thought it would come to this. Keir, I –'

'You'd better go,' said Keir, sounding tired. 'Oh, and by the way, tell the people you'll be seeing that the cabinets here contain only copies. I spent all of yesterday parcelling up the originals. They're lodged in banks all over the place. If we were burgled tonight, it wouldn't matter a damn.'

518

Seventeen

An entry in Elizabeth Wharton's diary.

I awoke this morning. How unremarkable that sounds, yet there were times yesterday when it seemed doubtful. In fact I awoke with a scream. The first thing I saw were lights through the porthole. They looked like the lights of a building, stacked up above each other in neat rows. I shrieked that we had drifted and were almost aground, then raced up to the deck – only to find we hadn't drifted at all. What had looked like a small town were the lights of a ship. A French warship about two miles away. Then I saw Joe in the cockpit where he had been all night, wrapped up in thick sweaters and oilskins, calmly smoking his pipe and staring across at the ship as if defying it to come nearer. Apparently, it had been there most of the night. It was huge, stationary and silent in the mist, like a ghost ship.

The others had followed me up on deck and they stayed there when I went below to brew coffee. I felt much better. Clearly they wouldn't explode the Bomb with their own ship in the area. The others agreed. We were all in vastly better spirits than yesterday. After breakfast we thought we'd say hello to our new neighbours. After all, although we could see them, *The Dove* is so tiny it was unlikely they could see us. Eric and Pete fixed our position as eighteen miles off-shore and the ship was seaward of us, so there was no danger of trespassing into the twelve miles of territorial waters. Hoisting the sails, we set off. Immediately we began to move, a puff of smoke emerged from the ship's funnel. They ran away. Not far, but it was soon obvious that we were not to be allowed to get close to them. When we stopped, they stopped. When we moved, they moved. Eventually we stopped trying. Nick called them a lot of stuck-up bastards and went back to his radio. He spent another hour this morning trying to raise Tahiti or Pitcairn or Rarotonga, with the usual lack of success.

By noon it was obvious something was happening on Mururoa. There was a lot of activity. Helicopters buzzed back and forth over the atoll, and several aircraft came and went. Whenever one flew over us I flinched, fearing a repeat performance of yesterday's nightmare. Thankfully they left us alone. We also saw several ships, all French warships except one, which was a very peculiar-looking affair. Painted brilliant white, she had a huge radar dish on her bow and fairly bristled with antennae. We got close enough to identify her. She wasn't French at all. She was American. The US Victory ship, *Wheeling*. It does explain why the Americans abstained at the Stockholm Conference. When the United States signed the Nuclear Test Ban Treaty last year they agreed not to conduct any atmospheric nuclear tests. Yet here was an American instrumentation ship – well within the French cordon – obviously letting the French do their dirty work for them. We didn't see a British ship, but that doesn't necessarily mean one isn't here. God, the hypocrisy makes my blood boil!

By early afternoon, our earlier optimism began to fade. Mururoa, which yesterday had been brooding and quiet, was so alive with activity that it must mean they are getting ready to blow the Bomb. We had returned to our position, about fifteen miles out, with the French destroyer stalking us like a sea cow stalking a sprat. With nothing better to do we settled down for a game of cards (except Joe, who was sleeping), but none of us could concentrate. Without saying it aloud, we were all asking the same question: 'When are they going to come for us?' It was four o'clcock by then. The horizon was empty. So were the skies. Clearly Mururoa was ready. Staring through binoculars, I made out a sort of box-like contraption hanging below the balloon. Blood froze in my veins when I saw it. Was that the Bomb? A box, not much bigger than a coffin. We took comfort from the destroyer nearby, and all said the same thing – They won't blow the Bomb with their own ship in the fall-out area. Then we looked at each other again. Will they? we asked, seeking reassurance.

At five o'clock this afternoon, they finally came for us, although not in the way we expected. Another ship appeared, coming from Mururoa, smaller than the destroyer but mountainous compared with *The Dove*. Cutting through the water fast, she headed directly for us. So quickly did she arrive that I went down to fetch the camera and by the time I started back up the hatchway all I could see was the huge, grey-white wall of her bow. A uniformed man leant out over the rail, shouting through a megaphone. His voice boomed, 'We have a letter for you.' Within minutes they had lowered an inflatable and four seamen clambered aboard it by climbing down rope ladders. When they started the outboard and puttered across the calm water to us, we were quite sure the message about the letter was a fake. 'They're going to board us,' said Joe, and we were all of the same mind. Eric hurried below and returned clutching our document about our legal rights to remain in these waters. The men in the inflatable looked capable of murder. If they're anything to go by, the French are furious with us. When they came alongside, one of them threw Pete a rope which he made fast to the rail. Instead of boarding us, however, the officer fumbled in his pocket and brought out a brown envelope which he handed to me. I immediately gave it to Eric. Taking it, he handed our legal document to the Frenchman who examined it in amazement. I thought he was going to give it back at first, then he shrugged and stuffed it into his pocket. Then he untied the rope from the rail and sat down in the inflatable. Next moment they were on their way back to the ship.

Eric opened the envelope, which contained one sheet of paper on which had been typed two paragraphs. The first was in French. The second, in English, read –

From: Admiral Commanding Nuclear Tests Force.
To: *The Dove*.

A nuclear explosion will be detonated in this area tomorrow. You are required to sail immediately to a point beyond the cordon. Having given you this due and proper notice, we cannot be further held responsible for your safety.

Maintenance of your present position places your vessel and crew in mortal danger.

By the time we had read the message, the men in the inflatable had rejoined their ship and were scaling the rope ladders. The uniformed officer with the megaphone returned to the rail. 'This time tomorrow,' he boomed, drawing his finger across his throat, '*fini!*' The sneer on his face infuriated us. Eric immediately responded by lifting *The Dove*'s sails to take us closer into Mururoa.

We are there now, hove-to, fifteen miles out, in direct line of the fall-out from the Bomb. We are now quite alone. The destroyer and the other French ship waited to see what we would do. When it became clear we had no intention of moving, they put in for Mururoa, passing dangerously close to us, their rails lined with seamen jeering and shouting and shaking their fists.

Nick composed a message which he has been trying to get out on the radio – FRENCH INFORM US NUCLEAR EXPLOSION IMMINENT. PLEASE CONVEY OUR NEED FOR IMMEDIATE ASSISTANCE TO THE GOVERNMENTS OF THE UNITED STATES, GREAT BRITAIN, CANADA AND NEW ZEALAND. Poor Nick is quite hoarse from repeating this over and over again, calling Tahiti, Rarotonga and Pitcairn.

There is no question of us going. We came here to protest. We can hardly set sail simply because the French tell us to. What kind of protest is that? They have no legal right to tell us to do anything. Things haven't worked out as we expected but we really would be guilty of letting people down if we sailed now. So we stay. There was no need even to discuss it. In an odd sort of way we feel relief for knowing that tomorrow is the last day. No more trying to guess the enemy's intentions. They intend to blow their Bomb, and we intend to stay. The battle lines have been drawn.

I've spent the past hour in the cockpit with Joe. For some reason, I suppose because the possibility of death has been on my mind, I asked him again about my father. When I was a child I was forever asking him, and he always replied,

'Your mother will tell you one day.' Tonight I said, 'Keir's my father, isn't he?' When he offered no reply, I added, 'I *know* he's my father. I've known for a long time.' Which made his face crinkle into a smile. 'Why bother to ask, then?' he said. I said because it seemed silly to make a mystery out of something so obvious. I said I worked it out ages ago. And he said, 'Yes, I thought you might. They wanted to tell you on their wedding day, but we all know what happened to that.'

He told me everything then, Joe did. My grandfather! All about the old days. My mother sounds incredible. He said Edith thought she was a fast woman, a trollop for leading her son astray. I was astounded. I mean my mother's so proper! Joe says it was hard in those days for a girl with her looks. Other women, especially older ones, thought they were mantraps. Some of them were because that was all they could do. For a girl to have a career was almost unheard of. He said it took a lot of courage for her to achieve what she has. He's very proud of her, which is more than he is of his son. Poor Joe, the gulf between him and Keir is wider than ever, though he softened a little when I said I was pleased to have Keir as my father and him as my grandad.

He's still there, up in the cockpit, settled in for the night, clad in sweaters and oilskins, smoking his pipe and glaring across the water at Mururoa. He's got the portable radio for company and will spend the night tuning in to news broadcasts wherever he can find them. When I hugged him goodnight he ruffled my hair in the way he used to when I was a kid. I must have looked sad because he said, 'Cheer up, Liz. Remember what I said. Those people in Christchurch won't give up on us. Neither will Edith and Bob and Emlyn and Angie . . . and there are thousands like them. I bet they're giving the French hell . . .'

My dear, wonderful, brave grandfather. Even at this eleventh hour, he thinks the French will be forced to back down, that they will abandon their nuclear tests. Or perhaps he just said that to keep my spirits up?

When I returned below, the others had turned in for the night. I was glad because I don't much feel like talking. It's a

523

funny feeling to find out who you are the day before you might die.

I've been lying here thinking about what Joe said. Looking up at that huge warship today and seeing the hatred in those men's faces sent a chill up my spine. Why hate us? What's in it for them if they contaminate the Pacific with radioactive fall-out? How do they benefit if babies are born deformed? Not that I mentioned such thoughts to Joe. He's so convinced we shall win in the end I hadn't the heart to point out that, in our case, the end may be tomorrow.

Where, oh where, is his army of the good?

Eighteen

It was coming. The cry of outrage was growing. In villages and towns and cities along the rim of the Pacific, petitions were being signed, meetings were being held. In Peru, a hundred thousand women carried placards through the streets – 'Stop the Tests'. In Australia, thousands demanded that the French reveal *The Dove*'s whereabouts. In New Zealand, Eric Searle's father was leading a deputation to Wellington. In Samoa, in Tonga, in Fiji and the Solomon Islands, people were holding meetings in dusty streets and cramped village halls, demanding that their rulers 'do something'.

The cry of outrage was growing. Even as Liz wrote her diary, ninety thousand people were marching through Paris, chanting and shouting their opposition to nuclear tests. For once the French riot police were in retreat.

And in London, the cry of outrage was growing. A groundswell had been building. Circumstances, events and people were combining in a way that was truly unique. For weeks past, Angie and Betty and others had been distributing leaflets. Housewives on busy high streets, people in bus queues, fathers taking sons to football matches, were reading about the voyage of *The Dove* long before the story made headlines. Student friends of Pete and Nick at the Regent Street Poly, Eric's friends from the LSE, had been spreading the word. Trade Union officials, friends of Bob Cooper, had been handing out leaflets at branch meetings. The CND had been raising funds and campaigning . . .

By the time Ray Cox had become involved, a great deal of work had already been done. One of the most experienced publicists in the business, even Ray had never experienced the like of those ninety-six hours which culminated in the Trafalgar Square rally. From the moment he called his first media contact about *The Dove*, from the moment of the first headline, Ray was swamped with offers of help. People just arrived at his office, sent there by Edith or Angie; all sorts of people from all walks of life, with little in common except a sneaking regard for an old man and a girl and three young men who had sailed thousands of miles into the path of the Bomb. Olga Bjord arrived from Oslo and took charge of the rally. 'You get the media there,' she told Ray firmly, 'and leave the people to us.'

Working through the night, posters were printed – WHERE IS *THE DOVE*? SAVE *THE DOVE*! STOP FRENCH TESTS NOW! FRENCH MURDER PLAN IN THE PACIFIC! More leaflets were run off. In a race against time, every second counted. Students literally ran from one letter box to the next, distributing leaflets door to door around London. They raced into blocks of flats, taking the stairs two at a time.

And so, that day, they came into Trafalgar Square. The involvement of some was predictable. Joe was widely known in the Peace Movement. Liz had grown up on CND marches. Friends rallied as never before, arriving from all over the country. From further, because as well as Olga Bjord, Gunter Hess and his wife flew in from West Berlin and Olaf Peterson brought a party of sixty people from Copenhagen. So many students came that the LSE and Regent Street Polytechnics were left virtually empty. Politicians came, the Church came, and because of Dawn Wharton, half the cast of every production running in the West End came too. Political activists found themselves joined by people who had never attended a public meeting in their lives. Shoulder to shoulder they protested outside the French Embassy, and they linked hands as they picketed the House of Commons. They raised their voices, chanted and bayed beneath the windows of the Foreign Office. Then they marched into Trafalgar Square . . .

They came in their hundreds, their thousands, and their tens of thousands. Market traders from Berwick Street market came to support Nick and Liz, Pete and Angie. Half of Arcadia Gardens came to support a man they had scorned in the past. The press came: reporters, commentators, cameramen representing papers and radio stations and TV stations from all over the world . . .

And into a Trafalgar Square overflowing with a hundred thousand people came Dawn Wharton and her husband Keir Milford. It was an alien world for them both. Most of all for Keir, to whom even a press conference would have been a new arena. He had spent his life behind the scenes pulling strings and opening doors for Sam Pickard. In a race against time he would have avoided the rally and gone directly to Heathrow, where the jet he had managed to hire was due in from Zurich. Ray Cox had insisted, 'You *must* appear on that platform. I've got the world's press there; TV, radio, everyone. We want last-minute pressure, agree? So what hurts the French most? You boarding a plane at Heathrow, or you joining a protest being heard all over the world?'

They had left Lord North Street, with John Westwood driving the Daimler and Barbara waving a tearful goodbye from the door. Edith was with them, as tired and frightened as they were. Ray, Harvey and Eric raced ahead in a cab.

Next to John in the front, Edith had opened her handbag and drew out two cheaply made white metal badges. Circular in shape to represent the unborn child, they bore a broken cross to symbolize the death of man. Edith turned and offered one to Dawn. 'Liz would want you to wear it,' she said. Wordlessly, Keir had taken the other badge from his mother's hand and pinned it to his lapel.

So they came into that crowded arena, desperately worried, exhausted from lack of sleep, nervous and confused about what they would say. On the platform other people were already addressing the crowd. Dawn was more recognized than Keir. Hurried introductions were made. Hands were shaken – not always possible in every case, like the woman who had both her arms in plaster casts. Dawn kissed the woman's cheek before turning to face the vast sea of faces and the blizzard of placards held high – SAVE *THE DOVE* – WHERE IS *THE DOVE*? – STOP THE TESTS!

Keir spoke first, and not well. He talked of legalities. He spoke of the international law of the sea. He said *The Dove* had every right to have sailed into those waters. It was the wrong line for such a meeting. Caring little for technicalities, people in the huge crowd were concerned only for the plight of *The Dove*. It was to save five people confronting terrible odds which had brought them out onto the streets.

Dawn held their attention from her first faltering words. 'You have heard the French may murder my daughter,' she began uncertainly. 'They may have done so already. I have no means of knowing. The only thing I know is that I will not plead for her life.'

Exclamations of shock arose throughout that huge assembly.

'Oh, no.' Dawn shook her head. Her voice rose strong and clear. 'I will not plead. Liz wouldn't want that. Neither would my father-in-law, nor the young American, the young Canadian, and the young New Zealander aboard *The Dove*. I will not plead for their lives. If these five people must be put to death, then so be it, for their fate will have been decided by those who rule over us –'

Shouts of, 'What about the French?' came from the crowd.

'They, too,' Dawn agreed, 'but make no mistake – the French act with the approval of the governments of America, Britain, Canada and New Zealand.' She gathered her strength and plunged on, expressing for the first time conclusions that had formed in her mind over the preceding agonizing weeks. 'Our governments know what they're doing. They look after us. They protect our way of life. Remember this, we have freedoms denied to those poor unfortunates who live in totalitarian states. So of course we must be strong. That's why we need nuclear weapons. Without those weapons we would be defenceless and our way of life – including those precious freedoms which we sometimes take for granted – would vanish!'

Dissenting voices were raised in one corner of the Square. From others came shouts of disagreement and surprise.

Dawn quelled them with a wave of her arm. 'That's what I've always believed. That's what I've been taught to believe. Yet these past six weeks have opened my eyes. I thought one of our basic freedoms was the right of peaceful protest. See that woman there . . . that's right, the lady with her arms in plaster

527

casts and bruises on her face. The French government did that to her when she tried to walk into France carrying a placard.'

Dawn took a deep breath, and raced on. 'I was taught to believe that one of our basic freedoms was the right to communicate with each other without let or hindrance. That woman there, Mrs Milford, whose husband is in peril on *The Dove* at this moment has had her phone tapped by MI5 for years. They've opened her mail. They've searched her house. For what? For bombs? She's opposed to bombs! For arms? She's opposed to arms. So who does she threaten?'

The crowd was with her now. For a moment people had doubted. They had hesitated. But not any longer.

Dawn's voice rang out, clear and challenging. 'One of our basic freedoms is the right to sail a boat in international waters. Yet five weeks ago a French admiral told my husband that this is a crime punishable by death!' She hurried on. 'One of our basic freedoms is the right to appeal to our governments for protection. Yet where is the British government in my daughter's hour of peril? I'll tell you. In Brussels, more concerned about trade than matters of life and death. Where is the Canadian government in Peter Grimshaw's hour of need? I'll tell you. In Paris selling uranium to the French for their precious nuclear bombs. Where is the New Zealand government in Eric Searle's hour of need? In Marseilles and Lyons and every grocer's shop in France, selling them butter! And where is America's government in Nick Grant's hour of need? I'll tell you, selling arms to the rest of the world!'

The roar of agreement which arose all over the Square rocked Dawn back on her heels. She finished where she had started. 'No, I will not plead for the lives of those brave people on *The Dove*, because if the French kill them they'll have to kill me. And if the French kill me, they'll have to kill my husband. And if they kill him they'll have to kill all the thousands and millions of people who will rise up and demand an end to this madness!'

Then the dam broke. All the worry and tension of the past weeks had brought Dawn to the edge of her strength. She choked up. Unable to utter another word, tears shone in her eyes. She swayed on her feet. Keir was at her side in an instant, supporting her. The roar, rising from thousands of throats, died and faded to almost a whisper. Some cheered and others applauded, but those nearest the platform cried out in concern. Dawn's deep distress was evidence enough that they had no reason to cheer. No victory had been won. Those aboard *The Dove* were still in grave danger. For a moment the mood of that vast crowd was irresolute and uncertain. Dawn's passion had reached out and touched them without giving them a way to respond. And then, at the end of the platform, a man rose to his feet. He began to sing. It was a hymn he had known from childhood: 'For Those in Peril on the Sea'. And to his voice, haltingly at first, others were joined. Slowly people who might not have been to church for years found the old familiar words coming back to them.

> Eternal Father, strong to save,
> Whose arm hath bound the restless wave . . .

The volume rose as others found their voices:

> Who bidd'st the mighty ocean deep,
> Its own appointed limits keep . . .

Thousands more knew the next lines:

> O hear us when we cry to Thee,
> For those in peril on the sea.

Keir was already helping Dawn from the platform. Edith, her eyes wet with tears, followed, fumbling into her handbag for a handkerchief. By the time they reached the car, the voices of thousands were sending the pigeons high into the sky above the Square. And as John edged the car slowly through that part of the crowd that had spilled over onto the road – as Dawn and Keir and Edith left to begin their desperate dash to Mururoa – one hundred thousand people gave expression to what they felt in their hearts:

> O hear us when we cry to Thee,
> For those in peril on the sea.

On *The Dove* tears streamed down Liz's cheeks. Clinging to Joe, she heard those voices hiss and crackle through the static from the other side of the world.

O hear us when we cry to Thee,
For those in peril on the sea.

She gulped hard, and dabbed her tears with the back of her hand. 'Oh Joe, wasn't she wonderful?'

A burst of static threatened to obliterate the words of the Radio Australia commentator as he shouted above the noise of the crowd in Trafalgar Square '. . . still no news of *The Dove*. While admitting they may have been mistaken about their earlier sighting, French officials maintain that the boat is not in the vicinity of the Mururoa test site . . .'

Static screeched and howled, rendering the transmission unintelligible for a moment. Then the newscaster returned '. . . count-down has started at the test site. French spokesmen refuse to say whether the first test will be made within hours or days, but the tests will definitely go ahead . . .'

Another deafening blast of static shrieked from the radio. Joe twiddled the dial, desperately trying to improve reception. More crackling and hissing tormented them before they heard '. . . that's the scene here in London. Dawn Wharton, star of a dozen Hollywood movies, threw away her sugar-coated image today. We witnessed a woman of chilling dignity . . . fighting for the lives of loved ones . . . we saw a cold, new Dawn Wharton . . .'

The rest of the words drowned in a sea of static and when reception was recaptured it was the voice of the Radio Australia newcaster back in the Sydney studio with the rest of the early morning news. Joe switched the set off and cradled Liz in his arms.

'I'm not really crying,' she sobbed, 'I'm just so proud . . .'

They were all on deck, crouched over the radio. Liz fought her tears long enough to give Nick a shaky smile. 'That was my parents! Weren't they great!'

Joe was astounded about Keir. 'The way he defended us. He was marvellous. And Edith was there on the platform. She must have been from what Dawn said. And, by God, didn't Dawn lash into them –'

'She was in tears at the end,' said Liz, her voice quivering. 'The man said so –'

'So were you,' said Joe, hugging her, 'and I wasn't far off tears myself when they started singing that hymn.'

The truth was they had all been moved by the broadcast – and encouraged, for despite the frightening news that the count-down had started, they no longer felt so alone.

'Did you hear that feller, Nick?' Joe grinned. 'He reckoned a hundred thousand people were crammed into Trafalgar Square.'

Nick nodded. 'And he said just as many were marching through Paris.'

Joe chuckled gleefully. 'The French won't like that, will they?'

'I should think most of them *were* French.'

'Oh yes,' Joe agreed, 'but they were *our* French, not *their* French.'

Nick laughed. Then Pete chuckled. Eric's grin broadened, and he too started to laugh. Liz began to giggle, then Joe saw the funny side of it, and the next moment all of them collapsed into convulsions. Anyone who could have seen them at that moment would have taken them for five holiday-makers out for a sail before breakfast. What a difference some good news made. To learn that *The Dove* had not been forgotten. To know that people were demonstrating on their behalf half-way across the world. For a moment they were blind to the balloon hanging over the atoll. The luxury of laughter made them forget the count-down had started and that they were in grave danger. The extent of their peril was savagely brought home to them a moment later.

Eric was at the helm, doing what he loved most, sailing his boat. He was so proud of *The Dove* – with justification after the way she had weathered that storm. And it was a fine morning for sailing. The wind had increased slightly. A few whitecaps touched the sea. Overhead thin tracers of white cloud scattered across the sky. It was Pete who looked back at Mururoa. 'Hello,' he said. 'Here comes the minesweeper. The one they sent out yesterday.'

Nick shielded his eyes from the sun. 'Perhaps we've got another letter,' he said cheerfully.

'She's coming up at a hell of a lick,' said Pete.

Joe hoisted himself up by his arms to improve his view. The minesweeper was long and low by the standards of warships, built for speed in coastal waters. Yesterday had given him a good

531

view of her lines. Now, with the minesweeper directly behind them, he could see only her bow, pushing fast through the water. 'She's certainly moving,' he agreed.

The laughter of a few moments before was forgotten. All five of them tensed expectantly. 'I think this is it,' said Nick, 'this is the boarding party.'

With the wind full in her sails, *The Dove* was racing through the water but might have been at a standstill from the way the minesweeper was closing the gap. Eric glanced over his shoulder. 'Bloody hell! What are they playing at?'

The French ship was less than fifty yards behind; dangerously close with the swell that was running. Joe squinted upwards and saw a group of officers standing under a canvas awning on the bridge. He counted the storeys down to the superstructure. The bridge was four complete storeys above the minesweeper's deck. Eric shouted, 'She's too close.'

Pete and Nick began to wave frantically, indicating that the French ship should veer off. The minesweeper came relentlessly on. An officer appeared at the railings over the bow. He laughed and shouted something over his shoulder to someone behind him.

Nick screamed with temper. 'You stupid bastard!'

The gap narrowed to forty yards. They could hear the minesweeper's engines. The bow wave racing ahead of her was so close that it sent beads of spray over Joe.

Thirty yards.

Pete yelled, 'They're going to ram us!'

Twenty-five yards.

Liz screamed, looking up in horror as the vast grey bow loomed high over *The Dove*.

'Get the lifejackets!' Nick roared at her. 'Move!' he bellowed when she hesitated.

Ten yards.

Joe looked up, and could no longer see the wheelhouse and the bridge. The huge, upward wedge of the minesweeper's bow filled the sky. Crouched over the tiller, Eric threw his weight sideways in a desperate attempt to turn *The Dove* out of the ship's path. *The Dove* faltered. Losing the wind from her sails, her speed fell away.

Joe was under a huge black shadow. He could see nothing

except the bow of the warship rising higher and higher. Then it came down.

Eric threw himself forward with the impact. *The Dove* shuddered as the warship smashed down on her stern. Timbers groaned and cracked. Deck planks sprang apart as they fractured. A section of rail snapped, sending vicious splinters screaming through the air like bullets.

Emerging from the hatch, life jackets in her arms, Liz staggered and fell backwards into the cabin. Nick landed on his knees beside Joe. Eric, winded by his fall, heard the groans of tortured joints and splintering beams, and knew without a shadow of doubt that his beloved *Dove* was sinking. Joe, dazed and incredulous, could think of only one thing. Where, oh where, was the army of the good?

Nineteen

As the Daimler raced down the motorway to the airport, Keir was making frantic calls on the car telephone. Speaking to the Swiss pilot of the hired jet waiting at Heathrow, he met with another setback. Yes, the aircraft was fuelled and ready for take-off, but the pilot would fly them only to New Zealand. His company would not permit him to fly into the nuclear test zone around Mururoa. Cursing furiously, Keir instructed him to radio ahead and appeal for a volunteer crew and aircraft to be standing by in New Zealand. Keir's next call was to Chuck Hayes. He went white as he listened.

'I don't know if they've been sunk,' Chuck admitted. 'That was the original order.'

'For Christ's sake! Those murdering bastards –'

'Hang on! We spent the whole night twisting arms. You name them, we called them. The Pentagon, Ministry of Defence –'

'Has that order been changed?'

'Yes –'

'Thank God for that –'

'But I don't know if it got there in time –'

'You don't *know*?'

'Keir, we're dealing with a chain of command. You know what these things are like –'

'And you know what I've got in those filing cabinets. I swear –'

'I know that. Everyone knows that. Christ, you don't have to threaten anyone. The French are desperate to reach your people. Paris is taking so much flak about this. Every newspaper, every TV station in the world is running this story –'

'I'll call you from the plane,' Keir shouted angrily. 'You tell those bastards to sort out their chain of command!'

Keir slammed the phone back into its cradle and his eyes went to the road ahead as John swung the car off the motorway onto the approach road to the airport. Protestors were gathered along every inch of the verge. Banners and placards were everywhere – SAVE *THE DOVE* – STOP THE TESTS – SAVE *THE DOVE*.

The deadly French attack had been swift and efficient. Even as *The Dove* began to sink, inflatables were being lowered from the minesweeper and men were scrambling down rope ladders. Reversing its engines at the moment of impact, the French ship backed slowly, its bow embedded in *The Dove*'s rigging. Dazed and terrified, Liz fought her way up the hatch, screaming, as water poured in. Behind her, the cabin was already knee deep. The boat lurched horribly as she reached the deck. 'Joe!' she screamed, seeing him. He was releasing his safety harness. Left on, the harness would drag him down with *The Dove*. The deck tilted again. Liz stumbled. When she looked again, Joe had vanished over the side. 'Joe!' she screamed as the deck rolled. She lost her footing. She was falling, falling. The sea engulfed her. She was drowning. Drowning. Gasping for breath, she rose to the surface. Arms gripped her. Hands reached for her. She saw the sky. Strange faces. French voices. Sodden, she was dragged over the side into an inflatable which was already wheeling away from the wreck. Choking sea water from her lungs, she attempted to sit up. Hands restrained her, turning her face down, pounding her back. Struggling to her knees, she lifted her head and saw the French ship directly in front of her. Next moment a seaman hoisted her over his shoulder like a carcase of beef, and she was being carried up a rope ladder with the sea yawning beneath her. On deck she found her feet just as Nick was carried over the side in similar fashion. Breaking loose from the man holding her, Liz stumbled over to him and flung herself into his arms. 'Oh, Nick! Thank God. I saw Joe go over the side –'

'He's there. Look.'

She turned and saw Joe propped against a bulkhead, with Eric and Pete crouched over him. On rubbery legs, Liz lurched across the deck to fall down beside him. His face was grey with exhaustion, but he was alive. They were all alive. Liz found herself touching all of them to make sure they were real and not ghosts. Dazed and soaking wet, the boys tried to respond while Joe clutched her hand.

'Good morning,' said a voice, 'I am the captain.'

They all craned their necks to see a man in an officer's white uniform. He was of medium height, with dark hair, and a bronzed face, and the immaculate appearance of a superior being come to look at what had been dragged from the sea.

It was too much for Eric. He had been brought up in sailing boats, and taken to sea before he could walk. The law of the sea was sacred to him. For the French ship to have deliberately run down *The Dove* was a crime ranking with murder in his book. Uncoiling from his crouch, he brought his fist up from the deck. Arcing upwards, every ounce of outraged fury was thrown into that punch. The captain jerked backwards too late. The uppercut smashed into his jaw to send him reeling backwards onto the rails.

A dozen men threw themselves at Eric. Nick and Pete leapt valiantly to his aid. Liz screamed as Nick was clubbed to his knees in front of her. Pete was bent double by a blow. Moments later they were being dragged inside the ship – Joe too, his useless legs smashing into steel uprights and bulkheads. They were flung into a large cabin furnished with two bunks, a table and four chairs, where they heard bolts drawn across the door behind them.

Eric's nose was bleeding. A cut had been opened above his left eye. Nick had an egg-sized bump rising behind his right ear. Pete was in agony from a kick in the crotch. All wringing wet, they were angry, frightened and bewildered by the speed of

535

events. In less than thirty minutes *The Dove* had been sunk and they had been taken prisoner.

Joe was recovering. Colour had returned to his face and his breathing was easier. But as Eric dabbed at his bloody nose, his temper returned. 'Bastards! Fascist bastards!' Liz found herself trembling as she tried to calm him. Nick and Pete were as angry as Eric, but they were better at controlling their tempers.

A moment later, the bolts were drawn and the cabin door opened. Several seamen entered, followed by the captain, flanked by four other officers. The large cabin was suddenly very crowded. The captain held a piece of paper in his hand. 'You will sign this,' he said, looking at Eric. Liz realized they obviously knew that Eric was *The Dove*'s skipper. She wondered what else they knew.

'I'm not signing anything,' Eric growled, looking with satisfaction at the swelling on the side of the captain's face.

Joe raised himself onto one elbow on the bunk. 'I demand you inform our governments of our whereabouts and that you have taken us prisoner.'

The Frenchman looked at him coldly. 'You will be released when you sign this.'

'What about my boat?' Eric roared.

The captain glanced at the paper in his hand. 'You were well inside our territorial waters and refused to obey our lawful demands to stop –'

'That's a lie and you know it,' Eric interrupted.

The captain shrugged, his eyes still on the paper in his hand. 'We were compelled to intercept you for your own safety. Unfortunately, you resisted and a collision occurred –'

'You expect me to sign that?' Eric's voice shook with outrage. Pushing back his chair, he rose to his feet. Immediately two seamen put themselves between him and their captain.

Joe spoke. 'We have the right to medical attention and dry clothes –'

The captain's face mottled with anger. 'You have no rights!' he shouted. 'Unless your captain signs this paper –'

'Shove it!' Pete shouted, springing up from his chair.

A seaman turned and hit him in one movement. As Pete crashed backwards, Nick lurched towards the captain, only to be fended off by a dozen arms. The captain stepped backwards and

536

retreated from the cabin, with his entourage backing out after him. The door was slammed and the bolts crashed back into place.

Liz helped Pete to his feet. 'I'm okay,' he said, wiping blood from his mouth with the back of his hand. 'Hey, you're shivering.'

She was shaking uncontrollably. No tears made her eyes wet, but she was unable to stop trembling. Nick ripped a blanket from the other bunk and wrapped it around her shoulders.

'She's in shock,' said Joe, 'get her over here.'

Everything was forgotten in the concern for Liz. They all got her to the bunk and crowded round her, offering encouragement and comfort. Pete dropped to his knees and began rubbing her hands. 'Come on, Liz, you've been great, absolutely fantastic, don't give up now.'

As Joe hugged her, his hand brushed against the chain of the St Christopher around her neck. He drew the medal out from her shirt and made her take hold of it. 'Hang on to that, Liz. Remember who gave it to you?'

Liz stared with blank eyes. 'Mabel Flint.'

'Right,' Joe said nodding, 'and there are hundreds of Mabel Flints working flat out at this moment, hammering away at the French government for all they're worth.'

For once, Liz failed to respond. She shook more than ever.

'*Thousands* of Mabel Flints,' Joe insisted. 'You heard them in Trafalgar Square. They won't let us down. What was that song they were singing? That hymn?'

Liz looked at him with blank eyes; her body was still trembling beyond her control.

Joe began to sing. 'Eternal Father, strong to save.' He broke off, looking at the others for support. 'Come on,' he said, 'all of you.'

Self-consciously, Nick began to hum the tune. Eric cleared his throat and went back to the first line. 'Eternal Father, strong to save.'

Pete took over. 'Whose arm hath bound the restless wave.'

Nick sang, 'Dah, de dah dah dah . . . its own appointed limits keep.'

Joe led them on as he clutched his shaking granddaughter to his chest,

O hear us when we cry to Thee,
For those in peril on the sea.

The jet was already screaming through the blue skies above
southern Spain. Dawn was weeping, despite the comforting arm
of Edith around her shoulders. Opposite, Keir leaned forward
to take her hands. Three minutes before, Chuck's voice had
come over the radio: the crew of *The Dove* was safe!

As he held Dawn's hand, Keir said gently, 'They're taking
them into Mururoa. From there they will fly them to Tahiti, then
back to New Zealand. Darling, with any luck they'll be landing
at Christchurch only a few hours after we get there.'

Edith, desperate to believe, looked at her son with hope in her
eyes, the first hope she had dared allow herself in weeks. 'It is
definite, isn't it? No more tricks, no more lies –'

'Lies!' Keir's laugh was shaky with emotion. 'They wouldn't
dare. Not if they want a French Embassy left standing.'

Edith's eyes brightened until they shone with pride. 'That
crazy, stubborn old man,' she whispered.

Twenty

The news hit the morning TV and radio broadcasts in New
Zealand, causing an eruption. Christchurch had eight hours to
get ready. Bells rang from every church steeple. Old men ran out
the flags. Kids played hookey from school. Typists invented
head colds and took a day off from the office. Others persuaded
grandmothers to die to provide a convenient funeral. Everyone
wanted to be there when the plane from Tahiti arrived. People
came from all over South Island, others flew down from
Auckland and all parts of North Island, and more people came
from distances even greater than that. Ten came from Samoa,
eight from Fiji, sixteen came from the Solomon Islands. Fifteen
came from the New Hebrides and seven came from the Gilbert
Islands. They brought good wishes from every village and town

threatened by fall-out from the French bomb. They wanted to say thank you. They wanted to see for themselves the old man and the girl and the three crazy young men who had taken a tiny sail boat thousands of miles into the face of the Bomb.

They made garlands of flowers and designed placards and posters and – strangely, perhaps – they felt very proud. In their thousands they came, to stand in the sun, craning their necks for first sight of that plane. Mr Searle polished his spectacles and stared expectantly upwards.

'Listen,' Dawn whispered. Straining their ears above the hum of excitement around them, the distant sound of an aircraft could be heard faintly on the breeze. An eagle-eyed youth spotted a dot moving high in the sky. He raised his arm and pointed. Keir checked his watch. Three rows behind him, squinting into the sun, a young girl cried, 'Here it comes!' Seconds later others could see the speck growing larger. As she patted her hair, Edith cast a quick smile at her son. She turned and smiled at her daughter-in-law. Then, as the cheers began to ring out, as cars around the airport perimeter began tooting their horns and flashing their lights, Edith linked arms with Dawn and Keir and together they walked down the red carpet, out onto the apron . . .

Author's Note

COLD NEW DAWN is fiction. On the other hand . . .
The French conducted their nuclear tests on Mururoa that year. Once again, radioactive fall-out poisoned the beautiful shores of the South Pacific. And the following year, 1973, another huge mushroom-shaped cloud rose over Mururoa. But the world finally called a halt. Such was the outcry, such were the protests and petitions and boycotts, that the French were compelled to bow their heads to public opinion. Since then, no nuclear bombs have been exploded into the atmosphere over Mururoa – although to this day the island remains an underground test site for French nuclear weapons.

COLD NEW DAWN is fiction. On the other hand . . .
The Lockheed scandal first hit the headlines in the summer of 1975, when a US Senate sub-committee, under the chairmanship of Senator Frank Church, opened the first of a series of hearings into the company's affairs. The proceedings had scarcely got under way when Lockheed were compelled to admit that they had paid two hundred and twenty million dollars in 'consultancy fees' and 'assorted commissions' from 1970 to 1975. When pressed to agree that much of this sum could be classified as bribes, Lockheed officials prefered the words 'kickbacks', 'pay-offs' or, quite simply, 'questionable payments'. Later (in May 1977) Lockheed acknowledged this figure was a gross understatement and that the real figure was almost twice as large, even without counting bribes paid out during the fifties and sixties.

Lockheed was not alone. Northrop, Boeing, McDonnell-Douglas and various other weapons contractors were compelled (by Senator Church) to admit to involvement in corruption. Many will blame American businessmen, but to do so would be a false judgement, for although the American system has its faults it is without doubt a more open society than, for instance, that of

Great Britain. Given the draconian powers of the Official Secrets Acts and the absence of a Public Information Act, the unfortunate citizens of Great Britain face a much harder task when trying to unearth the truth. Sadly, they have no Senator Church at the head of a powerful US Senate Committee. Perhaps the morality of British big business is of a much higher order? The answer to that was given by the prominent industrialist Sir Frederick Catherwood who, when commenting about the Leyland affair in 1977, said, 'If you don't pay some kind of money, you don't get the business. Politicians can get up in the House of Commons and say this must not happen, but they do not live with the consequences . . .'

So there!

COLD NEW DAWN is fiction. On the other hand . . .

Mention is made of some very real people. Franz Josef Strauss to name one, and Ernest F. Hausser to name another. Mr Hausser has in fact written a book, *The Lockheed European Caper* – and has told of his dealings with Herr Strauss on many occasions, not least among them in a lengthy interview on Granada TV.

Prince Bernhard of Holland, of course, is another very real person. Following Senator Church's revelations about Lockheed in America, other countries called upon their governments to instigate similar enquiries. The one in Holland was presided over by Judge Donner of the European Communities Court of Justice. Faced with Prince Bernhard's denials that he ever received money from Lockheed, Judge Donner was forced to conclude that HRH's statements 'cannot be reconciled with established facts'. He further commented that the work of his enquiry had been 'repeatedly hampered by HRH's poor memory' and finally reached the conclusion that the Prince

> showed himself open to dishonourable requests and offers [and that he] allowed himself to be tempted to take initiatives which were completely unacceptable and which were bound to place himself and the Netherlands' procurement policy in the eyes of others in a dubious light.

Thus disgraced, the Prince resigned his hundreds of directorships and retired from public life. Had he not done so it is quite possible that the Dutch monarchy would have fallen.

542

Corruption involving the arms dealers reached across the world. In Italy (in May 1977) parliament reached a decision almost without precedent – to indict not one, but *two* former Ministers of Defence for collecting bribes.

In Japan, former Prime Minister Tanaka was arrested in 1976 and charged with accepting bribes amounting to more than one million dollars.

But need I go on about corruption in high places? What about, as is suggested in COLD NEW DAWN, the persecution of quite humble people like Joe Milford by the State? Telephone-tapping, interference with the mail, break-ins and harassment – surely that can't be true of Great Britain. Sadly there is massive evidence to the contrary. Cathy Messiter, herself an intelligence officer at MI5 for more than twelve years, revealed (in March 1985) that MI5 had tapped the telephones of several people active in CND. And Cathy Messiter's allegations are widely supported. Were it not so serious, so sad and so sinister it would be almost funny. After all, no Russian 'moles' have been discovered in CND, whereas MI5 seems fairly riddled with them.

Finally, no commentary of this type would be complete without mention of David McTaggart who twice made courageous voyages into the French nuclear test zone at Mururoa. Joe and Edith, Liz and Nick, Eric and Pete would have loved David McTaggart. Without doubt, Joe would have made him a general in his beloved army of the good.

So, as I said at the outset, COLD NEW DAWN is fiction. On the other hand . . .

Ian St James